Defender of Jerusalem

Defender of Jerusalem

A Biographical Novel of Balian d'Ibelin

Helena P. Schrader

Defender of Jerusalem: A Biographical Novel of Balian d'Ibelin

Published by Wheatmark®
1760 East River Road, Suite 145
Tucson, Arizona 85718 USA
www.wheatmark.com

ISBN: 978-1-62787-273-7 (paperback)
ISBN: 978-1-62787-274-4 (ebook)
LCCN: 2015908915

rev201601

Contents

Cast of Characters vii

Genealogical Charts

- The Ibelin Family in the 12th Century x
- Kings/Queens of Jerusalem 1131–1212 xi
- The Greek (Byzantine) Emperors in the 12th Century xii

Maps

- Map of the Holy Land Today (Modern Israel) xiii
- Kingdom of Jerusalem xiv
- Baronies of Jerusalem xv
- City of Jerusalem in the Twelfth Century xvi

Introduction and Acknowledgments xvii

Defender of Jerusalem 1

Historical Note 494

Note on Leprosy 507

Glossary 510

Additional Reading 514

Also by Helena P. Schrader 517

Cast of Characters

(Names in **bold** are historical figures.
Names with * appear more than once.)

Royal House of Jerusalem

Baldwin IV, King of Jerusalem, 1174-1185

Agnes de Courtenay, his mother by **King Amalric**, and widow of **Hugh d'Ibelin**, her second husband

Maria Comnena*, Baldwin IV's stepmother, Dowager Queen of Jerusalem, great-niece of the Byzantine Emperor **Manuel I**

Sibylla of Jerusalem, Baldwin IV's sister, widow of the **Marquis de Montferrat**

Isabella of Jerusalem, Baldwin IV's paternal half-sister, daughter of **Maria Comnena*** and King Amalric

Baldwin V, King of Jerusalem, son of Sibylla by Marquis de Montferrat, nephew of Baldwin VI

House of Ibelin

Balian, third son of Barisan, 1st Baron of Ibelin, Lord of Ibelin from 1177, known to the Arabs as Ibn Barzan (son of Barisan)

Maria Comnena,* Dowager Queen of Jerusalem, his wife

Helvis, John, Margaret, and **Philip**, their children

Baldwin ("Barry"), eldest surviving son of the 1st Baron of Ibelin, older brother of Balian, Lord of Ramla and Mirabel

Elizabeth, his second wife
Eschiva*, his daughter, wife of **Aimery de Lusignan***
Godfrey, his son
Thomas, his son

Henri, youngest son of the 1st Baron of Ibelin, younger brother of Balian and "Barry"
Eloise, his wife

Household of Balian d'Ibelin

Rahel, a Coptic serving woman
Beth, a converted Muslim
Mathewos, an Ethiopian, marshal of Ibelin
Dawit, his son, Balian's squire, 1176-1181
Tsion, his daughter, Dawit's sister
Daniel, Balian's squire, 1176-1181
Ernoul*, Balian's squire, 1181-1188
Gabriel, Balian's squire, 1181-1187, Tsion's husband
Father Michael, Balian's confessor
Roger Shoreham, senior sergeant, father of Daniel, Gabriel, and Father Michael
Georgios, a groom of Greek descent
Centurion and Thor, Balian's destriers
Rufus, one of Balian's palfreys

Knights of Ibelin and Nablus

Sir Bartholomew, feudal tenant of Ibelin
Sir Arnulf, feudal tenant of Ibelin and father of Balian's squire Ernoul*
Sir Adrian, son of Sir Arnulf and older brother of Ernoul*
Sir Galvin, a household knight of Scottish origin
Sir Walter, a household knight, formerly Balian's squire
Sir Constantine, Constable of Nablus

House of Lusignan

Aimery*, third son of Hugh, Lord of Lusignan, Constable of Jerusalem
Eschiva*, his wife, daughter of the Baron of Ramla, niece of Balian d'Ibelin
Guy, fourth son of Hugh de Lusignan, second husband of Sibylla of Jerusalem,* Count of Jaffa from 1180, King of Jerusalem from 1186

Other Barons of the Crusader States

Bohemond III, Prince of Antioch
Theodora Comnena, his wife, sister of Maria Comnena*

Maria of Antioch, his sister, wife of **Manuel I, Byzantine Emperor***

Raymond, Count of Tripoli, Lord of Galilee
Eschiva, his wife, Lady of Tiberias
William and **Ralph**, Eschiva's sons by her previous marriage

Joscelin de Courtenay, brother of Agnes de Courtenay,* titular Count of Edessa

Humphrey de Toron II, Constable of Jerusalem
Reynald de Châtillon, Lord of Oultrejourdain
Stephanie de Milly, his wife, widow of Humphrey de Toron III, son of the above Constable, and widow of Miles de Plancy
Humphrey de Toron IV, her son by Humphrey III, and husband to Isabella of Jerusalem*

Reginald, Lord of Sidon

The lordships of Beirut, Sidon, Botron, Gibelet, Jubail, Scandelion, Nazareth, Haifa, Caymont, Caesarea, Bethsan, Arsur, Blanchgarde, Bethgibelin, and Hebron existed historically, so reference to lords of these baronies is accurate, although details of names and personalities are lacking.

Members of the Militant Orders and Church Leaders

Odo de St. Amand, Grand Master of the Knights Templar, 1171-1179
Arnold de Toroga, Grand Master of the Knights Templar, 1179-1184
Gerard de Ridefort, Grand Master of the Knights Templar, 1184-1189
Roger des Moulins, Grand Master of the Knights Hospitaller, 1177-1187
Heraclius, Archbishop of Caesarea and Patriarch of Jerusalem, 1180-1190
Sister Adela, a Hospitaller nun

Saracens

Salah ad-Din Yusuf, Sultan of Egypt and Damascus
Al-Adil, Salah ad-Din's brother
Farrukh-Shah, Salah ad-Din's nephew
Al-Afdal, the eldest of Salah ad-Din's seventeen sons
Husam al-Din Lu'lu, admiral and emir

Other Characters of Note

Ibrahim, a slave serving the King of Jerusalem
Godwin Olafsen, a Norse armorer

The Ibelin Family in the 12th Century

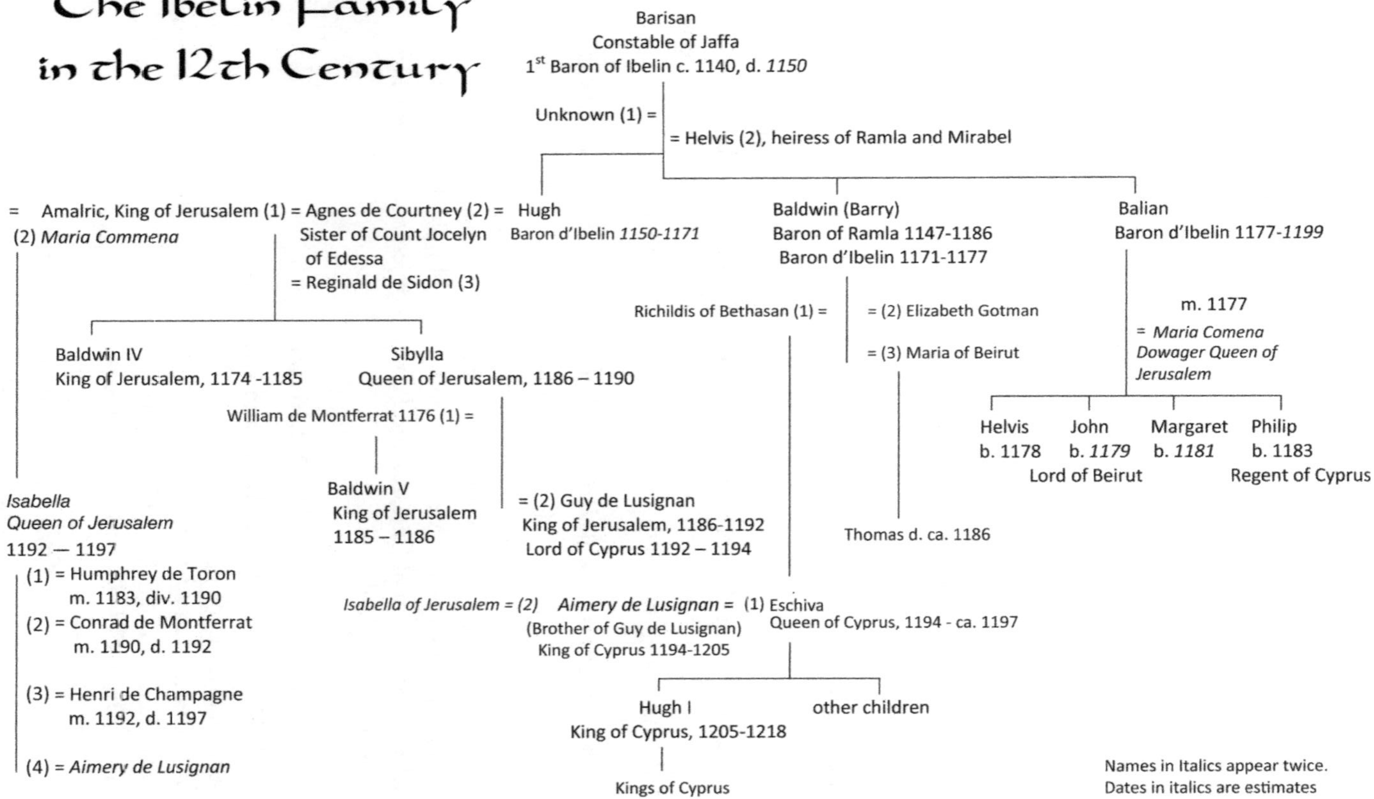

Kings/Queens of Jerusalem 1131 – 1212

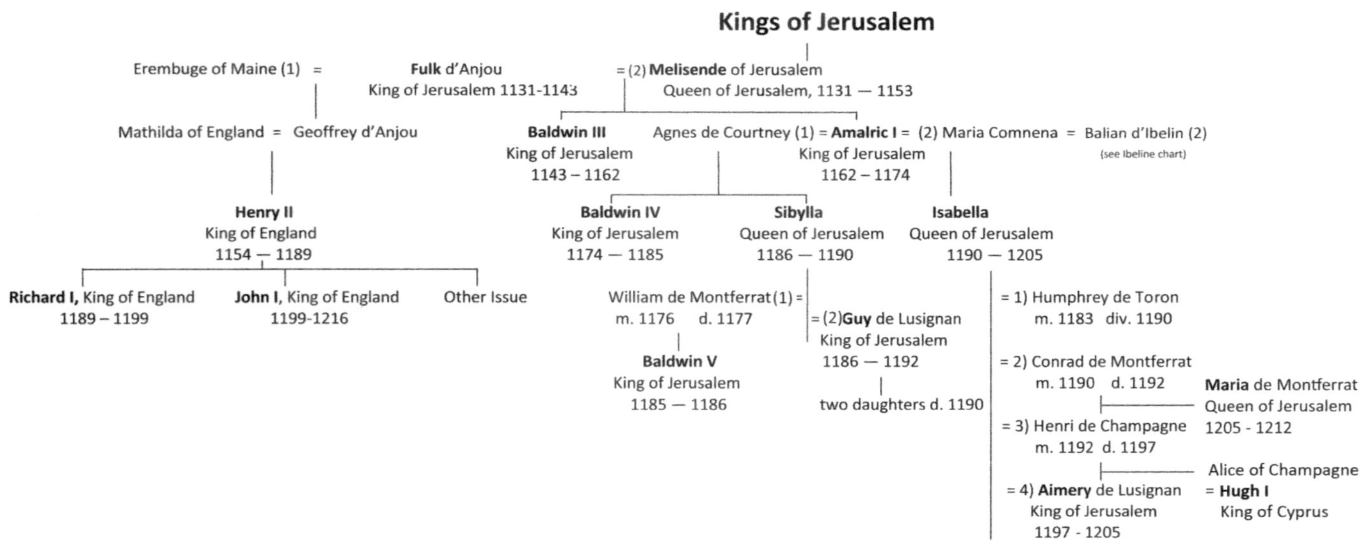

Names in bold are ruling monarchs

The Greek (Byzantine) Emperors in the 12th Century

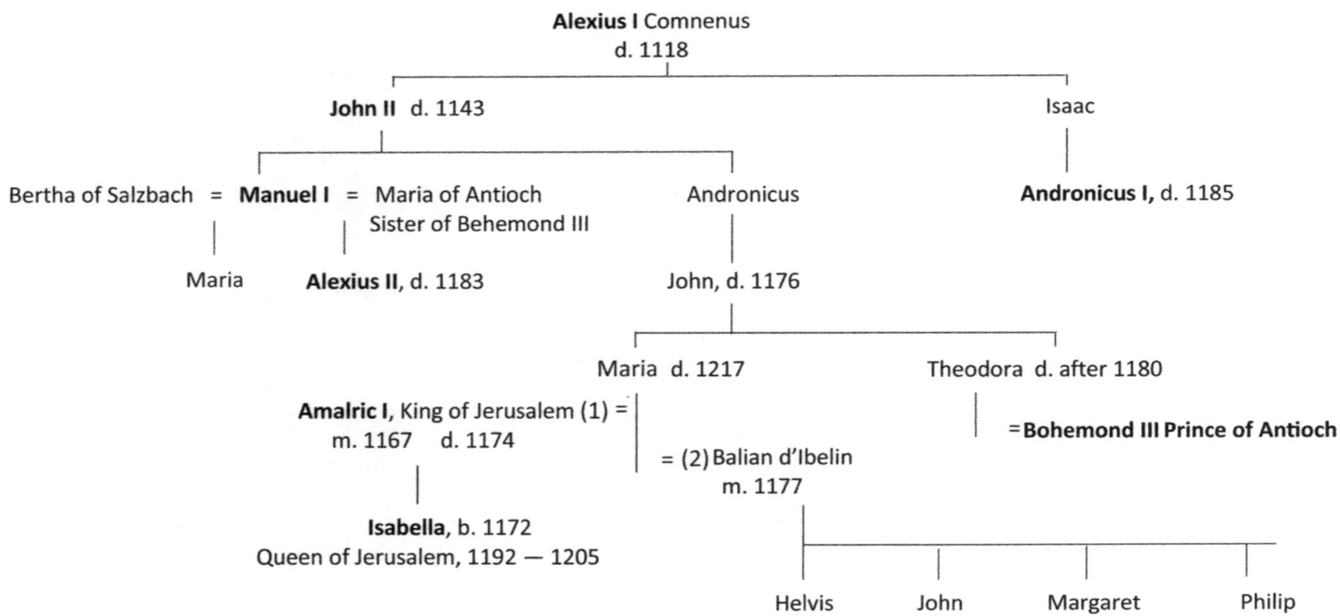

Names in bold are ruling monarchs

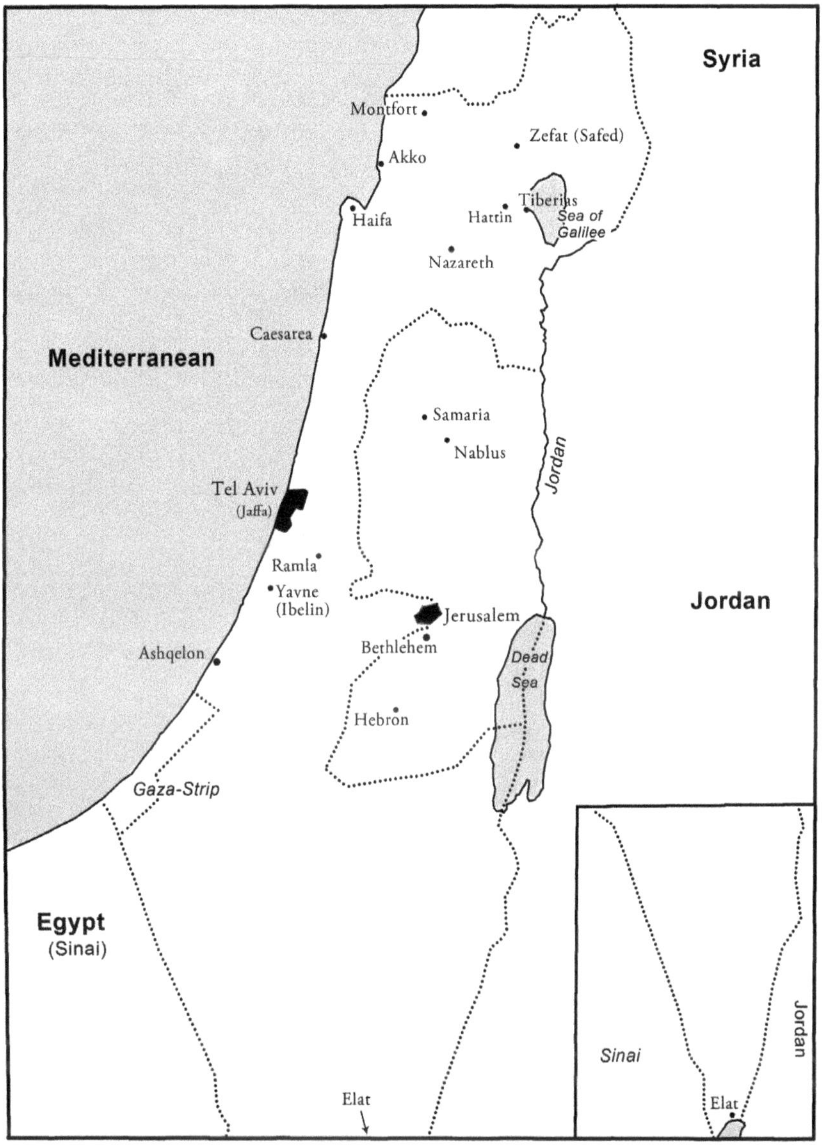

Map of the Holy Land Today (Modern Israel)

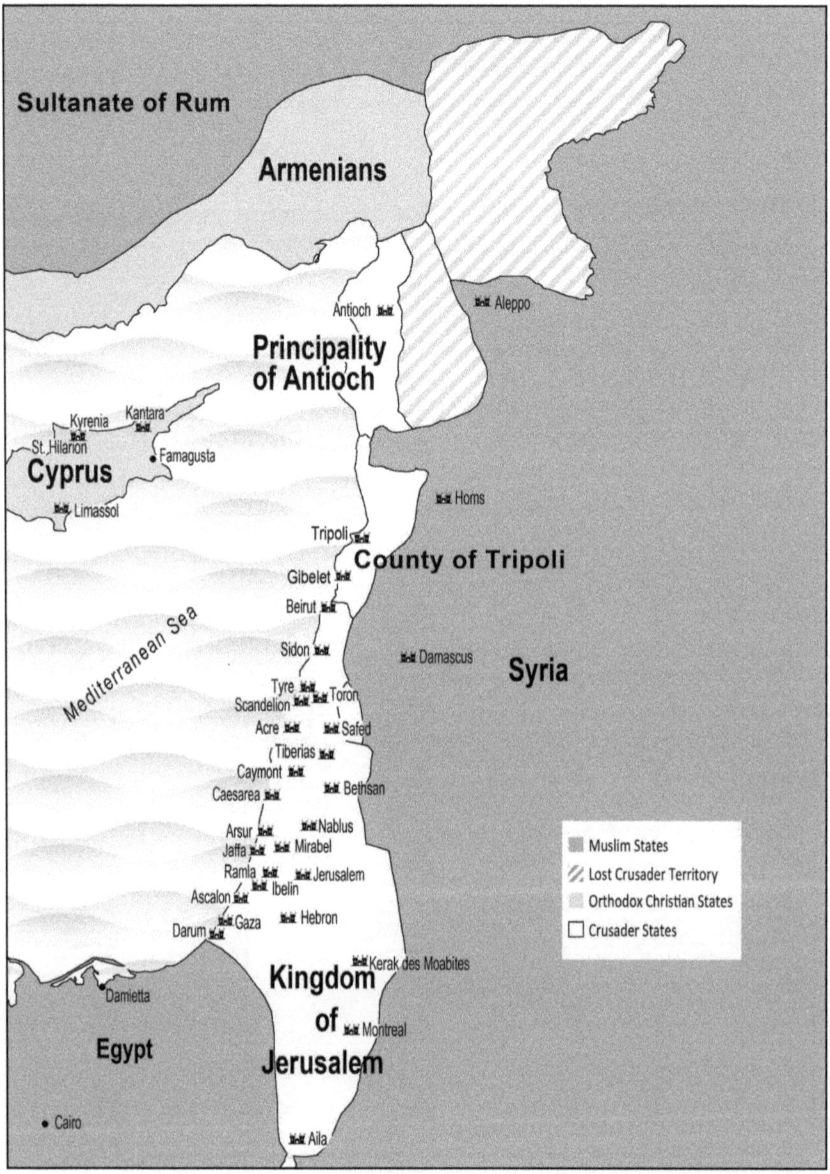

Kingdom of Jerusalem

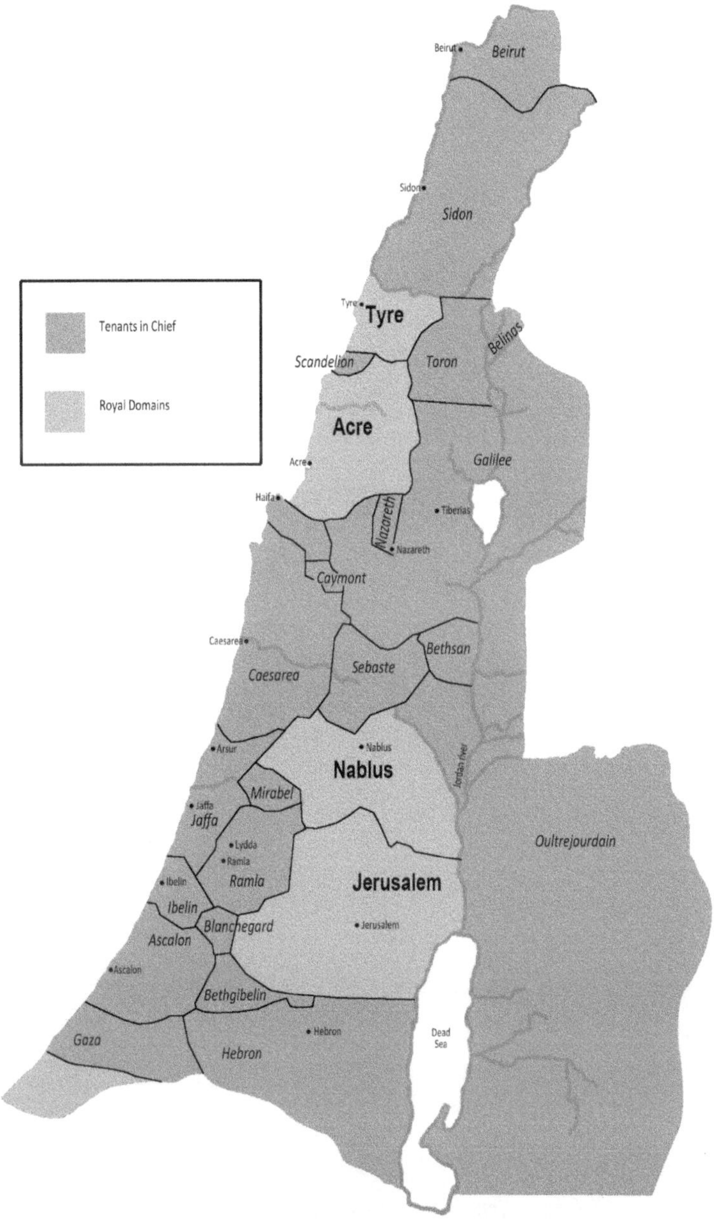

Baronies of Jerusalem

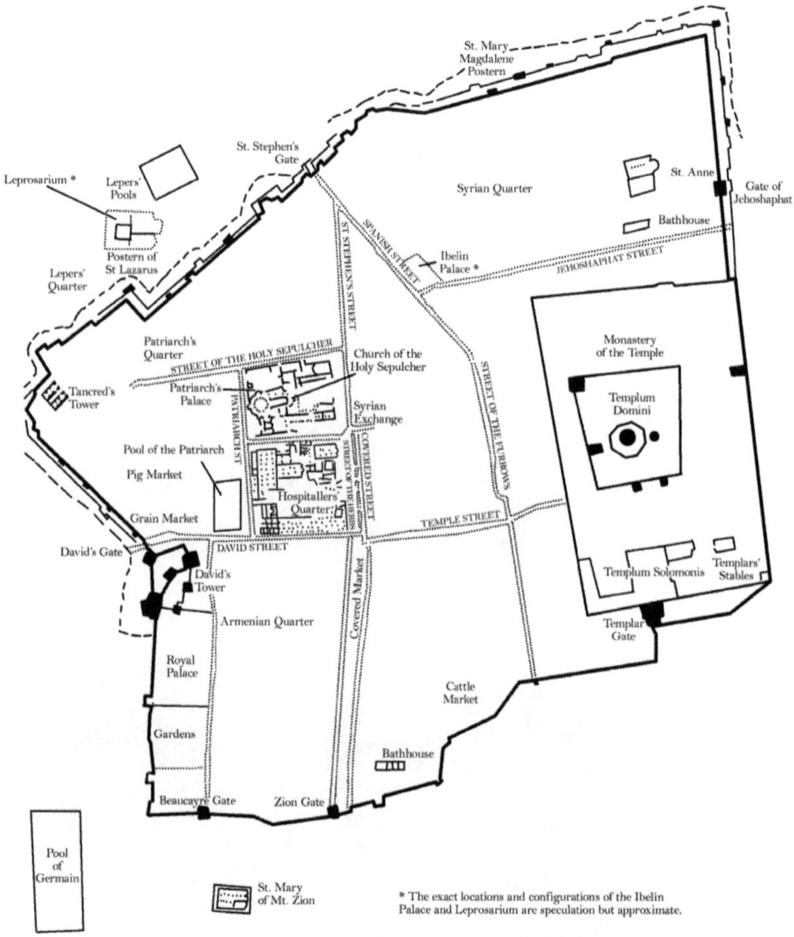

City of Jerusalem in the Twelfth Century

Introduction and Acknowledgments

THIS IS THE SECOND BOOK IN a three-part biographical novel of the historical figure Balian d'Ibelin, based on the known facts about his life. The first volume was published under the title *Knight of Jerusalem* and covered the period 1171–1177.

The historical Balian was born in the mid-eleventh century in the Christian Kingdom of Jerusalem. He was the younger son of the first Baron of Ibelin, and as such did not inherit land or title. Volume I of this biographical novel describes how Balian, as a landless knight, seeks his fortune at the court of King Amalric I of Jerusalem. The King offers him the dubious honor of serving in the household of Prince Baldwin, a boy afflicted with leprosy. Balian accepts the post, and thereby becomes one of the few friends of the isolated prince. In this capacity he meets Queen Maria Comnena of Jerusalem, a young Greek princess who is King Amalric's second wife, but their relationship is formal and platonic.

When King Amalric dies unexpectedly, the leper boy is crowned King Baldwin IV, but so long as he is a minor little changes except that the widowed Queen Maria retires to a convent. In 1176, however, on reaching the age of fifteen, Baldwin takes over the government of his realm, dismissing the Regent Raymond Count of Tripoli and welcoming back to his court his disgraced mother, Agnes de Courtenay, as well as his stepmother Maria Comnena. Balian is rewarded for his years of devoted service with the constableship of the city of Ascalon, and he takes over the defense of this vital border outpost. Here Queen

Maria seeks him out and they become lovers—but Balian, conscious of his lowly status, does not believe they could ever receive the necessary permission from the King for a marriage.

In November 1177 the Kurdish leader, Salah ad-Din, who has seized control in both Cairo and Damascus, invades the Kingdom of Jerusalem from the south and marches on Ascalon. King Baldwin rides with 376 knights (according to contemporary chronicles) to relieve Ascalon and is immediately trapped in the city by the overwhelming numbers of the enemy. When the King realizes, however, that Salah ad-Din has taken the bulk of his army farther north, apparently heading for Jerusalem itself, he sorties out of Ascalon and joins forces with the Templars from Gaza. Although the towns of Lydda and Ibelin (historically Ramla) are sacked, on November 24 Frankish forces overtake Salah ad-Din and decisively defeat him at the Battle of Montgisard. Salah ad-Din has to flee on a camel, and almost all his troops are killed or captured. Balian and his elder brother play a decisive role in this critical battle.

Meanwhile, Queen Maria has become pregnant and Balian, unwilling to let his child be born a bastard, is forced to request permission from the King to marry Maria, expecting that he and the Dowager Queen will instead be forced to flee to her family in Constantinople. King Baldwin, however, loves Balian well and approves the marriage. Furthermore, he puts pressure on Balian's elder brother to transfer the comparatively insignificant barony of Ibelin to Balian in exchange for permission to set aside his blameless wife, Richildis. In May 1178, Maria gives birth to a daughter, Helvis.

Thus at the end of Volume I, Balian is no longer a landless knight but Baron of Ibelin, husband of the Dowager Queen of Jerusalem, and father of his first child. This volume opens in June 1178.

I wish to thank my test readers for their careful and constructive criticism of the draft manuscript, my editor Christy Dickson for her meticulous and professional editing, and Mikhail Greuli for his inspired cover!

Helena P. Schrader
Addis Ababa
2015

Defender of Jerusalem was awarded "Silver" for Christian Historical Fiction in the Readers' Favorite Book Awards 2016. It won "Silver" for Spiritual/Religious Fiction in the Feathered Quill Literary Awards 2016. It placed "Best in Category" for Historical Fiction set in the Dark/Middle Ages in the 2015 Chaucer Awards. It was a finalist for the M.M. Bennetts' Award for Historical Fiction 2015, and was a B.R.A.G. Medallion Honoree.

Helena P. Schrader,
October, 2016

Chapter 1

Jerusalem, June 1178

"Jerusalem is dying," the Patriarch murmured in a low, grave voice, pitched not to carry beyond the man he was addressing. The gold-encrusted robes of office seemed too heavy for the frail old man, causing him to stand hunched over. So many rings adorned his gnarled fingers that the one with the crosses of Jerusalem was all but lost among the shine and gleam of the others.

"That's why I came," the man answered vigorously. The speaker, Balian d'Ibelin, was exceptionally tall, dark-haired and well tanned. He was not yet thirty and was dressed for riding in leather hose and boots, a hauberk of chain mail, and a marigold-colored cotton surcoat emblazoned with the red crosses paté of Ibelin. Beside him his slender wife, swathed in flowing white gauze to protect her from the Palestinian sun, waited anxiously. Both were coated in dust from the road.

"Yes, it is good for the High Court to gather," the Patriarch conceded, with a glance to the other men waiting in the anteroom to the King's chambers.

"I wish to see His Grace," Ibelin insisted.

The Patriarch shook his head firmly. "That's not possible. He has been shriven."

"It's no use, Ibelin," Raymond, Count of Tripoli and former Regent of the realm, interposed, pushing himself off the window seat facing the inner courtyard of the royal palace. "We've all been denied access." He gestured toward the men in the room, all of whom were important barons: the Constable Humphrey de Toron; the King's maternal uncle, seneschal of the Kingdom and titular Count of Edessa, Joscelin de Courtenay; and the lords of Hebron, Caesarea, Jubail, and

Caymont. "Your brother was here earlier, but he too was turned away. He was in no mood to wait."

Ibelin did not answer. He could well imagine that his older brother, Baron of Ramla and Mirabel and known to his family as "Barry," had not wanted to wait. Barry was not a patient man. Instead of answering, Ibelin led his wife to a large carved chest, where she could sit down and unwrap the veils that had protected her face from the burning sun. Automatically the men in the room turned to watch her, enjoying absently the beauty of her well-proportioned face. From the day she had arrived at the court of Jerusalem as the bride of the then King, Amalric I, her classical Greek beauty had aroused admiration. She was a princess of the Imperial Greek family, Maria Zoë Comnena.

Her expression now was worried. "Who has given the orders to isolate the King from his most important counselors?" she asked. "His doctors?"

"Ah," Tripoli opened with a cynical smile, his eyes reflecting admiration for the Dowager Queen's ability to slice to the heart of the matter. "No, not his doctors." He paused before adding in a sour tone: "His mother."

Queen Maria Zoë drew in her breath and held it, but her eyes glinted with indignation. There was arguably no one in the world she hated more than her first husband's first wife, the mother of the now dying King, Agnes de Courtenay.

"My sister has only the best interests of my beloved nephew at heart," the Count of Edessa hastened to rebuff the unspoken accusation that hung in the room. Edessa was an empty title. The county had been lost to the Saracens almost half a century earlier, and Joscelin had distinguished himself only by gorging himself both literally (on sweets) and figuratively (on the royal treasury) ever since his nephew had appointed him Seneschal of Jerusalem. He was only in his early forties, but he was both balding and flabby.

"No doubt," Tripoli agreed with sarcasm before adding caustically, "As we can see by the fact that she's kept *you* away from him."

Queen Maria Zoë looked down to mask her smile, but Ibelin frowned slightly, while Edessa spluttered in indignation and the aging Constable Humphrey de Toron made reproving noises in his throat.

"Excuse me," Ibelin broke in. "We've been riding since daybreak. I need to seek out a privy."

The others nodded absently as he withdrew, and Tripoli turned to the Dowager Queen. "You should not have risked such an arduous journey so shortly out of childbed, my lady, although you look the picture of health," he noted honestly and admiringly. His own wife was much older and would not have been up to the exertion. "Your daughter is well?"

"Yes," the Dowager Queen answered proudly; the disappointment of giving birth to a daughter had faded rapidly in light of her husband Balian's delight. If he did not care, why should she? "We've named her Helvis, after my lord husband's mother."

Beyond the door Ibelin made his way not to the closest garderobe, but to the large gardens that backed up against the southern wall of the royal palace. The gardens were enclosed by the massive city wall to the west and a tall protective but not defensible wall to the east and south. Ibelin had served for five years in the royal household and knew the royal palace intimately—including the fact that there was a narrow stairwell that led directly down from the King's apartments to the garden. The dog-toothed, pointed arch over the door to this stairwell opened in the northwest corner of the garden, nearly hidden behind three tall cypress trees that stretched heavenwards.

Ibelin made his way to this door and tried it. To his relief, it was not locked. He slipped inside the stairwell and closed the door behind him. Here he stood for several seconds, letting his eyes adjust to the dark. Then he started up the stairs, feeling his way by using the tip of his boot to find the next step, one at a time. Eventually he reached the landing and found the door with his hand by feeling for the wood set firmly in the stone frame. He found the iron handle and pushed down on it. The handle moved but the door did not budge; it was locked.

He knocked firmly. As expected, there was no answer, but after a pause he knocked again.

"Is someone there?" an anxious voice asked through the door.

Ibelin felt a surge of relief; the voice was familiar. It belonged to Ibrahim, the Syrian slave who had served the King almost his entire life.

Ibelin leaned toward the wooden door and spoke in a low voice. "It's me, Balian d'Ibelin."

"Lord Balian? Allahu Akbar!" The key turned in the lock and the door opened to reveal the old slave in his long kaftan and Muslim skullcap, bowing over his hands in welcome. The room behind him was in shadow. All the shutters had been closed over the windows, although the intensity of the afternoon sun ensured that it was not really dark. At this time of year, the shade could not entirely block out the heat, either, and without fresh air the temperature was stifling. The room smelled badly, too—of sweat and medicine and stale air.

"I came as soon as I received word the King was ill, but I was denied access—"

Ibrahim silenced him by holding a long, elegant finger to his lips. "I understand," he assured Ibelin. "His mother guards him jealously, but he has asked for you. He will be pleased—no, grateful—that you have come. Only—" Ibrahim looked anxiously over his shoulder toward the large four-poster bed, enclosed in heavy damask curtains,"he is—is losing consciousness. Or rather, it comes and goes. Sometimes he seems to know what is going on around him. At other times he is oblivious. And other times still, he sees things we do not. He has spoken to his father as if he were in the room with him. And once he reared up in his bed and gasped out: 'My lord, I am unworthy to be the defender of Your tomb'—as if he thought the Prophet Jesus stood in front of him."

"Let me see him, Ibrahim, whatever state he's in—before I am discovered and tossed out again by Dame Agnes."

Ibrahim nodded and turned to lead the way to the bed. He stepped up on the raised platform on which the bed stood and leaned through the curtains to whisper gently, "Your grace, Lord Balian has come."

"Balian?" The voice was so weak and dry—almost dusty—that the sound of it wrenched Balian's heart.

Ibrahim simply stood back with a smile and gestured Ibelin forward.

Ibelin stepped up onto the platform and leaned over the bed. It was overflowing with cushions and comforters, the latter ridiculous in the summer heat, and the King lay on top of all, wearing only a thin cotton nightshirt. Even so he was sweating visibly, and his hands and feet, naked of bandages, were discolored. The fingers of his right hand were starting to deform as the leprosy consumed them, and he had lost several of his toes, so his feet were stubby and misshapen. His face, while untouched by the disease, was deathly pale and almost skeletal. His lips were chapped and dry and his eyes were sunken in their sockets, but they sought out Balian's face as if they wanted to consume it. "Balian!"

"Your grace—"

"Call me Baldwin, like you used to."

"Baldwin. Queen Maria Zoë and I came as soon as we heard you were ill."

The ghost of a smile wafted over the King's face and his head lifted very slightly, as if he were trying to see beyond Balian. "Is Tante Marie here?"

"She is in the anteroom. They would not let us pass. I came up from the garden, but I left her there as a diversion."

Baldwin's head shifted on the pillow: a nod of understanding, acceptance. "Balian, I—I think I'm dying."

Balian could see the fear in the young King's eyes and heard it in his whisper, too. He tried to reassure his former pupil and protégé. "You have nothing to fear, Baldwin. Christ is waiting to receive you into his arms."

"I—I—I'm not sure. Jerusalem—so many have—died—suffered—" Baldwin's head began to roll from side to side, his breathing coming with obvious difficulty.

Balian tried to calm him. He reached out his hand and laid it on Baldwin's sweat-soaked shoulder. "It's all right, Baldwin. The barons of Jerusalem know their duty. We will not fail Jerusalem."

"Sibylla—is not strong. Not like—Tante Marie." For a fragile instant, Baldwin almost seemed to smile at the comparison. "Tante—a Queen."

"Yes, she is every inch a queen," Balian answered proudly; at times like these he still found it hard to grasp the generosity of God and this king in giving him such a high-born bride. He did not see that he deserved a dowager queen, but he was grateful that God had seen things differently.

"You will—recognize—Sibylla—" Was that an order or a question?

Either way, the answer was the same: "Yes, Baldwin."

"Burgundy," Baldwin gasped out, baffling Ibelin, who looked to Ibrahim. Was he asking for Burgundy wine?

Ibrahim was waiting, but not with wine. He had a cloth dipped in cool water and he wiped the sweat from the King's face, then offered him chilled water from a silver chalice.

Baldwin had to lift his head to sip, and this seemed to exhaust him. He sank back into the pillows, but his hollow eyes sought out Balian. "Tell—Tante Marie—love her."

"Yes." Balian looked at Ibrahim and the older man nodded. It was time to go. "You are in our prayers, Baldwin."

Already the lids had fallen over Baldwin's eyes and his breathing was deep but labored.

Ibelin drew back and stepped down from the platform supporting the bed. He turned to Ibrahim with a sincere but subdued "thank you." It was hard to see Baldwin like this, and Balian now felt certain this was the last time he would see Baldwin alive.

"I thank *you*, my lord," Ibrahim answered with a deep bow. "If—if a slave may ask a favor?"

"Of course."

"When—when it is over. Would you have a place in your household for an old man?"

"Of course!" Ibelin reached out a hand and laid it on the old man's shoulder. "You have a home at Ibelin, Ibrahim." He glanced toward the bed. "Whenever it is time."

Ibrahim went down on his knees and bowed his head to the ground. "Thank you, my lord. Thank you."

Balian reached down to help him back to his feet. "Come. None of that. We have been through too much together. But now I must go."

Ibrahim nodded and started for the door to unlock and hold it for the Baron of Ibelin. He turned the key and stepped back to let Ibelin into the darkness of the stairwell. Just as Balian crossed the threshold, a rasping voice cried out from the bed; whether the King was calling to Ibelin or was simply speaking in delirium was not clear. But the words were clear. "Jerusalem!" he cried out. "Must defend Jerusalem!"

"Your son commands your presence, madame," the doctor murmured in a low voice, bending close to speak directly into the ear of the King's mother, Agnes de Courtenay.

The Queen Mother had dozed off during her night-long vigil and started when the doctor's voice dragged her from her sleep. She struggled to right herself and looked hard into the doctor's weary face. He was a highly respected physician, trained at universities in both West and East, and quite elderly now. His younger assistants hovered in the background, dressed in the black robes and caps of their profession. "Is he . . . ?"

"He is lucid, madame, and asked to see you and the Marquise de Montferrat." The doctor nodded in the direction of Princess Sibylla, who was in the chair beside her mother, also struggling to wake up.

"Will he live?" Princess Sibylla asked anxiously. The dark circles under her eyes and the splotches of pimples on her face were testimony to her vigil at her brother's bedside.

"The fever appears to be receding," the doctor answered carefully, "and I think the worst is over for the moment. However, he is much weakened, and we cannot know yet what impact this will have on the leprosy."

"Dear God!" Agnes crossed herself, regretting her past—all her vanities, infidelities, and intrigues. Maybe if she hadn't been such a selfish and greedy woman, her son might not have been so afflicted. . . .

As long as she had been banned from court, Agnes had given little thought to the son her husband had taken away from her and raised as his own. She had not even been terribly interested in him after his father's death; he had appeared no more than Tripoli's puppet then. But after Baldwin came of age, welcomed her to his court, and gave her a place of honor, Agnes started to care about her offspring. Slowly she had overcome her aversion and fear of his disease—and now, after two years, she faced the astonishing fact that she had come to love him. She had had three husbands and twice that many lovers, but none of them meant as much to her anymore as the little finger of her son's hand.

"Come, Sibylla," Agnes urged her daughter as she pulled herself to her feet.

Sibylla was eighteen and already a widow. Her husband William Marquis de Montferrat had died of malaria before they had been married a year, and the son of their union had been born after his father's death. While Agnes had been sexually attractive in her youth and the object of male desire, Sibylla's charms were considerably more common. She was buxom and blond, but her features lacked elegance and her lips were too wide, her eyes too closely set. She looked particularly poorly at the moment with unkempt hair and naked of rouge, and she rose with trepidation.

It wasn't just her profound fear of leprosy or the shadow of death that made Sibylla reluctant to face her brother. It was also a sense of guilt. In the last two days, when it looked as if her brother might die, she had remembered all the times she had thrown temper tantrums, screamed and cried, or simply ignored his wishes or rejected his requests. He had always forgiven her, but Sibylla found it very hard to forgive herself.

The sight of his body servant, the Muslim slave Ibrahim, bending over Baldwin and wiping sweat from his face, only added to her discomfort. Ibrahim had been the witness to a stupid scene, shortly after her son's birth, when she had screamed at her brother that she would never marry again—arguing that she had done her duty to Jerusalem by giving birth to Montferrat's posthumous son. Now she knew that her brother's illness had taken a turn for the worse shortly before she had confronted him. Ibrahim had tried to tell her that, but she had struck him and ordered him to be silent. The sight of him now—and the accusing look he sent her with his dark eyes—only made her more agitated.

Agnes de Courtenay stepped on to the sideboard of the bed, and she reached out for her son's hand. He was not wearing gloves while in bed, but his hands and arms had been bandaged past the elbows.

Baldwin turned his head to look at her when she took his hand between both of hers. "Mama," he whispered.

"Sibylla's here, too. The doctor said you wanted to see us."

Baldwin nodded and tried to sit up straighter. Ibrahim at once set down the silver bowl with the linen cloths he used to wipe away King Baldwin's sweat and gripped his master under his left arm to help him sit up. He pounded and folded the cushions behind the King's back until they gave the invalid better support, and then re-wet the linen facecloth in water to wipe away the sweat streaming down his master's face.

Sibylla held the ends of her veils over her mouth and nose in horror. The room stank horribly—a mixture of bedpans, sweat, and medicine. But even worse than the smell was the sight of her brother: his blond hair hung in limp, greasy strands around his pale face, and he had a rash of pimples on his neck below his right ear and isolated pimples on his forehead and beside his nose. He had always been such a beautiful boy. . . .

"We need to discuss the succession," Baldwin rasped, shattering her thoughts.

"Not now," his mother protested. "The doctor said the worst is over."

"Only temporarily," Baldwin countered. "I could fall ill again at any time. We need to discuss the succession *now*." His gaze shifted to his sister. "Sibylla, the year of mourning is over. It is time to find you a new husband."

Sibylla nodded earnestly, remembering her cruel words in this very room six months ago. "Of course, Baldwin," she assured him.

"I promised you I would not make you marry against your wishes," Baldwin continued. Sibylla felt tears welling up in her eyes and closing her throat—because he had indeed promised this, although she didn't deserve it. "You know, too," her brother continued in his rasping voice, "that the Kingdom is in great peril, surrounded as we are by the forces of a man who has—against all the odds—managed to put down every rebellion against him and now controls Egypt and most of Syria. You know how weak we are."

Sibylla nodded as the tears slipped out of her eyes and started down her face.

"Will you, for the sake of Jerusalem, take the Duke of Burgundy as your husband?" Baldwin asked her, his eyes fixed on her face.

Sibylla nodded. "Yes, Baldwin, I will," she announced firmly.

"Even though it makes you cry?" Baldwin asked, his voice gentle and his expression sad at the sight of his sister's misery.

Sibylla shook her head. "I'm not crying for myself, or because of the marriage. I'm crying to see you so miserable!" She half choked on a sob at this admission, and Agnes removed one hand from her son's to put an arm around her daughter's shoulders.

"By all reports, he is a good and comely man," Baldwin assured her.

Sibylla nodded, wiping her tears with the ends of her veils. "He wrote me a lovely letter. Very courtly and fine." She was not lying. The Duke of Burgundy, unlike the Count of Flanders, had made a point of writing to the bride that came with the Kingdom, and he had done it very well. He had been polite and respectful, but hinted too at hope for "true affection" and "conjugal contentment." Sibylla was truly not opposed to this alliance. The Dukes of Burgundy, after all, were very rich and powerful; this was no insult, as Flanders' obscure candidate had been.

"You are certain?" Baldwin pressed his sister.

She nodded firmly. "Yes. I am certain."

"Then we must send for the Chancellor so that an embassy to Burgundy can be commissioned and provided with the necessary documents—"

"This can wait until you are a little stronger," Agnes tried to protest again, but Baldwin shook his head firmly.

"I may never get stronger," he countered, and gestured for Ibrahim to send a page for the Chancellor. "From now on," he continued to his mother and sister, "we will add Sibylla's names on charters, and she must be seen at my side during state occasions. Even before Burgundy arrives to take up the role of consort, people must get used to recognizing Sibylla as the rightful heir to Jerusalem."

Agnes tightened her hold on her son's hand as she realized the significance of what he was doing, but Baldwin couldn't feel her grip. "My dear boy," she murmured, "my dear boy."

Jerusalem, August 1178

"When was the last time you were at court?" Reynald de Châtillon, Lord of Oultrejourdain, barked at his household knight Henri d'Ibelin. Châtillon was no longer young, and certainly no longer the handsome man who had seduced the Princess of Antioch into a marriage. Fifteen years in a Saracen dungeon had left their mark, and since his release Oultrejourdain had adopted the custom of shaving his head completely, rather than be reminded of the lice that had once crawled in his unkempt mane.

"A long time ago," Henri admitted vaguely, breathless with trying to keep up with his lord as he pounded up the steps of the Tower of David two at a time.

"The King has been deathly ill and they say the leprosy is spreading again, but don't underestimate him," Oultrejourdain warned. "He's got more balls than Tripoli, Antioch, and the pack of them put together."

Henri wasn't entirely sure who belonged to "the pack," but he guessed pretty much everyone who wasn't one of Oultrejourdain's own men. Which meant both his surviving elder brothers, of course. Henri had been raised by his mother and stepfather after his father's death, while his brothers had remained at Ibelin. His relationship to them was, in consequence, far from close. The eldest, Hugh, had never been more than a name, and he was dead. The second, Barisan "Barry" of Ramla and Mirabel, was the object of intense resentment, because he had kept the entire paternal and maternal inheritance for himself on Hugh's death. Balian was the only one that Henri had any affection for, and that was tepid at best. Balian seemed to be Barry's lap dog most of the time—an impression reinforced by the fact that Barry had been persuaded (under considerable pressure from the King, it was said) to give Balian the smallest and poorest of his three baronies, that of Ibelin, after his spectacular marriage to the Dowager Queen. That marriage was now a barrier between them; Henri bitterly envied his brother such a wealthy, well-connected, and beautiful bride.

Oultrejourdain had reached the landing and paused only long enough to cursorily brush some dust off his surcoat and kick mud off the soles of his boots. Then he strode into the vaulted chamber of the ancient tower with Henri in his wake.

Henri scanned the crowd for anyone he knew and noted that except for the Bishop of Bethlehem, the clergy was conspicuously absent. On the other hand, damn near the entire High Court was assembled here, including both his brothers. Barry, as always, cut a fine figure, in chain mail trimmed with bronze and a surcoat bearing the arms of Ramla quartered with those of Mirabel, both edged in gold thread. He wore his blond hair longer than was fashionable, almost to his shoulders, and he had a mustache that drooped to the bottom of his chin. He was hale and hearty—and he avoided Henri's eye.

Balian was smaller and darker, a shadow of his more flamboyant elder brother, but Henri could sense the change in him now that he was a baron in his own right and had access to the revenues of wealthy Nablus through his royal wife. Balian might dress more modestly, but he was a force to be reckoned with. And he did not avoid Henri's eyes.

As their eyes met across the room, they exchanged nods. No more than that. No pretense of joy or affection, just an acknowledgement of the other's presence—and the blood tie that neither of them could alter. Blood is thicker than water, Henri told himself, content to think that whatever happened, he could count on Balian honoring that fact, even if arrogant Barry did not!

Oultrejourdain had reached the throne, and he dropped heavily on his right knee to bow his head to his sovereign. "Your grace!" his voice boomed out as it always did. "You sent for me."

As he straightened from his own bow, Henri had a chance to study the King.

Baldwin wasn't a pretty boy anymore. He was seventeen, Henri calculated, and he was suffering from acne that badly disfigured his face. Henri sympathized because, unlike his more fortunate elder brothers, he'd suffered from the same condition during puberty. The King, furthermore, looked slighter and less healthy than he had two years ago, apparently the result of his recent illness—or because he was growing faster than he could put on muscle, since he could not partake in the usual sports of hunting or jousting.

"My lord of Oultrejourdain, we wanted your advice along with that of our other tenants-in-chief," the King answered. "Come!" The King rose and led Oultrejourdain across the room to a table set up before the glazed window overlooking the street. On this table was spread a large and detailed map showing the crusader states and their immediate neighbors of Armenia, Syria, and Egypt. The cities were marked by little icons depicting walls, castles by pictures of crenelated towers, ports by miniature ships, and so on.

As the King led Oultrejourdain to the map, the other men in the room converged on it as well. Henri stood in the second row, but he still had a good view. "My lords," the King addressed them all, "unto our hands has been given the sacred task of defending the Holy Land."

A murmur of "Amen" went through the crowd, and several of the men crossed themselves.

"I want your advice on how we can best accomplish that task in face of the ever-growing strength of our enemy."

Almost before he had finished speaking, Oultrejourdain spoke up. "The best defense is a good offense, your grace."

"Don't be ridiculous," Tripoli tried to cut him short. Tripoli had been Regent during the King's minority, and furthermore was the wealthiest and most powerful nobleman in the Kingdom. Indeed, the County of Tripoli was only nominally subject to the King at all, and his position was somewhat analogous to Henry II and King Louis of France, with Tripoli in many ways more powerful than his liege. Nevertheless, he fell silent when the King held up his hand for silence and nodded to Oultrejourdain to continue.

"This Kingdom only exists today because our forefathers were prepared to fight for their faith no less vigorously than their Muslim enemies. We stand today in the Tower of David because they did not hesitate to strike, *despite* their few numbers. Our forefathers liberated Jerusalem by taking the offensive, not the defensive," Oultrejourdain reminded the assembled barons.

"A hundred years ago it was possible to take one city at a time, because the authority of the caliphs had crumbled to impotence and Sunni fought Shia. Indeed, every Seljuk prince was fighting with his brothers, cousins, and neighbors—only too anxious to make peace with us if we would help him against his kin. Today, Salah ad-Din controls his territories with grim efficiency and rules through his brothers and nephews, who are slavishly loyal to him," the elegant Tripoli countered condescendingly. There was no love lost between Tripoli and Oultrejourdain.

"Exactly! And Salah ad-Din has vowed to drive us into the sea! He has mobilized fanatics among his followers, who preach *jihad* in the mosques at Friday prayers. These are not men you can reason with, my lords; they are men who want to die for Islam because they believe it will bring them faster to heaven."

"Fifteen years in a Saracen dungeon has understandably embittered you, my lord," Tripoli sneered at Oultrejourdain, "and apparently they have also blinded you to the fact that our enemies are men like us: with ambitions but also fears, and above all an acute appreciation of their self-interest. They can most certainly be treated with. The history of this Kingdom is a history of treaties with various Muslim leaders."

"Yes, that too—when it suits them. But why should they treat with us, if they think us weak? Have you forgotten that Jerusalem is the most sacred place in Christendom? Here Christ died for our sins and rose again from the dead to offer us a means to our salvation. And what is it to the Muslims? Did their Prophet live or die here? Did he even set foot here? No! He had a *dream*—or claimed to have a dream—of rising to heaven from here!" Oultrejourdain scoffed.

"Get to the point," Tripoli snapped.

"The point, my lord," Oultrejourdain sneered back at his peer, "is that despite its only secondary importance to them, the Saracens will not let us live here in peace, because they feel strong enough to push us out." Reynald de Châtillon, former Prince of Antioch and now Lord of Oultrejourdain, took a step forward and stabbed his finger on the map at a point far south of the Kingdom of Jerusalem to underline his point. "Mecca!" he told his fellow barons, "Mecca is the holiest city of Islam. If we held Mecca, do you think they would care about Jerusalem?"

Oultrejourdain's suggestion produced an uproar. Not only Tripoli but most of the other barons erupted into protest. Tripoli called the parvenu Châtillon mad, while the Lords of Sidon and Beirut remonstrated that they didn't have the means to defend themselves, much less attack and seize a city a thousand miles away.

Châtillon silenced them all with a sharp gesture of his hand and an incisive: "Of course we can't take Mecca—at least not today or in the foreseeable future. But we can make the *Muslim* pilgrim routes unsafe—just as Muslims for so long threatened and harassed Christian pilgrims. Furthermore, in so doing, we can force Salah ad-Din to look to his rear. We can put *him* on the defensive and thereby end his dreams of destroying us. In short, we attack him where *he* is weak."

"And in return, he will attack *us* where *we* are weak," Tripoli scoffed.

"Then let us build up our defenses—and then strike him," Oultrejourdain insisted. "Salah ad-Din is not invincible. King Baldwin sent him scampering back to Egypt like a stray dog with his tail between his legs at Montgisard!" Châtillon reminded them with a smile at the young King, who was listening avidly to the debate.

"Exactly what are you proposing, my lord?" the King asked eagerly, his eyes fixed keenly on Oultrejourdain, and his bearing buoyed up by the rough baron's flattery.

"I'm proposing that we launch a fleet of war galleys in the Red Sea and sink every pilgrim vessel we can lay our hands upon. We can raid the coastal towns for good measure, pillaging and burning at whim—since the cities have no walls and there are no Arab fighting ships in the Red Sea."

"The moment we do that, all of Islam will unite against us! They will bury their internal differences and fight with greater fanaticism than ever before." This time it was Reginald de Sidon, rather than Tripoli, who protested the loudest.

"First of all, they already *are* united against us—except for Aleppo and Mosul. Second, they conquered *our* Holy Land by the sword and demolished the most sacred shrine in Christendom—the Church of the Holy Sepulcher. Why shouldn't they taste a little of their own medicine?" Châtillon countered, adding: "The only thing the Turks respect is force!"

"I agree with you in theory," replied the distinguished but aging Constable of Jerusalem, Humphrey de Toron, "but we don't have the manpower for such an enterprise."

"And while you're getting slaughtered in the Red Sea by the Egyptians, the army of Damascus will sweep across the Jordan and pillage and burn its way to the sea," Tripoli added.

"The key to preventing that is here!" declared the burly and bearded Templar Grand Master Odo de St. Amand, stepping up to the table and stabbing a thick finger at the map. He pinpointed a place on the Upper Jordan between the Sea of Galilee and Lake Huleh. "This is Jacob's Ford," the Master intoned, "and it is the gateway to Galilee—only a day's ride from Damascus."

"Your castle of Safed is only ten miles southwest," the Hospitaller Master pointed out.

"Exactly! Ten miles too deep into our own territory. By the time the Saracens wash up against foothills below Safed, they have laid waste to some of the most fertile land in the Kingdom. If we could stop them here—on the Jordan—we could protect the entire valley."

"Before we start building anything new, we ought to look to the state of the defenses we already have. The walls of Jerusalem are no longer in the best condition," Humphrey de Toron pointed out. "And Castelneuf is also in poor repair. I have seen cracks as wide as my fist in some of the towers, and the entire drawbridge is rotting, along with the chain works for it and the portcullis."

The King started and asked, "Why did I not hear of this before?" But he did not wait for or expect an answer; he was not interested in who was to blame for hiding the state of his defenses, too conscious that it was his own weakness that had prevented him from seeing things for himself. Instead he continued in haste, "Those things must be repaired at once! I do not trust Salah ad-Din and I do not trust this truce. The Sultan is arming, and as soon as he has put down the rebellion in Baalbek, he will try to avenge his humiliation at Montgisard."

"Then let's support the revolt in Baalbek," Tripoli suggested, adding with a sneer in Oultrejourdain's direction, "It costs us much less to stir up internal troubles than to launch fleets five hundred miles across the desert!"

Before Châtillon could reply, King Baldwin interceded, "One action does not preclude the other, my lords." To Tripoli he added the question: "You are in contact with the rebels?" His raised eyebrows suggested he expected this was the case.

"I have lines of communication," Tripoli conceded.

"Then use them!" the young King ordered firmly, turning next to the aging Constable. "My lord, I am ashamed I did not know of weaknesses in our defenses. I trust that you will make an assessment of the cost of repairs and present the bill to me no later than the Feast of St. Helena. We will raise new taxes if necessary, but we must secure our existing defenses before undertaking anything new. Make no mistake, I am determined to keep the Holy Land safe for Christian settlers and Christian pilgrims. In face of the threat Salah ad-Din poses, we cannot afford to simply wait for him to attack." The King turned pointedly to the Templar Master. "A castle at Jacob's Ford makes sense to me. I wonder that we did not build it long ago."

"There were attempts in the past, your grace," Sidon admitted, "but the position is exposed and, as mentioned, it is only a day from Damascus. The Saracens can rapidly deploy troops that slaughter the workmen."

"Then the workmen must be protected by the army," the King concluded with the simplicity of youth. "How long will it take to build?" he asked, looking to the two Grand Masters of the militant orders; they had the most recent experience in castle building.

"That depends, of course, on the design and how many workmen are conscripted to build it," the Hospitaller Master demurred.

"Once the harvest is in, your grace, you could conscript every working man from Galilee and Bethsan. If we opt for a roughly quadratic design that makes use of the natural contours of the land," Odo de St. Amand had evidently already surveyed the site and given this matter considerable thought, "with towers at the corners and flanking the main gate, we could get the main fortress built in a six-month. The outer works—a larger perimeter wall with towers at suitable intervals—could take maybe another year. But the inner fortress with a strong garrison would be in a position to protect the workers on the perimeter wall."

"And the Templars are prepared to provide the manpower to defend this border outpost, Master?" the King pressed him with raised eyebrows.

"We are, your grace. Build me this castle, and I'll guarantee a garrison of five hundred men, including eighty knights."

There were some raised eyebrows at that: such a huge force sounded like bravado.

"What do you plan to do?" the Hospitaller challenged his rival. "Denude every other castle you have?"

"Hardly!" Odo de St. Amand scoffed. "Our commanderies in France, England, Provence, and Sicily are overflowing with recruits. If we send the word out now, before the end of the sailing season, recruits will flood the Holy Land come spring." No one wanted to dispute this assertion, because the Templars were riding a tidal wave of popularity in the West at the moment; there seemed no end to the number of fighting men there who longed to don the white mantles of the Temple and join their fight to defend the Holy Land.

"Then let it be done," King Baldwin intoned. "We will call up the workmen to build this castle once the harvest is in, and I will summon the feudal host to defend it. By next spring, when your recruits arrive, Master de St. Amand, a castle will be ready to receive them."

Jacob's Ford, April 1179

There had been far too little rain through the winter, and the drought that had started the previous year was intensifying. Just beyond the reach of irrigation from the Jordan, the land was parched and spread out like a gray-brown carpet devoid of life. The wind stirred up tiny cyclones that spiraled to the heavens, and the horizon was hazy with lingering dust from every passing caravan and every gust that blew the loose earth sideways.

The weather was exceptionally hot as well, the sun remorseless as it burned down on the laborers. Most worked wearing only a loincloth, and dirt clung to their sweating bodies.

The Baron of Ibelin, returning to the army camp protecting the construction site after almost a month's absence, was amazed by how much progress had been made in his absence. Where before there had been a low lump of masonry hardly distinguishable from the bluffs around it, walls and towers were now clearly taking shape. Four big round towers guarded the corners of an irregular rectangle, and two additional towers flanked what was obviously the main gate. It looked as if all that was needed for the exterior framework was the crenelation. So the Templar Master had been right, Balian admitted mentally: they would have the main castle finished in just six months. And hopefully, his thoughts continued, the Templar recruits to man the castle had also started to arrive; the sailing season had opened and the first ships crammed with pilgrims had started to clog the harbors of the Kingdom. With luck the promised Templar knights and sergeants would soon be here to defend the castle, and the army could go home. . . .

Ibelin dismounted stiffly from his weary palfrey Rufus. The big red horse, like the workmen, was coated in dust that stuck to his matted, sweat-damp hair. He snorted and shook his head against the flies, sniffing about for water. Ibelin flung the reins over his head, and his Ethiopian squire, Dawit, who had jumped down at the same time, took them from him at once. "I'll water them, my lord," he offered.

Meanwhile Daniel, his other squire, was unlashing their saddlebags and flinging them over his shoulders. Both youths had come a long way since Balian had taken them into his service at Ascalon two years ago. Now they were a good, well-trained team with complementary strengths: Dawit was a centaur whom the horses trusted instinctively, while Daniel had grown exceptionally broad and muscular for a youth of just seventeen. Dawit could fight mounted as well as any Turcoman, while Daniel, if he could stand on his own two feet, was a superb swordsman unlike the more delicate Ethiopian.

Daniel led the way to Ibelin's red-and-yellow striped tent, which housed the knights of Ibelin. The barony owed ten knights to the feudal levy, but several of the knights here were not, in fact, tenants of Ibelin. Several of the older tenants had the right to send sons or brothers as proxies, while Ibelin could now afford to engage five household knights at his own expense as well.

The baron's arrival brought all fifteen knights from their various pursuits with a welcoming cheer; the boredom of this assignment made almost any distraction welcome.

"Well, don't keep us in suspense, lad!" Sir Bartholomew boomed out. He was easily the oldest man among them, already in his fifties, and it would have been normal for him to let a son fulfil his feudal duties at this stage in his life, but he had no sons. His heir was his grandson by his eldest daughter, a boy not yet six. More important, however, he had been a close friend and companion-in-arms of Balian's older brother Hugh—and the closest thing to an uncle that Balian had ever known. As a result he was allowed certain liberties, including calling his lord "lad" at times like this. "Was it a son or another daughter?" Sir Bartholomew pressed his lord.

Balian broke into a wide smile. "A healthy boy, and his mother's well." Maria Zoë said it had been her easiest birth yet, and she was bursting with pride to have a son at last. "We've christened him John, after his maternal grandfather," Balian answered the unspoken question.

"Something to celebrate!" Sir Walter, Balian's former squire and now one of his household knights, suggested at once.

"You'd celebrate *anything*," one of Balian's aging tenants, Sir Arnulf, shot back, and they all laughed.

Soon his knights had opened a cask of wine, and the squires set about filling cups for their lords. Balian sank down on his traveling chest, and Daniel brought him a brimming goblet. "Shall I go fetch fresh bread?" he asked.

The camp defending the construction workers had been designed to last for months. It was effectively a tent city, with bakers and butchers, cook shops and taverns, smithies, armories, moneylenders, and every other amenity necessary to keep almost five thousand men healthy and content for an indefinite period.

Balian assented, adding, "Take enough coin to buy stew as well. I have no desire to move outside this tent until morning." He had been in the saddle twelve hours this day, and he was ready to just relax.

"To John d'Ibelin!" Sir Galvin called out, raising his silver cup. Sir Galvin had taken service with Ibelin as a household knight just this past winter. He had killed a man in a drunken brawl in his native Scotland, and a pilgrimage to Jerusalem had been his penance. Having absolved his sins, however, he felt no inclination to return home and so had offered his service to Ibelin. He was somewhat ponderous of brain, but powerful of build, his preferred weapons being the ax and the mace, and—except for when he had drunk too much—he was good-humored and kindly. Balian smiled and lifted his cup in response.

"And his sire!" Sir Arnulf reminded the company sternly.

"Hear! Hear!" the knights shouted and drank.

"And my lady," Balian suggested, "the Dowager Queen of Jerusalem!"

"To the Queen!" his knights thundered back in good spirits, only too happy to toast the Lady of Ibelin. Their lord's wife had not only done her duty by providing an heir to the barony, after all, she had also brought him a fortune with her dower portion of Nablus. The latter was something they all profited from, since it enabled Ibelin to pay good wages to his household knights and provide extra equipment and supplies for his tenants as well. Furthermore, Nablus greatly added to their lord's prestige, since the barony of Nablus owed no less than eighty-five knights, half of whom Lord Balian had called up for service and were housed separately in three tents of their own.

The wine and the occasion were loosening tongues, and everyone seemed to be talking at once. Ibelin soon learned that the King, accompanied by the Constable and several other lords, had gone to seize Saracen cattle that were grazing on the already overly dry pastures of Galilee. They needed that grass for their own herds, and the army and workmen would welcome some fresh meat as well, Sir Walter explained. But soon the conversation turned to other things: the birth of other children, the name John, the drought, and the revolt at Baalbek.

Ibelin was contentedly nodding off to sleep when suddenly Dawit shook him furiously. "My lord! My lord! Lightning! Come quick!"

"We can use the rain," Ibelin answered, frowning, but the Ethiopian shook his head, his eyes wide with alarm. "Lightning! The King's stallion! He's just galloped in, drenched in sweat and blood!"

"Jesus, Mary, and Joseph!"

"Holy Cross!"

"St. George!"

They fell out of the tent in a pack, Ibelin leading only because he was more panicked than the rest. The day his brother Hugh died in a riding accident flashed through his head. But the King …

By the time they reached the horse lines, the King's big white stallion had been caught and was surrounded by dozens of agitated men. Other knights and barons, including Balian's brother of Ramla and his knights, were converging on the horse lines. Ibelin recognized the Bishop of Bethlehem and the lords of Caymont and Jubail, neither of whom were particularly young.

"Dawit! Saddle up Centurion!" Ibelin ordered, and Dawit darted away to prepare his lord's destrier, while Ibelin's knights scattered to find their own grooms and horses.

Daniel, however, had already tacked up the destrier while Dawit sought out their lord, so he was brought before the others returned. Ibelin, in no mood to wait for the others, swung himself up into the saddle. As he took up the reins, Daniel grabbed his leg. "My lord! You can't go unarmored!"

Balian hesitated. Something had caused Lightning to bolt, and he had smears of blood on his shoulder and haunch. The fact that none of the King's household had returned with the terrified horse suggested there had been an ambush or engagement that had pinned them down.

The decision about arming was taken from him by shouts upriver, followed by a surge of men in the same direction. Ibelin shook free of Daniel and cantered through the crowd to the cause of the commotion. Staggering toward them were five men, carrying a cloak between them in which something lay. Balian recognized one of them men as Sir Tancred, who usually rode as the King's "shield" on his left. Even as he watched, they set their burden down on the matted grass. It was the King.

Balian crossed himself and jumped down to kneel beside the lifeless figure. The King was in full armor under a white-and-gold surcoat with the arms of Jerusalem. His knights had removed the helmet with the gold crown upon the steel brow. The King's face was bloodless, his eyes closed. Balian unlaced the aventail over his neck and chin and slipped his hand inside as the men around him held their breaths. Balian felt the tremor of a pulse, and he breathed out. "He's alive," he announced to the audience crowding around. Then he looked up at the men who had carried the King back to camp. "What happened?"

"We were ambushed by Saracens—"

"Salah ad-Din's nephew—"

"Farrukh-Shah—"

"—took us by surprise—"

"They outnumbered us five to one—"

"Who had time to count?"

"The King's horse bolted!"

"He reared up, spun about, and bolted so fast, no one could stop him."

"The Saracens tried to cut him off, and the Constable rushed forward, killing several of them—"

"He decapitated one man, and the head bounced off the shoulder of the King's horse—which made him swerve and run faster still."

"None of us could catch him—"

"Besides, the Saracens were blocking the way."

"We had to fight our way out."

"By the time we'd—"

The sound of horses and riders, approaching at a fast pace, interrupted them. Everyone looked north and saw the approaching horde of riders. The banners of Oultrejourdain and Sidon fluttered in the breeze on upright lances, but in the center two riders were trying to carry a man between them. He was apparently unconscious and drenched in blood.

"It's the Constable!" someone gasped, and the crowd rushed toward the returning riders.

Balian left them to it, his concern still focused on the King. "Did you see him fall?" he asked Sir Tancred, who had also stayed behind. Balian was visualizing King Baldwin's plight: unable to use either hand, he had no means of reining his stallion in. Nor could he grasp the mane or the pommel to hold on. He could only cling to the stallion with his legs—effectively urging the horse to go faster. As long as the horse went straight, he would have been able to keep his balance, but any sudden spring to the left or right would have flung him from his precarious perch.

"No. We found him lying unconscious on the side of the road."

"He was already unconscious when you found him?"

"Yes."

There was no way of knowing how seriously injured he was until they got him to his tent and the surgeon examined him, Balian concluded, and looked around for the best means to get him there. Although his own knights crowded in offering help, a Hospitaller knight was shoving his way forward with six of his brothers and a stretcher. They efficiently lifted the King onto the stretcher and carried him away, trailed by the Bishop of Bethlehem.

Ibelin did not try to follow. He could not help Baldwin now. Instead he turned to the other commotion, but here too the Hospitallers had taken charge, and the Constable was being carried up to a large infirmary marked with the white crosses on black of the Hospital. He was trailed by a dozen wounded knights who could still walk, at least with assistance. There was nothing more Ibelin could do for him, either, he decided. So he remounted and rode slowly back to the horse lines.

"My lord? The King requests your attendance." The messenger was one of the royal body squires, and he spoke softly and respectfully. It was the middle of the night, and at least some of the other men in the tent were sleeping, their soft snores and deep breathing filling the chilly air.

Ibelin reached down and shook Daniel awake. The youth groggily helped him dress, then lay down and went right back to sleep.

As he followed the King's squire, Ibelin asked, "Is it true his grace has had no serious injuries?"

"That is correct, my lord. He was miraculously unharmed—not a single broken bone or even a concussion." The youth sounded awestruck in the darkness. Balian suspected that Baldwin had already lost consciousness by the time he was finally thrown and so had landed completely limp—the best way to avoid injury, as he had learned long ago on the tiltyard.

They reached the King's tent, and the sentries bowed their heads to the Baron of Ibelin and opened the flap. The interior of the tent was luxuriously furnished with dyed straw mats in bright patterns, cushions on the chairs and chests, and billowing striped silk hangings that cut off the view to the King's bed. A lamp behind the silks made them luminescent, and Balian could see shadows moving around the bed.

"It's me, your grace, Balian d'Ibelin," he announced as the squire dissolved in the darkness. "You sent for me?"

"Balian! Come in!"

Balian pushed the silk hangings aside and approached the King's camp bed. The King was propped up against the pillows, wearing only a nightshirt and a cap over his head, tied under the chin. His arms were freshly bandaged, and on the far side of the bed Ibrahim was stuffing the used bandages into a cotton sack that, Balian knew, would be burned.

"The Constable is dead," the King announced in a voice heavy with sorrow. "His wounds might not have killed a younger man, but his aging heart could not bear them. It gave out just before Matins. The good Bishop of Bethlehem was with him."

"I am sorry, your grace," Ibelin answered sincerely. He had not known Humphrey de Toron well. The Constable had belonged to the generation of Baldwin III and Amalric, and he had fought beside Balian's father in Egypt. Nevertheless, he had been on the High Court of Jerusalem for over forty years and Constable of the Kingdom for more than ten. He had been well educated, courageous, and a voice of reason, respected by all his peers. The Kingdom would miss him, Balian thought.

"He gave his life for me, Balian," the King continued in a voice strained by the intensity of his emotions. "If he had not come between me and the Saracens, they would surely have taken me captive."

"Then he gave his life for *Jerusalem*, your grace, for we cannot afford to have our King fall into the hands of our enemies," Ibelin corrected him, adding firmly: "You should not take such risks, your grace. Cattle raiding is for bachelor knights, squires, and men-at-arms, not kings."

"We can't just let them graze their herds in our territory, either!" Baldwin countered. "The drought is terrible, and many of our own cattle will starve if they do not find enough fodder. We can't afford to share our grass with the cattle of our foe. My mistake was putting too much trust in Lightning. Misty" he referred to the gelding Balian had selected for him and on which he had learned to ride, "would never have run away with me like that."

Ibelin agreed, but he knew that the aging gelding was no longer a suitable mount for a king, either—and it was not easy to find and train a horse to the leper's needs.

The King continued, "Oultrejourdain is right, Balian. The Saracens will wear us down and slowly overwhelm us if we just sit here. They have lost their fear of us. We must reawaken it—make them respect us again."

"You won't do that by chasing cattle," Ibelin countered in admonishment.

"If I had been a healthy man, there would have been no particular risk," Baldwin replied stubbornly.

"Salah ad-Din is healthy," Ibelin countered, "but we nearly captured him at Montgisard." Baldwin liked being reminded of that, Balian knew. When he had Baldwin's attention, however, he added, "But at Montgisard, Salah ad-Din was leading an army of invasion. Had he been killed or captured at Montgisard, it would have been for reasons of state. Risking death or capture for a cattle raid is not kingly."

Baldwin IV frowned in irritation, but then sighed deeply and considered Balian thoughtfully for another moment before finally conceding. "You are right to rebuke me, Balian. But don't you see? Jerusalem needs a king who can defend her—not keep to his bed all the time."

"You are the King God gave us, your grace," Ibelin retorted.

"But what if I am not strong enough to bear the cross of Jerusalem, Balian? What if I *can't*?" The King paused to let this sink in, adding softly, "You saw me when I was laid low by fever last summer. I was so close to death I could smell the incense of my own funeral in the curtains of my bed. And now—now a good man has died because I was too weak to play the role God gave me. Humphrey de Toron was a good man."

"I know. May God have mercy on his soul." Ibelin crossed himself.

"His son died half a dozen years ago," the King continued. "His heir is his grandson—a boy no more than twelve or thirteen."

Ibelin nodded absently; he was tired and sleepy.

"I have been thinking," the King announced in a soft voice. "I have been thinking that the best way I can thank the Constable for his decades of service and for his final sacrifice would be to elevate his heir to a position of greater prominence." The idea he was about to broach with Ibelin had been planted months ago by his mother, but at the time Baldwin had not been particularly focused on rewarding Toron.

"If he's still a youth, do you know that he is worthy, your grace?" Ibelin asked. He could not imagine why they had to discuss this in the middle of the night.

"Who can judge the mettle of a youth?" the King answered. "I do not think my father would have expected me to fight—and win—at Montgisard."

"No, your grace," Ibelin conceded with a rueful smile.

"And I would not appoint him to a high office he is not able to fill, but I thought I could include him in my family." Before Ibelin could work out for himself how that could happen, the King declared, "I think he would be a suitable husband for my sister Isabella; don't you?"

Ibelin was blindsided. Isabella was Maria Zoë's only child from her marriage to King Amalric of Jerusalem—and she doted on her.

"She's four or five years younger than young Toron," the King continued, oblivious to Balian's shock, "and if they are introduced to each other early, they might become fond of one another." That was what his mother had told him when she proposed the scheme a few months back.

But Balian was thinking of his brother Barry's marriage to poor Richildis. They too had been married as children, but that had not stopped his brother from setting Richildis aside when he wanted to marry someone else. Balian's instincts told him this proposal had nothing to do with a happy marriage for Isabella, and everything to do with the fact that Isabella, as the daughter of a Byzantine princess, was seen by many in the Kingdom as a more legitimate heir to the throne of Jerusalem than Baldwin himself. Someone, Balian sensed, was trying to take control of Isabella away from Maria Zoë to ensure that they could use her for their own purposes. But who? It could hardly be the boy Humphrey.

Humphrey's mother, however, was Stephanie de Milly, Balian remembered, and she was now married to Reynald de Châtillon; a more ambitious man had never walked God's earth. Balian protested with the first argument that came to mind. "She has not yet reached the age of consent."

"There's no need to rush the marriage," the King answered reasonably. "Next year or the year after will be soon enough. Now that his grandfather is dead, young Humphrey will join his mother's household in Kerak and learn knighthood from the Lord of Oultrejourdain."

"Oultrejourdain doesn't know what chivalry is!" Balian countered sharply, his suspicion apparently confirmed that the notoriously brutal and immoral Reynald de Châtillon was behind this suggestion. Oultrejourdain, to the surprise of many, had been a bastion of Baldwin's throne, throwing the full weight of his barony behind the King and demonstrating more respect for the young King than many another. But he remained fundamentally a brigand with a barony, and Balian did not trust him. He did not know why he wanted control of Isabella, but he was sure it was not for her good.

Meanwhile Baldwin answered Balian's objection by pointing out rather proudly, "But he knows how to defend my Kingdom."

"That's not the same thing as being a good stepfather to a child!" Balian countered, more hotly than was polite to a king.

"This isn't about being a good stepfather," the King answered coldly; "it's about the marriage of my sister—and heir. I did not call you here to ask your advice, my lord; I merely wanted to show you the courtesy of telling you in person what I am planning."

The rebuke sat, and Balian had no choice but to bow and remark, "Thank you, your grace." He was acutely conscious of his helplessness; the King was Isabella's guardian, and, as such, he could dispose of her in marriage as he pleased.

"You must understand, Balian," the young King pleaded with his mentor, distressed by the resentment Balian was exuding. "I am terrified of what will happen to the Kingdom if I do not live long enough for the Duke of Burgundy to take up my cross. Or what if something prevents the Duke of Burgundy from arriving at all? We need to be sure that Isabella, at least, is married to a local baron, a man who understands our needs and our limitations." That was how his mother had put it to him. "Would you rather I married Isabella to a grown man? A man old enough to be her father or grandfather?"

"Of course not," Balian admitted, thinking of his bright-eyed, impish stepdaughter. He always imagined that his wife had been like Isabella — before she was sent to a strange land to bed a King three times her age.

"I am trying to do what is best for everyone, Balian. At least give me credit for that," Baldwin pleaded.

Balian was not immune to the King's plea, but he could not shake off his instinctive sense of alarm. Defensively he pointed out, "You would have no need to marry off a child if you had given Sibylla to my brother instead of promising her to Burgundy."

Raising the issue of his brother's suit for Sibylla instantly backfired. Baldwin retorted irritably, "We've been through all this before! Salah ad-Din gets stronger year for year with new conquests. We need fresh blood! We need crusaders! If Sibylla marries your brother, we are not one knight stronger, but if she marries Burgundy, he will bring hundreds of knights with him!"

"But you want Isabella married to a local baron. Why not make it the other way around? Marry Sibylla to my brother and promise Isabella to Burgundy?"

"Burgundy will not come out here for a woman who is not certain to be

Queen! You know that!" Baldwin retorted, his anger stoked by Balian's stubbornness. His mother had warned him the Ibelins were ambitious. He hadn't wanted to believe her, but the more Balian argued, the more he wondered if his mother might be right about them after all. She'd been married to one, after all. "Nor will Burgundy come out here to marry a child! We *need* Burgundy sooner rather than later." Baldwin's fears were mingling with his irritation. "Balian, don't you understand? I'm failing!"

There was so much anguish and reproach in Baldwin's voice that Balian was temporarily silenced. Then he thought of his wife and how she would react to the news, and he made one last appeal, hoping to exploit the King's affection for his stepmother. "Your grace, it will break Maria Zoë's heart if you take Isabella away from her—no matter where you send her."

Baldwin stiffened, holding his breath. For a short moment Balian thought he had won, but then the King slowly let out his breath and noted, "I was torn from my mother's arms when I was barely two years old—to make way for Maria Zoë."

Christ on the Cross! Balian thought, understanding at last: this is Agnes' revenge.

"That is the fate of royalty," the King continued: "to serve the higher interests of the Kingdom, no matter how much it hurts. I'm sure no one will understand that better than Queen Maria Comnena. Besides, who said anything about taking Isabella away? I only said I would betroth her to young Toron. She may, for now, remain with her mother."

Balian recognized that he was trapped. He had no arguments left, and he could sense the King's budding resentment. If he were to retain the King's goodwill and affection, he had to back down now. He bent his head in submission. "Yes, your grace."

"Then you will make this sacrifice for Jerusalem?" Baldwin pressed him.

"I will make *any* sacrifice for Jerusalem, your grace," Balian countered.

Chapter 2

Ibelin, June 1179

"The King has summoned the army *again*?" Maria Zoë asked, unable to keep the anger from her voice. In eighteen months of marriage, Balian had spent less than a year with her. He had barely made it home in time for the birth of his son, and had returned almost at once to the camp at Jacob's Ford. After the skirmish in which Humphrey de Toron was killed, he'd accompanied the funeral cortege to Toron, and he had returned barely three weeks ago.

"The Saracens are trying to destroy the harvest in the lordships of Beirut and Sidon. The drought has resulted in severe food shortages as it is," Balian made excuses for his King. "We can't afford to let the enemy ruin what's left of the harvest. We have to face them."

Maria Zoë came from a royal family and she understood the logic, but that did not reconcile her to her husband's departure. "In Islam, a wife has the right to divorce a husband who abandons her for more than forty days at a stretch," she noted sharply.

"And you'd make such a good Muslim wife—never talking back to your husband nor setting foot outside the harem!" Balian snapped.

"Feudal levies in every kingdom of the West are only required to serve for forty days as well," Maria Zoë continued, ignoring his remark.

"Because they are only at war with their Christian neighbors, and all that is at stake is dynastic privilege. The King of Jerusalem has the right to keep his vassals in the field for a full year, because we are at risk of complete annihilation if we don't face our enemies. What would you prefer? To have me defending you in Beirut or here in Ibelin, when it is already too late?"

Maria Zoë clamped her teeth together, because she had no response. She had seen the destruction wrought by Salah ad-Din's last raid. She would not have wanted to be in her sister-in-law's shoes when Saracen troops plundered the town below the castle while she, with an inadequate garrison, cowered in the keep with her little children—especially her girls.

Balian softened his tone in response to her silence. "Do you think I want to spend my days in the heat and dust and saddle rather than here with you?"

"No," Maria Zoë admitted, although she was still angry. "No, but *you* be the one to break it to the girls. They have so looked forward to having you back, and they will not be happy to see you go away again so soon."

Maria Zoë had converted the southwest tower of the castle's encircling wall into the nursery. Here the children could play and shout on the rooftop (weather permitting) without getting underfoot of the garrison or household. Just below, there was a bedroom divided by a wooden partition into two chambers. The first was the nursery proper, with two cribs and pallets for the wet nurse and nanny for John and Helvis respectively, Maria Zoë and Balian's two children. On the other side of the partition was the bedroom of the older girls: Isabella, Maria Zoë's daughter by her first marriage to the late King of Jerusalem, Balian's niece Eschiva, who had lived with them ever since her father had set aside her mother to free himself for a more lucrative marriage, and Beth, the Muslim convert and orphan that Maria Zoë had adopted after the raid on Ibelin in November 1177. On the first floor a day room/classroom was located, and here the girls were taught their letters, to sing, and to sew. Here there were also a miniature castle made by the carpenter and a large (and growing) collection of dolls. The ground floor retained its original function of carpenter shop.

Edwin Shoreham, the eldest son of the garrison's senior sergeant Roger Shoreham, was methodically shaving wood off an object as Balian entered. Procrastinating, Balian stopped to ask the carpenter what he was working on. "Kneeling benches for the chapel, my lord," young Shoreham answered readily. "My lady says it's uncomfortable to kneel on the stone floor."

Balian nodded. It was just like Maria Zoë to want comfort even when praying. "You've finished repairing everything damaged or destroyed in the raid?"

"All that I can do, my lord," Edwin assured him. "I don't have the equipment for the screws of the oil and wine presses, but everything else is pretty much finished: shutters, doors, window frames, shelves, and the like."

Eighteen months after the raid in which Salah ad-Din's troops had plundered Ibelin town, burning down a goodly portion of it in the process, Ibelin seemed back to normal—at least on the surface. Yet the shock sat deep with the people.

The suspicion of treachery, the belief that someone had opened or intentionally failed to bar the southern gate to the town, poisoned the atmosphere. Hostility to the small Muslim community had caused several families to leave. Those Muslim families that remained kept more to themselves than ever before, and the Muslim women had started to wear black robes and veils that completely covered their faces, something they had not done before.

But Maria Zoë had also received reports of insolence and threats on the part of some of the younger Muslim youth directed at Christians. The Armenian priest complained that several times someone had shouted at him from the darkness: "Salah ad-Din will return!" and Father Vitus said he'd found a shard scratched with a similar threat on the steps of St. George's. The atmosphere was charged with a latent hostility between Christians and Muslims that Balian could not remember from his childhood. Nor was there anything he could do to defuse it, because it was fed by Salah ad-Din's successes.

Not everything had changed for the worse, however. The Armenian, Latin, and Syrian Christian communities had come closer together in the aftermath of the raid. The Armenian church had been the most badly damaged in the raid, and the other churches had taken up collections to help rebuild it. Balian had noted that the rebuilding of the weavers' quarter had likewise been a joint effort, with everyone pitching in regardless of their particular form of Christianity. Meanwhile Sergeant Shoreham was forging a militia from the entire male Christian population, and the common drills and common duty seemed to be reinforcing a sense of common identity across the Christian communities. Balian felt comfortable leaving Maria Zoë and his children in the care of Sergeant Shoreham and his militia while he took the knights and squires of Ibelin north again.

Leaving the carpenter's shop behind, he mounted the stairs carved in the thickness of the walls up to the first-floor chamber. The high-pitched chatter of children met him long before he reached the landing. The stout walls kept the tower relatively cool compared to the heat outside, and the open windows allowed for cross-ventilation.

As he entered he saw Beth, the Muslim girl who had been gang-raped by the Nubians during the raid and then rejected by her family, sitting demurely beside the cradle with his infant son, singing and gently rocking it with her foot. She still wore her hair covered in the Muslim fashion, but at least her face was visible.

His niece Eschiva at fourteen also had strong maternal instincts and was growing up rapidly; she had small breasts and a slender waist. Although she had her mother's brown hair, she had been lucky to inherit her father's fuller face and height. She was not a beauty but she was pretty, with unblemished skin and large, doe-like eyes.

Just the night before, Balian and Maria Zoë had been speculating about how much longer her husband, Aimery de Lusignan, was going to let her wait. Maria Zoë had speculated that he was looking for a way to set her aside, and asked Balian if he had a new mistress he was loath to part with. Balian pleaded ignorance of Lusignan's liaisons and motives, but pointed out that Lusignan had been appointed Toron's successor as Constable of Jerusalem. Under the circumstances he had a lot to think about other than his child bride.

As Balian entered, Eschiva had his daughter Helvis by the hand and was encouraging her to take a step. Helvis, sucking her thumb, appeared more interested in Isabella, who was playing with her dolls. Eschiva caught sight of Balian and broke into a smile. "Uncle Balian!" she exclaimed. "Have you come to take us for a ride?"

Balian had promised the older girls that he would take them for a ride, but the summons from the King had distracted him. "Later," he promised, going on to his heels to face Helvis. She frowned at him over her thumb, still not sure what to make of him, but Isabella at once left her dolls in disarray and rushed to take his hand. "Uncle Balian," she started, turning his signet ring, with the cross of Ibelin engraved on the shield-shaped onyx, and leaning against his arm coquettishly. "Aren't I old enough for a puppy *now*?"

"How old are you?" Balian asked, as if he didn't know.

"I'm six years, eleven months, and two days," she told him solemnly.

"Then you'll have to wait at least another seven months minus two days," Balian decided arbitrarily to delay the discussion. "No girl can have a puppy before she is seven and a half."

"Can boys have them sooner?" Isabella wanted to know.

"No, they have to wait until they are eight," Balian declared spontaneously, to Isabella's evident satisfaction.

Meanwhile, Eschiva had been thinking. "If you aren't here to take us riding, why are you here? Did the messenger bring news from my husband?"

So she had seen the rider in the King's livery.

"Yes, Eschiva, he did." Balian straightened, leaving Helvis' eye level for Eschiva's. As Constable, Lusignan called up the feudal levies in the King's name. "I came to tell you the King has summoned the army again. I will have to leave Ibelin tomorrow morning for Beirut."

"But you only just got here!" Eschiva protested, the disappointment in her voice flattering Balian.

Isabella at once joined in. "Yes! You only just got here, and you have not done *half* the things you promised yet!"

"What is so urgent that you must go already?" Eschiva wanted to know, a frown of worry darkening her brow, and he could sense the fear behind it. She had been here during the raid, her chamber had been lit by the lurid flames of the burning town, she'd heard the captured girls screaming for help and mercy, and she had befriended Beth.

He glanced at the latter and saw the fear in her eyes, too, before she dropped her head modestly. He answered honestly nevertheless: "The Saracens are trying to prevent us from bringing in the harvest in Beirut and Sidon."

"But why do you have to defend Beirut?" Isabella put the question bluntly. "Did Beirut come to defend us when the Saracens attacked Ibelin?"

Balian looked at her bemused as he answered, "Well, he would have, if there had been time. Even if I leave tomorrow, I will come too late for some towns and villages in his lands. But we must respond. The harvest in Beirut and Sidon feeds half the Kingdom."

Isabella frowned and asked in a peeved voice, "Will it never end?"

"What?"

"The war!" Isabella answered, stamping her foot for emphasis.

"In the Name of God, I wish it would," Balian answered sincerely, glancing out of the southern window to the pomegranate orchards that spread south from the town. This was such a beautiful piece of earth, he thought, and it had been fought over since the Old Testament. It was a land of blood as well as milk and honey.

Syrian Border along the River Litani, June 1179

"Keep up the pressure! Don't let them get away!" Ramla screamed at his brother above the clamor of the battlefield. He was making circular motions with his sword over his head. The sword was already red with blood, and the trapper of his stallion was soiled with it.

Ibelin, however, pulled up his stallion. "We don't want to get drawn across the Litani!" Balian warned his brother, pointing to the river only a couple of hundred yards ahead of them. "Salah ad-Din's main forces are somewhere nearby!"

"The Templars are dealing with them!" Ramla countered. "Forward! Kill them as they try to cross!"

There was some logic to what Ramla wanted to do. Since the river at this time of year reached only to the bellies of the larger European horses, the Franks could ride into it with ease. The smaller Saracen horses, on the other hand, were struggling—plunging and jumping as they tried to find their way to the far shore.

Ibelin looked for the King's standard and saw it well to the rear, surrounded by royal household knights. He decided his brother was right. They should kill as many of the enemy as they could here, at the ford. He put his heels to Centurion, and the grey destrier sprang eagerly after Ramla.

Ibelin and his knights splashed into the brown waters of the river, which were already turning red. The water was refreshingly cool on his chain-mail-encased legs. Centurion undoubtedly felt refreshed, too, Ibelin thought as he dropped the double reins on the stallion's neck and slung his shield onto his back. With the enemy well routed, which meant they were hardly fighting, his shield had become superfluous. Instead, he clasped both hands on the hilt of his sword to increase the force of each blow.

Swinging the sword methodically, first left and then right, he was killing men from behind as they tried to reach the far bank of the river. The river was the border between the Kingdom of Jerusalem and Syria, but at the moment there was nothing on the far side to save the fleeing Saracens. It was an illusionary refuge.

Still, Ibelin couldn't shake a sense of unease. The King had been far too eager to engage this raiding party led by Salah ad-Din's nephew Farrukh-Shah, even though Lusignan and Tripoli both warned him it was not the main Saracen force. The King, however, was anxious to wipe out the humiliation of his last encounter with Farrukh-Shah, and had not been prepared to listen to words of caution.

The results so far had proven the King right. There was precious little left of Farrukh-Shah's forces, most of whom lay littered on the field limp and soaked in their own blood or struggling in the reddening waters of the Litani. Furthermore, Lusignan and Tripoli appeared to have cut off Farrukh-Shah's escape. The Sultan's nephew was easily recognizable by his brightly caparisoned stallion, his uniformed bodyguard, and the purple-and-gold banner streaming out behind him. He had turned north to ride around the Christians blocking his escape across the river, but Tripoli and Lusignan were keeping pace so perfectly that he could not slip past them. Even as Ibelin watched, Tripoli and a handful of his knights closed with the Saracen leader and surrounded him. The horses came to a seething, circling halt and the emir's banner sank down to disappear in the swirling dust, trampled under by the horses of the men who had taken him captive.

Ibelin had reached the far bank of the river. His brother was already far ahead of him, still in hot pursuit of the fleeing remnants of Farrukh-Shah's raiding party, but Balian's instincts made him sit back and take up his reins to halt his stallion. As the horse came to a grateful halt and dropped his head to drink deeply, Balian looked around to assess the situation again.

His squires Daniel and Dawit immediately closed with him. "Aren't we going to pursue?" Daniel asked, disbelieving, glancing over his shoulder at the Lord of Ramla and his knights, who were still slaughtering. Ibelin shook his head, as more and more of his knights rallied around him in ones and twos until the entire Ibelin and Nablus contingent of a hundred knights and their squires was collected in the river. The others, like their lord, removed their helmets to wipe sweat from their faces with their surcoats and let their horses drink the flowing but bloodstained water.

Some Saracen stragglers were still plunging into the river and splashing past them, but Ibelin and his knights let them go. Dawit nudged his horse next to Balian's to offer his lord a wineskin filled with water. It was warm, but nevertheless refreshing. Balian drank deeply, but handed it back half full and nodded to Dawit to drink himself.

"It's rare to see the Templars arrive late for a battle," Sir Walter noted with a short laugh, pointing to a Templar galloping on to the field from their left. They all turned to watch with bemusement. The Templar pride at always being first in battle grated on their nerves to some degree. As they watched, more Templars appeared, also at a full gallop but not in any kind of formation. At almost the same instant, they collectively realized these Templars weren't attacking: they were fleeing.

Ibelin automatically looked left to see what the Templars were fleeing from, and gasped: "Holy Cross and St. George!" A wide line of Saracen horse had crested the hill with all their banners fluttering. Salah ad-Din's banner was the largest, in the middle of the host.

Ibelin jammed his helmet on his head, pulled his shield back onto his left arm, then grabbed up his reins as he put his spurs to his stallion. Around him his knights frantically did the same without being ordered. It didn't take a genius to recognize the danger they were in: the Christian army was scattered all over the field. Ramla was across the river; Tripoli and Lusignan had been lured fully two miles to the north in their maneuver to cut off Farrukh-Shah's escape. And even those knights still on the battlefield were, like Ibelin and his hundred knights, dispersed and partially spent.

Fortunately, Centurion had been refreshed by the drink and the soothing coolness of the running water on his legs and belly. He responded with alacrity. Once he was out of the river and onto the firmer ground of the plain, Balian stood in the stirrups and leaned forward, urging him onwards. Soon the stallion was going flat out, leaping over the bodies of man and horse in a mad dash to rejoin the King's forces.

On his right, Lusignan and his knights were also racing back to rejoin the King, while Tripoli took charge of the valuable prisoner and with a handful of his knights rode west for the coast.

The sound of the approaching Saracen charge became an increasing rumble. The Saracens could see their foe spread out and vulnerable before them—and could see Ibelin and Lusignan rushing to regroup. They, too, spurred their mounts forwards. Neither army had mustered infantry for what on the Muslim side had been a raid, and on the Christian side a counter-raid. Nor did Salah ad-Din appear to have the usual contingents of mounted archers; they had apparently been deployed with Farrukh-Shah. The Saracen horse thundering down toward the scattered Frankish forces were heavy cavalry armed with lance and sword. They shouted battle cries, the wind fluttered the pennants on their lance tips, and the sunlight caught on their raised swords. Centurion laid his ears flat back on his head as he raced, determined to escape the onslaught from his left.

But they weren't going to make it. The enemy was advancing too fast.

They could not risk being run over from the side.

Ibelin flung out his left arm toward the enemy to indicate they had to turn into the attack. He could not take the time to look over his shoulder to see if his knights understood him. Instead, he reached forward and with his left hand took hold of the bridle directly behind the bit. Then he leaned with all his weight on his shield arm and pulled Centurion around—more by the strength of his will than his arm. He barely managed to sit back in the saddle before the lines of horses clashed.

Centurion was thrown on his haunches by the impact from the first lance, and Balian felt blows raining down on his shield, helmet, forearms, and thighs. As the enemy swept past him, each Saracen within range tried to kill him without actually stopping.

That was what saved his life. After their lances shattered, the slashing strokes of the Saracens' swords as they swept by could not penetrate his chain mail. It took a direct, piercing blow to penetrate the linked steel rings, and none dared slow long enough to deliver that kind of thrust.

Ibelin huddled behind his shield, his head down to protect his face and eyes, making no attempt to fight until Centurion recovered his balance and began staggering and stamping his way forward, with a dogged determination that testified to the stallion's own will to survive. At once Balian straightened, and screaming to reawaken his own courage, he started fighting—even if this consisted of little more than warding off the blows still directed at him, using both his shield and his sword.

Finally the wave of Saracen cavalry rolled over them, and the knights of Ibelin and Nablus emerged from the clouds of dust billowing up behind the enemy. Like islands in the swirling dust, clusters of mounted fighting men emerged. They were scattered across three hundred yards. Immediately beside and behind Balian, the knights of Ibelin still made up a coherent body of men, while the knights of Nablus formed a half-dozen distinct clumps.

But there were also a score of unhorsed men staggering out of the clouds of dust, stumbling, coughing, holding their hands to their bleeding wounds or cradling broken wrists, dislocated elbows, and wrenched shoulders. As the dust settled further, the trampled corpses of horses and a half-dozen other men emerged, while the piercing screams of a wounded stallion struggling to get to his feet despite two broken legs blotted out all other sounds.

Dawit was down before Balian could stop him. He personally put the injured horse out of his misery with a quick slash to his jugular. This action brought Balian to his senses. Behind them the Saracens had fully engulfed the King and his body of knights. This was no time to sit around staring.

"Get those men mounted!" Ibelin ordered, gesturing for the dazed squires behind him to pick up the unhorsed men. "All of them! Take them back to camp!"

"Wait!" Sir Bartholomew countermanded, laying a hand on Balian's arm. The gesture had a calming effect, and the older man's troubled eyes met Balian's. "Have the wounded that still have horses take the unhorsed men. We need every unharmed fighting man we have—even the squires."

"Yes," Balian recognized the wisdom of the older man's advice and smiled his thanks. "Any of you not fit to fight, take a rider behind you and return to the camp. Everyone else, form up!"

As the remaining fourscore knights and their squires formed a conroi around him, Ibelin saw Lusignan arrive from the northeast and start fighting his way through the enemy to reach the King. They would have to do the same thing. "A Ibelin!" Balian roared as he asked the now drooping Centurion for yet another charge.

Around him they answered "A Ibelin!" and "A Nablus!" even "Jerusalem!" and started forward at a lumbering, weary canter.

If they'd had lances, it would have been comparatively easy. The Saracens were focused on the King and Lusignan, not expecting cavalry to attack them from the rear. But without lances they could not cut a swath through the enemy;

they had to fight their way through. The only good thing was that they were fighting cavalry; there were no Saracen foot soldiers stabbing at the bellies of their horses or trying to drag them down. Ibelin and his knights could drop their reins and urge their horses forward with their legs as they used their shields and swords to clear a path through the enemy to the compact body of knights around the King.

It seemed to take forever to kill their way forward, but they had almost made it. No more than two or three Saracens still separated Ibelin from the King when one of the Saracens, an exceptionally large man, stood in his stirrups and brought his sword down on Sir Tancred's head so hard that it sliced open the helmet. Blood spurted like a fountain, coating and temporarily blinding his assailant, but as Sir Tancred's heavy body fell sideways off his horse it fell upon the shoulder of the King's stallion, causing him to rear up and spring sideways just as he had done in the last engagement.

Balian saw the King lean forward in an attempt to stay seated, but now the enemy was stabbing Lightning in the belly and the stallion flailed out with his front hooves, squealing in pain and terror. The King didn't stand a chance; he lost his stirrups and fell backwards onto the ground.

The knights of Ibelin and Nablus burst through the enemy and turned to face the Saracens to shield their lord as he jumped down and dragged King Baldwin into his arms.

"We're lost!" Baldwin gasped, dazed and bewildered.

"Not yet, we aren't!" Ibelin answered stubbornly. He pulled Centurion close and urged the King to mount. Baldwin, however, could grab neither the reins, the stirrup, nor the pommel with his lifeless hands, and the blood-mad stallion danced away from the strange rider again and again.

Ibelin was aware of men around them grunting, cursing, killing, and dying. Young Sir Adrian let out a blood-curdling scream as a Saracen sword gutted him. Blood spurted and then spilled in a stinking gush over Ibelin and the King. It was only a matter of seconds before their protection would be slaughtered. Balian had to get the King off the field, but he could not hold Centurion still and lift Baldwin up at the same time.

Suddenly Daniel was beside him on the ground. "I'll carry him off!" the squire shouted.

Ibelin didn't have time to think, much less contradict. Daniel was pulling the King's lifeless arms around his own neck and hooking his arms through the King's knees. Then he jogged away in a crouch, slipping almost unnoticed between the horses as the horsemen struggled with one another.

Balian grabbed Centurion's reins, pointed his foot in the stirrup, and hauled himself back into the saddle, but he'd lost his shield in his efforts to help the King. The next instant he looked death in the face as a turbaned horseman charged at him, pointing his sword at his unshielded chest.

Then the hand holding the sword spun through the air with the longsword still in its grasp. The bleeding stub hit Balian in the chest before the rest of the body slumped down and fell between their horses. The knight who had saved him wore Sidon's livery.

Sidon had been left holding his castle of Sidon. If he was here now, it meant he had reinforced the Christian forces with fresh knights. Indeed, Sidon's knights, most of whom still had lances, were pushing the Saracens back, giving the exhausted men of the King's bodyguard—and Ibelin—a chance to escape.

Ibelin had no illusions about his ability to fight effectively any longer. He had no lance, no squires, and no shield. The best he could do was live to fight another day, and as he turned a weary Centurion away from the battle, he was followed by what remained of his troop: some threescore knights and less than half a hundred squires.

The muffled sound of screaming coming from the surgeon's tent suggested that one of the survivors was having a limb amputated or cauterized. Balian thanked God it wasn't he. He could not move his left arm without sharp, crippling pains shooting up through his shoulder socket. He was covered with bruises and had a gash in one leg, but no serious injuries. That was more than he could say about the rest of his surviving men. Of the roughly 170 knights and squires of Ibelin and Nablus who had survived the battle, more than a dozen had broken bones or dislocated joints, including Sir Walter, whose thigh was broken. While these men would recover to fight again, there were seven who had lost (or were losing) limbs, five with internal injuries that were likely to prove crippling if not fatal, and Sir Lucius had a gaping hole in his abdomen that wouldn't stop bleeding. Sir Galvin's squire had lost an eye, and the distraught Scotsman had only just managed to still the youth's whimpering with wine—and then taken to drink himself. Balian was badly shaken.

Objectively, the engagement had been a Christian victory. The Syrians, who had been burning and plundering inside the Kingdom of Jerusalem, had been forced to withdraw across the Litani. Furthermore, the casualties on the Saracen side were, as always, significantly higher. But Ibelin did not feel like he had just won a victory; this was no Montgisard.

Although the Christian losses were numerically lower, they were more damaging, because Jerusalem had fewer manpower reserves. On a personal level, moreover, the losses were devastating: of the fifteen knights of Ibelin, four were dead and two were seriously wounded, while the casualties among the squires had been even higher: seven. To be sure, Walter would recover. But Sir Adrian had been very young, standing in for his aging father for the first time, and Sir Lucius was his father's only son. Balian did not look forward to the grim task of facing their fathers with the merciless news.

And then there was the uncertainty about his brother's fate. Neither the Lord of Ramla nor any of his knights had returned. They had been too far to the east to regroup behind Sidon's knights and fall back to Sidon with the rest of the Christian army. Barry was either dead or captured—and with him some fifty knights and an equal number of squires. The Kingdom as a whole might have manpower reserves, but Ramla-Mirabel's strength had been decimated—and Balian dreaded telling Eschiva that her father was sitting in a Saracen prison, or dead.

At least her husband had survived, Balian noted, as the Constable poked his head inside the tent inquiring, "Ibelin?"

"I'm here," Balian answered, struggling to sit up.

Lusignan ducked into the tent, stepped over the wounded stretched out on mats on the floor, and dropped wearily down beside Balian on the bed he had been lying on. To cool off his overheated body, Ibelin had stripped off not only his armor but his filthy undergarments as well.

Lusignan, on the other hand, was still wearing his armor, although his head was bare. Blood stained his surcoat and coated the lower arms of his hauberk; hardened mud clung to the chain mail of his leggings. His hair was encrusted with salt, and he smelled rank.

"I thought you'd want to hear the news," Lusignan explained his presence. Ibelin just waited warily for him to continue. "A Saracen herald just rode in to ask whether the King would receive an emissary empowered to negotiate an exchange of prisoners."

"He wants Farrukh-Shah back that badly?"

"He does, and apparently he thinks he has the right bargaining chip."

"My brother?" Balian asked hopefully. That would be the grace of God indeed: if Barry had not only survived, but the Sultan was also willing to release him in exchange for his nephew.

"Maybe," Lusignan admitted. "We don't know, but the messenger suggested that the Saracens had a number of high-born prisoners. I think there's a chance

Ramla is one of them. He was easily recognizable by his armor as a valuable prisoner. The Saracens would have tried to avoid killing him."

Balian nodded; that was his hope, too.

"The King will receive the Sultan's emissary shortly. I presume you want to be there?"

Ibelin nodded. "Give me five minutes to dress." He signaled to Dawit to bring him a complete change of clothes.

The King, too, had changed into court attire for the Sultan's emissary. He wore white silk hose and shirt, over which he wore a short-sleeved robe belted at the waist and garnished with broad bands of gold embroidery at the collar, cuffs, and hem. Ibrahim had washed the King's hair as well, so although it was damp it was fine and drying to bright blond. He wore the crown on his brow and was seated in an armed chair with a baldachin over it bearing the arms of Jerusalem. Given the situation he was in and what he had just survived, he looked remarkably good, Balian thought, as he slipped into the tent and bowed his head to his sovereign.

The King smiled at Balian across the other men crowding the room, then leaned over and whispered something to Ibrahim, who at once gestured Balian closer. Balian pushed his way through the crowd with murmured apologies. When he reached the King's side and went down on one knee, Baldwin leaned forward. "I wish to reward your squire for rescuing me. I have asked the Constable to knight him."

Ibelin nodded. "He deserves it."

"And you will retain him?"

"I have need of every knight I can get," Balian answered honestly.

There was no time for further discussion. Outside the horns were blowing, announcing the Sultan's emissary. With a flashy display of horsemanship, a Kurdish Mamluke galloped up, halted, and vaulted to the ground. His turban was gold brocade, as were the sleeves and skirts of the tunic that emerged below the hem and sleeves of his scaled leather armor. Camel-leather boots came up over the knee to disappear below the folds of his tunic. His belt was jewel-encrusted—not something he wore in battle.

The royal knights flanking the entrance to the King's tent drew back the flap and admitted the emissary, and the men inside the tent parted to make way for him. He strode forward with the confidence of a victor, and made a flourishing bow before the King of Jerusalem. As he righted himself, his eyes fell on Ibelin and he smiled. Switching to Arabic he announced, "Ah, Balian Ibn Barzan, I have a message for *you* as well."

With dismay Balian recognized the man he had bargained with over the release of three Saracen youths captured at Montgisard. His stomach churned as he realized he was going to pay a high price for his earlier greed.

"But first, your excellency." The Kurdish emissary switched back into French and bowed again, if a little less formally, to King Baldwin. "I have come with greetings from the Sultan Salah ad-Din." He proceeded to list off all the Sultan's many titles before finally continuing, "The Sultan congratulates you on your success today. He regrets that he did not arrive at the party a little sooner, but hopes you will forgive him." The emissary was smiling genially, but the men around him were not amused. Only the King inclined his head slightly in acknowledgment. "The Sultan was delayed by the Knights of the Temple, as they call themselves, who blocked his way," the emissary continued conversationally. "Now the Grand Master of the Knights Templar is enjoying the Sultan's hospitality."

A shocked rumble of exclamations surged across the tent as men turned to their neighbors, asking how that was possible. Templars were expected to die for their faith. Certainly it was against the Templar Rule to pay ransom. It was unthinkable that a *Grand Master* had let himself fall into the hands of the Saracens alive.

The Saracen emissary understood the shock of his audience and was clearly enjoying it. As the flurry of exclamations died down, he continued, "The Templar leader was knocked unconscious in a fall from his horse. A half-dozen of his men died defending what they thought was his corpse, but when we removed his helmet, we discovered—to our astonishment—that he was still alive."

A new rumble of murmurs swept the room, while the emissary continued, "We also took several other prisoners of note." He smiled significantly in Ibelin's direction. "But however much my master enjoys the company of these gentlemen, he would rather dine with kin. So he suggests that you return to him his beloved nephew Farrukh-Shah in exchange for the Master of the Temple." The emissary bowed again.

"For the Master of the Temple alone—or for all the prisoners of note?" the King asked sharply.

"For the Master of the Temple, your excellency."

"Templars cannot be ransomed," Tripoli protested angrily.

"This isn't ransom; it's a prisoner exchange," the King corrected his mightiest vassal, and looked pointedly around the room. "Does anyone here think we could have won Montgisard without Master Odo de St. Amand?"

Balian wanted to point out that they couldn't have won Montgisard without his brother, either, but he didn't quite dare shout it out; it would have sounded too selfish and self-serving.

The King looked pointedly at the Count of Tripoli, who stood just behind his left shoulder. "What say you, my lord? Has Odo de St. Amand ever left us in the lurch when we needed him?"

Tripoli pressed his lips together in obvious disapproval, but under the gaze of the young King he capitulated. "If that is your wish, your grace," Tripoli answered stiffly. "But shouldn't we listen to the names of the other prisoners first?" He glanced significantly at Ibelin.

"No," the King insisted firmly. "We cannot decide based on whom we love best. Salah ad-Din has made us an offer. We take it or leave it."

Tripoli shook his head in disagreement, but Lusignan, Sidon, and other barons spoke up at once in favor of Odo de St. Amand. The King called for silence and turned back to the Sultan's emissary. "We agree to these terms."

The emissary bowed deeply in acknowledgement and came up smiling to turn his gaze on Ibelin. Still speaking French for the benefit of the audience, he announced, "My lord of Ibelin, your brother sends his greetings and assurances of his well-being, while the Sultan sends his compliments on your courage."

Ibelin dutifully acknowledged the compliment with a nod of his head and waited for the ax to fall.

"Such a brave and noble prisoner is of great worth to the entire Kingdom," the Mamluke continued, bowing to the King and smiling to the others in the room, "but to no one more than his beloved brother, I am sure."

Balian wanted to tell him to stop drawing out the torture and spit out the price, but he managed to bow and smile instead.

"The Sultan would be delighted to return your brother, the Baron of Ramla and Mirabel, in exchange for two hundred thousand bezants."

The gasps of the others in the room made it unnecessary for Balian to reply. The price was absurd. It was a king's ransom, not a baron's. It was Salah ad-Din's revenge for his tough bargaining over three youths of no importance. The Sultan would no doubt argue that if mere boys of good family were worth ten thousand bezants in Balian's book, then barons—and brothers—must be worth ten times that amount—or twenty times, as the case now stood.

Balian smiled and bowed deeply to the emissary. "My brother is indeed worth two hundred thousand bezants," he said to the mutters and whispered exclamations of his peers. "Whether Ramla and Mirabel can pay two hundred thousand bezants is another story. Your master will hear from me after I have had time to assess the resources at my disposal."

The emissary bowed deeply, and moved on to name the other prisoners and their prices, but Balian wasn't listening. His ability to listen was blocked out by the rushing of blood in his ears and the lameness of his brain. He was overpowered by the knowledge that he could not possibly raise that kind of money—not even if he pawned his own and his brother's barony, not even if he sold every movable thing he owned, not even if he sold himself and his soul. The thought of Barry chained in the darkness for the rest of his life was so intolerable, however, that he felt as if he could not breathe.

He turned and pushed his way blindly out of the tent, ignoring the protests and complaints of those he shouldered aside. Outside, the air was not rank with the smell of unwashed bodies, and he went around to the back of the tent where there was a lengthening swath of shade.

This is what comes of greed, his conscience preached at him. Because you wanted money to make yourself feel more equal to your bride, your brother may never see the light of day again.

"There you are!" a voice declared loudly, and a moment later the stink of sweat and dried blood moved within range of Balian's nose. It was Aimery de Lusignan: the last man on earth that he wanted to see at the moment.

Balian refused to even look at him.

"Don't think you can just plunder my wife's inheritance as you please! I will take you before the High Court of Jerusalem if you seek to exercise control of Ramla and Mirabel. Barry's heir is his only child, Eschiva, and as her husband I—and no one else—control the income and people of Ramla and Mirabel in your brother's absence."

Balian turned slowly and leveled a cold look at Lusignan. "Go to Ramla and tell them that." Balian was quite confident that Lusignan, completely unknown and an immigrant from France, would receive a cold reception from his brother's vassals.

"What do the people of Ramla have to say about it? The High Court will back me!"

"Maybe," Ibelin conceded, and he smiled faintly. "Are you saying you will take responsibility for raising my brother's ransom, then? You'll send word to the Sultan that *you* will pay it?"

"Don't be ridiculous! Two hundred thousand gold bezants is more than *anyone* can pay! If they'd taken the King himself, the Sultan wouldn't have asked for more. In fact, I daresay he'd wouldn't have dared ask so *much*—for fear we wouldn't pay it and he'd be stuck with a leper for the rest of his life!"

"What are you saying?" Balian asked through clamped teeth as he tried to keep his temper under control. Lusignan, after all, had once called his brother "friend."

"I'm saying that's a ransom Salah ad-Din doesn't expect *anyone* to pay. It's a price so high he knows we won't pay it. He's giving notice that he intends to keep your brother—God knows why. Or maybe . . ." Lusignan hesitated and then suggested, "Or maybe, he didn't expect the King to agree to the exchange for Odo de St. Amand. Maybe he expected us to reject that offer, and Ramla was the prisoner he *expected* to exchange for Farrukh-Shah. When the King agreed to give up Salah ad-Din's nephew for St. Amand, however, it took the emissary by surprise. The man had to improvise a price for Ramla, and didn't want to risk naming a price his master would have deemed too low. He named a price that even the Sultan could not expect in order to give himself time to get instructions from his master."

Ibelin gazed at Lusignan warily. A moment ago he had wanted to kill him for his callousness to Barry's fate, but what he said made a certain amount of sense—especially since the emissary had negotiated with Ibelin before. He had enjoyed tormenting Ibelin while he thought through his options and decided on a figure that would, as Lusignan said, not risk the anger of his master and give Ibelin a taste of his own medicine at the same time.

If Lusignan was right, he could at least hope the Sultan would be willing to bargain. With time the Sultan might be negotiated down to something more reasonable.

Balian took a deep breath and replied, tight-lipped, "Perhaps. We will see."

Ibelin

"Dawit's just ridden in!" Isabella shouted as she burst into the solar, where her mother was dictating a letter in Greek to Father Angelus.

Maria Zoë caught her breath and stopped her pacing. (She always paced when she dictated; it seemed to help the words flow better.) Since the day before, the taverns of Ibelin had been full of rumors about a battle with many Christian casualties and several high-born captives. Sergeant Shoreham had reported what he could find out, but those who talked of the battle were never the people who'd actually been there, and no one had been able to say for sure whether the Baron of Ibelin was alive or dead, captive or free.

Maria Zoë reached for a silk veil, wound it expertly around her head, and then started down the stairs to the ward at a dangerous pace. Isabella had a hard time keeping up with her.

By the time she reached the ward, Dawit had already dismounted and turned his winded horse over to his younger brother Eskindar, while he spoke to his father in a rush of Amharic. When he caught sight of Maria Zoë, he broke off and went down on a knee before her. "My lady, my lord and the Constable of Jerusalem are only two hours behind me. He sent me ahead to warn you."

"Thank you!" She reached out and touched his arm in gratitude for bearing the good news. Gesturing for him to get up off his knees, she added: "Please, go refresh yourself. Mathewos, you'll need to make ready for—" she broke off and turned back to Dawit. "How many men are with my husband?"

"We left the wounded in Sidon so we could travel faster, and the tenants-in-chief have headed for their own homes. So there are just three Ibelin household knights with two squires and Daniel—Sir Daniel, that is—with my lord, and the Constable has just two squires with him."

Maria Zoë registered both the severity of the losses and that Daniel had distinguished himself, but she preferred to save her questions for Balian. More important, Maria Zoë had no doubt that if Aimery de Lusignan was riding in with her husband, then he had come to claim his bride—and two hours was precious little time for the girl to prepare herself.

The spacious, if old-fashioned, second-story chamber of the keep was always used for high-ranking guests, and Maria Zoë gave orders for the entire chamber to be swept and scoured, the bed made up, and woven mats to be laid out on the floor. "Make it ready for a bride," she told the servants. Then she sent for Eschiva.

Eschiva entered the solar, breathless. "Is it true? Uncle Balian is on his way home and Daniel has been knighted?"

"That's what Dawit said, yes," Maria Zoë answered calmly. "Now come with me."

Eschiva was a dutiful maiden, and she obediently followed Maria Zoë up from the solar to the bedchamber on the floor above, but she couldn't help asking: "Is something wrong, Tante Marie?"

"No," Maria Zoë answered simply. "Sit down there." She pointed to a stool before a dressing table laden with beautiful inlaid boxes and elegant little flasks containing scents.

Eschiva's eyes widened. "What is it?"

"Your husband is with mine. I think we can assume he has come to claim you—and consummate your marriage."

Eschiva flushed at once, and her eyelids dropped over her eyes modestly.

"Rahel is organizing a bath for you," Maria Zoë announced, referring to her Coptic waiting woman, "but we won't have time to wash your hair. I'll dress it for you."

Stunned, Eschiva sank down on the stool, as the Dowager Queen of Jerusalem stood behind her like a handmaiden. Maria Zoë unbraided Eschiva's long tresses, and then started to gently and methodically comb out her hair. Eschiva was in shock. She had waited for this day for so long that she couldn't believe it had finally come.

Behind them two servants brought up the cork-lined tub, and other servants brought buckets of water from the well in relays. There was no time to heat the water and little need, given the heat of the summer day. Maria Zoë tied up Eschiva's long hair in a linen towel so she could bathe without getting it wet. She handed Eschiva olive-oil soap from Nablus, and after Eschiva was clean and dabbed dry, Maria Zoë had her sit again on the stool. Maria Zoë then massaged rose-scented oil onto Eschiva's shoulders, arms, and even her nubile breasts. Eschiva blushed as her aunt worked, but they did not speak.

Maria Zoë went to her chest and removed a silk shift that she slipped over Eschiva's head. Meanwhile Rahel brought from the girls' chamber the pretty red linen gown and yellow silk surcoat that Eschiva had been working on for months. The embroidery was not quite finished at the hem of the latter, but it was the prettiest and most flattering outfit she owned. Maria Zoë helped her dress and had just tied one of her own ruby-studded belts around Eschiva's hips when the sound of arriving horses wafted through the window.

Maria Zoë turned at once to Rahel. "Tell my lord to take the Constable directly into the hall. Tell him we will be down shortly, but that he is not to come upstairs."

Eschiva, however, jumped up and rushed to the window. Kneeling on the window seat and holding on to the window frame, she could just manage to see a corner of the ward. She caught a glimpse of horses clustering together as their riders dismounted. There were so many men in armor getting in each other's way that she could not identify anyone at first. Finally she located her uncle; he was taller than most men and rode a tall red stallion. From here she could not see his face, only his dark hair and the Ibelin arms on the trapper of his palfrey. Beside him was a man riding a stallion with a blue-and-white striped trapper. Her heart started beating faster. That must be him! His hair was brown, almost like hers, only lighter from exposure to the sun. If only she could get a look at his face!

But he did not look up. Instead he swung himself down, and with her uncle walked out of sight. Eschiva let out an unconscious sigh, and only when Maria Zoë gently touched her shoulder and urged, "Come, let me fix your hair," did she realize her aunt had come to stand behind her in the window niche.

She looked up at the beautiful Greek princess her uncle had brought home and whispered, "Tante Marie, do you think . . ." But she couldn't put all her hopes and fears into words.

Maria Zoë smiled and put her arm around the girl's shoulders to lead her back to the stool before the dressing table. She took the towel off Eschiva's head and started to comb out her hair again. When she was satisfied, she opened one of her boxes, removed long, narrow strands of braided gold threads, and started to deftly weave these into Eschiva's hair, using them to loosely bind it. As she worked she started talking.

"I was younger than you when I came to Jerusalem to wed King Amalric. He was old enough to be my father, going bald, and already very fat. I had been told about the fundamentals of procreation—as I presume you have?" She paused to look more closely at Eschiva, who nodded vigorously, blushing.

Maria Zoë nodded knowingly. "Now, you may also have heard that that act is very painful and humiliating." She paused to see Eschiva's reaction. The girl was biting her lip. Maria Zoë patted her shoulder reassuringly. "Well, it can be. I admit I never, not once, found pleasure in Amalric's bed. He was just too fat and unappealing. Aimery de Lusignan, on the other hand, is still a young, vigorous, and attractive man—far more like your uncle. And your uncle—although he was not a king or even a baron when we married—proved the troubadours right."

Eschiva twisted around to look up at her aunt hopefully. "You mean . . . ?"

"Yes," Maria Zoë smiled. "A woman can find exquisite pleasure in a man's bed, and she can find respect and comfort and safety in a man's arms. I know your mother's marriage was not happy, at least not in the end—and I will be honest with you, Eschiva, I do not know what kind of husband Aimery de Lusignan will make—but whatever he is, he is only one man, and he need not be your last."

"But—but I *want* to be a good wife, Tante Marie," Eschiva protested, looking up at her with wide eyes. "Tell me how I can best please him."

Maria Zoë stroked Eschiva's soft cheek with the back of her hand, feeling ancient although she was just barely twenty-five. "You can please him best just by being yourself—unblemished, full of hope, gentle and dutiful and anxious to please. Remember, too, you can confess anything at all to Beth. She will go with you to your new household, and she has seen the very, very worst that men can do. Nothing you tell her will shock her, so if you have cause—which I hope you won't—you will not lack a shoulder to cry on. But most important," Maria Zoë grasped Eschiva's shoulders so firmly that her fingers almost hurt, "if Aimery should ever fail to show you the respect you are owed as his wife and the daughter of a baron, you can come home to me and your uncle. I know!" She held up her hand to stop Eschiva's protest. "You can go to your father, too—but if you prefer, you can always come to me."

Eschiva flung her arms around her aunt and hugged her close. "Thank you, Tante Marie! Thank you!"

For a moment they clung to one another, sharing a bond that was stronger than their formal relationship. They were more than relatives; they were friends. Maria Zoë felt tears in her eyes. Eschiva was so young, and Aimery had been so indifferent to her up to now. She was so afraid for her, but she did not want to show it. She forced herself back behind her façade of cool efficiency. "Come. It's getting late and I must show you how to wrap a wimple. I'll give you one of mine, as you'll want to wear one in the morning."

"Does your lady always keep you waiting this long?" Aimery asked, drumming his fingers impatiently on the linen-covered high table.

"Actually," Balian remarked, leaning back in his chair and turning the goblet between his fingers, "never. She's a very punctual woman, but we didn't give her much warning."

"Dinner is ready," Aimery retorted, indicating the ushers and pages and cooks already in position. The tables behind the screens were groaning under the burden of platters piled high with roasted geese, stuffed hens, and grilled goat, not to mention the beans, peas, carrots, and lentils in various sauces, and the bread piled high in baskets. The meal was ready, and the squires had already had a healthy share of it in the kitchens before taking up their stations behind their lords, ready to pour wine and water and serve. But the lady of the house was absent.

"Have some more wine," Balian replied, signaling Dawit forward to pour for their guest.

Even as he spoke, however, Maria Zoë emerged from the screens and stood at the far end of the hall facing them. Since she had been in the bedchamber, to get to the screens meant she'd actually gone down into the ward and taken the outside steps, which at first puzzled Balian. Then he realized she was waiting for someone else. A moment later a lovely young lady stepped out of the screens, and Maria Zoë looped her arm through the other lady's elbow as they started forward together.

"Who's that with your wife?" Aimery asked, staring.

"*Your* wife," Balian answered, amused, although he too had had to look twice before he recognized his niece.

"That's what I thought; I just wanted to be sure before I did or said something inappropriate," Lusignan answered, admitting after a pause, "I wouldn't have recognized her in a different setting."

Balian couldn't resist commenting, "Well, whose fault is that? You were always welcome to visit more often."

Aimery just grunted in reply and touched his face with his hand, feeling the four-day beard. Without taking his eyes off his approaching bride, he asked urgently under his breath, "How do I look?"

Balian laughed. "You look like you've been campaigning for a fortnight, and smell like you haven't bathed in a month."

Aimery frowned and leveled an annoyed look at Balian. "You don't exactly smell like a bed of roses, either!"

Balian only had time to laugh before he pushed back his chair and welcomed his lady to the dais. After kissing her on both cheeks, he turned to Lusignan and announced with relish, "My niece, Eschiva de Ramla and Mirabel," as the latter fell into a deep curtsy before the Constable, her husband.

The water in which Eschiva had bathed had warmed to room temperature by the time Balian stepped into the tub and sank down with a sigh. Behind him Rahel helped Maria Zoë out of her surcoat and gown, and then withdrew. Dressed only in a loose, sleeveless silk shift, Maria Zoë settled herself on the towels around the base of the tub and soaked a sponge in the water before she began to wash her husband methodically with the olive-oil soap.

It was Balian who had taught her the pleasure of this task in the early days of their romance, by insisting that she send Rahel away and let him bathe her. It had since become a ritual between them, a way of enjoying each other's body without the frenzy of lovemaking or sleepiness getting in the way.

Zoë loved Balian's firm, muscular body, but this evening as she worked by the fading light of dusk, she didn't like what she saw. "Blessed Virgin Mary! Is there an inch of you that is not bruised or cut?" she exclaimed in growing alarm as she ran her hand gently down his back, charting the various hues of black, blue, red, green, and yellow left by the blows of men who had tried to kill him. One huge bruise spread from his shoulder halfway down his arm, and from the crusted cuts on his forearm she could read just how intense the fighting had been—how close he must have been to a fatal wound, to death.

"Probably not," Balian conceded grimly.

Zoë stopped stroking him and laid her hand on his arm in a gesture of sympathy. With alarm she realized that he was tense rather than limp with languid pleasure as he should have been now that the danger was past. At dinner he had joked about it. He should have been in the mood for coddling and feminine flattery. But he was not.

She studied his beloved face, darkened now with an unfamiliar growth of beard, and she saw beyond the cut on his cheek to the dark circles under his eyes and the chapped lips. More important: he did not meet her eyes.

"What aren't you telling me?" she asked, certain that she was not going to like the answer.

"At dinner we made light of it," he answered, and Zoë thought he meant the battle. Lusignan and he had certainly made it sound like a lark, a great adventure, a close-run race but a Christian victory. They had guffawed together about how ridiculous the Templars had looked—"fleeing like a bunch of geese with outstretched necks," Lusignan had claimed—and they had laughed so hard that Zoë had known it could only have been from pent-up tension and relief. "You mean how close the King came to capture?" she ventured.

"That, too," Balian admitted. "And Daniel earned his knighting, by all that's holy—though I'm not sure he's really ready for it. But . . ." He sighed. "What I meant was that I didn't want to upset Eschiva. She's got enough to adjust to just now."

Zoë nodded, glancing over her shoulder to the window that looked toward the keep. She could not see from her current position whether the light was still burning in the bedchamber there, but Lusignan had been eager to take his bride to bed. Now all she could do was pray. She looked back at Balian wordlessly.

"There's only one reason Lusignan came with me—although I daresay he's not regretting it," he added, with a glance in the same direction as Zoë the moment before. "But he had no recollection of Eschiva as a person. He only came to secure control of Ramla and Mirabel—and to keep my greedy hands off them."

"What do you mean? Is your brother dead?"

"Not yet, but there's precious little I can do to save him." Balian bent and splashed water into his face and then rubbed it vigorously with his wet hands, as if he could wash away his guilty conscience.

"Let me," Zoë urged. She squeezed water into a sponge and then rubbed it against the bar of olive-oil soap until it was well lathered. Then she started gently but firmly rubbing the sponge in circles under Balian's ears, down his neck, and across his shoulders, filling the sponge with more soap as needed. When she finished with his back, she gently pushed him against the padded rear of the tub and started to work on his chest and arms.

Very gradually he relaxed enough to confess. "The Sultan has set a ransom I cannot pay, Zoë. A ransom I could never pay, even if I plundered Eschiva's inheritance, as well as everything my father gave his life to win."

"How much?" Zoë asked practically.

"It's not a ransom, it's a death sentence. The Sultan is punishing me for bargaining so hard about those three worthless youths!" Balian burst out, the wine and the exhaustion and his nakedness combining to rob him of his self-control and exposing his raw feeling.

"How much?" Zoë repeated.

"You don't want to know."

"Yes, I do. Tell me."

"Two hundred thousand bezants."

Even after his prelude, the sum took Maria Zoë by surprise. She had thought Balian was being melodramatic to prepare her for bad news. Now she realized that he had been deadly serious: it was a ransom Ibelin, Ramla, and Mirabel could not pay. A ransom they would not be able to pay even with help from her dower lands of Nablus.

"Lusignan thinks the Sultan may be negotiated down."

"I should think so!" Maria Zoë answered indignantly. "He must know we cannot pay such a sum. Ibelin can't raise a tenth of that after what he did to it! Ramla and Mirabel—maybe fifty thousand, Nablus another fifty thousand. Do you think the King . . ." She fell silent, but her hands continued absently to rub the sponge in gentle circles.

Balian slid down and dunked his head under water. He re-emerged, brushing his wet hair back from his face, and shook his head. "If the King offers, I'm not too proud to accept, but I cannot ask him."

"Um. I was thinking of something—someone—else. Princess Sibylla."

"Sibylla?"

"He's been courting her, hasn't he? I mean, I know she's agreed to marry Burgundy when he finally gets here, but she's been dallying with Barry in the meantime—and no doubt the Sultan knows that."

"How could the Sultan know something like that?"

"Don't be naive. Oriental rulers always have a network of spies. Didn't you once tell me King Baldwin was served only by Muslim slaves? How much do you think it would take to persuade one of them to send little messages back to the great Defender of the Faith? Besides, regardless of how he knows, it explains everything."

"Forgive my Frankish simplicity, but I'm not following you."

"Salah ad-Din believes he holds in his hands the next King of Jerusalem—

and he's asking a king's ransom. You're quite right that he doesn't expect Ibelin, or Ramla and Mirabel, to raise two hundred thousand bezants, but not because he wishes to see your brother dead. He simply wants to see the Kingdom of Jerusalem poorer—maybe even divided and internally weakened—by raising such a huge sum for a man who is not yet crowned or anointed. Alternatively, he may even hope to expose Sibylla's relationship with Barry and thereby discourage Burgundy from honoring his promises."

Balian looked at his wife with a kind of wonder. It was now almost completely dark and it was hard to see more than contours and shadows in the corners of the room, but light from the moon caught on Zoë's oval face, and she had never looked more beautiful to Balian. She had cleaned more than the dirt from his body; she had taken the sense of guilt from his conscience.

She smiled at him and added in an almost playful tone, "And if Sibylla won't pay, we'll send your brother to my great-uncle. He'd like the idea of the future King of Jerusalem being deeply in his debt."

"Until he finds out Barry won't be the next King of Jerusalem, Burgundy will be."

"Maybe."

"What do you mean, 'maybe'?" Balian pressed his wife, looking at her hard. "The King has already agreed to his terms and sent his ambassadors bearing gifts. He'll come as soon as he can."

"For a man who has been offered a kingdom, he seems rather slow to seize it."

"He must settle his affairs in Burgundy first."

"Of course," Maria Zoë agreed lightly, for it made little difference to her if Balian saw things her way in this matter or not. "I am probably wrong—but so long as Salah ad-Din and my great-uncle think as I do, we can exploit the situation to your brother's advantage."

"That's a pretty daunting trio to dare question," Balian noted wryly, before reaching up a dripping arm to pull her to him. The sudden motion caused water to slosh over the edge of the tub. Zoë let out a stifled cry of surprise before their lips touched in the darkness. Then, framing Balian's face in her hands, she kissed him passionately.

Yet even as he lifted her up to carry her to the bed, she had space in her mind to pray that Eschiva, too, would enjoy this night.

Chapter 3

Jerusalem, Ash Wednesday 1180

Barry was looking remarkably good for a man just released from Saracen captivity. Clearly he had not been confined to a dungeon, for his skin was coppery brown and his hair a lustrous, bright blond. Nor had he been on short rations, for he was as broad-shouldered and vigorous as ever when he jumped down from his stallion and took the steps of the Ibelin residence in Jerusalem two at a time before his brother could come down to greet him.

They all but collided on the landing of the courtyard gallery, and Barry exuberantly flung his arms around Balian. "Good to see you at last, little brother!"

"And you!" Balian answered, overwhelmed by relief that no last-minute hitch had prevented Barry's release.

The ransom, after all, was still not paid in full, but Salah ad-Din had agreed to let Ramla return to raise the remainder of his ransom himself, in exchange for a down payment of fifty thousand bezants and the return of his nephew Farrukh-Shah. The latter was still in Christian hands because Odo de St. Amand—with admirable steadfastness—had refused the agreed exchange. Templars, he insisted, could not be ransomed, not for flesh any more than gold.

Salah ad-Din, however, considered the Baron of Ramla worth more than his nephew and insisted that, even after the return of Farrukh-Shah and the payment of fifty thousand bezants, Ramla still owed him one hundred thousand bezants. Ramla had agreed—confident that Sibylla would help pay some of the sum and that the rest could be raised in Constantinople with his sister-in-law's help.

As he caught sight of that sister-in-law now, waiting at the entrance to the main reception room for the brothers to complete their greetings, Ramla left his brother to sweep her a low, courtly bow. "Madame, what a pleasure to see you again as well." He lifted her hand to his lips. "To set eyes on a woman's face is as exhilarating as a whole pitcher of wine—especially a face like yours. That was truly the worst of it," he added over his shoulder to his brother, "not seeing women even from a distance! Seriously. The accommodation was better than many a place I've slept while on campaign—at least it was dry and reasonably clean. The food was actually quite decent, once you got used to so much rice. But not seeing a woman—not even when we were allowed to walk around Damascus—was hell! Nothing but these walking shrouds that hid everything of interest! Still, we were so starved of feminine company that we turned and stared after the billowing sheets, trying to imagine something lovely underneath."

Balian nodded understanding but urged, "Come inside."

Barry shook his head, and instead strode back to the gallery railing to shout down to his squire: "Bring up my saddlebags!" Turning back to his brother and sister-in-law, he announced, "I didn't come entirely empty-handed. Wait till you see what I've brought you!"

"You are the only gift we need, Barry, and to see you looking so well is a huge relief. I did not trust what you wrote in your letters, knowing every word was written in the presence of your jailers. You would not have dared complain."

As they spoke, they entered a long chamber that opened on the far side to a loge overlooking the Street of Spain. The floor was paved with marble tiles in a black-and-white checkerboard pattern and the walls were faced with polychrome marble tiles up to about three feet, both remnants from the building's past. Hugh d'Ibelin had bought this palace at about the time King Amalric set Agnes de Courtenay aside. At the time, Hugh had been enjoying the revenues of Ramla and Mirabel as well as Ibelin, but Balian still suspected King Amalric had helped finance the purchase in gratitude to Hugh for taking Agnes de Courtenay back. In any case, it was one of the more prominent residences in Jerusalem, occupying the wide northeast corner of the oblique intersection of the Street of Spain and Jehoshaphat Street. It had clearly been the residence of a prominent man during the Fatimid occupation of Jerusalem, and the mosaics on the ground floor dated to the Byzantine period, suggesting that it had been a wealthy man's residence even before the Muslim conquest. Its proximity to Pontius Pilate's palace, furthermore, led some churchmen to hypothesize that it stood on the ruins of a Roman residence.

Because the room opened on to the gallery on the inside and the loge on the outside, the doors and windows admitted fresh air already cooled by the shade, and no direct sunlight even in the hottest summer heat. Today, however, had seen intermittent showers, and it was the warmth of the fireplace that drew Barry inwards. He sighed audibly as he flung off his still-damp cloak and dropped himself into an armed chair before the slow fire.

"I can't tell you how good it is to be here!" he exclaimed, looking around the familiar room, which was furnished sparsely in the Frankish manner. "The Sultan killed all the Templars except St. Amand," Barry told his brother and sister-in-law as they settled themselves in chairs on either side of him. "Just executed them whether they were wounded or not, without a second thought. He snapped his fingers and their heads were off. He put St. Amand in chains in a dungeon as well, so you can imagine how nervous the rest of us felt. However, the Sultan ordered all the secular knights housed in a vaulted stone chamber of the citadel that was above ground. We were allowed out into the courtyard every day for an hour or two of exercise, and were given chess sets as well, and—"

His squire appeared hesitantly in the doorway with the saddlebags, and Barry gestured for him to come. "This is Stephan. You don't know him, since he served one of my Mirabel knights who was killed. Since I lost both my squires, Salah ad-Din allowed me to buy his freedom along with my own. Stephan, my brother Balian, Baron d'Ibelin, and his wife Maria Comnena, Dowager Queen of Jerusalem."

The youngster bowed his head politely to the exalted personages, and kept his eyes down. He looked very thin, pale, and fragile to Balian, who surmised the captured squires had not enjoyed quite the same level of hospitality as the captive lords.

Balian addressed his brother's squire. "Stephan, if you find your way to the kitchens, you can eat your fill. Then ask for Dawit and he'll show you around the house." Turning back to his brother, he added, "I've prepared our old room for you."

"Fine," Barry agreed, bending over to open his saddlebags and remove some objects. "This is what I brought for Eschiva," he remarked, setting the still-wrapped package on the floor beside the chair and digging deeper as he asked, "Is she in Jerusalem?"

"Yes, she and Lusignan said they would stop by later today in anticipation of your arrival. Or should I send a messenger to her now?"

"No, no, later's fine. Here!" Barry stood and walked over to hand his brother a magnificent curved dagger of Damascene production. It had an elaborately carved ivory handle and a bronze-reinforced hilt. Balian was taken aback by it. "Was this a gift from the Sultan?" he asked, thinking such a magnificent weapon must have belonged to a man of great wealth. He drew the blade to test the edge on his thumb and confirm that the cutting edge was as fine as its dressing suggested.

"No, no," Barry waved the thought aside. "After the fifty thousand bezants were delivered to the Sultan and he had word Farrukh-Shah had crossed into Muslim territory, he returned my armor, but not my arms. However, he allowed me access to the city of Damascus—with an escort, of course. I borrowed five hundred bezants back from him so that I would not return like a beggar. Here! This is for you, beloved sister-in-law." He brought Maria Zoë a blue silk scarf that shimmered with gold and was edged with gold embroidery.

Maria Zoë caught her breath at its beauty, but she cast Balian a frown of disapproval. Didn't Barry realize just how difficult it had been to raise those fifty thousand bezants? His tenants had been pressured repeatedly and intensely, but with the drought now going into its third year, many people had literally nothing to spare. Furthermore, so many of Barry's knights and squires had been taken captive with him that most families were hard pressed to pay the ransom of their own relatives, much less contribute to the ransom of their lord. Maria Zoë had donated the bulk of the fifty thousand bezants from her Nablus revenues, and she had done it willingly to prevent greater hardship on Ibelin, Ramla, and Mirabel, but she found it incongruous that Barry was spending money lavishly.

"And here is what I brought for Sibylla!" Barry announced proudly, unveiling a beautiful box inlaid with mother-of-pearl, which he opened to reveal a ring set with rubies in a circle around a sapphire. Maria Zoë gratified Barry by gasping, and he beamed with pleasure, thinking it was a gasp of envy. In fact, Maria Zoë was shocked: Sibylla had no need of more jewels—certainly not at a time when many laborers on Barry's lands were on the brink of starvation. She and Balian had spent hours talking about what they could do to help, torn between the need to contribute to Barry's outrageous ransom and their pity for people in desperate straits through no fault of their own. Again she glanced at Balian, but he shook his head at her. Instead, in a blatant ploy to change the topic of conversation, he remarked, "What's all that noise outside?"

Balian left his chair to step on to the loge and go to the corner, where he could see down both the Street of Spain and Jehoshaphat Street. This was a busy corner at any time, but on Ash Wednesday the crowds were always particularly thick. Furthermore, Easter fell late this year after a mild, dry winter, so the first of the pilgrim ships were already disgorging their passengers at all the coastal ports. From the coast, pilgrims hired hacks or mules if they could afford them, or trudged on foot along the roads that converged on Jerusalem. Most carried tall walking sticks and wore rough-woven capes with crosses sewn on their shoulders. Some came in little family groups, but many pilgrims formed companies along the way and traveled together with others who shared their tongue, so the continuous flow of people broke into clumps of French, Spanish, German etc. speakers.

Today was no different, except that so many pilgrims were squeezed into the narrow streets that it was almost impossible for anyone to move in either direction. Several pilgrims were carrying wooden crosses as they tried to push their way to the Chapel of the Condemnation to begin retracing Christ's steps from condemnation to crucifixion. Almost everyone in the crowd had drawn crosses on their brow with ashes, and a few men and women were flagellating themselves in an excess of penance that Balian had seen too often to take seriously. There were also a score of Benedictine novices singing their way up Jehoshaphat Street, and a madman screaming "Repent!"

The shouting that had drawn Balian outside, however, was coming from the other direction, the Street of the Furriers. Balian leaned over the railing to try to get a better view and saw mounted Templars pushing their way through the crowd, the Beauséant flapping from an upraised lance.

"That's how they make enemies," Barry remarked as he came up beside his brother.

Balian agreed with a silent nod, and together they watched as the Templars all but trampled the foot-folk under the hooves of their destriers. They were riding four abreast, which was as much as the street would allow, and it was a very long column. It was odd for them to be in this part of the city, since their headquarters stood to east and south of the Ibelin palace, on the site of the Temple of Solomon. As they came nearer, however, Balian recognized that the lead rider was wearing the insignia of the Grand Master. "Ah, that's what this is about," he surmised. "The new Grand Master has just arrived in Jerusalem, and he's anxious to visit the Mount of Olives on Ash Wednesday for the first time in his life."

"Have the Templars chosen a new Master already?" Barry asked, astonished. "St. Amand only died two months ago."

"Didn't you hear? No, I suppose your jailers would have no reason to tell you. When St. Amand refused to be ransomed, he also sent word to the Marshal that he was 'dead' and ordered the election of a new Grand Master. They held a Grand Chapter last fall and elected Arnold de Toroga, formerly Master of the Temple in Spain." As he spoke, Balian tried to get a better look at the man who would now wield huge power and influence in the Kingdom of Jerusalem. Toroga was white-haired and his long white beard hung to the middle of his chest. His face was long, thin, and deeply lined. An old man, an administrator more than a fighter, Balian surmised, unsure how he felt about this.

Barry leaned his elbows on the railing and watched the Templars ride past. "Is it true we lost the castle at Jacob's Ford, after all the trouble we went to build it last winter?"

Balian nodded grimly without looking at his brother. "We lost it."

"How?"

Balian took a deep breath. "The King called for the army to muster at Tiberias, but many knights were slow to react. The spring harvest had been terrible because of the drought, and the autumn harvest promised to be even worse. Men were more worried about how to feed their families than about defending a new castle. The Templars were at Jacob's Ford, men told themselves. The Templars had eighty knights and two hundred fifty sergeants at Jacob's Ford. Why did the whole army have to muster *again*?" Balian could hear the words in Maria Zoë's voice in his ear.

"When we did muster, the King fell suddenly ill. Another fever. Again, it looked as if he were going to die. His mother and Princess Sibylla made a mad night ride from Jerusalem with the True Cross to be at his bedside. By the time he recovered, it was too late. Salah ad-Din had mined under the walls of the castle, and—on the second attempt—brought down a huge section of the masonry. The Templar commander flung himself into the flames when he realized the situation was hopeless." Balian crossed himself and muttered, "May God have mercy on his soul."

"And the rest were also slaughtered, no doubt," his brother added grimly, crossing himself as well.

Balian nodded. "They slaughtered most of the garrison on the spot, being Templars, but even the lay workmen—the masons, carpenters, cooks, and smiths—were massacred. Not immediately, I admit, but while being marched back to Damascus to the slave market. I don't know why exactly—just religious fervor on the part of the common soldiers, it seems."

"They have that," Barry confirmed, tight-lipped, his eyes turned inward to his memories. After a moment he added, "When you hear them chanting their slogans of hatred, calling for death to all Christians, for the 'cleansing' of a land that was never holy to them until we took it from them, you realize that there is no reasoning with them. They are determined to exterminate us."

Balian studied his brother, and a chill went down his spine. He tried to chase his fears back into his subconscious. "Over the last century, they have spent far more time fighting each other than us."

"Yes. So long as Egypt was Shiite, they were divided. Even now, the rulers in

Aleppo and Mosul view Salah ad-Din as a usurper, while the Nubians hate him for the slaughter of the Caliph's guard, and the Egyptians only support him as long as he brings them loot. He can never quite be sure there won't be a revolt somewhere. But that's exactly why he's let the genie '*jihad*' out of the bottle. He clothes himself in piety to disguise his earthly ambitions, to justify his conquest of Muslim territory—and to unite his diverse subjects in a common cause against a common enemy.

"Make no mistake," Barry continued, turning to look his brother squarely in the face, "Salah ad-Din is an intelligent man. Very well-educated and somewhat scholarly. Surprisingly short and no longer young," Barry couldn't resist adding, "but he is first and foremost a ruthless ruler determined to establish his own dynasty in the largest possible territory. And he wants the Kingdom of Jerusalem not for any religious reason—for what the hell is Jerusalem to them? The venue of a dream!" he scoffed. "No, he wants Jerusalem because he wants the *ports* we control. He has no iron, you know. He has to import iron for all his weapons and armor from the East or the Greeks."

"Or capture them from us," Balian noted with a snort, adding, "They say he took a thousand suits of mail at Jacob's Ford. What on earth were the Templars doing with a thousand suits of mail in an unfinished castle?" He asked the question rhetorically directed toward the column of Templars still blocking the street below.

Looking down, however, Balian caught sight of a party of riders waiting in the Street of Spain for the Templars to turn up Jehoshaphat Street. Balian recognized his niece and her husband and nudged Barry. "There's Eschiva and Lusignan now."

Barry followed Balian's finger and his face broke into a wide smile. "She's all grown up! What a proper young lady!"

Eschiva did look grown up in her white silk wimple under an embroidered, crown-like hat, and she sat the bay mare Lusignan had given her very well. She also looked quite small and fragile to Balian, flanked as she was by two armored men on tall horses. The men were talking to each other over her head, and for a moment it looked as if they were ignoring her. Then the stranger bent and addressed her directly, making her draw back as if in shock, while her husband laughed. At last the Templars had passed and Eschiva's party advanced to dismount in front of the Ibelin palace, while Balian and Barry returned inside.

"I'll go surprise her," Barry announced, and moved out onto the gallery while Balian and Maria Zoë hung back.

The guests mounted the stairs from the courtyard, and then with a startled "Papa!" Eschiva ran to her father's arms.

He lifted her off the floor and spun her around. "My little bird! You're all grown up! Was I really away so long?"

Balian and Maria Zoë exchanged a look. He hadn't been away so long; he had simply taken no time for his daughter even when he was in the country. Barry set his daughter down and turned to face his son-in-law. "Lusignan, I understand you helped raise part of my ransom. I am grateful."

"For my wife's sake," Aimery answered coldly, making it very clear he still begrudged Barry his efforts to disinherit Eschiva, even if she chose to ignore the slights to herself and her mother. "I don't believe you've met my younger brother Guy," he continued, indicating the knight beside him.

"No," Barry conceded with a stiff nod in the direction of the younger man. Aimery de Lusignan was Constable of Jerusalem and so could not be slighted, but his younger brother was of no consequence.

Maria Zoë, however, as hostess, gestured for the newcomers to come into the hall, promising refreshments. At the sound of her voice Guy de Lusignan turned in her direction, and Balian saw his eyes widen. A moment later he was bowing over Maria Zoë's hand with an elegance that made Barry look like a callow youth. "Madame de Ramla, I presume—"

"No," three male voices corrected him at the same time.

"Ibelin," Maria Zoë introduced herself with a regal smile, removing her hand from his slowly, but pointedly nevertheless. She knew exactly how to put distance between herself and others, Balian noted—with approval.

"Dowager Queen of Jerusalem," the Constable hammered the point home, taking his younger brother by his upper arm and steering him firmly past Maria Zoë into the room beyond.

Maria Zoë raised an eyebrow at Balian, but then turned to go and tell the staff they were ready for refreshments, while Barry, his arm still around Eschiva, followed the Lusignan brothers into the solar.

"So when did you arrive, sir?" Balian asked the younger Lusignan as he joined the others.

"Today," Guy admitted cheerfully. "I landed at Jaffa five days ago, but it took me a couple of days to find suitable horses."

"You didn't bring your own?" Balian asked, surprised. The Holy Land was always short of horses, and most knights brought their own if they wanted to be sure of having a powerful mount.

"Oh, horse transports need to be booked *so* far in advance—particularly at this time of year. I was lucky to get a cabin at all. In fact, I would have had to come steerage like the poor, if some old merchant hadn't developed the runs at the right moment."

"Were you in such a great hurry?" Barry asked. "It makes it sound like you were running away from something."

The elder Lusignan snorted. "Guy is *always* running away from something—usually his own bad judgment," Aimery quipped, adding, "Guy has managed to be on the *losing* side of every squabble between the King of England and his sons, between the Plantagenet princes, and between Plantagenet and Capet—not because he's been loyal to anyone in particular, but rather because he has a knack for changing masters just before they go down in humiliating defeat. No," Aimery insisted, "Guy is not the most successful member of the Lusignan family—but having made himself persona non grata in France, Normandy, Brittany, England, and Aquitaine, he has come to make the Holy Land unsafe as well."

"We don't need any help with that," Balian remarked dryly. "Salah ad-Din has made it unsafe enough as it is."

"I daresay my brother is exaggerating," Guy countered. "I've actually done quite well on the tourney circuit," the younger man bragged.

Barry and Balian just stared at him.

"They don't have tournaments here," his brother enlightened him.

Guy gaped at him, shocked.

"No need," Balian explained. "We spend too much of our time fighting in earnest to need to play at it."

"So," Aimery changed the subject by turning pointedly to Barry and asking, "Where and how do you plan to raise the remaining hundred thousand bezants?"

Barry thought it wise not to mention his hopes of getting a handsome sum from Sibylla, and instead bowed toward Maria Zoë and answered, "My beloved sister-in-law has been kind enough to plead my case with the Greek Emperor. He has agreed to see me and hear me out, so I will leave for Constantinople almost at once." Just as soon as I've seen Sibylla, he added mentally. "I'll make first for Tripoli to thank Raymond for releasing Farrukh-Shah for my sake and forfeiting a sizeable ransom himself. Then I'll continue on to Antioch and, after paying my respects to Prince Bohemond and Maria Zoë's sister Theodora," he nodded again to Maria Zoë, "I'll take ship from there. I hope to be back by Easter.

"Now a question for you, Aimery." Barry turned the tables on his son-in-law, "Since you are Constable and so the man responsible for organizing the defense of the Kingdom of Jerusalem: just how much longer can you leave the fate of the Kingdom in the hands of a leper?"

"What sort of question is that?" Aimery shot back, shocked, while Balian spluttered in equal amazement, "Barry! Baldwin IV is our anointed King."

"That he may be, and I've sworn homage to him no less than the rest of you, but he's no longer capable of leading the army. You know that better than I do. He's worse than an infant or a woman!" Balian winced at the analogy, but it wasn't inherently wrong. Barry was only saying out loud what many men thought in silence. "If we had a child or a girl on the throne, *you* would lead the army in their name, Lusignan. But by insisting on coming on campaign despite his handicap, Baldwin undermines your authority, prevents you from doing your job, and gets in everyone's way, endangering us all. Twice now, his inability to stay on his horse has cost us a battle that would otherwise have been won."

"Hardly," Balian felt compelled to defend Baldwin. "It was the Templars' rashness in attacking Salah ad-Din's larger forces on their own rather than falling back and fighting with the King and the rest of us that cost us the victory on the Litani." He could have added that if Barry had not crossed the Litani, he too could have rallied around the King and broken the Saracen charge, but he didn't want to get into a fight about that, certainly not in front of his niece and the Lusignans.

"I'll give you that, Balian. The Templars made a bad decision and it cost them dearly, but the fact remains that twice in a row—three times, if you count the loss of the castle at Jacob's Ford—the King's health has cost us victory. How much longer can we afford to lose battles and castles because of the King's health? When will he see reason?"

"What do you mean by reason? Baldwin has long since agreed to abdicate to his sister's husband, as soon as she marries a man of proven military ability," Balian pointed out. "It's not his fault that the Duke of Burgundy reneged on his promise!"

The news that the Duke of Burgundy would not be coming out to marry Princess Sibylla and assume the role of heir apparent of Jerusalem had arrived with the first pilgrim ships of the season, proving Maria Zoë's instincts correct. The King of France had had a paralyzing stroke and his fourteen-year-old son was fighting down a rebellion—not to mention facing the perpetual threat from the Plantagenet. Under these circumstances, the Duke of Burgundy felt he could not leave France, and sent his regrets to his future brother-in-law and bride.

"The Duke of Burgundy is the third Western prince who has promised to take up the defense of the Holy Land—only to change his mind. We cannot look there for help any longer," Aimery declared. "We must find a husband for Sibylla among the experienced men already in the Kingdom."

Balian glanced toward his brother, and Barry grinned. This was the opportunity he had been waiting for: what had before been little more than dallying with a princess was about to become serious politics and an open bid for the throne.

"The Baron of Ramla is a comely man," Stephanie de Milly probed cautiously, as Princess Sibylla paused by a stall selling carpets in the market.

Stephanie was the Lady of Oultrejourdain in her own right. She had inherited the border barony from her father and had bestowed it on three husbands in succession. Her first husband, the hapless son of the former Constable Humphrey de Toron, had died young in an accident, leaving her with an infant named for his father who was rapidly taken away from her by her father-in-law. Her second husband, Miles de Plancy, had been a man after her own heart, fierce and ambitious. When he had been assassinated in the streets of Jerusalem, she had vowed revenge on the man she suspected (but no one else credited) with the murder—the Count of Tripoli. To that end she had taken her third husband, the infamous adventurer Reynald de Châtillon. The latter had seduced his way into the Crown of Antioch, but had lost it again when his wife died and his stepson came of age—while he was rotting in a Saracen prison. Reynald and Stephanie shared a passion for power, a contempt for weakness, and utter disregard for law and religion.

Madame d'Oultrejourdain was taller than most men, heavy-boned, and well-padded with muscle and fat. She disdained "female vanities" and dressed in practical linen dresses of solid colors, although she no longer wore only black. She used neither makeup nor perfume and tended to smell rather bad most of the time. She was an unusual companion for the vain Sibylla, but Sibylla had been bored, and Stephanie had been the only other woman willing to come shopping with her.

The traders in the covered market were all natives and spoke Arabic, Armenian, or Greek. Despite the crowds and the cacophony of voices haggling, quarreling, and gossiping around them, they had more privacy here than in the royal palace—and Stephanie had been asked by her husband to find out if it was true Sibylla planned to marry the Baron of Ramla now that the Duke of Burgundy had jilted her unseen. In the short space of time before Ramla departed for Constantinople, he had made no secret of his suit for Sibylla. He had brought her a beautiful ring from Damascus and had showered attention on her, hardly leaving her side by day—or night.

"What did you say?" Sibylla asked, without taking her eyes off the rich carpet as she absently traced its intricate patterns with one of her fingers. The shopkeeper extolled the quality of his wares in a constant flood of Arabic spiced with French words.

"I said, the Baron of Ramla is a comely man."

Sibylla nodded curtly and admitted, "He is"—but with less enthusiasm than Stephanie would have expected. "I'm not just interested in a pretty face," Sibylla added, turning away from the carpet to look accusingly at the Lady of Oultrejourdain. "Why does everyone think the only thing I care about is the way a man looks?" It was a rhetorical question, and the Lady of Oultrejourdain wisely ignored it. "I like Barry because he's *more* than a pretty face," Sibylla insisted. "It was he, you know, not my brother, who actually won the battle of Montgisard." As she spoke she moved further along the narrow alley, which was shielded from the sun by a vaulted brick roof. "My brother was in the rear, surrounded by his knights; it was Barry that led the charge."

Stephanie de Milly noted that this version of the battle ignored the role played by the Templars, but she had no reason to dispute with Sibylla. Let her think what she liked.

The next stalls offered shawls and veils, but Sibylla shook her head at the shopkeepers and continued up a couple of steps in the pavement. It was the steps, more than anything else, that made the market unsuitable for horses and forced even princesses to walk. At a shoe shop she paused again.

Sibylla pointed to a pair of slippers hanging out of reach on the wall of the little shop, and the shopkeeper eagerly got a long pole with a hook at the end with which to lift them down by the strap binding them. He presented them to the princess on his palms, grinning and chattering happily. They were polished leather, with designs painted on them in gold, and very pretty. Sibylla absently kicked off one of her shoes to try the new slipper, while her brain remained focused on Barry.

There was really nothing she could say against Barry. He was handsome, virile, brave, rich, educated, and—well—perfect. She knew her brother favored him as a suitor for her hand, while everyone seemed to think that the High Court would find him acceptable as her consort and future king. He certainly wasn't domineering like Montferrat had been, or insulting like Flanders. And Burgundy might have written fine letters, but he was all words and no deeds!

No, Barry was the best of the lot—so why didn't he excite her? Like this pair of shoes: they fit, and yet somehow they didn't. Sibylla took the pretty slipper off and handed it back to the shopkeeper, shaking her head. The shopkeeper tried to interest her in another, similar pair, but she shook her head and kept walking.

It wasn't even that she could complain about Barry's lovemaking; he was a skilled lover. Maybe too skilled. She couldn't forget that he'd been unfaithful to his first wife—and then discarded her. But what did she expect? A saint who was also a brave knight, good in bed, and a baron acceptable to the High Court?

Sibylla and Stephanie emerged from the market on the Street of Palms, very close to the entrance of the Church of the Holy Sepulcher, and suddenly a horse was hauled to a stop so abruptly that it skidded on the paving stones, lost its balance, and upset a stall selling fresh pomegranates and oranges. While the fruit rolled in all directions and the shop-keeper screeched in protest, the rider alighted with a swirl of cloak and a glitter of chain mail. He bowed deeply before Sibylla. "Your grace! No sooner do I emerge from the holiest of churches than I am granted the sight of an angel—or in this case, the most beautiful of mortals!" Stephanie rolled her eyes, disgusted at such blatant flattery for the rather plan Sibylla, but Sibylla beamed. The knight continued, "It can only be a sign from heaven that my sins have been forgiven! May I beg the boon of accompanying you wherever you are headed—even if it is to the gates of hell?"

Sibylla's blood was racing and her heart was beating; she could hardly breathe. Why didn't the Baron of Ramla make her feel like this? she asked herself before she queried the knight, "And who might you be, sir? I do not recall ever seeing you before."

"That is a dagger to my heart, madame! For I have had eyes only for you ever since I came to Jerusalem three days ago. Surely you remember now? I'm the younger brother of your brave Constable."

"Of course." Now she remembered vaguely, but she hadn't taken much note of him at the time; Ramla had been beside her whispering remarks about the young man being a "troublemaker" and a "ne'er-do-well"—banned, he had claimed, from the King of England's realm. "Guillaume, was it?" she ventured.

"No, madame, Guy: Guy de Lusignan."

"If he has dared debauch a princess of Jerusalem, I will see him hanged!" King Baldwin raged, springing up from his throne. His face was purple with outrage, and his mother was genuinely distressed for his health. She was convinced that stress increased the spread of the leprosy.

"Calm down, Baldwin," she urged, making soothing motions with her hands. "There's nothing that can be done about it now—"

"I can hang him!" Baldwin insisted, adding in fury, "He's nothing! Nothing at all! The fourth son of a Poitevin noble who has only distinguished himself by rebelling against his feudal lord! He's little better than an outlaw. He's been banned from the Plantagenet's lands. My *cousin* calls him traitor and murderer! And you want me to calm down? You want me to accept his sinful relationship with my sister? To bless a union that is despicable to God and an insult to Jerusalem? Never!"

Agnes de Courtenay had never seen her son so furious, and she was a wise and practical woman. She beat a tactical retreat and advised her daughter to give her brother a day or two to calm down.

Sibylla, however, couldn't wait that long and approached him on the following afternoon. He tried to escape her. "I know what you're here for," he warned, backing away from her. "I don't want to hear it. I *won't* hear of it. That wastrel, that traitor, that *fornicator*, will not wear the crown of Jerusalem!"

"Then so be it," Sibylla answered, dropping to her knees. "I will renounce my right to the throne. I do not want the throne of Jerusalem if it means living without Guy."

That was not an option for Baldwin. He was starting to go blind. He needed to retire from the world and prepare to face God. He needed Sibylla to marry a fighting man to whom he could turn over the Kingdom in good conscience. He could not wait for little Isabella to grow up. So he asked instead: "What on earth do you see in Guy de Lusignan? It wasn't a month ago that you were happy with the brave Baron de Ramla!" Baldwin was genuinely baffled.

"I can't explain it, Baldwin. I wish I *could*! I *wanted* to love Ramla—because I know you think he would make a good king. And probably he *would* be a good king. I don't question that he is a fine man—brave, wise, decisive, and pious. But I don't—can't—*love* him! Not now that I know my heart belongs to Guy. Do you want me to marry one man while being in love with another?"

"It happens all the time," Baldwin threw back at her bluntly.

"But do you want *me* to suffer that fate?" she asked, her big blue eyes already brimming with tears.

Baldwin kept his face rigid and refused to answer. Sibylla's face slowly crumpled into a visage of perfect misery, and she held up her clasped hands in a gesture of desperate pleading.

Baldwin turned his back on her, because he could not bear to see her so miserable. This was not like that terrible night when she had screamed at him, oblivious to his own pain. She had grown up since then. She had been beside him whenever he was ill. She had nearly killed herself when her horse stumbled in the dark as she rode through the night to bring the True Cross to him in Tiberias.

"I will not marry against your wishes, Baldwin," she spoke to his back in a choked voice. "I will marry whomever you choose. But it will break my heart if you give me to anyone but Guy. It will break—" She broke down into miserable sobbing, and if Baldwin had been able to control his arms he would have put what was left of his hands over his ears. All he could do, however, was refuse to turn around until she had withdrawn from his chamber, her sobs slowly becoming fainter until he could not hear them at all.

The following day Baldwin summoned the Baron of Oultrejourdain to the Tower of David. Assuming it was a public meeting of some kind, Oultrejourdain arrived accompanied by a small entourage, but he was told to leave the others in the courtyard. He mounted the stairs to the Tower of David by himself, and found the King entirely alone. He bowed curtly. "You sent for me, your grace?"

"Yes. I did. Come closer so that I do not need to shout."

Oultrejourdain obliged warily. He had never had a personal audience with Baldwin IV before, and he could not imagine what the cause for this unexpected summons might be. He kept combing his conscience for something he had done recently that might have been so outrageous as to arouse the royal ire. Surely it had nothing to do with the beating he'd given his worthless stepson, Humphrey de Toron, did it? How could the King have heard about that?

"My lord," Baldwin was speaking. "It was not so long ago, in this very chamber, that you expounded upon how best to defend the Kingdom. You were overruled, indeed ridiculed, at the time."

Oultrejourdain's shaved head reddened at the memory. Not that he wasn't used to ridicule and scorn from the likes of Tripoli, but he was agitated by the thought that they had wasted two years building—and then losing—the castle at Jacob's Ford. "I remember well, your grace," he answered simply.

"So do I," Baldwin answered. "And I liked your ideas," he added. "I think they make sense. We have proved too weak to defend ourselves against a determined enemy. But maybe if we attack him where *he* is weak, he will have less time and inclination to attack us."

"Exactly my thinking, your grace," Oultrejourdain agreed, at once astonished that the leper boy shared his thinking and smug to have his positive assessment of the sick King proved right. Hadn't he warned his knights and his stupid wife that the leper might have a disintegrating body, but he still retained a proud, fierce heart and a sharp intellect?

"Tripoli made much noise about an attack on the Mecca pilgrims bringing all the Muslims together in joint outrage, but—except for Aleppo and Mosul—Salah ad-Din already rules all the Muslims of Egypt and Syria. How can his power become greater?"

"It won't. I promise you. Rather, if we prey upon the Muslim pilgrims as they have preyed upon Christian pilgrims in the past, it will discredit him instead. If Salah ad-Din can't protect the pilgrim routes, many of his subjects will question why he should be Sultan at all."

Baldwin nodded. "Yes, that's the way I see it, too. So how do we go about it?"

Although taken by surprise, Oultrejourdain immediately focused on the problem and marshaled his arguments. "We have two options: first, we try to capture Eilat on the Red Sea and hold it long enough to build ships—we'd have to import the shipwrights, of course. Or we build the ships in, say, Ascalon, then disassemble them, transport them by camel to someplace along the shore of the Red Sea—not necessarily a walled city—then reassemble and launch them."

"The second option sounds considerably more practical to me," Baldwin conceded. "Attacking Eilat could be difficult, which means we'd have to pull together a substantial force, and that would inevitably leave other parts of the Kingdom inadequately protected. Furthermore, all that would alert the enemy to our intentions."

"Quite right, but the second option will require very skilled shipwrights. Italians of some sort. And they won't come cheap."

"I know," Baldwin agreed. "Nor will their crews."

"Oh, the crews won't be a problem," Oultrejourdain declared with a confident wave of his hand. Then he paused and added, "—provided you don't expect the loot?"

"I'm not following you, my lord," Baldwin admitted.

"Simple. You want to attack the pilgrim routes to Mecca for political reasons—to weaken and discredit Salah ad-Din. Am I correct?"

"Yes, we just discussed it," Baldwin answered, slightly irritated.

"Do you care about the plunder and prisoners, the girls and slaves, our ships capture in the process of discrediting Salah ad-Din?"

"No, of course not. You mean the crews would do this for the plunder?" Baldwin sounded so astonished that Reynald de Châtillon broke into a wide grin.

"Your grace, it does you credit to sound so amazed—but, believe me, I can man a hundred ships with men I can trawl out of the ports of this Kingdom alone. Tell most sailors they can keep the booty and do what they like with the girls, and you'll have volunteers banging your doors down."

Baldwin still looked skeptical, but he was willing to believe Oultrejourdain, because he wanted to. "So if I were to finance the building of these ships—"

"— And their transport across the desert to Eilat," Oultrejourdain interjected.

"You would be prepared to recruit the crews and oversee the launch of the ships on the Red Sea?"

"With pleasure, your grace!" Oultrejourdain was bursting with excitement. This was a challenge equal to his energy and vision. It was damn near as good as raiding Cyprus (he'd never really intended to hold on to it, after all), and it would give him greater experience in naval warfare—something that might prove useful in the future. By God, if they could take one or two of the cities on the Red Sea, even if only for a few weeks or months, it would flood his coffers for the next decade. Of course, he dared not be too prominent in this adventure, but Henri d'Ibelin was hungry and driven by jealousy now that both his elder brothers were barons. He would jump at the opportunity to lead this expedition.

"Because of the truce I signed with the Sultan, no one must learn that I am behind it," Baldwin hastened to warn Châtillon. "I must be able to swear to Salah ad-Din that I had nothing to do with it."

"Of course, your grace," Châtillon replied. "Upon my naked head," he said, knocking his shaved skull with his knuckles, "you can place all blame and shame. I can take it." Châtillon grinned. "My reputation as a rogue needed a little refurbishing; I've been tame for too long."

Baldwin was somewhat uncomfortable with the baron's pride in his own misdeeds, but he needed him. "Then we are agreed? You will make what plans are necessary and secretly let me know the costs?"

"I'll send you a friar now and again to collect alms for the abbey I want to build in Sinai."

"Yes. Very good!" Baldwin agreed.

"St. Nicholas, I think."

"The patron saint of seafarers." Baldwin understood the symbolism at once, and smiled.

"And pilgrims!" Oultrejourdain added with a laugh. "For all the pilgrims to Mecca!" And he guffawed until tears were squeezed from his eyes.

Baldwin could not join in, because his heart was filled with pity; they might be the misguided pilgrims of a false prophet, but among them there would be many simple men like Ibrahim, not to mention women and children, who did not really deserve the fate Oultrejourdain's mercenaries would deal them. But he kept his face impassive, afraid to show his weakness to the infamous Reynald de Châtillon.

Eventually Châtillon's laughter subsided and he asked, "Was there anything else, your grace?"

"Well, yes; there is another matter on which I would appreciate your counsel as—as an experienced military commander, a leader of men."

Châtillon could see how uncomfortable the King was, and noticed that he had lowered his voice even further than before. He narrowed his eyes in concentration and held his breath in anticipation. He no longer expected to be chastised for some sacrilege or offense, but he could not imagine what advice the young King could want from him that he could not ask publicly.

"My illness—it makes it almost impossible for me to fulfill my—my duties as King."

"You've done a damn good job of it so far, your grace," Châtillon admitted, and the sincerity in his voice made Baldwin's eyes shine with pride.

"I—but—you know—I had to be carried off the field by a squire—and—"

"And how many of your knights and nobles would dare ride into battle without being able to wield a sword or hold a shield? You have more courage than the rest of us put together, your grace. Myself included."

Châtillon's words were a balm to the bleeding wounds of the King's pride, and Baldwin felt tears of gratitude forming. "Thank you, my lord. Thank you. But—it's getting worse, not better. I can't go on much longer. And my barons, the High Court, even my confessor and my mother, urge me to turn command over to the Constable or—better yet—to my heir."

Châtillon burst out laughing. "I'd rather follow you into battle than your sister Sibylla any day!"

"Not Sibylla, but her husband."

"Ah!" At last Châtillon sensed which way the wind was blowing. "Whether I would follow Sibylla's husband into battle depends on who her husband is," Châtillon admitted, adding mentally that it was good thing Tripoli was already married.

"I was hoping for the Baron of Ramla."

"Ramla?" Oultrejourdain weighed his head from side to side. Aside from Oultrejourdain himself, Ramla was arguably the best leader of troops in the Kingdom—certainly better than Tripoli. But that was the problem with him from Oultrejourdain's point of view: he was already powerful, and the fact that the Greek Emperor had agreed to pay one hundred thousand bezants of his ransom suggested his younger brother's alliance with the Dowager Queen had yielded support from the mightiest ruler in the world. If he became heir to the Kingdom through Sibylla, he'd become insufferable—and hard to stop. Oultrejourdain did not like overly powerful monarchs. They might get in his way. To Baldwin he said simply, "Ramla is too heavily indebted to the Greek Emperor. By letting Emperor Manuel pay his ransom, he's become his client, his puppet. If you don't want Jerusalem to become a vassal of Constantinople, you can't let Ramla marry your sister."

Baldwin was nineteen years old. Although wise for his age, he still had a lot to learn about intrigue. He was taken by surprise at the suggestion that Ramla might be compromised by taking money from the Greek Emperor, and did not see through Oultrejourdain's motives for raising doubts about Ramla's independence. It never occurred to him that one of his barons would give him anything but honest advice. He protested weakly, "But Manuel has been a staunch ally. A good friend. I'm sure he only paid the ransom out of love for his niece, my stepmother."

"Maybe, but how old is he? Will his son be such a good friend? Or will he start calling in the debt—if not in gold, then in favors?"

"But his heir is the son of *your* stepdaughter, Mary of Antioch!" Baldwin protested. Oultrejourdain's first wife had been Constance of Antioch, and her daughter by her first marriage was the current Greek Empress and mother of the Crown Prince.

"Indeed, and *Mary* will certainly do all in *her* power to make her son a friend of Jerusalem." Oultrejourdain was scrambling to find arguments that supported his sham reasoning without revealing his real motives for opposing Ramla's marriage to Sibylla. "But we both know how easy it is for regents to get replaced—dismissed—by other powerful factions. A woman is particularly vulnerable to such maneuvers."

Baldwin frowned. He did not like what he was being told, but he had to give credence to what Châtillon was saying. Châtillon had (not always by choice) had considerable contact with the Greek court. At last he burst out, "But he would surely be better than Guy de Lusignan!"

"Guy de Lusignan?" Châtillon was taken fully aback. "You mean that boy Aimery brought out here to save him from the rage of the Plantagenet?"

"Yes, that's exactly who I mean. He's not at all suitable to be King of Jerusalem. Is he?"

Oultrejourdain had no ready reply; the thought was too surprising. He hadn't actually seen much of Guy de Lusignan. He played for time as he tried to form an opinion. "He's very young. No experience in Outremer, either—although to be fair, his grandfather crusaded here, and his father died in a Saracen prison just before I was incarcerated. His brother has certainly proved competent. Indeed, the Constable would have been the perfect choice for Princess Sibylla. A pity he's already married. I don't suppose there's some way to set the Ramla girl aside, is there?"

Baldwin shook his head. "She's with child already."

"That didn't stop your father from setting your mother aside," Châtillon pointed out hopefully, but Baldwin firmly shook his head, his lips pressed together. His mother had convinced him that his father had done an evil and sinful thing when he discarded her. Which reminded Baldwin that Ramla was no better. Ramla's first wife, just like his mother at the time of his father's second marriage, was still alive; that could make any second marriage vulnerable to challenge. It would be child's play for future opponents of Ramla or his policies to find clerics willing to declare his marriage to Sibylla invalid. Baldwin started to have doubts about forcing Sibylla into a marriage that might be deemed bigamous.

"Well, think about it," Oultrejourdain suggested, not knowing where the King's thoughts had led him. "Aimery de Lusignan is intelligent and competent, without being the sort of man to take what isn't his." What Oultrejourdain meant was that Aimery de Lusignan would never dare confront him. Under Aimery de Lusignan, he'd have as much freedom to do what he liked as under Baldwin himself. Indeed, the more he thought about it, the more he liked the notion of Aimery de Lusignan becoming the next King of Jerusalem.

"Antioch, Tripoli, and Ramla are due to arrive in Jerusalem on Palm Sunday—and that's not a coincidence," Agnes de Courtenay told her son. "They expect to be greeted with hosannas!"

"What do you mean?" Baldwin asked irritably. Ever since his sister had broached the subject of marrying Guy de Lusignan just over a week ago, he had slept poorly, had had little appetite (particularly for Lenten fare), and was becoming increasingly short-tempered. His thoughts seemed trapped in circles. Guy de Lusignan was not suited to become King of Jerusalem. He was not of high enough birth, let alone character, and he had no qualities whatever to recommend him. Of that, Baldwin was certain. But he was no longer certain that Ramla was the ideal candidate, either. There had to be other eligible barons in the Kingdom, but noblemen married early and often died young. There were always more widows than widowers.

Besides, he had given his word to Sibylla that he would not force her into a marriage she did not want—and she wanted no one but Guy. So it didn't matter who he selected, she would be miserable. But if he let her marry Guy and renounce the throne in favor of her son by Montferrat or Isabella, he would be forced to remain king for many more years, regardless of how helpless and weak he was or became in the future.

Would Guy de Lusignan really make a worse king than a youth whose limbs were rotting away?

If he could abdicate even *some* of his royal duties, he could rest more. He craved rest. The only time he ever got enough rest was when he was so ill that they closed the doors to the antechamber and let in only the doctors and the priests—and his mother. Sometimes he thought God was telling him he needed rest when he sent the fevers.

Dear God! he cried out in his heart. What do You want of me?

"You haven't listened to a word I've said," his mother concluded irritably.

Baldwin turned bloodshot eyes to her and admitted, "No. I was not listening. Tell me again."

"I'm telling you that Ramla thinks he is riding to his wedding with Sibylla, and the moment she is his wife he will turn around and depose you."

"Why would he do that?" Baldwin asked wearily. He was tired of his mother ranting against Ramla. The baron was her brother-in-law; he would have expected her to favor the match.

"Because he's greedy and not content to be heir," Agnes insisted. "Have you forgotten I raised him as a child? I know his character very well indeed. He always hated and snubbed me!"

There was some truth in that, Baldwin conceded with a sigh. Even Balian admitted that his older brother had detested their sister-in-law and shown her little respect when they were children.

"Furthermore," Agnes pressed her case, "the Lusignan brothers heard him say you were no longer fit to rule and needed to be deposed in favor of someone healthy."

"Where did Ramla allegedly say that—within hearing of both Lusignans?" Baldwin asked wearily. The claim was too ridiculous to take seriously.

"In his own home and in the presence of not just the Lusignans but his brother, his wife, and your stepmother."

Baldwin stiffened. He might long for rest and dream about retiring to a monastery where he could focus on preparing his soul for God, but he did not like *other* men presuming he was not fit to rule. He looked his mother in the eye and declared firmly, "I don't believe you. Balian would *never* speak against me."

Agnes knew better than to criticize Balian. She might not particularly like him herself, but she could not deny that he had been a friend to her son when he had had no others. Nor had he been rude to her, as Barry had been when she married their older brother Hugh and tried to assert her authority a lady of the house. She hastened to assure her son, "No one is suggesting he did! Quite the contrary. According to Aimery, Balian sharply rebuked his brother, and so the conversation turned to other things. But you *must* see the danger. Ramla is coming here with the backing of the Greek Emperor, Antioch—who is brother-in-law to the Greek Emperor—and Tripoli, who from the start wanted to see Isabella crowned Queen. It's a conspiracy."

If he could have controlled his hands, Baldwin would have dropped his head in them. He was so tired. So utterly exhausted. He felt as if he didn't have the strength to think, reason, or resist anymore.

"Ramla will send you to the Brothers of St. Lazarus and steal your kingdom from you the moment he has secured Sibylla."

And what would be so wrong with that? Baldwin asked himself. Wasn't it really what he wanted? To just retire from the world and live among people who weren't repulsed by the sight of him? People for whom he did not need to dress in bandages and fine robes? Why didn't he rejoice at the thought? But he didn't. So he answered wearily, "We don't know that he would do that, Mother. Only God knows."

"And only God knows if Guy de Lusignan would make such a bad king. He's still very young. He needs time to learn about the Holy Land, I admit that, but while he's learning you would still be King."

Baldwin looked warily at his mother. He could not entirely dismiss the thought that her opposition to Ramla was based on nothing more than her fear that *she* would lose power and influence the moment Baldwin stepped down. On the other hand, could he blame her for fearing that? It had happened to her once before when his father set her aside, and he had heard that Tripoli had argued that both he and Sibylla be passed over in favor of Isabella. His mother had every reason to feel insecure—and reason to think it ominous that Ramla was traveling in the company of Tripoli and Antioch and some five hundred knights, if reports could be believed.

Baldwin closed his eyes and tried to think. It rankled that Ramla had called him unfit to rule, after all the effort he made to be a good King. He'd been prepared to give him the keys to the Kingdom by allowing him the privilege of marrying Sibylla. Shouldn't Ramla be grateful for that, rather than turning around and biting the hand that fed him? Maybe his mother was right. It was true she had known him all his life.

Agnes de Courtenay spoke right into his thoughts. "Don't confuse Barry with Balian—they are very different men. Even as boys they were different. Barry was impudent and mean to me; Balian was reserved, but never cruel or rebellious. Balian would never betray you. He's proved that over and over again. I'm sure he hasn't a clue about his brother's plans. Ramla would not dare tell him, because he too knows that Balian would never support him. There's a conspiracy against you, my dearest son, but Balian d'Ibelin is not part of it."

"What are you asking me to do, Mother? Order the arrest of the Prince of Antioch, the Count of Tripoli, and the Baron of Ramla on suspicion of treason?" Baldwin's tone emphasized how absurd the notion was. Antioch and Tripoli ruled the other two remaining states founded by the first crusaders. They were independent rulers in their own right, not vassals of the Crown of Jerusalem. No one would follow such orders—certainly not from a feeble nineteen-year-old youth rotting away from leprosy.

"No, Baldwin," Agnes said in a gentle voice, resting her hand on his arm as she rarely did. "No, all I'm suggesting is that you let your sister marry the man she loves."

Chapter 4

Jerusalem, October 1180

A SUDDEN BUT HEAVY RAIN SHOWER had induced Ibelin to seek shelter under an arch until the worst of the downpour was over. The delay, however, made him late. To make things worse, on arriving at the Citadel he was told that, contrary to custom, the High Court of Jerusalem wasn't meeting in the Tower of David. The session had been moved to the hall of the royal palace.

Ibelin cursed, wondering if his brother of Ramla knew of the change of venue. Neither of them had been at court during the last six-month; they had withdrawn to their respective baronies to protest Sibylla's marriage to Guy de Lusignan. Ramla had been stunned to discover that the woman he had courted (and seduced) had transferred her affections and favors to another in such a short space of time. But that insult might have been endured as the faithlessness of a shallow woman had not the King seen fit to bless the marriage—and then raise the landless seducer to the rank of Count. Worse: he had made him Count of Jaffa. Ramla, Ibelin, and Mirabel were all technically components of the County of Jaffa, but ever since the last count, Aimery, had become king almost two decades ago, the fiefs had been held de-facto from the crown. Now, with a single blow, both Barry and Balian had been demoted from "tenant-in-chief" to the king to sub-tenants of the Count of Jaffa. That was too much. The brothers had demonstratively removed themselves from court and Jerusalem to express their outrage.

But they couldn't ignore a direct summons from the King to attend a session of the High Court. They had ridden together from Ramla and arrived the previous night. Barry, however, had wanted to meet with Tripoli in advance of the High

Court session and so had left the Ibelin palace several hours ahead of Balian, before the rain started.

Cursing to and at himself, Balian made his way down the street to the palace entrance. He was unable to hurry on the wet, slippery cobbles, but at the palace he left his stallion with his squire and took the steps two at a time from the courtyard to the first-floor gallery — only to come close to colliding with the King.

The venue for the High Court session had been changed because the King's spreading leprosy now made it impossible for him to go up and down stairs unaided. He could not walk unaided, either, but the faithful Ibrahim was strong enough to keep him upright on a level path, just no longer strong enough to carry the nineteen-year-old King on the stairs. The aging servant had his shoulder under the King's arm and held the King around the waist while the young monarch flung one limp leg forward after another. They were moving forward painfully slowly, one small, sloppy step at a time, when Balian almost careened into them as he bounded up the last step.

"Your grace!" Balian exclaimed in surprise. Thinking the High Court was already session, the last person he had expected to meet on the gallery was the King. But Balian's shock was magnified by the sight of the King's face and increased frailty.

"I can read on your face, my lord of Ibelin," the King answered slowly, "that the leprosy has reached my own."

It was true. In the six months Balian had stayed away from Jerusalem, the disease appeared to have accelerated. Notably, it had reached Baldwin's face; he had lost his eyebrows and the skin on his chin was discolored, although not yet disfigured.

Balian was both horrified by what he saw and struck with a pang of remorse for keeping his distance. Some part of his brain thought irrationally that this decline in health was the result of the bad company the King was keeping.

His next thought, however, was that God, or more likely the ever-merciful Mother Mary, had arranged this chance meeting as a means to enable a reconciliation. Even if Sibylla's marriage to Guy could not be undone, it might still be possible to get the King to make amends of some sort—at least to the deeply offended Barry. In any case, it was never wise to be at odds with a king.

So Balian slipped his arm under Baldwin's other shoulder in a gesture calculated to remind the King of how close they had been in the past—and assure the King that despite their differences, they were still friends.

"Balian, you don't have—"

Balian cut the young King off. "I think Ibrahim is getting too old for this," he suggested, taking the weight of the King from Ibrahim with a smile to the old slave and adding, "Do you want me to carry you?"

"No, no. Stop! It is good that you came upon me here before we face the others. There are things we need to discuss in private."

Yes, Balian thought; thank you, Mother Mary.

"Your brother of Ramla," King Baldwin started. "He has not yet vowed fealty to the Count of Jaffa."

Balian nodded and answered steadily, "You ask too much, your grace."

"*You* have taken the oath," the King countered.

"True, but my situation is different from my brother's. I was not born to my barony and can better suffer the humiliation of being only a sub-tenant. More important, however, I was not offended in the same way as my brother. First you took his bride and his prospects away from him, then you degraded him, and now you expect him to pay homage to the man who has insulted and mocked him."

"What else could I do?" Baldwin asked back defensively. He did not want the break with Balian; he had missed him these past six months. But Baldwin felt trapped and blameless in the whole affair. "I had to maintain the status of my sister!"

That was Agnes speaking, Balian thought bitterly. If the King was so concerned about his sister's dignity, he should not have let her marry a man without a title in the first place! But he bit his tongue. If the gracious Virgin had granted him this opportunity to speak to the King in a situation evocative of past trust and affection, he did not want to squander it with recriminations. He tried to find some means of reconciling the King's concern for his sister's status with his brother's need for the restoration of his pride and dignity. "Could you not give Guy de Lusignan another barony?"

"There is nothing else vacant," the King protested.

"Then create a new barony," Balian pleaded. "It is your right."

"But the royal lands are already much diminished!" Baldwin protested—and Balian heard the whining of the ever-greedy Count of Edessa, whose only talent appeared to be enriching himself at his nephew's expense, echoed in the King's voice.

The thought of Edessa angered Balian enough to make him snap, "Not so diminished that you could not have found enough for the likes of Guy de Lusignan!" No sooner were the words out, however, than Balian recognized that insulting Lusignan would get them nowhere. Reining his emotions in, he pleaded, "Try to see things through my brother's eyes, your grace. By making

Lusignan Count of Jaffa, you not only degraded him, you are asking him to take an oath to the very man who stole his bride from him!"

"They were not betrothed," Baldwin countered stubbornly—precisely because he was not proud of what he had done.

"You led him to believe you favored his suit," Balian reminded the King, stopping and making the King stop, too. Balian was remembering the day Barry had returned from Constantinople, full of joy for having raised his ransom and eager to see the woman he thought would be his bride—only to be told his "bride" was another man's wife. The memory of the way his ever-confident brother's face had frozen, then filled with a look of disbelief, and finally the utter bewilderment in his eyes, sharpened Balian's tongue. Unconsciously, he removed his arm from the King's waist and faced him as he protested despite his best intentions, "Yes, you encouraged him—but the moment his back was turned, you gave your sister to another!"

"Is that the way you see it?" Baldwin retorted, lifting his chin and clamping his teeth together. He hated being reminded of the way he had been tricked and pressured by his sister and mother.

"Is there any other way to see it?" Balian asked back, meeting his eyes.

"There were rumors that Ramla was plotting to depose me!" Baldwin flung at Balian in self-defense.

"And you believed such slander?" Balian snapped back, outraged. He could not fathom that after all the years he had served Baldwin, the King could give credence to such lies—undoubtedly from the mouth of his poisonous mother. "What have we ever done to deserve such mistrust?" Balian demanded.

"There were witnesses that said he had called for me to step down," Baldwin countered, feeling cornered.

"You were lied to, your grace," Balian answered steadily, meeting his eye. "It's true my brother suggested that you should not lead your armies in person any longer, but he never suggested that you abdicate!"

Baldwin considered this answer carefully. It was possible that his mother had exaggerated Ramla's words—but just as possible that, as she had said, Balian had no idea about his brother's true intentions. He took refuge in his second excuse, the one he used to convince himself he had been in the right in the whole unsavory affair. "Your brother is still married to Richildis in the eyes of many. If challenged, your brother's marriage to Sibylla might have been ruled bigamous. I could not risk that—"

"In the name of the Almighty, your grace, *you* were the one who gave my brother permission to set Richildis aside," Balian reminded him.

"Yes, but I was young and inexperienced, and I did it for *you.* I wanted you to get Ibelin. I thought the only way to persuade Ramla to part with a third of his inheritance was to offer him the chance to marry another heiress—including my sister. I see now that I was wrong to do what I did," Baldwin told Balian bluntly, physically distancing himself from his former mentor by taking a step back into Ibrahim's arms. Having decided that his mother was right and Balian wrong, he declared, "There is something else we must discuss."

Balian waited tensely. So far this encounter had not gone well. If the Virgin had facilitated it, somehow he had failed to exploit the opportunity. Too late, Balian registered that it had been a mistake for him to withdraw from Jerusalem. At the time it had been a relief to get away from the gloating of Agnes de Courtenay, but in retrospect it was clear that by withdrawing from court, he had handed the King's mother and uncle more opportunity to poison the King's mind.

Baldwin was speaking. "I think it's time my sister Isabella joined her future husband—"

"Toron's with his mother at Kerak!" Balian protested, with a sense that he was sliding rapidly down an abyss to utter destruction.

"I know," Baldwin answered stubbornly, "but he's to be her husband, and it's better for young people to get to know one another when they are still children." Baldwin's mother had convinced him that if only Sibylla had been married as a child, she would not have become infatuated with Guy de Lusignan. Baldwin was certain (and his uncle of Edessa whispered in his ears) that Sibylla had been led astray by Guy de Lusignan only because she was of an age to be susceptible to sexual attraction. He did not want Isabella to fall into the same trap. He wanted her securely and safely married to a man of his own choosing before she was old enough to know carnal desire.

But Balian recognized Agnes de Courtenay's hatred of the Ibelins—and of his wife—behind the King's plans. The Queen Mother was taking revenge for being set aside by Amalric when he took the crown, for being forced to return to a man she did not love, and for being replaced by Maria Zoë. But the King appeared to have fallen completely under this mother's spell, making it pointless for Balian to expose the Queen Mother's motives.

Instead Balian argued, "You cannot seriously intend to turn a tender princess over to the keeping of a notorious brute like Reynald de Châtillon!"

"You're being unreasonable, Ibelin. Châtillon may have his unsavory side, but I have never heard it said he is anything but extraordinarily courteous to ladies. After all, he won both the Princess of Antioch and the Lady of Oultrejourdain by his charms. There is absolutely no reason to suspect he would be anything less than exemplary in his treatment of my sister."

"Isabella is only eight years old! She's a child," Balian reminded the King.

"I *know* how old my own sister is, Ibelin," Baldwin answered coldly. He was determined to go through with this, and Balian's resistance was only convincing him his mother had been right to warn him about the Ibelins. She had warned him Balian and Maria Zoë would try to retain control of Isabella—because, his mother said, they wanted to have a puppet they could raise up in his and Sibylla's place.

Baldwin was as blind to his mother's motives as Balian thought he was, but he now realized that by letting Sibylla marry the younger Lusignan and alienating Ramla, Tripoli, and Antioch, he had undercut his own legitimacy. He saw that those who did not want to see Guy de Lusignan crowned King would likely argue that *both* he and Sibylla were illegitimate. Sibylla's marriage to the upstart Guy had abruptly turned Isabella into a threat to his own throne. He could not risk having her in hostile hands. Not that Balian himself was hostile, of course, but Balian had just made it abundantly clear that he sided with his brother in the dispute over Sibylla's marriage. And Ramla and Tripoli were far too friendly, while Antioch's wife was Maria Zoë's sister and so Isabella's maternal aunt. A dangerous clique, his uncle of Edessa warned him.

Balian made one last desperate appeal to Baldwin's affection for his stepmother. "Your grace! Maria Zoë dotes on Isabella! She could not bear to be separated from her."

Baldwin was not prepared to be moved. He resented the way his mother and sister had maneuvered him into sanctioning Sibylla's marriage, but what was done was done. Now he was determined to prevent something like that from happening again. He was determined to ensure Isabella married the man of his choosing—and was firmly controlled by a man utterly opposed to Tripoli. In answer to Balian's protest he replied coldly, "I'm astonished to hear that, my lord. After all, she has two children by you already, and a third on the way."

The King's tone and the use of "my lord" should have warned Balian not to continue the argument, but Balian was desperate. "Isabella is her firstborn," he tried to explain. "Maria Zoë has said more than once that she does not want to see Isabella married as young as she was—"

"The decision is not hers to make," the King reminded his vassal. "Isabella is my sister and my ward. *I* will decide when she marries." His tone brooked no further argument.

But Balian knew that on this point he, too, could not bend. "Think hard, your grace, before you take Isabella away from her mother," he warned. "The bonds between mother and child and between husband and wife are made by God, not man!"

Baldwin felt the blood flushing his face, turning his un-sickened skin a vibrant shade of cooked-crab red, while the damaged skin remained uncolored and so highlighted. He had always defended Balian to his mother—always insisted that Balian would never be disloyal—but here he was all but declaring outright that he would withdraw his loyalty just because they were taking Isabella away from him. His mother had been right all along. The Ibelins planned to use Isabella against him. They were plotting with Tripoli and Antioch against him! Baldwin wanted to fling this accusation at his former-friend, but shouting erupted from the chamber beside them, distracting the King's attention.

It was Guy de Lusignan, and he shouted hotly. "No! You forget who *I* am! I'm not your little brother! I'm Count of Jaffa and heir to the Kingdom of Jerusalem! If you don't show me the respect I'm owed, you won't be Constable another day!"

Aimery de Lusignan shot back at his brother, "I'm appointed by the King—not the likes of you!"

"The King?" Guy sneered. "He's a walking corpse! Have you seen his face lately?"

Balian saw the King stiffen and then stagger a little, as if he'd been physically struck, but Balian made no move to support him. Guy was his choice for brother-in-law when he could have had Barry! It was time Baldwin learned that the loyalty of even the truest vassal had limits. Taking an eight-year-old child away from her mother and sending her to live with a notorious brute was going much too far. "You've made your bed, your grace," Balian murmured in a low growl. "See how you like the company you've chosen to share it with."

Ibrahim cast Balian a shocked, then a pleading look, but Balian's face was harsh with bitterness.

Baldwin averted his own face from his former friend, the pain of this break much greater than he wanted to admit. He clung to his mother's words about Ibelin ambition and treachery, telling to himself that Balian had just revealed his true nature. The old slave propelled him past the room where the Lusignans were squabbling and on into the great hall.

Kerak Castle, November 1180

"I'm going to tell Uncle Balian what you did!" Isabella screamed, red-faced and streaming tears. "I'm going to tell Uncle Balian what you did, and he'll make you pay! He'll make you sorry! He'll make you—"

Stephanie de Milly had had enough of Isabella's temper tantrums; she slapped her across the face, then took her by the shoulders and shook her until she fell silent. "Call your *Uncle* Balian!" she sneered as soon as she had the child's attention. "Call just as loud as you can! I don't care if you scream for him from the ramparts. He can't hear you and he can't help you!"

Isabella was shocked enough to calm down, and she stared at the Lady of Oultrejourdain with hate-filled eyes. "I'll tell him when I go home for Christmas," she declared determinedly.

"What makes you think you're going 'home'—if that's what you call Ibelin—for Christmas?"

"My mother promised me!" Isabella retorted indignantly. "She said Humphrey and I could come for Christmas and stay until my baby sister or brother is born."

"That was very foolish of your mother," the Lady of Outrejourdain sneered ominously. "She shouldn't make promises she can't keep."

"Why can't she keep it?" Isabella wanted to know.

"Because, you stupid little brat, your mother doesn't control you. *I* do." Stephanie de Milly could not keep the smile off her face as she said this. Revenge had been a long time coming, and it was not yet complete, but having deprived Tripoli of control of Princess Isabella (for the Ibelins were Tripoli's creatures) was clearly a significant victory on the way to humiliating him. To Isabella, however, she replied smugly, "You can't go anywhere I don't let you go, and you will go wherever I send you—which at the moment is to the crypt."

"No!" Isabella screamed, this time in terror rather than outrage.

"Yes!" Madame d'Oultrejourdain insisted, grabbing Isabella by the wrist.

Isabella resisted with all her eight-year-old strength, digging in her heels and leaning back with the weight of her whole body. She had been forced once before to spend the night in the crypt below the chapel, and she was convinced it was haunted. She was terrified of the crypt of this castle, which perched on a mountaintop above a desert and was so much harsher, more brooding, and more ominous than Ibelin in its blooming orchards.

Stephanie de Milly was at the end of her patience. She had put the bug in the Queen Mother's ear about the need to "rescue" Isabella from the influence of Maria Comnena and the Ibelins. She had harped on the fact that Ramla would surely seek revenge for being thwarted in his ambitions to become King via Sibylla and might try to raise up Isabella in place of Agnes' children. The only way to prevent that, she had argued to wide-open ears, was to get physical control of Isabella and ensure she had no further contact with her mother or stepfather. The plan to bring her to Kerak had seemed so simple, as it was an impregnable fortress far from Ibelin and even farther from Nablus.

But Stephanie had not reckoned with Isabella herself. The girl was a spoiled brat: willful, stubborn, and disobedient. It was obvious to her that Queen Maria and Balian d'Ibelin were totally incompetent guardians—probably because they paid no attention to Isabella at all and let her lord it over servants afraid of saying no to a princess. Stephanie saw it as her duty to teach her future daughter-in-law manners, discipline, and respect for her elders.

With a single whopping smack to Isabella's backside, she broke the little girl's stance. She grabbed her second wrist as Isabella tried to claw her with her free hand, and with both the child's wrists in her large hands, she wrenched them behind Isabella's back. Even though the eight-year-old writhed and struggled, Stephanie could now push her toward the stairway.

Isabella realized she was too weak to resist the massive Madame d'Oultrejourdain, so she went completely limp and dropped to the floor.

"Oh, don't think *that's* going to stop me," Stephanie sneered, as she proceeded to drag Isabella by her arms out the door and down the steps.

Now Isabella was screaming with pain as her bony hips hit the stone steps one at a time. "Stop! Stop!" she screamed.

The sound of footsteps rushing upward made Stephanie pause, but not let go of Isabella. A young knight careened around the corner, clearly responding to the screams of the young girl. When he nearly collided with the chatelaine, his eyes widened, first in surprise and then horror at the scene before him.

"Don't just stand there, Sir Henri!" Stephanie snapped. "Help me! The little princess has been a terrible girl, and she is going to the crypt to beg forgiveness on her knees. Since she refuses to walk, I have no choice but to drag her, but you're strong enough to carry her. Pick her up!" Stephanie ordered, standing back against the curved stone wall of the spiral stairs.

Isabella was too bruised and terrified to resist. Besides, Sir Henri was Uncle Balian's brother and had never done anything to hurt her. He picked her up easily and followed Madame d'Oultrejourdain without further ado. Isabella put her arms around his neck and buried her face in his broad, warm chest. She kept her eyes closed, only peeking now and again to check on their progress. When they reached the vaulted passageway leading to the chapel, however, Isabella started to squirm. "I don't want to go to the crypt," she whispered. Then as the chapel drew nearer, she raised her voice and asked, "Why can't I pray in the chapel?"

"Because the rest of the household will gather in the chapel for Vespers, and the priests will read the Mass at Nocturnes, but *you* aren't to see or speak to anyone until *I* decide," Madame d'Oultrejourdain answered pointedly.

Isabella looked up hopefully at Henri d'Ibelin, but he kept his face neutral, proceeding into the chapel and then down the stairs beside the high altar into the crypt below.

"Set her down!" Madame d'Oultrejourdain ordered, and Sir Henri bent and lowered the arm under Isabella's knees, so that her feet touched the floor even as she continued to cling to his neck.

"Don't leave me here!" she whispered desperately into his cheek.

"Don't let the little bitch seduce you, Sir Henri! She pretends to be a sweet little girl to you and even to my husband, but inside she has a dark, vain soul. If she were my flesh and blood and not a princess, I would have her flogged, not simply make her spend a night in prayer."

Henri extricated himself from Isabella's arms and backed away from her to follow Madame d'Oultrejourdain up the stairs, but just as he turned to go up the stairs, he looked back at the crestfallen child—and winked at her.

It gave her a moment of hope, but then she heard the key turning in the door to the crypt and realized she was indeed locked inside with the dead. She hugged herself and began moaning in a low whine of misery and protest that she knew no one could hear or heed. "Please, Mother Mary! Help me! Protect me!" she begged as she looked wide-eyed at the catacombs around her. There was no light down here except what seeped under the doorway and down the stairs from the chapel above. The catacombs seemed to stretch eternally into the darkness. While the most recent tombs were of stone with proper effigies on top, there were older tombs that were just vaults carved out of bedrock on which the dead had been laid out. Isabella was convinced these were the bodies of outlaws or Muslims or other people who hadn't received a "proper" Christian burial. *Their* souls, therefore, were still at large.

Isabella was sure the ghosts were going to come and get her, and she had no place to hide. All she could do was curl up at the base of the altar and keep praying. That was what Madame d'Oultrejourdain meant when she said Isabella would pray all night.

The hours crept by. Whenever Isabella started to nod off to sleep, one of the ghosts would breathe on her or make a sound, and she was startled back into consciousness. She had some short relief when the chapel overhead filled for Vespers and she could faintly hear the Mass being read. The ghosts, she told herself, wouldn't dare come out during Mass.

But after that the silence was all the more ominous, smothering her with fear, now made more painful by her increasing thirst and hunger. Feeling sorry for herself, Isabella finally cried herself to sleep, only to be torn from oblivion by the sound of footsteps. She sat bolt upright and froze in terror. The footsteps were very soft, but they were more distinct and solid than any of the earlier noises. And they were coming toward her.

Isabella was so terrified that she could not even scream. She felt liquid between her legs as she urinated in fright. A shadow separated itself from the stairwell and stopped. "Bella?" a soft voice called.

"Humphrey?" Isabella asked back, hardly daring to believe it might be her husband-to-be.

"Yes. Where are you? I can't see anything in the dark."

"Here!" Isabella scrambled to her feet and ran to her betrothed, flinging herself at him. His warm, soft arms closed around her back and he laid his cheek on the top of her head. "Sir Henri told me you were here," he explained. "He said my mother ordered you locked in here for the night, and—and I thought you might like company."

"Oh, Humphrey!" Isabella looked up at him, her eyes huge. "Would you do that for me? Will you stay with me?"

"Of course, Bella. That's why I'm here. I'm sorry I couldn't bring you anything to eat, but . . ."

"I don't care," Isabella assured him. "I can go without dinner, but there are ghosts down here. I'm sure of it."

Humphrey squeezed her in a gesture of reassurance, and they walked together back to the altar and sank down to sit at the base side by side, Humphrey still enclosing Isabella in his arm. She snuggled up against his chest. "I had a terrible fight with your mother," Isabella confessed to Humphrey. "She's banished Gluttony to the kitchens. First my dog and now my cat."

Humphrey nodded in sympathy. He knew how much Isabella loved her pets, and he felt sorry for her. But all he could say was, "I don't like it here, either."

"And now your mother says we can't go to Ibelin for Christmas. She says she won't let us go, but Uncle Balian will come for us. I'm sure he will."

"I hope so," Humphrey murmured, stroking Isabella's arms. With Humphrey warm, comforting, and protective beside her, Isabella's exhaustion overwhelmed her, and she fell sound asleep in his arms.

When she woke up again they were curled up on the floor, with Humphrey still holding her. Light was seeping down the stairs and into the crypt again, and overhead the priest was reading Mass. Isabella sat up, feeling very stiff, and looked over her shoulder at Humphrey, who was still asleep. She gasped. His face was dreadfully swollen and starting to turn blue in several places—notably his lips and his left cheek and eye. "Humphrey!" she exclaimed, unable to control her distress.

He started out of his sleep and sat up sharply.

"What happened to you?" Isabella wanted to know, now that she had his attention.

He looked down, avoiding her eyes. "I fell off my horse," he mumbled.

"I don't believe you! A riding fall wouldn't leave those bruises," Isabella told him knowingly. "Oultrejourdain hit you again, didn't he?"

Humphrey just kept his eyes down in shame and muttered, "Because I fell off my horse."

"I hate him!" Isabella declared furiously. "I hate him!" Then she flung her arms around Humphrey, holding him to her flat chest and promising, "When Uncle Balian finds out, he'll take us away from here. I'm sure he will!"

"Maybe you, Isabella," Humphrey answered despondently. "But he can't take me away from my mother and her husband. They are my legal guardians. I'll have to stay."

"Oh, Humphrey!" Isabella cried in distress, as she realized it would be terrible and cruel to leave him behind.

Her sympathy was too much for Humphrey. It broke his resolve more than all the taunts of the other squires. Their gibes just made him stubborn, but Isabella's tenderness unmanned him completely, and he croaked out, "Please don't leave me, Bella." He fought back tears of his own as he clung to her. "You're the only friend I have in the whole world. Please don't leave me."

Isabella took a deep breath, straightened her back, and consciously grew up. "You're my husband, Humphrey—or almost. I won't ever leave you. If Uncle Balian and my mother can't find a way for us *both* to stay at Ibelin, then I'll stay with you here—until we're old enough to have our own household. And *then,"* she added defiantly, "Oultrejourdain will learn what it means to make an enemy of a princess of Jerusalem!"

Ibelin, Christmas, 1180

"It is traditional for the lords to grant reasonable requests from their tenants at Christmas," Sir Arnulf reminded his younger son. "All you have to do is present yourself to the Baron of Ibelin, remind him that your older brother was killed on the Litani defending him and the King, and ask that he let you learn the trade of arms at his stirrup."

Ernoul swallowed down his panic. His father owed knight's service to the Barons of Ibelin for the small manor the family held from them, but Sir Arnulf was nearing fifty and had been relieved when his elder son, Adrian, had been knighted and had taken over his feudal duties. Unfortunately, Adrian had been killed in the battle on the Litani the previous year. This left Ernoul as Arnulf's heir, but until his brother's death Ernoul had been destined for the Church. Ernoul knew precious little about the use of arms, and wasn't even a very good horseman.

Now Ernoul stood before his parents wearing his maternal uncle's chain-mail hauberk. His mother's brother, who had never married, had been much taller than Ernoul was at thirteen and almost twice as broad, so the mail hung loosely on Ernoul's frail body. The limp but heavy sleeves reached well beyond his knuckles and the hem fell below his knees. It was also in poor condition, rusty and torn in several places, but even so it was in better shape than the helmet. The helmet looked a century old and had probably been handed down to his uncle from an even older ancestor. It was conical with a gigantic nosepiece that all but blinded Ernoul. There was no shield, since the inherited shield had long since been misplaced or rotted away, and his brother's equipment had been lost to the Saracens in the aftermath of the battle. By the time the Christians had returned to the field, they found all the bodies stripped of valuables. Sir Arnulf and his lady counted themselves lucky that their son's body had been found and returned for burial. Thus, for a sword, Ernoul again had only his uncle's nicked and slightly corroded weapon. Ernoul was acutely aware of what a ridiculous figure he would cut at Ibelin.

"There's nothing to be afraid of," his father insisted, frowning, annoyed by his younger son's lack of enthusiasm and deeply depressed by the loss of his older boy, who had been so much more promising.

"No, sir," Ernoul answered stoically. There were a thousand things to be afraid of that he could think of, but he knew better than to think about them.

"Here." His mother stepped forward and lifted a small wooden crucifix on a chain. Ernoul dutifully bent his head and let her put the crucifix around his neck. "Remember to say prayers for your brother's soul every night," she urged him.

"Yes, Mama," Ernoul promised absently.

"Now, you'd best be on your way," his father urged. "You want to be one of the first to ask a favor, as those who come late rarely find their lord in a generous mood anymore."

Ernoul turned and walked the length of the short, familiar hall. The entire manor was nothing more than a rectangular stone structure consisting of a kitchen and a vaulted storeroom on the ground floor, a long hall and a smaller "great chamber" on the first floor, and a second floor under the roof-beams, which was partitioned into three rooms by wooden walls.

Ernoul exited the hall onto the landing at the top of the external stairs that led down to the stableyard. At the foot of the stairs, the kitchen clerk emerged with a satchel that he handed over to Ernoul with tears in his eyes. "Just a little something to keep you from starving along the way," he told his erstwhile pupil. In addition to being the household clerk, this cleric had taught Ernoul his letters in preparation for his service in the Church. The clerk was deeply distressed to see Ernoul wearing arms, as he thought Ernoul was much too intelligent and sensitive for life as a fighting man.

Ernoul was too numb with his own trepidation to notice the clerk's distress. He took the offered parcel with a mumbled "thanks" as he turned to face his father's gray-muzzled palfrey, which one of the village boys had led from the small adobe stables.

The palfrey still had straw clinging to its bushy tail and stable stains on its hocks and haunches. Ernoul knew he ought to complain and order the boy to brush the horse down, but he didn't have the energy for a fight. Instead, he tightened the girth and tried to mount up. The aging gelding expertly backed away from the inept rider, leaving Ernoul hopping on one leg after him. The clerk came over to hold the horse still—but even so, in all his unfamiliar and heavy armor, Ernoul couldn't manage to pull himself into the saddle until the third try, and he nearly pulled the saddle off in the process. Ernoul remembered the way his older brother Adrian could just swing up into the saddle in a single fluid motion, and he knew he was going to be the butt of ridicule in Ibelin—assuming Lord Balian took him on at all.

Once in the saddle, the clerk handed up the satchel, which Ernoul had let fall in his struggle to mount. "Thank you," he said more distinctly and loudly this time, and their eyes met. Now Ernoul registered the older man's sadness and it almost made him break down and cry, but he resisted the impulse and managed a wan smile instead.

"Don't forget Brother Bernard, will you?" the clerk asked hopelessly.

"No," Ernoul promised. "I'm going to keep a diary—if I can find something to write on—so I don't forget how to write."

The clerk smiled sadly, not believing it would ever happen, and patted his leg. "Good boy."

Ernoul turned his horse away from the stables, and it instantly balked. He had to kick it hard several times before it reluctantly decided it was less unpleasant to walk than to endure more kicking.

Outside the stableyard the road passed directly in front of the parental manor. Opposite the manor sat the flat-roofed church. Ernoul crossed himself and said a quick prayer for help, then turned his reluctant horse down the road through the village. This was made up of a dozen flat-roofed stone houses that stood along both sides of the road. Wheat and barley fields backed right up against the houses on the north side of the road, and olive orchards backed up on the houses to the south. At the far end of the village there was a common bread oven, a well, and a corral for the cattle and donkeys of the sub-tenants. That was all. There wasn't even an olive mill; Sir Arnulf had to take his olive harvest to Ibelin for processing. But it was home.

Ernoul had rarely been outside this village. He'd been taken to Jerusalem once so he could pray at the Church of the Holy Sepulcher in the year of his first communion, and he'd been allowed to accompany his mother when she went to Jaffa to meet one of her cousins, who had come on pilgrimage two years ago. He'd been to Ibelin three or four times, too, with the olive harvest or to purchase pottery, cloth, or harness with his father. That was all.

Ernoul was heavy of heart as he rode between the houses of the village. He knew the names of each cottager, their wives and children, and even the names of most of the dogs. The villagers were, with one exception, all descendants of settlers come out from Burgundy or Lorraine to start a new life in the Holy Land roughly half a century ago. The one exception was a Syrian Christian, who had been enslaved for a number of years before he was freed by the old Baron d'Ibelin in some engagement. He had married the widow of one of the settlers and now attended the Latin church, so he was accepted. As Ernoul rode by, the women came to stand in their doorways and wave to him, their toddlers hanging on their skirts. Toward the end of town the boy who had been tending the village sheep called out to him cheerfully, as if he thought Ernoul were going on some great adventure.

It was a gray day, threatening rain, and it promised to be a cold ride. With considerable effort Ernoul managed to coax his father's old horse into a shuffling trot, both to warm himself up and to get it over with faster. The sooner he got to Ibelin, the sooner he would know his fate.

A stiff gale-force wind off the ocean was driving rain horizontally by the time Ernoul finally reached Ibelin. The palms were swaying and waving their great feathery leaves like hysterical sailors in distress, and the pomegranate orchards seemed to roar and threaten him with their frantically waving branches. Flashes of lightning lit up the darkening horizon, and the growl of distant thunder promised worse to come. Ernoul was already soaked to the bone, and his father's horse was dripping water from mane and tail while mud covered its ample pasterns and fetlocks.

The guard at the drawbridge gate was only willing to crack the peephole and call out: "Who goes?"

"I'm Ernoul, son of Arnulf, and I've come to see Lord Balian."

Ernoul didn't catch exactly what the man mumbled, but it didn't sound very friendly. Still, he signaled the barbican on the far side of the moat, and by the time Ernoul had crossed the bridge, the barbican outer doors were creaking open. After he had passed through the L-shaped, vaulted entrance under the main gatehouse, a man in a conical helmet not so different from his own gestured Ernoul to one of the half-timbered buildings backed up against the inside of the wall.

This turned out to be a stable. Ernoul dismounted stiffly and led his horse inside. No sooner was he out of the rain than he stopped to gape, because he had never seen stables like this before in his life. To his left was a large room with a fireplace in it, exuding warmth. There saddles were resting on wooden arms that extended out of the wall in neat rows, three layers high. Bridles hung on hooks beside the saddles, and there were open boxes crammed with brushes, picks and combs, and even benches for the grooms to sit on while they cleaned the tack. There were also ladders at the far end of the room leading to a loft where the grooms evidently slept. To his right the horse stalls stretched in two rows, and each was big enough for the horse to turn around and lie down in. Most amazing of all, the rainwater was being funneled straight from the roof into a narrow trough that ran along the wall under the windows and ended in a deeper trough at the far end of the stables. The horses could drink the running water as it went by or, when the rain stopped, be led to the large trough.

As he stood in amazement in the entryway, a man called out to him: "Bring your horse down here!"

Ernoul dutifully tugged at the bridle and led his horse toward the voice. It was dark from the storm and the gathering dusk, and Ernoul was startled when he came face to face with a man as black as coal. Ernoul would have suspected he was a Saracen except that he wore a large, elaborate wooden cross on his chest; that reassured him somewhat.

"Miserable day to be out riding about, young man," the groom addressed him in a soft, almost sympathetic voice.

"I've come to ask a boon of Lord Balian," Ernoul admitted, too tired, cold, and wet to dissemble.

The black man nodded solemnly, but did not press him for more details. Instead he said, "I'll see to your horse; he looks old enough to be your grandfather."

"He's twenty-four, I think," Ernoul admitted.

The black man nodded and urged, "Go across to the hall and ask for Dawit."

"Dawit?" Ernoul asked; it was a name he'd never heard before.

"Yes, that's Lord Balian's squire and my son. He'll find you some dry clothes before you are presented to the baron."

"Thank you—ah—" Ernoul suddenly realized he didn't know how to address this man. He'd assumed he was just a servant, but if his son was squire to Lord Balian, then maybe he was someone important after all.

"My name is Mathewos," the tall black man helped him out. "I'm marshal of Ibelin."

That sounded important. "Thank you, sir."

Because of the rain, more people than usual were crowded in the hall. Mostly they clustered around the fireplace that stood in the middle of the outside wall. The fireplace had a massive stone hood that sucked up the smoke, leaving the rest of the room almost smoke-free, although warm. Knights and sergeants were sitting astride benches and playing backgammon or dicing. Women were sitting side by side on benches backed up against the wall, darning and gossiping. Several young children were chasing after a dog that had something in its mouth, and they in turn were being followed by a nurse with an indulgent expression on her face. In a far corner two men appeared to practicing on a lute and a flute, with a great deal of bickering and discord.

It took a moment before anyone took any notice of Ernoul, and when they did they dismissed him as unimportant. Eventually a man sauntered over and asked him, "You looking for someone, lad?"

"Da—De—" He couldn't remember the strange name.

"Dawit?"

"Yes!"

The man turned at the waist and shouted across the room, "Anyone seen Dawit around?"

Eventually they tracked the lord's squire down, and Ernoul was confronted by a slender youth as black as his father and very well kitted out in low leather shoes, red woollen hose, and a woollen gown that fell to his shins and was belted at the waist. His gown had short sleeves over his long silk shirt, with very nice embroidery bands trimming both the sleeves and hem; the belt looked like it had cost at least a bezant. "You were asking for me?"

"My name is Ernoul, son of Arnulf, and I'm here to see the Baron of Ibelin, but your father, the marshal—" by this point, Ernoul couldn't remember the strange name of the man in the stables, either—"told me to ask for you. He said something about dry clothes before being presented to my lord," he added hopefully.

Dawit smiled and nodded. "Come with me."

Five minutes later, Ernoul was stripping off his wet clothes in front of a fire and Dawit was handing him dry things to wear, while Ernoul spilled out the whole story. He told about his brother being killed on the Litani, and becoming his father's heir, which meant he also had to take over his father's military duties, but, he told the patient Dawit, he had no training—and probably no aptitude at arms.

Dawit listened silently, only nodding now and again.

"Do you think Lord Balian will hear me out?" Ernoul asked at last, when he was fitted out in soft, warm clothes—better than any he'd ever worn before.

"Of course," Dawit assured him. "He listens to everyone."

"Do you think he'll send me packing?" Ernoul asked next, not sure if this was the worst or the best possible outcome.

Dawit shook his head. "I don't know. Now come with me to the kitchens for something warm to eat, while I go tell my lord you are here."

"Ah." Balian recognized Ernoul's name at once when Dawit reported his presence and quest. He glanced at Maria Zoë. She was in her eighth month, and as a result less mobile than she usually was. "His brother was killed defending me as I tried to get the King remounted on the Litani."

"Then we will have to find a place for him," Maria Zoë answered without hesitation. "What about with Sir Daniel? Doesn't he need a squire? He's been making do with his brother for over a year now, and that's not a good thing for either of them."

"Yes," Balian nodded agreement. Much as he respected his brother and stood by him in his dispute with the King, the last thing he would have wanted was to be Barry's squire—and had he been, it would have ended in an ugly fight at some point. "Good idea. Dawit—what is it?"

Dawit looked as if he had just seen a ghost. "Hasn't he told you, my lord?"

"Told me what?"

Dawit looked at the Dowager Queen as if for help and then back at Ibelin, licking his lips. "I—I don't think I should be the one to say anything. If he hasn't told you . . ."

Balian narrowed his eyes and insisted, "What is it?"

Dawit looked down at his feet and mumbled.

"What did you say?" Balian demanded more sharply. It was rare for Dawit to be disobedient.

"He's lost the feeling in the fingertips of his left hand, my lord."

Dead silence descended on the room, except for the sound of the rain pelting the shutters and gurgling in the drains. Finally Balian asked, "On the Litani. When he carried the King off the field. Did he help the King undress after he brought him back to the camp?"

Dawit swallowed as he looked up and met his lord's eyes. "Yes, and he—he picked up the dirty bandages after Ibrahim had changed them. Ibrahim was angry with him when he saw what he had done, but—but it was just natural for him. He didn't think anything about it."

"Holy Mother of God," Maria Zoë whispered in the background. She had come to believe the King was not contagious at all, and suddenly this. She shuddered.

"He—Daniel—I mean Sir Daniel," Dawit stuttered, "says he wants—with your permission, of course—to join the Brothers of St. Lazarus."

Balian shook his head in denial of the whole situation. How could he have served Baldwin for years and still be completely healthy while Daniel, who had only been in close contact with him for a few hours, was afflicted? It wasn't fair.

"Daniel—Sir Daniel—says that a runaway baker's apprentice was never meant to be a knight. . . ."

"Nonsense!" Balian snapped. "He may go to the Brothers of St. Lazarus if that is his wish, where he will certainly receive the best medical treatment available—but he goes a knight!"

"Yes, my lord," Dawit answered contritely, as if he were the one who had earned this rebuke.

"And you, too, have earned your spurs," Balian declared. "I'd planned to tell you in a more—What is it *now*?" he asked, exasperated, as Dawit shook his head.

"My lord, I know it is a great honor. I know! But I don't want to be knighted."

The thought was alien to Balian. "Your grandfather may have been an exile from your royal court for supporting the old line of kings, but he was a great nobleman, marshal to the rightful kings of Ethiopia. That qualifies you by blood alone. And you have served me well, if less spectacularly than Daniel did."

Dawit was still shaking his head.

"What is it?" Balian demanded.

"If I am a knight, then I will have to fight, but I can't bear it—the suffering of the horses, I mean. So many are killed or so terribly wounded that they have to be put down afterwards! The Saracens even target the horses, because knights are so well protected by their armor it is much easier to kill a horse than a knight. But they are innocent, my lord. They are only trying to please us. They trust us. And we take them to be slaughtered. I can't bear it. Remember when you first took me for your squire? You asked my father if he would *lend* me to you. It is time for me to be returned to my father. He is not getting any younger, and your stables keeps growing. He needs me, and in time I would be honored to follow in my father's footsteps as your marshal." The words came in such a rush from the usually quiet youth that Balian suspected he had spent hours, days, even weeks—maybe ever since the Battle on the Litani—trying to justify his decision to reject the honor of knighthood should it ever be offered to him.

Balian took a deep breath. "If that is what you wish, then certainly you may take up duties under your father—but I hope you will first train a new squire or two."

"Of course, my lord!" Dawit assured him, relieved to have this issue resolved.

"You and Daniel were a good team," Balian reflected sadly, still unable to fully accept that Daniel had contracted leprosy.

Dawit looked down, embarrassed. Then he looked up and met Balian's eyes. "Give Ernoul a chance, my lord, and Daniel's younger brother Gabriel."

"Gabriel? He's more impudent than Daniel ever was."

"But it would be a consolation for Master Shoreham," Dawit argued. "He would like nothing better than for you to make Gabriel your squire." Balian nodded absently, remembering how proud Roger Shoreham had been when Daniel came home a knight. Roger looked as if he'd grown six inches—and his wife, it was said, bought a new gown and a new set of bed linens to celebrate. Yes, it was only fair to give his younger son the chance of knighthood, too.

Dawit was still singing the youth's praises. "Gabriel rides well and he's big for his age, and he'll have the strength of his brother and father. Besides, he's half trained already, having served his brother this past year."

Balian was not inclined to argue, and he nodded absently. Dawit smiled. "I'll fetch Ernoul, then."

Rahel helped Maria Zoë undress, brushed out and braided her long hair, and then folded back the covers and helped her climb, awkwardly, into the high bed. Only after she had withdrawn did Balian leave the antechamber where Dawit and the new squire Ernoul had helped him out of his clothes and into a woollen nightshirt. A fire had been lit to warm the room before they arrived, but it was now slowly dying. Balian climbed into the far side of the bed and snuggled up beside his wife, laying a hand on her distended belly. "Is he active tonight?"

"No, he's very still," Maria Zoë answered, putting her own hand over her husband's. "Balian?"

"Yes?"

"I'm worried about Isabella. I know Stephanie de Milly said it was only a small fever and nothing to worry about, but I *do* worry."

Balian could understand that, but he didn't see what they could do about it. "You can't travel to Kerak," he told his wife firmly. "I won't have you risk our unborn child."

"I didn't intend to!" Maria Zoë snapped, resenting the fact that he seemed to think he had to tell her what was good for their child. "And before you tell me off, I know *you* can't leave Ibelin in the middle of the Christmas season, either. What I was thinking," Maria Zoë added before they quarreled, "was that now that you have a new squire, we could send Dawit with the pony we were going to give her."

"Are you so sure the Lady of Oultrejourdain will let a groom into her daughter-in-law's sickroom?"

"No, of course not. But he could stay until she is well enough to come down to the stables—and meanwhile, learn a great deal just from listening to the talk of the servants. Dawit's so unassuming, people hardly notice him. He's bound to hear a lot that was never intended for him, and he listens very well."

Balian smiled to himself. He was frequently surprised by his wife's deviousness. He supposed it came more naturally to women, who often could only obtain what they wanted by indirect means. Or maybe it came from growing up in a court infamous for intrigue. "Is it that you fear Isabella is sicker than Madame d'Oultrejourdain claims, or that you suspect she's not sick at all?" Balian asked cautiously.

Maria Zoë had reacted to the news that she must send her daughter to Kerak with such intense fury that it had sparked the worst fight of their married life. She had instantly seen that the Queen Mother was behind the move and that her intentions were remorselessly evil—but once the initial shock wore off, Maria Zoë had also recognized that her husband was not powerful enough to confront the Queen Mother head on. Tripoli was their only hope, and Tripoli was too far away—if not outright indifferent to Isabella's fate. Tripoli appeared to have completely reconciled himself to the rule of not only Baldwin, but Sibylla and Guy de Lusignan. Or maybe he was just preoccupied with trying to deal with the aftermath of the drought, a new marriage, and other personal affairs. Anyway you looked at it, Maria Zoë reckoned the Queen Mother had the upper hand.

"I think Stephanie de Milly is doing the Queen Mother's bidding, and *she* doesn't want Isabella to *ever* come visit us. At best, she wants Madame d'Oultrejourdain to turn Isabella against both of us," Maria Zoë confided to her husband.

"And do you think she might succeed?" Balian asked, astonished. He found it hard to imagine that Isabella would ever turn on her mother.

"Children are so very vulnerable!" Maria Zoë warned him. "They are malleable and easily deceived. They can be made to hate almost anyone! And I haven't even said what the worst is: I think the Queen Mother wants Isabella dead!"

Abruptly, Balian realized she was crying. He pulled her closer and kissed the side of her face that was wet with tears to try to calm her. He had only physical comfort to offer, because he too feared the Queen Mother wanted Isabella dead. She could not risk having any easy alternative to her own children ready at hand—not after she'd let Sibylla marry a man like Lusignan.

After a bit, Maria Zoë seemed to have cried herself into a calmer state, and Balian promised, "We'll send Dawit now, and we'll make a surprise visit to Kerak ourselves at the first opportunity."

Maria Zoë hiccupped and patted his hand. "Thank you, Balian. I know I'm not the easiest wife to live with."

"No," he admitted, "but I would not trade you for anyone." It was what she wanted to hear, of course, but it was also true. The longer they were married, the more Balian was coming to value his wife's political acumen, her common sense, and her willpower. She was far more than a pretty bedmate, a source of wealth, the mother of his children, and a companion: she was his most important ally.

Chapter 5

Jaffa, May 1181

It was good to be back on the coast, Sister Adela thought, taking a deep breath of tangy air spiced with the scent of salt, fish, and wet sand. Beyond the crowded harbor, waves were breaking on the rock ledge where, according to legend, the Ethiopian Princess Andromeda had been chained, a sacrifice to the sea monster. The story of her rescue by the Greek hero Perseus had always been one of Adela's favorites when she was a child growing up here in Jaffa—second only to the very similar story of St. George and the dragon.

Adela's father held a money fief from the Count. She and her seven siblings had lived in a large three-story, but rather cramped, townhouse just behind the citadel, and they had often (or so it seemed in her memories) escaped their tutors to come down to the port to watch the coming and going of galleys, busses, and dhows. It was especially exciting at this time of year, when the first pilgrim ships from the West arrived with their cargoes of iron, copper, chain mail, horses, and best of all, bewildered Westerners.

Today, too, Adela was here to meet Westerners, but now she came in her official capacity as the Head Sister at the Hospital of St. John in Nablus. She had joined the Hospital of St. John almost twenty years ago, at the age of eighteen. As the fourth daughter of a nobleman with only modest means, there had been precious little left for a dowry, and the Hospital was one of the few orders that expected little in material wealth from its novices. That had not been the principal motivating factor for her joining the Order, however. She could have taken service with the then Countess of Jaffa instead. In fact, her father had already broached the matter with Count Amalric. Adela, however, had seen enough of his vain and proud wife, Agnes de Courtenay, and recognized that the position would bring her only misery. Not without a little arrogance (Adela admitted in retrospect), she had told her father that she would rather serve Christ than "a selfish woman."

She had taken her vows and completed her novitiate at nearby Lydda, but spent her first fifteen years of service at the large Hospitaller establishment in Ascalon. She had been there during the siege of 1177, when the city was flooded with refugees fleeing in panic before the invading army of the Sultan of Egypt. She had witnessed the dramatic arrival of King Baldwin and his knights from Jerusalem, and watched tensely from the ramparts as they sortied out of the beleaguered city, riding out to the stunning victory at Montgisard.

It was during that siege that Sister Adela had come to the attention of her superiors for her calm and levelheadedness in the midst of a crisis. Two years later she had been entrusted with the responsibility of running the large and always busy women's ward at the large hospital and hospice complex in Nablus. The Nablus Hospital of St. John housed nearly a thousand beds, four hundred of which were reserved for women. No less than 130 sisters worked there to provide medical care, food, and emotional support to the female patients and the many children that the patients, often widows or abandoned wives, brought with them. While the bulk of the female staff were lay sisters of native birth, mostly Maronite and Greek Christians, there were forty-two Sisters of the Hospital as well. Sister Adela had supreme authority over all these women, and, as was common in the Hospital of St. John, a voice in the Chapter alongside the male officers.

Sister Adela had been sent to Jaffa with an escort of two Hospitaller sergeants and six Turcopoles to collect six new sisters who were assigned to their house. These women had volunteered for service in the Holy Land and had been selected by their respective superiors as sufficiently devout and skilled to be suitable for such service.

Sister Adela was skeptical. Too often in the past, women sent East by superiors ignorant of the real situation were completely out of their depth once they reached Outremer. Some could not adjust to the climate, others had stomachs that rebelled against the diet, and many more simply couldn't cope in a cosmopolitan society in which multiple languages and diverse forms of Christianity lived side by side—not to mention accept the presence of large Muslim and Jewish minorities.

"There's the ship, madame," one of the sergeants announced, drawing her attention to a sleek galley with a black hull and white trim. The sail, which had been hauled up but still hung loosely in the tackle, was also black with a (now largely concealed) white cross. The ship was maneuvering alongside the dock by oar. A sharp command rang out, and with noisy clunking but amazing dexterity the oars were shipped along the port side. The galley glided the last few yards to thump gently against the quay. Immediately a half-dozen men sprang ashore, with lines that they pulled tight and then deftly made secure on the bollards of the quay.

The sailors were still making up the ropes fore and aft when the gangway was run out. At once the passengers moved down from the poop toward the waist of the ship. Two knights of the Hospital were the first ashore, and with only the briefest nod in the direction of Adela, one started pushing his way through the crowds in an obvious hurry. The second, however, turned back to offer his hand to the first of the nuns timidly making their way over the gangway on unsteady legs.

Adela moved along the quay to stand opposite the gangway, but remained three yards back so she didn't get in anyone's way. The first nun was young, pretty, and eager. She looked about with wide, intelligent eyes and an expression of obvious delight, as if she were already enchanted by her new world. Adela liked that. If she came with an open mind, she would find it much easier to adapt. The nun behind her, however, was already more problematic. She was red-faced and waving a little fan as if she couldn't bear the heat, when it was actually quite pleasant here on the coast with the breeze off the sea. Behind her came an ugly woman who collapsed on to her face the minute she stepped off the gangway. To Adela's horror, she realized the nun was kissing the quay and then sitting up to offer a prayer of thanks. Apparently it had been a bad crossing.

Her sisters helped her to her feet and pulled her out of the way of the remaining two nuns, one of whom looked around with large, dazed eyes—hardly more promising than the two before, Adela thought with a sigh. But the last nun, although she moved with the awkward gait of a woman with a hip or knee injury, was helping a couple with a crippled child.

The father of the child, a tall, well-built man with the long blond hair still popular among the Norsemen, took his crippled son upon his back, while his pretty blond-haired wife nagged at him to "be careful." As if he wouldn't be on his own! Adela hated women like this, who couldn't stop giving everyone useless advice. With approval, she saw the last nun distract the woman by offering to carry the boy's crutch and one of the woman's parcels. By the way this nun moved without self-pity or self-consciousness, Sister Adela decided she had probably been born with her defect. Many children born with a physical handicap were promised to the Church as children. While the Hospital did not take child oblates, a girl who had been raised in another order could transfer to the Hospital as an adult.

But that was only five. One was missing. So she waited a bit longer, watching absently as the Norseman set his son down on one of the bollards and returned aboard ship to fetch their sea trunk. Meanwhile, his wife approached Sister Adela and started asking about where she and her "poor boy" might find a safe place to sleep. "Not with heathens or other riffraff!" the woman insisted.

Sister Adela suggested a good (but expensive) inn near the Jerusalem gate, and then turned her attention back to the five nuns who had come ashore. They were busy chattering among themselves, but her low, melodic "Welcome to Outremer and the Kingdom of Jerusalem" made the newcomers spin around. They quickly recognized a woman of authority, and dutifully dipped their knees and bowed their heads. "Weren't there supposed to be six of you?" Sister Adela asked.

Her words produced a stunned silence, until the crippled woman, up close the eldest of the lot, nodded and explained. "Sister Millicent was taken with a fever and died before we could reach port. She was buried at sea."

"It was something in the terrible food, if you ask me," the nun who was fanning herself announced—only to be told pointedly by the crippled nun: "No one is asking you."

"It was terrible!" the nun who had kissed the ground seconded her rebuked companion, closing her eyes and crossing herself. "We nearly all died!"

"But now we are walking the very stones Christ walked!" the awestruck sister answered, her mouth open in wonder. A religious fool, Adela noted mentally before bringing her back to earth with a matter-of-fact: "Hardly. King Amalric built this quay while he was Count of Jaffa, not more than twenty-five years ago. I was around to see it being built. I'm Sister Adela, by the way, and I'm here to collect you and bring you to Nablus."

"We will go by way of Jerusalem, won't we?" the awestruck newcomer asked. "We will go to the Holy Sepulcher first, won't we?"

"You will do as you are *told*, sister," Adela answered sternly—to remind her that it was not her place to make demands—before adding, "but, yes, it is customary to allow new arrivals to pray at both the Church of the Nativity and the Church of the Holy Sepulcher before taking up their duties. You'll be able to visit Nazareth and other shrines later. Now, if you'll follow me, we can take a meal at the Hospital here while your things are offloaded." She gestured with her hand toward the head of the harbor and the stairs leading to the sea gate in the city wall before leading them away.

Behind her the women followed in varying states of wonder, confusion, and curiosity. The very air seemed different here, heavy with humidity and heat, while the palms waving their arms above the red stones of the fortifications were wonderfully exotic. Not more exotic, however, than the half-naked, dark-brown men in turbans hauling on the ropes of a large dhow that was making ready to cast off, or the sight of wheelbarrows full of oranges and lemons for sale. This was a very different world from Dublin. . . .

Ibelin, September 1181

The tiltyard, where the knights and squires honed their skills, was located on the edge of the coastal sand dunes, within sight of Ibelin castle but separated from it by nearly a mile. It was little more than a barren field, moderately level and fenced off to keep the stray animals away. There were no spectator benches, much less bleachers, although sometimes people gathered to watch the knights spar with one another. Even the Dowager Queen had been known to come down now and again when Lord Balian was practicing, but she usually stayed mounted while she watched.

There were now eleven knights in the Ibelin household, including the younger sons of two barons who preferred service for pay with Ibelin over unpaid service to their fathers or brothers. When Ibelin joined them that made for two teams of six, and so they sometimes clashed in simulated melees, practicing the art of riding in close formation—and withstanding such an attack.

It was more common for pairs of knights to fight each other with sheathed swords or to joust with reed lances without iron heads. That way they practiced the thrusts and parries of combat without risking serious injury to either party. Even more often, individual knights tilted with a dummy outfitted with shield and mace and suspended at the end of a pole: the quintain.

Only after all the knights had had enough and had retired from the tiltyard, and their horses and equipment had been cared for, could the squires take the tiltyard over for their own exercise. In the summer months this was often after the sun had started to burn oppressively, and in the rainy season it meant the yard was already badly torn up and muddy. Sometimes knights stayed to train and coach the squires; sometimes they were without supervision.

Ernoul had soon learned that, demanding and critical as Lord Balian could be, it was better to have him or another knight looking on than for the squires to be left on their own. Without the knights watching, the rivalry and competition among the squires often got out of hand. Twice in the past year, dares had escalated to the point where serious injuries had been incurred. Although Ernoul was immune to dares, he suffered from the ridicule lavished on those less skilled. Such insults took on a sharper and more hateful tone when the squires were unsupervised.

After he had been unseated for the third time in a single morning, to the hoots and mockery of the others, one of the other squires chased his horse away rather than catching it for him. Ernoul, red-faced as much from frustration as exertion, limped back toward Ibelin to the catcalls of the others.

He'd been with Lord Balian nine months now, and most of the time he liked his life at Ibelin. He certainly liked the food and music offered in his lord's hall, both so much more sophisticated and diverse than what he'd known at home. Even the dormitory he shared with the other squires was comparatively comfortable, located in the loft above the eastern tract of storerooms and workshops. But best of all, he had discovered that the Baron of Ibelin had almost a dozen books. Half belonged to the Dowager Queen and were in Greek, and one was a magnificent psalter with a carved ivory cover inlaid with gold—a legacy from Balian's godmother, an abbess—but there were also a translation of a Greek book about a war that had taken place in ancient times and a book in Latin by a Roman general.

Because of his interest in these books, Ernoul had made friends with Balian's confessor, Gabriel's elder brother Michael. Father Michael had agreed to give him scrap papyrus, the kind used for taking dictation before a letter was copied into a fair hand, on which to write his diary. He also let Ernoul keep his diary hidden in the sacristy, where it was not at risk of someone finding it. Ernoul didn't want anyone else seeing what he wrote down there, because that was where he vented all his contempt for the other squires—half of whom, like Gabriel, couldn't even read and write!

A horse was suddenly beside him. Ernoul looked up warily, half expecting his tormentors to have followed him from the tiltyard, but it was only Gabriel. Gabriel jumped down easily and threw the reins over his horse's head so he could lead him. His coarse brown hair had bleached in the summer sun and stood up in all directions. He'd obviously run his fingers through his sweat-damp hair after shoving the chain-mail hood off to hang down his back. Gabriel was broad-shouldered for a fourteen-year-old, and freckled. He fell in beside Ernoul. "You've got to relax more," he advised the still over-slender and dark-haired Ernoul. "Being stiff is what makes you fall off all the time."

Ernoul looked at Gabriel with dark eyes filled with exasperation. "How can I relax when I know I'm about to be knocked off the horse again?"

"Look at it this way: What bounces higher, a stone or a pillow?"

"I'm neither!" Ernoul protested. "I'm human, and it *hurts* when I fall off. I've got bruises all over my body!"

"I can't help you if you won't let me," Gabriel pointed out, starting to get annoyed. He tried to defend Ernoul to the others, but they ridiculed him for siding with the "acolyte," as they referred to Ernoul.

Ernoul looked over at Gabriel, torn between resignation and hope. "How can you help me?"

"You need to ride better before you can joust. You should ask Lord Balian's permission to spend time more time riding every day. I can cover for you while you're away."

The idea made sense to Ernoul, but he was hesitant nevertheless. It was one thing riding the ancient horse his father had given him, but the Ibelin marshal had rapidly relegated the parental horse to the pasture, and Ernoul had been given a younger palfrey that, until it was entrusted to him, had been ridden mostly by messengers. This horse still had enough energy and temperament to spook and bolt now and again. Ernoul was a little afraid of him.

"Look, Ernoul. I know you're the darling of the ladies because you can recite poetry and tell tales so well, and I know you can serve my lord better at table than I can, but that's not going to get you knighted—or stop you from being killed, as your brother was, in your first encounter with the Saracens."

Ernoul looked down miserably and sighed. He was not really afraid of following his brother to an early grave, because Lord Balian had made it very clear he would not be allowed to take part in any muster unless his skills improved substantially. But he hated the thought of disappointing his parents by failing to win the accolade of knighthood. His family had never been more than poor gentry, not even at home in Normandy—which was why they were all the prouder of being knights.

The boys had reached Ibelin and passed through the gate to walk up the cobbled street toward the castle. Just ahead of them, a rider on a clearly exhausted mount was clattering over the drawbridge.

"Who's that?" Gabriel asked, raising his head.

"Arms of Antioch," Ernoul read the heraldry immediately.

"Antioch?" Gabriel asked, puzzled. "That's at the other end of the Kingdom."

"And the home of Queen Maria's sister, Theodora." Ernoul might not be the most adept youth in the tiltyard, but his family had been in Outremer almost a century, and like any well-brought-up gentleman, he knew genealogy and who was related to whom.

Gabriel, coming from yeoman stock, was not so well versed in the family ties of the nobility. "What is a Greek woman doing there?" he wanted to know.

"She's married to the ruling prince, you dunce: Prince Bohemond III."

"Oh." Gabriel looked after the rider, who was disappearing inside the gate.

"How old was he?" Balian asked his wife, referring to the Greek Emperor, Manuel I. It was the news of his death that Antioch herald had brought to Ibelin. "He ascended to the throne before I was even born—1143, wasn't it? He must have been getting very old."

"That's not the point," Maria Zoë told her husband sharply. "The point is that his heir is only twelve years old and very vulnerable." Maria Zoë could sense from her husband's expression that he did not grasp the gravity of the situation.

Balian confirmed her assessment by replying with a shrug, "And Baldwin was only thirteen and a leper when his father died."

"You do not understand the court in Constantinople, Balian," Maria Zoë countered, taking a deep breath to muster her patience. "The High Court of Jerusalem acknowledged Baldwin as King immediately, and all tenants-in-chief swore an oath to him the same day his father died. Furthermore, those oaths *mean* something. When you swear an oath, you are more likely to keep it than not. That's not the case with my countrymen. They'll swear to anything, even while—or especially while—plotting the opposite. Well," she moderated her statement, "maybe the great lords take oaths seriously, but it's not the great landowners that control Constantinople. The bureaucracy and the mob control Constantinople—and oaths mean nothing to them."

Balian tossed her a skeptical look. "The mob? Of course oaths mean nothing to the mob, but you can't mean to tell me that the *mob* rules the most civilized city on earth," Balian protested.

"Well, along with the court officials," Maria Zoë conceded. "They are the people who actually run the Empire—the tax assessors and collectors, the bookkeepers and archivists, the chroniclers and musicians, the almoners and paymasters, et cetera, et cetera. All the people who control revenue and patronage, and so have the means of buying influence, hold power in Contantinople. They are often eunuchs, by the way, and rarely men of high birth. In Jerusalem such functions are filled by clergy, but our priests do not dirty their hands with such secular tasks."

"You're telling me these castrated clerks are powerful enough to endanger the legitimate male heir of the Emperor himself?" Balian clearly did not believe it.

"Yes—not on their own, of course, but although Maria of Antioch is technically the Regent along with my uncle Alexius, they are not popular. Furthermore, my great-uncle Andronicus has returned, and he hates both of them. He has been poisoning the ears of the influential bureaucrats and buying the favor of the mob for months in anticipation of my great-uncle's death."

"Andronicus? Isn't he the man who ran off with the Dowager Queen Theodora and took service with Nur ad-Din?"

"Exactly! You see how treacherous he is! He is a man of very low morals but excessive ambition. Although we could never prove it, my father was convinced he poisoned my grandfather. Don't look at me like that, Balian. I'm not making this up. I know you Franks are more candid—blunt or crude, my countrymen would say. If you get angry enough, you tend to throw a gauntlet in another man's face, or simply raise an army in rebellion. My people are more subtle and devious."

"You're telling me there is a chance Andronicus will try to murder your young cousin?"

"There's nothing 'chancy' about it, Balian. Andronicus will try to murder the young Emperor Alexius, and he will try to kill my uncle Alexius as well. They both stand between him and the Imperial Crown. That's why we must prevail upon King Baldwin to send his assurances of support. He must send ambassadors at once, renewing the alliance and promising mutual defense."

"The King takes no heed of my advice!" Balian answered bitterly. His breach with the King was a festering wound. Furthermore, he was uncomfortable offering assurances of aid to Constantinople when their own borders were so vulnerable.

"Balian, without the support of Constantinople, Salah ad-Din has no reason to fear attack from the rear when next he falls on Jerusalem. Jerusalem needs Constantinople far more than Constantinople needs Jerusalem."

Balian shrugged. "You're probably right, *Αγαπημενη μου*." His use of the Greek term of endearment eased Maria Zoë's tension somewhat even as Balian continued, "But what do you want me to do? The King does not listen to me anymore. Indeed, whatever I suggest, he is likely to do the opposite!" The acidity in his tone testified to how deep the wound was. "Maybe if you write a letter, impressing upon him the urgency and the risks, he would listen to reason." He paused before adding, "We can send a messenger at first light tomorrow, if you like."

"Thank you, Balian," Maria Zoë answered; the tension her sister's letter had ignited started to die away as Balian came and kissed her on the forehead. She caught his hand and kissed the palm passionately.

"What was that for?" he asked, bemused.

"Just a thank you for being such a good and loving husband to me," Maria Zoë answered. With her great-uncle dead, she was intensely grateful that Balian had married her for herself and not for her connections—unlike Bohemond and her sister Theodora.

Montreal, Oultrejourdain
December 1181

"Emperors, kings, and princes—all dying like flies. It's a good time for the vulture," Reynald de Châtillon declared to himself with satisfaction, squinting as the sun lifted itself over the horizon like a burning copper ball. It bathed the desert below his castle of Montreal in cold orange light. The land to the southeast was a barren wasteland of rocky hills and gravel valleys, dotted with parched thorn bushes too dry for even camels to eat. He smacked his hand down on the parapet, then turned and bellowed down into the castle ward: "Mount up!"

His knights had been roused after Matins, told to prepare to ride at dawn and to pack enough provisions for ten days. While the knights and sergeants were milling about checking their equipment and tightening their girths, the squires were loading the mule panniers with provisions, and servants were fastening water casks on the camels. By the length of the camel train, the fighting men could guess that wherever they were going, Oultrejourdain expected them to be away from water for a long time.

At the base of the stairs, Stephanie de Milly awaited her husband. She walked with him to his waiting palfrey, held by her son and her husband's squire, Humphrey.

"We'll stay here," Stephanie told her lord simply.

"You'd be safer at Kerak," Reynald growled back at her. He had no intention of ordering her to go anywhere, since she was likely to ignore him anyway.

"I don't care," she answered. "I like the change of scene—and Ibelin, with his bitch of a wife, is less likely to come here trying to interfere with Isabella." She deeply resented the fact that Balian and Maria Zoë had twice visited Kerak; she was convinced that they reinforced Isabella's innate rebelliousness and stubbornness. They certainly made her proud and impudent, and it took her months to badger the girl back into submission after they left.

"Don't underestimate Ibelin," Oultrejourdain warned. "He's tougher than he looks."

"Maybe, but his Greek wife loves luxury too much to come out here."

Oultrejourdain wasn't so sure, but he didn't really care. Isabella and the Dowager Queen were his wife's problem. It had been her idea to force Isabella into an early marriage with her son because, she argued, it robbed Tripoli of his best weapon. Her determination to humiliate and, if possible, murder Tripoli had not diminished over the years, although Châtillon himself had lost interest in the feud. He had promised to kill Tripoli only because it was Stephanie's condition for marrying him, but now that he was safely installed as Lord of Oultrejourdain, he was attracted by more lucrative enterprises—like the one he planned to undertake today. So he gave Stephanie a brusque kiss and then swung himself up into the saddle.

She held up a richly decorated goblet to him, and he flung the contents down his throat, then demonstratively smacked and licked his lips, declaring, "Last wine we'll taste in a while, I wager." He handed the goblet back to his wife, took a crumpled straw-brimmed hat from his pommel, and jammed it on his bald head before putting his heels to his stallion. The horse jumped forward so strongly that Humphrey was nearly trampled underfoot.

Oultrejourdain signaled his men to follow, and Humphrey scrambled to get to his own horse. The young stallion was so agitated, however, that he wouldn't stand still. Humphrey ended up hopping around in circles, trying to stop his horse from following the others long enough for him to pull himself into the saddle, and it wasn't until Isabella grabbed the bridle from the offside and with a firm jerk ordered the horse to "stand still!" that he managed to mount.

By then the bulk of Oultrejourdain's force had already filed out of the inner ward to cross the rocky outer ward to the main gate. Oultrejourdain himself was leading them out through the barbican to the gravel path that wound its way down the steep slopes of the barren hill to the desert below. Humphrey had no time to kiss his betrothed goodbye as he spurred to get ahead of the camels that were just about to go out of the gate.

Indeed, the path was too narrow for him to get past the other riders until they were at the foot of the hill, and then he cantered past the trotting main body of troops to fall into his place just behind his lord. Beside Oultrejourdain rode Henri d'Ibelin, who was speaking loudly enough for Humphrey to hear what he was saying.

"If we continue on this course, we'll soon cross out of Christian territory."

"Brilliant observation," Oultrejourdain quipped sarcastically.

"The King signed a four-year truce with Salah ad-Din barely two years ago." Sir Henri looked significantly over his shoulder at the roughly three hundred mounted fighting men in their wake.

"Did he? Doesn't interest me."

"Funny. I seem to remember you swearing an oath of allegiance to the King."

Oultrejourdain turned and stared at the household knight. Henri d'Ibelin had been one of his most trusted and most reliable supporters up to now. He answered with deliberate slowness, "And *you*, if I remember correctly, swore an oath to *me*."

"So I did," Henri confirmed with a shrug, "and I will follow you to hell itself, if need be. But tell me *why*," Henri challenged, looking his lord boldly in the eye.

Oultrejourdain snorted, and it sounded almost like approval to the baffled Humphrey, who would never have dared challenge Reynald de Châtillon as Sir Henri had just done. "I swore an oath to Jerusalem, and I intend to *serve* Jerusalem. That's not the same thing as respecting every piece of parchment sniveling clerks cover with fancy phrases. Prince as-Salih, Nur ad-Din's rightful heir, has died in Aleppo. On his deathbed, he named his cousin Izz ad-Din Mas'ud, the Lord of Mosul, as his successor. Now in case you don't know, Izz ad-Din is a fighting man, unlike the unfortunate as-Salih—and if he gains control of Aleppo, he will pose a serious threat to our friend Salah ad-Din because he is a true Seljuk prince and not a Kurdish upstart. He is also our natural ally, because with Izz ad-Din in Aleppo, certain of the Sultan's subjects in Homs—and even Damascus—might feel less loyal to the usurping Kurd. So, what would you do if you were Salah ad-Din?"

"I'd make damn sure Izz ad-Din didn't establish control of Aleppo," Sir Henri replied emphatically.

Châtillon nodded slowly in answer before adding, "The only problem with that strategy is that Salah ad-Din is in Cairo at the moment."

"Farrukh-Shah is in Damascus, and he's up to the job of seizing Aleppo," Sir Henri countered.

"Ah, but he won't *be able* to do that if there is a Frankish force threatening Eilat, will he?"

"Eilat? That's on the Red Sea!"

"I've heard from very reliable sources that its defenses are in ruinous condition," Oultrejourdain countered, grinning in the shade of his straw hat.

Henri looked over his shoulder again, this time at the camels rather than the fighting men. "We don't have enough water to get that far!"

"We don't have to," Oultrejourdain answered smugly. He pointed ahead of them to what he had seen with satisfaction from the tower. "Look at the color of the sky up ahead. That's rain. By the time we meet up with our Bedouin guides, it will be pouring, and the desert will start to turn green."

Arabia, December 1181

Henri had not expected to enjoy campaigning in enemy territory as much as he did. All his previous experience had been defensive—or at best, chasing off raiders. This raid, however, drove deeper and deeper into the desert, which, as Châtillon had predicted, was suddenly sprouting so much grass that their horses fed themselves wherever they paused or camped for the night. They camped, they rode, they fought—always with the advantage of surprise, always against a panicked enemy. They had Bedouin guides, who were clearly enjoying themselves as much as if not more than the Franks, reveling in taking revenge upon men who looked down on them as savages.

They killed anyone who crossed their path, and took whatever they wanted from the houses and villages they overran. When they reached Eilat, they found the defenses were indeed useless, so they swept through the town spreading terror in all directions. They were too few to kill the whole population, and most people escaped into the surrounding countryside to spread the word that the Franks had come to Arabia.

But they didn't stop. They couldn't. They had to keep moving or risk being overwhelmed. They were just sixty knights and twice that many sergeants, three hundred men counting squires and servants. So they kept riding south, deeper into the Arabian Peninsula.

If Eilat's defenses had been in poor repair, Tarbuk had none at all. The city just spread across the desert as if God had spilled adobe houses from a bucket. The domes of the mosques and the needles of the minarets dominated the skyline, and the streets were lined with shops catering to pilgrims traveling down from Syria to Mecca. The sudden appearance of Frankish cavalry was completely unprecedented, and the ensuing panic was so complete that most of the inhabitants just got in each other's way as they tried to seek shelter in their houses or flee.

They were now 130 miles south of Eilat and totally dependent on their Bedouin guides to find their way from place to place—and back home. Their horses might find fodder in the short-lived blooming of the desert, but the men were only eating what they could seize and drinking where the Bedouins led them. Henri was becoming increasingly uneasy over that dependency, and he couldn't shake the fear that they might be betrayed at any moment.

"Here all the spoils go to the Bedouin!" Oultrejourdain announced abruptly into his thoughts, and Henri smiled to himself, thinking this was how Oultrejourdain retained their loyalty. One of the sergeants was less charmed by his lord's strategy, however, and spat in disgust. Oultrejourdain spurred into the ranks and smashed the man full in the face, breaking his jaw. "The spoils go to the Bedouin!" he repeated, more loudly than before. "You'll get your reward later! Today all we do is kill, so we leave behind a ghost town that the Bedouins can plunder at leisure in our wake!"

And so they did.

Shortly after the sack of Tarbuk, a desperate messenger arrived on a foundering horse from Montreal with news that Farrukh-Shah had led a cavalry force into Oultrejourdain and was laying waste to the towns in the north of the barony. From Châtillon's perspective, his mission had been accomplished: Farrukh-Shah could not be threatening Aleppo if he was in Oultrejourdain. Stephanie de Milly, the messenger reported, had ordered every fighting man left in the barony to muster at as-Salt, but the remaining men were infantry and sergeants for the most part, since Oultrejourdain had all his knights with him on the raid. Her situation was desperate, the rider told his lord.

Châtillon grunted. "Did she say that?"

"No, my lord. She thinks she can manage Farrukh-Shah by herself—but it's not true."

Châtillon laughed and clapped the man on the shoulder with pride. "Don't underestimate her! She very well might—and I'd love to see the bastard's face when he finds out he's been bested by a woman!"

But Châtillon was satisfied that they had accomplished what they set out to do, and not a little uneasy about the trustworthiness of the Bedouins himself, so he ordered his men to turn for home.

By then the rains were letting up and the desert was turning brown again. The Bedouins were notably less keen to help. Henri was glad for every mile closer to home, and then they crested one of the endless hills—and spread out below them, following the course of a drying wadi, was the long, swaying file of a camel caravan laden with the riches of Egypt. Oultrejourdain's eyes lit up under the ragged brim of his straw hat, and he declared, loud enough for the first several ranks to hear him: "The answer to my prayers!" Then he threw away his straw hat and screamed over his shoulder at Humphrey: "Helmet!"

Oultrejourdain's men were as eager as their lord. They knew that their lord intended to give them this; it had no strategic value, and the Bedouins had been rewarded already. This was theirs, and it had everything to turn a man's head: there were young horses evidently on their way to market, there were heavily-laden camels with (surely) spices and ivory, gold and incense—and best of all, at least a score of camels were carrying the swaying, completely enclosed tents in which the Muslims moved their women from place to place. Probably women on pilgrimage.

"How many women do they squash into those tents?" one of the younger knights asked an older colleague excitedly.

"Usually two—sometimes three, if we're lucky," the veteran answered.

"That's almost half a hundred!"

"Enough to go around, if we share. No one has to sleep like a monk tonight."

Someone in the caravan had caught sight of the wide line of Frankish cavalry on the crest of the hill. There were shouts and frantic riding to and fro on the part of the guards. But their situation was so helpless that Oultrejourdain didn't feel compelled to hurry. In fact, he dismounted to take a piss and drink water from a skin Humphrey brought him before remounting and demanding a lance.

By the time Oultrejourdain was ready, the caravan had passed in front of them at a jog and the guards were looking over their shoulders, thanking Allah and thinking the Franks were going to respect the truce. But now, at their leisure, the Franks were ready.

"I'll have no fighting among ourselves!" Oultrejourdain announced. "We kill the men, herd the animals and women together in the middle, and then divide them and the cargoes up. Each man will get his share of the loot: that is, 50 per cent is mine and I choose it, 20 per cent belongs to the knights, 20 per cent goes to the sergeants, and the last 10 per cent goes to the squires. Once you have your shares you can start haggling among yourselves, but not before. And you can haggle all you like, but keep it civil. If I see two men fighting over a woman or a horse or a damned piece of shit, I'll personally kill you both! Do I make myself understood?" The older men were nodding. They knew the routine. Oultrejourdain had always been strict about dividing the spoils equally; that's why they served him.

The horses were dancing around, stepping forward and back, so eager were the men to attack. Oultrejourdain let his gaze sweep along the line of helmeted men, and he liked what he saw. This was raw power. Armored men who had been fighting a month now. They were filthy, stinking, sleek, and hard. Not even his sop of a stepson looked like a prissy courtier anymore, he noted with approval. He was blooded, too, for Châtillon had personally seen him run his lance into the belly of a man who tried to defend his home in Tarbuk.

"I'll let you have my woman when I'm done with her," Oultrejourdain decided generously, punching his stepson in the arm. "It's time you lost your virginity, or you'll be no use to that minx the King so generously gave you." If Oultrejourdain had had sons of his own, he would have found a way of eliminating Humphrey and ensuring that some of his own blood could claim the Crown of Jerusalem by siring sons on Isabella. But since he did not, Humphrey would have to do.

He turned back to his other men and grinned at them. "Ready?"

"Oultrejourdain!" they shouted in unison in reply, and as a wild pack they plunged exuberantly down the side of the barren hill, causing a cascade of small stones and gravel and sending a plume of dust into the air.

Humphrey didn't know where to hide. No matter where he stumbled in the darkness, he came across men fornicating loudly and brutally. The screams of the women had given way to whimpering and begging as their resistance was broken. Now the only sounds they emitted were sobs or hoarse gasps for water or a minute of respitet between rapes. Their outrage and fear at the beginning had been hammered into pain and sheer exhaustion. Even if he had not been able to understand Arabic, he would have understood their misery from their tones and gestures alone.

But he did understand Arabic. He knew that not one of these women was a whore or a slave. They were honest wives and virgin daughters: women returning from the hajj full of a sense of purity. These women had known nothing but the perfect shelter of protective fathers and husbands. Nothing had prepared them for this night of brutal gang rape. The barbarity of it, the heartlessness of it, the unending nature of it because there was only one woman for ten men, appalled Humphrey to the marrow of his bones.

He wandered as far as he dared from the camp. He put his hands over his ears, but he could not block out the memories of what he had already heard. He tried to pray, but he was too ashamed. Without having touched one of the women, he felt as besmirched with sin as the perpetrators, simply for being one of them—and being unable to stop them.

It wasn't supposed to be like this. Men should *never* use women like this. It wasn't right. It offended against God and nature. Christ had been born of the Virgin Mary, and there was nothing more virtuous than perfect chastity. Yet God had also made woman to be man's companion, to be his helpmate, and to propagate the human race, so the sacrament of marriage had been devised to join a man and woman together in God's holy name. Within marriage, women were the precious vessel in which children were conceived and nurtured. Women were weaker than men and so in need of constant protection. That was what his grandfather had taught him, and it was what chivalry dictated: women should always be treated with courtesy and respect.

Did it matter that these women were Mohammedans? As women they had no choice in the matter. They were what their fathers made them.

Something stirred ahead of him. In horror Humphrey realized that a girl was trying to crawl away from the camp. She was completely naked, her long black hair a tangled mess filled with dust and thorns. She saw him at almost the same moment he saw her, or perhaps he had emitted a gasp. She looked up at him with huge black eyes, and his innards twisted in agony, because she was as young as Isabella.

"Kill me!" she gasped out. "Please kill me!" She was pointing to the sword he still wore at his hip.

But from the camp a man was shouting, "Hey! It's my turn!"

"Please!" the girl pleaded more urgently, looking over her shoulder at the man staggering toward them, naked from the waist down but pouring wine or water down his throat as he came after her. "I can't take it again! I can't! Please kill me! If you know what mercy is, sir, kill me!"

Humphrey backed away from her in horror. He could no more kill her than he could protect her. He was utterly helpless—and ashamed of his helplessness.

The man had reached the girl at last, and he grabbed her by the arm and started dragging her back toward the camp. She let out a high-pitched scream that pierced the desert night and would follow Humphrey the rest of his days—but all he could do was turn on his heels and flee deeper into the darkness.

Chapter 6

Jerusalem, April 1182

In the narrow confines of the Tower of David, where the High Court had met before the King's illness had worsened, the Court had seemed to crowd the room. The great hall of the modern palace, however, was much larger, so the barons and bishops were widely dispersed, chattering to one another in small groups. Balian spotted his brother standing with the Count of Tripoli near one of the tall, peaked windows that overlooked the walled garden south of the palace. He joined him there.

A moment latter, the herald announced the King of Jerusalem. When Balian turned with the others to look at the dais, Baldwin was already seated on his throne, his gloved hands resting on the arms, his back straight as a lance. With horror, however, Balian saw that the discoloration of his skin had almost reached his eyes, and the skin on his chin was starting to become deformed with hideous growths. Balian's heart quavered, and he felt his anger and bitterness toward the King falter. He was the victim of Agnes' evil influence, Balian found himself rationalizing. If they could just speak again in private! He had failed last time, but he would beg for a second chance. Surely if Baldwin knew that Oultrejourdain and his lady were not even allowing Maria Zoë to visit her child, he would be persuaded he had made a mistake.

"My lords!" the King's voice rang out sharply. It had started to rasp, as lepers' voices so often did, but it was forceful enough, and the mumbling and chattering ebbed away. "I have summoned the High Court to consider an embassy from the Sultan Salah ad-Din." That got the attention of most of the men in the room, while the King paused and focused his eyes on the bald-headed Lord of Oultrejourdain. "The Sultan Salah ad-Din demands the restoration of all goods seized illegally from a caravan crossing south of Montreal, *and*—most important—restitution for the cold-blooded murder of thirty-two men and forty-seven women and children."

Oultrejourdain shrugged demonstratively. "Can't be done. My men have already consumed or gambled away most of their plunder."

"The Sultan demands one hundred pieces of silver for each man, and fifty for each woman and child," the King continued as if he had not been interrupted.

Oultrejourdain snorted. "Bah! He doesn't expect to see an obol of it! He's looking for an excuse to attack us."

"He doesn't have to *look* for an excuse to attack, since you've already *handed* him one on a silver platter!" Tripoli snapped in a voice loud enough for all to hear.

"What I did, Tripoli, was prevent Salah ad-Din from seizing Aleppo!" Oultrejourdain retorted, twisting at the waist to fling this over his shoulder contemptuously at his fellow baron.

"You could have done that without attacking and plundering the caravan!" Ramla countered hotly in support of Tripoli.

"Well, I had to give the men *something*, or they wouldn't be keen to fight next time. And there is *always* a next time," Châtillon reminded them.

"What is more important to you? Keeping your *men* happy or your *King*?" Edessa asked sternly—but his fat, balding figure hardly evoked respect from anyone, much less Oultrejourdain.

"Asked like that, Edessa: my men," Oultrejourdain retorted, causing some of the men in the room to shake their heads in disapproval or disgust, but others to smile. One of the latter was Guy de Lusignan. He was clearly amused by the remark and cast Oultrejourdain an approving look. Balian looked sharply from one man to the other. That would be an unholy alliance if ever there was one, he thought. A ruthless man like Oultrejourdain would make a vain but spineless man like the younger Lusignan dance to his tune!

"Well, I hope, my lord, you find it equally amusing to learn that a Christian ship with 1,676 souls on board has been seized by the Sultan's men, and all are being held captive," continued the King, drawing the attention of his barons back to the issue at hand.

"What? Has the Sultan taken to piracy? I didn't think he had a navy." Oultrejourdain sounded surprised but not contrite.

"The ship went aground off Damietta in a storm that had blown her off course."

"God's will be done," Oultrejourdain intoned, harvesting a crop of reproaches and admonishments from the clerical members of the High Court—but everyone in the room knew that Reynald de Châtillon didn't give a damn for the opinion of the Church.

"So, my lord, you will not pay restitution?" King Baldwin pressed him.

Oultrejourdain spread out his arms dramatically. "Will restitution bring back the dead? If the Sultan wanted an eye for an eye, then he'd keep the same number of prisoners as I killed—less than a tenth of those he holds—and let the rest go free. But believe me, he does not want restitution; he wants war."

"And whose fault is that?" Tripoli taunted again.

"Not mine!" Oultrejourdain rejoined. "The Sultan has wanted war ever since he was strong enough to confront us."

"Silence!" the King called from the dais, and then waited until the muttering and side conversations had died out again. When silence had settled upon the room, he addressed the company. "You have heard the Lord of Oultrejourdain, my lords. He will not pay restitution, not even to save 1,676 Christian souls from Muslim slavery. So, will the rest of you raise the money between you?" Baldwin asked, his eyes sweeping the room for reaction.

"Better to save the money to prepare our defenses, your grace. Whether Oultrejourdain should have done what he did nor not, the dye is now cast. There will certainly be war," the lord of Caesarea remarked heavily, earning nods across the room.

"My lord bishops?" Baldwin challenged the clerical members of the High Court. "What say you?"

"Your grace," the Bishop of Bethlehem spoke up, "if I believed Salah ad-Din would release the Christians for any sum of money, I would willingly contribute my share, but I fear that what the Lord of Oultrejourdain has said is right: Salah ad-Din wants war."

King Baldwin looked across the room until his eyes came to rest on Balian and his brother. He couldn't bear to look at Balian, because of his guilty conscience; he felt guilty about taking Isabella from her mother, and even guiltier about turning his back on the man who had been his only friend in his youth. So he focused on Ramla instead. "My Lord of Ramla, you have met Salah ad-Din face to face. What say you? Will he negotiate with us, or does he want war?"

"If we held anything of value to him—like his nephew or Eilat—he would surely negotiate, but he does not need our gold or silver. Of both he already has far more than we. For mere coin, he will not abandon his *jihad*."

The King nodded slowly. "Then, my lords, let us arm ourselves."

Balian and Barry rode back to the Ibelin palace together. To avoid the covered markets between the palace and the Holy Sepulcher, they took David Street past the large Hospitaller complex, riding single file to let one of the almost daily funeral corteges of paupers pass. Too many pilgrims came to the Holy Land to die, or simply underestimated the strains of the long journey and fell ill on arrival. The Knights Hospitaller maintained a hospital for the sick and dying that reputedly had two thousand beds. Every day some of those patients inevitably died and were taken by the good brothers of the Hospital for burial beyond Mount Zion.

When the funeral cortege had passed and the brothers again rode side by side, Barry caught Balian's arm to draw his attention. "You talked to the King alone after the High Court adjourned. What was it about?"

Balian sighed. Although the conversation had started well, with the King asking about Daniel, in the end the exchange had only increased their breach. Balian had begged the King to use his influence to allow Isabella to come home, at least to visit, and the King answered by insisting that Barry take an oath to Guy de Lusignan as his overlord. For his brother he reduced the conversation to the issue of the oath of loyalty he owed to Jaffa.

"I will never swear! Never!" Barry answered and spat onto the street in disgust. Although it had been two years since the wedding of Princess Sibylla to Guy de Lusignan, Barry could not get over the insult. He had married another heiress, Elizabeth of Beirut, and she was already pregnant, but his hatred for Guy seemed to be increasing rather than diminishing with time. This had nothing to do with love for Sibylla, Balian recognized; it was injured pride, not thwarted love, that so impassioned his brother with hate.

Balian agreed that Barry had been grievously slighted and unjustly treated. He also agreed that Guy de Lusignan was not suited to be Count of Jaffa, much less King of Jerusalem. Yet what bothered him most was the degree to which his brother had become consumed by hatred. Father Vitus had taught him as a boy that a man must forgive his enemies, because "hatred is like taking poison and expecting someone else to die from it." This was exactly what was happening to Barry. His hatred for Sibylla's husband had no effect on the debonair and increasingly self-assured young Frenchman, but it was eating Barry up from the inside. He looked ten years older and he almost never smiled, not even for his new wife. Before he could say any more, however, Barry grabbed Balian again and exclaimed, "What's going on?" He pointed to what appeared to be a mob besieging the Ibelin palace.

The crowd completely blocked the street, and it was obviously agitated. The men were making angry gestures and speaking in loud, threatening voices, while the women were keening and tearing their hair as if at a funeral. The brothers' hands went instantly to their hilts as they urged their reluctant horses forward. Barry's eyes focused on the men, watching for the first that dared draw on him, while Balian's searched the first-story loge to be sure none of his family were exposed. Helvis, at four, couldn't seem to stay in one place and often got away from her nanny, while three-year-old John followed her everywhere. Fortunately, the loge was empty.

Then they were into the crowd, wading through it as their horses shook their heads and danced in agitation. The crowd turned on them. "We want news! We demand more information! We have a right to know what has happened to our loved ones!"

"What are you babbling about?" Barry barked irritably.

"The massacre! We demand to speak to the messenger!"

Barry and Balian looked at each other, more mystified than ever. Then, from the front door, a half-dozen Ramla and Ibelin knights burst forth. They pushed back the crowd long enough for the brothers to get into the courtyard of the house, the heavy wooden door thumping shut behind them and dimming the roar of the enraged mob.

Maria Zoë was already running down the stairs from the gallery, her hair and veils streaming behind her. "Balian! Barry! Andronicus has seized control in Constantinople! He blinded my uncle Alexius and imprisoned Maria of Antioch along with her son. The mob—with his approval, if not at his instigation—ran rampant and slaughtered the entire Latin population of Constantinople. Thousands of people, including women, children, and priests." Maria Zoë's distress was raw, but it wasn't about the atrocity alone. "Oh, Balian! Jerusalem has lost the protection of Constantinople! Salah ad-Din is sure to move against us at once!" It was only then that Balian truly realized how much his wife had put her faith in Greek protection rather than in the strength of Jerusalem itself. It was a chilling insight.

As he did every week, Father Michael made his way to the Leprosarium of St. Lazarus, located just outside the northern wall of Jerusalem. He had brought a couple of live chickens in a basket and some salted fish as a gift for the kitchens. As usual, after he had handed these over to the cellarer, he asked after his brother.

The cellarer sighed. "He's doing penance again."

"What for this time?" Michael asked. He had tried to warn Daniel that he was not suited to the life of a monk, but at the time Daniel had not been willing to listen to him. Indeed, Michael had concluded that the more he tried to reason with him, the more stubborn Daniel had become. So he'd given up, and Daniel had taken his vows as a brother-knight of St. Lazarus more than a year ago. The problem was that the longer Daniel lived among the Brothers of St. Lazarus, the more his rebellious nature came to the fore.

"He complained about the food and then threw his bowl across the room at one of his brothers," the cellarer explained.

"I beg pardon for him," Michael pleaded humbly and sincerely.

"He's getting more and more aggressive by the day," the cellarer warned, shaking his head.

"Then send him to me, for the King has requested his service, and it might be the best thing for everyone."

A few moments later, Sir (Brother) Daniel emerged. He was wearing a sullen expression, a black habit without insignia, and sandals. The robes seemed incongruous on his tall and powerful body.

"What did they do?" he growled. "Send word to you about my transgressions so you could come and lecture me?"

Michael sighed. All his life he had tried to be a friend to his young brother, but Daniel insisted on being resentful of his well-meant advice. "No, Daniel," Michael answered steadily. "I'm here at the request of Lord Balian."

Daniel stiffened. The happiest years of his life had been those three years as Lord Balian's squire and household knight. He had felt he was somebody then. He had been proud and confident and buoyed up by a heroic vision of himself.

Until God had punished him for his pride.

"Let us go where it is quieter," Michael urged. Some of the lepers were fighting among themselves, while women lepers were chattering and laughing loudly as they hung out the laundry.

Daniel fell in warily beside his brother, and they walked along the outer edge of the dry moat surrounding the city until they came to the road leading north to Nablus, Nazareth, and Tiberias. Here a number of enterprising shopkeepers had set up stands selling refreshments and souvenirs, and a little beyond them was a sheep market. The pilgrim season had only just started, so the shopkeepers had a shortage of customers and they called out to the brothers as they passed, trying to interest them in their wares. It was not possible to tell by looking at Daniel that he was afflicted with leprosy, for his skin was not yet discolored, much less ulcerous or deformed.

Michael was finding this conversation much more difficult than he expected. Lord Balian had charged him with finding out what Daniel wanted and had made him promise not to try to influence his brother one way or the other. But Michael knew that influence could be very subtle. Simply the way he approached the topic might affect Daniel's response. "Lord Balian saw the King yesterday, and they spoke of you."

"The King still remembers me, then?" Daniel answered in a voice that crackled with bitterness.

"He knows you saved his life, Daniel. He mentioned it again yesterday." Michael paused. "Daniel," he repeated and stopped, turning to face his brother. They were now beyond the shops and the sheep market, although the bleating of the sheep was still audible. "The King can hardly walk anymore."

Daniel shrugged. "It was bound to happen." Now that he lived in the leper hospital, he had seen many men far worse off than the way he remembered the King.

"Ibrahim is too old to carry him, and the King will not let anyone else touch him—because of what happened to you."

"That's silly!" Daniel answered, raising his head. "The healthy brothers of St. Lazarus often carry the lepers on their backs, and they are not afflicted."

"But you were."

"Not from carrying him. It came from handling the bandages when my own hands were covered with broken blisters and cuts from the battle. I know that now. If only I had known it then!" he blurted out wretchedly.

"Then you would not fear carrying the King again?"

"What is there left to fear?"

"How would you feel about being the King's knight—a household knight, living in the palace, in attendance directly on the King, ready to carry him if needed?"

Daniel stared at his brother in disbelief. He was offering him an escape, the opportunity to live among healthy people again, to set eyes on beautiful people up close and every day, to live in luxury and eat the best food that money could buy. As a leper. That was unimaginable. "You're sure he would have me?" Daniel asked skeptically.

"Why wouldn't he, Daniel? You two are brothers—joined by the grace of God."

Le Forbelet, July 15, 1182

The heat was insufferable. In all his thirty-three years, Ibelin had never experienced anything like it. He felt as if he were being slowly cooked in his own sweat. His underclothes, from his braies to the quilted gambeson under his hauberk, were drenched. Sweat had saturated his arming hood under his coif and now ran down across his forehead, collected on his eyebrows, and then spilled into his eyes. Sweat from his chin and throat under the closed flap of his aventail had soaked his chest until the water oozed out between the links of his chain mail onto his surcoat. One could almost envy the infantry in their linen aketons and open-faced helmets.

But such envy would be misplaced, Ibelin reproached himself, with a look at the bodies carpeting the field in front of them. The King, commanding from a litter, had brought up the army from the springs of Sephorie, where they had mustered, to relieve the Castle of Bethsan, which Salah ad-Din was besieging. They had not realized just how large Salah ad-Din's army was, however, until they caught sight of it. The messengers, of course, had spoken of "overwhelming" forces, but that was only to be expected. Seeing it here, spread out before them, was something else again.

In retrospect, the siege of Bethsan had merely been bait; the Saracen army was very short on siege equipment and long on troops. This was an army of invasion, complete with a huge baggage train still safe on the east bank of the Jordan. Hundreds of camels waited there patiently, ready to move forward and start collecting loot—just as soon as the back of the Frankish resistance was broken.

But the resistance wasn't broken yet. Salah ad-Din had been subjecting them to showers of arrows for hours now, and although most men wore more than one arrow embedded in their shields or caught in the weave of their horses' trappers, they had not had a significant impact even on the infantry, who simply crouched behind their large shields with their heads down.

Roughly an hour earlier, Salah ad-Din had either grown tired of waiting or overestimated the impact of his archers, and had sent the first wave of infantry against them. The Saracens had charged at them, their swords raised, screaming the greatness of Allah, and had been cut down with appalling efficiency by the small but well-disciplined band of 270 Genoese crossbowmen the King had hired and brought along.

Salah ad-Din had sent in his cavalry next, but horses don't like charging at fixed pikes, and the Christian footmen had planted their shields before them with their pikes bristling out between the wall of shields. Time and again the Saracen horse rushed the Christian line, only to have their mounts abruptly rear up or wheel around when they got too close—thereby colliding with the horses behind them and causing mass confusion. More than one Saracen cavalryman was trampled to death by his comrades.

Salah ad-Din pulled his cavalry back and sent in the second wave of infantry. These were Nubians, and they ran forward fast enough and in such numbers that they overwhelmed the ability of the Genoese to stop them. As they clashed with the Christian infantry, the first hand-to-hand fighting of the day began. One on one, the infantry of West and East were well matched. Footmen on neither side wore metal armor, and the sturdy linen aketons of the Christians, like the leather of their opponents, could withstand a great deal of slashing and hacking. Eventually, however, the numbers began to tell, and the Christian front line was hacked to pieces and overrun. The Saracens began stepping over or on the bodies of the Christian dead to reach the second rank.

At that point King Baldwin ordered his knights to drive off the enemy. The Constable conveyed the order along the line. "Just drive the enemy foot soldiers off! Don't pursue! Just drive them off and return to your positions."

The shouted orders to the infantry to let the knights through was enough to break the momentum of the Saracen infantry. The moment they saw the Frankish knights go into motion, they broke and ran, fully conscious that they could not survive a direct encounter with a charging knight. Either that, Ibelin reflected, or they had orders to break and run in a deliberate attempt to lure the Frankish knights out from behind the protection of the infantry.

Responding to the frantic bellows from the horns calling the retreat, Ibelin galloped back through the Frankish lines, his knights around him, and then swung Centurion to face the enemy again from behind the safety of the infantry. When he looked again at Salah ad-Din's army through the slit in his visor, he registered that it was surging forward. He looked left and right, counting men in the red-and-gold surcoats of Ibelin and beyond them the men in the blue and gold of Nablus. His eyes met those of Sir Bartholomew doing a like survey. They exchanged a nod of satisfaction. All his knights were still with them.

A handful of other knights, however, had either not heard or refused to heed the call to retreat. Within minutes they were overwhelmed and overrun, man and horse both, by the onslaught of Saracen cavalry, followed closely by Saracen foot soldiers running in the dust of their cavalry, ready to kill anything the cavalry left alive.

The dust was thick in the air and rising slowly but steadily toward the heavens, turning the sky a murky yellow. It also restricted vision like a heavy fog. The infantry was coughing in it, and someone was calling for water. Yet even as Ibelin registered the oppressive heat and the dryness of his throat, he also sensed the enemy approaching in an unrelenting mass.

"Here the bastards come," Sir Galvin growled, his Scottish accent mangling the French and eliciting a laugh from Sir Walter. Balian was glad the younger knight could still laugh, and glanced again at Sir Bartholomew, amazed that a man nearing sixty could withstand the exertions in this heat.

Someone jostled his elbow, and startled Ibelin looked down to find Gabriel at his knee, offering him a water skin. He shook his head furiously and waved his squire back. "Get out of here! To the rear!" he shouted.

Almost before the words were out of his mouth, a barrage of arrows from the advancing enemy fell among them. The arrows worried Ibelin little, but Gabriel had only a hauberk and his helmet was open-faced, exposing his eyes. Balian had seen too many men take arrows in their eyes. Even if the wound itself was not fatal, the pain was excruciating and the loss of an eye horrible.

Centurion squealed and leapt sideways as an arrow thudded into his thigh, and Ibelin reached down and broke off the shaft, then leaned forward and patted the stallion's throat reassuringly. The loose canvas trapper had sapped the strength of the arrow and the wound was not deep.

Meanwhile the front line of Christian infantry was going down again under the onslaught, and the knights were growing uneasy. All up and down the line horses were shifting, turning, stepping forward and back; they shook their heads or lashed out with their heels in agitation that reflected their riders' mood.

Ibelin looked over his shoulder toward the litter covered by a baldachin with the arms of Jerusalem on it. He could see Daniel standing tall and proud at the King's shoulder, awaiting orders. Just beyond the King's litter stood three canons of the Holy Sepulcher, surrounded by a troop of ten mounted Templars in close formation. One of the canons held aloft a tall gold cross encrusted with gold and jewels. At the heart of the large reliquary was a fragment of the True Cross. This relic was always carried with the army of Jerusalem when it marched out to face the Saracens. Usually the Patriarch or one of the bishops carried it, but the Patriarch was too ill to travel and Bethlehem preferred to fight with his mace rather than hold the cross, so today the canons were alone. Balian hoped that would not mitigate the efficacy of the Cross. They needed Divine help if they were to withstand this much longer.

A slight wind had sprung up from the northwest and was blowing the dust away from the Christian lines, revealing the carnage already wrought and still ongoing. The carpet of bloody, still-writhing bodies was five to six yards wide already, and the Saracens walked on corpses and dying men, screaming their curses and insults as they flung themselves at the notably thinned line of Christian infantry. The Genoese were either all dead, out of quarrels, or afraid to shoot now that the enemy was so close. Immediately ahead of him, Ibelin saw a man in the back row of the infantry fall over backwards without any wound on him; with apprehension Balian realized he'd collapsed from heat stroke alone. Looking along the infantry line, he realized there were several men stretched out behind the line in a similar state of heat-induced unconsciousness.

Ibelin glanced again at the litter. The Constable was leaning down from his horse to hear what the King was saying. He nodded just as one of the canons beside the True Cross collapsed from the heat. The Constable spurred over to Ibelin and shouted the order to form up into a conroi. They were going to charge at last.

The charge was the most effective weapon the Christians had, but it could rarely be used more than once in a single engagement. If used too soon, it would bring utter and total defeat. Jerusalem had only managed to muster seven hundred knights, because neither Tripoli nor Antioch had responded to the King's call: Antioch because of the threat from the north now that the Greek Empire had turned hostile, and Tripoli because the County had not yet recovered from the devastation of the last Saracen raid. The Templars, however, had brought about one hundred sergeants in addition to seventy knights, and the Hospitallers one hundred ten knights and sergeants combined. That put the effective fighting strength of the Christian cavalry at roughly one thousand heavy horse.

They were facing close to thirty thousand Saracens, Ibelin estimated, but the odds did not particularly bother him. His ancestors had reclaimed this land against these odds. They had won at Montgisard against these odds. They could win here today—if God willed it. He glanced once more at the True Cross and crossed himself. "In the name of the Father, the Son, and the Holy Ghost."

Aimery de Lusignan had corralled the knights and sergeants into a compact body. The Templars and Hospitallers appeared to be fighting over the honor of leading. The Templars had the larger body of heavy horse, including sergeants, but were led by their Marshal rather than their aging Master; the Hospitaller Master, in contrast, was personally present. The Constable rode over and settled the dispute by sending the Templars to form a separate conroi on the right wing of the Christian army and sending the Hospitallers to the left to form a third conroi. This left the largest body of knights, the secular knights, in the center. Ibelin nodded to himself, pleased with the deployment, regardless of who had devised it.

The Constable rode to the front of the conroi of secular knights, with the royal banner held upright by a knight on his flank. His brother, the Count of Jaffa, took up a position directly beside him with his knights (including Ramla although he still hadn't paid homage to Jaffa) stretched out to the right. Oultrejourdain meanwhile swung his ninety knights into position at the left of the Constable. Altogether they made a front roughly one hundred forty horses wide. Caesarea and Sidon, each with nearly eighty knights, made up the second rank. Ibelin, with his twenty-two knights from Ibelin and eighty-odd knights from Nablus, was joined by Nazareth and some of the other smaller barons to form the third rank, the remnants making up the rear.

Ibelin looked forward past the two rows of riders ahead of him to the battlefield they were about to charge, and realized he couldn't see it: it was completely blotted out by the dust. While it was intimidating to charge into a dust cloud, he supposed that the enemy could not see them, either, which meant they probably did not know the Franks were about to charge—much less in three conrois.

Aimery de Lusignan stood in his stirrups and twisted around to shout at them: "For the greater glory of Christ—and the safety of our wives and children! Jerusalem!"

The knights behind him roared "Jerusalem!" and set their horses in motion. The charge was slow at first because some of their infantry were so dazed, exhausted, or injured that they were sluggish getting out of the way of the horses. Ibelin found himself trotting almost ten yards before the way was clear to break into a canter.

The sound of battle grew louder with each stride. The banner of Jerusalem was just barely visible above the cloud of dust, and Ibelin and his men could no longer see the first rank, only the tails of the horses in front. For another five strides they swept forward, then they crashed into a wall of resistance. Horses piled up into one another, whinnying and rearing up. Centurion lost his footing, tripping over a body.

Ibelin guessed that the enemy had realized a charge was coming when they heard the shout of "Jerusalem" from a thousand throats and had pulled back fifty yards or so, but now they had collided. The knights of the first and second rank had already expended their lances and were laying about with their swords. Ibelin managed to kill one man with his lance, but it drove so deep that when the corpse fell sideways off his horse, the lance snapped in two. He threw the useless stub aside and drew his sword.

In the dust his attackers were indistinct and almost surreal—until their swords and axes crashed down on him. With his shield, helmet, and sword he deflected some of the blows, but Balian felt something drop on his shoulder so hard he cried out involuntarily, and a stinging pain in his thigh warned him he'd been stabbed there, too. He fought back, his sword bloody to the hilt. But while the Saracen cavalry tried to kill the knights, the Saracen infantry were trying to kill the horses. Balian dropped the leather-encased chain reins on Centurion's neck so the stallion could defend himself, biting and kicking, while Balian focused on his own assailants.

Ibelin felt as if he were completely enveloped and utterly overwhelmed by the enemy. He was suffocating in the dust, and his sweat-soaked undergarments were so heavy that it took extra effort to raise his arms. It was like swimming in honey. Within a short space of time he felt as if he could not possibly respond to the blows coming at him from all directions for more than a few minutes more. The odds *did* make a difference, after all.

Suddenly screams of terror could be heard on both flanks, and the resistance of the enemy broke like a dam. The fighting monks had taken the enemy on both wings completely by surprise. Saracen morale shattered and turned to panic in a heartbeat. One moment Ibelin was being attacked from all sides, and the next moment he was not being attacked at all. The enemy was dissolving into the filthy clouds ahead of him.

"À Ibelin!" he called, raising his sword, as he pushed Centurion after the retreating enemy. Amazingly, he felt knights cluster around him, and the little conroi bounded forward together. They caught up first with the fleeing infantry, but did not slow down. Some fleeing Saracens looked over their shoulders at the sound of hooves; Ibelin saw their terrified faces, mouths wide with screams, and he hacked them down or rode over them as they stumbled and fell.

Centurion was galloping with his ears laid flat on the back of his head, his neck stretched out, racing with the other horses. Beside Ibelin his knights were trying to keep up with him. Ibelin saw lance tips and realized some of the Nablus knights still had lances. He reached down, picked up the reins, and checked Centurion's stride, signaling the men with lances forward. Centurion did not like this in the least and fought for a free rein again, dragging his head down and bucking once, but the check had been enough. The three knights with lances had overtaken the lead and smashed into the fleeing Saracen cavalry, slicing through it easily since they were stabbing men in the back.

The remaining knights of the conroi followed in the space the lances cleared, expanding the wedge on both sides as they killed men, until their horses began to stagger from sheer exhaustion and they could no longer lift their arms. Around them the dust was slowly settling.

Centurion came to a halt, swaying back and forth in rhythm with his breathing, his head hanging. Balian could hear only the sound of his own panting and the pounding of his pulse inside his helmet. He flung the visor open to gulp in air. His tongue and throat were so dry it hurt to swallow. The dust in the air he was breathing in only made it worse, however, and he started coughing. He would have given anything for a single sip of water.

Gradually his breathing became more regular, and Ibelin looked at the men immediately around him to make a head count. Sir Galvin grinned at him. The man seemed happiest in a fight; he had a violent demon bottled up inside him that he could only release (without endangering his soul) in battle against the enemies of Christ, Balian reflected. Sir Walter, in contrast, looked faint, as if he could not hold up much longer. Sir Arnulf was screwing up his face in obvious pain and resentment at being here at all; he counted the days until Ernoul would take his place. Sir Bartholomew, in contrast, looked exhausted but satisfied—whether with himself for holding up where younger men were clearly fading, or with Ibelin as a troop. In short, Ibelin had lost not one of his knights, although the horses looked the worse for wear. Their coats were completely matted with dust turned to mud by their own sweat. Streams of moisture were dripping off their bellies, and like Centurion, the other horses were utterly winded.

Extending his gaze, Ibelin saw scattered bands of Frankish knights all over the field; some were still actively killing, but most, like his own troop, had come to a halt. With a start Balian realized that the River Jordan was no more than a hundred yards ahead of him, and this was where the Constable was rallying a growing number of knights under the King's banner, his brother among them.

At least Ramla had the sense to stay west of the river this time, Ibelin noted, although by the look of things, that fool Jaffa was urging them to pursue. He was making wide, sweeping gestures that everyone else, including Jaffa's brother the Constable, ignored. A large band of Templars, still collected around the Beauséant, rode up while Ibelin watched, and the Templar Marshal and the Constable of Jerusalem consulted one another in apparent harmony, for they were nodding their heads.

Casting his gaze beyond them, Ibelin registered that the Saracen army was re-forming on the far side of the river, and despite the dead littered over the field, they seemed as numerous as ever. Worse, the signs of panic were dying out. On the fringes some men still fled, but at the center, around the Sultan's banner, the Kurdish Mamlukes were drawn up in ranks and files as immobile as a rock. Even as Ibelin watched, other units fell into place beside them. Salah ad-Din still had the bulk of his army intact, and the Frankish charge was exhausted. They had not yet won.

Turning to look behind him, Ibelin was astonished to see that the Christian infantry, or what was left of it, had moved down from their position on the low slope of the hill and were systematically executing or taking the Saracens captive, depending on the extent of their injuries and prospects for ransom. Behind the ragged line of foot soldiers staggered the canon with the True Cross still held high, and beside him, lurching unsteadily as the bearers stepped over or around the dead and dying, came the litter with the King, Daniel striding proudly beside it.

Slowly now, conscious of the aches and pains of his many bruises and the gash in his thigh, Ibelin coaxed a walk out of Centurion and led his men to meet up with the King and escort him to the Constable. The King was dressed in armor, a helmet with the crown upon his brow. The aventail fastened across his chin hid the deformed skin on the lower half of his face. He almost looked whole—except that he could neither walk nor ride—and his eyes were filled with distress when they met Balian's.

They reached the other leaders, and the Constable rode straight to the King. "They're re-forming, your grace."

"Then so must we. We'll put the infantry ahead of us again. Pull back to just in front of our original positions."

Aimery nodded, and trotted back to start chivvying the infantry into position, while the rest of the cavalry drew back warily, with one eye on the enemy beyond the river. By the time they reached their starting position, their squires were waiting with water and, for those lords with more than one destrier, fresh horses. Despite the wound in his leg, Balian managed dismount and turn the exhausted Centurion over to Gabriel. Pointing to the arrow in the horse's thigh he ordered the youth to have the horse doctor see to the wound and reminded him not to let the stallion drink too much at once. He then wet his own mouth with water, and savored it before swallowing. He took another sip, resisting the temptation to gulp down the entire water-skin. But when he turned to mount his replacement stallion, he couldn't lift his wounded leg high enough to reach the stirrup — and it wouldn't have been strong enough to lift the rest of his weight either. Only with the help of Sir Galvin, who dismounted to lift him up and hold him while he flung his sound leg over the cantle, was he able to remount and take up his shield and lance again.

Looking again across the field at the enemy, Ibelin tried to estimate the casualties on both sides. The Christian infantry had suffered sorely. At a rough estimate, there were a thousand or more corpses marking the front of their previous position, now behind them. Despite these losses, there were still more than enough Christian foot soldiers to protect the cavalry, however.

Across the field itself, most of the dead were Saracen. There were maybe five times as many Saracen dead as Christians and not, as far as Ibelin could see, more than a dozen knights lying beside their crumpled, motionless horses. But, of course, that hardly diminished the odds against the Christians. There were still some twenty-five thousand Saracens drawn up on the far bank of the Jordan. In short, both sides still had the wherewithal to renew the battle.

Ibelin glanced back over his shoulder at the sun, trying to judge the time of day and how long before darkness would deliver them from the heat and the threat of a renewed attack. The sun was more than halfway down the sky, but that meant they were still four to five hours from darkness—and the heat was, if anything, worse than ever.

Suddenly cries went up all along Christian battle line. Ibelin swung his attention back toward the enemy, but they seemed as immobile as before.

"There!" Sir Galvin pointed. "The True Cross!"

Ibelin followed the Scotsman's pointed finger, and to his horror saw that the canon who had been holding the precious relic had fallen face-first to the ground. Daniel and one of the Templar escort had apparently just managed to catch the cross itself before it hit the earth. They were holding it together off the ground while another canon bent over his fallen brother. The whole army watched, mesmerized. Even across the distance and in miniature, Ibelin could feel the intensity of emotion played out before them as the canon realized his brother was dead. He saw the priest fall on his knees with outstretched arms. Fortunately the Templar had the wit to hold up the Cross in both hands above his head to show the army it was still with them, while the King ordered Daniel to pick up the dead monk and lay him on the litter.

The army was abruptly alive with chatter. Men were arguing about what this meant. Had God abandoned them? For surely, to strike down the very man carrying the True Cross could not be a good omen. But others were quick to argue that the Cross itself had not touched the ground, and some even made much of the fact that a Templar had rescued it at the very last moment. Was it a warning perhaps? Or had the *bearer* of the Cross been unworthy in some way? It was not the Patriarch, after all, nor even a bishop—although now, when it was too late, the Bishop of Bethlehem rode up and took the Cross from the Templar. Now that the men had had some water, the arguments were endless. Ibelin, however, kept his eye on the enemy, while the vultures and other carrion-eaters descended on the battlefield and began to feast, and the flies gathered in sickening swarms.

"We fought him to a standstill and he withdrew; that's what I call victory!" Barry insisted loudly. He had come to the Hospitaller infirmary tent, where one of the monks was tending his brother's thigh wound. The Baron of Ramla was still in his hauberk and dirty surcoat, but he'd washed the blood and dirt from his face and hands.

Balian was feeling too weak to argue. The gash in his thigh was surprisingly deep and long, as his anonymous attacker had managed to stab right through the chain mail of his chausses. He'd lost a lot of blood before Gabriel had dragged him out of the saddle and, together with Ernoul, carried him to the Hospitaller tent. "Do we know where the Saracen army went?" he asked his brother instead.

"Back where it came from," Barry answered, gesturing vaguely to the east.

Ibelin would have felt better if they had had a handful of Turcopoles to shadow the enemy and verify the direction Salah ad-Din's army had taken, but they had no Turcopoles with horses fresh enough to keep up with the Saracen cavalry. And that was what unsettled Balian.

Salah ad-Din might have decided it was too costly to confront the collected might of Jerusalem on the open field again tomorrow, but his army was in much better shape than King Baldwin's. At least his cavalry could move rapidly, and Ibelin was acutely aware that most of the castles in the Kingdom were, like his own, only sparsely manned. He'd left just five of his knights behind in command of the citizen militia of eighty men at Ibelin, and fifteen knights at Nablus, where the militia was more numerous but less well organized and not as well led. His children were at Ibelin, but Maria Zoë had insisted on taking command at Nablus. Both garrisons were strong enough to fight off marauding bands of undisciplined troops such as had attacked Ibelin in '77, but neither Ibelin castle nor the citadel of unwalled Nablus would be in a position to withstand a serious siege if Salah ad-Din concentrated his forces. Balian wasn't particularly worried about Ibelin at the moment because it was so far away, but Nablus might seem temptingly close—and it was on the road to Jerusalem, if Salah ad-Din thought he could outflank the Christian army and steal a march on them while the Franks licked their wounds and rested their horses.

To his brother, however, he chose to remark, "Daniel tells me that the King was pleased with your deeds this day." When word had reached the King that Ibelin was injured, he had sent Daniel to check up on him. Daniel had left only just before his brother arrived, and he had reported that throughout the battle the King had demanded that Daniel be his eyes—since his own were too weak to penetrate the distance, much less the dust. Daniel, Balian suspected, had loyally emphasized the fighting prowess of his former employer and his brother, because he had proudly reported that the King had been "most impressed" by Ramla and Ibelin and wished to thank them both.

Barry snorted derisively. "Enough to absolve me of refusing homage to Jaffa?" It was a rhetorical question, really, and Balian could only sigh in answer, inducing his brother to continue. "He's my King, and I will serve him for the sake of the Kingdom, but I cannot love him after what he's done!"

Balian realized he was looking for signs that the King was less under the influence of his mother. He wanted to be reconciled with him. "At least admit King Baldwin led us well today," Balian urged.

Barry snorted again. "From a litter!"

"Yes, from a litter."

"Aimery could have led us better if he *hadn't* been tied to that litter," Barry insisted.

"And would his brother have obeyed him if the King hadn't been there looking on?"

"Guy!" Ramla exploded, his hatred too great for expression. "I will *never* bend my knee to him—not as Count of Jaffa or, God forbid, King of Jerusalem. I swear to God!" He lifted his hand dramatically to make this oath.

Balian took a deep breath and nodded, unwilling to argue with his brother, although he wondered what alternative Barry would have when the time came. For now, while the wound in his thigh was not in itself life-threatening, he'd seen too many men die of wound fever not to realize he was still in danger. If he should die, Maria Zoë and his three small children would be dependent on Barry's goodwill—and it would be better if they didn't quarrel in the meantime.

Barry seemed to be having similar thoughts, because his expression softened and he put his hand on Balian's shoulder. "Come. Let's not talk of Guy. We both hate him. You need to save your strength so you can recover faster—and get home to that beautiful wife of yours and your litter of children."

Even when he was trying to be kind, a touch of bitterness crept into Barry's voice—for Maria Zoë had given Balian three healthy children, including a son, and Barry still had only one living daughter.

Chapter 7

Jerusalem, August 1182

Eschiva was frightened. She had miscarried the first child Aimery had sired on her, and she had prayed fervently for this new child to ripen. Yet now that her prayers had been answered and she was near her time, she was terrified of giving birth. She could remember all too well Maria Zoë's screams at Helvis' birth, and even her own miscarriage had been horribly painful. If it hurt so much to lose a tiny, half-formed infant, how could she withstand the pain of bringing a fully grown baby into the world? All she had to do was compare the size of her belly with the exit from her womb to know it was going to be terrible.

It did not help that Aimery was still with the army. Although Salah ad-Din had been forced to withdraw after sustaining severe casualties at Le Forbelet, he had not dispersed his army. Instead he had marched north, keeping to the mountains of Lebanon, until his fleet had sailed up and blockaded Beirut. Then his army descended from the heights and laid siege to Beirut. The King at once moved the Christian army to Tyre to prepare the relief of Beirut, and that was where Aimery was now, hiring Christian fighting galleys to challenge the Saracen fleet.

Without Aimery, Eschiva felt very lonely in Jerusalem. Her mother had buried herself in a convent and refused to come out. Her mother-in-law, whom she had never met, was in France. She had no sisters and only two aunts, the wife and widow of her father's brothers respectively. The former and her favorite aunt, Maria Zoë, however, was in Nablus, defending her dower lands from a possible invasion, while the latter, Agnes de Courtenay, terrified Eschiva. To make matters worse, her only other female relative in the city was her brother-in-law's wife—Princess Sibylla. No one made Eschiva feel more insignificant or pitiable than the Countess of Jaffa.

Eschiva would have preferred it if both these ladies ignored her. Then she could have buried herself in her own rooms until it was all over. Beth knew where to find a midwife, after all, and everything was prepared as best it could be. But no, the Queen Mother and the Princess of Jerusalem insisted on taking an interest in "poor, dear Eschiva."

The royal ladies made much of the fact that Eschiva lived in a tower of the citadel, the official apartment of the Constable of Jerusalem, rather than in a comfortable palace. It was true that these quarters, with their thick walls, narrow windows, and ancient floors, were cramped, dark, and oppressive by August, when the heat had penetrated the thick walls and turned the interior almost into an oven. Eschiva did not like these rooms herself, but when she had complained about them to Aimery, he had told her bluntly that they could not afford to rent, much less buy, anything more comfortable, because her dowry had gone to pay her father's ransom. She felt, therefore, that by drawing attention to her poor lodgings, her sister-in-law and aunt were really trying to remind her that her father had been "foolish" enough to get captured.

Furthermore, being "invited" to the royal palace, ostensibly so she could get away from these "dreadful rooms," meant she had to wash and dress and then walk, all things she would rather not have done in her condition. Eschiva had never considered herself a beauty, and she felt even less presentable with her waist bulbous, her breasts heavy, and her feet swollen. Sibylla was bound to make some remark about what she was wearing and promise to send over some material to make something "pretty"—which, of course, she would never actually do. It was just her way of drawing attention to Eschiva's humble wardrobe.

But there was no way to refuse a woman like Agnes de Courtenay, so Eschiva dutifully dragged herself from her bed and let Beth sponge the sweat from her body and dress her in a gauze shift, over which Beth pulled on a lightly woven cotton gown with long, flowing sleeves and finally a sleeveless silk surcoat tied loosely at the sides. The needlework was Eschiva's own, and no doubt Sibylla would comment on it in feigned admiration, "Oh, did you stitch it all *yourself*? I never have time, and you know the professional needlewomen are *so* good." Or perhaps she would remark that many of the professional needlewomen were ex-prostitutes trying to reform their sinful lives and in need of patronage. Either way, it would make the other women look at Eschiva as the poor country cousin.

Beth expertly brushed and bound Eschiva's hair under a wimple of loose-woven gauze and asked, "Would you like to wear the turquoise pendant Lord Aimery gave you at Christmas?"

Eschiva nodded absently, thinking of Aimery. He was a good husband, always courteous and patient. He had not reproached her for the miscarriage, shrugging it off as "perfectly natural" at her tender age. But she was no longer a "tender age," not at eighteen, and Aimery was almost thirty-five. He wanted an heir. He deserved an heir. She put her hand to her belly, seeking some sign of life. Nothing would be more horrible than tearing her guts out to bring forth another dead child—or a girl. Tears sprang to her eyes as she felt the full weight of her own worthlessness. It was because she was a girl that her father had never been able to really love her.

Beth rubbed her shoulders in a mute gesture of sympathy. Beth knew her fears because she had spoken of them candidly, but Beth could not allay them. She had not gone through childbirth herself, and she shared Eschiva's sense of worthlessness.

With a deep sigh Eschiva pulled herself to her feet, and Beth at once offered her an arm to lean on. Together they left the cramped constable's quarters and crossed out of the citadel by the drawbridge into the city. They turned into the Street of the Armenians for the short walk to the palace.

The street was busy. It was a main thoroughfare, and farmers from the surrounding countryside used it to bring their wares to market. The pig market was just north of David's Gate, and two straw-hatted, barefoot men with skin like leather were chasing a herd of trotting pigs up the street, while an Armenian wedding procession was making its way in the opposite direction. Between these, pilgrims with staffs wended their way looking lost, bewildered, and a little disappointed. Eschiva had often observed that expression on the faces of pilgrims, as if they had expected streets paved with gold and archangels hovering in the air.

Just a hundred yards down the street, Eschiva and Beth reached the northern entrance to the royal palace. The palace itself had been started by Fulk d'Anjou and finished by Baldwin III. It made no pretense of being defensible; in an emergency, Jerusalem's walls were expected to withstand attack long enough for the royal family to seek refuge in the citadel. The palace was consciously designed to be comfortable, with large glazed windows to let in light and air, marble floors, tile walls, bubbling fountains, and potted palms.

The sentries recognized Eschiva. She was admitted without hesitation, and advised that the Princess Sibylla was in the enclosed garden south of the palace. Eschiva resignedly climbed a flight of stairs to make her way down the long gallery to a second flight of stairs that led back down into the garden beyond. At the top of the stairs she paused to cool off (for already she was damp with sweat) and to collect her courage.

Below, seated on cane chairs in the shade of a canvas awning, were Princess Sibylla, Agnes de Courtenay, and a dozen other ladies of the court. Conspicuously absent, Eschiva thought, was Stephanie de Milly, who was holding her husband's castle of Kerak against possible retaliation by Salah ad-Din—and holding poor Isabella hostage there as well. Eschiva had received two desperate letters from Isabella, begging her to come visit, but Aimery had not been inclined. "Leave things alone," he'd told her. "The King has good reasons to think your Greek aunt is plotting against him and wants to see her own daughter on the throne. It's better for Isabella if she doesn't have such notions whispered into her ear day and night. She'll be happier in the long run if she accepts Sibylla and her son by Montferrat as the rightful heirs to the throne."

Eschiva had wanted to protest that Maria Zoë wasn't like that, and that even if she was, it wouldn't hurt for *her* to visit Isabella. But she didn't dare challenge Aimery, certainly not when he was as firm as he had been in this case. She had written Isabella instead, but she gathered from Isabella's next letter that her own had never been delivered. Isabella, it seemed, had someone she could trust to smuggle letters out, but no way to stop her mother-in-law from intercepting what came in. The thought of Isabella imprisoned by Stephanie de Milly reminded Eschiva that her own fate was not that bad, and so she took a deep breath and started carefully down the stairs into the walled garden.

Eschiva couldn't see the steps because of her belly, and that made her feel unsure of her footing. She put her left hand on the rough wall while Beth held her other arm.

Beth had been raised in a harem, and she had an instinct for female intrigue. She had only to cast one look at the women gathered in the garden to know that Eschiva was a lamb come to the slaughter. Sibylla had been married to Guy de Lusignan for two and a half years already, but her womb had yet to quicken. People were starting to snigger that Guy was not virile enough or speculate that God opposed the marriage. Both interpretations infuriated Sibylla, and she hated seeing Eschiva's full belly. Beth saw the looks she flung at Eschiva whenever the latter's head was turned, and knew her sugary smiles and the kisses on both cheeks she would soon deliver were a tawdry façade. Beth was certain that if Sibylla had the chance, she would actively induce another miscarriage.

The Queen Mother was less hostile, Beth sensed. She was indifferent to Eschiva as a person, but she resented the fact that her former lover had settled down with his child wife. By the time Aimery consummated his marriage, Agnes had again been sharing her bed with Heraclius, and Beth had heard her waiting women whispering excitedly that the latter had learned some truly exotic love-making techniques in Constantinople that made Aimery look rather tame. Still, Beth sensed that it bothered the Queen Mother that Aimery seemed so *happy* with his child bride.

The other women were insignificant; there was no one here who would stand up to the royal women for Eschiva's sake. The strong-willed women like Stephanie de Milly and Maria Zoë Comnena were commanding the defense of castles and towns, while their husbands prepared the relief of Beirut.

Eschiva and Beth had reached the bottom of the steps when with an audible squeal Sibylla exclaimed, "*Poor* Eschiva! There you are *at last*. You look *exhausted* and *red*. Come have a seat beside me. Girl!" she addressed Beth, who she knew was of lowborn, native blood. "Go fetch some sherbet for your mistress."

Beth was not sorry to leave such company, but was reluctant to leave Eschiva alone in this viper's nest. Still, she could hardly refuse an order from the Princess of Jerusalem. Bowing her head slightly, she withdrew through the door under the stairs they had just descended, which led into the kitchen tract below the great hall.

As always, the great kitchens were terribly hot and hectic. Scullery boys and pages were running every which way, except for the poor slaves condemned to turn the spits in the fireplaces, on which skewered pigs were slowly browning and dripping fat. In addition to the roasting pigs, cauldrons were steaming and iron skillets were sizzling. A cacophony of smells assailed Beth's senses, from the fresh onions being chopped on a large board to the garlic-scented steam wafting up from one of the skillets.

Sweat beaded on her brow, and she knew the precious ice used for sherbet was stored behind the wine cellars at the other end of the palace. She could get there by the interior passages through the pantry and buttery, or by taking the street and re-entering the palace by the northern portal. The problem with the interior path was that it took her past a guardroom and the men there exuded barely harnessed brute force, so Beth opted for the street.

She exited by the door at which deliveries were made and alms distributed, and started up along the familiar street. As she had learned to do as a child, she kept her eyes down, watching where she was going rather than looking at the people around her. She had almost made the northern entrance when her way was abruptly blocked. People were piling up around some sort of obstacle, and someone was cursing. She glanced up timidly, and by pure chance her glance led between the backs of the people ahead of her to a little donkey that had collapsed under a heavy burden. Its huge eyes connected with hers as it struggled to right itself. Its knees were already bloody, and its nostrils were wide and red. The eyes were full of despair. It did not understand why someone was beating it when it could not go another step.

Beth could not stand it. In that split second she saw herself in the donkey's wide, uncomprehending eyes as the Nubians fell over her. She gave an inarticulate cry and shoved the youths ahead of her aside. "Leave her alone!" she shouted furiously at the man with the cane. "Leave her alone! Can't you see she can take no more?"

Such a spirited defense of a stupid donkey aroused laughter from the surrounding crowd, but Beth didn't care. "Stop it!" She put herself between the donkey and the man beating it and stared him in the eye, even though he was a man and she nothing but a worthless girl.

The donkey owner was old, with an ugly wound on his face. He was filthy and stinking and his clothes were little better than rags. He had overburdened the donkey and was now venting his anger at its collapse because he had so little. "Get out of my way or you'll feel this cane yourself!" he shouted at Beth, shaking the cane over his head.

"No! I'll buy the donkey from you!"

"You?" the man scoffed, but he also let his arm drop so he wasn't threatening her, clearly interested in any way to turn a profit out of this catastrophe.

The only thing of value Beth had on her was a gift from Eschiva, a belt with little silver weights at the ends. She unbound this and shoved it in the mule driver's face.

The man snatched the belt from her with his filthy hands and narrowed his eyes as he inspected the silver balls. Although they were hardly worth a fortune, the donkey was finished anyway, so he closed his fist over them, then bent to remove the heavy panniers from the donkey. With an audible grunt, he hefted these over his own shoulders. He muttered something about "stupid females" as he turned away, and the crowd dispersed, leaving Beth in the street with the dying donkey.

The donkey looked at her with its big brown eyes, which still did not understand what was happening. Beth put her hand on its neck and felt the fluttering pulse under its sweat-damp hide. Now that she was squatting down beside the poor beast, she could see that she was bleeding from a half-dozen cuts opened by the cane. Her haunches were covered with scars of earlier cuts as well. Her knees were bleeding, and her bony rib cage was heaving up and down. The donkey was dying, and there was nothing Beth could do for it. She didn't even have a way of getting it out of the street.

Then she felt someone beside her. A shadow fell over her, and a moment later another hand joined hers on the donkey's neck. It too stroked the neck in a gesture of comfort and sympathy, and it was a black hand. Beth gasped and drew back, instantly terrified. But as she looked up, her eyes met a familiar face. "Dawit!" she exclaimed. "Where did you come from?"

"We just arrived from Nablus on our way to Ibelin, and my lady went to the citadel to see the Lady Eschiva. We were still at the gatehouse when I heard you cry out. I thought I recognized your voice."

Beth looked beyond Dawit and saw a party of horsemen milling about in front of the gate to the citadel. There were a least a dozen Turcopoles with their round shields and reed lances, and two knights in chain mail and longswords wearing the Nablus arms. The Ibelin marshal (Dawit's father) and other familiar servants were also in the train. At the center, on a magnificent black mare, was the Dowager Queen of Jerusalem. To protect herself from the sun, Queen Maria Zoë wore loose white robes and veils that covered her face and hands no less than the best Muslim women—only her robes and veils were white instead of black, and edged with the gold crosses of Jerusalem.

Beth felt a surge of relief go through her. "Eschiva is so near her time and so frightened!" she admitted in a rush to Dawit. "The Queen will stay with her, won't she?"

Before Dawit could answer, Maria Zoë turned her horse, and the crowd parted before her as she rode toward Beth. She threw back her veils to reveal her face as she drew up beside them. "Beth! What are you doing out here? Where's Eschiva?"

"She's at the palace, my lady. Princess Sibylla sent for her." Beth stopped there, too intimidated by the Dowager Queen to say what she had just said to Dawit.

"I see; then we'll settle into the Ibelin residence first and—"

Beth's intake of breath was enough to stop her. Maria Zoë looked more closely at Beth. "What is it, Beth?"

"Madame, please go to her. She's in the gardens with the Queen Mother and Princess Sibylla. She's very frightened, madame."

The Queen's face was unreadable, although she was obviously far from pleased. Her lips tightened and her eyes narrowed, but she nodded and turned to order her escort, except for the two knights, back to the Ibelin residence. Then she and her two knights rode through the main gate of the palace into the inner courtyard, to a flurry of shouts and a trumpet blast in honor of the Dowager Queen.

As the others clattered away, leaving only Dawit, the Ethiopian spoke softly to Beth. "I will take the donkey to our stables and see if I can nurse her back to health."

"Oh, Dawit! Would you?" Beth asked, tears stinging her eyes in gratitude. "Could you?"

"Of course, Beth. I will see what I can do for her." He bent and gently lifted the exhausted donkey into his own arms. He staggered a little as he laid her across the saddle of his horse. The donkey was too broken to resist or even bray in protest at this unusual treatment. Then he took the reins and started across the city on foot to the Ibelin residence.

Beth was left alone in the streets, where more than one person was giving her curious glances. She'd caused a commotion by interceding for a mere donkey, then had talked to a queen without apparent awe. She was dressed like a Frank, but dark like a native. She was neither fish nor fowl. She took a deep breath and proceeded to the northern service entrance to fulfill her task of bringing sherbet to her mistress.

A page rushed ahead of the Dowager Queen to announce her, but she was too close on his heels for the Queen Mother or Princess Sibylla to do anything more than look up in astonishment. After all, she had lived in this palace seven years and she knew exactly where she was going, even if she had avoided it since the disastrous Easter court two years ago when Sibylla had married Guy de Lusignan. Certainly she had not set eyes on Agnes de Courtenay since the Queen Mother had connived to steal Isabella away from her.

Maria Zoë had no doubt whatever who had instigated the theft of her child. She knew that the King was not really the originator of the idea, and she was convinced that neither the King nor even Balian, good man that he was, fully understood what was at stake. They both saw in Isabella a potential contender for the throne of Jerusalem who needed to be "controlled" —but Maria Zoë recognized that to Agnes de Courtenay, Isabella was a threat to her *children*. While Maria Zoë was certain that Baldwin meant his half-sister no harm, she remained convinced that Agnes was plotting Isabella's death behind her son's back.

Maria Zoë had made no less than five trips to Kerak in the last two years, but on the last two occasions she had been told that Isabella was "away"—allegedly on pilgrimage in one case and at Montreal on the other. Maria Zoë believed none of it. If it hadn't been for Dawit's regular reports on Isabella's physical health and fierce determination to survive her imprisonment, she would have been frantic enough to take desperate measures. What measures, she didn't know, but she knew she was capable of doing things no one expected of her.

One of them was walking straight up to the King's mother and sister and holding out her hand for them to kiss her coronation ring. It was a gesture so haughty that all the ladies in the garden gasped. Maria Zoë knew at some level that such gestures did not make her popular, but she was in no mood to seek the approval of others. This was the ring of Jerusalem that had been placed on her finger at her coronation. She was an anointed queen—something neither Agnes de Courtenay nor Sibylla could claim. Agnes was a baroness, Sibylla Countess of Jaffa; Maria Zoë outranked them both.

Flushing with fury, Agnes just stared at her, while Sibylla threatened, "I will tell my brother about this."

"Please do!" the Dowager Queen answered, turning to look at her coldly. "King Baldwin understands the significance of being an anointed monarch. He will not be pleased by your insult to *his* Crown."

Agnes choked on something she wanted to say, and Sibylla leapt up and ran away from this woman, who always made her feel so inadequate, worthless, and small.

That suited Maria Zoë. She was now face to face with her hated rival. "So, madame, whose child are you planning to steal today?" Maria Zoë asked. Agnes turned even redder, but still could not seem to find her tongue. "If it is my *niece's* unborn child," Maria Zoë continued with only the barest glance in Eschiva's direction, "think again. Aimery de Lusignan is not as susceptible to your poisonous whispers as your poor, pious son. Oh, but then you must *know* that—since you knew Aimery so *very* well."

"How dare you?" Agnes de Courtenay had found her tongue at last and jumped to her feet in outrage, her fists clenched.

"How dare I what, madame? Draw attention to your morals? But they are common knowledge." Maria Zoë made a gesture of innocence that included all the other ladies, who gawked at them in shock. Then she added in a voice as hard as steel, for all that it was barely more than a whisper: "Everyone knows you have as much virtue as a *bitch in heat*."

Agnes tried to slap Maria Zoë across her face, but Maria Zoë was faster. She caught the Queen Mother's arm before she could strike and held it, her fingers digging into her Agnes' wrist until she whimpered in pain. "Let me go!"

Maria Zoë dropped Agnes' arm, and they stared at one another. "Don't think you have won," Maria Zoë warned. "Isabella may be a child, but she has friends far more powerful than you and your vultures."

"You can't mean my ineffectual brother-in-law," Agnes sneered.

"No, of course not," Maria Zoë answered, refusing to be provoked. "We both know my husband is too honorable for the games *you* play." Maria Zoë was bluffing about having powerful friends. Her great-uncle was dead, her relatives murdered or chased into exile, but she could see the fear that suddenly shot through Agnes' eyes, and that was satisfying enough for the moment.

The fear, however, made Agnes bluster, "You are not welcome here. I order you to leave at once."

"I'll leave when I want to," Maria Zoë countered. "And don't think your *son's* guards will lay a hand on me! They know the difference between an anointed queen and a king's whore—"

"Get out of here!" It was Sibylla who shrieked this, coming back to defend her mother at last.

"With pleasure," Maria Zoë answered. "I do not like the company of sluts—or fools." The latter remark was directed at Sibylla.

"Baldwin will hear of this!" Sibylla shrieked, louder than ever.

"I wonder whose side he'll take?" Maria Zoë answered evenly. It was not so much that she seriously believed Baldwin would approve of her calling his mother a whore—much less a bitch in heat—but she was, in fact, so furious with him for letting his mother steal her child that she wanted to hurt him. And perhaps, just perhaps, if he learned what she had done, he would be shocked into understanding just how deeply she had been hurt and how dangerous a mother animal in fear for her young was. Maybe, just maybe, he'd begin to see that his mother was not his best adviser, and that engendering the hatred of those who had loved and served him best was stupid—and could be very dangerous as well.

With this thought she turned to a pale, wide-eyed Eschiva and ordered, "Come with me, child. You'll be far more comfortable at the Ibelin residence, and I'll be with you until your time has come and you are safely delivered of the child in your womb."

Beth had fled the birth chamber. She loved Eschiva far too well to be indifferent to her screams, and she was superfluous anyway, now that the Queen Mother and her ladies were in attendance. She sought instead the stillness of the stables and the donkey she had rescued. Dawit had put her in a stall filled with straw, and when Beth first found her she thought she had died, for she was lying on her side with her legs stretched out and her eyes closed. But at Beth's cry of distress, the gentle eyes opened and the donkey pulled her legs under herself, as if she wanted to get up. Her strength abandoned her at that point, however, and she dropped her head back on the straw with a sigh. Beth ran to the feed room and scooped out a handful of oats, then ran back to offer it to her donkey. As she reached the stall door, however, Dawit emerged out of the shadows and gently shook his head. "Give her hay, not oats. She is not used to oats."

Beth returned the oats and when she came back to the stall, Dawit handed her a flake of hay and held the stall door open for her. She stepped inside and knelt down beside the donkey, who raised her head in alarm. Beth held out the hay, and the donkey's nostrils flared as she sniffed sharply before she at last risked taking a little bite. Once she started eating, however, she became quite greedy, and together Beth and Dawit fed her three flakes of hay, before she lay down her head again with a contented sigh.

"Will she live?" Beth asked Dawit anxiously.

"After the way she just ate, I think so," he answered, with a smile fixed on the now sleeping donkey.

"How can I ever thank you for helping her?" Beth asked.

Dawit shook his head. "I wanted to help as much as you. I think if I were a rich man, I would start a hospital for all the wounded and abused horses and donkeys in the world."

"Is it true you turned down knighthood because you did not want to see horses suffering on the battlefield?" Beth blurted out—she had heard this story from Rahel the evening before, but could hardly believe it.

Dawit nodded slowly. "I am not ashamed of that, and I do not regret it. God gives each of us different gifts, and He expects each of us to serve Him in our own way. There is not only one path to honor—or to heaven."

Beth sat back in the straw and clutched her knees in the circle of her arms. She felt warm and safe here in the stables, with the little donkey breathing deeply beside her and Dawit speaking in his soft melodic voice. It was inexplicable to her that of all the men she had met since the night of her shame, she trusted this young black man most—even though it had been black men who had ravished her and killed the girl she had once been.

"Dawit?" she asked timidly. "Do you believe that applies to women as well as men?"

"Of course it does," he answered firmly.

"Even for girls like me?" she asked, holding her breath and not daring to look at him.

"Why wouldn't it?" he answered steadily. "God must love you very much to have brought you from the errors of Islam to a good Christian household like this."

Beth thought about that a moment, her chin resting on her knees and her eyes on the little donkey. She knew in her heart that she would have preferred not to be raped by four men, even if the price had been never to find Christ. "So you think some women are never meant to marry? That it is good enough for some of us to be only half a woman?"

She could hear Dawit shifting uneasily behind her, and the stall door creaked as he leaned on it. She had almost despaired of an answer when he said softly, "If I did not know you must despise me for what the Nubians did to you, I would be honored to make you my wife."

Beth caught her breath and held it, afraid to shatter the enchantment. Then she looked up over her shoulder at Dawit. "Truly?"

Before Dawit could answer, shouting broke in on them. Mathewos was calling for his son. "Dawit! Quick! Tack up Lulu! A messenger must go at once to the Constable at Tyre! He is the father of a fine son!"

Chapter 8

Kerak, March 1183

The Armenian merchant at the high table was worldly as well as wealthy. He knew the customs of the Franks no less than those of his own people, the Greeks and the Turks, so he gallantly shared his trencher with the Lady of Oultrejourdain, and cut her meat for her as he regaled her and her husband with the latest news.

"So Salah ad-Din has been forced to give up his siege of Mosul?" Reynald de Châtillon pressed his informant.

"Yes, Mosul remained beyond his reach," the Armenian agreed, nodding as he gnawed on some duck bones. "But he's still extended his power. Both Amida and Mardin now acknowledge him as sultan. On the other hand"—the Armenian was clearly the kind of man used to seeing all sides of an issue, and matching his narrative to the taste of those he was seeking to please at any one point in time—"On the other hand," he repeated, "his reputation as the defender of Islam was decidedly tarnished by the Christian pirate ships that got loose in the Red Sea. They are said to have captured over two score merchant ships, burning most and turning the oared vessels into auxiliaries of their own fleet. They sacked Aden and even sent raiding parties inland to capture unarmed caravans on their way to the port. But that could have been put down to brigandry had they not then landed between Medina and Mecca. Panic ensued in both cities, and many Muslims were convinced these raiders intended to desecrate the tomb of their prophet at Mecca itself."

Reynald de Châtillon raised his eyebrows at that and grunted in apparent skepticism.

His guest reached for the bowl filled with wheat rolls and helped himself liberally before continuing. "Of course, Salah ad-Din's brother in Cairo wasn't idle. He managed to drag a fleet of warships overland from Alexandria to the Red Sea. His admiral, I believe it was Husam al-Din, tracked down the Frankish ships at al-Haura and penned them into the harbor. When the pirates realized they were completely outnumbered and there was no way to break out by sea, they abandoned their ships—and indeed their captives and plunder—and fled inland. It took the Egyptians five days to finally track them down in a narrow ravine and kill most of them."

Châtillon grunted and nodded again, apparently satisfied.

"But the Egyptians took over a hundred and fifty of the Franks captive," the Armenian noted, signaling to the squire behind his chair to refill his goblet. Humphrey jumped forward to comply, his ears red with embarrassment and pent-up anger as he glanced at his stepfather.

Châtillon was frowning. "Captive? What kind of fools *were* they?" Châtillon was willing to take the overall credit (or blame, depending on how you looked at it) for the expedition, but he didn't trust mercenaries not to say too much—especially when being tortured.

"You can say that again!" the Armenian agreed, as he set his cup down and dabbed his lips on the back of his sleeve. "Islam may prohibit the murder of captives who voluntarily surrender, but Salah ad-Din had no scruples about having these Franks executed anyway. He probably argued that they had forfeited their right to mercy by threatening Mecca, but his real motive would have been that they had learned too much about sailing the Red Sea. Most important, of course, he needed to allay accusations about being more concerned with his own power than with the safety of pilgrims to Mecca. After all, all this havoc had been wrought while he was fighting fellow Muslims, all of whom have a better claim to rule than he does. By sending two of the captives to each of the important market towns of the Arabian peninsula and having them publicly executed, he hoped to divert attention from his own greed."

Châtillon again grunted approval and nodded vigorously, throwing back his own wine and gesturing impatiently to Humphrey for a refill.

"Most of the captives had their heads cut off in one public square or another, but two of the Franks—one presumes, the men identified as the leaders—were taken to Mecca itself, and there, at the place where the Muslim pilgrims usually offer animal sacrifices, they slaughtered these two poor Christians—like human sacrifices to Allah." From the Armenian's tone of voice, it was clear that he was torn between fascination and horror. "They say the crowd went wild with religious fervor as they watched the Franks bleed to death."

Isabella, sitting with her mother-in-law's ladies and the household knights at one of the lower tables, had not been able to hear everything the guest said, but this part of his tale came to her with frightening clarity. She gasped and put down her knife in distress. The man leading the expedition had been Sir Henri, Uncle Balian's younger brother.

Later, after the meal was over, Isabella went in search of Humphrey. She found him on one of the wooden benches before the armory in the ward, where he was diligently oiling Oultrejourdain's sword and scabbard. The rag in his hand was filthy, as were his hands, and he sat hunched over his work. He had grown a lot in the last year and was now a fraction taller than Oultrejourdain himself, but because he hadn't filled out at the same time, the effect was not beneficial; he looked skinnier and more awkward than ever.

"Humphrey! Did you hear what that man said at dinner?" Isabella pounced on him, making him start.

"Isabella! What are you doing down here?" Humphrey looked around at his surroundings uncomfortably. Here by the armory the men-at-arms loitered, drank, and gambled. It was no place for Isabella.

"I needed to talk to you alone," she answered simply. She had no fear of any of the men here; unlike Humphrey, she had not seen what they could do to women in their power.

"We're not alone!" Humphrey protested, nodding to the men lounging about and casting curious and amused glances at the noble children.

"Better than talking to you in the presence of your mother and stepfather," Isabella retorted. "Did you hear what that Armenian said? That the leaders of the Red Sea raid were slaughtered *like animals* in Mecca." Isabella stressed "like animals," because the slaughter of animals was something she had witnessed and so could visualize—unlike battles, which in her mind remained shrouded in clouds of chivalry and heroism.

"Well, they deserved it!" Humphrey snapped back, remembering what he had witnessed on the raid of Tarbuk.

"How can you say that?" Isabella protested in outrage. "They were *Christians*!"

"Yes, and some Christians are *barbarians*," Humphrey told her, tight-lipped, his eyes on the sword he was polishing. He could not forget that girl in the desert, and it made him hot with shame to think of her while Isabella was standing so near, soft and blooming—and no less vulnerable.

"But it was Henri d'Ibelin!" Isabella could not understand Humphrey. "Sir

Henri isn't a barbarian! He's Uncle Balian's brother! He's a good man and a fine knight!"

"You don't know what you're talking about, Isabella!" Humphrey snapped, remembering that Sir Henri had taken his share of the "spoils" just like the baser men. "Now go back to your Latin lessons and lute playing! You have no business being down here!"

Humphrey had never spoken to her like this before, and Isabella was both hurt and offended. She put her hands on her hips and drew a deep breath to give her (future) husband a piece of her mind. Humphrey forestalled her. "Isabella! If you don't do what I say, I'll tell my mother about Dawit!"

"Humphrey!" Isabella gasped, flabbergasted. "You wouldn't!" Nothing in the world meant more to her than the bimonthly visits of the faithful Ethiopian. He brought her not only letters from her mother and pomegranates or other sweets from her stepfather, he brought her all the gossip from home. Through Dawit she felt connected to her real self and the real world; Kerak was not "real" to her, it was an aberration.

Humphrey knew he did not have the heart to betray her, but he wanted her to obey him, and so he set his face and repeated, "Go back to your lessons now, or I will tell her!"

Isabella spun on her heels furiously and ran away. Humphrey let out a long breath and resumed his task. He knew Isabella would be angry with him for days after this, but eventually they would make up. They always did, because they needed each other.

Kerak, April 1183

The lookout on the southeast tower signaled approaching riders, and Oultrejourdain mounted the spiral steps to the roof to take a look for himself. The news that Oultrejourdain was behind the "pirate" raid in the Red Sea had spread far and wide by now. Châtillon had reliable reports from his Bedouin friends that Salah ad-Din had vowed personal revenge—while, as planned, King Baldwin had washed his hands of the whole affair and declared his innocence. Châtillon and Châtillon alone was to be held responsible for the highly successful sortie into the Red Sea, and he suspected he was about to pay the price.

From the tower he could make out a large body of armed men moving purposefully at a steady but not neck-breaking pace, sending up a plume of dust. It was impossible, however, to distinguish the heraldry on their banners against the glare of the sun, or to make out if their shields were round or triangular or if the riders wore turbans or helmets. After squinting into the sun for a few minutes, Oultrejourdain gave up the vigil and returned to the ward, with orders for the lookouts to shout down a report when they could see more.

Then he strode through the barbican to the outer ward and started kicking men-at-arms awake. "Riders approaching out of the desert! Puke up the rest of last night's wine and arm yourselves!"

Châtillon had repeated his advice about last night's wine at least a dozen times before shouting drew him back into the main ward. Here a man leaned over the parapet of the tower and shouted down, "Franks!"

Châtillon snorted. That wasn't much better, since he didn't know who these visitors might be, and he distrusted everyone. After all, except for the King, his peers assumed he had acted on his own and for his own gain. While the bishops blustered about excommunication, men like Tripoli and Hebron had been quick to condemn him for breaking the truce with Salah ad-Din and "imperiling" them all. The asses! As if they weren't imperiled already!

Still, he couldn't be openly hostile to his fellow Franks, so he had to be all the more wary. Saracens he could meet with arrows, insults, and defiance; his fellow Franks had be treated with apparent courtesy, even if they were trying to stab him in the back.

He frowned and looked around at the roughly triangular ward of his castle, as if looking for lurking assassins. The southern tip of the ward was blocked by the chapel, while against the wider northern wall stood the bakery, brewery, smithy, and other workshops. The stables were to the west and storerooms lined the east flank. The storerooms were not as full as he would have liked when facing the prospect of a siege, and he was loath to share what stores he had with a large host of visitors, but the laws of hospitality in the desert were immutable.

"Ibelin!" A shout came down from the lookout.

Just what he needed! "How many men?"

"Upwards of a hundred, my lord."

Cursing under his breath, he turned away and collided with his wife. "The bastard's here to interfere with Isabella again!" Stephanie de Milly exclaimed. "You've got to deny him access."

"Deny access to a baron of Jerusalem with a hundred mounted men? You're out of your mind, woman!" On previous visits Ibelin had come with his wife and only a small domestic escort; that made it obvious his business was private. A baron traveling with a hundred mounted fighting men was not on private business, and Oultrejourdain had no intention of provoking a clash over Isabella. Indeed, he very much doubted this had anything to do with Isabella at all.

"I don't know where Isabella is right now," his wife complained. "The minx has slipped her snares again, and I can't guarantee Ibelin won't run into her someplace if you let him in."

"In case it's escaped your notice, we're on a hostile frontier, and I may desperately *need* Ibelin and his hundred fighting men to save my own hide in the near future! I'm not going to insult him just because you've met your match in Isabella of Jerusalem!"

"What do you expect me to do? Chain her in the dungeon?" Stephanie screamed at her husband. Her frustration at her inability to break Isabella's resistance was a sore spot, compounded by her husband's repeated warnings not to do anything to the girl that would incur the King's wrath. She felt her hands were tied and all her efforts undermined by the men around her.

"Just stop worrying about what that chit of a girl might do or say, and see to your duties as chatelaine! We have a hundred guests for dinner!"

Oultrejourdain was in the ward to greet Ibelin as he drew up, his men flooding in and spreading out behind him. "Welcome to Kerak, my lord. What a pleasant surprise." Although there was no obvious sarcasm in his voice, Ibelin still smiled cynically in return before continuing the charade in an equally sarcastic voice. "We regret any inconvenience, my lord. We had intelligence that Salah ad-Din is again raising his army, and the King requested I conduct a reconnaissance in force to try to ascertain his goal. Now that we are satisfied he is marshaling his forces to attack Aleppo rather than Jerusalem, we are returning to Nablus." As he spoke, he swung himself down from his stallion.

The story was plausible enough, although decidedly vague. Oultrejourdain didn't entirely believe it, but it offered no basis for a direct challenge. He let it stand.

"But, of course," Ibelin continued, now that he was standing face to face with Châtillon in the center of the cobbled ward as his men dismounted around them, "the *real* reason I'm here is to find out about my brother."

"Your brother?" Châtillon was taken completely by surprise.

"Yes, my brother. You do *remember* my brother Henri, I presume?"

Châtillon was unsettled by two things: first, that Ibelin was taking an interest in his younger brother, something he had not noted before, and second, that Ibelin apparently knew Henri had been involved in the Red Sea raids. He reacted defensively. "Stupid question! Of course I remember Henri—I'm just surprised that *you* do!"

"Blood, my lord, is thicker than water. Henri may be your knight, but he is still my brother. I have a longing to speak to him." Ibelin was staring Oultrejourdain straight in the eye, watching for Châtillon's reaction.

Châtillon's conscience was too guilty to meet Ibelin's gaze. Instead, he shrugged and glanced around the ward as if looking for someone. "No idea where he is at the moment. He comes and goes as he pleases."

For the moment, the ruse seemed to work. Ibelin let the topic drop, thanked Châtillon for his hospitality, and turned to see that his men took their horses into the stables in an orderly fashion, but Châtillon suspected the topic was far from closed.

Isabella had heard the lookouts announce her stepfather and had slipped into the stables to hide herself there. No sooner did Balian enter leading his horse than she jumped up from her hiding place among the bales of straw and ran to him. "Uncle Balian! Uncle Balian! Have you come to take me home?"

At ten and a half Isabella was too big to be swept up and carried in his arms, so Balian bent to hug her and hold her fast for a moment. "I wish I could, sweetheart. You know that. There is nothing your mother wants more than to have you come home. I'll have to tell you about the confrontation she had with the Queen Mother because of you." He laughed at the memory, but Isabella had heard the subjunctive in his answer. He *wished* he could, but he couldn't. She gazed at him with wide, trusting hazel eyes. "Why *can't* you take me home, Uncle Balian?"

"Because the King has ordered you to stay here, precious. I am his subject and so subject to his will."

Isabella refused to be satisfied with this facile answer. She knew she was here on the King's orders, but they didn't make sense to her. "But *why* does he want me to stay here?" She had asked Dawit the same question more than once, but accepted that he was just a servant and could not answer. She expected an answer from her stepfather. Balian was supposed to have all the answers.

"He wants you to grow up with your future husband so you will love him more," replied Balian, trying to give her an explanation that was not frightening.

"But Humphrey hates it here, too!" Isabella pointed out, suddenly filled with hope. "If it's just about me being with Humphrey, then we can both come with you!"

Balian was shaking his head.

"Why not?" Isabella demanded to know.

"Because Humphrey is still subject to his guardian's—Oultrejourdain's—will until he is fifteen."

"But he'll turn fifteen in two months!" Isabella protested.

"Will he, now?" Balian looked at his stepdaughter sharply. That was very valuable and welcome information that had long been lacking. Since Maria Zoë's confrontation with Agnes de Courtenay, she and Balian had decided their best hope for Isabella was to convince the King to install Humphrey in his lordship the day he came of age. Their hope was that the King remembered his own minority sharply enough to sympathize with a young man's desire to be free of tutors and guardians. However, they had not known Humphrey's actual date of birth and so the date he would come of age.

"Yes, on St. John's!" Isabella told her stepfather. Birthdays were important to ten-year-olds.

"Good. That's not so long to wait, then, is it?" Balian asked Isabella with a hopeful smile.

"You mean we can leave then? After Humphrey comes of age?"

"Yes. That's the promise your mother and I are going to get from the King."

"But you haven't got it yet," Isabella noted perceptively.

"No," Balian admitted, wishing for once that she wasn't quite so bright. "But we will do everything we can to extract it from him." This was much easier said than done, Balian knew, but it was all he had to offer. He tried to distract Isabella. "Look! I've brought you a whole parcel of gifts from your mother." He indicated the saddlebag behind his saddle, which had already been removed by Gabriel and hung over the stall door.

Isabella glanced at it, but her disappointment was too great to be really interested in things. "Uncle Balian, it's not just about me and Humphrey being together, is it?"

Balian took a deep breath. "No, it's not."

"What is it, then?"

"Well," he took another breath, "some people fear that you could be used to challenge the succession of Princess Sibylla. The King is very sick, as you know, and when he dies he wants his sister Sibylla to succeed him, but he and his mother and Sibylla herself fear that some men in this Kingdom might try to have you crowned instead."

"Oh." Isabella appeared not to have thought of this, and Balian could almost hear her brain working as her eyes narrowed under a furrowed brow.

"I'm sorry, Isabella," Balian said softly and sincerely—for while Isabella was just a threat to Agnes de Courtenay and a tool to Raymond de Tripoli, she was a little girl to him.

"It's all right," she told him, taking a deep breath and standing up straighter. "I'm glad you told me the truth. Now I can understand better." What Isabella understood was that she might be Queen one day, and fear of that was what made her jailers keep her so closely under control. She at once determined she was going to be cleverer than they. She reached out and took Balian's warm hand in hers and smiled up at him. "You can tell Mama not to worry about me. Humphrey loves me very much, so if you can get the King to recognize him as Lord of Toron in his own right, then he'll take me away from here and we'll be free. Then we can visit you at Ibelin or Nablus, and you can come to Toron. Just as soon as Humphrey is recognized as an adult." Balian understood that Isabella had found something concrete and measurable to look forward to, and it was now up to him to ensure that the King really did set Humphrey free at his majority.

At dinner Balian studiously showed no interest in Isabella at all. Instead he raised the issue of his brother again. Since the entire household was clearly gathered, after pointedly surveying the lower tables where the knights and the men-at-arms were seated, Balian asked Oultrejourdain where Henri was. Châtillon, meanwhile, had had time to consider his options and had decided on candor. "Your brother volunteered to take command of the mercenaries I sent to the Red Sea."

"Volunteered?" Balian asked back. "What did you promise him?"

"The Lady Eloise of Amman. She's not much to look at, but she's the heiress of a fief that owes me fourteen knights—more than Ibelin."

Yes, Balian thought to himself, nodding. That was significant. For while he commanded upwards of a hundred knights, most of those knights owed service to Nablus. He only commanded them because Nablus was his wife's dower portion during her lifetime. He would lose them at her death—which, of course, might occur at any moment. What he held in his own right was a fief worth ten knights. It would mean a lot to Henri to be able to say he had a larger barony than Balian, even if it still did not equal that of Barry.

"And what have you heard from my brother lately?"

"Not a thing!" Oultrejourdain spread out his hands in a gesture of helplessness. "I'm sorry to say. Not a thing."

"In short, you sent him to his death and have washed your hands of him."

"He was a grown man, Ibelin. He knew the risks he was taking." Châtillon dropped his pretense of regret.

"Greed sometimes makes a man blind," Balian pointed out, thinking of how Henri had been willing to alienate Barry for the sake of what he considered his "fair share" of their inheritance. This raid, offering the prospect of loot and treasure—and an heiress at the end—would have appealed to Henri. He did not doubt that, but he found it hard to forgive Oultrejourdain for exploiting his brother's weakness on such a dubious mission. This raid had been in clear violation of the existing truce. It targeted unsuspecting civilians. And it dragged Christians down to the same level as their Muslim enemies, who had for so long preyed upon Christian pilgrims. Balian acknowledged the raid's tactical utility, but he did not like to think of his brother being a part of it.

Balian had been absently turning his empty wineglass, and an attentive Humphrey de Toron, standing behind his own lord, sprang forward to fill it. Balian thanked him over his shoulder. So far he had not been much impressed with Isabella's future husband. To be sure, he was almost as tall as Balian himself, but he kept his eyes down and hunched his shoulders, more like a servant or a whipped dog than the heir to an important barony. He had woolly blond hair, an almost invisible adolescent beard, a smattering of pimples, and big blue eyes. Had he been more bold and self-confident, maidens might have found him attractive, Balian speculated, but his bearing made him seem insignificant. Indeed, he seemed to want to melt into the background.

Balian would have liked the opportunity to speak to him alone, but he had little legitimate reason to seek out Châtillon's squire. Seeing him now, however, gave him an idea, and he signaled Ernoul forward.

"My lord?" Ernoul asked eagerly.

Balian lowered his voice and spoke directly into Ernoul's attentive ear. "Try to befriend Toron, will you?"

Ernoul grinned and bowed deeply. "At your service, my lord."

Ernoul had grown into his duties over the previous two years, and even if he was still the butt of laughter in the lists, his savvy at table and in other duties was universally acknowledged. If the other squires wanted a favor of their lord or lady, they sent Ernoul to make the plea for them. If someone broke something or stained something or a horse got injured, Ernoul was the one to break the news to whomever was most likely to get angry. If Maria Zoë's children were getting too loud, Ernoul was more likely to calm them than their nurses, and if the household was bored on a rainy night, Ernoul could be counted on to tell a story with so much drama and feeling that everyone, from the ancient laundresses to the wildest of the squires and the hardest knights, were soon sitting on the edge of their benches, mesmerized.

After the meal the squires were released from serving, and Ernoul caught Humphrey by the elbow and asked with apparent eagerness, "I heard your grandfather saw the inside of the Caliph's palace in Cairo!"

"That's true," Humphrey replied cautiously, unsure where this question from the strange squire might be leading.

"How exciting! Tell me about it!" Ernoul urged, pulling a crude chair closer and swinging his leg over it to sit astride, with his arms resting on the back.

"What is there to tell?" Humphrey replied uncomfortably. No one at Kerak had ever shown the slightest interest in his grandfather and his deeds. He'd had the feeling ever since he got here that his mother didn't want to be reminded of her marriage to his father, and that his stepfather despised his grandfather for some reason.

"But don't you know? I've heard that when the Franks were led through the first gate, they found themselves in a vast menagerie filled with exotic wild animals—not just peacocks and monkeys, like you see all over the place here, but striped horses, and beasts as tall as palm trees with necks like swans but legs like cattle. And there were not just lions, but striped lions as well." Ernoul was off. Humphrey hardly realized that he'd sat down, too, and was listening to Ernoul as he told the very tale he'd asked Humphrey to tell him.

"And so," Ernoul came to the climax, "the Caliph with a smile removed his glove and shook hands with an infidel to seal the treaty! I wish I could have been there!" he ended. "Don't you?"

"Yes," Humphrey admitted, adding with tentative pride, "I read Arabic, you know." When he made this last admission he kept his head down and his shoulders hunched, but his eyes darted sideways to see how his fellow squire reacted.

"You do?" Ernoul sounded amazed, and that made Humphrey sit up a little straighter. "Not even Lord Balian can do that! He speaks it fluently, but he can't read it, though he's often said it would be useful. It must terribly hard to learn—all those squiggles!"

"Yes," Humphrey agreed, nodding vigorously. His grandfather had taught him that it was important to understand one's enemies, but Oultrejourdain dismissed the notion. Oultrejourdain had said: "The only language the Saracens understand is force! Learn to hit 'em hard, and hit 'em where it hurts, and you'll be far ahead of anything you can gain with words!"

"My grandfather," Humphrey ventured, "had a collection of poetry books in Arabic. Poetry and some medicine books."

"Poetry? I love poetry! I've found this incredible poem in Greek about a war that took place a thousand years ago!" Ernoul admitted enthusiastically; his pretense of friendliness was slowly melting into the real thing without him even noticing.

"That must be the *Iliad*," Humphrey agreed, proud to show off his knowledge to someone who seemed to appreciate it.

"Is that what it's called? About the siege of a place called Troy?"

"Yes! That's the *Iliad*. And there's a second book by the same poet, Homer, about how the Greeks get lost trying to sail home—well, not lost, but blown off course—and they have all these adventures trying to get back."

"Do you have a copy of that book?" Ernoul asked eagerly.

"No, my grandfather only told me about it."

"I wonder where we could find a copy?" Ernoul speculated. "I suppose I could ask the Dowager Queen. She has a whole library of books in Greek. Oh!" Ernoul stopped and looked at Humphrey. "I just remembered. She'll be your mother-in-law! If you ever marry Isabella, that is."

"Why shouldn't I marry Isabella?" Humphrey demanded defensively.

Ernoul shrugged, surprised by the sudden anger in Humphrey's voice. "I don't know. You're just both so young. Anything could happen."

"No! Isabella and I are betrothed, and as good as married in the eyes of God. As soon as I'm of age, we're going to formalize it. We've promised each other that. We're going to marry so no man can ever separate us!"

"OK." Ernoul backed off, raising his hands as if in surrender, and Humphrey realized he'd overreacted. He tried to calm himself down, but he was breathing hard at the mere mention of "something happening" that might take Isabella away from him. The fact was, he was far too aware of all the things that *could* get in the way of their marriage—starting with a change of whim on the part of the Queen Mother. Humphrey knew perfectly well that his role was to keep Isabella from becoming the bride of a man more ambitious and powerful than himself. He was only going to be allowed to keep Isabella if he played his role and did what Oultrejourdain and the Queen Mother told him to do—he hoped.

Balian had escaped from the great hall, where the drinking had started in earnest, and cautiously followed the vaulted passage that ran north from the chapel to the underground postern. Part of it was curiosity, for he was interested in the defenses of every castle he visited, but mostly he was seeking solitude so he could think. Isabella had been sent to bed long ago, before the entertainment became too crude, but the touch of her lips on Balian's cheek as he said good night still lingered like a reproach. She knew he planned to depart without her in the morning, and although she had said she understood, it was hard to leave her here.

It was always hard to leave her here, of course, but previous visits had been before the Red Sea raids. Now, when Balian looked out across the hall, he was reminded that many of the men sitting at the tables and sharing their meals with Isabella were mercenaries—and capable of all the atrocities attributed to the raiders. Like Oultrejourdain, Balian and Maria Zoë had their informers. Greek traders with strong ties to Alexandria had provided them with some very gruesome details of the raids—and of the fate of the survivors. The reports had all spoken of "mercenaries" and sailors from the gutters of the Levant—led by a blond knight of great height and strength, with a nose that hung straight from his forehead like the nosepiece of a helmet.

Height and strength were always attributed to an opponent who was difficult to subdue—it increased the reputed prowess of the victors in the end—and most Franks were considered "blond" by their Arab foes, but the detail about the nose had led Balian to believe Henri had been the leader of the raid. Barry and Henri both had a nose like this, but it was most pronounced in Henri's case. Barry's face was otherwise harmonious and attractive, so that the dominant nose didn't jump out at you as much; Henri's hunger for land, fame, and fortune had carved out his cheeks and left his nose more prominent than ever.

Out of the darkness that face emerged to confront Balian. It was blackened, however, as if burned, and encased in a Bedouin headdress. Balian caught his breath and stepped back, certain he was facing a ghost.

The ghost, however, laughed. "Afraid of your own brother, are you?"

"Henri! Where have you come from?"

"Hell," came the simple answer.

The answer seemed to corroborate that this was his brother's soul, but at the same time the image seemed far too substantial. Dust soiled and weighed down the hem of the Bedouin robes, and the smell of sweat—thick and masculine—oozed from his brother as he blocked the passageway. Surely ghosts wouldn't smell?

"Châtillon tells me you went voluntarily," Balian ventured an answer.

His brother laughed harshly. "Oh, that I did, and the heaven part came before the hell. Ever make love to a harem slave? I assure you, it's like nothing else in the world!" He laughed again. "And they have wine in Aden, Balian, like the nectar of lotus that drove Ulysses' men mad. You can't imagine what it's like to lick that sweet wine from the thighs of dancing girls. And the treasure, Balian, the treasure was more than we could carry. The men started paying their whores with ruby rings and ivory bracelets. I could have bought Ibelin ten times over with what I had in my sea chest alone."

"Ibelin is not for sale," Balian replied, certain now that this was no apparition but his brother, very much in the flesh, who had somehow managed to disguise himself as a Bedouin and escape the vengeance of the Egyptian authorities.

"No? I'm not so sure. Even our saintly little leper might have been tempted by the treasure I could have lain before him. It was surely enough to build a wall all around the Kingdom of Jerusalem—or pay a thousand knights from the West."

"He might have been tempted," Balian agreed, "if you had managed to keep it and bring it here."

"They trapped us, Balian." The tone of voice changed from triumph to bitterness. "We were betrayed! I killed a dozen of the Pisan bastards—just to set an example—but it was too late. We had to abandon all we had—the ships, the treasure, the girls—and head inland. But the Bedouins led us into a ravine with no escape and then tried to disappear among the rocks. I chased after them while the rest of the fools fought off our pursuers. The rock crevices were so sharp, they cut like the edge of a knife." He opened his hands and looked down on them as if amazed by the jagged, scabbed lines that now deformed them.

Balian waited, torn between shock and sympathy.

"I finally brought one of the bastards down, cut his throat, and took his robes. I dressed his corpse in my armor and kicked it over the edge of the cliff. It rolled its way back into the ravine to land at the feet of the Egyptian troops, the face so smashed and ravaged by the rock edges that they never even suspected the deception. When they looked up, I waved back to them, clenched my fist over my head, and shouted "Allahu Akbar! Allahu Akbar!" The idiots answered with similar shouts and never even tried to come after me."

"I'm surprised the Bedouins didn't get you," Balian observed, still trying to sort out his feelings; he was glad Henri was alive, and yet ashamed of what he'd done.

Henri just laughed. "So am I. Of course, I still had some gold in my purse that helped with some of them. The others I had to kill."

"You have a lot to confess, it would seem," Balian concluded. After all, it was not his place to judge his brother; that was for God to do.

"Don't preach to me, Balian. You haven't been where I was."

"No, and I hope I never am."

"Barry always said you weren't ambitious enough."

"I'm a baron of Jerusalem and an honorable man. That's good enough for me."

"Yes, I know. But not for me. Did Châtillon tell you about the little girl he's going to give me?"

"Yes, with a fief worth more than Ibelin; I know. You're welcome to it, Henri, because you are right: I would not have done what you have done to get it. May God have mercy on your soul."

"That sounds rather like you are washing your hands of me."

"Does it?"

"Yes." Something in Henri's tone sounded distressed, as if some last flickering remnant of decency, or maybe just affection, had flared up in him. Or maybe he was just suddenly afraid of losing Balian.

Balian heard it, but it was too faint to sway him. "You are beyond my help, Henri. Go collect your earthly reward from Châtillon, and see that you enjoy it, for the Day of Judgment will not be far behind, and I do not want to be in your shoes."

Balian turned and walked back in the direction of the chapel.

Henri called after him. "Nor I in yours, Balian! Nor I in yours! For all your goodness will not help you when Salah ad-Din comes!"

Chapter 9

Kerak, July 1183

"Humphrey! You're fifteen! You're grown up! You don't have to put up with this anymore!" Isabella argued furiously with her future husband.

"If I don't do what Oultrejourdain says, he'll break my face in!" Humphrey countered just as angrily.

"He doesn't have the right to do that! You're his *peer*!" Isabella insisted indignantly. "You're the Lord of Toron!"

"What does that have to do with anything?" Humphrey wanted to know. "It's all very well for you to talk about my *rights*," Humphrey sneered; "he's never laid his fists on *you*!"

"Because he wouldn't dare! Don't you see, Humphrey? You have to make him respect you!"

"Why the hell should he respect me when he's so much stronger than I am? I'm not even a knight!"

"The King has never been knighted, either," Isabella pointed out. "But people respect him, don't they? Even Oultrejourdain respects him. And you can't say he's stronger than Oultrejourdain, either. They say he can't even walk anymore."

"But he's the *King*," Humphrey pointed out in exasperation.

"And you are the Lord of Toron! If you don't remind Oultrejourdain of that and insist that he treat you according to your rank, we'll never get out of here!"

Humphrey stared at her. "What are you talking about?"

"Do you want to stay here forever?" Isabella demanded. "You are Lord of Toron! We should be living in Toron as lord and lady, not imprisoned here!"

"Oultrejourdain says I'm not ready," Humphrey conceded, red with shame.

"Because he likes having your income! He's never going to *willingly* give you your inheritance. You have to *make* him give it to you!"

"You make it sound so easy!" Humphrey protested. "If you think it's that easy, *you* tell him!"

"All right, I will!" Isabella decided, and with clenched fists she turned and started striding toward the great chamber, where Oultrejourdain was consulting his household officials.

Humphrey ran after her. "Isabella! Don't!"

"Why not?"

"We don't know what he'll do to you!"

Isabella could see real fear in Humphrey's flushed face, and she knew he was genuinely afraid for her. She appreciated that, but she was convinced that sometimes you had to be brave. She had had enough of being a prisoner. She was not prepared to wait any longer for her freedom. "I don't care what he does to me," she told Humphrey stubbornly. "I'm going to confront him!"

"Isabella! I'll tell him about Dawit!" Humphrey used the threat that had worked before.

But Isabella was beyond being blackmailed. Her stepfather had reminded her that she was not a helpless child, she was a princess of Jerusalem, and she had more right to the throne than did Sibylla, the daughter of a bad woman. It was because people were *afraid* of her that she was kept imprisoned here.

Isabella swept into the great chamber with Humphrey in her wake, but the adults paid no attention to them. Humphrey seized the chance to try to pull her back, whispering loudly for her to come with him. Isabella broke free of his clasp angrily and burst out in a loud, demanding voice: "I want to speak to you, my lord of Oultrejourdain!"

"I'm busy," he retorted without even looking up from the document he was reading. "Later."

"No, now!"

Humphrey gasped, and the men of the household snorted.

"You'll do as you're told!" Oultrejourdain growled, looking up and frowning threateningly.

Isabella stood her ground. "I'm Isabella of Jerusalem, and you can't order me around!"

Oultrejourdain burst out laughing and leaned back in his chair, crossing his arms over his chest in bemusement. The fact that a chit of a girl, barely eleven years old, was willing to stand up to him like this amused him. Of course, he could have brushed her aside with a single backhanded flick of his wrist. He could have picked her up with one hand, dumped her in the deepest and vilest of his dungeons, and left her there without food or water until she begged his forgiveness, or he could have simply hit her until she was broken and streaming with tears. But what was the point of demonstrating his power over someone so weak? He used his strength to keep strong men from challenging him and to make weak men stronger, but he saw no point in employing brute force against a girl who would never be strong and never be a threat to him—at least not physically.

"So, Madame de Jerusalem," Oultrejourdain asked with an amused smirk, "just what is so important that we have to discuss it now?"

"My husband—my future husband—turned fifteen last month," Isabella told him, starting to feel afraid now that she was face to face with Oultrejourdain and he was staring at her so intently. His eyes seemed to communicate a mixture of malice and amusement.

"Did he?" Oultrejourdain asked back, feigning surprise. Then he turned on Humphrey and asked as if he could not believe it, "Is that true, boy? Did you turn fifteen?" Before Humphrey could answer, Oultrejourdain continued in a tone of utter contempt, "I never would have guessed. You act more like *five* than fifteen!"

"But it's true!" Isabella insisted. "He's fifteen, and so he is an adult! He is now Lord of Toron."

"A lord who needs an eleven-year-old girl to speak for him!" Oultrejourdain countered sharply, shaking his head in a mixture of disbelief and scorn. "When he's man enough to argue his own case, Isabella, I'll hear him out. For now, go back to your nursery and take the little boy with you!"

That night when Oultrejourdain prepared for bed, he pointed out to his wife, "The problem is, she's right. Humphrey's technically of age, and we have no legal grounds for keeping him here."

"When did the law ever interest you?" Stephanie snapped back.

"The law *always* interests me, woman. It's important to know exactly what the law says, so one can decide when to use it to one's advantage and when it is more sensible to break it. What do we gain by keeping Humphrey here? It's not as if he's adding greatly to the strength of my garrison!" Oultrejourdain scoffed.

"We keep Humphrey here to keep control of Isabella—and so thwart Tripoli."

"Tripoli. Of course. I'd forgotten about Tripoli." Oultrejourdain was rather bored by his wife's obsession for revenge against Tripoli. He'd agreed to kill the man because she wouldn't have married him otherwise, but he'd been her husband for eight years now and she could hardly dismiss him. His control of Oultrejourdain was absolute.

"He killed your predecessor!" Stephanie de Milly reminded him shrilly, all too conscious of his waning enthusiasm for the task she had set him.

"For which I ought to be indebted to him," Oultrejourdain replied flippantly.

Stephanie reared up furiously, her eyes wide with outrage. "If you think you can go back on your promise to me—"

Oultrejourdain backhanded her easily, drawing blood from her nose, and when she shrieked and lunged at him, trying to dig her fingernails into his face, he grabbed hold of her wrists and forced her back onto the bed, pinning her down with a knee to her belly and holding her wrists on either side of her head. She continued to struggle, spitting at him and shouting insults that would have made a whore blush, but Oultrejourdain was quite used to that. They'd had more than one of these marital spats over the years.

"Hysterical woman!" Oultrejourdain sneered, silencing her instantly. She hated being called hysterical.

Although she had gone completely still, her eyes glinted with hatred, and Oultrejourdain knew better than to release her. Instead he increased the pressure on her belly and her arms. He could tell he was hurting her, although she was too proud to beg him to stop. "I am Oultrejourdain now. Don't forget that. I *am* Oultrejourdain. If you want me to do your bidding, then think about finding ways to make me want to."

Stephanie de Milly's breathing was shortening as his knee dug deeper and deeper into her belly. She fought against admitting the pain she was in, but she gasped once. "Get off me!"

"Maybe. Will you be an obedient wife if I do?"

"Get off!"

"You can do better than that."

"Off!"

"No." He increased the pressure.

"Stop it!"

"Will you be a good wife from now on?"

"Yes! Yes!" she gasped and then started sobbing as he removed his knee, released her wrists, and stood up staring down at her. She whimpered miserably, as much from the defeat as the pain.

Châtillon felt no pity for her. She was an ugly bitch, and she used other people for her own purposes. He'd used her to get a barony, and when he'd married her after fifteen years in a Saracen prison, he'd even found a certain pleasure in her bed. But that was long ago. Now he took his pleasure elsewhere, and he doubted she much cared.

"I'm fed up with having Humphrey around, and tired of having responsibility for Isabella. Let him go to Toron and take her with him," Oultrejourdain declared.

"If you let her go, Tripoli might try to make her Queen!" Stephanie shouted at him, infuriated by his betrayal.

"What's so bad about that? If I have to bend my knee and swear fealty to a woman, then I prefer Isabella, who's guided by what's between her ears, over Sibylla, who's guided by what's between her legs. Besides, if Isabella's Queen, then your son, you stupid bitch, would be her king and consort."

That stunned his wife for a moment. Stephanie de Milly hadn't really considered the fact that her son might one day become King. She had wanted control of Isabella to prevent Tripoli having control of her. She knew that her scheme to take Isabella away from her mother had resonated with the Queen Mother, who hated her rival Queen Maria Zoë, and it was good to be on the good side of a woman like Agnes de Courtenay. The latter had even suggested, obliquely of course, that it would be so easy to put something in Isabella's food that led to a "tragic stomach ailment."

Oultrejourdain had sharply resisted the suggestion. "She's too valuable to kill," he'd told his wife bluntly, and the subject had been dropped—even if Stephanie had often wished she could kill the little bitch, and once or twice considered just pushing her down a flight of stairs.

She had been so focused on *preventing* Isabella from becoming Tripoli's puppet queen that she hadn't given a thought to the advantages of Isabella being crowned. She found herself frowning in perplexity at her own stupidity. How could she have been so dense? She didn't have any more respect for Humphrey than Châtillon did, but he *was* her son. And if he became King, then she would be in Agnes de Courtenay's position. That was not a bad position to be in. As Queen Mother, it would be easy for her to take revenge on Tripoli. As Queen Mother, she wouldn't even need Châtillon anymore. Then she remembered something. "They aren't legally married."

"Then let's put on a wedding! Let's wine and dine all the nobility of Outremer right here and have them witness Humphrey taking her to wife!"

She smiled to herself, rubbing the bruises on her belly, before announcing in what sounded like a sullen voice, "Well, if that's what you want, then let's do it. Just give me a couple of months to stock what we need for a proper feast and to ensure as many people come as possible."

"Good," Châtillon agreed without even looking over his shoulder. Neither of them was the least concerned that the bride would still be only eleven years old.

Barony of Ibelin, mid-September 1183

It was Ramadan. When two Muslim boys driving their goats home at the end of the day spotted an old man lying at the side of the road, they assumed he had simply collapsed from lack of food and drink, because it was obvious from his beard and clothes that he was Muslim. Hassam bent over the old man and shook his shoulder. "Hey, Uncle!" he spoke to him respectfully in Arabic. "Come and join us for the Iftar!"

The old man reared up, startled, and looked around in bewilderment. He seemed not to know where he was. But the boys coaxed him to come with them, Hassam picking up his pathetic bundle of belongings and slinging it easily over his shoulder. To share the evening meal with beggars and travelers during Ramadan was an important act of charity, and the boys knew their father would be pleased with them.

"It's not far," Hassam assured the bewildered stranger. "Just over that hill, and our mother is a good cook!"

The old man nodded and thanked the boys many times, but he seemed so unsteady on his feet that Omar offered his arm while Hassam took care of the goats.

When they reached the boy's adobe house with its flat roof and the rough animal pens around it, the sun was very low over the horizon, a bright orange ball sinking into the haze over the sea twelve miles further west. The boys' mother, wearing a black abaya but no face veil, stood in the door of the house as they came into the yard. At the sight of the stranger, she turned and called to her sister-in-law to fetch a hand bowl. The pregnant girl scooped water from the trough so the old man could wash the dust of the road from his face and hands.

While the stranger washed, the boys shooed the goats into the pen, closing the swing gate with a loop of twine, then they washed their hands and faces in the trough. Their father and uncle could be seen striding in from the cabbage fields, mud on their bare feet and the edges of their rolled-up, baggy trousers. They owed service to Ibelin, but they also had a small plot of land for themselves and made money selling goat's cheese, cabbage, carrots, and onions in the local markets.

The men and boys sat down cross-legged in front of the house, under a crude roof made of woven rushes and held up by raw poles, while the boys' mother, aunt, and sister served them water laced with mint leaves, still-warm flatbread, and then cucumbers in yogurt sauce, little meatballs, and crushed chickpeas in olive oil. They were ravenous after the long day and ate in a hurry at first, but after their initial thirst and hunger were stilled, their tongues were loosened, and the boys excitedly told how they had found their visitor on the side of the road.

The old man nodded and thanked his hosts profusely for their hospitality, bowing his head over his folded hands many times.

"You are not from these parts," the boy's father and head of the household observed cautiously.

"No, I was born in Aleppo," the old man admitted, clearly feeling better after partaking of the good food.

"Aleppo?" the boys and men exclaimed together, while the women risked little glances at the stranger from the door of the house, all equally amazed by this news.

"I was taken captive when still a youth—hardly older than Hassam here," the old man narrated, with a smile to the elder boy.

"You are a slave?" Hassam asked, wide-eyed. As the son of a native peasant in the Kingdom of Jerusalem, his contact with slaves had been very limited.

The old man sighed deeply as he nodded. "Most of my life I was a slave. Now, when I am a free man, I wish I were a slave again."

"How can you want *that*?" Omar asked, earning a frown and gestures to be still from his elders.

But the old man did not seem offended. "Well you might ask," he said to the boy sadly, "and for a young man, slavery is terrible. But an old slave cannot be sent away when he can no longer work. A slave must be cared for and fed even in his old age."

"You have been turned out?" the boys' uncle asked, frowning.

"Yes. I have been turned out." Tears were shining in the old man's eyes, and the wrinkles of his face seemed deeper than ever.

"Have you no family?" the boys' father asked.

The old man shrugged. "Who knows what is left of my family now? I have not seen and heard from them since the day of my capture half a century ago. You see, I came from a house like this," he indicated the simple adobe dwelling, "and none could pay a ransom for me."

The boys' father and uncle exchanged an alarmed look. They were poor men, and while they welcomed a traveler for a shared meal during Ramadan, they did not relish a permanent guest. Their income was limited, and now the younger brother's wife was pregnant; they would soon have yet another mouth to feed.

"I never married, of course, and I gave all my love to my master." The stranger's tears shone now on his leathery skin as they slipped down his face.

The brothers exchanged an even more alarmed look, but this time the old man intercepted it and told them: "You need not worry. I seek charity of a man who loved and served my master almost as well as I did, although he too was sent away thanklessly by those who poison my master's ears. But once, long ago, he promised to care for me if my master died before me, and I hope he will care for me even if my master is still alive." The tears had turned into a veritable flood that dripped off the man's wrinkled chin, and the little family gazed at him, gripped with pity.

After the old man's tears had ebbed, the head of the household asked gently, "Who is the man you seek?"

"Sir Balian, the Lord of Ibelin."

"The Lord of Ibelin?" the men gasped. "Himself?"

"I knew Sir Balian when he was still a landless knight, a servant to the King."

"You have served the King?"

"I have served him almost since the day he was born, but most closely since he became stricken with leprosy and the other servants were afraid to serve him."

"Are the rumors true that he has fallen ill again?" they asked.

The old man nodded sadly. "So ill he has taken what the Christians call the 'Last Rites,' and the Patriarch of Jerusalem hardly leaves his side. His mother and sister are with him constantly, too—and the Count of Jaffa." He fell silent, staring into space.

"Hassam!" the boy's father called sharply. "Finish up, then run to Ibelin and tell the Baron that—" He stopped and addressed the old man. "Who should we say begs the Baron's charity?"

"Ibrahim. Just Ibrahim. He will know who I am."

Ibrahim was so overwhelmed by the arrival of the baron himself at the little peasant house that he fell on his knees and kissed Balian's feet—to the intense embarrassment of the latter. When Balian lifted him up, he burst into tears, overwhelmed by a confusion of emotions. Except to say he'd been "thrown out," he could not answer any of Balian's questions coherently.

"Is the King dead?" Balian asked him repeatedly, but Ibrahim shook his head, only to burst into tears again. Finally Balian tipped his tenants for their kindness, coaxed Ibrahim onto the old gelding he'd brought, and led him back to Ibelin.

It was the middle of the night and at Ibelin almost everyone was abed, but Mathewos helped Ibrahim wash his feet and Ernoul found him a clean kaftan before escorting him to the solar, where Maria Zoë and Balian waited for him alone. Gabriel had laid a fire and brought food, wine, and water, but he was dismissed as soon as Ibrahim entered.

Balian indicated a chair by the fire, but Ibrahim first insisted on going down on his knees and bowing his head on the floor to Maria Zoë. "My lady, thank you for taking in an old and worthless man."

"Ibrahim." Maria Zoë cast Balian an alarmed look. "A man's worth is not measured by the strength of his body, but by the quality of his soul. Come, sit and tell us what has happened." She helped Ibrahim to his feet and guided him to the chair Balian had prepared for him between their own.

Ibrahim lowered himself slowly into the chair and dropped his face into his hands. Maria Zoë and Balian again exchanged a look. But then Ibrahim lifted his head and spoke clearly. "The King is dying, Sir Balian. He has taken the Last Rites, and the Patriarch hardly leaves his side. Perhaps, even as we speak, he is already dead."

Balian and Maria Zoë looked at one another.

"I—I always thought I would be with him when he died. . . ." The tears started down Ibrahim's face again. "Do not be angry with me, my lord. But I—I beg Allah to forgive him for being a Christian. I always thought . . ."

Maria Zoë and Balian waited for him to collect himself.

After a moment he continued. "I always include him in my prayers, of course, but I thought to be there at the end. . . . But she threw me out."

"Who?" Maria Zoë asked, so sharply that she raised her husband's eyebrows.

"The Countess of Jaffa. She barred me from his chamber. She told me I was no longer needed. She said my 'stink' was unwelcome, and that Sir Daniel could look after the King without my help." Ibrahim's pain was sharp enough to give his words strength.

"Surely she just wanted you to get some rest," Balian suggested cautiously.

"No! She told me to leave the palace, my lord. She told me to go away and never come back! She said she never wanted to set eyes on my 'ugly face' again."

"The little bitch!" Maria Zoë declared, incensed. "She's hated Ibrahim from the day he witnessed her inexcusable behavior before our wedding!"

Balian frowned—not because he did not share his wife's opinion, but because he feared Maria Zoë's too-public expression of her opinions had already been damaging to both of them. He asked, "Who else was with the King?"

"His mother, of course, the Patriarch, and the Count of Jaffa."

"The *Count* of Jaffa?" Balian asked in alarm.

"Yes, the Countess brought him with her."

"Did she bring her son?"

"No, the risk of infection was too high."

"Was the Constable there?"

"He, the Grand Masters of the Templars and Hospitallers, and the Bishop of Bethlehem were in the hall, but they were not given access to the King."

"And Salah ad-Din, smelling weakness, is raising another army. . . ." Balian whispered to the room.

The Springs of La Tubanie, September 29, 1183

"Jerusalem and an annual income of ten thousand bezants is all the King retained for himself—and the title of King. The Count of Jaffa is Regent," Ramla informed his brother, as the knights and Turcopoles of Ibelin and Nablus pitched their tents beside those of Ramla and Mirabel.

The new Regent of Jerusalem, Guy de Lusignan, had summoned the feudal host to face yet another invasion by Salah ad-Din. As always, this invasion was stronger than the one before, because Salah ad-Din had successfully subdued yet another of his Muslim opponents while not engaged in *jihad* against the Christian states. This summer it had been Aleppo, the city that had so long eluded him. On the other hand, the Regent had persuaded both Tripoli and Antioch to muster with the army of Jerusalem, and thus he had impressively pulled together the largest Christian army ever seen in Outremer. It was spearheaded by nearly fourteen hundred knights, backed by three times that number of native light horsemen, and ten thousand foot soldiers.

The forces of the Ibelin brothers made up a significant portion of those numbers. With his vassals and household knights, Ibelin could field one hundred and five knights and two hundred seventy-five Turcopoles, despite leaving ten knights each at Ibelin and Nablus to stiffen the backbone of the garrisons there. His older brother, who felt Ramla was indefensible, had left his new wife and infant son at Mirabel with a garrison of just fifteen knights, to field a force of one hundred twelve knights and two and a half times that number of Turcopoles. Finally, for the first time, their youngest brother Henri was now also a banneret, leading a contingent of fourteen knights as part of Oultrejourdain's force of one hundred sixty-two knights.

"Where is the Regent?" Balian asked his brother, as he dropped down from his palfrey Rufus and turned him over to Gabriel. He had not encountered Guy de Lusignan since the latter's elevation to Regent, and he was dreading the meeting. The Count of Jaffa was bound to blame him for Maria Zoë's attack on his wife and mother-in-law—especially since, based on Ibrahim's account, the younger Lusignan owed his current position to the fact that Agnes de Courtenay and Sibylla had badgered the desperately ill and frightened King into naming him Regent. The decision had certainly not been made in council with the High Court of Jerusalem—an omission the Count of Tripoli suggested made the decision illegal.

Illegal or not, when Salah ad-Din crossed the Jordan in force, the barons of the Kingdom recognized that this was no time for quibbling over legalities. They were all here, even Ramla and Tripoli, giving their backing to the young and untried Guy de Lusignan in the hope that he would prove their doubts unfounded. At some level, they dreamed he would surprise them all and demonstrate the leadership they so desperately needed. After all, hadn't young King Baldwin surprised them at Montgisard?

"Oh, you can't miss him!" Ramla replied to his brother's question. "He's in the largest, gaudiest, most extravagant tent you can imagine—all red satin and glittering gold. They tell me he brought a half-dozen little page boys, too, to serve him on their knees. The latest fashion in Cairo."

Balian drew a deep breath and looked at his brother with a hint of reproach in his eyes. Barry's hatred of Lusignan, rather than diminishing with time, was still eating him up from the inside.

"I'm just telling you what I've heard. I'm staying clear. I'll fight my damnedest for Jerusalem, and you know it, but Jaffa's an upstart. Regent or not."

Balian nodded in fundamental agreement. "Has there been a council yet?"

"No, he appears to be waiting until everyone has arrived. We're still missing Beirut and Sidon. That, or he's afraid to call a council, which might just point out that his appointment has not been confirmed and so is not yet valid."

Balian nodded ambiguously and avoided taking sides on the issue. "Do we know exactly where Salah ad-Din is?"

"Last I heard, he was beleaguering Bethsan again."

"With how many troops?"

"Does it matter? A lot more than we have—but they're largely feudal levies, just like our force but with less motivation. Except for the fanatics, most Saracens don't give a tinker's damn about Jerusalem. They'd rather be home with their wives and children."

"As would we," Balian noted.

"But we're fighting for our survival; *they're* fighting for the aggrandizement of their insatiable master. There is a difference."

"I hope so."

"Come join me for some refreshment. It'll take your squires at least a half-hour to set everything up."

Balian glanced over to where Sir Galvin was forcefully (and none too gently) taking advantage of his unusual stature and bulk to stake out the perimeter of the Ibelin-Nablus camp, while Gabriel and Ernoul were together rolling out his tent and preparing to erect it. He nodded, and followed his brother inside the latter's tent.

Inside, he sat down on one of the folding stools Barry indicated. The Baron of Ramla did not scorn creature comforts while on campaign. There were woven straw mats on the floor to level the surface and keep the mud at bay. There were stands on which his heavy armor could be hung—and cleaned—and a half-dozen wooden chests containing silver utensils for dining, as well as clean clothes and bed linens. He had a collapsible bed with thick covers for the increasingly chilly nights, and folding tables and chairs. The Ibelin tent was outfitted in roughly the same way, the only real difference being that Barry's things tended to be somewhat more ornate and costly.

One of the Ramla squires brought Balian a silver goblet with cool water in it, and he drank it gratefully, holding up the goblet for a refill almost immediately before asking his brother, "And how are Elizabeth and little Godfrey?"

At last Barry smiled. "Godfrey is a fine boy. He screams as lustily as a lion cub. Big paws, too! He's going to grow up as tall as we are. He's not going to die on me like the runts Richildis gave me."

Balian sighed, glad that his brother had been blessed with a healthy son at last, but sorry that he felt compelled to insult his first wife and dismiss her suffering as if she were to blame. Richildis had surely suffered more giving birth to those sickly sons, who died before seeing a single birthday, than Barry had in making and losing them.

"And your Philip?" Barry asked back, more out of courtesy than interest.

"He's dark like Maria Zoë, with eyes that seem wise beyond his years. John is rather jealous of him at the moment, as he was not of his sister Margaret, but I hope they will grow up to be friends like we are."

"Yes, and friends with my Godfrey, too. Cousins can be as close as brothers."

"You heard Henri's wife is pregnant?" Balian asked cautiously. Henri and Barry usually acted as if the other didn't exist, but Henri had been understandably proud of siring a child on his bride, Eloise of Amman, within the first month of their marriage. It was said she was no beauty and had been promised to the Church until the untimely death of her brother turned her into an heiress overnight. By then she was already twenty-something, and Oultrejourdain had seen her value as a reward and controlled her jealously, apparently leaving her in the convent until the very day of her wedding. Balian hoped his younger brother had been gentle with her under the circumstances, but he doubted it.

"Yes, he couldn't resist telling me," Barry answered Balian's question. "But who's to say the child will be carried to term or won't be a girl?"

"You know," Balian remarked, smiling a little provocatively, "I rather like my girls—and yours. Eschiva is an attractive and sensible woman."

"Yes, thank God for that. Aimery seems pleased with her—but then, she's given him a son. They've named him for Aimery's father, Hugh, did you hear?"

Balian nodded. Maria Zoë had been there, after all. He stretched and got to his feet. "Time for me to return to my men. I think I'll wait to be called to our friend the Regent. There's safety in numbers, after all."

Barry laughed. "I'll be right beside you, Balian." He added, "You know, your wife may have exceeded the normal bounds of propriety in her attacks on Agnes and Sibylla—but, by the Cross, she had the rights of it! They are a diabolical duo, with no more brains between the two of them than a peahen. I wish to God your wife had given the Kingdom a male heir; then we might have had an alternative to rally around."

"There *is* Isabella," Balian noted.

"Ah, yes. Isabella—and Humphrey de Toron? Don't make me laugh, Balian. The boy's more feminine that some girls I know—his mother, for a start. You have to wonder if he isn't, you know, a sodomist."

"Barry! Where do you get such ideas? You hardly know the boy. When was the last time you saw him?"

"Not so long ago as you might think. I too stopped at Kerak on my way back from reconnaissance. If anyone could make a man out of a boy, it's that bastard Châtillon, but Humphrey's still—I don't know—*soft*."

"Ernoul says he can read and write not only Latin and French, but Arabic."

"A lot of good that's going to do him!" Barry scoffed.

"Speaking it certainly has its advantages, and reading it is valuable, too—for one thing, we'd be able to read intercepted messages, particularly when we shoot down their carrier pigeons." Balian was speaking from experience. His archers had brought down a Saracen carrier pigeon the week before, but his entire garrison had stood about, baffled and frustrated. Ibrahim did not come from a class of men who had learned to read and write, and Balian had been forced to seek out Ibelin's remaining imam and ask him to translate. He was not convinced the man had been honest about it. The translated message had been too bland and vague. Balian had the distinct feeling that the imam had hidden something from him. Then again, the messages entrusted to carrier pigeons might also be encoded in some way. How would he know?

"No one would object to Humphrey being a scholar," Barry pointed out, "if he also had his grandfather's courage and political acumen. The old man could also read and write Arabic, if I remember correctly, but he was a lion on the battlefield and a fox in negotiations as well."

"The boy's only fifteen," Balian defended Isabella's fiancé.

"And at fifteen I had seized my inheritance and joined in the invasion of Egypt at the head of my troops. Humphrey and the knights of Toron, in contrast, are fighting under Châtillon's banner as if the boy were still a child!"

Balian abstained from pointing out that his brother had actually been sixteen before he took part in the first invasion of Egypt. Instead he nodded and took his leave.

Outside, his camp had been set up with his own tent in the center, surrounded by no less than ten smaller tents shared by the knights under his command. The Turcopoles and foot soldiers had no tents, but each troop had a fire over which they could cook food, and they had spread out mats around these on which to roll out their bedding. Ibelin inspected his camp, greeting the various knights and sergeants, by name if he could remember them, or with a smile if he could not.

The smells coming from the various pots were strong and savory, since at this stage in the campaign the men were still living on the food they'd brought from home. Garlic and onions in abundance, of course, but plenty of pork fat and seasoned lamb, too. Some of the stews even contained fresh produce like leeks and carrots. They'd get to the lentils with salted meat when the fresh things ran out.

In his tent, Gabriel and Ernoul had unpacked the mats and furniture and made up his bed, while his knights had spread out their pallets around the edges of the tent. In the center was a collapsible table. His thirst quenched with his brother's water, Ibelin asked for wine as he sank down on one of the folding stools. They'd spent the previous night at Nablus, collecting the knights and troops of his wife's lordship. This meant they'd slept and fed themselves well in the rich and fertile valley and were not particularly tired from the modest ride today. The horses, particularly, were in good form, because the weather had started to cool and some sporadic rains had produced fresh green grass for grazing after the dryness of summer fodder.

Ernoul, as usual, was quicker than Gabriel when it came to serving, and he handed Balian a goblet brimming with a wine the delicate color of translucent rubies. "May I have permission to go find Humphrey de Toron, my lord? I've got something to give him." Maria Zoë had tracked down a copy of the *Odyssey* via a Greek book-dealer in Jerusalem, and she had translated part of it for Ernoul. He had carefully noted down her words onto a roll of papyrus and made a copy as a gift for Humphrey.

"Are the horses watered?" Balian asked back.

"Of course, my lord. I'm not a novice anymore." Ernoul frowned with annoyance at the implication he would have neglected one of his most elementary duties.

"We'll see about that," Balian growled, glancing at Gabriel, who nodded reassuringly. "All right, go see if you can find him, but be back before darkness."

"Yes, my lord!"

Ernoul was gone before his lord could change his mind, and Ibelin signaled to Gabriel to come help him out of his hauberk. Before Gabriel could respond, however, shouting erupted outside. Frowning, Balian stood, waving Gabriel aside, and went to look out the tent flap. A troop of royal Turcopoles were cutting through the Ibelin-Nablus camp at a rash pace, causing men to curse and complain. Balian stepped out of his tent to demand that they slow down, but then he recognized the commander: it was the very man he had once commanded during the Homs expedition eight years ago. "Amos!" he called out sharply. "What's going on?"

"Salah ad-Din is trying to seize the springs at La Tubanie!" the Maronite shouted back. "I've got to warn the Regent!"

Balian waved him on, then turned and ducked inside his tent. "Helmet! Then go tack up Centurion!" he ordered Gabriel before turning to Sir Bartholomew. "Bart, muster my knights and Turcopoles!"

With his helmet under his arm, Balian hurried across to his brother's tent. "Salah ad-Din's trying to take the springs at La Tubanie!" he announced without preamble.

"How do you know that?" Ramla asked, but it was a rhetorical question; he was already snapping his fingers at his squires to bring his armor as he downed the rest of his wine. His knights reared up from whatever they were doing and started arming without an order being given.

Because the men of Ramla, Ibelin, and Nablus had been at ease, it took nearly half an hour for them to arm, tack up their horses, and muster. By then the Constable had already led a strong force of royal knights out of the camp. They followed at a good but not breakneck pace—until the unmistakable sounds of battle wafted over the contours of the low hill ahead of them.

Ramla and Ibelin were riding side by side at the head of their mounted troops. They heard the squeal of horses and the clang of weapons at the same moment. They looked at one another and then spurred forward together, their horses racing each other as they urged them forward.

As they came around the bend in the road, they saw chaos. The level area nearest the springs was littered with Saracen corpses, suggesting that the Saracens had already seized the springs by the time Aimery de Lusignan arrived. Now, however, the elder Lusignan was surrounded by enemy troops, and his knights were going down with appalling regularity as the Saracen archers targeted their horses from close range.

Ramla didn't even look back to be sure his men were with him. He couched his lance and spurred straight into the melee. Ibelin took a moment to ensure his knights were ready, checking Centurion as he tried to sprint after Ramla's stallion. Centurion hated seeing the tail of another stallion, and he responded to his rider's checks by rearing up in frustration. Within a quarter-minute, however, Sir Galvin and Sir Sylvester, a new and ambitious young knight, had spurred forward. When Centurion dropped back onto his forefeet, Ibelin could drop the reins and give the horse his head as he pulled his shield into place and couched his lance.

They smashed into the thin line of Saracens separating them from the Constable and rolled right over them. Their heavy horses knocked over the smaller Arab horses while they killed or unseated the Saracen horsemen. They swept through and past Ramla and his son-in-law, both fighting furiously against more than one opponent, and crashed into the Saracens beyond. Ibelin's lance glanced imperfectly off the first shield he aimed at, but embedded itself in the second and snapped, and he dropped it to draw his sword.

By now some of the momentum of the charge had dissipated, but Ibelin could sense uncertainty in the enemy. The riders around him were fighting halfheartedly, as if unsure if they should fight or flee. The Saracen troops were not fighting coherently, leading Ibelin to suspect that either the Constable or Ramla had managed to bring down the commanding emir. Even as he parried fierce blows with his shield and sword, he sensed other riders spinning away, refusing combat.

A glance to the right to verify this impression almost cost him his life. An exceptionally large Saracen managed to get around his shield-guard and lunge at him. Ibelin flung himself to the right to avoid the thrust, and Centurion jumped sideways to get his weight back under his rider again. That leap enabled Ibelin to swing his right arm across his chest and sever the arm holding the sword that had nearly killed him before its owner could lift it again. Then he used his shield to knock the stunned man off his horse and continued forward, wielding his sword with brutal efficiency as his heart pounded in retrospective panic. Around him other knights surged forward, leaving him momentarily alone in the eye of the storm.

From this perspective of temporary calm, it was clear that the enemy had indeed been routed. Hundreds of riders were streaming eastward. There were so many, in fact, that the road was becoming jammed, and riders were taking to the hills on either side.

As Ibelin watched, some of the Frankish knights started after the fleeing Saracens—only be cut off by the Constable, who put himself between the Frankish knights and the retreating enemy. He thrust one man halfway off his horse to get him to obey. Although Ibelin was too far away to hear what he was saying, he was gesturing to the men not to pursue. Ibelin nodded mental approval. Control of the springs was the strategic issue at stake; all too often in the past, pursuing Frankish knights had been led into an ambush.

Ibelin sat back and picked up his reins to signal to Centurion it was time to halt. Those Saracens who had been slow to disengage were now being slaughtered systematically by the better-armored Frankish knights. Ibelin felt no pressing need to take part in that. They had secured the springs, and that was all that mattered.

The Constable trotted up beside him. "Well met, Ibelin," he remarked with a weary smile, his eyes in the shade of his helmet and its nosepiece.

"We were bored," Ibelin quipped back.

"Well, thank God for that!" The Constable dropped his chin, and with his right hand raised the front of his surcoat to wipe the sweat off the lower part of his face.

Ramla trotted over, grinning under the nosepiece of his helmet. "Well, that was pretty easy. Let's hope it was a prologue of things to come."

"No. Let's hope *not*," Aimery answered grimly, taking the brothers by surprise. They stared at him, puzzled; they had almost no casualties to hundreds of Saracen dead and wounded all across the floor of the valley—and control of the vital springs.

"My ass of a brother didn't have a clue about how important these springs were! If I hadn't happened to be with him when the Turcopoles reported what was happening, and if I hadn't happened to have a hundred men already mounted, we might have lost the springs. You notice *he* didn't reinforce me!"

Ramla and Ibelin exchanged a look of foreboding mixed with déjà vu; this news only confirmed their low opinion of the younger Lusignan.

Aimery's near brush with death made his tongue loose. "Guy's in love with the trappings of command, not the substance. He doesn't have an ounce of competence! He panics under pressure and he dithers. He's a bedroom hero and nothing more!"

Jerusalem, early October 1183

"Look," Daniel coaxed. "Doesn't it make even me look comely?" He held the silver mask over his own face and confronted the King, who was lying in bed, propped upon pillows.

"You're always comely, Daniel," Baldwin replied, with a weary smile that only made his deformed face more hideous.

"Your grace, your hands and feet are covered with bandages and clothes; why shouldn't we cover your face as well? If you don't like this particular mask, we can commission another one. You can choose whatever visage you like—you could even change it from day to day!" Daniel suggested eagerly.

Baldwin sighed. "The only face I want is the one I had before. . . ."

"We asked the silversmith to try to reproduce it," Daniel admitted, looking down at the mask in his hand, "but he wasn't skilled enough. Or maybe he just couldn't remember what you looked like before. . . ."

"I'll wear it if you can't stand the sight of me anymore," Baldwin offered, "but otherwise, now that I've turned over the affairs of state to my brother-in-law, why do I need to hide?"

"It's not for me," Daniel hastened to assure him. "It's just that your sister thought . . ." Daniel looked nervously down at the mask again. The Countess of Jaffa had charged him with making Baldwin wear this. She'd told him she couldn't bear the sight of her brother's face another day. Daniel knew she would blame him for failing to convince the King to wear the mask, and Princess Sibylla could be hell on earth when she was displeased.

Baldwin caught his breath at the mention of his sister, and after a moment he repeated slowly and deliberately, "My sister." It wasn't a question by the time it came out of his mouth, because now that it was out in the open, it was so obvious. His sister was somehow ever present—yet never really at hand. His mother had repeatedly assured him she was here, but she had never come close enough for him to see her with his dimming eyes.

"My sister wants me to wear the mask," he concluded.

Daniel nodded vigorously. "She—she says she loves you too much to see you like this."

"Yes," Baldwin said stoically. "Too much."

Sibylla had always been attracted to beauty, he reminded himself, striving for the thousandth time to find an excuse for his sister. But the words rang falsely even in his own head. If she loved him so much, then surely she would see beyond his deformed face to his heart and soul? Surely she would care more about what he was feeling than what she was seeing? Like Ibrahim.

Baldwin suddenly realized he had not seen or heard from Ibrahim in days. The thought distracted him from his sister's pseudo-love. "Daniel, where is Ibrahim? He hasn't been with me for days. He hasn't fallen ill, has he? He didn't catch the fever, did he?" Even as he spoke, Baldwin was seized with fear that Ibrahim might be dead. Old people, like children, were the most vulnerable to fevers, and Baldwin could distinctly remember Ibrahim at his bedside during the worst stage of his fever, when he had been half mad and had thrashed around in the bed trying to escape his worthless body. Ibrahim had come and calmed him, cooing to him in Arabic.

Daniel looked up in alarm. This was the first day in a month that they had been alone together. It was the first time Daniel had seen the King lucid and completely free of fever. "Didn't . . ." Daniel started.

"Didn't what?" Baldwin asked.

"Didn't the Countess of Jaffa tell you?"

"He's dead?" Baldwin asked, rearing up from his pillows in alarm, his grief so great that it gave him strength.

Daniel shook his head vigorously.

Baldwin sank back onto the pillows, exhausted from even this little rush of adrenalin. "Christ be praised for that. But where is he, then? Is he ill?"

"No," Daniel admitted, "no, the Countess of Jaffa complained that he only got in the way and underfoot—"

Baldwin was sitting bolt upright again. "She didn't—she *couldn't* have said that!" he protested, yet his tone and expression belied his words. It was as if he were hearing these very words again in his memory, as if he had recorded them in his subconscious and they were echoing now in his conscious mind.

Daniel could not meet his eye, because he was ashamed he had not done more to defend Ibrahim at the time. He muttered, "She said he's too old to serve, and sent him away."

"What?" Baldwin protested in shame and outrage. "Sent him away? Without my consent! And where? Where is he now?" Baldwin demanded.

"I don't know, your grace," Daniel mumbled shamefacedly.

"But how could you just let him go?" Baldwin wanted to know. Reproach was in the King's words, making Daniel realize that his lord knew how jealous he had been of the love the King showed the old Muslim slave.

"I—I was too concerned about you at the time, your grace," Daniel defended himself lamely. "We all thought you were about to die."

"All the more reason to ensure poor Ibrahim was not thrown out! He has no family like you have, Daniel. He has no one in the whole world. No where to go. You must find him. You must go—" Baldwin had been about to order Daniel to go to the hospice of the Hospital—but then he realized Ibrahim would never seek solace in a Christian institution, and there was no mosque or Muslim community in Jerusalem either.

"I think he might have gone to Ibelin," Daniel ventured. "He said Lord Balian had promised to take him in. . . ."

Baldwin leveled reproachful eyes on Daniel. "Ibelin is fifty miles away! How is poor Ibrahim supposed to get there? He's at least seventy years old!"

Daniel looked down at his feet.

"Daniel, I hold you responsible for Ibrahim's welfare. You must send a man to Ibelin at once to see if Ibrahim is safely there. If Balian has given him a home, then we will let him be—but in the name of the Virgin Mary, if he is *not* there, I will not let you rest until you have found him and brought him back to me."

"Yes, your grace," Daniel muttered.

"Leave me," Baldwin ordered, lying back on his pillows and closing his eyes.

"But, your grace—" Daniel protested, knowing that without Ibrahim there was no one but himself to help the King do anything, now that he had lost the use of all his limbs and was almost blind.

"Wait outside the door. I'll call if I need you," Baldwin insisted, without opening his eyes or stirring until he heard the door close behind Daniel.

When he was alone, Baldwin tried to sort out his thoughts.

It had seemed so natural to give up the burden of ruling when he was ill. It had been such a relief. "Yes, Guy can be Regent," he had told his mother—anything but the smothering sense of a duty he could not fulfill. He had just wanted to rest, to die in peace, without the guilty conscience of leaving the Kingdom ungoverned.

"You'll retain Jerusalem, of course," his mother had promised. "And an annual income of ten thousand pieces of gold."

What did he want with an income of ten thousand gold pieces when he was dead? And of course he would retain Jerusalem, because he would be buried beside his father and uncle in the Holy Sepulcher.

Only he wasn't dead yet. He drew a deep breath. The room smelled slightly foul—from unchanged sheets, a dirty garderobe, and rotting bandages. Ibrahim had never left his bandages lying around, nor let the garderobe get dirty, either. Daniel—Daniel was strong still and devoted to him, but he hated cleaning the garderobe and, not unnaturally, he hated touching the used bandages, too.

How could it have taken him this long to register that Ibrahim was missing? Baldwin reproached himself. How long had it been? A week? Two? Even three? Christ, forgive me! He squirmed uneasily in his guilt, and then went still with a paralyzing sense of fear.

He was alone. Utterly alone. Everyone who truly loved him had been chased away. The Archbishop of Tyre, after being passed over for the post of Patriarch of Jerusalem to make way for his mother's lover, had withdrawn to Tyre and never attended on him any more. Tante Marie had been turned into a bitter enemy because they'd taken her little girl away from her—to please his mother. Balian had been alienated first by the insult to his brother, and then by the loss of his stepdaughter. And now poor, harmless Ibrahim—thrown out in his old age without so much as a pension.

Baldwin felt cold, but he could not pull up the covers on his own. He lay on the bed feeling the chill gnawing at his rotting bones, but he did not cry out for Daniel, because he felt God's wrath in the cold around him.

"You have created this cold by your own faithlessness," God said in his conscience. "You have replaced those who loved you with those who love only the power they derive from you. You have turned your back on love and basked in its counterfeit."

Baldwin felt the urge to cry, but he had long since lost the ability to shed tears. Instead he began to writhe in silent agony. With a clarity and vividness that only existed in his mind, he remembered how Ibrahim had come to put him to bed the day the doctor suggested he had leprosy; the other servants were all in hiding or had run away altogether, but Ibrahim had smiled at him and tucked him into bed. Next he remembered the day Balian had come into his life and put his arm around his shoulders—risking his own health and life to give comfort to a frightened child. He remembered, too, the day his father died and he had been so terrified of becoming king, but Balian had knelt and offered him fealty, telling him he could be king without the use of his hands. "You will be king by the force of your mind and the courage of your heart," Balian had said. Even when the leprosy had attacked his face, Balian had helped carry him—with Ibrahim. They *loved* him. They would not have asked that he hide behind a mask.

Baldwin was racked with dry sobs as he thought next of Tante Marie. She had kissed his hands the day she returned to court, making his mother and sister gasp because *they* had not dared. She had brought little Isabella to him, while Sibylla insisted she could not risk her son's life in his presence. And how had he rewarded Tante Marie? By taking Isabella away from her.

Baldwin's writhing was becoming more violent, and his breathing came in gasps. How could he have done that? How could he have let his mother and Sibylla talk him into such an act of cruelty? What were Tante Marie and Balian going to do to or with Isabella that was so dangerous to him? Nothing! *They loved him.*

Maybe it was good to marry Isabella to Humphrey before she was old enough to be driven by sexual desire like Sibylla, but why hadn't he ordered Humphrey to go to live with Balian and Maria Zoë, rather than tear poor little Isabella away from the people she loved and who loved her? How could he destroy a family after suffering so much from the destruction of his own?

The voices of his mother and sister seemed to be everywhere around him—chattering, nagging, vowing their love to him while cooing poisoned advice and begging him to reward their lovers. Guy, Heraclius, Guy, Heraclius. He had made their men the most powerful men in the Kingdom: the head of the State and the Church respectively. And where were they now? Probably in bed with their lovers, while he lay here alone in the growing stench of unchanged bandages and linens and a dirty garderobe. He was starting to shiver and his teeth began to chatter—but he still did not call to Daniel, because he had brought this upon himself. God was right to punish him.

Abruptly, he felt warmth returning.

He went still. Where was the warmth coming from? He had managed to wriggle under the covers a little, but he was sure it was more than that. He could sense someone was in the room with him.

"Hello?" he called out, trying to see into the shadows. "Who's there?"

No one answered, but he still felt the presence of someone gentle and benevolent. He closed his eyes to feel it more intensely. He felt her—he was sure the presence was feminine—approach the bed, and he felt her touch his hideous face and stroke his deformed cheeks. He felt her kiss his forehead, and he knew it could only be the Virgin herself, for no other woman would kiss a leper like this.

She didn't speak, but he understood her nevertheless. Love did not die, even if it was rejected. He did not have to be alone. It was up to him whom he chose to favor. He was still the King—by the force of his mind and the courage of his heart.

Chapter 10

Jerusalem, late October 1183

ALTHOUGH HE HAD RESISTED THE MASK at first, Baldwin was beginning to appreciate it. Daniel fixed it to his face with white linens that encased his throat and brow, and then set the crown of Jerusalem, which had once graced his helmet, upon his head. The effect was unquestionably impressive—Baldwin could tell by the looks of those who encountered him in his mask.

Guy de Lusignan was no exception. Baldwin could not remember a time when the handsome Frenchman had not looked on him with a twisted mixture of pity and disgust—until he was confronted by the mask.

Guy valued his own looks highly, of course. After all, he owed his extraordinary rise from obscurity to Regent of a kingdom to his looks alone. At least, Baldwin had been unable to discover any other quality that explained Sibylla's devotion to him. And because he was vain, he spent a great deal of time and expense on his appearance, particularly since he had been too poor to afford finery in his youth.

His long blond hair was freshly washed and brushed until it was as fine and light as corn silk as it hung to his shoulders on either side of his clean-shaven, well-molded face. He wore a surcoat of the finest purple silk trimmed with gold embroidery, over a long-sleeved blue silk shirt with elaborately embroidered cuffs. His sword belt was decorated with gold plaques bearing the crosses of Jerusalem. The scabbards of his sword and his dagger were encased in silver filigree work, obviously of Damascene origin. The sword itself had a large polished lapis lazuli in the pommel. His over-the-knee suede boots were dyed purple to match his surcoat, and his gold spurs glittered as if studded with crystals of some kind. He wore rings on all his fingers.

Baldwin had summoned the Count of Jaffa two days ago, as soon as the army of Jerusalem had dispersed after Salah ad-Din withdrew across the Jordan. There had been no battle beyond that first skirmish by the springs of La Tubanie. Instead, the two massive armies had camped opposite each other for three weeks, and then both had returned from whence they'd come.

The Count of Jaffa had been summoned two days ago, but the Count had not come. Instead, he'd sent word that he had to "attend his wife"—who, it seemed, was pregnant at last. However, he'd arrived today without warning, and had been annoyed to be kept waiting while the King was dressed to receive him. Baldwin had heard him bullying the guards at the entrance to the audience chamber, demanding entrance "immediately" and threatening to just burst in upon the King. "Damn it! I'm the Regent! You have no right to stand in my way!" But the guards were used to impertinent barons and pompous bishops and had stood their ground.

When at last Jaffa had been admitted, he'd been flushed with fury and ready to vent his anger on a man he considered worse than useless. Baldwin was certain that Guy de Lusignan thought his leper king ought to be—and would be better off—dead. However, instead of a lump of deformed flesh sweating and gasping on a bed, as Jaffa had last seen him and expected now, the Regent was confronted by a man sitting on a throne, dressed in beautiful court robes and wearing a crown over a silver mask.

Guy de Lusignan's eyes widened as he froze. "Who are you?" he demanded.

"King Baldwin IV of Jerusalem," Baldwin answered steadily, his voice echoing inside the mask.

"How do I know that? Anyone could wear a mask and a crown!" Guy countered.

"But not speak with my ruined voice. You know my voice, Jaffa." It was not a question.

Guy abandoned the pretense of not believing this was the King, and his eyes flickered covetously to the crown before he lifted his chin and declared resentfully, "You sent for me."

Baldwin considered demanding that Guy address him more respectfully, but decided against it. "Yes. Don't you want to give an account of yourself and this last campaign against Salah ad-Din?"

"Why should I?"

"Because many voices have been raised in criticism."

"What voices?" Guy demanded angrily. "Who dares?"

"This is not a kingdom populated by cowards, my lord. Men who risk their lives as often as my barons and knights do are not afraid to say what they think. And they, my lord, are men with more experience in war than you. They tell me you made many mistakes, showed very poor judgment, and cost us a possible victory."

"Really? How easy it is to criticize! What have you been doing? Listening to the whining of Raymond de Tripoli? He's a disloyal coward," Guy declared dismissively.

Baldwin did not bother to answer the self-serving accusation against Tripoli, preferring instead to note: "I have been told that you did not bring provisions to maintain the army in the field. After the ten days of rations the men carry had run out, they had nothing to eat."

"I'm not a butler! I'm Regent," Guy retorted haughtily.

"When the royal army is called up on feudal service, it is the responsibility of the Crown to provide provisions."

"Nobody told me that."

"Your brother the Constable did," Baldwin corrected him.

"Salah ad-Din had already crossed the Jordan! The important thing was to muster the army and face him."

"You had ten days to procure and deliver the provisions, while the men were still eating what they had brought with them."

"I had more important things to do."

"Such as?"

"Such as! Such as! I was commanding the army!"

"An army that was disintegrating before your eyes as men's rations ran out and they deserted."

"If men deserted, it was because their lords weren't maintaining discipline. If I caught any of the royal men deserting, I had them flogged 'till their bones showed through what was left of their flesh!"

"Yes. I heard that. First you let your men starve, and then flogged them for seeing to their stomachs. My barons were outraged by your lack of foresight, and my bishops by your lack of compassion."

"Well, I didn't have any choice if the army wasn't going to disintegrate altogether."

"You had the choice of fulfilling your duties and bringing up provisions. I understand Ibelin brought up over a hundred wagons from Nablus to feed his own and his brother's troops, while Tripoli brought provisions from Tiberias for his troops as well."

"Well, there you are. If everyone had done their duty, there wouldn't have been any problem."

"Correct—because it was *your* duty, my lord of Jaffa, no one else's, and if *you* had fulfilled it there would indeed have been no problems. Ibelin and Tripoli are within their rights to submit a bill to the Crown for the provisions they provided."

Guy shrugged. "Fine. Is that what this is all about? A couple of whining barons who want to be paid—probably at a nice profit—for bringing up supplies? Really, you didn't have to send for me to present procurement bills."

"No, you're right, my lord. The more serious accusation comes from the Grand Masters of the Temple and Hospital, supported by the Bishops of Bethlehem and Nazareth. They tell me that two monasteries and one convent were sacked and burned by Salah ad-Din's troops while you sat idly by with the largest Christian army ever mustered in Outremer."

"The churchmen understand nothing about strategy."

"The Templars and Hospitallers know nothing about strategy?" Baldwin replied, incredulous. "You are presumptuous, my lord."

Guy de Lusignan continued as if he had not been interrupted. "Salah ad-Din attacked the monasteries to provoke me. He was trying to lure me away from the wells and springs around which we camped. He thought he could cut me off from water and then destroy us all. But I was too clever for him; I refused to take the bait."

"At the price of one hundred thirty-three monks' lives and the freedom and honor of twenty-eight nuns."

Guy shrugged. "What do you think our casualties would have been if we'd been cut off from water?"

"The lives of fighting men rather than men and women of God. The Master of the Temple was particularly outraged. He said his Order has vowed to come to the rescue of any Christians attacked by Saracens, but you physically prevented him from doing his duty before God. You stopped him from riding out of camp to the rescue of these men and women who have devoted their lives to the service of Christ."

"How could I allow such a large contingent of troops to separate from the main body? It would have invited attack by Salah ad-Din—either on the Templars or on the rest of us, while we were separated."

"The Grand Master reminded me that the Temple does not answer to any secular authority, and that the participation of his Order in any muster is voluntary."

"I know. He shouted that at me, too, but I'm not interested in legal technicalities. I restrained the Master and his senior officers in my tent until it was too late to do anything. I'm not ashamed of that; it was the only way to keep the army intact."

"A starving army is not intact," Baldwin countered.

Guy groaned and rolled his eyes. "Back to bickering about full bellies, are we? Next time I'll be sure to bring the senior clerk of the household with me on campaign!"

"Hopefully, you'll do more than that. Hopefully, next time you will be sure your troops and their horses are adequately provisioned."

"Yes, yes, God, yes! If only to keep you and my nanny brother happy!" Guy promised in exasperation.

"Good." Baldwin hoped Guy had learned his lesson. "Then there is one more thing."

"Really?" Guy asked impatiently.

"Yes. When I turned over the Kingdom to you, it was agreed I would continue to hold Jerusalem for my own use."

"Yes, I remember," Guy answered, bored.

"But the cold here is much more painful to me than the gentle coastal climate. I would like to swap Jerusalem for Tyre."

Guy was completely unprepared for this request, and he asked in disbelief, "Tyre?"

"Yes. When I was there this past spring, I felt better than I have for a long time. I came down with the fever when I returned to Jerusalem."

"Tyre is the richest city in the Kingdom," Guy noted.

"That's not the reason I want it," Baldwin protested. "It's—"

Guy cut him off. "It may not be the reason *you* want it, but it's the reason *I* do! I'm not going to give you Tyre for Jerusalem! That would mean giving up the largest source of income I have! No, absolutely not! My God! First you call me here to insult me, and then you expect me to do you a favor! To give up my best source of income!" Guy de Lusignan was working himself into a rage of righteous indignation. "No! You may think I'm incompetent, but I'm not going to be tricked into giving up the greatest prize I have! Sibylla will be outraged when she hears you tried to take from her the place she likes best in the entire Kingdom! She'll—"

"How *is* Sibylla?" Baldwin broke into Guy's tirade.

"What?" Guy asked, bewildered to be interrupted when he was in full swing.

"How is Sibylla? I don't think I've seen her since the day you were named Regent."

"She's pregnant and taking care of herself."

"Of course. I see. If that's your final word?"

"On Tyre, you mean? Of course it is."

"Then there is nothing more to talk about for now. Leave me."

Guy had no desire to stay, but he was just as obviously annoyed to be dismissed like this. With an audible snort, he turned and stormed out of the audience chamber. Wearily, Baldwin leaned his head on the back of his chair and closed his eyes. It was getting so cold in Jerusalem. . . .

Kerak, mid-October 1183

Guests had been arriving for days. Oultrejourdain's vassals and their ladies had come not only to join in the wedding celebration but to fulfill various functions, while the wealthier burghers and settlers from across the barony came bearing gifts with an eye to gaining favor. Soon, rooms long left vacant or used for storage were filling up with people, while the stables were overflowing with beasts. The castle began to feel crowded, although only the Count of Edessa with his sister the Queen Mother and his niece Princess Sibylla but none of the other prominent guests had yet arrived.

Eloise of Amman had been given the honor of acting as Isabella's maid of honor and tasked with helping fit her wedding dress, because Stephanie had no time or inclination for the task. Eloise, on the other hand, was very adept with a needle, having spent so much of her life wielding one in the convent. She worked diligently, trying to make the gown Stephanie had worn at her marriage to Humphrey's father fit the much slimmer, shorter and younger Isabella. She held the pins between her lips and worked silently, only hissing in disapproval if Isabella fidgeted or fussed.

Isabella was at an age when clothes did not particularly interest her—certainly not a gown that Stephanie de Milly had once worn. Indeed, the entire wedding interested her far less than what would happen afterwards. Oultrejourdain had announced that after the wedding, Humphrey could set up his own household.

Eloise put in the last pin and sat back on her heels. "That will have to do. Take the gown off carefully so I can get to work on it."

Isabella tried to wriggle out of the gown and promptly succeeded in pricking herself. "Ow!" she exclaimed loudly and irritably.

"Be careful!" Eloise admonished.

Isabella was going to protest that she *was* being careful, when a furious knocking on the door interrupted her and Humphrey called through the wooden barrier: "Isabella! I think they're coming!"

"Come in and help me!" Isabella answered, anxious to get out of the gown as fast as possible.

"Stop!" Eloise shouted to Humphrey. "Your lady is disrobed!" Then, turning on Isabella, she scolded in a deeply shocked voice: "You shameless hussy! What were you thinking of?" As she removed the pinned gown herself, she added, "Do you want a man to see you in nothing but your shift?"

"Humphrey's seen me in my shift before—and he'll see me in less after the wedding," Isabella answered matter-of-factly, provoking a vivid blush from the older woman, who turned away and concentrated on collecting fallen pins rather than answering.

Isabella grabbed the gown she had been wearing before the fitting and pulled it hastily over her head. "I'm coming!" she shouted to Humphrey, looking around desperately for her shoes. At last she spotted them under the bed and pulled them on, hopping on one foot after the other before bursting out of her chamber to join Humphrey.

By the time Isabella and Humphrey reached the triangular inner ward, the lead horses were already through the barbican and the usual bustle of grooms, squires and household officials had seized the ward. But Isabella had already spotted her mother and she plunged into the chaos, oblivious to fractious horses and protocol. "Mama! Mama!" she shouted as she ran.

Maria Zoë flung herself off her mare and opened her arms just in time to catch Isabella.

"Mama! Mama! I can't believe you're here at last!" Isabella clung to her, but no tighter than Maria Zoë held her daughter.

"Sweetheart! Sweetheart!" Maria Zoë muttered repeatedly into Isabella's chestnut curls until she loosened her hold and begged, "Isabella! Let me look at you!" She took a step back to hold Isabella at arm's length, only to pull her close again. Isabella had grown so much, and she was so thin, that Maria Zoë would have questioned if she had been getting enough to eat, if it hadn't been for the strength of her embrace and the rich color of her cheeks. Isabella looked and felt healthy. She was just eighteen months older than she had been when Maria Zoë had seen her last.

A shadow fell over them, and Maria Zoë looked up into the sneering face of Stephanie de Milly. "My, my," the Lady of Oultrejourdain exclaimed dismissively.

Maria Zoë raised her eyebrows. "What's the matter? Have you never seen filial love before? No, probably not—since you clearly never earned it!"

Isabella giggled in delight as she looked up at her tormentor and stuck out her tongue. She knew she was being childish—but with her mother here, holding her, she felt she could afford to be a child again, even if only for a moment.

Meanwhile Maria Zoë pulled herself upright, still holding Isabella protectively in her left arm, and held out her right hand with the coronation ring of Jerusalem, until Madame d'Oultrejourdain dutifully dipped a curtsy to her and muttered, "Welcome to Kerak, madame."

Maria Zoë was too furious to answer this woman who had stood between her and Isabella for three years. She turned her back on her hostess and addressed Isabella instead. "Do you know where I am to stay?"

"In my chamber, in my bed, for tonight, anyways, while—Where's Uncle Balian?" Isabella noticed belatedly that her stepfather was missing.

"The King has summoned the High Court to Jerusalem. Balian had to go, of course, and Uncle Barry, but I've brought your new aunt Elizabeth and Eschiva." Maria Zoë looked behind at the rest of her entourage.

Because she commanded the knights of Nablus, she was in a position to provide a strong escort, a necessary precaution when venturing into Oultrejourdain. Both Eschiva and Elizabeth had been more than happy to take advantage of that escort, as soon as it became clear their husbands must first attend the High Court. "We all hope the High Court will not meet for long and that our husbands will make it down in time for the wedding," Maria Zoë commented.

Isabella wasn't listening. She had spotted Eschiva and ran to her childhood friend exuberantly. "Eschiva! Eschiva!" Eschiva felt ancient compared to the still childlike Isabella, and she smiled a little condescendingly, but Isabella didn't notice. She was continuing, "Oh, I can't believe you're finally here! As soon as the wedding's over, Humphrey and I are going to Toron! I'll be a real lady then, and you can come and visit!"

"This is your Aunt Elizabeth," Eschiva answered with gentle reproach, because Isabella was ignoring the stranger. Isabella dutifully turned and offered Elizabeth a kiss on both cheeks, but then she turned back to Eschiva. "Is Beth with you?"

"Yes, there, on the little donkey." Eschiva smiled as she pointed, for the slender maid looked a little ridiculous on the tiny donkey beside the tall horse Dawit was riding.

Brought up like a good Muslim girl, Beth had never learned to ride, and she had a fear of horses that not even Dawit had been able to take from her, but the donkey she had rescued was so devoted to her that she trusted it completely. Eschiva thought the donkey would rather die than harm Beth. Isabella ran to Beth, and the girls hugged each other fiercely.

"I wanted to come to you, Isabella!" Beth whispered. "And so did Eschiva, but the Constable wouldn't let us."

"I understand," Isabella replied generously. That was the past. Her ordeal was over. She was back among the people she loved, confident that she was never going to be separated from them again.

With so many guests and still more arriving by the hour, it was hard to get a moment alone with her daughter. But finally, after the elaborate dinner, Maria Zoë managed to pull Isabella aside on the pretext of showing her the donkey Beth had rescued. They made their way to the stables, away from the other women. There, despite the bustling of the grooms and squires offloading, watering, and feeding, they found a corner where they could sit together on a few bales of straw, ignored by the busy servants.

Maria Zoë could not keep her arms off her little girl. She held her close, and Isabella snuggled against her just as she had when she was much younger. Indeed, Isabella quite unconsciously was acting younger than she had for years. It felt so good to be a child again.

"Princess," Maria Zoë opened, kissing the top of her head. "I'm so grateful that this wedding has given me a means to visit, but—but you're *so* young!" Maria Zoë could not get over the fact that her daughter was two years younger than she had been when she went to her marriage bed. There was a huge difference between eleven and thirteen!

"It's the only way we can get *away* from here," Isabella told her, her childishness dissolving as she set her mouth. All her longing—indeed her determination—to escape was naked in her voice.

"Yes, I suppose it is," Maria Zoë agreed, "but—but do you know what marriage means?"

"You mean the consummation?" Isabella asked bluntly without a trace of embarrassment. "Humphrey's promised he's not going to do that until I'm older and ready."

Maria Zoë was taken aback. "You mean you've talked to him about it?"

"Of course," Isabella told her candidly. "Who else should I have talked to?

Not Madame d'Oultrejourdain! Besides, Humphrey and I are friends, and he'd never do anything to hurt me. He promised me that."

Maria Zoë had seen too little of her future son-in-law to know how good Humphrey de Toron's promises were, but it was reassuring to think that he did not *intend* to rape his little bride. "I'm very, very pleased to hear that," she told her daughter honestly.

"You'll like Humphrey," Isabella assured her mother. "He's nice. It's just that Oultrejourdain badgers him. Once he's in Toron, you'll see. He'll surprise everyone. He's a true and gallant knight—oh, except Oultrejourdain hasn't knighted him. Uncle Balian could do that for him, couldn't he? He should be knighted, you know. It would mean a lot to him."

"Yes, sweetheart," Maria Zoë assured her, stroking her rich, long tresses, which she would soon have to cover under scarves and wimples. It seemed so ridiculous at her tender age! "Balian would be happy to do that—if not before—"

"My lady! We've been looking all over for you!" Rahel exclaimed breathlessly. "Eschiva and Elizabeth want to see Isabella's wedding gown before retiring for the night."

They left the stables and went together to Isabella's chamber in one of the towers of the castle.

"This is what Madame d'Oultrejourdain wants me to wear," Isabella said with a peeved expression. "She said she wore it at her wedding with Humphrey's father."

"Do you want to wear it?" her mother asked, feeling the silk between her fingers. It was of inferior quality to the silk she had brought—almost raw—and it had faded and frayed along the folds from nearly twenty years lying folded in a chest. In was as if Stephanie de Milly wanted Isabella to look shabby at her own wedding!

"Not particularly. I don't like the color," Isabella admitted.

"It's a fine gown," Eloise de Amman objected. She had invested so many hours getting the gown adjusted that she felt personally insulted by Isabella's rejection.

Maria Zoë turned to look at this sister-in-law she had not met before. Eloise's face was overly long, with a much too prominent nose and close-set eyes. But all those disadvantages could have been overcome by a sunny temperament or a ready wit. Eloise had neither. She seemed both dull and morose.

"When is your child due?" Maria Zoë asked gently, nodding toward her sister-in-law's swelling belly.

"In January, the end of January."

"You're welcome to come to Nablus for the lying-in, or Ibelin. Whichever you prefer. You'll find either castle more comfortable than here." Maria Zoë looked pointedly around the barren tower room to which Isabella had proudly led her. She had thought Ibelin was an inhospitable fortress the first time she saw it, but Ibelin was a pleasure garden compared to this. From the tower chambers of Ibelin one was only sixty feet above the ground, and looked out across the surrounding orchards or past the palms and the dunes to the brilliant blue of the Mediterranean. The view from here, in contrast, was a dizzying drop to the desert floor hundreds of feet below, and then a cracked and barren landscape of rocky hills and dry gullies across which only scrub brush grew.

"Thank you, madame," Eloise replied stiffly. "I will lie in wherever my lord husband orders."

Maria Zoë looked at her with a slight frown, but Eloise wouldn't meet her gaze.

"I'll talk to Henri," Maria Zoë decided, and then turned to pull out of her traveling bag a gown of shiny copper-colored silk with a golden sheen on the back side. "I thought you might like to wear this," she announced, as she shook out the worst wrinkles and spread the gown on the bed to gasps of delight from Isabella, Beth, and Eschiva all together.

"It's beautiful!" Isabella exclaimed as she held it up to herself, stroking the long sleeves lined with gold-colored silk.

"Oh, but I've made it too short!" Maria Zoë exclaimed in distress. "You've grown so much!"

"Surely we can fix that," Eschiva declared practically, leaning forward to check how large the hem was.

"What was that?" Elizabeth, sitting in the window seat overlooking the courtyard, asked in alarm.

"What?"

"There's something going on out in the ward." She leaned and unlatched the shutter to peer out.

"Probably just more guests arriving," Eloise surmised.

"Maybe my brother the King is coming to my wedding," Isabella suggested, revealing a hope she had harbored silently for weeks.

But with the shutter open the noise from outside was more distinct, and it was clear the shouting was angry or alarmed. Then a horn started blowing. "What does that mean?" Elizabeth asked. Trumpet signals were standardized throughout the Kingdom to ensure there was no confusion in time of war.

Maria Zoë answered soberly, "That's the signal calling the garrison to arms."

Elizabeth looked at Maria Zoë in shock and then hastily got out of her way, as Maria Zoë stepped into the window niche and bent forward to look out of the window. Torches were being lit and handed out as men poured through the barbican and spread out to the various tower stairs. Before long they heard men's feet pounding up the spiral stairs of the tower. There must have been a half-dozen men on the stairs, and their breathing was heavy and rasping as they hurried past.

Maria Zoë crossed briskly to the other side of the chamber and flung open the shutters of the window that looked out across the desert. The sight before her made her catch her breath and hold it. The desert was not empty, as it should have been. It was crawling with men and horses and fluttering banners lit up by torches.

"What is it?" Elizabeth demanded, fear making her voice unnaturally sharp.

"Yes, tell us what's going on." Eloise echoed in a frightened whine.

Maria Zoë looked over her shoulder at her daughter, and then back out at the host gathering in the darkness, as fear crawled its way up her spine. In her mind she was trying to calculate just how many men they had gathered here. Oultrejourdain, at least, had all his knights, and she had brought sixty fighting men from Nablus. Edessa would not have come with his sister and the Countess of Jaffa without a substantial force. Maybe three hundred men?

In a castle like this, that ought to be enough to fight off an assault—but in a siege the large number of wedding guests, with their escorts and servants, would devour stores at an alarming rate, maybe ten times faster than the garrison alone. Even more dangerous, the cisterns of a desert castle might be overtaxed by the number of people gathered here. Maria Zoë fought back from her consciousness the tales told of besieged garrisons reduced to eating rats and drinking dirty water until they died of disease like flies. She tried to focus on what she could see outside, trying now to estimate the size and character of the force besieging them. In the darkness it wasn't really possible, so she drew the shutters closed and turned to face the others.

She opened her mouth to speak, but something clattered on the wall just beside the window. The sound was so close and loud that Beth screamed in terror and Eschiva pulled her into her arms, as much to comfort herself as her maid. There was loud shouting from overhead as the noise repeated itself. A pair of feet tore down the stairs. A fist pounded furiously at the door and a man shouted, "Keep the shutters closed, for Christ's sake! They're shooting flaming arrows at us!"

"Who is shooting at us?" Elizabeth wanted to know.

"Salah ad-Din—with his entire host."

Tower of David, Jerusalem, late October 1183

Baldwin sat upon the throne with the baldachin of Jerusalem over his head, the crown on his brow, and his face concealed behind his silver mask. He could not move his limbs, and Sir Daniel stood behind the throne ready to respond to his slightest request. Despite the rain drenching the walls and gurgling in the gutters, the Tower of David was hot, and Baldwin was sweating under the bandages and layers of clothes designed to disguise his claw-like hands and toeless feet.

The recriminations against the Regent came fast and furiously, and Jaffa was decidedly at a disadvantage in the absence of the Count of Edessa and the Lord of Oultrejourdain, who usually took his side. The King, watching from his vantage of distanced neutrality on the throne, noticed that not only were the Count of Tripoli and the Lord of Ramla hammering away at an apparently helpless Guy de Lusignan, but the Constable of the Kingdom was eloquently silent. Aimery did not take part in the attacks upon his brother, but he made no move to defend him, either. That said everything.

The King knew that Ramla and Tripoli hated the younger Lusignan for their own reasons, but Aimery de Lusignan had backed his brother up to now—at least in public. Baldwin sighed, remembering how Oultrejourdain had once suggested Aimery would make a better husband for Sibylla than his younger brother. How very true! Aimery was a brave man—but more important, he was capable of thinking through the consequences of any action, and he knew how to make friends. Aimery was no less an outsider than Guy, but when he had been captured by the Saracens shortly after his arrival, King Amalric himself had paid his ransom. He had won the respect of the barons of Outremer by showing them respect first. Even as Constable, he listened to their counsel, took their sensibilities into account, and never acted as if he thought himself superior to them.

Even Ramla, Baldwin reflected, as he watched Balian's older brother gesture grandly and then point an accusing finger at the ineffectual Guy, would have made a better king. If nothing else, Ramla had the bearing of a king—he was tall and muscular, with a strong face. He was proud but not haughty, and more important, he was vigorous and decisive, unafraid of making mistakes.

Baldwin asked himself how he could have made such a fatal error as giving his sister to Guy de Lusignan. With both his mother and sister absent, it was as if the very air had cleared and he could see better. He could certainly see that Guy de Lusignan was not fit to wear the crown of Jerusalem, and that Tripoli, despite being slight of stature, pedantic, and cautious by nature, was no traitor. How could he have let that evil seed, planted by his mother, grow? Yes, he had resented being under Tripoli's tutelage as a youth; Tripoli had made it all too plain that he didn't expect Baldwin to live for long. But that was a far cry from being power-hungry and disloyal!

"Water," Baldwin whispered, turning his head to Sir Daniel.

Sir Daniel at once stepped back to the window niche behind the throne to pour from the waiting pitcher into a goblet. The niche looked out over the gate of the citadel, and Daniel's attention was distracted by a commotion near the gate. He frowned and knelt on the window seat to get a better look out of the narrow loop window. It looked for all the world as if a Bedouin had forced his way into the ward and was fighting off the men who tried to stop him. An assassin? Sir Daniel thought with alarm, but calmed himself. There were plenty of guards out there.

He drew back out of the window niche and brought the water to the King. He leaned across the arm of the throne, shielding the King from view, as he lifted the mask and held the goblet to Baldwin's lips.

The shouting from the ward was becoming audible in the audience chamber, and several of the men nearer the door turned to look over their shoulders. A moment later the door crashed open and a Bedouin burst in on the High Court of Jerusalem, his white robes drenched with rain and mud staining the skirts all the way to the knees. With a furious gesture, the man reached up and tore off his headdress, exposing the familiar but heavily bearded face of Henri d'Ibelin. Chatter erupted around the room while Sir Henri strode towards the throne and went down on one knee before the King.

"Your grace! Kerak is under siege. Salah ad-Din has brought his army from Damascus, completely investing it. He took the town in the first assault, and—"

The room exploded with curses and exclamations that drowned out Sir Henri. Some men demanded more information, while others insisted it could not be, and still others shouted that it was what Reynald de Châtillon deserved.

"Silence!" roared the Constable. "Hear Sir Henri out!"

"We barely managed to take in most of the townspeople, but we had to destroy the bridge across the fosse under the very feet of the men holding it against the enemy. We lost a dozen brave men." Henri's report elicited a grim response from his audience. All the men gathered in this room knew that the castle of Kerak was perched on the tip of a mountain ridge, protected on three sides by steep cliffs that fell hundreds of feet to the valley floor. They also knew that the town of Kerak sat on the same ridge to the north of the castle, and that an assault on the castle would invariably come from the north through the town. To prevent this, a man-made fosse roughly thirty feet wide and four hundred feet deep separated the castle from the town; the fosse could only be crossed by a wooden drawbridge. The men in the Tower of David understood that if the bridge was not raised in time, it would be necessary to destroy it, but they also sympathized with and admired the men who had died to hold it long enough for it to be hacked out from under them.

Henri d'Ibelin continued, "Salah ad-Din has deployed four siege engines in the town that keep the castle under continuous bombardment."

"What about the wedding?" someone thought to ask. Balian was too stunned to ask himself. He was torn between hope that the siege had started before Maria Zoë arrived and horror at the thought that Isabella was undoubtedly trapped inside.

"The marriage took place under enemy fire. Madame d'Oultrejourdain sent out part of the wedding feast to Salah ad-Din by lowering it down in a basket from one of the eastern towers. In return, the Sultan sent word he would not bombard the tower where the nuptials were taking place, if she would identify it for him with a white flag. It was during this exchange that I was able to slip out of the postern, disguised as you see me now. I made my way across the desert in the dark. With wedding guests and townsfolk crammed in the castle, I doubt food and water will last more than a month."

Other men were asking about their wives, while Barry clasped Balian on the shoulder and muttered, "Thank God Elizabeth left Godfrey behind."

"Is your son all you care about? Eschiva and Elizabeth are both trapped there, along with Maria Zoë and Isabella."

Barry answered irritably, "Of course I care about Eschiva and Elizabeth, but I'm still glad that at least Godfrey isn't there."

Balian had no chance to answer, because Guy de Lusignan was dramatically calling for the collected barons to take horse and rush to the relief of Kerak. His demand was as melodramatic as it was self-serving. He was clearly most interested in distracting attention from his miserable performance in the past campaign. Guy had, as usual, misjudged the temper of the men around him. His call to arms was met with deafening silence—broken only by a cool question from the Count of Tripoli: "Under your command, Jaffa? Never."

"What are you saying?" Guy asked back, incredulous. "I am Regent. A critical castle is under siege! Not just that, but half the fair ladies of the realm, including *both* of the royal princesses, are trapped inside. We cannot let Kerak, the princesses, the Dowager Queen," Guy made one of his elaborate French bows to Balian, "the Queen Mother," he now bowed to the King, "and all the other fair ladies fall into Saracen hands! Why, they'd be turned into harem slaves!"

His last dramatic claim earned only a contemptuous snort from Tripoli. Into Jaffa's baffled face the Count of Tripoli remarked, "Salah ad-Din is much too civilized—and self-interested—to enslave noblewomen. He'd hold them for ransom, nothing more."

"You can't honestly mean you're just going to sit here and let Kerak—with all the highest ladies of the land—fall into the hands of the Saracens!" Guy de Lusignan could not fathom what was happening.

"Of course not," Tripoli replied, and the silence of the others underlined the degree to which he had tacitly been accepted as their spokesman. "We will relieve Kerak—as soon as the King appoints a different Regent." As he finished he turned pointedly to King Baldwin, leaving the younger Lusignan gasping like a fish out of water, while his brother Aimery raised his eyebrows in evident amusement.

Baldwin sat up straighter in his throne and lifted his head to meet Tripoli's gaze. Things were taking an interesting turn.

Guy was blustering, "Regents can't just be appointed and dismissed! I was—"

"—not legally appointed," Tripoli interrupted him. "You never had the approval of the High Court."

Shouts of "Hear! Hear!" and "True!" erupted from across the room as other members of the Court voiced their support for Tripoli's audacious move.

"Silence." Baldwin tried to draw attention to himself, but he could not make himself heard above the acrimonious accusations that were passing furiously between Jaffa and Tripoli and the general uproar among the other members of the High Court. Sir Daniel, however, had heard him, and he bellowed into the room: "Silence!"

Startled, the members of the High Court looked at the throne and gradually fell expectantly silent.

"My lord of Tripoli, do I understand you to mean that, in your opinion, I had no right to appoint a Regent without the consent of the High Court?"

"Your grace, not even a *king* can be crowned in Jerusalem without the approval of the High Court," Tripoli countered firmly. Tripoli was not as imposing a man as Ramla; he was much smaller and slighter, with a somewhat hawkish nose. However, he was arguably more intelligent than Ramla, and certainly more intelligent than Jaffa. In the name of the merciful Christ, Baldwin asked himself, why had he named Jaffa Regent rather than Tripoli? Just to please his self-centered sister? Or because he had felt slighted and disdained during his minority? He had not liked—and still did not like—Tripoli, but what did that have to do with appointing a Regent? Good kings appointed men to positions of power for their capabilities and virtues not their congeniality.

"My lords." The King lifted his gaze from Tripoli to the entire room. "If it is your opinion that no Regent could be appointed without the approval of the High Court, then we *have* no Regent." Baldwin's eyes watched the reactions closely, and there was widespread agreement with his statement. Notably, the bishops were nodding and the Templar and Hospitaller Masters were in rare agreement, while Aimery de Lusignan just shrugged, as if washing his hands of the whole business.

When the occupants of the room had settled down and turned again expectantly to the King, he announced: "In that case, Constable, light a fire on the roof of this tower to hearten the defenders of Kerak, and summon the army to Jerusalem that we may go to the relief of Kerak."

To his disappointment, his words were not met with a thunderous cheer of approval. Instead Baldwin, too, was met by stunned silence. It was Aimery de Lusignan who put the question on everyone's mind into words. "Do—ah—do you want *me* to command the army, your grace?"

"No, I will command it myself," Baldwin answered.

Now everyone started speaking at once. Jaffa's voice, of course, was loudest in protesting that this idea was preposterous—but Tripoli, too, seemed far from pleased by the idea, and there could be little doubt that Aimery de Lusignan was disappointed. These were the three men who thought they should command the army, and so their voices and arguments moved Baldwin not at all, but he was distressed to realize that the Grand Masters of the Temple and Hospital and the Bishop of Bethlehem were also shaking their heads. They certainly did not expect command, so what was their objection? Baldwin was hurt and confused by this rejection of his command when he had, after all, never led the army of Jerusalem to defeat in all the years he had commanded in person.

Baldwin sought Balian d'Ibelin in the sea of faces, and their eyes met. Across the distance, Baldwin pleaded voicelessly with his friend for forgiveness and support. His eyes said: I was wrong! I know I was. Forgive me, Balian—and please intervene. Please speak up for me!

Balian started forward, to the irritation of the men around him, but then they fell silent as they saw him gently push his younger brother Henri aside and go down on one knee before the King. "Your grace, do not mistake our reluctance to see you take command of the army for mistrust in your leadership. We—my brothers and I—have fought with you at Montgisard, on the Litani, and at Le Forbelet. We know you are capable." He paused to let this sink in before adding, "But we fear for your health. Each time you take to the field, you are left weaker than before. Can you afford to take the field again? Now? So shortly after recovering from near-certain death?"

The silence in the room was brittle, as if men were holding their breath.

"My lord of Ibelin, that you care for my health I do believe," Baldwin answered steadily, his eyes fixed on Balian, trying to convey how deeply he regretted the hurt he had done him in the past. "But it is a King's duty to put the welfare of his Kingdom ahead of his own. The Count of Jaffa is right to say we cannot let Kerak—or my sisters—fall into Salah ad-Din's hands."

"But, your grace," the Bishop of Bethlehem replied, moving up behind Balian. "In your condition—"

"I can be carried in a litter," Baldwin assured him.

"Yes, of course—but, your grace, if, as the good Baron of Ibelin says, the exertions of this campaign render you—incapacitated—who then is to rule the Kingdom?"

"According to the Count of Tripoli, that is for this High Court to decide. What does it have to do with me?"

"Your grace!" the Bishop protested, with a scowl in the direction of Tripoli. "The kings of Jerusalem have always designated their heirs; the High Court then reviews that recommendation and ensures that there are no impediments."

"My heir is my nephew and namesake, my sister Sibylla's son," Baldwin answered, pointedly looking at the Count of Jaffa.

"The boy is six years old!" Jaffa protested in exasperation.

"Then he will need a Regent—when the time comes," Tripoli replied coolly, harvesting exclamations of support that silenced Jaffa.

"If it would please this High Court," Baldwin spoke into the chatter that gradually stilled as they waited for him to continue, "we can crown my nephew King—anoint him in the Church of the Holy Sepulcher—so no one can challenge his right to rule when I am dead—which we all know will not be so long from now."

"Your grace!" the Bishop of Bethlehem gasped, but then fell silent, as the silver mask swung in his direction and Baldwin's burning eyes fell on him.

"I may be dying, my lords," Baldwin told them coldly. "But I will die a *king*—and not a discarded and disregarded fool!" He looked pointedly at Jaffa as he spoke. "I will be Regent for my nephew as long as I live, and I will tolerate no Regent to be placed over me as long as I draw breath. God is my witness!"

The High Court muttered a collective "Amen," greatly subdued by the King's stance.

"So light the fire, Constable, and summon the army. I *will* lead it to Kerak."

"After your nephew has been crowned," Tripoli added with an audacity that surprised many in the room.

"You can't crown the boy with his mother trapped in Kerak!" Jaffa protested. But the other barons loudly overrode his protest and insisted on a coronation at once. This need be no grand affair, the Templar Master noted; the boy would only be a co-monarch, after all. The Patriarch protested, however, that he wasn't ready, and that the sacred oil and vestments were locked away. The boy needed to be prepared, taught his lines, and spend time in prayer, the Bishop of Nazareth added.

"A week from now, then!" Ramla concluded to widespread applause. "Kerak can be held that long at least. Indeed, much longer. There is no rush."

Baldwin had stopped listening and had returned his gaze to Balian, who was still on his knee before him. There was so much that needed to be said—to right the wrongs he had committed, to thank him for taking in Ibrahim, to beg forgiveness and support in the days, weeks, maybe even years ahead. There was so much Baldwin wanted to say, but he didn't have the strength to say it all.

Balian pulled himself to his feet and approached the throne. He laid his hand on Baldwin's arm, which lay dead upon the armrest of the throne. "I am still your knight, your grace. You need not doubt it."

"And your wife my step-mother? Will she, too, forgive what I have done?"

Balian drew a deep breath, for he could not honestly speak for Maria Zoë. "I do not know, your grace. Much will depend on how she finds Isabella."

Baldwin closed his eyes in shame and whispered, "God forgive me." Then he opened them and looked again at Balian. "Tell her—tell her that she was right to attack my mother and sister. Tell her that it was that desperate cry of a wounded mother that finally penetrated the walls of lies they had woven around me. I did not comprehend it until I had recovered from the fever, but I heard it and remembered it. And tell Ibrahim that I did not throw him out, that I miss him every day, every hour, but I do not deserve his love and care. My punishment for not having had the strength to prevent my sister from dismissing him is to live without the comfort of his care."

"I will tell him, and Maria Zoë—as soon as we have lifted the siege of Kerak."

Kerak, December 3, 1183

Beth sought to flee the stench and misery of the crowded courtyards by seeking fresh air upon the ramparts. It had been roughly six weeks since the start of the siege, and while the food seemed to be holding out, water had long since become rationed. There was little enough to drink and nothing whatsoever for bathing. The masses of humanity crammed into the inadequate spaces not locked against them (for Oultrejourdain had no intention of letting people live amidst his stores or armory) stank abominably. More and more of the children were becoming ill, vomiting and defecating wherever they happened to be, while even the adults hardly made the effort to go to the filthy battery of latrines in the outer ward.

Obviously the nobility lived above the squalid courtyards, but with so many guests, conditions even here were crowded. Beth shared a small tower room with Eschiva, Maria Zoë, Elizabeth, Rahel, and Elizabeth's waiting woman, Martha. The noblewomen shared the bed that had been Isabella's until her marriage, while the waiting women slept on pallets on the floor. At least they had their own garderobe, but Beth sometimes needed to get away from the others. Elizabeth was increasingly on edge and very short-tempered, and her maid Martha looked down on the base-born Beth and ordered her around like a scullery maid. Meanwhile Eschiva had fallen into a deep depression that left her listless. Beth had done all she could to try to cheer up her mistress, but what was she supposed to say? She was more terrified of the future than any of the others.

Her only solace was Dawit. His mere presence in the castle was a comfort to Beth, and they met in the stables, where he was desperately trying to protect the Dowager Queen's horses from being deprived of water or losing all condition from standing still. They usually met there, but when she had expressed her longing for fresh air, he had offered to take her to the ramparts.

He led her up a narrow, twisting stair to the top of the southeast tower that she would not have known about—much less risked visiting—on her own. Beth held her skirts in her right hand, seeking her footing cautiously and uncertainly, for the stairs narrowed to little more than three inches wide on the inside where they joined the central stone column running up the center of the stairs. Beth might have been safer clinging to the outer wall where the stairs were wider, but that would have meant letting go of Dawit's hand. Beth was still very shy of touching him, and grateful for occasions like this when she could hold his hand "innocently."

"Just a few more steps," Dawit promised her, hearing how she gasped for breath after the steep climb.

Beth nodded, too out of breath to speak. She was tired of climbing, but part of her did not want the climb to end, because then she would have to let go of Dawit's hand. The stairwell, however, was getting steadily lighter as they approached the top. It darkened briefly as Dawit blocked the door while exiting, and then she stepped out onto the roof of a small tower that jutted out from the rest of the walls. There were two sentries here, but they just looked dismissively over their shoulders at the Ethiopian and the serving girl.

Dawit gestured Beth to follow him to the wall, and when she stepped up beside him and looked down between the parapets, she gasped and caught her breath. The view was breathtaking and dizzying. They were hundreds of feet above the valley floor, which fell off in a sheer cliff to a lazy, muddy stream below. The tents and camp spread out on the floor of the valley at the foot of the precipice were tiny, and the figures moving between the tents looked more like little insects than men. Even the horses and wagons looked like toys from here.

"They don't look so threatening from here," Dawit remarked with a quick, reassuring smile that seemed, as always, to understand exactly what was going through her head.

"No," Beth agreed with a smile of her own.

"Look." Dawit was anxious to show her what he knew. "Do you see that large tent over there, surrounded by smaller tents and flying the very long banner?"

Beth leaned closer to Dawit in a pretense of straining to follow his outstretched arm. "Yes."

"That is Salah ad-Din's own tent. And that green tent," Dawit changed the direction of his arm, "You see the one with all the black banners?"

"Yeees," Beth agreed, not entirely sure if she was looking in the right place.

"That is the tent of al-Adil, the Sultan's brother. He's the one who arrived almost two weeks ago with the army of Egypt."

The arrival of the Egyptian army had caused considerable consternation among the defenders, since it had tightened the noose around Kerak and ensured that the siege was utterly impenetrable. Before the arrival of the Egyptian army they had managed to get several men out of Kerak, and others had slipped in as well, including Sir Henri with the news that the barons had refused to march until Guy de Lusignan was dismissed as Regent and Baldwin V was duly crowned in the Holy Sepulcher, a process that had taken longer than expected.

The mention of al-Adil thus led Beth to admit, "Oh, Dawit, I'm so frightened."

"There's nothing to be afraid of," Dawit assured her; "the relief army is on its way. We've seen the fires at night."

"But the fires were lit over a month ago," Beth protested. "What is taking it so long?"

"It takes time to muster an army and collect the provisions. Coming into Oultrejourdain isn't like going to Bethsan. They have to transport water for the men and horses in big wooden barrels on wagons. Horses need twelve gallons a day each. Loaded wagons can't move more than six or seven miles a day," Dawit explained knowingly.

"But we're almost out of water here," Beth protested. "I've heard many of the women say we can't hold out much longer."

"Of course we can," Dawit insisted. He pointed to the reservoirs at the foot of the castle walls, which were still hundreds of feet above the enemy. "See, they aren't near empty yet." Yet he did not sound as confident as he would have liked. Dawit's fear was that they would soon kill the horses to save water, and he couldn't bear the thought.

Beth, however, had other fears. She drew a ragged breath of clean air and admitted to Dawit, "If—if we surrender, Dawit, they'll kill me as an apostate."

Dawit looked over at her sharply, and although she did not dare meet his eye, he judged her mood correctly and risked putting his arm around her. She did not shrink back from his touch or even wince. Instead, she leaned against his warm, strong body in instinctive search of protection. "How would they know you were once Muslim?" he asked.

"They'll know! They'll know!" Beth insisted irrationally. "Or someone will betray me. Martha hates me." Although this was an exaggeration, there was little doubt that Elizabeth's serving maid considered herself much better than the Syrian convert, and in the stress that would follow surrender and capture, there was no way of knowing what anyone might do.

"But if it comes to a surrender, then I will be with you," Dawit assured her. "I'll tell everyone you are my wife."

"Oh, Dawit," Beth nestled closer. "I wish that that were true—even though it would not stop them from killing me. In Sharia law, a Muslim woman who marries a Christian must be stoned to death just like an adulteress, because Christian marriage isn't recognized. To them," she nodded with her head to the Saracen army at their feet, "I am a whore and a traitor and something only to be spat upon and kicked to death. The women would do it to me even if the men didn't. There is no one in that whole army who would feel so much as a whisper of pity. They will tear me apart alive." All her pent-up terror was pouring out.

"No, they won't," Dawit insisted, holding her more firmly. "They won't because I won't let them—ever. And they won't because this castle isn't going to fall. Even if we have to kill the horses, we'll hold out until the army comes."

"No, Dawit!" Beth knew just how much he loved the horses and what it took for him to say this. "We won't have to kill the horses—just turn them loose. They," again she indicated the Saracen army with her head, "would rather tear a girl apart limb for limb and trample on her belly until her guts come out of her mouth than harm so much as a hair on a horse's body. You can let the horses all go free and they will be well fed and watered and groomed." Tears were running down her face as she spoke—for much as she wished the horses well, it hurt to be reminded that she was worth less than even her donkey to the men outside the castle.

Dawit, on the other hand, was reassured to think the horses might not be slaughtered after all. He nodded to himself and held Beth closer. They stood like that in silence, content to be together and (comparatively) alone. But then the sentries shattered their moment of peace.

"What the hell's going on there?"

"Messenger of some kind."

"They sure the f**k look upset about something."

"They're mounting up—the whole lot of them."

"Better report to Oultrejourdain."

One of the sentries ducked down the stairs while Beth and Dawit stared at the camp below. The agitation was clearly spreading, like the ripples from a stone thrown in a still pond. The disturbance had reached al-Adil's tent, and a moment later several men emerged from it and gestured dramatically until horses were brought. Al-Adil rode straight for his brother's tent, and soon men emerged from Salah ad-Din's tent as well. Although from this distance it was impossible to guess which was the Sultan himself, they could be sure he was there, that they were seeing him. Meanwhile horns were being sounded, and they appeared to be answered from within the castle. Going to the other side of the tower, Beth and Dawit looked down into the ward to see Oultrejourdain storm out of the tract of buildings south of the chapel, trailed by a least a dozen other men. They crossed the inner courtyard and plunged into the ward, lost from view behind the chapel. But more men were streaming out of all the buildings around the ward, most of them donning helmets and girding on swords as they ran.

"They're going to assault!" Beth concluded in alarm.

"We better get back inside," Dawit decided and hustled Beth down the stairs.

He escorted her to her chamber, and when she entered she was received with reproachful cries of "Where have you been?" and "I've been frantic with fear!"

Dawit backed away, and Beth faced the deluge of censure alone. She didn't care what they said or thought, because the moments with Dawit had been worth it all. If she was going to die tonight or tomorrow, it would be knowing that Dawit loved her.

And then the Dowager Queen swept into the room and ordered everyone to be still. "The northwestern lookouts are reporting the banners of Antioch and Tripoli at the head of a large force. They estimate as many as two thousand horse with infantry behind."

"Hail Mary!" Elizabeth dropped on her knees and started offering profuse thanks, but Maria Zoë cut her off. "Stop that! The army has come, but the outcome of the battle that must now ensue is far from certain. We are about to have the dubious pleasure of watching our husbands fight—maybe even die—to rescue us." That Balian and Baldwin, not to mention the Constable of Jerusalem, were in the approaching host was beyond doubt.

Elizabeth's jaw dropped, and Eschiva clapped her hand over her mouth in horror. Neither of them had given a thought to the fact that the arrival of the army did not necessarily mean rescue. It just meant the confrontation that had failed to take place in September had been postponed and relocated. Only now, the Christian army did not occupy a spring.

Oultrejourdain was not so naive as the women. He called his own and the visiting knights and lords together in the great hall. Maria Zoë attended because she commanded the largest single body of knights after Oultrejourdain himself, those from Nablus. Not that she could personally lead them in combat, but they technically took their orders from her, and so she had the right to attend the council of war. Maria Zoë was not prepared to renounce her rights, nor was Stephanie de Milly. Of Agnes de Courtenay and the Countess of Jaffa, on the other hand, there was no sign.

"We'll know by morning where the Constable—or Antioch, whoever is in command—has decided to deploy," Oultrejourdain opened. "If I were the Constable, I would bring the army past Kerak, where it can camp without worrying about bombardment from the siege engines. Wherever the royal army deploys, however, it will have only the water it has in the train—and that won't be enough to last for long, so the relief force will have to attack. The sooner the better."

Oultrejourdain paused to see the reactions of the men around him. Most were nodding agreement, although Maria Zoë thought her new son-in-law Humphrey looked decidedly nervous.

"Our duty," Oultrejourdain continued matter-of-factly, "is to be ready to sortie the moment the royal army launches its attack. If it has deployed to the south, as I hope, we will be able to sortie out of the southern postern, and it may be possible to cut right through the enemy to join up. If we can do that, we should be able to feed enough infantry out of the postern to provide protection for our cavalry to regroup and launch a second attack."

Maria Zoë was impressed despite herself. She hated this man with all her heart, but he clearly understood war.

"If, however, the Constable deploys to the west or east, we'll have a much harder time joining up with him, and should therefore concentrate instead on a diversion."

"What about the northern postern?" Henri d'Ibelin asked. He was leaning against one of the pillars that supported the vaulting of the roof, his arms crossed over his chest. The fact that he had managed to escape the invested castle, reach Jerusalem, and return through the enemy lines had greatly increased his stature, and indeed his allure. Maria Zoë had noted many of the ladies cooped up here taking an inordinate interest in him—all except his wife, that was.

"Ah, Sir Henri!" Oultrejourdain was clearly pleased with his protégé. "I expected that question from you. The northern postern is far too steep for horses, but we could send men-at-arms down that slope, ready to break out and cause havoc at an appropriate moment. Don't you think?"

Sir Henri nodded. "I'll select a hundred men and take them down tonight under cover of darkness. We can wait in the base of the fosse until you give us a signal."

"Excellent. We can discuss the details in private," Oultrejourdain responded, and Maria Zoë suspected she did not want to know those details.

"Does anyone else have any questions?" Oultrejourdain scanned the room, his eyes coming to rest on Maria Zoë with a smirk. "Madame d'Ibelin, perhaps?" He meant to mock her.

"To ensure you have the maximum number of men ready for the sortie, why don't you assign some of us to lookout duty?" Maria Zoë suggested spontaneously. "We may not be able to fight, but our eyes are as sharp as yours, my lord."

There was a surprised reaction among the knights—some grumbling, some casting amused or deprecating smiles at the ladies, others shrugging and saying, "Why not?"

Stephanie de Milly silenced them all. "I'll take charge of that. We women will post the lookouts starting immediately, so the men can get a good night's rest."

Oultrejourdain shrugged in answer to indicate he did not object, and that was the end of it. War could make strange bedfellows, Maria Zoë concluded, as she and her bitterest enemy, Stephanie de Milly, went together to make a roster and assign volunteers.

Sentries had been a part of Marie Zoë's life as long as she could remember—well, at least since she'd come to the vulnerable and threatened Kingdom of Jerusalem—but she had never actually stood watch before. She was surprised to discover how hard it was to stay alert, particularly after her feet became too tired to pace. Yet it was impossible to sleep, either, knowing that battle was likely to be joined on the next day.

It was bad enough knowing that a battle was imminent when Balian took their troops to join a muster far away. But at least before, she had had her duties and her children to distract her thoughts. The thought of looking down from these very walls and watching the ebb and flow of battle, watching men hack each other to pieces, watching horses wild with pain and terror, did not appeal to her. Part of her wanted to hide under the covers of her bed with a pillow over her ears until it was all over. But she wouldn't be able to stand that, either, she concluded with a deep sigh.

As the night passed, the campfires on the valley floor gradually died out. Because Maria Zoë had not been on watch before, she did not realize this was unusual and therefore significant. She did not report it.

Instead, she wrapped her cloak more firmly around her shoulders and forced herself to pace some more, while her mind insisted on thinking through scenarios. The worst one was that the Christian army would attack but be beaten back with heavy casualties. They would then have no choice but surrender, and would all face Saracen imprisonment with only a distant prospect of ransom. Maria Zoë did not fear personal abuse—she was of too high rank—but she feared for Beth and Rahel. And of course, in such a scenario there was no certainty that Balian would not be among the killed, wounded, or captured.

Another possibility was that the Christian army would succeed in driving off their besiegers, but that Balian might still be among the dead or dying. He had the best armor money could buy and he had a remarkable stallion, but no man was invincible. The thigh wound he'd taken at Le Forbelet was testimony to his vulnerability.

Maria Zoë knew she would survive Balian's death. She had five children who still depended on her protection and care because, married or not, Isabella was still her little girl, and what she had seen of Humphrey had not impressed her. Not that he didn't have his good qualities. He seemed genuinely fond of Isabella. He was certainly gentle with her, and he was very well mannered and well educated, too. Certainly Isabella would be better off at Toron with Humphrey than here in Kerak under the control of Oultrejourdain. Nevertheless, Humphrey did not strike her as the kind of man who would stand up to the likes of Agnes de Courtenay or Guy de Lusignan when it came to Isabella's rights. He was still young of course, at fifteen, and he might well grow into a more forceful man, but meanwhile she remained Isabella's strongest advocate.

So for the sake of Isabella and Balian's children, she would not break down or withdraw from the world if she lost him. But what a bleak and desolate place this world would be without him!

Was the horizon becoming lighter? Surely the contours of the land were becoming more distinct? Maria Zoë strained her eyes in the murky light, frowning as she looked for the familiar outlines of tents. She couldn't seem to make them out, although looking in the other direction, back toward the castle, she could clearly see various features of the now all-too-familiar stone structure: towers, stairs, arches. She looked again toward the desert, first with a sense of irritation because the patterns of light and dark that had marked the besieging army weren't visible.

And then her sleep-starved brain began to understand: Salah ad-Din's army wasn't there! It had melted away in the night!

They opened the gates and flung down an improvised bridge made of beams lashed together with ropes and cross boards nailed down on top. Maria Zoë didn't like the look of it and did not relish the thought of crossing on it—a sentiment the horses of their rescuers shared. Neither Antioch nor Tripoli could persuade their horses to cross the fosse on such a precarious contraption, and so the Prince and Count were forced to dismount. While they were doing that, however, people surged out of the castle to swarm around them in jubilation.

It was the commoners who fled first, their confinement having been so much more unpleasant. Besides, they had been housed down in the lower ward anyway, near the gate that opened on the improvised bridge. They swarmed past the vanguard of the relieving army and into the town they had been forced to abandon in haste six weeks earlier.

It was thus the common people, not the knights and nobles that followed them, who first found the King of Jerusalem. When they realized that the King himself, carried on a litter, had come to the relief of Kerak, the people of the town started cheering so wildly that in the castle it sounded as if there'd been some kind of ambush.

Then those like Maria Zoë, watching from the northern wall walk, saw a horde of people surge back toward the castle—and in their midst, carried upon what seemed like a hundred shoulders, was a litter. It was covered by a white canopy with the gold crosses of Jerusalem glittering in the morning sun. And upon that litter sat a small man, likewise dressed in white-and-gold robes, white gloves, and a silver mask.

"Jerusalem!" they shouted in a frenzy of joy as they carried him into the castle in triumph. "Jerusalem!"

The great Sultan Salah ad-Din had fled at the mere approach of the Leper King.

Chapter 11

Jerusalem, April 1184

"There has to be some grounds for annulling the marriage!" the King of Jerusalem protested to the collected princes of the Church. The learned bishops had been arguing in Latin over Church law for hours, and King Baldwin had had enough. He had rarely felt so helpless, and all his frustration with his illness, his paralysis, and his approaching death was echoed in his voice as it rang out, loud if distorted, from his silver mask. "My sister's marriage to Guy de Lusignan threatens the very existence of this Kingdom! The marriage *must* be dissolved!"

"Marriage vows are sacred, your grace!" the Patriarch Heraclius retorted primly, harvesting laughter from his fellow prelates and a muttered "So are a priest's vows of chastity" from the Archbishop of Tyre.

Baldwin looked with affection (lost behind the mask) at his old tutor. The Archbishop was too principled and prickly to forgive Baldwin the insults he had suffered, and Baldwin accepted that, but Baldwin was glad to have his voice of reason in the council again. He was further warmed to have him so uncompromisingly behind his efforts to dissolve Sibylla's marriage.

Meanwhile, the Archbishop of Caesarea deflected discussion away from Heraclius' scandalous lifestyle with a warning frown at his fellow archbishop as he insisted, "That is a topic for a different day." Gregory of Caesarea personally shared William of Tyre's outrage over Heraclius' flaunting of his mistress, but he felt equally strongly that the Patriarch's morals should not be discussed before the secular authorities.

"Indeed, but the sacredness of vows is something we must not lose track of here, my lords. Intensely as I sympathize with your grace's desire to be rid of

Lusignan," the Bishop of Acre addressed himself to his King, "marriages cannot be dissolved at whim." The pomposity of the young bishop harvested rolling eyes from some of his more worldly colleagues, but vigorous support from the Patriarch, who added, "We are not godless Mussulmen who can simply say 'I divorce thee' four times to be rid of a wife."

"Guy de Lusignan is the last man who wants to be rid of his wife," Tyre retorted sharply.

"Unfortunately Sibylla does not want to be rid of her husband, either," the Archbishop of Nazareth pointed out with a weary sigh.

"This isn't about what Sibylla or Guy *wants*!" the King reminded them in an angry outburst. "It's about the Kingdom of Jerusalem! We are endangered as we have never been before since the very founding of the Kingdom. We are surrounded by a united Islamic state under a competent and charismatic leader. We *must* stand united behind a leader *capable* of leading the defense. That man is *not* Guy de Lusignan!"

His words were greeted by silence until the practical Bishop of Bethlehem tried to explain. "The problem, your grace, is that the usual grounds for dissolving unwanted royal marriages—consanguinity—just don't apply here. Lusignan is not related to any royal house, much less your own."

"What about bigamy?" the Bishop of Lydda suggested hopefully. "Surely Guy de Lusignan was married or betrothed to *someone* in France before he came out here? Most crusaders are."

"I've looked into that," the Bishop of Hebron reported with a deep sigh. "Unfortunately, as a fourth son, he was too poor to marry—which did not stop him from fornicating and committing adultery, of course. Nevertheless, no father was prepared to give his daughter in marriage to Guy unless Hugh de Lusignan, Guy's oldest brother and Lord of Lusignan, settled land on him. The elder Lusignan, however, does not appear to have had much affection for his youngest brother, and is on record saying he'd rather give land to the devil."

"Wait," Tyre sat up straighter. "Guy may not have been married before, but Sibylla was!"

"William de Montferrat was dead long before Guy even set foot on our shores."

"But the Baron de Ramla was not," Tyre pointed out, harvesting astonished looks from his colleagues.

"You can't dredge up that old story!" Heraclius protested shrilly, and everyone in the room stared at him.

"Everyone knows that Princess Sibylla had promised herself to the Baron of Ramla," Tyre pressed his case in a reasonable tone. "Why, even Salah ad-Din and the Emperor of the Eastern Empire had heard of it—otherwise they would not have set, much less paid, a ransom of one hundred fifty thousand bezants."

"It doesn't matter what she said to him," Heraclius insisted in obvious agitation; "their agreement was never blessed by the Church. They did not exchange vows!"

"How do you know that?" Bethlehem wanted to know.

"Her mother told me—"

"In bed, no doubt!" Tyre mocked, harvesting laughs from some of his colleagues and admonishments from others.

"Does it matter *where* she told me?" Heraclius flung back. "What's important is only the truth, and who knows better than the girl's mother—"

"I'd say the man she gave the vows to. No woman tells her mother *everything*."

"Careful, William. Ramla has remarried. If he exchanged vows with Sibylla, he *too* is a bigamist, and that would make his son Godfrey illegitimate. He may not like that notion," the Bishop of Lydda warned.

"Yes," the Archbishop of Caesarea pressed Tyre earnestly, "think carefully. Do you know for *certain* that Sibylla and Ramla exchanged vows?"

"No, but I'm saying we need to investigate."

"This is ridiculous!" Heraclius protested, his very defensiveness underlining how serious the charge was. "If they'd exchanged vows, Ramla would have protested before Sibylla's marriage to Guy. He would have stopped it!"

"How could he? He was in Constantinople at the time," Tyre pointed out smugly. "He returned to find the marriage celebrated *and* consummated—which undoubtedly curbed his appetite for his faithless bride."

"He still could have protested—"

"He did," the King reminded them, his whole body vibrating with newfound hope. "He *did!*"

"We can't take Ramla's word for this," Heraclius protested vehemently. "He will say they were betrothed just to get his hands on the Crown. His word is worthless."

"You exceed yourself, my lord," the King rebuked the Patriarch. "You have no right to call a baron of Jerusalem a liar."

"But if Sibylla denies it," Caesarea asked reasonably, "what then?"

"It will prove nothing, as the Lady of Jaffa appears singularly attached to Monsieur de Lusignan," Tyre answered dismissively.

"She is besotted with him!" Lydda agreed, shaking his head in disgust.

"So we can assume she will deny having exchanged vows with Ramla, even if she did, just as she evidently forgot all her promises to Ramla as soon as she'd become enflamed with passion for Lusignan," Caesarea concluded his argument. "That means it will be his word against hers, with *both* having strong motivation to lie."

"If they exchanged vows before a priest, then it should be possible to find the priest who officiated—or a written agreement," Lydda suggested cautiously.

"There were no such vows!" Heraclius insisted stubbornly.

"There's no harm in asking Ramla—and if he says he exchanged vows with Sibylla, then we can ask him to produce the priest who officiated," Tyre returned with a smug smile; he knew no one could oppose such a reasonable proposal. Around him his fellow bishops gave their vigorous assent, leaving the despised Patriarch stewing in his own anger.

The Baron of Ramla stood on the ramparts of David's Gate and looked eastward into the city of Jerusalem. From here he could see all the major landmarks, from the Tower of David on his right to the Patriarch's palace on his left. Behind the Patriarch's palace rose the dome of the Holy Sepulcher, almost dwarfed by the massive Hospitaller complex beside it. Farther away, the even larger dome of the Temple of God reared up against the luminous sky of dusk, while the Templar headquarters, housed in what had been the Al-Aqsa mosque, crouched to its right. Jerusalem.

On these streets, on the paving stones leading from the gate below him past the Hospitaller quarters to the old Jewish Temple, Christ had walked. Now tens of thousands of pilgrims followed in his footsteps. The Baron of Ramla watched as a slow-moving procession of pilgrims shuffled forward, singing a hymn and carrying candles. A couple with a crippled boy between them were making their way along the cobbles on their knees in evident hope of a miracle. A lone knight followed behind them, leading his horse in a clear gesture of penitence; his cloak, with a cross sewn on the shoulder, was ragged and filthy from the journey, and he seemed grayed and bent from the weight of his sins.

They came from the four corners of the earth, speaking many tongues and wearing everything from ermine to rags. They came at great expense through great danger, braving the uncertainties of sea travel or walking across two continents to reach this city. They had mortgaged or sold all they owned at home and had faced the threat of pirates, cutthroats, thieves, and slavers. They had endured thirst, hunger, exhaustion, and disease. They came for the redemption of their sins, in search of Divine forgiveness. They came to prove their love of Christ and earn their entry into heaven. They were drawn here by the sole desire to pray at the place where Christ had shed his blood for them—and risen from the grave again with the promise of everlasting life for those who followed him.

And it was all at risk.

Lifting his gaze slightly, Ramla's eyes traced the perimeter walls. White and tall, they enclosed the vibrant city like a mother's arms her child. The clean lines were punctuated by square towers and projecting gates, all topped with battlements and proudly flying the white-and-gold banners of the Kingdom. But Ramla was a military man, and proud as the walls appeared, Ramla could see their vulnerability. They might keep out the rabble at night, but they were not built to withstand a modern siege with the kind of engines Salah ad-Din could bring to bear against them, or the sappers he would send to undermine them.

Almost a hundred years ago, Jerusalem had fallen to the Christians in just six weeks. The Christians had had no siege engines and had been too few to enclose the city. By contrast, if Salah ad-Din managed to penetrate deep enough into the Kingdom to deploy his vast army against this city, he would be able to surround it many times. Furthermore, he would have catapults, mangonels, and trebuchets. The walls would break like eggshells under the force of those terrifying machines. The Saracens would pour triumphantly inside, slaughtering the entire population and desecrating the very tomb from which Christ had risen from the dead to bring salvation to the world.

That would happen if Guy de Lusignan became Regent for the young King Baldwin V—let alone if Baldwin V should die before he reached maturity and Guy were crowned King as Sibylla's consort. Guy de Lusignan did not have the instincts of a hunter, did not understand the art of war, and could not command men. If he were allowed to rule the Kingdom of Jerusalem, it would be lost.

The dying King understood that, and so did the bishops. Tyre had made it very clear: if Barisan de Ramla had plighted his troth with Sibylla of Jerusalem, then her marriage to Guy de Lusignan could be declared null and void. All he had to do was produce as a witness the priest who had officiated at their betrothal ceremony.

But of course, there hadn't been one. Ramla was quite certain that the good Archbishop of Tyre knew that perfectly well. The worthy churchman and his colleagues were, however, prepared to "believe" a lie as long as Ramla was willing to tell it.

It would not be difficult, Ramla reasoned, to find a destitute or venal priest willing to swear upon the True Cross itself that he had officiated at the betrothal of Barisan Baron of Ramla and Princess Sibylla of Jerusalem—for a price. The price probably wouldn't even be too high—the next free bishopric, perhaps, or a wealthy abbey. Nothing Ramla would not be able to pay from future revenues and patronage as King of Jerusalem.

No, the problem wasn't finding a priest corrupt enough to perjure himself: it was the thought of taking the false vow. Not only would he be bearing false witness, he would be denying his marriage to Elizabeth and discarding his little son. Little Godfrey was such a fine boy! He was already taking his first steps—fearless and eager, like a warrior trapped in a child's body. Ramla loved Godfrey more than anything else in the whole world. How could he discard the boy? Declare him illegitimate?

King Amalric had set the precedent of discarding his wife while insisting that the legitimacy of his children be recognized, but Tyre had already indicated that Ramla's position was too precarious to give him room to negotiate. Barry had to choose between Jerusalem and his son.

Darkness was spreading through the valleys that fell away from the walls of the city to the south and east, while the city itself was increasingly lit by torches and lanterns. The stars were becoming visible as the blue of the sky deepened, and over Bethlehem the evening star hung like a reminder of Christ's birth. "Will you forgive me, Lord, if I swear upon Your cross that I was canonically promised to Sibylla?"

Ramla waited a moment, but angels did not appear in the sky to answer him. Nor did a bolt of lightning indicate divine displeasure. So Ramla sighed and ducked into the stairwell to descend the spiral stairs of the gatehouse. He moved slowly in the darkness, feeling his footing more than seeing his way, until he emerged behind the gate, where his squire Stephan was patiently waiting with their horses. With a nod, Ramla indicated the squire should mount, and he took up his reins and swung himself up into the saddle. In silence they started up David Street, but as they came to the junction with Patriarch Street, Ramla suddenly changed his mind, turned left into the street, and drew up before the entrance to the Hospital.

Unlike the Templars, who were fiercely hostile to the outside world and guarded their headquarters against visitors like a fortress within a fortress, the Hospital was open to the public. Torches flanked the open door, and lay brothers manned a table under the arch to help direct the sick to one of the dozen different wards. Beyond the doorway, the courtyard was bustling even at this time of night; lay brothers brought meals from the huge kitchens to the east to the wards along the south wall, while other brothers watered mules and donkeys at one of the dozen cisterns, and a third group was laying out the dead who were to be buried the next day. Above the clatter of hooves on paving stones and voices from the wards, the sound of hundreds of male voices joined in plainsong wafted from the massive church of St. John along the north wall.

At the sight of Ramla and his squire, one of the lay brothers rang a bell. At once another brother emerged to take the horses, and a second, on hearing Ramla's request for an audience with the Master, led the way to the Master's quarters beyond the church of St. Mary Major. There were no less than four churches enclosed within the complex; two were reserved for the sick, one for the sisters, and the other for the brothers of the Hospital.

The Master of the Hospital lived in rooms on the first floor above the chapter house of the Order. A large double-light window encased with exquisite dog-tooth carving looked out from the audience chamber over the Street of Palms to the Church of the Holy Sepulcher. Ramla stepped up into the window and gazed out at the holiest church in Christendom.

St. Helena had located the tomb of Christ and the True Cross on this spot seven hundred years ago. The Emperor Constantine had built a church to mark the spot, but the Persians had razed it to the ground. Rebuilt by the Greeks after they recaptured the city, the church had been completely destroyed a second time by the Muslims two hundred years ago. After restoring Jerusalem to Christian rule, the Latin rulers had worked on the site for half a century to build a church worthy of Christ. They had incorporated much of the Greek foundations, but greatly extended the church complex to include a choir and ambulatory east of the Greek rotunda. The church now encompassed the rock of Calvary as well as the tomb of Christ, and between these two sacred sites were the tombs of the Kings of Jerusalem. Successive Kings and Patriarchs had engaged the best masons and craftsmen money could buy, many from Constantinople itself, so that the quality of the workmanship elicited amazement from the many pilgrims. On July 15, 1149, the fiftieth anniversary of the liberation of Jerusalem from Muslim control, the new church had been ceremoniously reconsecrated.

Ramla had been only two years old and not included in the festivities, but both his parents, his mother big from carrying Balian under her heart, and his elder brother Hugh had taken part in the solemn Mass. Hugh had always claimed that Balian's presence at that Mass as an innocent unborn child had given him a special place in Christ's heart—an idea that had greatly annoyed Barry when growing up. But even if true, Barry thought now, it was nothing to being anointed king in such a place.

To be crowned king in the Church of the Holy Sepulcher would be utterly enrapturing.

To do so based on a lie would be damnation itself.

"My lord?"

Ramla had not heard Roger des Moulins enter; he spun about, startled. He then hastened to step down from the window and cross to the Master of the Hospital. "Forgive this unexpected intrusion, my lord."

"You are always welcome, my lord." The Master of the Hospital indicated a small round table flanked by high-backed chairs where they could sit.

Roger des Moulins had come out to the Holy Land nine years earlier, initially as Grand Hospitaller, but he had been elected Grand Master two years later. Although of noble birth, he was not by nature a violent man, and he had advanced within the Hospital because of his administrative abilities and financial acumen rather than his military prowess. It was no secret that his principal task had been to restore the material fortunes of the Hospital after the disastrous leadership of his predecessor, Gilbert d'Assailly. The latter had borrowed huge sums of money and mortgaged important Hospitaller properties to hire mercenaries for the last invasion of Egypt. The invasion had been a disaster and the Hospital was left in a precarious financial situation, resulting in the resignation of Gilbert d'Assailly. Moulins had managed to raise the money owed by appealing to wealthy lords in the West, many of whom turned over their property to the Hospital in return for the salvation of their souls. He had increased the recruitment of knights as well, although he generally left the command of these to his marshal. Perhaps most important for the future of the Kingdom, he had amicably settled a series of disputes with the Templars. In short, Ramla and Moulins were of profoundly different temperaments. The monk was cautious, restrained, and open to compromise; the baron impulsive, passionate, and obstinate.

"How may I be of service to you, my lord?" Moulins asked, with a gentle smile under alert, almost suspicious eyes.

"I wish your advice on a moral issue."

Moulins' eyebrows twitched, but so slightly that Ramla did not notice.

"If, to save a great many lives and indeed things more valuable than life itself, a man were to tell a small lie, would you give him absolution?"

"If he truly repented, of course."

"But how can a man repent doing something that effects great good, not just for himself but for his fellows, his Kingdom, and his Church?"

"We all commit sins. It is the overall balance of good versus evil that matters—unless that sin is a mortal sin."

"A lie—indeed, more an exaggeration than an outright lie."

"But the motive matters," Moulins warned. "Is it pride, greed, lust, envy, or wrath that motivates the lie?"

"No, of course not! Only fear. Fear of what will come if this lie is not made."

"You are asking, then, if the end justifies the means?"

"Yes, I suppose I am."

"That depends on the end and the means, and whether there are alternatives," Moulins answered, adding with a cynical smile, "I suspect, my lord, I'm not telling you anything you don't already know."

Ramla took a deep breath. "I—I am deeply distressed about the state of the Kingdom."

"As are we all."

"Guy de Lusignan—" When he said the name out loud, all Barry's hatred of the man bubbled up in his voice. "Guy de Lusignan threatens to destroy us! It was bad enough that he debauched a Princess of Jerusalem and seduced his way into the County of Jaffa, but now much more is at stake. The King is dying, and his nephew is a fragile child! If Baldwin V should die, the Crown will fall to Sibylla, and she will give it to her lover!"

Moulins nodded. "I fear you are right, my lord, but what can we do to stop it?"

"If—if it could be proved that Guy is not Sibylla's lawful husband . . ."

"If that could be proved, my lord, it would be a great blessing." Moulins met Ramla's eye as he spoke. "For all of us."

Ramla nodded, and for a moment they sat in silence. Then Ramla got to his feet. "Thank you for taking the time to see me."

"My pleasure, my lord." The Hospitaller Master saw Ramla to the door of the chamber.

It was now completely dark, but the streets of Jerusalem were still crowded. It was the eve of Palm Sunday and pilgrims had poured into the city, filling the inns and hostels to overflowing. Wide-eyed pilgrims agog at the thought of being in the Holy City were accosted by cynical locals selling everything from meat pies to "relics." Many shopkeepers had lanterns on their tables and called out their wares to passers-by, while innkeepers with vacant beds called out their prices. In the Street of Bad Cooking, men spilled out of the corner taverns with tankards in their hands to get a breath of fresh air, while pickpockets and whores moved surreptitiously through the crowds, plying their trade.

The crowds in the narrow streets forced Ramla to ride at a walk, and he thought back to his trip to Constantinople. There the main streets were wide enough for chariots, and noblemen cantered through them rather than being reduced to a crawl. Nor was the city vulnerable to attack, Barry thought enviously, for it was protected by water on two sides and an amazing wall on the third.

The thought of Constantinople also reminded Barry of why he had been there: to raise his ransom so he could marry Sibylla. She had sent him on his way with kisses and whispered promises after a night spent in his bed. They had made love twice that night, and Sibylla had gasped and groaned in ecstasy as he teased her to sexual climax. There had been no question when he rode away in the morning that she intended to marry him on his return! She had even expressed hope that she was carrying his child under her heart—"a Prince Barisan for Jerusalem," she had cooed. Christ! Did it really matter that they had not said vows before a priest?

She had not said vows in the presence of a priest before she took Guy to her bed, either! The little highborn whore!

Ramla no longer felt an ounce of affection for Sibylla. He loathed her for betraying him, and if he were to carry through with this deception and she were forced to abandon her stupid little playboy and return to him, Ramla was determined to make her pay for humiliating him. He would treat her correctly in public, of course, but rape would be too kind a word for what he'd do to her in private.

They had reached the Ibelin residence, and Barry and his squire dismounted in the street to lead their horses through the gate into the courtyard. A lone torch burned at the stables entrance, and Stephan took both horses, while Ramla mounted the stairs to the first-floor gallery. He made his way toward his chamber, but then turned and went to the nursery instead to look in on his son. The nurse stirred sleepily and asked what was wrong. He hushed her, and went to stand over his son's cradle.

Godfrey was such a perfect child, with such big hands for his age. Barry bent and stroked the back of his son's curled fist. The skin was softer than silk. "Ah, Godfrey, you have nothing to fear," he promised, thinking that a king's bastard could be given titles and honors. Henry II of England had made one of his bastards an earl and another a bishop, after all.

Elizabeth . . . Well, she would just have to understand. This was for the greater good of the Kingdom. It was nothing personal. She would just have to retire to a convent and accept her fate as God's will.

Ibelin, May 1184

"Balian, you can't imagine it! The highest prelates of the realm, screaming at each other like two whores fighting over a coin! They actually came to blows!

Heraclius threw himself at William of Tyre as if he intended to crush the air from his throat with his thumbs. William flailed with his fists to defend himself, and the Bishop of Bethlehem had to thrust himself between them. Then Heraclius started screaming, 'I'll excommunicate you!' and Tyre scoffed back that he cared nothing for the threats of a debauched priest who lived in open sin with another man's wife.

"But Heraclius actually carried out his threat in a huge public show at the Holy Sepulcher the very next day—he clanged the bells and doused the candles and pronounced William of Tyre excommunicate! In the middle of Easter Week!" Barry's outrage expressed itself in the volume of his voice and the redness of his face.

"Barry, did I understand you correctly?" Balian answered cautiously, pressing chilled water on his overheated brother. Barry had just arrived at Ibelin with fifty knights and one hundred Turcopoles he was leading to Ascalon. Ibelin, too, had been summoned along with the rest of the feudal host, and the men from Nablus were expected shortly. Thus even as Barry spoke, the sound of men and horses pitching tents and setting up cooking pots poured through the open windows of the solar along with the humid summer air, hot from baking for hours in the sun. "You swore to William of Tyre that you and Sibylla had been legally betrothed?"

Barry flung the water down his throat, gratefully gulping the refreshing coolness, and then reached for the glazed pottery pitcher to refill his chalice as he answered, "It's what they all wanted—except Heraclius, of course. They were too cowardly to just declare the marriage invalid; they needed an excuse. I provided it in the form of a priest who swore he'd been present at Sibylla and my betrothal. But no one had reckoned with Heraclius' reaction. When Tyre declared smugly that now there was no question Sibylla's marriage was null and void—that Guy was an adulterer—he went stark raving mad. You've never seen anything like it!" Barry repeated himself, shaking his head and pouring himself a third helping of water.

"Barry, slow down," Balian cautioned.

"You're right," Barry agreed, thinking his brother was referring to the ice-cold water and his overheated body, which was streaming sweat and smelled of horse and leather; he shoved the chalice aside.

But Balian was still trying to absorb the implications of what Barry had said. "If Sibylla's marriage is invalid, then so is yours—and Godfrey is a bastard. You can't really have sworn that?"

"It was a necessary evil. I didn't do it lightly, and I would have made it up to Godfrey and Elizabeth after I was king, but Heraclius ruined everything.

He threatened to excommunicate all the bishops. He said he'd have the priest tortured until he told the truth. None of us had any idea just how closely he clung to Guy de Lusignan—but it seems Agnes de Courtenay is seriously ill, and Heraclius can no longer count on her patronage. He's completely dependent on Sibylla and Guy now."

"He's been anointed Patriarch; what more does he need?"

"How the hell should I know? I only know that when he reacted so violently, all the other bishops—except Tyre, of course—scuttled for the safety of the shadows. The next thing I knew, my priest had disappeared, too. I don't know if he got cold feet, if Heraclius got his hands on him and has him in some dungeon on the rack, or if one of the other bishops spirited him away to 'safety.' All I know is that within twenty-four hours Tyre was excommunicated, the other bishops wouldn't even meet with me, and my witness had disappeared, leaving King Baldwin completely in the lurch. He was the one who wanted this, after all!"

Balian poured himself some wine to steady his nerves.

"Meanwhile," Barry continued, "the King had summoned Guy and Sibylla to Jerusalem to face the Church Convent and hear the verdict, but they refused to come. Just flat-out refused to come! I presume Heraclius warned them of what was afoot—but still, can you imagine the effrontery? That's why Baldwin has summoned the feudal host to accompany him to Ascalon."

"Does Elizabeth know what you had planned?"

"No, I didn't tell her about it. She knew I was spending a lot of time at the palace, and she asked me what was going on, but I gave her only vague answers. Said it was affairs of state having to do with the Count and Countess of Jaffa."

Balian nodded, glad that his sister-in-law had been spared learning that her husband was prepared to perjure himself to discard her. Sometimes it was better not to know the whole truth.

"I know what you're thinking, Balian, but that's the difference between us: I'm willing to do what it takes to get ahead, and you let your scruples get in the way. That's why I have twice come within a hair's breadth of being King of Jerusalem, and you've got a ten-knight barony because I gave it to you and are dependent on your wife for your wealth."

"That's true," Balian agreed simply, unwilling to fight with Barry. He was not unhappy with what he had—and if it made his brother feel better to think he was superior, then he would let him.

Ascalon, May 1184

The entire feudal host was drawn up around the walls of Ascalon. For Balian it was a poignant moment, as he remembered how he had once held the city against Salah ad-Din. Indeed, the Christian army was now using some of the same ditches and earthworks that the Saracens had dug seven years ago. The city then had been crammed with refugees who had fled before the advancing Saracens. They had been preparing for a siege with a deep sense of foreboding, because half the barons and fighting men of the Kingdom were campaigning in the north. Then suddenly the young King had ridden to the rescue with his knights, and the city had gone wild with jubilation.

Now that same city had closed its gates and refused to admit their anointed King, their savior of just seven years ago. The gates not only remained closed when the royal herald rode up with the banner of Jerusalem held aloft, they had stayed shut when King Baldwin had his litter carried to the door and he had pounded with his fist, guided by Sir Daniel and encased in chain mail, on the door. The King's men had held their breath, watching for the slightest sign of yielding, but the city might as well have been dead. Nothing stirred. The King had raised his fist a second time and shouted through his mask, "This is Baldwin of Jerusalem, and I demand entry to my city of Ascalon." But the gates had not cracked or creaked.

Of course, the orders to close the city to the King came from the Count of Jaffa, whose banner fluttered defiantly from the battlements, but Balian couldn't help but wonder if Roger Shoreham would have followed Jaffa's orders. Shoreham was an honest man with his own sense of right and wrong. Shoreham, Balian thought, would have yielded to the King he respected rather than follow the orders of a man like Jaffa. But Shoreham no longer commanded the garrison; the new commander was, according to Sir Daniel, the very man who had had him flogged for being a few minutes late to work as an apprentice.

The question was: what to do now? The barons of Outremer had followed their King to Ascalon, as outraged as he by the defiance of his parvenu brother-in-law, but not one of them—including Ibelin—was prepared to assault the city that defied him. They could not afford this dangerous disunity when their enemies were so strong. They certainly could not afford to shed a single Christian life or weaken the defenses of one of the Kingdom's most exposed and critical cities.

"The King will see you now," Sir Daniel gently told his former lord, coming out of the King's tent and holding the flap open.

Balian cast a last look at the city that had been his home, his first royal honor, and his bridal bower, and then ducked through the flap into the King's tent.

The King had removed his royal robes, crown, and mask. He was dressed only in a loose linen kaftan, and two monks were busy at the back of the tent emptying the tub in which he had bathed. In the wake of Ibrahim's dismissal Baldwin had undertaken a reorganization of his personal staff, and he had readily found several monks who were not only willing but anxious to serve him. Unlike Sir Daniel, they were not men who had themselves suffered from leprosy, but rather penitents who sought salvation through service to the afflicted. The ease with which King Baldwin had found no less than five monks made Ibelin wonder if King Amalric had seriously tried to find Christian servants for his son, or if he had selected Muslim slaves for some reason of his own. It no longer mattered, Balian supposed, but he was gladdened to see Baldwin surrounded by devout Christians, particularly as the King drew daily closer to his grave.

Exposed as the King now was, Balian could see that he had no toes left on either of his feet and that his fingers were completely deformed. The lower part of his chin and face was covered with growths that distorted his face and the nose had started to rot away, while all his hair had fallen out and he was now bald.

"I can see the pity in your eyes, Balian," Baldwin greeted him. "Would you prefer I wear the mask?"

"No, your grace. You need to breathe freely and feel the fresh air. I will adjust to the sight of you—though it breaks my heart."

"Yes," Baldwin nodded, "I knew you would care more for my comfort than your own. The fresh air is indeed welcome after a day in this heat behind the mask. Please, sit beside me."

Balian took the vacant chair beside his king.

"Do you remember when I came to your relief seven years ago?" Baldwin asked wistfully.

"I do, your grace; that's exactly what I was thinking about while waiting outside."

"The whole city was bracing for a siege, and yet they flung the gates open at the sight of my banners, and they cheered and cheered."

"You were a beautiful sight, your grace, and you rode like a centaur."

"That was Misty," the King replied, recalling his destrier of seven years before. "You chose him for me and taught me to ride."

"Yes."

They were silent for a moment, remembering.

"Tante Marie was gracious to me at Kerak, but do you think she has really forgiven me?"

"You, yes—your mother and sister, no."

"My mother did not have an easy life," Baldwin tried to explain. "She was deeply hurt when my father set her aside and took a new wife."

"She made her own hell, your grace," Balian countered, "first by treating my brother like dirt because he was not a king, and then by seeking revenge on everyone who she thought had ever slighted her. She alienated half your court."

"I know that now," Baldwin admitted with a sigh. "But she is still my mother, and she loves me. Much of what she did, she did for love of me and to protect me."

Balian wasn't so sure. He thought Agnes de Courtenay was only interested in protecting her own position at court, but he did not want to offend Baldwin, so he held his tongue.

"I know you disagree, Balian, but she is dying now. I expect to hear word that she has crossed the spiritual Jordan any day now. Her intentions, motives, and soul will be weighed and judged by one more qualified than either of us. I hope you will have the charity to pray for her soul, Balian, but that is between you and your conscience. As for me, I will pay the canons of the Holy Sepulcher to say Masses for her in perpetuity." He paused, and Balian supposed he would have crossed himself if he had been able to move his hands.

Then taking a deep breath, the King continued. "My sister . . . My sister, on the other hand, has never loved me and does not love me now. She loves first and foremost herself, and then Guy de Lusignan." With each sentence Baldwin's bitterness was more pronounced and his voice grew louder, laden with hatred. "She does not even care for her little son, because she hated William de Montferrat and sees her innocent child as an extension of him. If she has a son by Guy de Lusignan, she will try to find a way to make him my heir."

"But little Baldwin is already crowned."

"Do you think that interests my sister? As his mother, she has access to him, and if she has a son by Guy, she will kill my namesake. So far, God in his great wisdom, has given her a girl instead, and she has no ready replacement. Still, she will try to rule *through* my namesake. You and the High Court must expect that and prevent it."

Baldwin's bitterness was all the greater because he had loved Sibylla so much, Balian supposed. Now he had turned on her completely, seeing evil intent even where it might not be. Since Balian could not fathom what went on in Sibylla's head, however, he was not inclined to defend her either. He answered simply, "Yes, your grace."

"Tomorrow I will declare Ascalon forfeit to the Crown, and then we will strike camp and advance to Jaffa. I will reclaim that for the Crown as well, whether it yields to me or not, and thereby strip Guy de Lusignan of all his titles and fiefs. I will then call the High Court to Acre to discuss the succession."

"I don't understand. Your nephew is already crowned."

"But he's weak, Balian, very weak, and Sibylla will have control of him. As I just explained, I don't trust her not to do him harm. Jerusalem needs a new king, a strong king."

"What are you thinking of, your grace?" Balian asked warily.

"England."

"England?"

"My grandfather, Fulk d'Anjou, was selected from among the nobles of France to rule Jerusalem when Baldwin II had no male heir. So why shouldn't my cousin, the King of England, who shares the same grandfather as I, send us one of his sons? He has too many, and they make him no end of trouble. Why shouldn't he send us just one of his sons? I have been told they are all fierce fighting men."

Balian had never thought of such a radical solution. Although when he thought about it, it was not so radical after all. All the early Kings of Jerusalem had been men from the West, and while some newcomers proved completely incapable of adapting (like Guy de Lusignan), others, like his elder brother Aimery, soon acclimatized and became valuable fighting men and leaders.

"The idea came to me after meeting a most extraordinary English knight," Baldwin confessed. "His name is William Marshal, and he is very close to the English King. He has convinced me to send an embassy to him asking for aid. He says King Henry vowed more than ten years ago to come to the aid of Jerusalem and has been setting money aside for that very purpose—only he is beset with rebellions by his sons that keep him at home. To be sure, he is half a century old, so it is his sons who offer greater promise. Young lions all. I have decided to send the Masters of the Temple and the Hospital—and the Patriarch," Baldwin added with a smile, for though his face was deformed it was still movable. "What do you say, Balian?" In that question was a trace of the youth Balian had once known and mentored, a young man anxious for his approval.

"It is a good scheme, your grace," Balian assured him. "Out of courtesy, you might send the same ambassadors to the King of France as well."

"I will send them to the Pope, the Holy Roman Emperor, Philip of France, and Henry of England. With luck, they will vie with one another for the honor!" Baldwin was clearly excited and inspired by his idea. "I will sent the keys to the Tower of David, the keys to the Church of the Holy Sepulcher, and a banner of Jerusalem with the envoys to make it clear what we are offering. Whichever king takes the keys and the banner and comes to us will be received as our next King. I'll make the High Court swear to recognize whoever comes."

Balian saw a thousand problems. Disputes between the Western kings, Western noblemen without any understanding of conditions in the East, and a divided High Court, not to mention Sibylla and Guy's opposition and the fact that Baldwin V was already crowned—but he didn't have the heart to discourage Baldwin. So he nodded and said, "It's worth a try, your grace. Certainly, worth a try."

Chapter 12

Nablus, September 1184

Maria Zoë was not pleased with the steward of the citadel at Nablus. It appeared that for some time now, the aging clerk had meticulously kept the books without physically inspecting the stores of the citadel. In consequence, the fact that the sugar had been infested with beetles; that something had died in one of the storerooms, causing an infernal stink; and that leaking water had rusted a dozen axes and some hauberks in the armory had gone unnoticed until she undertook an inspection herself. It was, of course, her own fault for not inspecting sooner, she told herself, but that did not make things better.

Salah ad-Din had taken advantage of the fact that the High Court of Jerusalem was meeting in Acre to attack Kerak a second time—and this time he'd brought rocks to fill the fosse that separated the castle from the town. King Baldwin had no choice but to lead the army south to the relief of Kerak, and so Balian was again in the field. Maria Zoë had first put Ibelin on a war footing under Master Shoreham's command, and then come north to Nablus to make sure everything was in good order here as well—only to find it was not.

In the early years of her widowhood Maria Zoë had been preoccupied with other matters, happy to reap the income Nablus offered without paying much attention to where it came from. Increasingly, however, she had taken an interest in the management of her estates. There was, after all, much she could do to increase her income, and with four children to provide for, she was keen to do exactly that. This matter of damaged stores, however, had less to do with loss of income and more to do with the preparedness of the castle in the event of siege.

After being trapped in Kerak last autumn, she was determined to ensure that her own castles were prepared.

It did not help matters that the steward was a Latin priest who clearly disliked working with her and did not respect her. He kept repeating that his lord (by whom he meant not Balian but Philip of Nablus, who had surrendered the lordship of Nablus to the Crown more than twenty years ago) had never found cause for complaint. Maria Zoë was determined to dismiss him, but she could not do that without knowing whom to put in his place.

She dismissed him mentally after he withdrew with the books, and went to the window. From this tower room she had a good view of the city of Nablus. It had long since burst out of its old walls, which had fallen into complete ruin. Now the city sprawled white across a broad valley between two hills.

Nablus was ancient and the population reflected that fact, with a sizable community of Jews, a substantial Muslim population, and a bustling and prosperous Greek Orthodox quarter. But Nablus had prospered under the Latin kings as well. The Premonstratensians had built a major monastery here, while the Hospitallers maintained one of their largest hospitals on this important crossroads. Over the last eight decades, many pilgrims not only passed through on their way between Jerusalem and Nazareth, but had also chosen to settle here, forming a large and vibrant Latin community concentrated in the west of the city.

Regardless of their religion, the citizens of Nablus were largely traders and tradesmen and many had accumulated substantial wealth, a fact reflected in the tall stone houses that crowded the narrow streets and the many cobbled squares. Arcades enclosing the squares offered shade to the shops selling, at this time of year, fresh apples and pears, black and green olives, lemons, crushed spices, and sugar cane. Nablus was also a major center for glassmaking and a bottling center for scents and spices, as well as a soap manufacturing town. It wasn't exactly Constantinople, but Maria Zoë found it livelier and less stifling than Jerusalem. Like Constantinople, it had layers of history and it was solidly Christian, but it was not so much of a mausoleum as Jerusalem was.

There was a knocking on the door, and Maria Zoë called "Come in!" as she turned and stepped down from the window niche onto the terracotta-tiled floor.

Her visitors were a dark man, with a dramatic streak of gray hair and a beard equally divided between dark and light, and a nun in the habit of the Hospital of St. John. The first was Sir Constantine, the constable of Nablus, and the latter the Head Sister of the Hospital in Nablus, Sister Adela. Maria Zoë smiled at the sight of both of them.

Sir Constantine was of Greek descent, although he had been born and raised in Nablus and spoke Arabic better than Greek. He had been recommended to her by one of the Greek ambassadors who had visited her shortly after she took up residence here in 1176. "A reliable man," the ambassador had assured her, and while she understood that meant Sir Constantine was in the pay of her great-uncle, it mattered little. Her great-uncle was dead, and Sir Constantine was here with her still.

As for Sister Adela, Maria Zoë had first made her acquaintance in Ascalon, where she had helped set up an orphanage that Maria Zoë supported financially. She had been delighted to learn that the competent woman had been transferred by her Order to Nablus, and they had had frequent contact with one another since. Maria Zoë valued this woman's common sense and unsentimental commitment to helping the sick and destitute.

"Madame, a pleasure to see you, as always," the constable exclaimed with a bow, a smile, and a glint in his eyes.

"Likewise, Sir Constantine." She indicated the chair vacated by the indignant steward before exchanging kisses on both cheeks with Sister Adela.

When they were all seated, Maria Zoë asked, "So, what brings you here today—and together?" She looked from one to the other.

"We wanted to welcome you home to Nablus, madame. We see too little of you since your felicitous marriage to the good Baron of Ibelin," Sir Constantine opened gallantly—and the women exchanged an amused glance, because this was so much a part of the Greek's character.

Maria Zoë replied with a smile, "Come now, I've been married nearly seven years, and I was here just last spring."

"Indeed, but without your children. We hardly know your children. It was a pleasure to see Lord John riding beside you when you arrived yesterday. A fine boy."

Maria Zoë smiled. John at five did not ride so much as sit on a pony on a lead, but he was very proud to do that. Helvis, although a year older, was still too timid to ride her own pony, and preferred to sit in front of Rahel on her tame mare. To Sir Constantine she answered simply, "Yes, he's growing up fast."

"Madame, since your last visit the Jewish community approached me with the request to establish a rabbinical college in the abandoned madrassa."

"Is there any reason why they shouldn't?" Maria Zoë responded, surprised by Sir Constantine's earnest tone.

Sir Constantine sighed. "Not that I could see, which is why I granted permission. But no sooner had the Jews taken possession of the building than they were attacked by some of the Muslim youth. An elderly rabbi was badly beaten."

Maria Zoë felt her stomach tighten. She had gone out of her way to grant Muslim residents of Nablus a number of privileges, including the right to the *hajj*. They had their own religious courts for all private disputes, and they were allowed their own prayer rooms, although she had drawn the line at allowing them to build a minaret.

"Were you able to arrest the perpetrators?" she asked Sir Constantine.

"Unfortunately not, madame. The rabbi was badly concussed and said he could not remember faces, only that they overwhelmed him; he claimed it was five or six young men. We made inquiries among the Muslim community, but they all denied any knowledge of the event. They accused Christian youths of being behind the attack."

"Is that possible?"

"Unfortunately, yes, madame. There are elements among the Latin community that have recently come from the West. Some of them think nothing of attacking or burning synagogues. We have had to intervene more than once to protect Jewish property and persons. But in this case, madame, I fear the trouble indeed came from the Muslims. You see, they also chalked sayings in Arabic on the walls of the building saying: 'Salah ad-Din is coming!' and 'Beware the wrath of Allah!'"

Maria Zoë's and Sir Constantine's eyes met. It was the same everywhere. Tensions were building between the religious communities within the Kingdom. Populations who had lived together harmoniously only a decade ago were suddenly simmering with mutual mistrust.

"And that's why I'm here, madame," Sister Adela spoke up. "These sayings have greatly incensed many people—including some of my brothers—but they frighten others. Several of my sisters have asked to be transferred to someplace 'safer,' while others have asked to be allowed to return to their homes in the West."

"And what do you tell them, sister?" Maria Zoë asked.

"I tell them they vowed obedience and that they are privileged to serve where Christ chose to be among us in the flesh!" Her tone was firm and indignant. But then she added, "Yet in truth, madame, frightened sisters make poor nurses. I feel strongly that we must put an end to this kind of anonymous threat. It undermines morale and weakens us. Sir Constantine does not share this view, and that's why we decided to take it up with you."

"What do you propose to do?" Maria Zoë asked her bailiff.

"I have suggested to the Jews that they find another suitable building."

Maria Zoë raised her eyebrows. "Is that not capitulating to bullying and vandalism, sir?"

Sir Constantine lifted his shoulders. "What is the alternative? Should I randomly take youth from the Muslim community and punish them? Or should I risk more incidents by letting the Jews go ahead with their plans?"

Maria Zoë looked to Sister Adela. "What do you say to that?"

"How many Muslim youth can read and write in any language? Those sayings could only have come from an educated man, madame. I fear it was agent of the Sultan, sent here from Damascus to spread fear and, far worse, to radicalize the native population."

That made sense to Maria Zoë, and she looked again to Sir Constantine.

"It's not that I disagree, madame, but we have already questioned the elders, and they are not betraying the man, or men. What do you want me to do? Torture them?"

"Of course not!" Sister Adela jumped in before Maria Zoë could answer. "I don't advocate torture, but I don't accept that we cannot find the perpetrators. I think we need to be more insistent about demanding that they be turned over to us. Furthermore, I think the imams should be called together and advised of what dire consequences there will be for them and their flocks if the hostile elements are not weeded out. I think you should cancel the right of the *hajj* for all Muslims until these agitators have been turned over to Sir Constantine for punishment. We cannot not allow ourselves to be threatened or mocked."

Maria Zoë looked back to Sir Constantine. "What speaks against this course of action, sir?"

Sir Constantine weighed his head from side to side. "We risk angering the Muslim community even more by denying them the *hajj*."

"And I say, it is while they are on the *hajj* that their heads get filled with notions of the greatness of Salah ad-Din and *jihad!*"

"Let me think this over," Maria Zoë urged. "Meanwhile—"

Another knock on the door interrupted her and Maria Zoë looked over, annoyed. The door opened and one of the pageboys announced, "My lady, there's a visitor here says he's from my lord."

Maria Zoë was already looking beyond the boy, expecting one of her husband's household knights or squires, but she was disappointed to see a total stranger. The man looked to be in his mid-forties, with dusty brown hair and beard. He was attractive in a mature way, with the bright red skin that betrayed he had only recently come from the West and was still unaccustomed to the

Palestinian sun. His chain mail was of good quality, and his belt and sword bordered on ostentatious, with enameled panels bearing some emblem—and yet his surcoat was plain, threadbare, and ragged, like that of a man who was down on his luck.

He came briskly into the room like a fighting man, but his bow was courtly and his French impeccable. "Madame d'Ibelin, forgive the intrusion. I am an English pilgrim who joined the host going to break the siege of Kerak. Unfortunately, the only horse I brought East missed his footing and came up so lame, we had to cut his throat. Your noble husband urged me to come here to obtain a replacement." As he spoke he drew a sealed letter from inside his aketon and handed it to Maria Zoë as accreditation.

Maria Zoë checked that the seal was Balian's and then turned to Sir Constantine, who was already on his feet, eyeing the stranger with the same interest as Maria Zoë herself. "Sir Constantine, there's no need for you to go, or you, sister," Maria Zoë added to the nun, who had also risen.

"I have many duties to attend to, my lady, so if you would not be offended, I will indeed take my leave now."

"And I," Sister Adela echoed, "but I hope you will visit the school my sisters and I have established for the children of the lepers. We opened it on St. Helena's."

"I'd be delighted to visit!" Maria Zoë assured her. "In fact, I can't wait. I will come tomorrow." Then she held out her hand to Sir Constantine. He bowed over it, nodded to the stranger, "Sir," and withdrew with Sister Adela.

"Please, be seated," Maria Zoë invited the stranger as she broke the seal and scanned Balian's short letter. Balian was always brief when on campaign. He said only that Sir William Marshal had served the late King Henry the Younger of England, and was in urgent need of horses and a squire so that he could "prove his worth" against the Saracens.

Maria Zoë closed the letter and smiled at her visitor. "Welcome, Sir William. Let me take you down to the solar, where I can offer you some refreshment. Do I understand correctly that you are traveling alone?"

"Thank you, my lady. Water would be most welcome. Yes, I came out to Jerusalem as a pilgrim." He paused, but Maria Zoë was looking at him so alertly that he felt obliged to continue. "I served the son and heir of Henry II Plantagenet, but he was seized by a violent fever and died miserably. He had taken the cross months earlier and asked me to fulfill his vow for him."

That still did not entirely explain why he came alone, but Maria Zoë let it be for the moment, and instead led Sir William down to the solar, where she sent for refreshments. The knight looked alertly around the room, taking in the tiled floors, the carved window frames, the silk-covered cushions on the window seat, and the Persian carpet before the naked fireplace. His gaze at last came to rest on the delicate mosaics on the tabletop, and he brushed his hand over the surface, remarking, "Byzantine craftsmanship."

"Indeed," Maria Zoë agreed with an amused smile, wondering if he knew who she was; many Western knights did not. "Did you pass through Constantinople on your way here?"

"No, I chose to come by sea. I've heard unpleasant things about the way Latin pilgrims are handled in Constantinople since the fall of Alexius and the murder of his mother." So at least he knew this much, Maria Zoë noted. "But Queen Eleanor had a table like this in her palace at Poitiers. I believe she purchased it in Constantinople when she passed through with her first husband, Louis of France."

"Ah." Maria Zoë understood perfectly that he was subtly informing her that his association with royalty was more than that of a servant of the now dead Young King. She smiled and remarked politely, "I understand Queen Eleanor is quite a remarkable woman. I heard it said at my great-uncle's court that she and her ladies dressed like Amazons and behaved most outrageously while allegedly on pilgrimage."

"I daresay the tales have become exaggerated over time. Queen Eleanor says that she and her ladies rode astride, of course, and several of them had coats of mail made to provide protection against sudden attack. I wouldn't call that dressing like an Amazon, myself."

"No, I suppose not—since none of us know how Amazons dressed, if they existed at all," Maria Zoë added with a light laugh. "And what is she like now, this Eleanor of England? She must be ancient."

"She is over sixty, but you wouldn't know it to look at her. She is still slender and remarkably fit. She can ride all day, and she still rides astride—just as women do here."

"Here it is largely from necessity," Maria Zoë pointed out.

"Yes," Marshal agreed simply, but his expression suggested he was thinking something else; he was certainly frowning.

Maria Zoë raised her eyebrows. "Is there something the matter, sir?"

"No. No, of course not. Forgive me, I was just remembering something. An incident from long ago."

"An unpleasant incident, it would seem," Maria Zoë concluded, but the arrival of refreshments distracted them both. The pages unloaded dishes of sherbet, pistachios and cashews, candied fruit, raisins, and fresh pears, along with a pitcher of chilled water and another of light white wine.

"Please, help yourself, sir," Maria Zoë urged.

Marshal thanked her and helped himself to the sherbet and the water, but then he sat back and remarked, "My lady, I must confess I am uncomfortable in your presence in my present rank state. I have not bathed in more than a week, and I saw a bathhouse just across the street on the way in. Would you excuse me so that I may make myself more presentable?"

"Of course, sir." Maria Zoë understood perfectly. She turned and called to one of the pages. "Take Sir William down to the Syrian baths, and stay with him there. They are the best," she assured Marshal in an aside. "Meanwhile, sir, I'll have a room made ready for you, and inform our marshal that you are in need of horses and a squire." They both stood, and Sir William bowed deeply to her before departing.

That evening they were together again. Marshal was scrubbed and shaved, and his hair, beard, and nails had been duly trimmed. He had set aside his armor, although he was still sweating in his woollen hose, shirt, and gown. "You need some lighter clothes," Maria Zoë observed, as they sat down and one of the pages came to pour wine for them.

"I need a lot of things, my lady," Sir William observed with a wry smile. "Starting with the means to pay for all the other things I need."

"Jerusalem is always in need of a good sword, sir. You'll have no trouble finding employment here. Indeed, I thought my husband had already offered you a place in his ménage." Maria Zoë had been operating on this assumption when she had welcomed him into her home and put one of the knight's chambers at his disposal.

"He was indeed so generous, my lady, but I have yet to *earn* my keep." He smiled a crooked, rather sad smile.

"I daresay you'll have ample opportunity to do that soon enough, sir, as soon as you are again properly mounted and served; the Kingdom is surrounded and in a precarious position at the moment."

"So I understand, which is why I am happy to stay and do what I can here, despite promising my liege that I would return. I believe . . ." His voice faded away.

"Yes?"

"I sincerely believe King Henry would want me to stay here and help his cousin, King Baldwin. His son . . ." Again Sir William's voice faded, and this time Maria Zoë simply pushed the pitcher of wine closer to her guest.

Sir William took the hint and poured for her and then himself with an absent smile. "My lord, the Young King, took the cross lightly, my lady. He took it on a vain whim, if you like, and despite his vow, he was more interested in squabbling with his father and too proud to make peace even when he could no longer pay his mercenaries." Sir William upended his goblet of wine and refilled it. "They—we—took to plundering churches, and when that still didn't yield enough, they—we—sacked the monasteries of St. Martial and Rocamadour." He paused and looked hard at Maria Zoë. "Those names may mean nothing to you, madame, but they are very sacred places in France. My lord paid the price by dying within days of the sack of Rocamadour—and I came here, not only to fulfill his dying wish that I bring his cloak with the cross representing his vow to the Holy Sepulcher, but to seek forgiveness for my own sins, madame."

Despite the cooling breeze that now breathed through the window into the solar as the night chilled, Sir William was still sweating heavily.

"You are not alone, monsieur," Maria Zoë pointed out softly.

"Every man is alone with his sin, madame," Sir William answered with a crooked smile as he refilled his goblet, raised it to Maria Zoë, and drank deeply again.

"True," she conceded, bowing her head.

"I have spent many months trying to understand how I could have sunk as low as I did, madame, because, whether you take my word for it or not, it is not my nature to sack monasteries. When my lord died so miserably, it was like waking from a nightmare. I looked around and did not recognize myself. I had always prided myself on my honor, and my word was so good that even the mercenaries accepted it as if it were royal writ. Yet out of loyalty to my young lord, I committed grievous sins." He paused; the eyes sunk in his well-featured face were pools of darkness. After a moment he admitted, "I used to think that loyalty was the highest of all virtues, yet my very loyalty led me to commit crimes and offend God. Loyalty to an unworthy lord is like loyalty to the devil." He spoke to his wine rather than to Maria Zoë.

She waited, but when he said no more she remarked softly, "There is truth in what you say, but there is also the devil in rebellion." She was thinking of her own homeland, sinking ever deeper into chaos now that the legitimate ruler had been murdered and a usurper was on the throne.

"Too true," Sir William agreed, thinking of the rebellions of Henry II's sons. He finished his wine, but rather than refilling his cup, he pushed it aside and looked Maria Zoë in the eye. "You have a worthy king. I wish that Young Henry had had half as much sense as King Baldwin."

"And we wish King Baldwin had half the strength and prowess at arms of his cousin King Henry."

Sir William shrugged. "Other men can fight for a king, but they can't think for him. There is, however, something that greatly disturbs me. . . ." he admitted.

Maria Zoë looked at him expectantly and waited.

"This afternoon, when we were talking about Queen Eleanor, I stopped short of telling you something."

"Yes."

"It is something you—your husband and your King—need to know, although I fear it will only add to your many concerns."

Maria Zoë waited; she did not need more bad news, but apparently she was about to get some.

"As I understand it, Baldwin's heir is his nephew by his sister Sibylla, and in the event of the boy's death, his sister Sibylla would become queen and her husband would rule as her consort."

"Yes. That is correct."

"Her husband . . ." He reached for the wine again.

"Guy de Lusignan," Maria Zoë prompted.

"Yes, Guy de Lusignan . . . I knew him before he came to the Holy Land—and far better than I would have liked. Indeed, I was once his prisoner."

Maria Zoë looked startled at that.

"It was twenty years ago, madame, and the Lusignans were in rebellion against the Crown—or against the Duchess of Aquitaine, to be precise. I was just a young knight then, recently knighted and serving my maternal uncle, the Earl of Salisbury. At the King's request, Salisbury was escorting Queen Eleanor across her own county of Poitou when we were abruptly attacked by the Lusignans. You have to understand, madame, that we were not expecting any such attack. It was a fine spring day, and we had stopped to water our horses in a little stream and removed our armor to cool off and take some light refreshment in the shade. The horses had been untacked. My uncle, recognizing the Lusignans and discerning their hostile intent, saddled his fastest palfrey and ordered the Queen to mount and ride it to the nearest castle, assuring her the rest of us would hold off her pursuers. She, as I said, had no trouble riding astride, and she was soon flying to safety, while the rest of us scrambled to don our armor and to catch and saddle our horses.

"But we were not fast enough. They were upon us before we were mounted. My uncle was just putting his foot in the left stirrup when he was pierced from behind. He had not had time to don his armor, because he had been seeing to the safety of the Queen. He was run through by a lance."

Maria Zoë caught her breath. "From behind?"

"Yes. He was skewered on the lance, and as the horse fled in terror, he fell at my feet with the tip sticking out of his belly, punctured from the inside. He looked at me with an expression of surprise, horror, and pain, and I flung myself at the man who had killed him, with all the fury of youth shaken out of innocence in a single moment.

"Later I was told that I laid about, killing several men, before I too was stabbed in the thigh from behind, brought to my knees, and overpowered. But for all my wild fighting, I had failed to avenge my uncle's murderer. The youth who had aimed the deadly lance evaded my sword with a triumphant smile as he spurred away, leaving his henchmen to finish me off." He paused. "It was Guy de Lusignan, madame."

Maria Zoë sat up straighter in her chair. "No! That can't be!" She did not want to believe that the man who might be King of Jerusalem was a murderer, devoid of all chivalry.

"He was a youth—and later, when I was dragged, wounded and a hostage, to the Lusignan castle, I heard his elder brother berating him for his stupidity. 'You were supposed to bring the Queen to me a captive,' Hugh de Lusignan shouted. 'You weren't given leave to kill prizes worth much more alive than dead!' Hugh backhanded Guy for his foolishness, and scoffed at him for bringing back a 'penniless bachelor knight of no value'—meaning me—when he could have held a peer of the realm for ransom.

"Perhaps it was these words that made Guy despise me, for he did not accord me the slightest courtesy, not even attention to my wounds. I would surely have bled to death or died of wound fever had not one of the ladies of the house taken pity on me and sent me hot water and bandages to clean and dress the wound."

Maria Zoë was still in shock. "Guy de Lusignan stabbed an English earl in the back when he was not wearing armor?"

"Yes, madame."

"And no one brought him to justice?" Maria Zoë was thinking that in her homeland, he would have been publicly tortured and executed for such an outrage.

"It is a complicated story, madame, but the loyalty of the Lusignans was too important to King Henry; to end their rebellion he had to make concessions. It was more profitable for him to agree not to take action against the juvenile Guy de Lusignan than to make financial or territorial concessions. Henry excused Guy's action as an excess of juvenile zeal. Although Queen Eleanor was indignant at first, she eventually saw the sense of it. He was not brought to justice, but he remained persona non grata in the Queen's court. His elder brothers might cross the threshold, but not Guy.

"For me, however, the incident was not about forgiving the murder of one vassal to secure the loyalty of another; it was about the murder of my kinsman, my patron, and my lord. I have not forgiven Guy, and had he ever crossed my path in a tournament, much less war, I doubt he would have lived—but Guy avoided me adroitly, even dropping out of tournaments or switching sides at the last moment to avoid giving me a chance for revenge."

"Would that you *had* served justice upon him, monsieur!" Maria Zoë exclaimed with feeling. "He is a curse upon this Kingdom—he mocks and defies King Baldwin, completely overestimates his abilities, and will take advice from no one."

"Yes, that is Guy," Marshal agreed, nodding slowly. Maria Zoë shuddered in the heat, as if the ghost of Salisbury had just walked through the room.

The horse trader led the bay stallion out of his box and into the stableyard, to trot him up and down for the Latin knight that Ibelin's marshal had brought. This stallion was no longer young, but then, nor was the knight—and like the knight, the stallion had a number of battle scars.

"His last owner was a young knight who felt he needed a prettier horse to impress the ladies," the horse trader explained in heavily accented French, "but there's nothing wrong with him."

Sir William walked around the horse, critically looking at his hooves, hocks, and knees, measuring the width of his chest with his eyes, and noting that the horse's elbows stood well out from his sides. He glanced at the Ibelin marshal, whom the Dowager Queen had sent along to help him find two suitable mounts.

The Ethiopian not only knew horses very well, as Sir William had rapidly discerned, he also knew all the horse *traders* in Nablus. He judged this man the most honest. Nevertheless, Mathewos went forward and pulled up the stallion's lips to check his teeth and then ran his hand along his back, pinching along the spine, watching for a reaction. The stallion twitched his ears in irritation and stamped his foot, but he gave no indication of pain. The Ethiopian nodded and looked back at Marshal questioningly.

"How old is he?" Sir William asked.

"Twelve," the horse trader answered.

John d'Ibelin, who had begged to come along with Mathewos and Sir William, had already lost interest in the old warhorse. He wandered over to the corral for ponies, looking for one he liked; he longed for one of his own, even if his mother said he was too young. The horse trader was located on the south-eastern edge of Nablus, where he had sufficient room for paddocks to hold his sometimes substantial herds. John looked at the ponies for a while, but then his eyes wandered to the countryside beyond and saw something funny. Frowning, he raised his voice to attract the attention of the adults, "What's that?"

Sir William was interrogating the trader, so it was Mathewos who turned to see what John was asking about.

John pointed across the paddock to the valley beyond.

Mathewos followed the boy's finger, aimed at the Samaritan village about five miles away. A thin column of smoke appeared to be rising from it. "A fire," he started to answer, and then his heart missed a beat and his pulse started racing, even as John irritably answered, "No! Not that, over there! Aren't those camels?"

"Holy Christ!" Mathewos gasped, and he grabbed John up into his arms and ran to their horses. "Saracens!" he called to Sir William as he ran past.

Mathewos had only one thought at that moment: to get Lord John back to the citadel and warn the Dowager Queen. Sir William and the horse trader, on the other hand, turned in the opposite direction to see what had frightened the Ibelin marshal. Sir William shaded his eyes against the sun and squinted. Out upon the plain southeast of them, there was movement. A column of riders and camels was advancing up the valley. The head of the column was already into the next village, and there was now a second plume of smoke rising into the still air of the September morning.

"Holy Cross!" the horse trader muttered under his breath, his eyes bulging in his pock-marked face.

"I'll buy the horse!" Sir William decided instantly, and he shoved a handful of gold pieces at the horse trader, took the lead of the stallion, and flung himself into the saddle of his borrowed horse to start galloping after Mathewos, who was already clattering up the road into the city.

"The alarm!" Sir William shouted to Mathewos as he caught up with him. "How do you raise the alarm?"

"We ring the church bells."

"Good. Take this stallion with you and have him tacked up with my gear as soon as you get back!" He turned the lead over to Mathewos and turned up the street, heading for the closest church.

Within minutes the bells were clanging throughout the city, and people ran out into the streets to see what was going on. Maria Zoë heard the bells long before Mathewos came clattering into the ward of the citadel with John on the saddle in front of him to announce: "Saracens! They're burning the villages southeast of us!"

Maria Zoë was conscious of the terror that gripped her chest. Nablus had no walls, and even the citadel had only a dry ditch about four feet wide and walls hardly more than six feet wide and twenty high. This was no Kerak, rearing up on a mountain ridge with a massive fosse to protect it. It had no natural defenses, only its walls and towers, none of which would withstand mining or siege engines for more than a day or two.

"Rahel! Take the children to the keep at once!" she ordered, grabbing her linen veils and starting down the exterior stairs into the ward as she wound them around her head and neck. In her mind she was damning her steward. They were about to endure a siege with half their weapons rusted and the sugar full of beetles.

"Dawit! My horse!"

"Madame, have you heard? The—"

"Yes! I know! I need to reach Sir Constantine as quickly as possible."

Dawit ran back into the stables. Sir Walter was taking the steps from the garrison tower two at a time. "Madame! You can't go out—"

"Damn it!" Maria Zoë answered. "I *have* to go out there! This city isn't defensible! We have to get the townspeople into the citadel, and I need your help. Tell my knights to mount up!"

Around her the twoscore men-at-arms and sergeants of the garrison were running to their positions on the walls and towers. Men were pulling on their aketons as they ran, or buckling their swords and kettle helmets. A sergeant opened the door to the armory and started forming a line to pass crossbows up to the men on the battlements. A boy was still yanking the bell of the citadel chapel with all his might.

Sir Walter had reached Maria Zoë's side. "Madame, let us round up the townspeople. Take yourself to the keep!"

"No!"

Dawit brought out her black mare, and Maria Zoë swung herself up into the saddle. "You can catch me up at Sir Constantine's."

Walter grabbed her reins. "Madame, your husband will kill me if anything happens to you. Wait for me to mount."

"Nothing's going to happen to me yet. Join me at Sir Constantine's." She put her heels to her mare, and Sir Walter jumped out of the way.

Panic had gripped the streets of Nablus. Men were shouting, women screaming, children howling, and dogs barking. People were running in all directions or throwing things out of their windows, apparently intent on flight with their valuables. Halfway to the constable's substantial residence, Maria Zoë ran into him coming the other way. "Madame! What are you doing out here in the streets? Haven't you heard—"

"I'm hardly deaf, sir! We need to get everyone into the citadel! Everyone! We must convince people to abandon their possessions and see to their lives!"

The Greek constable smiled cynically at that, but inspired by Maria Zoë's determination, he agreed, "We can try. Send one of your Latin knights to the brothers!" He pointed to the Premonstratensian monastery, which sat a little above the city on the slopes of the hill to the west. "Have them round up the Latin settlers. Meanwhile, I'll go to the Syrian quarter and do what I can to persuade them to make haste to the citadel. I leave you to persuade the Greeks, madame. If you can convince the Greek clergy to join you, you might just succeed."

Sir Walter, with five of her knights and William Marshal, clattered up and surged around her. Maria Zoë pointed them to the Premonstratensian monastery, but Sir William insisted on staying with her. He was fully armed and carrying a lance.

"We hardly need that yet," she told him. "The Saracens are at least five miles away, and they've stopped to sack the villages."

"Some of them have, madame, but if they are like any other men I've met, they know towns offer far greater riches than peasant villages."

"That is what I am counting on," she flung back at him. They both had to shout above the noise around them.

He frowned at her, uncomprehending.

"If we leave them all our riches, maybe they won't bother attacking the citadel to take our lives as well!" she explained in a shout, then spurred away, leaving Sir William riding hard to catch up with her.

The Greek quarter of the town was one of the oldest, and the streets here were narrow and roughly cobbled. The two- to three-story flat-roofed houses, built around interior courtyards, pressed in close. Many apparently confused people clogged the streets, while others hung out of their windows asking what was going on. Maria Zoë rode into the midst of the chaos, pointing and calling out: "Get to the citadel! Waste no time! Get to the citadel!" She was speaking Greek, and Sir William, who had no knowledge of the language, found himself frustrated by his inability to add his deeper, louder voice to hers. Her voice was too high and frail to make itself heard very far in this mess. It seemed that most people, particularly the women, were just pointing excitedly, saying, *Vasilissa! Vasilissa einai!*" or "*Vasilissa Maria!*" Fortunately, however, several male voices picked up her message, and her words began to be repeated first by one, then a half-dozen, and finally a score of voices.

To Sir William's amazement, the people milling in the streets started to turn toward the citadel. More and more people began grabbing up their children and shouting to one another, apparently saying "Come!" or "Hurry!" But here and there, others still seemed intent on hitching up a cart or collecting their valuables. Sir William shouted at them in French and pointed toward the citadel. Language no longer mattered. The situation by now was clear enough, but he was glad to see a burly youth in ragged, dirty clothes start to reinforce his message. The young man was on foot and he moved among the crowd, firmly turning and, as needed, pushing people in the right direction. As Maria Zoë and Sir William advanced deeper into the Greek quarter, he kept up with them, pleading, urging, and pushing people to go.

The population in the street was gradually thinning and so was the clang of bells, as church after church was abandoned. But then they came around a corner and found their way blocked by dozens of men and women on crutches or pushing themselves on handcarts; these were the inhabitants of the large Hospitaller infirmary and their caretakers.

"They'll never make it to the citadel in time!" Sir William warned in alarm. In his mind he calculated the distance from the village he had seen the Saracens entering more than an hour ago. He did not think the Saracen vanguard could be far away, and his concern for Maria Zoë was rising by the second.

Maria Zoë looked for Sister Adela but could not find her. She was probably seeing to the children, but that reminded her of the leprosarium. Pointing in the opposite direction from the citadel, she called to Sir William, "There's a leper colony just two hundred yards away. They'll be safe there." She turned back and called to the Hospitaller sergeant who appeared to be in charge. "Take them to the leprosarium! Hide them inside!"

A roar of protest erupted from the cripples. Maria Zoë tried to calm them, arguing, "You will be safe there! The Muslims fear leprosy."

"I'd rather be killed than catch leprosy!" someone shouted.

"There is little risk of catching it just from entering the leprosarium," Maria Zoë reasoned, but the patients of the Hospital were not listening. Instead, they were trying to go in the opposite direction, and the sergeants that should have stopped them seemed confused.

Fortunately, at that moment Sister Adela emerged from the Hospital, followed by her sisters with the women patients. "The Queen is right," Sister Adela called out. "There's no time to get to the citadel. Go to the leprosarium! Hurry!" She ordered the sisters around her, pointing. Then, raising her voice, she ordered, "Sergeant, get the men to the leprosarium immediately. There is no time to lose!"

There was still some grumbling, but now that someone in authority had made a decision for them, the Hospitaller sergeants and lay brothers started physically pulling and pushing the halt and the lame in the direction of the leprosarium, while the sisters hustled the women and children.

The bells on the citadel started ringing dramatically faster, screaming in alarm, just as Sir Walter and two other knights clattered into the narrow street from the other end, all but trampling the lame who were still limping forward. "My lady! They're on the outskirts of Nablus! You must return to the citadel!"

"Not until one of you takes that boy behind him!" Maria Zoë answered hysterically, pointing to the youth who had been helping them persuade the people to go to the citadel and was now guiding the sick and lame toward the leprosarium.

Sir William shouted, "I've got him, madame! Go!" He drew up and reached out his arm to the youth. Without hesitation, the boy placed a foot on Sir William's and flung his other leg over the horse's croup to land behind Sir William's saddle.

They were riding at far too fast a pace. The horses' hooves slipped on the pavement and more than once they stumbled, dangerously close to pitching their riders onto the cobbles. The houses sped by, but the citadel seemed no nearer. Sir William started regretting taking the boy onto his saddle. Without him, he would have been free to turn toward the approaching Saracens. If he could put himself between the leading Saracens and the Queen, he could stop one or two. The mere sight of their leaders being killed would give the others pause. Sir William had seen it happen dozens of times.

At last they turned into a wider thoroughfare that led straight toward the narrow drawbridge and gate of the citadel. The Queen and the knights around her started drawing away, their horses unencumbered by the weight of two and the footing under their hooves finally firmer. There were other stragglers, however, running on foot from various quarters. One man, carrying his old mother in his arms, was clearly at the end of his strength. A woman was struggling with a babe in arms and two toddlers on her skirts. A man was leading his blind father.

Sir William drew up and told his passenger, "Run for it! I'll hold the Saracens."

"Alone?" the youth asked, incredulous.

"Long enough for you and the others to get inside! Go!"

The youth jumped down and ran, sweeping one of the toddlers up into his arms as he caught up with the mother. His example inspired a dozen men-at-arms to dash out from the gatehouse and start helping with the stragglers, too.

Meanwhile, Sir William turned his horse around and took his lance from its sling. He couched it at the ready under his arm and turned his horse to face the streets to the south and east, listening.

Men were shouting from the citadel, but he tuned out their voices. He focused all his senses on the approach of the enemy. He had fought more than once in towns and knew that there could be no massed attack of cavalry. The streets funneled knights into parties of two and three. Furthermore, streets were never straight—they bent and curved, ended suddenly at intersections or in cul-de-sacs. The deeper an attacking army penetrated into a town, the more diffused it became. Inevitably, one or two riders got out ahead of the pack and came on alone.

Sir William's goal was to kill one or two of these before the rest caught up with them. The thought that he was likely to be killed in exchange did not bother him; he had come here to do penance for his sins. If he died defending unarmed Christians from Saracens, God might just forgive him for the sack of Rocamadour.

At last he could hear hooves and shouting from the direction he was facing rather than from the citadel behind him. Men were calling encouragement or advice to one another in an alien tongue that made the hair on the back of his neck stand up. An instant later a rider burst out from between two houses, his horse stretching out its neck as the rider held a javelin aloft.

Sir William's heart missed a beat as he registered the turban and the tight-fitting, long-sleeved, brightly patterned tunic hiding the man's armor. He was face to face with his first Saracen.

The man noticed Sir William only a split second later, and he at once sat back and slowed his horse in surprise. Sir William did not give him a moment to recover from that surprise. He charged.

His opponent did not stand a chance. Sir William's horse and lance were both heavier. As the Saracen's comrades burst out from between the houses, all they saw was a riderless horse bucking in panic and a bleeding man with a lance pinning him to the street. Sir William released the lance as he swept past the dead man and drew his sword as he turned to face the next three Saracens, but before he could engage, three knights swept past him with leveled lances and struck two of the three Saracens from their saddles.

By now shouts were going up from the enemy, and the Saracens who had started to emerge from other streets turned around, cantering back the way they'd come.

The knights of Nablus likewise turned and started back for the citadel, pulling Sir William with them in their wake. He had achieved his objective. There were no more stragglers to be seen. As he and the other knights raced across the drawbridge, the wheels began to clank on the drums as it was raised behind them. They were into the ward of the citadel, amidst a throng of terrified people who filled every nook and cranny of the little enclosure as far as the eye could see.

Smoke soiled the sky, turning the sun orange and drifting over the walls of the citadel to drop cinders and ash upon the thousands of refugees crowding the ward. The breeze also brought shouts, cries, and the raised voices of men quarreling, along with the sound of things being dragged, broken, and smashed. Many children were crying in terror, held by mothers hardly less terrified themselves, while priests chanted in a half-dozen languages, and men murmured and argued and looked anxiously to the thin walls around them.

Maria Zoë, who had been looking out of the interior window of the hall, drew back, closing the shutters. Her household knights, Sir Constantine and Sir William, were discussing urgently the best defensive strategy for the citadel, but there had not yet been an assault, and the fires suggested there would be none today. The Saracens appeared to have taken the bait of plunder over the risky business of attacking the citadel—no matter how weak it was. She had bought them time, but how much?

"Water, food, and latrines," she said out loud, turning back to face the men in the room. "How many people are sheltering here? Do we even have a head count?" For this she looked not to her steward, who was conspicuously lurking in the shadows trying to avoid her eye, but to her confessor Father Angelus and the Abbot of St. Sebastian, an energetic and competent man.

"A head count?" Father Angelus answered with a glance toward the abbot. "No, but we estimate eleven thousand."

"That would be the entire Christian and Jewish population of Nablus," Maria Zoë responded dismissively.

The churchmen looked at one another and nodded. "Yes, madame. Except for the Muslims, who consciously remained outside, the entire population is here: Christians, Jews, and Samaritans."

"We can't possibly feed eleven thousand!" Maria Zoë protested next, after she absorbed the magnitude of her own success at getting the residents of Nablus into the citadel.

"Not for long, no," Father Angelus admitted.

"For how long?" Maria Zoë wanted to know.

"The castle was stocked to feed fifty fighting men and twenty others for a year," Father Angelus answered. "That means we can feed eleven thousand for . . ." he pursed his lips as he did the math in his head, "three to four days at the most—on short rations."

"Is that long enough?"

"That depends on what has happened to the King's army," Sir Walter replied, coming up beside her with the other knights in his wake. "If the Saracens are here because they have already defeated the forces under King Baldwin, we cannot expect relief at all."

Maria Zoë had been far too focused on the immediate threat to think about that.

"How do we find out what has happened to King Baldwin?" she asked, carefully avoiding the question about her husband, brother-in-law, and son-in-law.

Silence answered her question, and as she looked from man to man, they dropped their eyes. "I see," she answered her own question. "Either someone comes to our relief—or they don't."

The churchmen and rabbis took over the task of organizing the refugees of their respective flocks: giving the men watch duties or having them help with chopping wood for the bakery and ovens, and mucking out the stables and the latrines. The women were likewise organized to clean the common areas and keep the children out from underfoot. For the moment everyone appeared to be cooperating with everyone else, the shock of the fires beyond the walls and the consciousness of common danger overcoming all rivalries and hostilities, even between the Jews and the Samaritans.

By early afternoon a pregnant calm had descended over the castle, and Maria Zoë made her way to the top story of the keep to check on her children.

Rahel had them occupied with games and they did not seem unduly alarmed, although Helvis asked at once, "What caused the fire, Mama?"

"Men set the fire, sweetheart," Maria Zoë answered, stroking her curly dark hair.

"It's Saracens, isn't it, Mama?" John asked next, his voice excited rather than frightened.

"Yes," Maria Zoë admitted. He had been the first to see them, after all. He understood why Mathewos had brought him home, why the bells had rung all morning.

Helvis sucked in her breath. "Are we under siege?" she asked, her arms tightening around her doll in fear. "Like you were last year?"

"Yes," Maria Zoë admitted, thinking how sad it was that a six-year-old already knew the meaning of the word "siege."

"Is Papa coming to get us out?" John asked eagerly.

"Yes, I'm sure he is, John. So look after your sisters and keep them from becoming frightened until he gets here, will you?"

"Yes, Mama." He held up his head and hooked his thumbs in his belt, as he had seen the sergeants of Ibelin do.

Returning to the great hall, Maria Zoë sought out Sir William, who was at one of the tables, evidently swapping war stories with Sir Walter and some of the other knights. At the sight of her approaching, the knights all got to their feet respectfully. Maria Zoë gestured for them to sit down again, but drew Sir William aside. "Sir, I have a favor to ask of you."

He bowed. "I am at your service, madame."

"This morning, when we were trying to persuade the residents to come to the citadel, a youth helped us. The youth you took behind you on your saddle."

"Yes—and the last thing I saw him do was pick up one of the straggler children and carry it across the drawbridge."

"I would like to reward him—but I don't know who or where he is. Do you think you could find him out there?" She gestured toward the ward.

"I will certainly try, madame. He seemed both resourceful and courageous, not to mention bilingual—the ideal candidate for a squire. So it would be very much in my self-interest to find him."

Georgios sat with his back against the rough outer wall, clutching his knees in the circle of his arms. The air stank of terrified humanity crowded together, and it was impossible to move without stepping on someone. It was clear they could not survive like this very long, even though the priests were trying to get water and bread passed out to everyone as the sun sank down in the sky. The day was at its hottest now, and flies plagued the sweating people crushed together in the ward, while fires continued to burn just beyond the walls of the citadel.

Georgios supposed they would all soon be slaves, unless they decided to die instead. He had not yet decided what he would do. The thought of slavery to a Saracen master was so terrifying that Georgios' first thought was that he'd rather die. But then, he told himself, ever since his father had died and his mother had remarried a Latin innkeeper, he was little better than a slave anyway. Things had only gotten worse when his mother also died this past spring, trying to give the fat old bastard yet another child!

Someone shook him out of his thoughts. "Georgios! Georgios! Over there! That Latin knight is asking for you!"

Georgios followed the pointing fingers of those around him and recognized the knight who had taken him on his saddle. He swallowed and pushed himself to his feet, unsure what to expect.

The knight was stepping over people, excusing himself as he inevitably trod on someone now and again. Finally he was opposite Georgios, and the youth saw his eyes widen as he registered the ugly red birthmark that disfigured almost half his face. During their frantic efforts to drive people to the citadel, the knight had not taken any time to actually look at him.

"Young man," the knight opened in French, "the Dowager Queen asked me to find you and bring you to her."

"Me?" Georgios answered immediately, looking around as if the knight might be speaking to someone else. "Why? I'm nobody."

"You're the young man who helped us this morning, aren't you?"

"Yes, sir, but . . ." He shrugged.

"She'd like to thank you," the knight told him, his eyes far too alert and penetrating for Georgios' comfort. Most people didn't like looking at Georgios at all, and so they averted their eyes.

"But I'm nobody," Georgios repeated, "and I'm filthy." He indicated his hose, baggy and soiled at the knees, and his ragged linen tunic, stained with all sorts of undefined filth.

"The Queen is looking for the youth who helped her this morning, not a courtier," the knight countered, adding in a tone of voice that did not brook contradiction, "Come with me." For emphasis, the knight clasped his hand around Georgios' upper arm and propelled him through the crowd, with everyone now staring and murmuring in wonder.

The hall was crowded with monks, priests, guild masters, and other "better" citizens and their wives and children. The Abbot of St. Sebastian was at the high table along with Sir Constantine and several other prominent citizens, including the chief rabbi and the Greek archdeacon. They all seemed to stare at Georgios as he was led through the hall, up onto the dais, and then through the door to the room beyond. Georgios was burning with shame, and the red mark on his face was aflame by the time he entered the smaller chamber and realized that the Dowager Queen was here.

Georgios' throat was so dry it hurt to swallow, and he was sweating so badly he was conscious of his own stink while absently wiping his filthy hands on his dirty hose. "This is the young man who helped us this morning," he heard the knight say, but he didn't dare look at anything but his big feet. Looking down, he realized that in all the running he'd done this morning he had managed to tear the side seam of one of his low leather shoes, and his little toe was hanging out. He curled his toes in his shoe to try to hide it.

"Come closer," the melodic voice of the Queen said in Greek. Georgios shuffled closer, keeping his face down, hoping his hair would hide the birthmark but knowing it wouldn't.

"What is your name and station, young man?" the voice asked next.

"Georgios, my lady. My father was Antonis the soap maker, but he died when I was seven, and my mother married the innkeeper Charles Lyon."

"Ah, yes; he owns the tavern near Sts. Peter and Paul, doesn't he?"

"Yes, my lady."

"You know, many, many people might not have made it to safety if you had not helped us this morning."

Georgios shrugged and shook his head. "All I did was repeat what you said."

"Adding a little physical persuasion as necessary!" the knight added with obvious approval, and Georgios risked looking up at him. The knight was smiling at him.

"Georgios," the Queen was saying, "I don't know if any of us will be free five days from now, for that is the longest time we can hold out here if we receive no relief—but I want you to know that if we have to pay a ransom for our freedom, I will personally pay yours."

Georgios was so astonished by this offer that he forgot himself and looked up. The Queen was so close he could see the gold sheen on her veils and the pearl earrings swinging on either side of her face. She was the most beautiful creature he had ever seen, and he was so lost in wonder that he stared at her.

She smiled at him, only making matters worse, and the knight laughed because he could tell exactly how Georgios felt.

"So, Georgios, have you ever been around horses?" the knight asked.

Georgios tore his eyes away from the beautiful Queen to look at the knight. "That's all my stepfather lets me do, sir, muck and feed and—if the customers pay extra—I groom them, too."

"Can you ride?"

"A little," he admitted.

"How would you feel about looking after my horses, my gear, and me—assuming I get out of here alive, that is?"

"You mean as your manservant, sir?"

Sir William shrugged and nodded. Even if the youth took on the duties of a squire, it would be wrong to call him that, since he would hardly be in training for knighthood, but a good servant was better than a bad—or nonexistent—squire.

Georgios didn't know what to say. It seemed a far too exalted position for the likes of him. "But I'm not of Latin blood, sir," he found himself stammering. "My stepfather is Latin—that's how I learned French—but my parents were both Greek."

"That makes no difference to me," Sir William assured him. "As long as you believe in Our Lord Jesus Christ and we can understand each other."

"Yes, sir!" Georgios assured him, smiling for the first time, as he registered that this was *real*: he was being hired by a Latin knight. The fact that their joint future was so uncertain at the moment didn't for a second cross his mind—and if it had, it still would not have diminished his excitement or his surge of pride.

John couldn't sleep. He slipped out of the bed he shared with his sisters and tiptoed past Nanny Anne, who slept snoring on a pallet at the foot of the great bed. He peeked into the cradle at his little brother Philip, who was sucking his thumb, baby that he was. At the door he reached up above his head to drag down the heavy handle. The door was so massive he had a hard time dragging it open, but he didn't have to open it all the way, just wide enough to slip out.

Wearing nothing but his nightshirt, which came to mid-calf, he started up the stairs, which were cut into the thickness of the walls. The stones were rough and cold on his bare feet, for the sun never reached them. He counted them in his head automatically, testing his ability to count to a high number: there were exactly eighty-eight steps from the nursery to the roof.

There was a door at the top of the stairs, but it had been left open, and John stepped out onto the roof of the keep. Around him the battlements stood out black against a pinkish-gray sky. Most of the fires had gone out sometime during the night, and the noise had died away as well. A lone sentry was stationed up here, but he was slumped in the corner, sound asleep. A part of John knew that was bad, but he was thankful for the man's incompetence at the moment. If the man had been awake, John was certain he would have chased him away.

As it was, John was free to cross the roof, clamber up onto the step that ran around the interior, and lean out between two of the merlons to look down into the town. John gasped: the fires had blackened everything and the roofs of many houses had collapsed, so that he could look right down into the rooms with their ruined furniture. There were dead dogs and pigs in the streets, too, because the Muslims hated both animals.

John wished he had a bow. He pictured himself up here picking off one Saracen after another. Unfortunately there were no Saracens in sight, or in his imagination they would have been dead men. He wondered where all the Saracens were. Could they all be sleeping?

Two floors below, the captain of the watch was trying to keep his voice down as he argued with Rahel, insisting that he be allowed in. "I must report to my lady!"

"She's only *just* fallen asleep. I will *not* wake her. Tell me what it is, and I'll tell her when she wakes."

"She would want to be woken for this news!" the sergeant insisted angrily, infuriated that a native woman was standing in his way of being the bearer of good news to the Dowager Queen.

"I'll be the judge of that," Rahel insisted firmly, standing her ground.

"Damn you, woman!" The sergeant intentionally raised his voice, hoping to wake the Queen so she would hear the news from him even if this Coptic woman refused to let him tell her face to face. "The Saracens have gone! Just slipped away in the dark of night, like the creatures of hell they are!"

His words were drowned out by the blowing of a horn. Although the sound was far away, it was penetrating, and both Rahel and the sergeant lifted their heads and listened.

"Holy Cross!" the sergeant exclaimed and started pounding down the stairs, leaving a bewildered Rahel behind him.

As he burst out of the keep, he nearly collided with other men pouring out of the garrison tower and tripping over the people in the ward. "Out of the way! Out of the way!" the sergeant-in-charge shouted furiously, not waiting for sleepy civilians to obey him before kicking them aside. He forged his way through the sea of refugees, indifferent to the wailing of infants and the curses of their parents.

The horn was answered by another horn from a tower of the citadel, and suddenly the Dowager Queen, shrouded in a fur-lined cloak, her hair loose, was standing on the landing of the stairs to the keep, as the sun crept over the horizon and bathed the sea of humanity in brittle morning light.

"Open the gates, you idiots!" the sergeant shouted. "Open the gates! Don't you recognize the horn? The Baron of Ibelin is approaching!"

Maria Zoë still wasn't properly dressed, but she had covered her hair with a wimple and veils, and she'd replaced the thick, fur-lined cloak with a linen surcoat as she waited for Balian's squires to finish undressing him. A bath was being prepared by the household servants, and their ears were long as they listened.

". . . So he broke off the siege and pulled out in the night, just as he did last time."

"Without a battle?" Maria Zoë asked anxiously. Balian looked very haggard and exceptionally dirty and unkempt.

"Without a battle, though we did some skirmishing with some of their patrols. The problem is that Baldwin was feverish again, so we didn't follow as hard on their heels as we should have done. Salah ad-Din rapidly took advantage of that fact to withdraw over Samaria rather than heading due north to Damascus. The Bishop of Sebastian saved the city from sack by releasing some eighty Muslim prisoners of war he held there, but the Saracens completely razed the Templar settlement at Zarin, slaughtering every man, woman, and child before driving off the livestock and scuttling back across the Jordan. As soon as we had word of the direction they'd taken, I got Baldwin's leave to bring a force to Nablus. We came as fast as we could."

"I'm sure you did," Maria Zoë assured him, stepping forward and gesturing for him to step into the bathtub. "Come, relax. I'll massage the back of your neck," she coaxed.

Balian nodded, but first he dismissed his squires. "Get some rest," he advised. "You can see to my armor and equipment in the morning."

Gabriel and Ernoul nodded to Maria Zoë and then slipped gratefully out of the room. Despite their youth, they too seemed finished, she noted, all but falling asleep on their feet. Maria Zoë shooed the other servants away and sank down beside the bath, handing Balian the olive-oil soap for which Nablus was famous.

Balian let out a sigh of relief as he sank into the warm water and dunked his head under it to get rid of the sweat and dust clinging to his hair. As he came up he started soaping himself down, remarking as he did so, "Humphrey brought the knights of Toron, but he couldn't lead them. It was downright embarrassing to watch. They just ignored him for the most part, doing as they pleased or taking orders from a certain Sir Cyrus. I don't know who he is exactly, but he was charismatic, loud, and self-assertive—everything that Humphrey is not."

Maria Zoë said nothing. She rather liked her son-in-law, but Balian had taken an instant dislike to him because he was weak and timid. Barry went even further, calling him "effeminate." Maria Zoë's feelings for him were colored by the fact that Isabella so obviously loved him and insisted he was good to her. To her husband she noted, "He's only seventeen."

"I know! Do you want to know what Barry and I were doing at seventeen?"

"Not really," Maria Zoë answered, smiling and gesturing for Balian to lean forward so she could massage the back of his neck. "Apparently young Frankish noblemen do many regrettable things when young," she remarked lightly. But then she paused and added in a serious tone, "Guy de Lusignan was murdering English earls."

"What?" Balian sat up so fast he splashed water out of the tub, and Maria Zoë gave a sharp cry of protest as she got wet. Then she told him the gist of what Sir William Marshal had told her about Lusignan and the Earl of Salisbury.

"Christ have mercy on us!" Balian exclaimed, staring at her.

"Yes. Now calm down and let me rub your shoulders. There's nothing we can do about Guy de Lusignan right now."

"How did we come to this?" Balian asked, rhetorically but with no less anguish.

"He's not King *yet*," Maria Zoë reminded him. "Maybe Baldwin V will grow up big and strong and throw his stepfather out of the Kingdom. You've heard that Agnes de Courtenay died?" Maria Zoë made no attempt to disguise her delight at this news. "Without her to poison the boy's ears, he stands a better chance of learning wise government while still young. His mother's never shown any interest in him and is too stupid to have much influence anyway, so he's under the wise tutelage of Tripoli. Meanwhile, Guy might get himself killed in some accident, as your brother Hugh did, or maybe he'll catch malaria as William de Montferrat did or dysentery as Amalric did. We don't know what will happen.

Who would ever have thought that a boy suffering from leprosy would be able to defeat the combined forces of Syria and Egypt again and again and again?"

"If only we *were* defeating them, Zoë, but we're not. All we do is chase them away, and they come back again when it suits them, stronger than ever. He's wearing us down, Zoë."

"That's your exhaustion speaking, my love. You'll feel better after some sleep."

Balian didn't contradict her. He took a deep breath and tried to relax, grateful for the feel of Maria Zoë's strong thumbs moving in small circles, rubbing the tenseness from the muscles on the back of his neck. Her fingers were soon working away his headache as they massaged the back of his head next. His eyes closed, he asked, "How did you manage to get everyone into the citadel? We didn't see a single casualty as we passed through town—or were they all in the north and west?"

"No, we cleared those quarters as well. Only the Muslims refused to come, and I don't know what happened to them."

"Fools! They were slaughtered in Ibelin!" Balian reminded his wife.

"I know; I visited shortly afterwards, remember? But we didn't hear any screaming in Nablus, as Richildis described at Ibelin. Either they did have an agent of the Sultan here, who guaranteed their safety—or, I suspect, they had the sense to slip into the countryside. Sir William Marshal killed the first Saracen to appear before the castle, by the way. You should have seen it. He lowered his lance, and three seconds later his opponent was dead. Then Sirs Gregory, Godfrey, and Martin reinforced him and they unhorsed or wounded another three of the leading Saracen cavalry, which convinced the others to withdraw and regroup. Our knights raced back into the citadel and we raised the drawbridge. But we couldn't have withstood an assault, nor did we have sufficient stores to feed so many people more than four or five days."

Balian could hear the doubt and uncertainty in his wife's voice, so he sat up and twisted around in the bath to look her in the face. "You did the right thing, Zoë. It's what Richildis should have done at Ibelin. Never forget: if you look after your people, they will look after you."

"But what if you hadn't come?" Maria Zoë asked him back, tears springing to her eyes as the tension of the last twenty-four hours overwhelmed her.

"Then you would have negotiated a surrender," Balian told her earnestly.

Maria Zoë bent and kissed him.

He returned the kiss, then drew back and held her face in his wet hands. "Zoë, as long as I live I will do all I can to protect you and our children, but we both know I may be killed any day. If that happens, you *must* then see to the safety of our children yourself."

She nodded, but the tears were now spilling out of her eyes. "I didn't have time to be frightened, but this citadel hardly deserves the name!"

Balian stretched forward to kiss her eyelids, then pulled her closer and held her in his wet arms. "But you saved every Christian man, woman, and child in Nablus! They won't forget that."

Maria Zoë pulled back to remark cynically as she wiped the tears away on her sleeves. "I'm not so sure. They are just as likely to blame me for the loss of their property."

Balian shook his head. "I don't think so. Now let's finish the bath so we can get to bed. I have missed you sorely these past weeks."

"And I you," she admitted, leaning to give him a lingering kiss that affirmed her desire. The danger she had just escaped made her desperate for the reassurance of his presence and his love.

Chapter 13

Jerusalem, March 1185

IT HAD SNOWED DURING THE NIGHT and the roofs were white, but the cobbles were black where the snow had melted and mixed with dirt and manure. The party of riders made slow progress on the slippery stones, and the shopkeepers lining the street took advantage of the fact to try to lure them inside with promises of flea-free beds and spiced wine. Eventually, however, they reached the large residence on the corner of Jehoshaphat Street and the Street of Spain. The broad stone façade of the three-story flat-roofed building had a large arched door giving access to the inner courtyard, and a battery of windows protected by iron grilles on the ground level. The third story was marked by double-light windows with delicate double pillars separating each pair. But the most distinctive and unusual feature was a loge on the second floor, supported by a line of simple Doric columns stolen at some forgotten date from a long-lost Roman structure.

The lead rider leaned out of his saddle and rapped on the wooden door with his mailed fist. Almost at once the double doors were thrown open to admit the twenty riders. They were wrapped so completely in fur-lined cloaks that it was hard to tell that the men were armored, or that there were two women in the middle of the group.

Inside the courtyard, Humphrey de Toron jumped down and went to help his wife dismount. He was wearing thick sheepskin boots that made no sound as he moved, and unlike the mailed feet of some of his retainers, they did not slip on the wet cobbles. He held Isabella's bridle and off stirrup so she could get down, and then turned the horse over to a young black youth who appeared out of nowhere and grinned at him.

"Eskindar!" Isabella recognized Dawit's younger brother. "You're all grown up!"

"I'm fourteen!" he answered in annoyance.

"Where's Dawit?" Isabella asked next, looking around the congested courtyard.

"I don't know," Eskindar answered indifferently. "I'll take Sultana. She'll be happy to be home." Isabella's mare had been bred, born, and raised in the Ibelin stables and had been a wedding gift from her stepfather.

"So am I!" Isabella announced. Indeed, she could hardly stop herself from throwing her arms around the Ethiopian in sheer delight, but she could feel Humphrey stiffen beside her. So she slipped her hand in his instead and flashed him a smile.

Humphrey could not begrudge his wife her joy at being home. He knew how miserable she had been at Kerak, and they had found Toron inhospitable, too. It was hard to feel "at home" in the cavernous but nearly unfurnished fortress. But he was jealous of her affection for her mother and stepfather, because the treatment he had received from his own mother and stepfather had been so different.

The Dowager Queen was already coming down the stairs into the courtyard, and Isabella let go of his hand to run to her. "Mama!" She ran to her mother so fast that her hood fell off her head, revealing her neat white wimple. Then Maria Zoë was clutching her firmly, exclaiming in dismay, "Child! You're as tall as I am!"

"I'm not a child anymore!" Isabella answered with a laugh, looking back over her shoulder at Humphrey.

Humphrey took the cue and duly advanced to bow to his mother-in-law.

"Come!" Maria Zoë responded. "Not so formal!" She touched her cheek to his, first left and then right. As she stepped back she urged, "Come inside; you're nearly frozen!"

The solar, warmed by a roaring fire, was overflowing with dogs, children, and servants bringing up hot spiced wine, meat pasties straight from the oven, and hot fig and raisin cream, Isabella's favorite sweet. Helvis and John greeted their unfamiliar half-sister politely as their mother had instructed them, and Nanny Anne brought the toddler Margaret and baby Philip for Isabella's inspection before spiriting all four children away, trailed by two of the dogs.

Isabella and Humphrey were urged to sit down in the chairs closest to the fireplace. They had hardly taken their places before Ernoul bounded in, grinning. At the sight of the squire, Humphrey smiled for the first time and stood to embrace him.

"Have you brought the poems you promised?" Ernoul asked, with a familiarity that made Maria Zoë raise her eyebrows slightly, but Humphrey was clearly not offended.

"Yes, everything is with my luggage. I'll bring them to you as soon as—"

"No rush!" the squire told the baron graciously. "But when you're settled I'll take you to St. Anne's. They have an amazing library."

"Ernoul!" It was the stern voice of the Baron of Ibelin as he entered the solar. "The Baron of Toron is here to attend a session of the High Court, not to gallivant around Jerusalem in search of romances and poetry with the likes of you!"

Ernoul bowed deeply to his lord and took a step back so that the barons could greet each other, but he was grinning, evidently indifferent to the rebuke.

Balian dutifully embraced his son-in-law, but both his wife and his stepdaughter could see the men were uncomfortable with one another. Humphrey's smile was gone, and Balian's expression was carefully guarded.

"When will the High Court meet? Do you know what this is about?" Humphrey asked as they pulled back.

Balian gestured to the seat Humphrey had vacated and took his own place beside his wife. "The High Court will meet as soon as we have a quorum. That should be tomorrow or the next day. Oultrejourdain, Beirut, and Sidon are not here yet. As to what it is about," Balian took a deep breath, "I think you can guess. The Queen Mother is dead, so the last voice favorable to Jaffa that the King trusted—rightly or wrongly—is silenced. Jaffa remains obdurate and has made not one gesture of reconciliation. The King is determined to exclude him from both the succession and the Regency."

"Can he do that?" Humphrey asked, frowning uncertainly.

"Legally, the High Court decides who will be King," Balian reminded him, adding, "even if there is a strong inclination to take the closest relative of the last King. The High Court selected Baldwin IV's successor when we crowned his nephew. So—no, King Baldwin cannot alone designate his successor's successor, but the High Court can."

"And—if not Sibylla and Guy—who, then?" Isabella asked in a slightly breathless voice, suggesting either fear or eagerness.

Balian looked intently at his stepdaughter. He remembered vividly how vulnerable and yet brave she had been during her captivity at Kerak. When he and the rest of the army had arrived to relieve the siege, he remembered thinking she looked like a child playing grownup in a wimple declaring her married status, but a body that was still wholly childlike. She was not so childlike now. Her chest was no longer flat, and her waist had narrowed. She was nubile, very pretty—and very alert. It struck him that while her body was not yet mature, her wits and heart had been forced to grow up rapidly—even prematurely—in the hostile environment of Kerak. Isabella might be only on the brink of physical maturity, but her brain and ambitions were far ahead of her body.

"I'll be honest with you," Balian answered his stepdaughter, with a very short glance at her husband. "King Baldwin favors a mature and experienced military leader from the West."

"But I thought his embassy to the West had yielded nothing," Humphrey complained.

"That is an exaggeration," Balian corrected him. "Henry of England has instituted a special tax, the 'Saladin Tax' they call it in England, and the proceeds of this tax are paid directly to the Templars and Hospitallers in equal portions so that they can finance the reconstruction of castles and hire mercenaries here."

"That hardly addresses the question of the succession," Humphrey pointed out, and Balian's lips narrowed. Humphrey was a puppy with soft down on his cheeks, but he spoke in a pedantic tone that got under Balian's skin.

"Not directly. I was simply pointing out that the embassy *did* yield us significant new financial resources. Furthermore, according to the Hospitallers, Henry II was far more tempted to come to Jerusalem than his final rejection would suggest. He called together a council of his barons. But then Heraclius poisoned the atmosphere by losing his temper and accusing Henry of deceit, saying he came from the devil and would go to the devil—hardly diplomatic behavior, not to mention that he thereby insulted the King of Jerusalem as well as the King of England."

Maria Zoë could tell that Balian was furious, but he kept his voice down. It was only the clipped way he spoke that betrayed him. Balian would never forgive the Patriarch for excommunicating the good William of Tyre, or for this latest blunder.

Balian had his temper on a curb rein, however, and continued. "The real reason Henry of England would not come to our aid, Sir William Marshal tells me, is that he fears his lands in France would be attacked by Philip of France the moment he left for the Holy Land. He would have liked to see his son Richard take the bait, however, as there is no love lost between them. Richard, on the other hand, according to Sir William, fears that if he sets out for the Holy Land, his father will snatch the Aquitaine away from him; he prefers a bird in the hand to one in the bush."

"So who does King Baldwin want from the West?" Isabella brought the conversation back to the point.

Balian sighed. "I don't know."

"So he doesn't tell you everything?" Humphrey asked, sounding rather satisfied by this fact.

"No King tells *anyone* everything," Balian answered, biting his tongue to stop himself from adding, "boy."

Maria Zoë felt it was time to intervene before the tension between her husband and son-in-law escalated further, so she turned to Isabella and asked: "Don't you want to change out of those wet shoes? Let me send for some warm slippers for you."

Humphrey frowned in annoyance, but Isabella was thankful for her mother's intercession, exclaiming, "That would be wonderful, Mama. It was such a cold trip! I can't remember anything like it." Balian knew exactly what Maria Zoë had done and why, so he calmed his own irritation, gesturing toward the refreshments and asking Humphrey if he didn't want some wine.

Ernoul at once jumped forward to pour, and the squire's proximity seemed to mollify Humphrey a bit. He and Ernoul exchanged a smile, and Ernoul added a wink that neither Balian nor Maria saw.

"Have you heard about the Templar election?" Balian asked his son-in-law, after Ernoul had withdrawn and Humphrey had taken a sip of the aromatic, hot, mulled wine.

"No. Has there been one?" Humphrey sounded surprised. "I know Arnold de Torroja died even before he reached England, but have the Templars had a Grand Chapter already?"

"Last week."

"And?" Humphrey pressed his wife's stepfather.

Balian took a deep breath and then drank deeply of the wine before answering. "A disaster. I honestly don't know what the Templars were thinking—or rather, who was paying them."

"Papa! Surely the *Templars* can't be bribed!" Isabella exclaimed, shocked.

"Hush!" Maria Zoë silenced her daughter. "The Templars are just men, and they too are corruptible—it seems."

"Why do you say that?" Humphrey demanded to know. "Whom did they elect?"

"Gerard de Ridefort." Balian made a grimace as he spoke the name.

"What's wrong with Ridefort?" Humphrey asked. "He was Marshal and led the Templar relief of Kerak, didn't he? He seemed to be a vigorous fighting man, better suited to leading the Templars than the aging Torroja." Humphrey's defense of the new Templar Master only lowered Balian's opinion of him.

"Ridefort may be a knight after your stepfather's heart—brutal and brainlessly brave—but he is a man without subtlety or the ability to compromise. Everything to him is black or white, good or evil, right or wrong; he knows no shades of gray, no nuance, and no self-doubt. That, my lord" (Balian hid behind formality to avoid calling his son-in-law "boy"), "is dangerous in a man in his position. On top of that, he holds a grudge against the Count of Tripoli for some ridiculous promise he alleges the Count made him."

"A lot of barons bear grudges against one another," Humphrey answered with a shrug.

"Raymond de Tripoli is likely to be Regent for Baldwin V. It is not good for the Templar Grand Master to be at odds with the ruler of the Kingdom at a time like this," Balian answered steadily, fighting hard to keep his temper. He did not understand how the young man could be so naive, and he found it disconcerting.

"Does Ridefort get along with the Hospitaller Master?" Isabella asked, distracting attention from her husband and earning a smile from her stepfather. At least *she* was thinking!

"Not at all. Moulins is more monk than knight, and he is everything Ridefort is not: a man guided by reason rather than passion, cautious and circumspect."

A soft knock on the door was followed by the appearance of Rahel with the slippers Maria Zoë had sent for. At a gesture from Maria Zoë, Rahel helped Isabella, while Maria Zoë exploited the interruption to change the subject. Turning pointedly to Isabella, she asked innocently, "How are you settling in at Toron?"

To her distress, Isabella's face closed and her lips tightened, and it was Humphrey who answered. "I've surrendered Toron to the King in exchange for a money fief. Isabella and I will buy houses here and in Acre."

"You did what?" Balian asked in disbelief, sure he had misheard something.

"I've exchanged the Barony of Toron for a money fief," Humphrey repeated, his lips a tight, defensive line, while he fixed his gaze on his wine to avoid looking at his father-in-law.

Balian opened his mouth and closed it again, casting a look at his wife to help him in his speechlessness. It was completely beyond his comprehension that a man—or even a youth—would give up a major barony worth eighteen knights for any sum of money. Taking money payments was demeaning; it put Humphrey almost on the same level as a groom in the stables or a purveyor of cloth!

"Reynald de Châtillon had completely plundered Toron!" Isabella came to her husband's defense. "The castle had almost no furnishings. Even the chapel was stripped!"

"I'm sure he sold all the movable goods to help build the ships he launched in the Red Sea," Humphrey complained, still evading Balian's eye. He was pleading his case with his mother-in-law instead, adding, "I couldn't ask Isabella to stay in

Toron. We had no proper hangings for the walls, and they bled moisture in the winter."

"Half the windows in the residence didn't have glass!" Isabella added. "And there were no glass lamps, either—just torches that smoked all the time. Not to mention the state of the latrines!" She made a face of disgust that shattered her mature image and made her look like a child again.

"Why didn't you tell me?" Maria Zoë protested, reaching out a hand to Isabella in her distress.

"But, Mama! We knew Nablus had been sacked! You don't have anything to spare."

"We could have found *something*—at least spare lamps and wall hangings," Maria Zoë insisted with a look at Balian, who shrugged agreement.

"We didn't want charity," Humphrey insisted firmly, frowning. "Taking the King's offer made more sense. He wants Toron as a border fortress, not a residence, and for that he doesn't need lamps and wall hangings."

"How did the King make this offer?" Balian wanted to know, remembering that the King had not left Jerusalem in six months.

"He made it through the Constable."

"Aimery de Lusignan," Balian noted, wondering if the King was even aware of the arrangement.

"Eschiva came to visit and brought little Hugh with her. He's such an adorable little boy!" Isabella told her mother enthusiastically, and the women again steered the conversation to uncontroversial topics.

The Templar and Hospitaller Masters were not technically members of the High Court of Jerusalem, but they were almost always included, and there were dozens of knights from both Orders loitering around in the inner ward of the citadel when Ibelin and Toron arrived. At the foot of the stairs leading up to the great chamber of the Tower of David, Oultrejourdain was standing in conversation with a man in Templar habit, and Balian felt his son-in-law recoil at the mere sight of Oultrejourdain.

The latter had replaced the straw hat he wore in the summer months to protect his shaved head with a cap made of bear fur he'd bought from a Russian trader. The man opposite him wore his well-lined coif up over his tonsure, but boasted a bristling red-and-gray beard that came halfway to his chest. He was a burly man even when standing beside the hefty Oultrejourdain, and he spoke

French with a heavy Flemish accent that sounded guttural and common to Ibelin's ear. It was Gerard de Ridefort.

Oultrejourdain caught sight of his stepson and smiled at him like a wolf sighting a sheep. "Ah, my dear boy! Have you met the good Grand Master de Ridefort yet?"

Humphrey didn't answer directly, just clung to Balian's shadow as the latter strode forward to greet Ridefort.

"Ibelin," the Grand Master growled, and turned his eyes on Humphrey as Oultrejourdain introduced him: "My stepson, formerly Baron of Toron, but he gave that up for money, so I don't know who he is anymore."

"I'm still Humphrey de Toron," Humphrey insisted, more like a surly teenager than a proud baron.

"Husband of the Princess Isabella," Ibelin reminded the other two men.

"Ah, how is dear little Isabella these days?" Oultrejourdain asked, with the same predatory grin.

"She's growing up," Ibelin answered with a warning look, and then led Humphrey past the other two men and on into the great chamber of the Tower of David.

The great chamber was already crowded, but Ibelin found his brother with Antioch and Tripoli and joined them, Humphrey still in tow. "Any sign of Jaffa yet?" Ramla asked him immediately.

"No. Do you honestly expect him?" Ibelin countered.

"Yes. I've heard he's in Jerusalem, though he left Sibylla in Ascalon with their daughter." Sibylla had still not given Guy de Lusignan the male heir he craved—very much to the satisfaction of those like Ibelin and his brother, who mistrusted him. "He lodged at the Patriarch's palace."

Balian mentally noted that "birds of a feather flock together" as he scanned the room and confirmed that Heraclius had not yet arrived. He gathered that Oultrejourdain and Ridefort were awaiting the Patriarch and with him, Guy de Lusignan. An unholy coterie if ever there was one, he thought to himself with an inward grimace. And then, as if on cue, the Patriarch of Jerusalem swept into the great chamber, glittering in white satin robes stitched with gold embroidery, with rings on every finger and a jewel-studded cross around his neck. In his wake came Guy de Lusignan, wearing a supercilious smile that betrayed his nervousness. He wore his blond hair long and flowing about his shoulders. His chain mail was fancy, with bronze edging, but obviously virgin too. His sword held a disk of lapis lazuli in the pommel, and was suspended on a belt of enamel panels. It was bound around a silk brocade surcoat so heavy with gold embroidery it would not have disgraced the Caliph of Baghdad. To finish the picture, Lusignan's spurs glittered with gemstones along the prongs enclosing his soft leather boots.

Compared to the two principals, Oultrejourdain and Ridefort looked like poor retainers in their simple armor, plain surcoats, leather belts, and iron spurs—but they were what made Lusignan dangerous. They might physically follow in his wake, but intellectually they led him by the nose. Their very pretense of "support" was a means of persuading Lusignan to do their bidding.

Ibelin's eyes met Reginald de Sidon's on the far side of the room, and for a moment they shared a grimace. Then Ibelin's eyes slid to Aimery de Lusignan, who went forward to greet the Patriarch with a deep bow and kiss his ring before he gave his brother a demonstrative embrace. Aimery's embrace was for the public, Balian calculated. Aimery thought Guy was a fool, but he was signaling to the rest of the baronage that he would stand by him now despite his personal feelings; his brother was his brother, and blood was thicker than water.

Balian cast his own brother a look and saw the tension around his eyes, while the bitter taste of hatred twisted his lips in a caricature of a cynical smile.

Finally, the herald announced King Baldwin IV of Jerusalem, and they all turned to stare at the doorway through which four knights of the Order of St. Lazarus were—with difficulty—carrying a narrow litter with long handles that enabled them to stand single file. They came slowly through the door, and the occupants of the room parted to make way, while all eyes focused on the man lying propped up on the litter, under white linens embroidered with the gold crosses of Jerusalem. The linen completely covered Baldwin IV except for his gloved hands, folded on his chest, and his masked face. But he wore the crown.

As he was carried between them, the men in the room went down on one knee, out of respect both for the sick man himself and for God, who had visited this king upon them and would soon take him back to his bosom. When the Knights of St. Lazarus reached the throne, the litter was set down, and knights together lifted Baldwin IV up and placed him on the throne, arranging the white sheets around him, putting the scepter in the lifeless fingers of his left hand and the sword of state across his knees. Then they took the litter behind the throne and positioned themselves to flank the King, two on either side. Sir Daniel was the knight closest to the King's right hand, Balian noted.

"My lords," the King spoke in a voice that echoed inside the mask and was now familiar to all of them. "I have summoned you—here—out of—deep distress—for the—the Kingdom—of Jerusalem. I will soon depart to—to whatever—reception Our Lord—has prepared for me. I am in His hands—more each day."

A mutter of "Amen" swept through the room; many of the bishops crossed themselves.

"My successor. My nephew Baldwin." The King was clearly having trouble speaking—whether from emotion or from physical weakness, it was impossible to tell. Balian felt the old urge to go to him, to tell him it was all right, that he need not say any more. Yet he could not. He was separated by a room full of more senior barons, by protocol—and by the knowledge that Baldwin had to continue, no matter how much it hurt him.

"My nephew—Baldwin—is very—young." Did he mean young or weak? There were rumors the boy was sickly, though Ibelin had no proof of it. "He—he will need a Regent—as soon as—I am gone. This Court must—today—decide on—who that will be. Today."

"I am the boy's stepfather," Guy de Lusignan started, only to be silenced by a cascade of hisses, boos, and protests.

"We know where your Regency would lead us!" someone shouted.

"Yes, to defeat!" someone else added.

"You are not Sibylla's legal husband!" Ramla bellowed. "You're nothing but a male whore! A—" Balian gripped his brother's arm and hissed at him to shut up.

Barry looked at Balian in outrage, and Balian shook his head. "Let the others bring him down," he said between his teeth, and nodded to the rest of the room.

There was a veritable storm of protest against Guy de Lusignan that included most of the bishops and all the barons except Oultrejourdain, who was looking bemused but hardly provoked. Only Heraclius was supporting Lusignan, shouting in an ever higher voice that it was only "natural" that the boy's mother be made Regent. "We have the precedent of Queen Melisende!" he tried to remind the High Court.

"She was married to a fighting man, not a fop!" Sidon barked.

The uproar was so loud that the King could not make himself heard above it, and Ibelin saw him turn his head to his escort. Sir Daniel opened his mouth and called for order in a voice that reverberated off the ancient beams overhead. Silence gradually fell on the room, and the High Court waited expectantly.

"The High Court has—made it clear—whom they—do *not* want. Now, decide who—it should be."

"Your grace, there can be only one choice," the Prince of Antioch stepped forward. "My cousin and yours—the Count of Tripoli."

Ibelin saw the new Templar Master start as if he had not expected this, but that hardly seemed likely. Tripoli was the obvious candidate, because he was himself a grandson of Baldwin II of Jerusalem and had ruled during Baldwin IV's minority. Fortunately, the Templar Grand Master did not have a vote.

Tripoli was speaking. "If it is the will of the High Court, your grace, I will take the burden of the Regency, but not guardianship of the young King."

Ibelin started. Why that? He looked at his brother, who knew Tripoli much better than he.

"I would not have it said," Tripoli answered the question himself, "if the boy should die before he comes of age, that I had a hand in it. I will rule the Kingdom in his name, but I will not bear responsibility for his person. Jaffa is welcome to—"

"No, he's not!" Ramla interrupted his ally, earning an astonished look. "Edessa should be guardian."

Although Jaffa resisted this at first, Ramla's suggestion found a majority, and within a few more minutes it was settled. The hubbub that had greeted the King's insistence on settling the question of the Regency immediately died away and everyone gradually fell silent, expecting the King to now dismiss them.

He did not. Instead, he drew a deep breath and announced, "My nephew—might not live long enough to—to rule. In the event—event that he dies—still—a minor—"

The room was deathly still. Every man, even Heraclius and Jaffa, hung on the words issuing from the immobile mask. At the back of the room, men were straining hard to hear what the King said, for he was not capable of projecting his voice very far.

"I want—the High Court—to swear—on the True Cross—" the mask nodded in the direction of the Bishop of Bethlehem. The bishop strode forward, holding the reliquary that was usually placed inside the larger cross when carried on campaign. The box, encrusted with precious stones, rested reverently in the palms of both his hands.

After the Bishop of Bethlehem had taken up his place immediately to the right of the King, facing the rest of the bishops and barons, Baldwin IV resumed: "Swear—to accept as your King—the man chosen—by His Holiness the Pope, the Holy Roman Emperor, and the Kings of France and England."

There was a moment of stunned silence before Oultrejourdain had the nerve to ask what they were all wondering: "And who is that?"

"I don't know," Baldwin answered, and Balian could almost imagine him smiling behind the mask.

"What?" Guy de Lusignan recovered first. "You want us to swear an oath of allegiance to an anonymous King? Swear loyalty without knowing the identity of the man we are swearing ourselves to? You want us to swear to a cat still in the sack?"

"It might be you, brother," Aimery pointed out, the word "idiot" hanging unsaid (but clearly thought) in the air.

"Swear—to accept—the choice of the Pope—the Holy Roman Emperor—and the Kings of England and France," King Baldwin repeated. "It does not—matter—whom they choose."

"The hell—" Guy started. Aimery stamped on his brother's foot so hard that Guy yelped and then stared at him in outrage, but fell silent.

"There is wisdom in this," the Hospitaller Master spoke into the stunned silence. "By swearing now, without knowing whom they will choose, we avoid all factionalism. It could just as easily be Guy de Lusignan as Raymond de Tripoli—or young Humphrey de Toron here." He gestured toward an astonished Humphrey, who took a step back as if horrified by the thought, thereby treading unwittingly on Ibelin's toe.

"Let us all swear this, and we swear to abjure all strife for the sake of the Kingdom." He continued, and he bishops joined in with hearty "Hear, hear" and "In the name of God" and the like, but there was a tangible resistance on the part of the fighting men to swear a blind oath.

"My lords," the King's voice cut through the atmosphere. "I am dying."

No one dared speak after that, and his words hung in the air.

"I am dying. You must swear—now—on the True Cross."

Reginald de Sidon dropped so heavily onto his knees that Ibelin winced for him, but beside him the Bishop of Nazareth also went down on his knee—and then, one by one, the other bishops and barons knelt and bowed their heads. "Swear on the True Cross," the Bishop of Bethlehem lifted his stentorian voice, "to accept as our liege lord and King whomever His Holiness the Pope, the Holy Roman Emperor, and the Kings of England and France in their wisdom, inspired by God, proclaim successor to Baldwin V, should he die without heirs of his body, so help you God."

"I do so swear." Ramla's voice led the rest, loud and clear and firm, and Ibelin glanced at him, a little surprised by his brother's willingness to accept this unnamed ruler. In the collective oath swearing, it was also impossible to know if anyone abstained, but Ibelin strongly suspected that Jaffa did, while Oultrejourdain would think nothing of breaking an oath and had scoffed at the True Cross more than once, calling it a "piece of old wood." Ibelin did not believe this oath was going to solve anything—particularly when one considered that the Kings of England and France were bitter enemies and unlikely to agree on any candidate. But the King seemed reassured by the collective oath swearing, and Balian noted that he relaxed somewhat on his throne.

Men were getting up off their knees, and again there was the expectancy of being dismissed, but King Baldwin had yet another surprise for them. He again turned to one of the Knights of St. Lazarus, and the knight went to the window behind the throne and signaled to someone outside. A moment later, the herald called for order, announcing, "King Baldwin V of Jerusalem!"

The boy was dressed in silk robes embroidered with the arms of Jerusalem and wore a small gold crown, evidently made for his still small head. He was blond and blue-eyed and very lovely—like a fragile glass vessel, Ibelin found himself thinking, containing the royal blood.

"Now," Baldwin IV announced from the throne, "my nephew will lead you—to the Church of the Holy Sepulcher—and we shall pray—together—for God's grace—upon this Kingdom—and upon my nephew. And we—shall—then go—together—" It was clear that the dying King could hardly find the strength to speak. He was struggling to get the words out: "to the—Temple—of God—" King Baldwin sank back and nodded to the Bishop of Bethlehem.

"It is the King's wish," the bishop continued in a voice that seemed to boom after the dry and fading whispers of the Leper King, "that his nephew formally offer his crown to God, as once the Christ Child was offered to God and was bought back by his mother. Baldwin V will offer his crown to the Christ in the Temple of God, and receive it back in exchange for your promises to serve him loyally." The High Court was feeling collectively manipulated, and men were exchanging looks of unease, but it was hardly possible to refuse. Furthermore, it appeared that several other bishops had been told about this last part of today's session, and they were starting to pull on their gloves and put on their miters, while Bethlehem told them to start forming up outside in the courtyard. "I will lead with the True Cross," he told them.

"Ibelin!" the dying King called from the throne.

"Your grace?" Balian, who had been turning to file out of the chamber with the others, stopped and looked back toward the throne.

"Take—my nephew—on your—shoulders—so he is—above all—as—he—should be."

Every man in the room suddenly went still and silent. All motion toward the door halted. Ibelin could hear intakes of breath, and protests waited on a dozen tongues. If the young King was to be carried, he ought to have been carried either by the highest-ranking nobleman present, the Prince of Antioch, by his future Regent, the Count of Tripoli, or arguably by his guardian, the Count of Edessa; even his stepfather, the Count of Jaffa, outranked Balian.

"Your grace," Ibelin started to answer, his eyes meeting those of Raymond de Tripoli, who was standing near the door, looking offended. "My lord of Tripoli—"

"Is slight—of stature," King Baldwin cut him off. "You are—tallest—tallest man—here."

That was not a plausible explanation of this unexpected honor, and Ibelin again looked to Tripoli, pleading with him to intervene. Tripoli frowned, his lips narrow with disapproval, but he waved his hand in a gesture of irritation that seemed to suggest it was of no importance.

From the throne the King said softly, as if it were a last farewell, "Balian—please."

Ibelin turned, bent down, and swept Baldwin V up onto his shoulders, warning the frightened little boy to duck his head as he strode toward the door.

It started drizzling as Maria Zoë and Isabella returned to the Ibelin palace and a visit with Eschiva, who was only just recovering from giving birth to her second son. Maria Zoë shooed her daughter up the courtyard stairs to the solar, where she threw two fresh logs on the fire before turning to remove her cloak. As she did, she was astonished to discover Isabella hugging herself as tears streamed down her face.

"Sweetheart! What's the matter?" Maria Zoë asked baffled.

"Oh, I know it's a sin," Isabella managed between sobs, as she dropped her head in her hands, "but I'm so jealous!"

"Of Eschiva?" Maria Zoë asked, astonished. She was pleased that Eschiva seemed content in her marriage, and she was relieved that Aimery was a courteous and kind husband, but it never occurred to her that her daughter might be jealous. Eschiva and Aimery's relationship was nothing like what she had with Balian. Indeed, from what she could see, Humphrey cared more for Isabella than Aimery did for Eschiva.

"I'd like babies of my own," Isabella admitted.

"Good heavens, child! You have plenty of time for that! You're much too young. You should be thankful—"

"I'm *not* too young!" Isabella answered firmly—only to have the effect shattered by a hiccup.

"Of course you are!" Maria Zoë insisted, leading her over to a chair by the fire and sitting her down there.

"I've started my flux!" Isabella countered.

"Which is well and good, but it's not the same thing as being ready to bear a child to term—much less survive childbirth. Believe me, there is no reason to rush this!"

"But I want to be Humphrey's wife in more than name!" Isabella protested, dropping her face in her hands and crying more strongly than ever.

Maria Zoë put her arm around Isabella's shoulders and let her cry herself out. Only after she'd settled down a bit did her mother bend and kiss her cheek and ask in a very soft voice, "Are you saying Humphrey still hasn't consummated the marriage?"

Isabella nodded without looking at her mother.

Maria Zoë used the tip of her linen sleeve to wipe Isabella's face dry of tears, and then kissed her again. "Does Humphrey know you want him in your bed?"

"Oh, we *sleep* together every night, but he—he doesn't show any interest in me. It's like we're just sister and brother."

Maria Zoë digested this information and tried to analyze it. It would have surprised her less if an older man, like Aimery, refrained from sexual relations with a child wife—but Humphrey was now seventeen, an age when most youth tended to be obsessively interested in sex. Balian had admitted (one evening after too much wine, when the escapades of Gabriel had gotten them onto the topic of youth and sex) that he had celebrated his knighting with two girls, sisters, who had vied with one another for his favor until they finally agreed to share him. More recently, Gabriel had managed to get Dawit's sister Tsion pregnant, causing a household crisis when the usually soft-spoken Mathewos demanded in a rage that Gabriel be castrated. They had eventually solved the crisis by insisting that Gabriel marry Tsion, but the incident highlighted how youths let their loins obscure their reason. So it did seem odd that Humphrey did not show any interest in his now nubile wife—especially since he was otherwise so devoted to her.

Cautiously Maria Zoë noted, "He did promise not to do it until you were ready. You told me that yourself. So maybe he's just waiting for some word from you?"

"But I've told him I have my flux! I told him! And I've tried to cuddle with him—you know—more, more maturely—face to face. But he just turns his back on me and pretends to go to sleep."

That didn't sound normal to Maria Zoë, and she resolved to speak to Balian about it—but for the moment she wanted to comfort her daughter, not increase her anxiety. "Sweetheart, I think this is just something that needs more time. After all, you have lived together as brother and sister for so long that Humphrey hasn't come to think of you as a woman yet." She stroked Isabella's arm as she spoke.

Isabella hiccupped. "I suppose not," she conceded before adding, "but you see it really was terrible at Toron, and—" Maria Zoë looked hard at her daughter, waiting. Isabella dropped her eyes. "It wasn't the castle, really. It was the knights of Toron. They didn't respect Humphrey. They—they ignored him and wouldn't do what he told them to do."

Maria Zoë remembered Balian had told her something similar more than a year ago, but she was still appalled. In her shock, she only managed to stammer out, "What—what did he ask them to do?"

"It didn't matter. If he told them to come on a certain day, they didn't arrive until much later. If he told them to send him the cattle that they owed him, all they sent were excuses. It was one thing after another. It was as if they were all still taking orders—or at least awaiting orders—from Châtillon. Aimery said as much to me. He said Oultrejourdain hadn't given up control of Toron—and he never would unless he was forced to. But how could Humphrey force him? Humphrey is still so afraid of him. . . ."

Maria Zoë stroked Isabella's back. "Then it is probably best that he did what he did and gave it up. Let Aimery deal with Châtillon. They are well met."

Isabella sighed. "Yes, I suppose. It's just . . ."

"What?" Maria Zoë asked gently.

"I just wish—I wish—that Humphrey would—would be *bolder*," Isabella admitted. "I wish he would be—more of a man."

Ibelin, April 1185

"Pay attention!" Father Michael admonished, cracking his wooden pointer on the reading pulpit for emphasis. John winced and frowned, while his sister Helvis cast him a reproachful look. Helvis loved their lessons. They set her and John apart from "the babies" (Margaret and Philip), who were still confined to the nursery and the care of Nanny Anne. Helvis and John, in contrast, had "graduated" to the care of Fathers Michael and Angelus, who had the unenviable task of trying to teach them their letters as well as their catechism.

Helvis was clever, and she could already form her letters neatly and clearly. She liked writing, taking time with each letter, her tongue sticking out of the side of her mouth as she worked with great concentration. On the chalkboard in front of her, Father Michael could clearly read the exercise: "Our FathEr WHOart in HEavEn. Holow BE ThY namE. ThY Kingdom comE, ThY Will bE . . ."

John, on the other hand, was impatient with writing and found it difficult to form the letters neatly. His chalkboard looked more like pigeon scratchings in the dirt of the dovecote. He had particular difficulty with round letters, nor could he sit still while trying to write. His feet were swinging under the bench, which was too high for him, causing the whole bench to teeter on the uneven floor with an incessant clacking sound.

"John's still a baby," Helvis concluded with the superiority of an elder sister. "He's not big enough to learn how to write."

"Yes, I am!" John shot back furiously. "But something's happened! Didn't you hear the herald arrive? And that was over an hour ago! Something terrible has happened! Salah ad-Din has probably attacked again! Or Nablus is under siege!"

"Master John! Your duty is to learn your letters so that you will one day be able to read and write messages, not sit here speculating," Father Michael replied sternly. At just twenty-six, however, he didn't really command the same respect as his colleague Father Angelus, who was twice his age and tasked with teaching the children Greek and mathematics.

"Yes, and I will learn," John answered earnestly, "but now I want to know what has happened! My lord father should have been here long ago!"

Father Michael could not contradict the boy, since the lessons had indeed run overlong, and he himself was wondering what had happened. Since the Lord and Lady's return from Jerusalem, Lord Balian had never failed to collect his son from the little classroom to take him for a ride. It was, Father Michael knew, the highlight of the boy's day—better even than meals. Helvis was still afraid of horses and preferred to trail after her mother in whatever she was doing, so that the afternoon rides were a time for John to be alone with his father.

Father Michael ordered John to finish his exercise, but he went himself to the window to see if he could discern anything unusual. All seemed calm and normal out in the ward, except that he could see one of Lord Balian's palfreys, the red stallion Rufus, tied to a post before the stables. He was already tacked with a black saddle blanket under the baron's fine leather saddle, waiting as impatiently as John. He kept stamping his feet at flies and lashing his tail back and forth, as much in a gesture of displeasure as to chase away the flies. As Father Michael watched, he started dancing about, jerking at his lead so angrily that Mathewos emerged from the stables and began walking the fractious stallion to calm him down. The Ethiopian, too, was casting anxious glances toward the great hall.

That was not a good sign. Unlike Father Michael, Mathewos knew where the messenger was from, and his unease suggested the expectation of bad news was well founded. Michael sighed and turned his attention back to his charges, going around behind John to offer, "Let me hold your hand and guide you while you form the letters."

Instead, John jumped up and clambered over the back of the bench. He ran to the door, and tore it open. Sure enough, his sharp ears had heard the approaching footsteps before the others, and his father stood in the doorway.

"Papa! What's happened?" John demanded, looking up at him.

"I'll tell you in due time. Are you finished?"

"Yes!" John exclaimed, even as Helvis and Father Michael denied it.

Balian walked over to his son's tablet, looked down at the scrawls, and smiled to himself before turning to his son and noting, "I'm sure you can do better than that, but I am late, and for today I think we can achieve no more. Come, children!" He held out both his hands, and Helvis and John readily each took one. "Your mother wants you to come to her, Helvis," Balian told his firstborn. "She will explain when you get there. John, we will take our usual ride."

At the foot of the tower, Balian bent and kissed his daughter on her soft cheek, then sent her scurrying toward the stairs up to the great hall with a playful pat on her backside. He then led John across to the mounting block, where Eskindar led Rufus. Balian used the block to swing himself up into the saddle while Eskindar held the off stirrup, and then John scrambled from the block into his lap, flinging his right leg across the pommel. When John was settled, Balian took up the reins, and Rufus at once picked up his head and ears.

They crossed the wooden drawbridge into Ibelin town, turned right, and rode down the cobbled street toward the southern gate. People recognized the baron and nodded their heads, doffed their hats, or called greetings to him, depending on their temperament. John held the pommel of the saddle firmly in both hands—not from fear, but rather pretending he was holding the reins—as he looked straight ahead between Rufus's ears.

Once they left the town they were in the pomegranate orchards, blooming with red flowers at this time of year. Most days, Balian turned east at the next crossroads and rode out of the orchards toward the tilled fields and pastureland to check on the state of his domain. Although he rarely intervened directly, his tenants had become accustomed to his watchful eyes following them as they plowed, sowed, harvested, and threshed. He often stopped at his mill, too, his presence reminding the miller that he was not his own man—and the tenants that any attempt to go elsewhere (at least too often) would be detected.

But today he turned away from the main road, following a narrow and uneven path that made Rufus's gait so rough that John held on to the saddle for real. Soon the horse was straining on a steep incline, the pomegranates gave way to figs and palms, and the soil became increasingly sandy. At last they crested the hill and John caught his breath: in the distance the sea glistened and gleamed, blue-green beyond the sand.

"Do you know what people in France call this place?" Balian asked his son as he drew up and took in the view himself.

John shook his head.

"Outremer—Beyond the Sea." He pointed with his right hand. "That sea."

"But they are beyond the sea to us," John noted, as if offended by the name.

His father laughed softly and nodded. "Indeed." Then he gave Rufus more rein and they started down the back side of the dune, the sand sinking and sliding under the palfrey's shod hooves. John saw a rabbit dart to safety amidst the scrub brush, and then looked up to the bird of prey wheeling lazily overhead. He did not know enough to know what kind of bird it was, only that it was looking for something to eat on the earth below.

When the footing became a little harder and flatter, Balian laid his right arm firmly around his son's waist, pulled him closer, and warned him to "hold tight" before taking up a canter. John loved it when they cantered, for the gait, particularly Rufus's gait, was fluid and easy to sit—although it was frighteningly fast if he looked down. John avoided looking down and concentrated on the sea, which came slowly nearer, as they raced between the low bushes and trampled the yellow wildflowers. Then the sea was right before them, crashing white upon the hard-packed wet sand of the beach, and his father drew up and let his palfrey shake his head and stretch his neck with a satisfied snort.

John could not remember being so near the sea before, not like this. He had been to Jaffa, of course, but a harbor full of ships and docks cluttered with people, cranes, carts, and draft animals was totally different. The sea there had been dirty and brown, filled with rubbish and floating waste. Here the water looked clear. He could see the waves heaving up and crashing down, and the smell on the air was salty and tangy, not foul. Overhead the seagulls cried. John looked up, shading his eyes against the glare of the sun. Father Angelus said that the souls of sailors who had gone to their watery graves unshriven were trapped in the bodies of seagulls, and that was the reason they cried out so piteously. John watched a seagull riding the wind overhead without ever a twitch of his wings, and wondered about the sailor he had once been.

But eventually he got tired of watching the seagull and looked up at his father expectantly and questioningly. His father usually talked to him on these rides: lecturing him about the crops that could be produced and the weather they needed to produce them, or about the different trees—the lemons and cherries, almonds and plums. Or he talked about the people that lived in Ibelin and why they spoke different languages and wore different clothes. It really didn't matter what his father talked about; John was happy just having his father's attention to himself. "What's the matter, Papa?" John asked when his father just kept staring at the sea.

Balian sighed and looked down at him with a sad smile. "Today we learned that a good man has died."

"Who?" John wanted to know.

"Baldwin, by the grace of God, King of Jerusalem and my liege lord."

"But he's been sick for a long time," John protested, not understanding his father's sorrow.

"Yes," Balian conceded. "That is my comfort: that he is now with Christ and he is no longer suffering, as he did for far too long. I am sure he is now whole and he can laugh and sing and, indeed, fly—like those seagulls there." Balian nodded with his head toward what was now a pair of seagulls, turning their heads from side to side as they glided effortlessly on the air currents rising from the sea. "He must feel elated and liberated to be rid of his putrefying body at last. I do not mourn for *him*," Balian told his son, "but for *us*. We are all poorer without him." He paused and ruffled his son's hair in an affectionate gesture before admitting, "I loved him like a younger brother."

John didn't see that that was so special, since he didn't feel all that much fondness for his younger brother Philip. He dismissed his father's feelings to ask, "And who is King now?"

"A boy only two years older than you are: Baldwin V."

"He can be king at only eight?" John sounded distinctly jealous.

"He has a regent, who rules for him—the good Raymond, Count of Tripoli—and a guardian, Joscelin, Count of Edessa, who will look after his lessons and ensure he learns his duties. Then there is your cousin's husband, the Constable Aimery de Lusignan, to command his armies for him, and the entire High Court to advise and guide him."

That sounded like way too much control, John decided. "When will he get to rule on his own?"

"When he is fifteen," Balian answered, thinking of another boy who had seized the reins of government at fifteen.

To John, turning fifteen was too far away to be imaginable, so he lost interest, but surprised his father with the perceptive question: "Do you think Salah ad-Din will attack us now that the King is dead?"

"I hope not, John. The Count of Tripoli does not want war, and he has said many times that we should make a new truce with the Saracens, but it can never be more than a truce," Balian warned. "The Sultan has vowed to drive us into that sea, and he will not rest until we are destroyed or he is dead. We can only hope to hold him off so long as he lives, and pray to God that when he dies his empire will fall apart under squabbling rivals to his throne or that his successor, if there is just one, is less intent on *jihad*."

John didn't understand all that, but it didn't matter. He had spotted something on the water. "Is that a sea monster?" he asked excitedly.

"No," Balian answered with a faint smile, all he could muster in his current mood. "That is the sail of a ship. Pray that it is a ship from the West, full of strong fighting men and steel weapons." Then he took up the reins and turned the head of his horse away from the sea to ride back to Ibelin, his heart still heavy, but his arm held firmly around his vulnerable son.

Chapter 14

Damascus, May 1185

The heat was oppressive. Ibelin felt as if he were slowly baking inside his armor, while the metal exposed to the sun was too hot to touch. Rufus was sweating, too, although they were only walking, and Balian suspected he would be as happy as his master to find some shade and stop. At least they were nearing the end of their journey. They had descended from the Anti-Lebanon Mountains and were approaching Damascus itself.

Their escort of twoscore Mamlukes had met them at the border and still surrounded the little party of Christian emissaries. The Master of the Knights Hospitaller, Roger des Moulins, led the little delegation, accompanied by one knight and one Turcopole from his Order. Ibelin traveled with Gabriel, the militarily more useful of his squires, and Mathewos, because of the latter's language skills and ability to blend into a Saracen society. Traveling under the banners of Jerusalem, they came at the behest of Raymond de Tripoli to try to negotiate a truce with Salah ad-Din.

One of the Mamlukes from their escort spurred ahead, apparently to clear the way and announce their arrival to the garrison of Damascus, while the rest of them plodded along the poorly paved and increasingly crowded road. Ibelin was feeling distinctly disappointed. Some of that was just the natural effect of the heat and his parched throat, but most was due to false expectations. He had been told by Ibrahim and others that Damascus was "like paradise on earth." It was, he had been led to believe, an oasis in the midst of the desert, but so far Ibelin had seen only desert. The back side of the Anti-Lebanon was so dry that the mountains were bare of vegetation—unless you counted dried-out thorn bushes.

The surface was carved with dry gullies and wadis filled with gravel. Ibelin had expected that, but he had also expected that once they left the mountains and reached the plateau on which Damascus was built, they would enter a green and fertile region similar to home.

Instead, the orchards around Damascus made a parched impression. The irrigation ditches contained at best a trickle of water. No weeds, much less a crop (as in Ibelin), grew between the trees. The surface soil was dry, and each breath of air blew up tiny cyclones that dusted the drooping leaves and choked the air. That said one thing to Ibelin: drought.

They entered Damascus proper by a square stone gate, not significantly different from those of Jerusalem or other Christian cities, and found themselves in a crowded, cacophonic city. With inward amusement Ibelin recognized that most of what was being shouted at them in Arabic was identical to what he would have heard in Jerusalem or Acre: offers of clean beds, good wine, cheap food. Only the offers of "succulent women" was new to the mix; Western pimps weren't quite so brazen, because Christianity frowned on commercial sex, whereas Islam did not. Now and again there were insults shouted at them as well, but the presence of the Sultan's personal bodyguard kept hostility at a minimum and a distance.

The deeper they penetrated the city, the more crowded it seemed to become. To Ibelin's eyes the near absence of women was notable, and what women there were, were completely shrouded in black. Their faces and sometimes even their eyes were covered, robbing them of any identity, much less personality, and they kept to the shadows and the fringes like frightened stray cats: heads down and shoulders hunched to make themselves even less visible.

The streets narrowed. Soon the buildings crowded so close to the uneven pavement that the balconies almost touched overhead. It became necessary to ride single file. Ibelin glanced curiously to the side, trying to get a glimpse through the latticework enclosing the balconies to what lay inside. All he saw were shadowy figures that drew back from the intrusion into their privacy.

Meanwhile the stench was getting worse. So much for Muslim cities being cleaner, Ibelin thought to himself. Just as everywhere else in the world, rubbish was thrown into the streets and chamber pots emptied into the gutters. It would be nightfall before the streets were swept down and the rubbish carted away to make them clean again.

At last they emerged out of the crowded Old Quarter, however, and found themselves in an attractive square, surrounded by impressive buildings with elaborate and ornate facades. One was clearly a major mosque, with no less than three minarets rising above the white stone walls that enclosed it. One of their escorts came back to ride beside Ibelin and, pointing to the mosque, told him it contained the head of John the Baptist. "If you convert," he added with a grin, "I will take you inside so you may see it."

Ibelin smiled back at him. "But if I *don't* convert, I will have the blessings of the Baptist's spirit, which are worth far more than the sight of his mortal remains."

The Mamluke countered aggressively, "I thought you Christian pigs worshiped things!"

"No," Ibelin answered steadily, "we believe in God the Father and in his only Son, Jesus Christ."

"Polytheist!" the Muslim dismissed him, and then changed the subject by pointing in the opposite direction to the tall, turreted walls of a citadel. "That is the Sultan's residence. You are welcome to stay inside—or, he instructed me to offer you accommodation in one of the best caravansaries. It is just up there!" He pointed to a street leading away from the square.

"What is he saying?" Master des Moulins demanded irritably. His face was bright red and glistening with sweat. Moulins had been in the Holy Land less than a decade and had never bothered to learn even rudimentary Arabic.

"We are offered accommodation in either the citadel or a caravansary," Ibelin explained to him.

"Ask if the latter is near a bathhouse. Salah ad-Din will have his spies all over the citadel."

"He will have his spies all over the caravansary as well," Ibelin replied cynically, but asked their escort about the baths and received the assurance that the caravansary was directly beside a bathhouse, so they proceeded there.

The owners of the caravansary had clearly been warned to expect important guests, and the owner and his sons were lined up outside to greet the visitors, bowing graciously and welcoming the ambassadors with broad smiles. Ibelin supposed Salah ad-Din had made it worth their while to host the Christians, but he was too relieved to get into the shade to care.

Their escort withdrew, promising to report their safe arrival to the Sultan. Ibelin dismounted to find a young man frowning at him. "You are wearing crosses!" the youth exclaimed, staring at Ibelin's surcoat, which bore the red crosses of Ibelin painted all over the background of marigold linen. "And that is a fine horse," the caravansary groom added, with admiring looks at Rufus.

"He is. Take good care of him," Ibelin answered, looking automatically for Mathewos, as he no longer trusted this groom.

"It is *forbidden* for Christians to ride horses!" the young man protested emphatically, frowning more fiercely.

"Not where I come from," Ibelin countered firmly.

The young man, however, grew even more indignant, declaring, "I'll teach you your place, you Christian pig!" He raised his hand as if to strike Ibelin.

Before Ibelin could respond, the innkeeper called out, "It's all right, Ayub! He's an ambassador from Jerusalem."

The young man looked at his employer in outrage, but the innkeeper now came over and put him in his place with a deluge of insults, interspersed with reference to Salah ad-Din and his safe-conduct. He concluded with the warning that if the youth didn't behave he'd be sacked. This silenced the groom, but he continued to cast hateful looks at Ibelin while Mathewos came and took Rufus.

The horses taken off their hands, the guests were rapidly shown to a suite of private rooms on the first floor of the caravansary. The floors were paved with white and brown tiles in a checkerboard pattern, and the furnishings, although showing signs of age and wear, were of good-quality wood, elaborately carved and outfitted with cushions in bright patterned covers. Best of all, however, there were two balconies, each fully encased in wooden latticework that blocked out the sun but let in a light breeze. Because they looked out on two different streets, they allowed for a welcome cross current.

Ibelin went at once to one of the balconies to get a look at the city from this raised perspective, and quickly noted that he could see the citadel. Behind him Moulins was stripping off his armor and replacing it with his simple monk's habit in preparation for going to the baths, while Gabriel and the Hospitaller Turcopole dumped the saddlebags on the floor.

The innkeeper made a second appearance, bowing deeply to Moulins and offering to have "some of his slaves" escort them to the baths. Moulins accepted with so much relief that Ibelin knew he should not dally any longer. He left the balcony, unbuckling his own sword, and ordered Gabriel to help him out of his mail.

"Are you sure you want to disarm?" Gabriel asked skeptically.

"I can't bathe in my armor," Ibelin countered.

"But you're vulnerable without it."

"We are protected by nothing but our diplomatic immunity," Ibelin reminded him. "If Salah ad-Din gives the order to kill us, even ten coats of mail would not save us."

Gabriel sighed. He had been excited to be selected for this mission and eager to see Damascus. So far it had been an adventure, but now that they were here, he was starting to feel frightened.

The baths were indeed adjacent to the caravansary, and a narrow passage led directly from one building to the other, where the visitors were again evidently expected. Ibelin stripped naked and then wrapped the towel provided around his waist before being led to the marble steam room. This chamber had a domed ceiling that let in light through round, glazed holes. Ibelin lay down and tried to relax his mind as well as his body.

Although he agreed with Tripoli's policy of trying to negotiate a truce for—if possible—the full six years it would take Baldwin V to reach his majority, he was less comfortable with being tasked to accompany Moulins. Tripoli had argued that his exceptional command of Arabic was invaluable, and Ibelin had countered that his brother of Ramla already knew Salah ad-Din and therefore had an advantage.

"Your brother is not a diplomat," Tripoli had replied bluntly. "If I want a man to lead a near-suicidal charge, I can think of no one better than Ramla—or Oultrejourdain; for delicate negotiations, you're the better man."

Which, Balian conceded, might be true, but he was still unhappy with this mission. He was certain the Sultan begrudged him for the hard bargaining he had conducted over the ransom of his captives after Montgisard, and he suspected the Sultan felt misled about Barry's prospects of becoming King of Jerusalem after the Battle on the Litani. With a sigh he turned over onto his back, his eyes closed, and tried to empty his head. He concentrated on the sweat forming and slowly trickling off the promontories of his body to drip on to the marble slab under him.

He was startled awake by a gasp, and his eyes flew open to see a youth standing over him, staring down. "Sir!" the boy exclaimed.

"What?" Balian asked, alarmed and wary.

"That—that's a cross! The Cross of Our Lord!"

Balian's hand went to the gold cross he had worn around his neck from the day he was knighted, a gift from Hugh. He had never taken it off since, although it was usually hidden from view by his clothes. He rarely thought about it, but it was always against his heart. "Yes, of course," he remarked cautiously.

"Are—are you Christian?" the youth asked in wonder.

"Yes."

"But I was told you were a great lord," the youth protested.

Balian almost laughed. "I am—in Jerusalem."

"You've come from Jerusalem?" The youth's eyes were growing bigger.

"Yes, my colleague and I have come from Jerusalem." Balian nodded to Moulins, who appeared to have dozed off on the other side of the room.

The youth lowered his head and whispered, "We are Christians, too."

"Jacobite?" Balian asked, and the boy nodded vigorously before asking, "And you?"

"Latin," Balian answered, then nodded for the boy to continue with his duties. The youth set to work with a will. He dipped his sponge into a bucket of water that was cool compared to the heat of the room, and started slowly but effectively wiping Balian's sweat away with all the grime it carried. Then came the soap, scented with balsam, which he vigorously rubbed between his hands to create suds before soaping Balian down and then sponging him off again. After that came a massage with oil.

Glancing over his shoulders and determining that all the other customers had left except Moulins, who was now awake and being sponged down by a second attendant, the youth confided, "I wish *we* lived in Jerusalem. The taxes on Christians here are terrible. No matter how hard we work, there is never enough to live on. And sometimes they attack us, too—when the Sultan is away. Six years ago, they said we were to blame for the drought, and they broke in and trashed everything! You can still see some of the damage they did!" He pointed to some chips and cracks in the marble. "My father is afraid they will do the same again if the drought continues much longer."

"You say they attack when the Sultan is away?" Balian asked the youth, as he was led to one of the washing basins for scrubbing down.

"The Sultan is a good man," the bath attendant said firmly. "He follows the Koran, which says we are 'of the book' and should not be killed or harassed. When he is here, no one attacks us." The boy shrugged. "But he is rarely here, and they teach hatred of us in the madrassas."

Balian nodded sadly.

"Tell me about Jerusalem," the youth begged, as he vigorously scrubbed the last vestiges of ingrained dirt from Balian's body before soaping it down a last time.

"It is a walled city like any other, except that it contains the sites of Christ's passion. Tens of thousands of pilgrims flood it each year as a result."

"And there are churches there?"

Balian laughed. "More than I can count."

"And they have bells? My father says that in Christian countries the churches have big bells that can be heard from far away and that they ring out more times each day that the muezzins call to prayer."

"Yes, that's right," Balian confirmed.

"And priests read the Mass *out loud* in them?" the boy asked skeptically.

"Of course," Balian answered. "That's what Mass is."

"Here no one is allowed to read the Christian service out loud—not in our meeting places, nor even in our homes. We have to read all holy texts silently; that way only literate people can learn Christ's word, and the poor forget their faith. Others convert to avoid the taxes." There was scorn in his voice.

Balian nodded as the youth poured cold water over him to wash away the soapsuds and the last of the dirt. It was good to be reminded of what was at stake, Balian told himself. If they failed to defend Jerusalem, all Christians in the Holy Land would again be oppressed like this, and the bells—even those of the Holy Sepulcher—would be silenced.

Their host recommended a place for dinner near the Great Mosque, but one of the bathhouse attendants said that another Christian owned a restaurant just a few blocks away, and he agreed to show the Christian emissaries the way. They would not have found it otherwise, since on the street there was no sign or other indication that here was a place to eat. Rather, they were taken into a shop selling spices and led between the open sacks of saffron and nutmeg, cumin and cinnamon, to a door at the back with a curtain across it. Beyond the curtain it was so dark that Ibelin instinctively dropped his hand to his hilt, but a youth with a glass lantern bowed deeply and led them deeper into the house. They emerged in a small courtyard open to the stars where half a dozen low tables had been set up around a small, gurgling fountain. The largest table was vacant, and they were led straight to it and asked to sit down.

Sitting involved lowering themselves onto cushions spread on the cobbles of the courtyard—but except for the elderly Moulins, they were used to that. They had hardly settled down before they were offered bowls of water to wash their hands and towels to dry them with. The proprietor emerged to welcome them heartily, bowing over and over as he expressed his honor to have them in his humble establishment. At last he inquired if they wanted wine, at once offering red wine from Armenia and rosé from Cyprus. After taking their drink orders, the proprietor offered a choice of lamb stewed with dates or cheese pasties, with rice or unleavened bread. They ordered and the proprietor withdrew, only to be replaced by a man in the long black-and-red robes and unique round black hat of a Jacobite priest.

"My lords," he bowed deeply, "I have been told you are from Jerusalem; may God's blessings be upon you."

Ibelin started to get to his feet out of respect as he translated for his companions, but the Jacobite priest gestured for him to stay seated, instead pointing to a spare cushion and asking if he could join them. Moulins agreed at once, and told his Turcopole to go after the landlord to order wine for the guest as well.

"It is a great honor to have you among us," the priest continued as he settled himself. "You come to treat with the Sultan, it is said?" The question was directed at Moulins as the oldest member of the party, and Ibelin translated for him.

"Yes, that is our purpose," Moulins agreed.

"Peace is sorely needed," the priest confirmed, nodding seriously. "The rains failed here for the third year in a row. There is hunger among the poor, and some villagers"—he gestured vaguely—"have nothing left. They are selling their wives and daughters—even their sons—to the Bedouins and the harems of the rich."

"Surely Christians do not do that!" Moulins protested indignantly after Ibelin had translated the Syrian priest's remarks.

"No, I was not speaking of Christians. Christian families are smaller and Christian communities more urban—and we help each other as much as we can." The priest smiled mildly, but his eyes remained sad. "And Jerusalem, is it suffering, too?" Rather than answer directly, Ibelin translated again for Moulins.

"Not so severely," Moulins reported. "We favor peace to let our King grow up, but if the Sultan gives us war, we are united behind a strong Regent." He was speaking on the assumption that the priest was one of the Sultan's spies. Although Ibelin was not so sure, he faithfully repeated Moulins' words in Arabic.

The priest nodded. "Will help come to you from the West?"

"There are always armed pilgrims from the West in Jerusalem, and my Order provides continuous support, as do the Templars," Moulins answered steadily when Ibelin put the question to him in French.

"Yes; but once, when I was a boy, kings came from the West and nearly liberated us from the Turks."

"I don't expect any repeat of that in the foreseeable future," Ibelin answered directly without translating for Moulins, glad that the arrival of the proprietor with their drinks provided a break in the conversation. Ibelin did not want to be confronted with pleas for assistance and support. The Christian kingdoms were far too weak to go on the offensive—and yet he found himself feeling guilty when confronted with the plight of Christians here.

The priest seemed to understand him, for he gave Ibelin a sad but understanding look, and Ibelin changed the subject. "Tell us more about Yusuf ibn Ayyub, who is called Salah ad-Din."

"Who is pleased to call *himself* 'Salah ad-Din,'" the Syrian Christian corrected Ibelin with a cynical smile.

Ibelin raised his eyebrows. "You think his subjects do not see him as Righteousness of the Faith?"

"The Shiites most certainly do not view the suppression of the Fatimid Caliphate as righteous, but they do not count for much in Syria. As for the Syrians . . ." The priest shrugged.

"What are you talking about?" Moulins demanded, irritated that Ibelin was carrying on the conversation rather than translating for him.

"About the Sultan's popularity among his people."

"Ah, good. Carry on and tell me later," Moulins conceded, leaning forward to focus on his food.

Ibelin asked the Syrian priest, "Surely the Syrians are impressed with the Sultan's successes."

The priest shrugged. "Impressed, yes, for with success comes the power to silence dissent, but do not mistake respect for admiration. The old elites despise the Kurds even more than the Turks, while the Turks resent the fact that he has beaten them at their own game—playing them off against one another, murdering where necessary, bribing where convenient. Yusuf ibn Ayyub has attained *power*—not popularity. He trusts no one but members of his own family and men like Imad ad-Din, who owes everything to him."

"But you believe he is firmly in power?" Ibelin wanted to know.

"Absolutely—at least for the moment. You see, Yusuf ibn Ayyub's greatest strength is his practicality: his ability to back down if the cost is too high, his willingness to postpone battles he cannot win. He is the consummate opportunist."

That boded well for this mission, Ibelin thought, but he couldn't resist asking, "Why do the 'old elites' despise him?"

"Because he is a Kurd, as I said."

"And that's all?" Ibelin found such an attitude bigoted.

"Among the Arab elites, both the Turks and Kurds are seen as barbarous peoples—like the Franks. People good at war, but little else. The Arab elites, remember, are no longer fighting men: they are Sufis and Qadis, who believe that knowledge of the Holy Koran is all a man needs. Nur ad-Din won their support by taking up their call for *jihad* and seeming to fulfill it—and, of course, by using some of his spoils to build new madrassas that preach this version of the Koran. Salah ad-Din is doing the same thing."

Ibelin did not like the sound of that. "That means that war against us is a vital component of his own legitimacy," he summarized.

The Syrian priest shrugged. "Yes, that's exactly what it means."

"He's saying Salah ad-Din will not receive you, my lord," Ibelin translated for Moulins.

"Why on earth not?" Moulins asked back indignantly.

"The Sultan, it seems, views Hospitallers and Templars as enemies of the Faith" (Ibelin chose not to translate 'pigs and defilers of the holy places' literally) "and says you cannot be trusted."

Moulins sputtered indignantly and insisted that Ibelin protest, which he did, but the Sultan's emissary was deaf to all arguments. He had his orders. Salah ad-Din would receive Ibn Barzan, but not the Grand Master of the Hospital of St. John.

"We could withdraw," Ibelin suggested uncertainly.

"Are you out of your mind?" Moulins countered. "We need a truce to give Baldwin V time to grow up. We need a truce to refresh our manpower reserves. The armed pilgrims from the West are just starting to trickle in, and the taxes levied by England and France won't bear fruit for another two to three years. We need breathing space! If Salah ad-Din won't talk to me, then you must go!"

"Alone?"

"Take your men with you, if you like."

Ibelin looked at Mathewos and Gabriel; the former looked worried and the latter excited. He nodded and sighed. "If that is what you wish, my lord."

"It is! Go, and go with Christ!" Moulins made the sign of the cross over Ibelin's bowed head.

Ibelin expected luxury in the Sultan's palace, and he had heard the old Baron de Toron talk of the stunning magnificence of the Caliph's palace in Cairo, but again he was disappointed. The citadel of Damascus was less luxurious than the royal palace in Jerusalem; it lacked pleasure gardens and domestic tracts. It was more like the Citadel of David, with high, defensible walls. Furthermore, the fountains were small, almost functional, while the absence of visible women contributed to the sterility of the ambiance as well. Without doubt there could be great beauty in a monastery, Ibelin reflected—but women brought into a residence not only children and laughter, they brought flowers and colors and an intangible brightness that he associated with optimism. This citadel reminded Ibelin of a Templar fortress—a not particularly complimentary comparison. From what Ibelin was allowed to see, the Sultan's reception hall was the only notable exception.

Here the entire floor had been paved with carpets as if it were a mosque or a place of prayer, and Balian wondered if that was because the Sultan's subjects were expected to kneel before him and bang their heads on the floor as they did before God. The very thought made him stand straighter and advance more vigorously—although he stopped in place when his escort collapsed into bows beside him. He stopped so suddenly that Gabriel almost ran into him from behind, while Mathewos opted to bow like the Mamlukes.

Ibelin was now about five feet away from a raised dais, also paved with carpets, where five men were seated on cushions around a low but beautifully carved table inlaid with mother-of-pearl. Four of the men were splendidly dressed in satin brocade tunics, camel-leather boots, and elaborate turbans, while the fifth was evidently some kind of scribe, who hung back and had writing utensils across his knees. The other men all had swords at their hips in magnificent scabbards, and jeweled rings on their fingers. Ibelin was glad he had dressed his best for the occasion. Not only had Gabriel oiled and scrubbed his chain mail until it gleamed, he was in black suede leather boots that folded back at the knee to reveal a camel-colored interior. His surcoat was white on the left side with the arms of Jerusalem embroidered in gold, and marigold on the right with the crosses of Ibelin in red. His sword belt consisted of enamel plaques with the Ibelin arms, and the pommel of his sword held a round gold disk in which a red enamel cross had been set; the scabbard, a gift from Maria Zoë, was of Byzantine craftsmanship with a beautiful cloisonné decoration.

On closer examination, it was clear that one of the fighting men at the end of the table opposite was more youth than man. He was perhaps the most splendidly dressed, but his face sprouted only down rather than beard, and Ibelin guessed he was the eldest of the Sultan's seventeen sons—the boy he had kept with him ever since he first went to Egypt, al-Afdal. The man at the other end of the table looked vaguely familiar, and was likewise too young to be the Sultan. Balian guessed he was Farrukh-Shah, the Sultan's nephew, who had been Tripoli's prisoner after the Battle on the Litani but had been exchanged as part of Barry's ransom. The other two men, however, were both mature men with tanned faces lined with life. By Balian's reckoning, the Sultan was approaching fifty years of age, and he suspected he might be the somewhat stocky man with the first shimmers of gray in his trimmed beard—but the other man hardly looked younger, just slightly less worn down. Since he was not sure which of them was the Sultan, Ibelin opted to simply bow deeply and greet them collectively: "My lords."

The man who answered was indeed the man with the sprinkling of gray hairs in his thick beard, but there was otherwise nothing remarkable about him. If anything, he seemed smaller and less imposing than the man beside him. "Monsieur d'Ibelin," he opened in French that was practiced rather than natural, "we meet at last."

Ibelin bowed deeply again. "My lord."

"Please, sit down." The Sultan reverted to Arabic and gestured to the vacant cushion on the front side of the table. Balian stepped on to the dais and settled himself cautiously on the cushion. Behind him Mathewos and Gabriel settled themselves cross-legged on the floor.

The Sultan snapped his fingers, and black slaves emerged with a silver tray laden with silver goblets and bowls, which were quickly placed before all five men at the table, including Ibelin, but not the scribe. The water that was poured into the goblets from the silver pitcher was so cold that condensation formed almost instantly on the exterior of the silver. The Sultan gestured for Ibelin to drink, and he did so readily, because he knew the rules of Muslim hospitality: theoretically, once a guest had been offered and had accepted water, he was immune from violence of any kind. That didn't mean that many a man hadn't been murdered despite the rules of hospitality, but Balian was happy to avail himself of any form of protection offered.

"So," Salah ad-Din opened, after sipping from his own goblet and smiling faintly at Ibelin. "How was the harvest in Ibelin this year?"

"Excellent, your excellency," Ibelin assured the Sultan. "And in Ramla and Mirabel as well. Nablus, I admit, was not quite so good, but good enough." Ibelin was telling the truth, and he knew the Sultan knew it. The drought was much worse to the east of the Anti-Lebanon.

"Tripoli, I believe, had a poor harvest."

"You did a good job destroying the orchards, your excellency, but the grain harvest was better because of the fertilizer from the fires you set."

Salah ad-Din smiled and nodded before noting somewhat sourly, "Tripoli would not have been so blunt, I think."

"That may be, and the good Master des Moulins is also more diplomatic than I. I am a fighting man, your excellency."

Salah ad-Din nodded and sipped his water, his eyes fixed on Ibelin. "So is your brother, but you are very different."

"Indeed, I am only a poor shadow of my elder brother," Ibelin countered, bowing his head in self-deprecation.

Salah ad-Din glanced to the man on his right, suggesting to Ibelin that this was one of his several brothers, perhaps even his most trusted lieutenant, al-Adil. Ibelin could not decipher any particular resemblance between them, however. Whereas Salah ad-Din was somewhat paunchy, the other man was slender, and while Salah ad-Din had a round face, the other man's face was sharp and hawk-like. But then, they would have had different mothers, Balian reminded himself.

"Your older brother must be very angry with Guy de Lusignan," the Sultan surmised.

"Yes, he is," Ibelin conceded.

"If a man had taken my intended bride to his bed, I would not have let either of them live." The Sultan's tone and expression left no doubt that he thought Ramla's failure to kill Sibylla and Guy reflected poorly on him—and all Christians.

"My brother is far too loyal to Jerusalem to let a personal matter endanger the fighting capacity of the Kingdom," Ibelin tried to explain.

"What harm would have come if your brother killed Guy de Lusignan—let alone this woman who has dishonored her family and your king?"

Put like that, Balian almost wished his brother *had* killed them both—it certainly would have solved many problems. But murder was still murder, and had Barry laid a hand on Sibylla, the King would have used all the power of his office to see him punished. Ibelin bowed his head to the Sultan and admitted, "I appreciate that you, my lord, have the courage to murder even viziers, but we Christians have greater respect for God's laws."

The men around the table stiffened at this, and al-Afdal's hand dropped to his hilt, his eyes fixed on his father, awaiting a command. Salah ad-Din waved him to relax. "Do not take Allah's name in vain," the Sultan admonished Ibelin. "Who are we to know His will?"

"I do not pretend to know His *will*, only His *commandments*: 'Thou shalt not kill.'"

"Yet you do kill," Salah ad-Din retorted calmly, if a little sharply. "I have seen with my own eyes how well you kill, my lord of Ibelin."

"I have killed many men in self-defense."

"At Ibelin?" Salah ad-Din raised his eyebrows, and his voice was almost mocking. "Were those men any threat to you?"

"At Ibelin, more than anywhere—for a man has the right to renounce his own self-defense, but not the right to fail to defend those who cannot defend themselves."

"But that is not the case of Guy de Lusignan, is it? He *can* defend himself. Your brother should have killed him for what he did—and your King should have had his sister stoned publicly for disgracing him and his entire family."

Ibelin knew it was pointless to talk about affection for a sister: the Sultan would not be able to understand it. What he called "honor" meant more to him than the life, much less the happiness, of any female. He would never be able to understand that King Baldwin had genuinely cared for his sister, despite her weaknesses. So he ignored the second half of the Sultan's suggestion and focused on the first. "What do you think my brother's son-in-law, Guy's brother Aimery, would have done, while my brother killed his? We are a small kingdom, your excellency, and we cannot afford to be divided among ourselves."

"And you are united now? Behind this boy?" Salah ad-Din sounded skeptical, not to say disbelieving.

"We are, your excellency," Ibelin told him, steadfastly and with conviction. The problem was not uniting behind Baldwin V, for even Guy could not oppose his stepson without alienating his wife, and Edessa had been bought with the post of guardian, which gave him ample opportunity to enrich himself from the royal treasury. The risk lay in what came *after* him—if he did not grow into a vigorous young man.

"Yet you come here begging for a truce," Salah ad-Din pointed out, with a faint smile that might have been derogatory.

Ibelin shrugged. "Personally, I would enjoy a truce. My sons are very small. It would be good to watch them grow up. There is much I could do in Ibelin and Nablus to make them richer places. But I do not *need* a truce."

"You hope that in five or six years your boy king will grow into a mighty warrior," Salah ad-Din speculated.

"Yes, we do. Wouldn't you, in our shoes?"

Salah ad-Din laughed at that, shortly. "Yes, but why should I give you that breathing space and risk facing a strong young king six years from now?"

"Because your soldiers are weary of war *now*. Because the rains have failed *this* year, and the prices in the markets are so high that there have been riots in many towns. Because you have not yet subdued Mosul, and it threatens your rear. And most of all, because we can *still* beat you on the battlefield anytime you invade—as we have always done in the past."

"Each time, your victory is less convincing," Salah ad-Din pointed out.

Ibelin shrugged and opened his hands. "I have more knights than ever before. The losses on the Litani have been made good. We still have untapped resources beyond the sea, and mighty kings who long to fight on our side for the greater glory of God and to defend the holy places of our faith. If you insist on war, your excellency, we will be ready for you. Me, my brother, and my fellow barons. We do not crave peace at any price, for *that* we could easily have."

Salah ad-Din raised his eyebrows in question.

"With surrender and conversion."

"Of course." The Sultan started to dismiss this thought and then paused to ask—almost hopefully, or at least whimsically—"And that is unthinkable?"

"It is!" Ibelin looked him squarely in the eye, with not even a ghost of a reciprocal smile.

Salah ad-Din nodded. "I will think about what you have said," he announced and rose to his feet, ending the interview.

Ibelin also stood, bowed deeply as he would have to his own king, took a step back and bowed again, and then turned and departed, with Gabriel and Mathewos in his wake.

When the Christians were safely out of hearing, al-Afdal protested hotly, "Ibn Barzan insulted you."

"How?"

"By referring to the murder of Shawar!"

"Never be offended by reference to your deeds," the Sultan advised his son. "To take offense is to suggest regret. I do not regret killing Shawar. He had lost his utility to us, and his murder paved the way for the reunification of Islam. Do you mean to suggest it is not a good thing that the heretical Fatimid caliphate has been destroyed?"

"Of course not!" al-Afdal protested. "But the Christian *meant* it as an insult."

"That is *his* problem." The Sultan dismissed the matter, adding, "I liked him."

Farrukh-Shah protested with a look of distaste, "Ibn Barzan lacks subtlety."

"Subtlety? Perhaps, but diplomacy does not consist of deceit, but rather in the art of finding common ground. In this case it is in both our interests to stop fighting for a bit. A truce is not a peace—and Ibn Barzan knows that as well as I do. Ibn Barzan is an honest man, and precisely because he did not try to flatter me or pretend to be my friend, I trust him."

"You think, then, that the Christians are united behind this boy king?" al-Adil asked skeptically.

"I think they are—because he is the lowest common denominator. It would seem that none of the other barons are man enough to put the boy aside." It was obvious to his brother, son, and nephew that Salah ad-Din was making a disparaging comparison between his own willingness to set aside Nur ad-Din's rightful heir and the reluctance of the Christians to depose Baldwin V. "I thought at first that Ramla was such a man—that he would take revenge on Guy de Lusignan for the dishonor of stealing his bride—but you saw Ibn Barzan's reaction. Ramla may hate Lusignan, but he does not have sufficient support among his peers to actually hold on to the throne if he were to set aside this boy and his stepfather Lusignan."

"Who is there to oppose him?" Farrukh-Shah asked. "Tripoli and Antioch are his friends."

"Yes," Salah ad-Din admitted, "but Oultrejourdain is his rival. And then there are the Templars. I've heard they now back Guy de Lusignan. If so, that changes the balance of power in Jerusalem. Don't forget these Christian fanatics have access to enormous resources in the West, and they can deploy as many knights as the entire Kingdom. It is significant that the Hospitaller Master was sent to make peace with us, but the Templar Master was not in the party."

"You would have been even *less* willing to receive him!" Farrukh-Shah pointed out.

Salah ad-Din laughed. "Of course—and it would have given me *greater* pleasure to refuse him. But the fact that he was *not* sent says a great deal. In the past, both Masters were sent on embassies."

"I have heard rumors that the new Grand Master hates Tripoli," Farrukh-Shah insisted.

"Good. Then your spies tell you the same thing that my spies tell me," Salah ad-Din told his nephew pointedly.

"So this is where the Kingdom starts to crack?" Al-Adil suggested uncertainly.

"Maybe, but Ibn Barzan is right: it has not cracked yet. Furthermore, our harvests have been poorer than theirs. *We* have bread riots; *they* do not. *We* have Mosul to contend with; *they* have only supporters in their rear. We have little to gain by attacking now, and waiting is likely to be more to our advantage than theirs."

"So you will give them a truce?"

"I think four years should be about right."

The others nodded in agreement. It would not be such a bad thing, after all, to have time to see to their own affairs.

Chapter 15

Acre, June 1186

Sibylla's sobs were starting to get on Guy's nerves. She had been crying nonstop for hours, clinging to the corpse of her little boy with more apparent affection than she had ever clung to him in life. Maybe it was a guilty conscience, for she had shown the boy little love over the years. Indeed, even in the last weeks she had spent more time chiding him for "whining" than comforting him in his ailments. She hated the fact that he vomited so much of the time, and might at any time spew up whatever he'd just eaten over anyone in range.

Guy hadn't liked being near the boy, either, but now he was dead and wouldn't throw up over either of them ever again. So what was the point of all this hysterical weeping? They ought, instead, to be thinking about what to do next.

Lusignan glanced across the room at his wife's uncle, the aging Count of Edessa. He was almost bald these days and decidedly overweight. He did not suffer from his great-nephew's weak stomach, it seemed; yet for all that, he was not looking well. There were deep bags under his eyes and his hair was stringy and oily, while dandruff dusted the shoulders of his velvet gown.

Feeling Lusignan's gaze, Edessa at once approached. "We have to do something!" he advised in an agitated voice.

"What?"

"To secure the treasury—the Crown. Tripoli is bound to try to have himself crowned."

"We all swore to send to the Pope and the Holy Roman Emperor," Lusignan reminded his wife's uncle.

"You can't believe Tripoli will respect that!" Edessa responded nervously. "That could take forever. Besides, the Kings of England and France are fighting each other. They'll never be able to agree on a candidate. We need to take control of things here before—before Tripoli makes his move, or the Saracens destroy us all."

"There's no need for panic," Lusignan calmed the older man patronizingly. "The last we heard, the Turks and Kurds were fighting each other over who should succeed the dying Salah ad-Din."

"Haven't you heard? The Sultan recovered and is swearing his life was saved only so he could complete the task of driving us into the sea! We must get Sibylla crowned Queen in her own right."

"Sibylla?" Guy asked incredulously. Pleasurable as he found her bed, she was the last person he would have wanted to vow fealty to.

"Only so she can crown you as her consort, of course," Edessa explained.

"Oh!" That made sense, of course.

"We need to get to Jerusalem ahead of Tripoli and his supporters, and get Sibylla crowned and anointed before they have a chance to call the High Court together. Heraclius will anoint Sibylla. I've already secured his support," Edessa promised his niece's husband. "It's all taken care of!" he added, when Lusignan looked nonplussed rather than grateful. He expected Lusignan's thanks for this *eventually*, but at the moment he was unnerved by the latter's apparent lethargy. "Once she's crowned and anointed, the High Court will be confronted with a fait accompli. No matter what Tripoli and his faction wants, we'll have an anointed Queen, and at least some of the bishops will not have the courage to oppose her."

Guy was astonished by how well thought out this plan sounded, but he supposed Edessa had been thinking about it ever since the boy had become fatally ill. He was most concerned about his own position, of course—but that mattered little to Guy, since his plan gave Guy what he wanted, too. So he just asked, "How do we do that?"

"We mustn't arouse suspicion," Edessa answered, automatically lowering his voice to a conspiratorial level. The need for discretion seemed self-evident to Lusignan, but it did not answer his question, so he continued to stare at Edessa, demanding an answer.

"I think," Edessa continued, licking his lips nervously, "I think I should ride to Beirut and tell Tripoli in person that poor little Baldwin is dead, and that his grieving mother and stepfather are escorting the corpse in slow stages to Jerusalem for a burial in the Holy Sepulcher on the anniversary of the seizure of Jerusalem, July 15. You and Sibylla, with a strong Templar escort, should do exactly that—but meanwhile, your brother should ride ahead and with the help of the Templars secure complete control of Jerusalem, while warning the Patriarch of what is expected of him."

"Yes." This definitely sounded like a plan to Guy.

"Before the others arrive, the Patriarch can crown Sibylla."

"What about me?" Guy asked back.

"The Patriarch will crown you—or if he won't, she will. She knows she can't rule without you."

That was true, Guy agreed. She'd said as much many times. He absently rubbed his shaved cheek as he thought through Edessa's plan, but while he could imagine things going wrong with it, he could not come up with any alternative. It was better than just sitting around waiting for the others to take action. He certainly didn't trust the Pope and the Holy Roman Emperor to name him King! Yes, the more he thought about it, the more sense Edessa's plan made. The Crown of Jerusalem, denied him by the pettiness of that leper boy, was within his grasp again at last.

Jerusalem, July 1186

Things hadn't gone exactly as planned, because most of the High Court had arrived in time for the funeral—although Tripoli had stayed away, allegedly out of fear of arrest or assassination. Still, Guy remained confident of his goal. "Everyone agrees Sibylla is the heir to the throne, and I am her husband. What could be simpler than that?" Guy demanded rhetorically of his brother.

Aimery didn't know whether he should roll his eyes or slap his stupid younger brother across his smug face. Curbing his anger, he tried to explain. "First of all, 'everyone' is a wild exaggeration. Three-fourths of the High Court have retired to Nablus to *discuss* the succession with the Regent. Just what do you think they are going to *discuss*?" When Guy only looked at him blankly, Aimery continued in an increasingly exasperated tone, "I'll tell you what: whether they should fulfill the terms of their oath to Baldwin IV by sending to the West for advice on the succession—while Tripoli remains Regent, of course. Or acclaim Tripoli himself King, because he is the closest living male descendant of Baldwin II."

"His claim is through the youngest sister and—"

"That doesn't matter!" Aimery cut Guy off in exasperation. "The supporters you have amount to 1) Heraclius, who keeps sniffling that he promised Agnes de Courtenay he would crown her "little girl"—nothing about you, mind! 2) Edessa, who fears Tripoli will cut off his revenues if he is crowned but could be bought if Tripoli pays him enough, and 3) the Grand Master of the Templars, who simply hates Tripoli. Even the Hospitallers are against you, with Moulins refusing to surrender the keys to the coronation vestments until he has orders from the Pope!"

"And Oultrejourdain," Guy insisted.

Aimery grimaced. "Don't count on Oultrejourdain. He's half inclined to muddy the waters by crowning Isabella, simply because he thinks he can control Toron easier than he can control you. His wife hates Tripoli, but if the choice is between you and her son, whom do you think she'll choose?"

"But the bishops favor Sibylla!" Guy protested.

"Some of them do—but only on the condition that she divorce you, just as her father divorced her mother in order to secure the Crown."

"She would never do that!" Guy retorted confidently, dismissing his brother's objections as if they were nonsensical. Aimery wondered how any man could be so certain of his wife's loyalty—especially with a crown at stake.

"Well, we know what side your brothers are on," Reynald de Châtillon remarked somewhat dismissively, as he launched a pottery jug along the wooden surface of the tavern table toward his retainer, Sir Henri. Henri deftly caught the jug and helped himself to the wine inside, filling the cheap, green, glass mug provided by the inn. Châtillon had wedged himself into a corner where the benches on the wall met and had propped his feet up on the table. Henri made himself comfortable against the threadbare and dusty cushions, but kept his feet on the floor.

"Just because my brothers have the sense not to back Sibylla and her play-king doesn't make the alternative more attractive."

Châtillon threw back his bald head and laughed heartily. He then raised his mug to Henri. "Here's to the brothers Ibelin! You're still one of them, no matter what you protest!"

Henri was annoyed at being lumped with his elder brothers, but he knew better than to show it to Châtillon. Instead he shrugged and repeated, "Better to be caught dead in good company than bad."

"Meaning me or Lusignan?"

"That depends on which Lusignan you mean."

"Ah, yes; if only I could have persuaded dear little Baldwin to wed his sister to Aimery instead of Guy. Of course, he would have had to discard your little niece—what's her name?"

"Her name's Eschiva, and I don't object to Aimery being my kin. Guy is another matter. The man's insufferable."

"He is, rather, isn't he? But the question is, if Sibylla were to cast him off, who then would she take in his stead? Probably some other pretty sop."

"Doesn't Tripoli have two or three unmarried stepsons?"

Oultrejourdain burst out into another guffaw. When the laughing fit was over, he shook his head, still chuckling as he drank more of the local wine, remarking, "Henri, I'd forgotten how amusing you could be."

Henri was not flattered, and he swallowed more wine to drown his own irritation with his lord. The bulk of the barons (and not just his brothers), along with at least half the bishops, had taken a clear stand against Guy de Lusignan by withdrawing to Nablus after the funeral. Henri did not like being on the losing side of any battle—particularly not ones at home.

Oultrejourdain, sensing his companion's mood, dropped his feet onto the floor, leaned forward, and got serious. "Look, I seriously considered the idea of crowning little Isabella. She's got guts and she's got brains. I like her. As for her husband . . ." Châtillon made a deprecating gesture and noise. "Nothing there. If we had a situation where the pack was lining up behind Sibylla and we could play king-maker with Isabella and Humphrey, I'd be breaking in to the Holy Sepulcher to pour the sacred oil over her head myself. Think what wax Humphrey would be in my hands! Why, our only problem would be the stink of shit whenever I barked at him!

"But that's *not* the situation we have, is it? It looks very much as if the bulk of the barons are going to opt for Isabella—"

"Isabella? I thought they wanted to crown Tripoli."

"No, they don't, and Tripoli's a wily old fox. He'd rather be the power behind the throne, manipulating things, than be too exposed. That means Isabella will owe her crown to Tripoli—and your two brothers, of course. The three of them together control four times the number of knights I do. Indeed, if Tripoli succeeds at getting the High Court to back his proposal, Isabella will owe her crown to damn near the whole High Court. With so many knights to protect him, Humphrey might even take it into his head to defy me. Not to mention that little Isabella for some reason took a dislike to my beloved wife, despite all her kindly upbringing. So why should the likes of us have any influence in Isabella's court?"

"Your wife truly did mishandle Isabella, didn't she?" Henri couldn't resist gloating a little. He had long since abandoned any loyalty to Stephanie de Milly—and if by chance he remembered swearing himself to her on that distant night when he brought her word of Miles de Plancy's murder, it was only to cringe at how wet behind the ears he'd been.

Châtillon shrugged. "The bitch had her uses, but you're right. She screwed up royally with Isabella. But there you are. Like it or not, that's the landscape. Isabella has no reason to love us—and Humphrey, who would normally be scared shitless of me, can now hide behind the likes of not only Tripoli, but your brothers as well. Ibelin's his father-in-law, for God's sake! I don't like that setup.

"If, on the other hand," Châtillon leaned closer and lowered his voice, "we prop up Sibylla and her puppet prince, they're going to be very indebted to us, aren't they?"

"Maybe," Henri answered warily. "Royalty has a reputation for short memory."

"True enough, but Guy's situation isn't going to get easier after his wife is crowned—assuming Heraclius goes through with it. She has promised to set Guy aside and remarry in order to win the support of half the bishops. Once she's crowned, the pressure for her to fulfill her promise will only increase."

"Which means Guy's crown will depend on his wife's whim—not something we have much influence over one way or another."

"Maybe not, but Sibylla's not at all keen to set him aside, and she'll cling to anyone—like us—who assures her it isn't necessary. We promise to stand by Guy long enough for people to start getting used to him, and here's the important part: we convince him his popularity depends on pursuing an aggressive policy against the Saracens."

"Ah." Henri leaned back and raised his drink to his lips, his skepticism in the curl of his smile, before he hid his face behind his glass mug.

"My strategy of taking the war to them works!" Oultrejourdain insisted.

"It didn't feel that way when I was trapped in a gully with five hundred men using me for target practice," Henri snarled back.

"That was a tactical setback. You have to look at the larger picture. Salah ad-Din was unable to intervene in Aleppo."

"He has it now. And Mosul."

"All the more reason why we need to take the war to him before he brings it to us."

Eschiva had been given the "honor," along with Stephanie de Milly, of carrying the Queen's train at her coronation. Everything was being done in a hurry for fear the barons meeting at Nablus might find out about the coronation, so Sibylla had no time to have a gown specially made. Instead, she was wearing the same coronation robes that her brother had worn a dozen years earlier over a white silk gown. It was oppressively hot, and the coronation robes, encrusted with jewels set in gold wiring, were immensely heavy. Eschiva could not lift the outer cloak on her own and needed Stephanie's help.

The Lady of Oultrejourdain stank, and she had bad breath. Eschiva shrank instinctively away from her. The older woman was in a foul mood, too, snipping and snarling at anyone and everyone—including the Queen. "Don't forget who put you where you are, Sibylla," the Lady of Oultrejourdain lectured.

"No, I'll never forget," Sibylla answered, her lips clamped together in resentment. From the expression on the Lady of Oultrejourdain's face, she didn't believe Sibylla any more than Sibylla meant what she said.

Eschiva kept her head down and hoped to keep out of the line of fire. She wasn't feeling well again and suspected another pregnancy. She was not keen on it; her little nursery seemed full enough already. Furthermore, while Hugh and Burgundia were both thriving, her second son, Henri, seemed to lurch from one colic to the next. He was not as big as he should have been because he couldn't keep enough food down to grow. She would have preferred to have more time to devote to him before having another child, but how was a woman supposed to deny her husband her bed? Then again, she supposed she ought to be glad her husband still wanted to share her bed. She did not imagine Stephanie de Milly suffered from her husband's unwanted attention! And poor Isabella still could not seem to attract the interest of Humphrey, either. . . .

"Stop daydreaming, you stupid girl, and give a hand!" Madame d'Oultrejourdain snapped, bringing Eschiva back to the present.

Sibylla was seated on a stool, waiting for her attendants to lower the gem-studded cloak over her shoulders. Eschiva took up her side of the garment, which was spread across the bed, and walked sideways facing Stephanie; together they brought the cloak to Sibylla and lowered it onto her shoulders.

Sibylla seemed to sink under the weight at first, and then she straightened her shoulders, lifted her head, and held out her hands, commanding: "Help me up!"

Eschiva and Stephanie dutifully each took one of her hands and helped raise her to her feet.

"A crown is quite a burden," Stephanie reflected. "So, who have you decided to share it with—once you discard Guy?"

"Guy."

"Yes," Stephanie answered sharply, annoyed by Sibylla's dullness. "After you discard Guy, who will you take to be your consort?"

"Guy," Sibylla answered again stupidly.

"But you promised to discard him!" Stephanie insisted, irritated.

"On the condition I could choose my own second husband, just as my father chose his second wife. And I'm going to choose Guy de Lusignan!" Sibylla was so pleased with her own cleverness that she giggled and would have danced for joy—if the coronation robes hadn't been so heavy.

Nablus, July 1186

Dawit felt he hadn't had a good night's sleep in three days—and all his meals were snatched standing up because the stables were overflowing with horses. They all needed to be fed, watered, exercised, and groomed, which of course the visiting squires took care of—but he had to help his father keep all these strange horses and squires from fighting with one another, hogging the troughs and grooming posts, or stealing hay and grooming tools. Everybody seemed to think that they (or their lord) were more important than everyone else, and that led to a lot of friction.

Dawit admired his father's calm in the midst of so much chaos, and likewise his soft-spoken authority. Although some of the squires tried to talk back once or twice, Mathewos could quell them with a look—something Dawit hadn't yet mastered. At the moment he was having trouble convincing Caesarea's squires that there were no box stalls available, and that if they insisted on such fine accommodations for their lord's horses they would have to seek it outside the citadel. "There's a reasonable inn just around the corner opposite St. James," he told the complainers, rather hoping they would take his advice. Yet even as he spoke, another party of riders clattered over the drawbridge and into the already overflowing ward.

Dawit felt like this was just too much, and was on the brink of saying so, when he recognized Sir William Marshal, Georgios, and—to his bewilderment—between them, clinging miserably to a hired mare, Beth.

Sir William had been left in Jerusalem to keep an eye on Sibylla and her party, but it was only Beth Dawit cared about. He forgot everything else that was going on and ran to her. "Beth! Beth! What are you doing here?" Dawit was beside her horse and reached up his arms to her. She looked utterly exhausted, coated in dust and damp with sweat.

"Dawit!" Beth exclaimed, and in that single word was unbounded relief. With obvious effort and discomfort, she managed to swing her right leg over the rump and slide down the side of the bony, ill-kept mare into Dawit's arms. She turned and laid her head on his chest, oblivious to all the strangers around them, the bustle, and the impropriety of her gesture. "Dawit! We've galloped all the way from Jerusalem! My lady has terrible news!"

"What, then?" Dawit asked, glancing automatically up at Sir William.

He answered for Beth. "Sibylla's had herself crowned in the Holy Sepulcher."

"Without the sanction of the High Court?" Dawit asked, shocked.

"Exactly," Marshal replied.

"But that's not the worst of it!" Beth interjected, looking up at Dawit intently. "She promised to divorce Guy and choose another man, but she intends to choose Guy as her *next* husband as well."

"The Templars are controlling access in and out of Jerusalem," Marshal explained impatiently. "I had to take lodgings at St. Lazarus, outside the city, but Georgios managed to slip in and see the coronation procession. I was just preparing to bring you word when Beth found me with this second piece of intelligence, so I brought her along. We must get word to the High Court," Marshal announced, clearly on edge. Unlike Beth, he did not see the groom Dawit as their destination.

"Must I go with you, sir?" Beth asked, clinging to Dawit. "You can tell them everything."

Marshal bowed his head to her politely and started at once for the stairs, leaving Beth with Dawit.

As soon as Marshal and Georgios were gone, Beth turned her face up to Dawit again and admitted, "Dawit, I don't want to go back to Jerusalem. Sibylla hates us, and now she is Queen. I'm afraid of what she will do to us—Eschiva and me."

"You don't have to go back. You are with me," Dawit assured her.

Maria Zoë found Isabella waiting anxiously in the small chamber she and Humphrey shared. With so many other high-ranking guests, they had not been given the most commodious nor the most luxurious accommodations; this room served normally as quarters for some of the garrison. It had only two narrow windows—more like arrow-slits—so the circular chamber got little light or fresh air, but the burning summer sun heated it like a bake oven.

At the sight of her mother, Isabella jumped to her feet. "Are they still arguing?" she asked anxiously.

"The discussions have been quite intense at times," Maria Zoë admitted; "not everyone is prepared to believe Beth's account of Sibylla's intentions. We've had word from three other messengers that she was crowned alone, the issue of a consort deferred to a later date. That makes some men hope Sibylla will divorce Guy after all. But the bishops argue there are no legal grounds for setting Guy aside, and Tripoli is adamant that without the approval of the High Court, Sibylla is a usurper, her coronation illegal and so invalid." Maria Zoë paused and glanced at Isabella.

Isabella sat very straight on the edge of her traveling chest, her hands folded neatly in her lap. She was still slim, but there was no mistaking the budding of her breasts or her poise. She also held her head high on a long and slender neck. Although she was still young and fresh, she was clearly not a child anymore.

"Tripoli has suggested that you be crowned Queen in the Church of the Nativity at Bethlehem—which, after all, is the place where Baldwin I was crowned. The Bishop of Bethlehem says he will perform the ceremony."

Isabella caught her breath and sat a little taller and stiffer, but it was from excitement, not surprise. Her eyes glittered in the darkness. "And will they, mama? Will they pay homage to me as they have not done to Sibylla?"

"That is a good question." Maria Zoë was pleased that her daughter recognized the difficulties and did not think a crowning was the same as ruling. "You can be sure that Tripoli, Ramla, and of course your stepfather, will do so. And you can be equally sure that Edessa and Jaffa will not. The question, therefore, becomes what the others will do. Bethlehem will, of course, crown Humphrey with you, so the barons will have a clear choice not only between you and Sibylla, but also between Humphrey and Guy."

Isabella's expression wavered slightly. She was acutely aware that many men did not think highly of her husband, but she was not prepared to admit this openly. "But there can be no comparison," she declared defensively, and Maria Zoë sighed inwardly as Isabella warmed to her argument. "Guy is a fool and an outsider. Humphrey understands us and our situation. He'll be much better at negotiating with Salah ad-Din."

"Perhaps, but many barons want a man who can also *defeat* Salah ad-Din on a battlefield."

"Humphrey's not a coward!" Isabella insisted.

"No one is suggesting he is—just inexperienced in command."

"So was Baldwin IV at Montgisard," Isabella retorted, so readily that Maria Zoë knew Isabella had practiced this response. She smiled wearily and put her hand on Isabella's.

"I fear you underestimate the burden of a crown," Maria Zoë told her daughter honestly. "I certainly did before my coronation—but at least I was only a consort, and my husband was a mature and experienced man, already well established on his throne and respected by his subjects. I honestly cannot say that I envy you the burden of the Crown." Maria Zoë paused, reflecting on that. She certainly did not long for her former existence as Amalric's doll-consort—but to be Queen in her own right, as Isabella would be? With Balian at her side? That was a very different prospect. Together, they could do so much! Baldwin had allowed his mother and uncle to plunder the royal treasury, but if she were Queen, she would hoard those resources to use them for the defense of the realm. Balian, meanwhile, would never squander men and horses in pointless aggression, but if the enemy dared to invade, he would show Salah ad-Din the power of Frankish arms! For an instant Maria Zoë allowed herself to dream, but then she called her own imagination to order. She was not being offered the Crown, and Balian was not going to be King. The best they could hope for was to be Isabella's advisers. And the best way to do that was to advise her well now.

"Isabella, if you are to be crowned as an alternative to Sibylla, then you will not have the Kingdom at your feet; you will have to win it by proving yourself more *worthy* than your rival."

"All Sibylla cares about is herself! And Guy," Isabella retorted hotly. "She doesn't have a brain in her head."

"That may be," Maria Zoë agreed with warning slowness, "but most of the men down there in the hall have no way of knowing that you are any different. To them you are nothing but a name. They will picture you like the fourteen-year-olds they know—their own daughters and younger sisters. Or they may picture you as they remember Sibylla at your age. It will be up to *you* to demonstrate that you are not like Sibylla, and that you aren't a flighty or frightened little girl, either. You will have to prove to them that you have the best interests of the Kingdom at heart."

Isabella frowned slightly and considered her mother. "How am I supposed to do that?"

"Well," Maria Zoë began cautiously. "For a start, you will have to be very careful about how you use royal patronage and royal revenues—and, most important, you must be careful not to provoke our enemies. The truce with

Baldwin V ended automatically with his death, so you will have to renegotiate with Salah ad-Din."

The look in Isabella's eyes was reassuringly frightened; Isabella was beginning to grasp the complexity of her future duties. "But Uncle Balian will help me treat with Salah ad-Din," Isabella decided, after absorbing the first shock of being responsible for something so dangerous.

"If that is whom you wish to entrust with the negotiations," Maria Zoë agreed cautiously. "But you must be careful not to appear to favor only one man, or one family, or one faction."

"Will I have a regent?" Isabella asked, frowning.

"No; you are mature in the eyes of the Church, and already married to a man over the age of maturity. You and Humphrey will not be placed under the guidance of a regent."

Isabella clearly looked pleased about that. "So we will be free to appoint our own advisers and officers?" she pressed her mother.

"Yes, you will," Maria Zoë assured her.

Isabella nodded, her lips pressed together firmly. "You'll see, Mama. We'll pick good men—men other men want to follow," she added with a hint of a smile.

Maria Zoë nodded and leaned forward to kiss her on her forehead. She was remembering the night her mother came to tell her the Emperor had signed a marriage contract with King Amalric of Jerusalem and she was to be his queen. The negotiations had been going on forever, and she knew other girls in the family had been considered. She had also known that she had gradually become the "favorite," and she had fantasized about being queen in a strange place—and about the husband she had never met. At least Isabella knew her husband, and whatever doubts Balian and other men had about him, Isabella loved and trusted him.

"I'm going to leave you now," Maria Zoë told her daughter. "God knows how long the men may yet talk, but when Balian comes, I want to be waiting for him—and you, even more than me, need time alone with your husband. In your shoes, I would ask God's guidance and protection in the days to come."

"Yes, of course, Mama!" Isabella instinctively put her hand around the cross at her throat.

Maria Zoë kissed her again tenderly, and then in a burst of emotion, pulled her close and held her tight. "Oh, child, these are tumultuous times, and only God knows what the future holds. Indeed, even He cannot see how each of us, with our individual decisions and free will, will shape the future. But with

His guidance and His blessings, we will weather every storm—or sleep in His embrace."

Isabella returned the hug, clinging for a last childish moment to the comforting warmth and softness of her mother. Then she consciously drew back, straightening herself and lifting her chin. "I swear, Mama, I will always try to be guided by Jesus Christ our Lord, and I will do my duty as Queen of Jerusalem for the good of the Kingdom and my subjects, as long as I live."

"I know you will, sweetheart," Maria Zoë assured her, tears stinging her eyes as she resisted the desire to hug Isabella again. It was better to leave her so, encased in her newfound dignity and determination. So she sank into a deep curtsy to show her recognition of Isabella's new status, and then turned and left the chamber.

Isabella tried praying, but her thoughts kept straying to all the things she would have to deal with. It was all very well to be crowned in Bethlehem; as the Bishop had said, that was the old tradition. But the Kings had then proceeded from Bethlehem to Jerusalem, and William Marshal said the Templars, who had thrown in their lot with Sibylla, controlled access to the Holy City. It would be unthinkable to try to force entrance to Jerusalem—that would discredit her. She would have to go somewhere else. Acre? Acre was the economic heart of the Kingdom, and it was in the royal domain. From Acre she would control the resources of the Kingdom. But it lacked symbolic power. Maybe it would be better to stay in Bethlehem? But Bethlehem was dangerously close to Oultrejourdain's territory.

The thought of Oultrejourdain sent a shiver down her spine. She didn't understand why he had decided to support Sibylla. Humphrey was his stepson. He should have been one of their staunchest supporters!

She was so lost in thought that she jumped half out of her skin when the door crashed open and Humphrey charged in. "Isabella!" he shouted, as if they were in a huge hall rather than a tiny tower chamber. Then his eyes found her and he rushed to fling his arms around her. "You won't believe what's happened!" he gasped out, all but crushing the air out of her lungs in his agitation.

"Mama said something about—" she started.

But Humphrey wasn't listening; he was bursting with the news. "The High Court has decided to crown us King and Queen of Jerusalem. But it's madness!" He broke his clasp of Isabella and started pacing about the room, gesturing in agitation as he declared, "The Patriarch has already crowned Sibylla. And she's the elder sister, anyway."

"But her mother's marriage was dissolved and—"

"You don't understand!" He stopped his pacing to stare at his wife in outraged disbelief. "Sibylla's *already* been crowned and anointed! She is Queen in the eyes of God, whether we like it or not. We *can't* oppose her. It would be a grievous sin!"

"But without the consent of the High Court—"

"I know, I know. I've been listening to Tripoli for hours!" Humphrey started pacing again, kicking at the furniture in fractious distress. "I *know* the High Court is supposed to agree, but they were here, and Sibylla's been crowned *in the Holy Sepulcher*! In the sight of Christ! On the very place He rose from the dead! Maybe she shouldn't have done it—certainly the Patriarch shouldn't have done it—"

"He only did it because he was Sibylla's mother's lover—"

"Isabella! Don't even talk of such things!" Humphrey scolded, frowning. "He's still the Patriarch—the most senior prelate of the Church after the Pope himself!"

"And he *still* has a mistress! A married woman, whom he keeps in his palace like a Muslim concubine—"

"Isabella! How can you say such things?" Humphrey was genuinely shocked that his little bride knew about this scandal.

"Because it's true!" Isabella shot back. "It's true, and it's true he slept with Agnes de Courtenay too! He's not fit to be a parish priest, let alone Patriarch!"

"But he *is* Patriarch, and Sibylla is now Queen. There's nothing we can do about it. Even if the High Court crowns us in Bethlehem, we *still* won't be King and Queen. We'll be nothing but puppets! Tripoli's puppets."

"No, we won't!" Isabella protested angrily. "We can rule in our own right! He won't be Regent anymore."

"Not officially, but you can't think he's going to have us crowned and then let us do what we please! He's going to control us!"

"Let him try! *I'm* certainly not going to let him control *me*! I was born to this, Humphrey. This is my destiny!" Isabella reached out to her husband, trying to both calm him and capture him for her vision.

Humphrey stared at her as if she had gone mad. When Isabella realized that he did not share her vision, it chilled her. How could he—her best friend and her husband—not want this for her?

"Have you forgotten that Oultrejourdain is supporting Sibylla?" Humphrey asked into the shocked silence, as Isabella's outstretched hand slowly sank back to her side.

"How could I forget that *your* stepfather is not standing by you as *my* stepfather is standing by me?" Isabella shot back, aware that it hurt Humphrey to have his stepfather compared to hers. That was why she said it: *because* he had rejected her as Queen, she *wanted* to hurt him.

"Oultrejourdain will tear us apart—eat us alive—if we dare to defy him!"

"How can he do that if we are King and Queen?" Isabella answered, her chin held high.

"Don't be naive!" Humphrey dismissed her. "Kings and queens can be stabbed to death no less than anyone else!"

"We'll be protected," Isabella countered.

"Not every minute, every second. Besides, he doesn't have to stab us. He can poison us instead, or have us shot by a crossbowman as we ride through the streets."

"Humphrey, you can't seriously mean you are *afraid* to be King?" Isabella demanded. She was on the very brink of losing her respect for her husband. She had defended him for so long. She had insisted he was not a coward, but here he was sounding as if he was indeed afraid to step up to his responsibility—out of craven fear of Oultrejourdain.

"I'm not afraid!" Humphrey retorted angrily. "I'm not afraid! But this is madness! No kingdom can have two kings, two queens. Sibylla shouldn't have done what she did, but now that it's done, we have to live with it!"

Isabella could see there was no point in arguing tonight. She took a deep breath and managed to get command of her voice. "You're tired, Humphrey," she told him. "It's been a long day. Let's get some sleep." She patted the bed beside her and smiled.

Humphrey dropped his face into his hands in utter despair. Not that, too! he thought in agony. She wanted to seduce him. She wanted him to lie with her and thought that if he did, she would be able to make him do what she wanted of him—like Sibylla and Guy, like Agnes de Courtenay and Heraclius. Why couldn't she just love him as before?

Isabella, stung, turned her back on him to start undressing herself. She wanted to cry, but she wouldn't let herself. She kept swallowing down her sobs, asking God what she had done wrong. Why didn't her husband want her? She wasn't ugly. She knew she wasn't ugly. She'd seen admiration in other men's eyes—the eyes of sergeants and squires and young knights. Why did her own husband despise her, then?

"Isabella." Humphrey was so close behind her, she could feel his breath on the back of her neck. She froze. "Isabella." He was stroking the back of her head gently and lovingly. "Don't be angry. I love you. I love you so much!" Humphrey put his arms around her from behind, and Isabella couldn't hold back her tears any longer. She dissolved into a flood of self-pitying sobs. Humphrey bent and kissed the top of her head as he swung her gently from side to side, swiveling from the waist. "Sweetheart, sweetheart, there's no need to cry. I love you more than anything in the world! It's *because* I love you so much that I don't want anything to happen to you. I don't want to see you hurt."

"But you *are* hurting me, Humphrey," Isabella managed to gasp out between sobs. "You're hurting me by rejecting me—again and again—and now you don't even want me to be Queen."

"I *do* want you to be Queen—if it wouldn't endanger your soul," Humphrey assured her, kissing the side of her face and licking at her tears. "But we can't fight this."

"Yes, we can!" Isabella insisted. "We have the whole High Court on our side!"

"Not the whole High Court, sweetheart, just some of it. Come." He turned her around in his arms and wiped away her tears with the flat of his hands, then bent to kiss her on the lips. "Trust me, sweetheart, I only want what's best for you."

"Then why won't you make me your wife?" Isabella gasped out, the tears bubbling up again. She loved him so much! She *wanted* him.

Humphrey pulled her back into his arms and gripped her to his chest. "Because—because it is horrible and filthy and—defiling!" He finally managed to put it into words, the images from the desert of Sinai crowding in around him. "I won't do it to you, Isabella! Never. I want to keep you pure—as pure as the Blessed Virgin. I never want to humiliate you like—like a bitch or a whore. You're too good for it, Isabella. Much too good for—for—" He shook his head. He would not even say the word in her presence. He couldn't.

Isabella's tears and sobs subsided as she grasped what he was saying. She was stunned and confused. She had never thought of consummation as something horrible—not between two people who loved each other and were married. But it was comforting to think Humphrey was not rejecting *her* or repelled by her. She drew a deep breath and nodded. "All right," she whispered. "All right. If that's the way you want it," she conceded, not sure what they should do about having children if he wouldn't consummate the marriage. And if they were to be King and Queen, then they would need to have heirs. Or was that the real reason he didn't want them to be King and Queen? There was too much to think about here. For the moment all that mattered was that Humphrey was here with her, holding her in his arms as he so often had before—comforting and protective.

"You understand now?" Humphrey asked tentatively, hopeful but hardly daring to believe she had indeed accepted what he'd said.

"Yes," Isabella assured him, nodding. "Yes, I understand. Now let's go to bed. You needn't fear. I won't be importunate. Not ever again," she vowed.

Humphrey stroked her hair, her arms. "I love you so much, Isabella. You do understand that?"

"Yes, I understand," she told him as she continued undressing and finally lay down on the bed, her back to Humphrey. She kept her eyes closed tightly as she heard him moving about the chamber, undressing himself rather than calling for his squire. At last she felt the bed sink under his weight, and then his arm around her waist again as he lay down behind her on the bed and pulled her into his embrace. It was just like when she had been eight and he had come to comfort her in the crypt in Kerak, she thought, and silent tears trickled down her face into the pillow.

To Humphrey it seemed to take forever, but eventually all the excitement and emotional strain overwhelmed Isabella and she fell into a deep sleep. Testing, he called her name gently, "Isabella?" Her breathing continued, deep and even.

Humphrey cautiously took his arm away from her waist, but still she breathed deeply and steadily. He slowly drew back from her and waited again. Still no reaction. He eased himself off the bed and then stood still beside it, holding his breath, afraid the jostling would have woken her, but still she slept. He tiptoed across the room to his heap of clothes. He had not been wearing armor, and he did not need it for what he intended now. He took his clothes in a bundle and inched to the door.

He had been in such a state when he arrived that he had not even bolted the door, so he did not need to unbolt it now. He slowly turned the big iron ring that controlled the latch and gently pulled the door inward. It creaked, and he caught his breath and held still. Isabella was still breathing regularly on the bed. He slipped out, pulling the door closed behind him. Only then, when he was out in the stairwell, did he dump his clothes and, finding his braies first, start to dress himself.

Dressed, he moved stealthily down the stairs to the ward. Here there were still some people about. The wagon to take out the "night soil" was being loaded with the kitchen refuse and the dirty straw from the stables at the postern. A couple of baker's apprentices were chopping wood in front of the bread oven, apparently preparing to fire it up. Was it really that late already? But it had to be. The High Court had debated long into the night, and then he'd had the fight with Isabella and it had taken her a long time to get to sleep. Yes, it was probably not much before dawn.

He made his way to the keep and started up the stairs slowly and cautiously. Many of the visitors were housed here, and he did not want to wake them—much less for them to see him. When he got to the top floor, however, he knocked lightly on the door. When no one answered, he knocked again, and was finally answered by a groggy, "Who's there?"

"Gabriel, it's me, Humphrey de Toron. I need to speak to Ernoul!"

He heard a clunk and then a startled, "What?" followed by the mocking comment from Gabriel, "The Lord of Toron requests the pleasure of your company."

"What? In the middle of the night?"

"Yes," Humphrey himself called, holding his head close to the wooden door and speaking into the crack.

A moment later a tousled Ernoul, dressed in a nightshirt, yanked the door open and squinted at him.

"I need your help, Ernoul, please," Humphrey begged.

The squire pulled himself together, gesturing for Humphrey to wait just long enough for him to tuck his shirt into a pair of braies, push his bare feet into his low boots, and pull a tunic over his head. His hair still in disarray, he came out of the antechamber, closing the door behind him. "What—"

Humphrey held his finger to his lips and led the way back down to the ground floor. He didn't stop until they were in the middle of the ward, far away from any possible listeners.

"Ernoul, I need your help."

"Yes. What?" Ernoul asked, still half asleep.

"I can't go through with this crowning," Humphrey said in a low voice.

Ernoul's eyes widened. "What—"

"Sibylla's been anointed. To oppose her is treason! Besides, how can we have two queens in one country? It will tear the Kingdom apart, and while we're fighting each other, Salah ad-Din will overwhelm us. You must see this is madness! No matter how bad Sibylla and Guy might be, fighting among ourselves is worse."

"But Sibylla didn't have the consent of the High Court," Ernoul protested.

"That doesn't matter anymore!" Humphrey cut him off. "The only thing that matters now is that we unite and fight together."

"What does Isabella say to this?" Ernoul wanted to know.

"She wants to be Queen, but that's just a childish notion. She doesn't know what it will mean. Not really. She thinks it's about being rich and powerful and independent. She thinks it's her 'destiny.'" Humphrey's voice belittled Isabella's feelings. "But this is about our very survival!"

Ernoul was frowning. He could understand Humphrey's logic, but the High Court had decided something else, and Balian supported Isabella. Could they all be wrong and Humphrey right? He didn't think so. The High Court was composed of the wisest men in the realm. Men with hundreds of years of experience combined, and men who had given their whole lives to the Defense of Jerusalem. Surely they could not all be wrong and the teenage Humphrey de Toron right? Besides, they had might on their side. Oultrejourdain had only sixty knights, after all, and Edessa maybe twenty. The Templars were the problem, of course, but the Hospitallers were with the High Court, and if the Pope ordered the Templars . . . Ernoul shook his head sharply to bring himself back to reality. "What do you want me to do?" he asked Humphrey.

"I'm going to ride for Jerusalem tonight and do homage to Sibylla—"

"Humphrey! You can't!" Ernoul protested.

"I must! I'm going to stop this civil war before it starts! But you've got to keep Isabella from sounding the alarm."

"I don't know what you mean."

"When she wakes up and finds me gone, she'll come looking for me, and even if she doesn't know—doesn't even dream—where I actually am, her asking about me may make others suspicious. All I want you to do is make up some story—you're good at that. Tell her waiting woman that you've taken me somewhere. Tell her we won't be back until after dinner, so she doesn't get alarmed until then."

"Humphrey, you're asking me to betray my lord, the High Court, and the Regent!" He added forcefully, "Lord Balian *wants* to see Isabella crowned—"

"Ernoul!" Humphrey laid his hands on Ernoul's shoulders and looked him in the eye. "You've been my friend all these years. My only friend. Please, as you love me, do this for me."

Ernoul didn't know what to say. He *did* love Humphrey. Who else in the world shared his love of books and poetry—of language itself, and the way it was used to tell a tale? Even if the days when the others made fun of him were gone, they still did not share his love. They were happy to hear his tales and songs once they were finished, but only Humphrey had ever helped him write them. His friendship with Humphrey was like nothing else, and Humphrey still treated him like an equal although he was a lord.

"You can't stop me from what I intend to do," Humphrey told Ernoul. "Not unless you are prepared to knock me down and call the watch! And even then, they will have to chain me in a dungeon to stop me. I'm going to do this for the good of Jerusalem. All I'm asking is that you make it easier on everyone. The sooner this is over with, the sooner the threat of civil war is over—because once I've done homage to Sibylla, they will have no alternative king anymore."

"Humphrey! Are you sure? What will Isabella say?"

"That is my problem, Ernoul," Humphrey told him solemnly.

"Humphrey, please don't do this!" Ernoul begged.

"Are you going to help me or not?" Humphrey answered, his lips pressed together, with a determination on his face that Ernoul could not remember ever seeing there before.

Ernoul took a deep breath. "I'll tell Isabella a tall tale—but I won't lie to Lord Balian if he asks me where you are."

"Fair enough," Humphrey agreed with a short nod. Then he flung his arms around Ernoul and held him close for a moment. "Thank you!" he murmured. "I will not forget this. Ever."

He released Ernoul and turned to stride toward the stables where his squire slept with the other visiting squires. Ernoul stood in the ward, stunned, half inclined to call the watch after all—or at least wake Lord Balian. Should he really let Humphrey go and ruin everything the High Court had decided? Should he allow Humphrey to make Guy de Lusignan king? Was civil war really worse than a bad king? A stupid, arrogant king? Ernoul wasn't sure.

Humphrey emerged from the stables leading his palfrey, his squire stumbling behind him still half asleep, straw caught in his long hair. Humphrey swung himself up into the saddle and ordered the gate opened. Ernoul took a step forward, a shout on the tip of his tongue, but the gateman didn't dream of saying "no" to the Baron of Toron. Already the gate was creaking open as the first sliver of orange announced the rising sun. A moment later, Humphrey was clattering out over the drawbridge into the town, spurring his sleepy stallion as he turned south for Jerusalem.

Chapter 16

Ibelin, October 1186

It was drizzling and almost dark by the time Maria Zoë rode into the ward at Ibelin. While Dawit took her horse and the rest of her escort saw to their own mounts, a boy was sent bounding into the hall to tell the lord that his lady was back. Balian emerged on the landing to the hall before Maria Zoë had wearily reached the top. She fell into his arms, and as he turned to lead her inside he noted, "That feels like bad news. Did something go wrong with the birth?"

"Worse," Maria Zoë told him with a heavy heart. "Elizabeth died giving birth to a tiny, weak little boy, but while we were focused on helping her, Godfrey came down with a raging fever. He'd been coughing and sniveling a bit when we arrived, but of course our attention was focused on Elizabeth. By the second night, however, we realized he was feverish as well. I told Eschiva to stay with Godfrey while I helped with the birth. Elizabeth delivered a very sickly-looking son just before dawn and died within the hour, exhausted from fighting to bring him into the world. Meanwhile, Godfrey's fever had increased. We tried everything we knew, and Barry sent for the Nestorian doctor everyone swears by. However, Godfrey could not keep any food or water down. Just before noon today he died."

Balian crossed himself, stunned. "How's Barry—"

Maria Zoë shook her head. "You must go to him. I only came so I could tell you the news myself, but tomorrow we must return. Eschiva's with him, but I've never seen a man grieve so, Balian. Never."

"Barry is a man of great passion," Balian remarked simply.

"Of course. I know, but . . ." she paused, "I fear he is on the brink of losing his sanity—if he hasn't already."

Balian looked at her questioningly.

"Eschiva and I had to drag him—literally—away from the altar. He had seized the cross and flung it across the room. Then he blew out the Eucharist candle and hurled the glass out the window, breaking the pane. He was cursing and screaming, vowing to convert to Islam, and—I honestly didn't understand everything he said."

Balian gazed at her in horror. "When will the funerals be?"

"I don't know for sure. Barry was saying he would not put his son in the ground. He said Godfrey didn't like the darkness. Godfrey had always wanted to fly, he said, so he declared his intention to build a kite for him and fly it over the ocean."

"Mother Mary help him!"

"Eschiva's at the end of her strength, too. She shouldn't go through an ordeal like this in her state. I'm very worried she could miscarry this latest child—and that, after losing little Henri, her stepmother and half-bother, could be utterly devastating. When we return, we must take Beth with us. Eschiva was very generous to let her marry Dawit and join our household, but for this crisis she needs Beth's support. I think—" She paused, unsure if she dared say this out loud, but then decided it had to be said. "It is particularly horrible for her to see her father so distraught—and to know he would not have grieved like this for *her*."

Balian didn't have an answer to that, but he noted, "We've been summoned to Acre, did you know?"

"No. By whom? What for?"

"Guy was crowned in the Holy Sepulcher last month, and most of us were pointedly absent. Now he has summoned all his vassals to Acre to take the oath of fealty—or forfeit our fiefs."

"That's just like Guy, isn't it?" Maria Zoë observed cynically, but then she stopped and stared at Balian with a new thought. "Barry won't do it! I'm sure he won't. Not in the state he's in."

Balian admitted, "The timing couldn't be worse, but I'll have to reason with him."

"There *is* no reasoning with him," Maria Zoë muttered wearily, shaking her head.

Balian put his arm around her shoulders and hugged her. "I understand, but this state he's in won't last forever. He'll burn himself out, and then I'll have to be there to talk to him. Come, you need rest."

Maria Zoë nodded. "I do—and your arms around me," she admitted. Then she stopped and frowned, "But I'm sure Guy set a deadline. What was it?"

"The end of the month."

"So, just over ten days," she calculated with a sigh. "Well, we'll have to try. The last thing we need is for Barry to refuse and for Ramla and Mirabel to fall to the Crown. We'd then be completely surrounded by Guy de Lusignan's lands."

"The knights and men of Ramla and Mirabel are not going to turn into our enemies just because they are technically tenants of Lusignan," Balian reassured her, but Maria Zoë still didn't like the idea. Sibylla hated her with a passion that was raw and violent. Guy, conscious of how dependent he was on his wife for all his honors, was inclined to indulge her. At least for once, Maria Zoë reflected bitterly, she needn't worry about Isabella, whose spineless husband had secured the favor of Lusignan with his betrayal of his wife and the High Court. Yet she had four other children, and she was uncomfortable thinking that they might be surrounded by people who owed allegiance to her enemies. Maybe she should move them to Nablus? She was getting ahead of herself. Barry might yet be brought to reason in time.

They had passed through the hall and on into the solar. At once John and Helvis jumped up at the sight of their mother and ran over, with Margaret and the toddling Philip trailing uncertainly behind. Maria Zoë sank onto her heels to accept the hugs of her four children, feeling like a mother cat with four frolicking kittens around her. She could not fathom how she should be so lucky and have such healthy children while Barry had lost all but Eschiva; this latest sickly boy seemed unlikely to live long. Eschiva, too, had lost her second son, Henri, and she seemed to feel guilty about being pregnant again so soon, though it was hardly her fault.

"Shhh!" Balian admonished his rambunctious children. "Quiet down! Your mother's very tired, and she has bad news for you all."

Slowly they fell silent and looked back and forth between their mother and father. It was Balian who spoke. "Your Aunt Elizabeth and your cousin Godfrey have both died."

"Little Godfrey?" Helvis gasped in a tone of innocent pity, while John frowned.

"You have a new cousin, though," Maria Zoë added, in an effort to cheer them up a bit. "A little boy."

"What's his name?" Helvis asked.

"Well, he hadn't been christened yet when I left, but we'll soon find out."

Ramla, October 1186

Balian rose before dawn, leaving Maria Zoë still sleeping heavily, and set out for Ramla with only Ernoul and his confessor Michael in attendance. It was a clear, warm day after the evening rain, and the freshly tilled fields smelled heavily of dung. They encountered few other travelers, as they were earlier than most, and they made good time, arriving at Ramla by midmorning.

Barry's residence here was a large, imposing townhouse two stories high, with decorative crenelation on the flat roof. It had clusters of double-light windows supported by central pillars of marble on the upper floors, and square grilled windows on the ground floor. A large wooden door at street level gave access for people only; the stables were around at the back.

Balian turned Rufus over to Ernoul and was admitted with Michael into the marble-paved entry hall by a familiar servant. "Thank God you're here, Lord Balian! Lady Eschiva is at her wit's end. My lord has locked himself in his chamber, and we can't get him to come out for anything. The chaplain had to christen the baby without my lord's presence or consent, as he seems sickly and like to die any hour now. And—" He would have continued at some length, Balian suspected, if Eschiva had not appeared at the head of the stairs.

"Uncle Balian?" she called out uncertainly, her voice strained from lack of sleep. "Is that really you?"

Balian answered by turning to his confessor and ordering in a low voice, "See if you can find my brother's chaplain and help any way you can," then he took the stairs two at a time to join Eschiva.

She looked much too thin for the size of her belly, and the dark circles under her eyes had transformed what should have been a pretty young face into a ghoulish apparition. "Oh, Uncle Balian!" she gasped out in distress as he caught her hands in his own. "I don't know what to do!" she confessed, tears brimming up in her red-rimmed eyes. "My father's locked himself in his chamber with Godfrey's corpse, and he won't come out or even answer me. God knows what he's done to himself in there! I'm terrified he's killed himself!" she admitted. "He was cursing God and denying Christ. I'm sure he didn't give a thought to his immortal soul in his grief. He just wanted to end it all. I pleaded with him through the door, but at first he just screamed at me to go away, then threw things at the door. After that there was a terrible crash and all went deathly still."

"Eschiva." Balian guided her to a chest and sat her down on it. "You need to rest and look after yourself. Where are your women?"

"I don't know. I sent them to bed long ago," she corrected herself. Balian frowned; it was now midmorning, and even if they had laid down to rest they should be up again by now, seeing to their mistress.

"When was the last time you ate anything?" he asked her next.

"Tante Marie forced me to eat, but I'm really not hungry."

"You may not be, but that child of yours is," Balian admonished, nodding to her belly.

"Uncle Balian, my brother Godfrey's dead!" Eschiva wailed in anguish.

"I know. There's nothing you can do for *him* but pray for his soul, but for the child under your heart you can do much more." Eschiva's hand fell to her belly, but her expression remained tortured; she found no joy in the life within her.

Balian changed the subject. "Maria Zoë said Elizabeth died giving birth to another son. Where is he?"

"With a wet nurse." Eschiva gestured vaguely down the hall. "He's very tiny. I don't think he'll live very long. We tried to get my father to tell us what he wanted to name him, but he just screamed at us that no one could replace Godfrey. We christened him Thomas, for Elizabeth's father and brother."

Balian nodded approval and then asked, "Now, where's my brother?"

"Right down here." Eschiva hauled herself to her feet to lead the way.

Barry's chamber was accessed through an anteroom, where two frightened squires and a whining dog waited in nervous confusion. Balian strode past them and tried the tall, pointed door, but it was indeed bolted from the inside. He lifted his arm and pounded on the door with the side of his gloved fist so hard that Eschiva started as the hammering reverberated. "Barry! It's Balian! Open the door!"

Everyone in the anteroom held their breath as they listened for some sign of life on the far side of the door. There was none.

"Fetch me an ax," Balian ordered over his shoulder to one of the squires. Eschiva sank down on the arm of a chair, her hand over her mouth and her eyes wide with horror.

The squire ran, but it took him several minutes to find and return with one of his lord's battle-axes. He was followed by Barry's household steward, two other clerics, and Michael, as well as a gaggle of other staff.

Balian took the ax and weighed it in his hand, getting a feel for it, while the other occupants in the room drew back out of his way. Then he drew an audible breath and swung the ax. The head landed just beside the door handle with a crunching thwack, embedding itself several inches into the door. Balian had to brace a foot against the base of the door to yank the ax free again. He raised it and brought it down a second time, close to the first blow. With a cracking sound, one of the planks gave a little.

Abruptly from the far side of the door Barry roared, "You don't have to vandalize my home! Damn you!" Then he wrenched open the door from the inside and glared out at the assembled company with wild, furious eyes. His haggard face was covered with stubble and framed by a tangled mane of dull gray-blond hair.

"Papa!" Eschiva jumped up and started to run to him in relief.

"Leave me alone!" he barked at her, gesturing for her to stay where she was, and then turned to shout at the rest of them. "What are you staring at? Get out!"

Balian did just the opposite. He moved into the doorway before his brother could close it again, and stared his brother down. "The priests have come for Godfrey's corpse."

"What are they going to do with it? Eat it?"

Balian didn't bother answering, just gestured for Michael and his colleagues to come and get the boy's body from behind Barry while he held his brother in place, the ax still in his hand. Barry made no move to stop them from taking the body away. He just stared at it listlessly, his whole form sagging with indifference born of despair. As soon as the priests were out, Balian moved deeper into the chamber and closed the door behind him to be alone with his brother.

"Godfrey," was all Barry said.

"Godfrey is with Christ, but you have a tiny newborn boy who needs you."

"I've lost count of how many newborn boys I've buried. Godfrey was the only one who lived long enough to be a *son* to me."

"You didn't know in the first forty-eight hours that he was going to live."

"I did, though," Barry told Balian firmly, if irrationally. "I could tell. But this boy won't live. His mother's dead."

Balian said a prayer for Elizabeth, who even now to Barry was only the mother of his sons.

"This is the end," Barry told him in a dull voice.

"What do you mean?" Balian asked in alarm.

"Can't you feel it? Smell it? The vultures are gathering for Armageddon."

"What I feel and smell is your grief, Barry," Balian answered steadily.

Barry shook his head. "No. The forces of evil are on the move. They are gathering their troops and sharpening their weapons. And Christ—" Barry made a deprecating gesture and snorted. "*Christ* is as effective as that pathetic stepson of yours. A powerless man of peace, when the gods of war are about to devour us alive."

Balian did not try to answer. He was certain that Christ would understand Barry's grief and forgive him. Instead, he silently pulled Barry into his arms and let him cry.

Acre, October 1186

King Guy was holding court in the Hospitaller Quarter of Acre. Although built to accommodate hundreds of knights and three times as many sergeants and serving brothers, it was still crowded to overflowing by the large number of barons who had come with their entourages to pay homage. King Guy even had the effrontery to fly his flag higher than the Hospitaller banner—a gesture the Templars would never have allowed, Balian noted mentally. Moulins had evidently trimmed his sails to the wind.

The approach of the Barons of Ramla and Ibelin side by side did not go unnoticed. Even in the streets outside the Hospitaller complex, the street urchins excitedly called out their names: "Ramla and Ibelin!" No doubt they made a game of it to see if they could identify everyone—and keep track of who came and who did not.

Inside the usually spacious courtyard they found themselves crushed and jostled by the other visitors, messengers, victualers, and tradesmen, not to mention the sick and their attendants. Yet even so, the arrival of "Ramla and Ibelin" created a ripple of excitement as the word spread that they had come. People turned to stare at them, dropping whatever else they had been doing.

Balian glanced at his brother warily. Barry was dressed at his most flamboyant, in a camel-leather cloak sewn with the red crosses of Ibelin and the ravens of Ramla, lined with fox fur. His boots were likewise soft camel leather, his surcoat silk with gold embroidery worn over gleaming chain mail trimmed with bronze links. His hair was freshly washed, but tousled by the ride, which made it fuller and more impressive. The long mustache disguised the fact that his lips turned down in a sour expression. His eyes were shaded, but when he felt Balian's gaze he managed a wan, mirthless smile—like the angel of death, Balian thought.

Hospitaller lay brothers ran forward to take the bridles of their horses as they drew up, and a royal squire was sent scurrying to tell King Guy that his most inveterate opponent, the man he had snubbed and humiliated, had come to bend his knee.

As Ibelin's feet hit the cobbled surface of the courtyard, Reginald de Sidon pushed his way through the crowd to grab Balian by the arm and clap him on the back. "Well done!" he murmured in a low voice with a glance toward Barry, before he held his hand out to Ramla and welcomed him.

Ramla nodded curtly to his fellow baron and took his hand, but he did not return Sidon's greeting verbally.

"Let's get this over with," Ibelin urged his brother, and Sidon nodded his approval.

A royal squire bowed and gestured for them to follow. He turned away from the series of sick bays along the ground floor, with their rank smell of ill humanity crowded together, and led them up a narrow flight of stairs. Ibelin automatically let Ramla take the lead and followed in his wake, his view largely blocked by his brother's broad back. People were coming down the stairs, but Ramla made no room for them, forcing them to back up against the wall to make way for him instead.

At the top of the stairs a knot of men was standing just in the hallway, but Ramla ignored them and turned to enter a cavernous refectory. "Uncle Balian!" a voice called out, causing Ibelin to falter in his stride. There were only two people left alive who called him "Uncle Balian": Eschiva and Isabella. But this was a man's voice, Toron's.

Ibelin had not spoken to Toron since he had betrayed his wife, the High Court, and the entire Kingdom by sneaking off in the dark of night to pay homage to Sibylla—and so put Guy de Lusignan on the throne of Jerusalem. Neither his grieving and humiliated brother nor he would be here today if it weren't for Humphrey's cowardice.

"Uncle Balian!" Humphrey tried again, closer now as he pushed his way through the crowd of men, who stood back for him, their eyes shifting back and forth curiously.

Ibelin clamped his teeth and refused to look at his stepdaughter's husband. He had recovered from his astonishment, and rather than waiting for Toron he pressed ahead to catch up with Ramla, leaving a wounded Humphrey ignored in his wake.

The refectory was gigantic, and the King was on the dais. The High Table had been put away, and he sat in the high-backed armed chair usually reserved for the Grand Master, in full view of everyone who entered the room. Sibylla was beside him on a similar but slightly smaller chair. They were the only two people seated. Both wore crowns and ermine-trimmed robes, and while Sibylla sat primly in her chair, Guy de Lusignan sprawled in his, his very pose a provocation.

The sight of him reminded Ibelin that William Marshal had taken his leave this past month, with the words that he could not remain in a Kingdom ruled by a "murdering fool." "When I came," Marshal had admitted, "I thought I had at last found the true use for the gifts God gave me. I had wasted my talent with sword and lance in foolish games, for self-gain, and most recently in the service of an unworthy boy—but here, I thought, I had found my destiny and the reason God made me such a formidable fighting man. When I helped your wife defend Nablus, I was exhilarated beyond description. I felt a sense of purpose and blessing that was more gratifying than the greatest tournament prize or the praise of Eleanor of Aquitaine. And now?" He had paused dramatically before declaring sadly, "Henry the Young King was foolish and unbridled. He had the Plantagenet temper and lacked his father's steadying sense of reality. He dreamed big and was frustrated when things did not go as he planned, but he was never truly evil. He knew self-doubt and remorse. He loved his father too much rather than too little, and if only the Old King had shown him a little more trust . . . But it doesn't matter. Guy de Lusignan is a totally different man. He does not know his own shortcomings, and he gloats over every victory—no matter how ill deserved."

He was certainly gloating now as he looked down the length of the huge hall, past the massive pillars supporting the fan vaults that seemed to grow out of them. He had recognized Ramla and Ibelin, and the smirk on his face was undisguised. He did not even have the courtesy to sit upright, but remained lounging in his chair, one foot thrust out and the other cocked under his throne. He leaned his upper body on his left elbow.

"You go first," Barry hissed at Balian, causing Balian to frown slightly. Barry was senior by both birth and titles, so it was not proper for Balian to go first. But Barry gritted his teeth and repeated, "You first, Balian! Do as I say. You'll see why."

There was no point in hesitating any longer. Already people were whispering, and Guy's eyes had narrowed. Ibelin strode forward and went down on one knee just before the dais. "Your grace, I have come to do homage for the Barony of Ibelin."

"You certainly left things to the last minute, didn't you, Ibelin?" Lusignan pointed out in a loud voice, harvesting snickers from the sycophants that always congregated near seats of power. Balian did not even bother trying to identify them.

"I was in no hurry," Ibelin answered.

"Yes, I can see." Guy lazily got to his feet and came to the edge of the dais. Ibelin held up his folded hands and waited as Guy dragged out the humiliation as long as possible, clearly enjoying the sight of Ibelin on his knees before him in a pose of prayer and pleading. Finally he deigned to put his hands over Ibelin's and accept the oath of homage. Ibelin stumbled over the words because he was remembering that day, more than a decade ago, when he had given this same oath to a frightened, tear-stained youth who had just lost his father. Baldwin had been so frightened of his Crown, but Balian's gesture had helped the boy recover some of his poise. When he had pledged himself to Baldwin, he had meant it — body, mind and soul. He had wanted then to protect Baldwin with every fiber of his body.

And Guy de Lusignan? Jesus God! What a terrible thing it was to swear an oath to an unworthy man! Again William Marshal came to mind; Marshal claimed he had agonized over committing sacrilege and banditry in the service of his young king. Surely God did not expect a man to uphold an oath to those lengths? Surely God did not expect a man to sacrifice his immortal soul for the sake of an earthly lord?

It was over, and Ibelin got back to his feet, his knees as stiff as if he'd been on them for hours. He bowed his head curtly and then backed to the side to make way for his brother. He turned to look at Barry, nodding slightly to encourage him.

Ramla had put a smile on his lips, although his eyes were deadly serious. He strode forward, his boots pounding loudly on the flagstone pavement as stillness descended over the room, and all held their breath to see Ramla pay homage to the man who had first stolen his bride and then the Kingdom itself.

King Guy had not sat down again after Ibelin's homage, and he waited full of anticipation. He too was smiling, and his eyes glittered with triumph.

Ramla came to a halt, but he did not drop down onto one knee. "I am here to publicly renounce all my lands and titles in favor of my son Thomas!" he announced in a booming voice that echoed in the arches overhead—and set off a veritable conflagration of wagging tongues. Everyone was talking at once except, it seemed, the principals: King Guy and the Baron of Ramla. Even Balian found himself saying, "Barry! You can't—"

"What did you say?" the King demanded ominously, cutting short the chatter around him.

"I said I would not demean myself by taking an oath to the likes of you! You may have seduced a stupid girl"—Ramla spat the words in the direction of an indignant Sibylla—"and bought the favor of fat old men"—he gestured toward Edessa—"or convinced vultures like Oultrejourdain and Ridefort that they can feast on your weakness"—his gesture took in the bald Oultrejourdain and the tonsured Ridefort, who (Balian thought) did look remarkably like vultures at that moment. "You have blackmailed the barons and bishops with threats to their lands, honors, and families"—his gaze took in his brother and the Barons of Caesarea and Hebron. "But there are two men in this Kingdom you can neither buy nor break: Raymond de Tripoli, Count in his own right, who will not come to heel, and I. I will take my sword where it will not be discredited, to Antioch."

This declaration ignited another ripple of exclamation across the hall. Balian was still stunned. If only Barry had told him what he planned to do! It wasn't that Balian didn't understand his brother. He could see that Barry did not want to stay in Ramla or Mirabel anymore. He had buried too many children, and neither of his marriages had been happy. This had as much to do with Barry running away from his memories, his mistakes, and his unfulfilled dreams as it did with refusing to bend his knee to Lusignan. Not that his hatred of the other man wasn't real, but he would surely have been able to overcome it if he had had something left in Ramla that he cherished—as Balian had at Ibelin with Maria Zoë and his small brood of children.

The problem was, Barry didn't have the right to leave his lands and titles to Thomas. The conditions of his divorce from Richildis had been that Eschiva remained his heiress—regardless of issue from subsequent marriages. Since Godfrey's birth, Barry had sought to find ways around that agreement, consulting various lawyers, and even putting pressure on Eschiva herself.

But Ramla was blindly continuing to the still stunned Guy de Lusignan, "When my son Thomas comes of age, it will be his decision whether he takes the oath of homage. That's fifteen years from now—and, God willing, there'll be a better man sitting where you sit now before *he* has to make his choice. Meanwhile, he and his lands will be under the guardianship of my brother of Ibelin." Ramla gestured to Ibelin, still standing to one side.

Balian started to protest, to remind him that Eschiva was his heiress and that Thomas, no less than his lands, fell to her keeping, but he bit his tongue. This was Barry's moment. Why detract from it? He would work things out with Aimery and Eschiva directly.

"I think that is all we have to say to one another," Ramla concluded with a smile that reached his eyes this time. He truly seemed relieved to have given away his entire inheritance, and with a spring in his stride he pointedly turned his back on King Guy and his entire court and strode out of the refectory with Balian, somewhat uncomfortably, in his wake.

"This is the *second* time your father has tried to disinherit you!" Aimery shouted in fury, as he paced the beautifully appointed room at the Pisan palace with its magnificent view of the port of Acre. His boots clicked on the marble paving, and the hilt of his sword flashed in the sun pouring through the open window.

"I don't care," Eschiva answered in a strained voice, seated in the cushioned chair beside the bed with its sumptuous hangings.

"What do you mean, you don't care?" Aimery shot back at her. "It's *your* inheritance! If your father is such a fool that he's prepared to throw it all away while still alive, then Ramla and Mirabel are *yours*! He can't go back on the agreement he made when he divorced your poor mother!"

"I don't want to disinherit my baby brother," Eschiva told her husband steadily, her hand on her belly.

"Your baby brother isn't likely to live very long," Aimery retorted practically. "It's your uncle who's profiting from this. My God! With Tripoli refusing to pay homage, if Ibelin controls Ramla and Mirabel, he'll become the most important baron in the Kingdom! He'll command the largest single contingent of troops in the entire Christian army! He'll have more knights than Caesarea and more than twice as many knights as Oultrejourdain!"

"What's so wrong with that?" Eschiva croaked out, her voice tight as she suppressed the sobs welling up from her chest.

Something in her voice caught Aimery's attention, and he turned to look at her. Tears were slipping out of her eyes, and Aimery finally saw what Balian had seen a few weeks earlier: she was far too thin, frail, and hollow-eyed for her twenty-two years. "Eschiva," Aimery exclaimed in a voice softened by shock, "are you all right?"

"All right?" she gasped back, a sob escaping with her words. "In case you haven't noticed, I've lost my youngest child, my stepmother, and my brother Godfrey in the last three months. And now my father's left the Kingdom, never to return, without bothering to say goodbye. I know that to *you* they were just vehicles for conveying property, but to me they were *people*. People I *loved*."

"Eschiva! That's not fair! I loved Henri as much as you did!" The look in her glittering eyes was so scornful that he corrected himself. "No, you're right, no one can love a child as much as a mother does, but that does not mean I do not grieve for Henri—and rejoice that you are with child again."

"Of course." Her lips twisted as she added bitterly, "One child or another, it's all the same to you—as long as it's a son, of course." She paused, watching her husband wince and draw back, alienated by her tone, before noting, "I used to think you were different from my father, but you're not. All you care about is having sons—even if it *kills* me!"

"Eschiva! That's not fair!" Aimery was truly taken aback by her bitterness. He felt he'd been very considerate of his child bride. He had waited until she was mature and ready for him before bedding her, and he'd never reproached her for miscarrying their first child. He'd lavished gifts on her when she'd given him little Hugh, and he'd been generous, too, at the birth of Burgundia and Henri.

"Yes, it is," Eschiva told him coldly, her tears dry now as she faced him down. She wasn't entirely sure what had come over her, but she was so very, very tired of grieving and crying. She felt as if she had wrung the last tear out of herself and was now drained of emotion. She was so exhausted by grief and disappointment that there seemed nothing left to lose. She found herself saying bluntly, "I wonder, sometimes, if you don't *want* me to die."

"Eschiva! How can you say that?" Aimery asked, flabbergasted. It was truly the farthest thing from his mind.

Eschiva shrugged. "Now that you're the brother of the King, no doubt you can get yourself a better, richer bride."

"Richer than Ramla and Mirabel? Hardly! It's your *father* who has again tried to beggar us! I don't understand why you aren't as angry with him as I am," Aimery admitted, his anger with her father re-ignited.

Eschiva thought about that. "I was always a disappointment to my father. That's just the way it was. I've never known him any other way. But I was so in love with you. I adored you."

Aimery was chilled by her words; she spoke in the past tense. At length he asked softly, almost apprehensively, "And what's changed?"

Eschiva looked at him with large, weary eyes, trying to understand her feelings herself. She decided, "I think it was as I watched my stepmother writhing in agony to give my father yet another son. I realized that one day the same thing would happen to me, because you're exactly like him. You see me as a means to gain property and produce heirs. You come to my bed to make children, and you take your pleasure elsewhere."

Aimery caught his breath at that, shocked to think she knew about his little liaisons. After all, he tried to be discreet about them.

Eschiva saw and noted his reaction with a small cynical smile, before assuring him, "I wouldn't mind, really, if you did it to spare me pregnancy or out of respect, but that's not why you do it, is it? You sleep with other women out of sheer appetite—just because they're there and they're willing. As far as you're concerned, it has nothing to do with me at all. I'm your wife, the mother of your children, the source of future properties and titles. What does that have to do with satisfying your sexual itch?"

"Eschiva!"

"Why are men so shocked to hear women describe them?" Eschiva asked him, leaning her head against the back of her chair in exhaustion. She gazed at him through half-closed eyes, and then she shrugged and took a deep breath. "It doesn't matter why you do it. Your sexual escapades don't really interest me. Go ahead and have them, but I'm tired of being pregnant. I'm tired of facing death. And I'm tired of being your claim to Ramla and Mirabel. If you want to know the truth," she found herself saying, lifting her head again and looking at him through narrowed eyes, "I'd rather that Uncle Balian had both. He's shown more concern for me and my welfare than my father or you ever did!"

"Would you beggar us both—not to mention your children? What about Hugh and Burgundia? What sort of future do you think they have if we are landless?" Aimery replied in outrage.

"Why *are* we landless?" Eschiva countered coldly. "Isn't your brother—your *younger* brother—King of Jerusalem?" She was completely calm now, too exhausted for any further passion. "And who made him King? Who made sure the Templars secured access to Jerusalem? Who found the keys to the royal vestments after Master des Moulins threw them out the window? Who calmed Guy down whenever he had an attack of nerves?

"You made him King, Aimery, even though you knew he was unworthy. Why, if it wasn't out of expectation of reward? Well, where are the rewards? Why aren't you Count of Jaffa and Ascalon?"

Her thrust went home, and it went deep. Why indeed? How was it that he was still only Constable of Jerusalem, a post he owed to Baldwin IV? Why did he have to fight with his father-in-law about his wife's inheritance? And why fight with Balian d'Ibelin, who was surely one of the more competent commanders and saner voices in the Kingdom? A man it would be far better to have as a friend than an enemy. Jaffa and Ascalon together were more valuable than Ramla and Mirabel—or indeed, Ramla, Mirabel, Nablus, and Ibelin put together.

For a moment Aimery stood stiffly, feeling only resentment and anger directed at his brother, and then the woman in front of him gradually penetrated his consciousness again. Eschiva, for all her brave words, looked so fragile and vulnerable, and he saw the fear etched on her face. She was truly terrified of childbed, and it was that fear that had spoken.

Aimery closed the distance between them and went down on his heels before his wife. "My little dove, forgive me! You are right: my affairs are meaningless, idle self-indulgence. The only woman I love is you. And I love you not just because you were supposed to bring me Ramla and Mirabel. That was the reason I married you, of course, but I have come to love you for yourself—for your smiles, the way you sing to our children in the morning, the way you curl up in my arms at night. Yes, I want to make children with you, but not just for the children. And, yes, I want heirs, but not at the price of losing you. I—admit that I underestimated your fears." He looked up at Eschiva with a contrite expression and asked, "Can you forgive me?"

Eschiva was moved almost beyond words. She had not expected this of him. She could certainly not imagine her father acting like this, humbling himself to his wife. Maybe Aimery *was* different. "Will you stop fighting with my family, then?" she asked in a small, uncertain voice, testing him.

"If that's what you want," Aimery agreed reluctantly.

Eschiva nodded. "Yes, it is." And she reached out and took Aimery's hand in hers and squeezed it. It would be so wonderful to go back to being in love with him.

In relief, Aimery leaned forward and kissed her on the lips. "I love you, Eschiva. Wait and see, I will make you happy again. I promise."

Jerusalem, December 1186

"How *dare* he defy me!" Guy raged, his outrage reflected in the rawness of his voice. He had no sooner renewed the truce with Salah ad-Din than the Lord of Oultrejourdain attacked and seized a caravan, making a complete mockery of his word. It was hardly surprising that Salah ad-Din was demanding reparations—and action against Oultrejourdain. "I am the King! It was the King's peace! Châtillon can't just ignore my peace—much less my direct orders to pay reparations."

"He always has in the past," retorted Henri d'Ibelin with a shrug. He had been tasked by Oultrejourdain with bringing his response to the King. King Guy had demanded that Oultrejourdain release all the captives, restore the treasure, and pay reparations as well; Oultrejourdain replied that he'd do whatever he damn well liked in his own territories.

Guy paused in his outraged pacing about the David Tower to stare at Oultrejourdain's messenger. "What do you mean?"

"The Red Sea raids were made during a truce, too. Surely you remember?" Henri pointed out.

"That was the leper's truce. Who could take a man halfway to his grave seriously? Of course Oultrejourdain did what he pleased, when all he had to answer to was that walking corpse! But I'm no corpse! I'm no leper! I am Guy de Lusignan!" He said it with great flourish, but it failed to impress the other two men in the room: Henri d'Ibelin and Gerard de Ridefort, Grand Master of the Temple. Henri just shrugged and leaned back against the wall with his arms crossed. Ridefort, rubbing his beard with his hands, seemed deep in thought. Guy looked from one to the other, baffled by their apparent indifference to his plight.

"You could declare his lands and titles forfeit," Ridefort decided at last.

Henri hissed in contempt. "You can't believe Châtillon would give a tinker's damn for such a pronouncement. He'd just thumb his nose at the King and say: 'Come and take them.'"

"Yes," Ridefort agreed. "I'm sure he would—but why shouldn't we oblige him?"

"You think you can take Kerak, where Salah ad-Din has twice failed?" Henri scoffed.

"When Salah ad-Din attacked, the army of Jerusalem came to Kerak's relief; this time it won't."

"And what do you think Salah ad-Din will be doing while we fight among ourselves?"

"Why should he complain? He has demanded that the King discipline Châtillon. If we move against him, we are doing the Sultan a favor. We'd return any prisoners and treasure we found after seizing Kerak—"

"Not much, you can be sure!" Henri scoffed, adding, "And why in the name of the loving Christ should we do Salah ad-Din a favor?"

Ridefort shrugged. "That's not the point. There's no harm in doing the Sultan a favor if it serves our interests as well. The Templars can take control of Kerak and ensure that the King's word is respected from now on."

Even King Guy looked skeptical at that, seeing that the Templars notoriously did not owe any fealty to the King of Jerusalem.

Ridefort countered by insisting, "No one is in a better position to guarantee the safety of Kerak than the Temple. With us in control of Kerak, your flank would be absolutely safe."

"And the barony of Oultrejourdain gutted," King Guy countered. He was by birth a nobleman, and his instincts were not to do anything that weakened his own class. The Temple was dangerously powerful already. He didn't like the idea of making them more powerful still.

"So what? Who is Oultrejourdain's heir, anyway?" Ridefort made a dismissive gesture before answering his own question: "That spineless sop Toron. He couldn't hold Kerak against a company of nuns, let alone the Saracen. He'll be happy to take another money fief and let the Templars hold Kerak."

"You'll still have to take it first," Henri reminded him.

"Why shouldn't we be able to take it?" Ridefort asked back, annoyed.

Henri just shrugged. "Be my guest. Throw your best knights and sergeants down the fosse. It won't bother me to see your dead piled up like firewood—or the Templars humiliated. But I daresay the *jihadists* will be even happier!"

"Stop this stupid bickering!" King Guy ordered. He had no intention of letting the Templars attack—much less hold—Kerak. "I need to think. Leave me!"

Henri dutifully stood upright, and with a mocking smile bowed deeply toward his King. Ridefort was far less gracious about being dismissed so peremptorily, and warned, "Don't trifle with me, Lusignan. My Templars are the only reliable troops you have as it is. What do you think happens to your Crown if I withdraw them?"

King Guy caught his breath and his cheeks flushed with indignation, but he was even less inclined to back down. "Leave!" he ordered.

Henri had barely reached the stables to call his squire and collect his horse when a page came rushing after him and ordered him to return to the King. Henri made a contemptuous sound in his throat, but he pulled himself together and returned to the audience chamber. By the time he entered, his face was impassive. "Your grace," he acknowledged as he bowed.

"Come closer," King Guy ordered, gesturing for him to approach the throne.

Henri obliged.

"Why did he do it?" King Guy demanded when Henri was right in front of him.

"Who do what?" Henri asked, confused.

"Your lord! Why did Oultrejourdain defy my orders and attack a damned caravan? He can't be that hard up for cash! Why risk war at this time? Why not let things be?"

"Because he believes the best defense is a good offense. He believes we weaken Salah ad-Din when we take the war to him."

"How?"

Henri shrugged. "Well, to be fair, in the past, Oultrejourdain's attacks discredited Salah ad-Din with his own subjects by making him look weak. They also prevented him from subduing his enemies by forcing him to face us. However," Henri shrugged, "I must admit I don't see the point of this particular attack, either. Indeed, if you ask me, I think Châtillon has lost his edge. Maybe, he spent too long in that dungeon, and even if he doesn't talk about it, he hates the Saracens in a visceral sort of way. He cannot make peace with them, so truces rouse his bile. The existence of any truce is to him a provocation. He looks for ways—and excuses—to violate them."

"Hmm." Guy considered that. He had no way of knowing if what Henri said was true, but it would appear to explain Châtillon. "But truces are good for the Kingdom," he suggested, sounding a little unsure of himself.

"Indeed," Henri agreed. "They generally benefit us far more than the enemy, because truces encourage trade and pilgrims, both of which enrich us—especially the royal treasury."

"Yes, of course," King Guy nodded agreement, feeling more confident.

Henri watched him carefully; this was his first opportunity to be alone with Guy de Lusignan since he'd become king, and to observe him so closely. Oultrejourdain had always dismissed Guy as weak and easily manipulated, but Henri had not formed his own judgment—until now. He paused and thought things through one more time and then, with a nod to himself, commented, "Ridefort made a valid point just now."

"What do you mean?" the King asked defensively.

"About you lacking knights devoted to you. You have your brother, of course, and your wife's uncle of Edessa—"

"Edessa's no knight! He's a fat old courtier, an intriguer." King Guy stopped himself just short of adding "parasite." Ever since Guy had been crowned, Edessa had been making demands on him, wanting this and that source of income, this and that honor. He was insatiable!

They all thought he owed his throne to them, and they were all trying to blackmail him! Guy hated them all.

"My sword's for sale," Henri put it bluntly.

Guy looked over sharply, astonished. "What?"

Henri shrugged. "As I said earlier: Oultrejourdain's losing his edge—maybe even his hold. I'm looking for something better."

Guy frowned. "And what's your price?"

"The first available barony," Henri answered.

King Guy laughed. "Really? Not modest, are you?"

Henri shrugged again. "My brother's brat won't live for long. Why not give me his when it falls to the Crown?"

"Ramla and Mirabel?"

"Yes."

"Now, that's a thought. First of all, my brother's wife—your niece—is the heiress to Ramla and Mirabel, as my brother pointed out to me. All that theater at Acre was just that: theater. Aimery, however, says his wife begged him not to disinherit her infant half-brother, and asked him to leave Thomas and his lands in Ibelin's care—for now. Aimery, God love him, is inclined to indulge her, since I have given him the income—if not the title—of Jaffa and Ascalon. I daresay, however, he'd take it very badly if I rewarded *you* with his wife's barony after the boy is dead."

"In that case, maybe another barony will come due. I'm not fussy or in a particular hurry—as long as you pay me well in the meantime."

"How 'well' would that be?"

"Three hundred bezants a year."

The King was taken aback by how ready the figure was on Henri's tongue. Had he been planning to propose this all along? But he'd been dismissed. How could he know he'd be called back?

"The best part of it," Henri pressed his case, "is that Oultrejourdain need never know I'm in your pay. I return as if we'd never had this conversation. You pay me secretly, and I keep you informed of Oultrejourdain's future plans—before they can embarrass you. If something should by chance happen to Châtillon (and his lady, of course), then you name me Baron of Oultrejourdain. I can hold Kerak just as well as or better than the Templars!" he noted with enough acidity to be convincing, at least to Guy de Lusignan, before adding, "Or if another barony comes vacant earlier, you give me that."

"Just what do I get out of all this?" King Guy wanted to know.

"First, information about Oultrejourdain. Second, a knight you can call on against all your other enemies. And third," Henri leaned close and dropped his voice, "a man without scruples or honor to do your bidding."

King Guy drew back at the last offer and gazed askance at Henri.

Henri laughed. "Think about it."

Chapter 17

Tiberias, mid-April 1187

Tripoli's palace at Tiberias had many features of a Roman villa. It sat on the west shore of the Sea of Galilee, with a long terrace paved with mosaics and partly covered by wine trellises facing the lake. Large amphorae sunk into the terrace held palms, oleanders, and hibiscus bushes, the latter budding but not yet in bloom. A fountain fed by the lake bubbled out of the wall at the back of the terrace through a terra-cotta lion's head into a small pool. The gurgling water provided a continuous gentle counterpoint to conversation.

On this early spring day the lord and his guests sat on the terrace enjoying the warmth of the sun, although Maria Zoë and Tripoli's lady, Eschiva of Tiberias, both wore woolen shawls to protect them from the fresh, chilly breeze off the Sea of Galilee. The men had no such need of extra clothing. Tripoli, his stepsons William and Ralph, and Ibelin were warm enough in their well-padded gambesons, chain mail, and surcoats.

Despite the pleasant surroundings, the mood was tense. "Salah ad-Din has sent out letters to all his vassals and allies," Tripoli reported, "ordering them to muster for an invasion. Al-Adil will be bringing up the Army of Egypt, and Husam al-Din Lu'lu has orders to bring the fleet to Damietta, presumably to then proceed along the coast as the Egyptian army moves north. Taqi al-Din was ordered to reinforce Aleppo—although I doubt he'll stay there, now that Bohemond has sought and received a separate peace for Antioch. It is far more likely he'll bring his forces to join Salah ad-Din in Damascus."

The others listened intently, although what Tripoli was saying was hardly news to his wife and her grown sons—or indeed to Maria Zoë and Balian. It was the reason they were here.

Ibelin nodded solemnly and considered the man before him intently. Tripoli was now in his late forties, and his dark-brown hair was salted with gray. Never a heavy man, he looked gaunt, and his face was leathery and lined. The permanent expression formed by those wrinkles reflected both disappointment and increasing bitterness.

Tripoli, Ibelin reflected, was an intelligent man, and whether or not he agreed with everything Tripoli had done over the years, the older man's policies had on the whole been sound. Yet Tripoli was a man singularly lacking in charm, and he had failed to win many friends. Barry, Balian thought wistfully, with his far more dubious aims and inconsistency of purpose, had always been better at winning friends and followers. People hadn't always taken Barry's opinions seriously, but they had for the most part liked him.

"My lord," Ibelin opened earnestly. Tripoli made an annoyed gesture to suggest that such formality was not necessary between them in this environment, but Ibelin remained deadly serious. "I have heard rumors that you *too* have made a truce with Salah ad-Din."

"I had no choice," Tripoli answered bleakly, without dissembling.

Ibelin held his breath to stop himself from expressing his dismay, then glanced at Maria Zoë, whose Greek network had provided them with the intelligence.

"Guy does not even command the respect of his supporters!" Tripoli explained. "You saw what Châtillon did the moment he had a chance."

"Châtillon has never respected anyone—not even the Greek Emperor. He has always acted on his own, and Salah ad-Din knows it. He has vowed his revenge, and no doubt he will eventually have it. What do *his* actions have to do with your own?" Ibelin demanded, still trying to fathom the depth of this betrayal.

"Châtillon has provoked this latest call to *jihad* and an invasion that is quite unnecessary."

"*Every* invasion is unnecessary, from my point of view," Ibelin remarked dryly.

"Correct, but in the past we had a king to rally behind; now we have a usurper."

"You're saying you would rather make a truce with Salah ad-Din than fight beside Guy de Lusignan," Ibelin replied, measuring his words carefully. For all that he could sympathize with Tripoli's contempt for Guy de Lusignan and recognize that he had the law on his side, Ibelin still could not stomach the consequences.

"Guy had the nerve to demand a reckoning of my Regency during the reign of Baldwin V!" Tripoli replied indignantly. "As if I were a clerk in his employ!"

Ibelin took a deep breath before answering as levelly as possible, "Which is galling and insulting, and certainly requires no response. Nevertheless, Salah ad-Din remains our enemy, and if we do not fight together, we will be devoured separately."

Tripoli's step-sons William and Ralph stirred uneasily, and Ibelin spared them a glance. William was now in his late twenties and a formidable fighting man. Ibelin had first seen him fight at Montgisard, when he had still been a very young and untried knight, but a keen one nevertheless. Ralph, on the other hand, was barely twenty, but what he lacked in experience he compensated for with passion. He had been only a boy when his father died, and Tripoli had been more of a father to him than the man who sired him. It was Ralph who burst out now, "You cannot expect my father to serve under Guy de Lusignan, any more than your brother did! Guy is *not* King of Jerusalem."

Ibelin considered the young knight and tried to keep his own emotions in check as he answered patiently. "I understand your feelings, Sir Ralph, but tell me this: do you honestly think that the County of Tripoli can survive if the Kingdom of Jerusalem falls?" Somehow it was easier to put the question to Ralph than to Tripoli directly.

Sir Ralph, however, only dropped his eyes and looked over at his stepfather, who was equally uncomfortable with the question. Tripoli drew back in his chair, his lips a firm line, as if he did not intend to answer, but then he remarked primly, "It is my duty to protect my people from war if there is any way I can do so."

"That doesn't answer my question," Ibelin returned, exasperation starting to creep into his voice. Tripoli responded by clamping his jaws together to suggest it was the only answer he was going to get, and Balian glanced at his wife in frustration.

Maria Zoë frowned. A sleepless night made her look older than her thirty-four years. When her informants had brought the news of Tripoli's betrayal, she had been outraged, and she and Balian had ended up talking all night before deciding they had to confront Tripoli face to face. She shook her head at Balian to indicate she was as speechless as he was.

Ibelin drew a deep breath and tried a different approach. "The County of Tripoli is arguably an independent and sovereign state for which you can make truces as you please, but Tiberias is without doubt a barony of Jerusalem. You cannot conduct an independent foreign policy for Tiberias."

"Tiberias is far more vulnerable than Tripoli!" Sir Ralph burst out hotly.

Ibelin ignored the young knight. "To suggest to Salah ad-Din that you can include Tiberias in a truce is," Ibelin paused and looked from Tripoli to his wife and then to Tripoli's stepsons, before returning his gaze to Tripoli and stating bluntly, "treason."

Ralph predictably exploded with denials, but William significantly did not, and Eschiva looked down at her hands in her lap. She was nervously twisting a signet ring around and around.

"If there *is* no king in Jerusalem, then I cannot commit treason against him, can I?" Tripoli shot back.

"We're not talking about a subject's treason to his king," Balian snapped, losing his temper, "but about betrayal of the Kingdom itself! The Holy Land, for Christ's sake! Jerusalem!"

"Guy de Lusignan betrayed Jerusalem!" Sir Ralph tried to argue, while Eschiva pulled her shawl more tightly around her shoulders, casting frightened eyes toward the citadel that sat at the top of the steep bank leading up from the sea.

"My lord," Maria Zoë addressed Tripoli directly, cutting through Ralph's protests.

Tripoli bowed his head to her to indicate she should continue, as the others fell silent.

"Your truce with Salah ad-Din: does it include clauses that would provide you *protection* against Guy de Lusignan?"

To their surprise it was Eschiva who now lifted her head and answered for her husband, "It does. Guy de Lusignan is a murderer. We know that. And he is a seducer and a usurper as well. I do not trust him *not* to attack us. Raymond could withdraw to Tripoli, but this—" she gestured to the Sea of Galilee and the rich farmland that swept down to it from all sides—"is *my* heritage. I will not abandon it to the likes of Lusignan."

"Nor I." Sir William joined the conversation for the first time, his voice deep and firm. "This is my father's heritage, and it is mine. My brothers and I are determined to hold it, with or without the help of my step-father. That he has stood by us is to his credit!"

Ibelin glanced at Tripoli and caught a fleeting smile that seemed to say: "So there you have it." Tripoli might have been content to withdraw to his county and let Jerusalem go to the dogs, but his wife and his stepsons were not prepared to abandon their hereditary barony.

Ibelin drew on all his willpower to sound reasonable. "I sympathize," he opened. "I do not respect Lusignan either, but I must return to my earlier question: Do you seriously think that you can retain your independence in Tripoli, let alone here, if the rest of the Kingdom falls to Salah ad-Din? If the Sultan defeats the army of Jerusalem, what will stop him from attacking you next? You can't believe a truce will hold him back forever."

Tripoli made a helpless gesture. "I don't have an answer for you, Ibelin. I don't like the options I'm given. But one thing seems clear: Salah ad-Din is more likely to keep his word than a man who murdered, seduced, and bullied his way into power!"

"How do you think Salah ad-Din came to power?" Ibelin shot back. "He's no less a usurper than Guy is! Compared to the blood he has on *his* hands, our kings have been saintly."

"Our *kings*, yes; not Guy de Lusignan." Tripoli countered, absolutely refusing to accept that Lusignan was *de facto* King of Jerusalem—no matter the legal situation.

Ibelin, on the other hand, couldn't ignore the fact that without the fighting men of Tripoli and Tiberias, the Kingdom was robbed of one-fifth of its strength. It made the prospect of stopping Salah ad-Din almost impossible. Furthermore, he was certain that Salah ad-Din would attack Tripoli as soon as it suited him. Salah ad-Din's strategy was clear as glass: divide and conquer.

Ibelin looked at the peaceful landscape around him. Plum and apple orchards bloomed on the far side of the lake, casting a delicate haze of pinkish-white blossoms over the landscape. On this shore the hills were a vivid green, as grass, weeds, and wheat sprouted from soft soil, moistened by the winter rains. Bees hummed about the potted oleander and hibiscus bushes. It was so beautiful—and so fragile.

Balian's eyes sought Maria Zoë's, but her expression reflected only his own incomprehension, mixed with growing desperation.

"In the past," Tripoli spoke again in a pinched, defensive voice, "I always did what was best for the Kingdom. I sacrificed my own interests, my health, my family, to the safety and prosperity of Jerusalem. And what did I get for it? Nothing! Worse: contempt and suspicion! Your brother was the only one who ever appreciated all I did for Jerusalem. Had King Baldwin kept his promise to let him marry Sibylla, we would have worked together. He would have made a splendid and vigorous King, and I would have been his Chancellor. . . ." All the bitterness of an underappreciated man was in his voice.

Balian could understand his frustration—but he could not understand Tripoli's refusal to save the Kingdom he had indeed served so well for so long. "My lord," he made a final plea. "With this separate truce, you withdraw from Jerusalem 20 per cent of her fighting power, and tear open a gap in our defenses that we cannot possibly make good. You are endangering hundreds of thousands of Christians and the Holy Land itself. Your defection may cost us Jerusalem! Can you face Our Lord—whenever your day comes—knowing what you have done?"

Tripoli would not meet Ibelin's eyes. Instead he got to his feet, walked to the railing on the edge of the terrace, and stared for a moment out across the Sea of Galilee. Everyone waited. Finally he turned around and announced, "Until I have some guarantee from the usurper Lusignan that he will not seek to diminish or humiliate me, will not lay a hand on my status or my possessions, or otherwise threaten me or my wife and her sons, I must protect myself any way I can—even if that means making a defensive alliance with Salah ad-Din."

Nazareth, April 1187

A stiff breeze buffeted the King's bright-red tent. Sometimes it seemed to get caught inside, making the fabric bulge and shiver. Then suddenly the wind was gone, and the tent sagged back down to its usual shape and size. The mood inside the tent was nearly as stormy as the weather. Having returned from Mass at the Church of the Annunciation, King Guy was appalled to find that his army had not been swollen with the expected new arrivals. Aside from the troops from the royal domains and the six knights of Nazareth, he could not identify a single baronial banner. "Just who *is* here?" he demanded of his brother the Constable.

"Toron arrived just before noon."

"Toron?" Guy asked back incredulously before adding, "The boy doesn't command any knights at all anymore, does he?"

"He brought a company of crossbowmen. Pisan mercenaries."

"Marvelous!" Guy rolled his eyes. "Is that all?"

"The Templars."

"The Templars came with us!" Guy shot back angrily. "Where are the Hospitallers? Where are the rest of the barons? They were summoned to muster by noon today at the latest! It's well past noon! Where are they?"

"The Hospital is no more subject to the Kings of Jerusalem than the Temple. You may request their support, but not command it. Master des Moulins sent word he would be here by dusk—no doubt to underline that point. Oultrejourdain sent word that he could not leave Oultrejourdain or reduce his garrisons by a single man so long as he was being harassed by Saracen raiding parties."

Of all the barons of Jerusalem, Guy supposed Oultrejourdain was the man with the best excuse not to come, but it still annoyed him.

"Where are Sidon, Caesarea, Haifa, Sebaste, Hebron, and Scandelion?" He started to rattle them off, as if his brother did not know the barons of Jerusalem better than he.

"They have no stomach for an attack on one of their own," Aimery retorted. "They advised you at the last meeting of the High Court that you should seek a reconciliation with Tripoli."

"That was before he committed high treason by concluding a truce with our worst enemy. The man must be taught a lesson. He must be brought to heel. He thinks he's better than me! That's what all this is about! He thinks himself above an anointed King! If I don't crush him, he will tear this Kingdom apart."

"No," Aimery corrected; "that is what *you* are doing by attacking him."

"Gerard de Ridefort made it very clear that if I don't teach him respect, others would start to imitate him!"

"Like Châtillon, perhaps? Who has already defied you? Or Ramla, who has already abandoned you?"

"Gerard de Ridefort—" Guy started again, but he was interrupted.

A squire pushed open the tent flap and bowed to his liege. "Your grace?"

"What is it?" Guy snapped irritably at the youth.

"My lord of Ibelin just rode into the camp!"

"Ibelin! Thank God for that! With his brother's and his wife's knights, he commands the largest contingent in the entire army after Tripoli himself. He must have nigh on three hundred knights, almost as many as the Templars." Aimery was about to correct his brother's exaggerated estimate: Ibelin, Nablus, Ramla, and Mirabel together owed only one hundred sixty-five knights, and with household knights might field two hundred or a tad more, but not three hundred. Before he could curb his brother's enthusiasm, however, Guy was already ordering the squire, "Tell him to camp to the left of the Templars."

The squire looked frightened and glanced nervously at Aimery, preferring to address the Constable rather than the King. "Ah, my lord of Ibelin is alone except for two household knights."

"What?" Guy gasped.

Before anyone could answer, Ibelin himself ducked through the flap and came to stand before a stunned Guy de Lusignan. For a moment they just stared at one another, Guy vaguely alarmed. Then Ibelin bent his knee and bowed his head so perfunctorily that it was almost insulting—before standing upright so close to Guy that he looked down on him from his greater height.

"Your grace, just what is the intention of this muster? Why were your vassals summoned to Nazareth with all their knights and Turcopoles?"

"To put an end to the treason of the Count of Tripoli!" Guy retorted, as he instinctively moved backwards so that he was not so directly *under* Balian's nose.

"Treason?" Ibelin asked with raised eyebrows, as if he didn't know what Guy was referring to.

"No vassal of Jerusalem has the right to make a separate peace with the Saracens! Tripoli may *think* he is an independent prince, but I will teach him differently. I will besiege him at Tiberias, and he will have to either kill himself or grovel on his knees before me."

"Think again," Ibelin warned, staring Guy down.

"What is that supposed to mean?" Guy demanded, lifting his chin defiantly.

"First, Tiberias is almost impossible to besiege, because the Sea of Galilee provides it with endless supplies of fresh water, fish to eat, lines of communication, reinforcement, and escape. Second, you have already driven away the finest knight in your Kingdom; it is stupid to lose the most powerful lord as well. In short, I am here to urge you to cease this madness. For the love of Our Lord Jesus Christ, in whose name we all serve, stop this war upon Christians and save your strength to fight the Saracens!"

Guy spluttered, repeating, "Tripoli is a traitor! He has made a separate truce with Salah ad-Din!"

"And why do you think he took such desperate measures?" Ibelin snapped back, causing Aimery to lift his head sharply.

"Tripoli has always favored accommodation with the enemy," Guy replied. "He's essentially a coward, afraid to fight."

"Don't be a fool!" retorted Ibelin, his face flushed with emotion. The Kingdom, the Holy Land, stood on a precipice—and if Guy could not be persuaded, harassed, or bullied into stopping his assault on Tiberias, they were all going to fall into that chasm and die. Not just the barons and knights of Outremer, but their wives and children, and the ordinary people in towns and villages across the Kingdom as well. Since his failure to convince Tripoli to accept Guy de Lusignan, Ibelin's sense of impending doom had increased to the point where it utterly blotted out all other thoughts. He had become a driven man.

Aimery understood. Before Guy could answer indignantly, he cut him off with a simple: "Ibelin's right. Tripoli is no coward! He's fought for this Kingdom more often than you. And he's no fool, either! So sit down and let's discuss this like civilized men." He pointed to the folding chairs, inlaid with mother-of-pearl, that furnished the royal tent. Turning to the terrified squire who stood stock-still just inside the tent flap, he ordered, "Breathe not a word of what has transpired here, and make sure no one else enters, but let us know if any other barons or the Hospitallers arrive."

When the squire was gone, Aimery confronted his brother. "Edessa's clever plan may have opened the doors of the Holy Sepulcher, and Heraclius and Sibylla between them may have put a crown on your pretty golden locks, but a fat count without a county, a stupid woman, and a debauched priest cannot keep you on your throne. More important: *they* cannot save your ass from Salah ad-Din! Do I make myself clear?"

Balian held his breath, knowing that Aimery was the only man in the world who could talk to Guy de Lusignan like this—even now the elder to the younger brother, no matter that the younger was an anointed king. Guy sat with his jaws clenched and his face flushed, but he did not interrupt or talk back.

Aimery continued, "You can either rip out your own guts by attacking Tripoli and leave two gutted carcasses for the Saracens to finish off, or you can reconcile with Tripoli and reunite this Kingdom."

"How the hell can I reconcile with a man who refuses to accept me as his king?" Guy shouted at his older brother. In that instant Balian saw Guy's fear and insecurity, and held his breath with hope.

"By begging him!" Aimery answered coldly, looking his brother in the eye. "Beg him on your knees if you have to. Tell him you need him. Thank him for his past service. Flatter him, cajole him, honor him, humor him. But stop treating him like an enemy, and make him an ally!"

When Guy did not answer, Ibelin risked speaking up. Cautiously, he noted, "I have spoken to Tripoli, your grace. He called his agreement with Salah ad-Din 'defensive.' His wife expressed sincere fear that you planned to attack her lands—"

"Nonsense! Why should I attack Tiberias?"

"Why, indeed?" his brother answered pointedly.

Guy glared at him. "What I *meant* is, I have no quarrel with his lady. It is Tripoli who has refused to pay homage. Until he does—"

"No! Stop! He's checkmated you with the alliance with Salah ad-Din. He does not *have* to come to heel under the circumstances. And Ibelin is right about how strong Tiberias is. With the forces you have, you'll hardly be able to invest it. You cannot force Tripoli to submit. You need to give him a *reason* to bend his knee."

Petulantly, Guy protested, "He was demanding Beirut, and refusing to give account for his expenditure as Regent—"

"Forget it! Forget all your grievances against him. Forget everything but the essential fact that you need his two hundred knights if you want to *still* be King six months from now!"

"You expect me to just capitulate? To grovel at *his* feet?" Guy whined, already sounding small and deflated.

Ibelin took a deep breath, and with a glance at Aimery noted gently, "That won't be necessary. Tripoli knows how damaging this fight is. He loves Jerusalem. If you demonstrate your goodwill by disbanding the army and returning to Jerusalem, and then give him a bridge to walk over, he will find his way."

"What do you mean?" Guy asked skeptically, with a glance at his brother, who nodded.

"Drop all demands that he account for his past offices, and offer him Beirut in exchange for his oath of homage," Ibelin suggested. He couldn't be sure Tripoli would accept this, but he thought it possible. He had to believe it was possible. He needed some shimmer of hope.

The Constable nodded firmly, as relieved as Ibelin that there might be some means of reconciling his brother with his most powerful vassal. "That makes sense," he reinforced Balian's words to his brother.

Guy did not look exactly pleased, but he appeared to sullenly accept the need for compromise when he, too, nodded.

Nablus, April 28, 1187

With William Marshal's departure, Georgios' glory days were over. He was no longer a squire in all but name, no longer responsible for a knight's weapons and equipment, no longer included on journeys and musters. In short, he was no longer *someone.* Instead, he had been relegated back to the stables—although, thankfully, to the lord of Ibelin's stables rather than his stepfather's inn.

But here he was just another groom among a dozen—and they didn't even assign him the best horses, he thought resentfully, as he filled the water bucket of the gelding belonging to Joscius, Archbishop of Tyre. As the bucket emptied, he looked across the stall door toward the massive black stallion that Gerard de Ridefort had ridden in on. Now *that* was a horse! Georgios thought jealously, as he pushed open the gelding's stall and then latched it shut behind him. The Hospitaller Grand Master was here, too, and he rode a lean chestnut palfrey with elegant lines and a proud face. The twenty horses of the Hospitaller escort, on the other hand, were a mixed and rather sorry lot, Georgios thought a little contemptuously. He preferred to forget his days of serving in his stepfather's inn, when such stallions—scars and spavins and all—would have seemed like magnificent destriers to him.

The Grand Masters and the Archbishop had arrived together in a party less than an hour earlier. They were on a mission to reconcile the King with the Count of Tripoli. Georgios hoped they would be successful. It was frightening to think that the King and the Count would rather fight each other than the enemy. Georgios had heard enough from William Marshal to know why Tripoli hated Guy de Lusignan, but it was one thing for the Englishman to ride away; it was different for Tripoli. They needed him if they were to stop Salah ad-Din.

Georgios returned the water bucket to the stack beside the trough. He dipped his hands deep into the cool water and rubbed them together to remove the last bits of dirt. Then he bent over the trough and splashed water into his face several times. He dried his face by pulling up his shirt so he could rub his face on the inside, and then dried his hands on the long tails. With a final look around, to see that all the horses were contentedly tugging at their hay nets or licking the last crumbs of grain from their feed bins, he made his way to the tack room.

As marshal Mathewos had a chamber in one of the towers, but he always took his evening meal with his sons here, and the Ethiopians allowed Georgios to join them. Eskindar, as the youngest, brought a tray from the kitchens with a loaf of bread, lard, a slab of cheese, and a jug of wine. Sometimes there was cold meat left over from the midday meal as well, or nuts and raisins. Today, however, the kitchen staff was focused on preparing a meal for the visitors, and all they had were the basics.

Georgios sawed off a chunk of bread with his knife and spread lard over it with a wooden spoon, automatically listening to the conversation.

". . . He's taking only Ernoul and Gabriel with him, but wants Ernoul mounted on Thor, as they will be riding very hard," Mathewos gave Ibelin's instructions to his sons.

Eskindar frowned and complained, "Ernoul can't handle Thor. He's as likely to bolt with him as not."

"Your job is not to second-guess Lord Balian!" Mathewos admonished his younger son. "They'll need two strong packhorses as well. I think we'll send Freckles and Blondy."

"Why do they need *two* packhorses?" Dawit asked.

"Gabriel is to travel with his own armor as well as his lord's, and lances. There are reports of Saracen patrols penetrating the border."

Dawit stirred uneasily, and his face was marked with worry. He had lived with the Saracen threat all his life, but things were different now that he had a wife. Dawit knew from his father what life under the Saracens was like, and he knew that as Christians and Ethiopians they would be discriminated against and taxed, but they would survive. It was different for Beth. She was apostate, and if the Muslims discovered that she had been born one of their own, they would stone her to death. It would not help that she was eight months pregnant. They would kill her and her child. The very thought of it made Dawit burn with fury. They had raped her and rejected her—yet if they learned she had found comfort in the arms of Christ and Christians, they would slowly and brutally torture her to death. He could not understand how people—any people—could hate women so much.

"Beth and Tsion are late tonight," Mathewos observed gently, breaking into Dawit's thoughts.

Dawit looked up sharply and out the door of the tack room toward the stables, trying to estimate the time of day by the light coming through the windows. His father was right. It was almost completely dark.

"It's probably the guests," Eskindar suggested cheerfully.

Dawit frowned. While his sister Tsion was lady's maid to the Dowager Queen, his wife Beth was not. "Beth has nothing to do with the guests," he reminded his brother sharply. "She was helping the wet nurse look after little Thomas."

Mathewos said nothing, but he too looked out into the stables, and his expression was worried.

They had finished off the bread, and Georgios stood to take the tray back as he did every evening, but Dawit took it from him. "I'll take it. It's not right to keep Beth late in her condition," he told the others indignantly. "She needs her rest!"

No one contradicted him: they agreed with him. Still Mathewos warned, "Don't make a scene, Dawit."

Dawit didn't answer. He took the tray with what was left of the cheese and lard and crossed from the stables to the kitchen. Once he'd handed over the tray to one of the scullery servants, he bypassed the hall, which was still well lit and full of people, and went up the stairs of the keep to the nursery.

Even before he reached the door, he could hear the wailing of an infant and the louder crying of a larger child. Clearly there was some kind of nursery crisis. As he entered, he saw Nanny Anne give Margaret a brisk smack on her bottom to make her stop fussing—provoking an even louder howl. This in turn brought John into the fray, shouting at his baby sister to "be quiet, you silly goose!" Helvis scowled at her brother and went over to comfort Margaret, while Philip started crying as if his brother had shouted at *him*.

Dawit took it all in as his eyes searched for his wife. After a moment he realized she must be in the inner chamber. "Beth?" he called, crossing the anteroom with the children's toys toward the chamber with their beds and cradles.

"Dawit?" Beth came to the door in the wooden partition. In her arms was the infant Thomas, and he was the one whining incessantly. Beth was trying to soothe him by bouncing him in her arms, walking and cooing.

"Beth, it's late," Dawit told her.

Beth glanced at the window as if she had only just realized how late it was. "We can't get him to sleep," she told Dawit. "We've fed and changed him, but he won't stop crying. Something is wrong."

Dawit, frankly, didn't particularly care, but he knew Beth did, so he tried to be patient. "I'm sure he'll be better in the morning."

"If only he'd stop crying," Beth answered, turning a concerned face to the infant.

"He's too heavy for you in your condition," Dawit protested. "Put him down."

Beth was tired, so she went to the crib, bent, and laid the infant in it. Immediately he started screaming more loudly than ever, kicking his feet furiously. Beth felt she had to pick him up again and reached for him.

Fortunately, Nanny Anne came and held out her arms. "Give him to me," she urged, "and go with your husband. I'll see to him."

With obvious reluctance, Beth turned the baby over to the nanny and let Dawit lead her out of the nursery. On the doorstep into the stairwell she paused and looked back, worried. Thomas was still wailing in the far room.

Nablus, April 29, 1187

Dawn was breaking, clear but hazy, promising a hot day, as Balian finished dressing. The nicker of horses being led out of the stables and the low jocularity of the Hospital escort mounting up could be heard from the ward.

Suddenly a violent knocking shook the chamber. Gabriel and Ernoul, who were buckling on Balian's sword and spurs, froze and looked over, shocked. Balian called out, "Not so loud!" He'd left Maria Zoë sleeping after a long night playing hostess to their visitors.

"My lord! My lord!" The voice was that of Nanny Anne, and she sounded panicked.

"Let her in," Balian signaled with a nod to Ernoul.

Ernoul finished buckling Balian's second spur, drew himself upright and crossed the chamber to open the door. The nurse all but fell into the room. She was dressed in only a nightdress covered by light woollen shawl over her shoulders; her gray hair spilled out of her nightcap in disarray. "My lord!" she wailed. "It's the baby! Your nephew! Little Thomas!" She broke down into tears, sobbing so hard it was impossible to understand what she was trying to say. But everyone could guess.

Balian stood stock still. Barry had predicted Thomas wouldn't live for long. Pray God he was not also right about the apocalypse! No, he mustn't even think about that. They were on their way to see Tripoli. There would be a reconciliation. But if Thomas was dead, Balian no longer controlled Ramla and Mirabel. Would that diminish his stature to the point where Tripoli would not heed him? Indeed, would the Grand Masters even accept him on this mission?

Maria Zoë emerged in the doorway to the bedchamber, her hair cascading about her shoulders. She saw the nanny racked with sobs and swept in, asking anxiously, "What is it? What's happened?"

"Baby Thomas, my lady," the nurse sobbed, and Balian could see the relief that swept over his wife as she realized it was not one of her own brood causing the nanny's distress. The next instant, she contritely put her arms around the nurse.

"This changes everything," Balian said out loud, as his wife guided the nanny to sit on a chest by the door.

Maria Zoë glanced over at him with a question on her face.

"Without Ramla and Mirabel, I'm not the most powerful baron in Jerusalem, and Tripoli may be less inclined to listen."

"There's no need for him—or anyone—to know just yet," Maria Zoë countered.

But just then hysterical, high-pitched screaming reached them from the floor overhead. A moment later a breathless John in a nightshirt, his bare feet sticking out from under it, crashed into the room shouting, "Thomas is dead! Thomas is dead!"

"Shhh!" Balian ordered his eldest son, but Maria Zoë jumped up and started out of the chamber to try to calm whoever was shrieking overhead.

"He's all blue!" John was insisting, terror still on his face.

"Gabriel! Go down to the ward and tell His Eminence and the Grand Masters to ride ahead. I'll catch up with them as soon as I can. *Don't* tell them what has happened; just say I have a domestic matter requiring urgent attention. Tell them that at the latest I will catch them up at the Templar castle of Le Fève—that's where we planned to spend the night—if not before."

"What if they ask what is happening, my lord?"

"Tell them you don't know. Just assure them I *will* join them as soon as possible!"

Gabriel did not look happy about his mission, but he started down the stairs, while Balian followed Maria Zoë up to the nursery.

In the ward the knights and squires of the Hospitaller escort were already mounted and had formed up, while the Archbishop of Tyre was being helped into the saddle by Georgios. At the sight of Gabriel, the Templar and Hospitaller Masters, who had been in discussion together, glanced over, and Ridefort called out irritably, "Where's your master?"

"He's got a—there's something he has to attend to. He's asked you to proceed without him, and he'll catch you up," Gabrielle stammered.

Ridefort frowned, but Moulins announced, "Well, let's get started, then. It's going to be a hot day, and we don't want to ride in the heat of it." He pointed his toe in the stirrup, and Gabriel automatically went to hold his off stirrup as he mounted.

"He's not backing out of this embassy, is he?" Moulins asked Ibelin's squire in a low voice as his seat hit the saddle and he collected his reins.

"No, my lord," Gabriel assured him earnestly. "He'll catch up with you at Le Fève at the latest, he said."

Moulins raised his eyebrows. "He better have a good reason!" he suggested, but he disdained to discuss the matter further with a mere squire.

Ibelin was only two hours behind the others when he reached Sebaste, but when they stopped to water their horses, the Bishop of Sebaste came out to speak to him. "My lord! We must talk!"

"Your grace, I am already behind the others. Can this not wait until after I return from Tiberias?"

"Of course not!" the bishop retorted indignantly. "It is because of your mission to Tiberias that we must talk urgently."

Ibelin looked at his squires, but they were in no position to contradict a bishop.

"Come with me!" The bishop took him by the arm and led him toward the imposing cathedral on the square. Although his palace was just beyond, the bishop took Ibelin to the cathedral itself. Monks were in the choir and the Mass was being read. Ibelin automatically went down on his knee and crossed himself. The bishop tugged on his sleeve and insisted they proceed deeper into the church. At the screens, the bishop left him with the admonishment, "Beg the Almighty's assistance for the success of your mission."

Ibelin could hardly protest. He bowed his head and tried to focus his thoughts on prayer. He *did* need God's blessings. Not just for this mission to Tripoli, but in what was to follow. He prayed, too, for the repose of little Thomas' soul and for the brother who had abandoned the boy, and for the sister-in-law who had died giving life to him. He prayed for his niece Eschiva, who had refused to disinherit her little brother, and he thanked God that she had been safely delivered of a second daughter, whom she had named Helvis after her grandmother.

When Mass was over, the sun was at its zenith and it made no sense to ride, so Ibelin accepted the bishop's invitation to dinner and let the churchman lecture him on the importance of peace between the barons of Jerusalem. By the time he departed, they were five hours behind the others and would have to ride hard to reach Le Fève by nightfall.

Pressing ahead after dusk, however, something spooked Thor and he bolted, dumping Ernoul in the process. Ernoul wasn't seriously injured, but it took them over an hour to recapture the errant stallion, and by then it was pitch dark. There was little point in continuing. They hobbled the horses where they were, built a fire, and camped for the night.

Le Féve, April 30, 1187

The sun woke them, stiff and unrested. Ernoul had fallen very hard on his shoulder and now could hardly move for bruises, particularly under his shoulder blade. Indeed, it hurt him to breathe, and he found it almost impossible to mount. After two futile attempts that left him cursing to stop himself from crying, Ibelin ordered Gabriel to take the supplies off the smaller of the two packhorses, transfer Ernoul's saddle to it, and put the supplies on Thor. Ernoul managed to mount the smaller and tamer horse, and they continued their journey as the sun cleared the mountains and started to burn down on them.

It was just after noon when they arrived at Le Fève, and Ibelin prepared to face a barrage of recriminations for keeping everyone waiting. Although the village at the foot of the Templar castle was eerily empty as they rode through, Balian presumed that was just because the inhabitants were seeking shelter from the noonday sun. It was considerably odder that the gate into the Templar castle was manned only by an old sergeant, who seemed to take forever to respond. Once inside, Ibelin was even more baffled by the stillness and calm.

Nothing seemed to be moving here, either. No groom came from the stables to take their horses, and no knight emerged to greet and escort them to the hall.

"Where is everyone?" Gabriel asked, putting his lord's thoughts into words.

Ibelin had no answer. He dismounted warily, his sense of apprehension growing, although he could not imagine what might have happened. Even if Ridefort and Moulins had decided to ride ahead, too impatient to wait for him, where were the rest of the Templars? Some eighty knights usually manned this critical castle.

Finally Ibelin spotted a man in Templar robes hobbling down the exterior stairway from one of the buildings that crouched against the enclosing wall. The man was evidently lame, as he took the stairs one step at a time, leading with the same foot. When he reached the bottom of the stairs, he lurched across the open ward on what was evidently a wooden leg. "My lord," he gasped out as he reached Balian. "You must be the Lord of Ibelin, Nablus, and Ramla."

"I am. Where is everyone?"

"We received word last evening that a large Saracen raid had crossed into the Kingdom. A thousand strong, they said. It was making for Nazareth, and the citizens sent to us for aid. The Master took command to meet it."

"What?" Balian couldn't believe his ears. "Ridefort was part of an embassy to the Count of Tripoli."

"He said this took precedence. He took the garrison of Le Fève and mustered the secular knights of the region as well, some forty knights altogether."

"That still only makes one hundred twenty knights, or one hundred thirty including the Hospitaller escort," Ibelin protested.

"Master des Moulins noted that as well, but Ridefort would not let this incursion go unanswered. Nazareth is the place of Christ's birth!" The Templar clearly sided with his Master, but Ibelin frowned. They were supposed to be effecting a reconciliation between the Count of Tripoli and King Guy. Fighting Saracen raiding parties should have been left to someone else—but it was too late to prevent it. "When did they set out?"

"At first light. Come in and we'll find you some refreshments," the man offered. "Only the halt and lame were left behind, but we'll manage to find you something."

Ibelin nodded absently. He was not particularly interested in refreshment at the moment. He was unspeakably nervous about this diversion. The urgency of the reconciliation with Tripoli had driven him ever since King Guy had agreed to it. His own delays had been bad enough, but he had hoped to press on immediately. Now he found himself wondering if Ridefort had allowed himself to be diverted because the Templar Master was not truly interested in reconciliation between the King and Tripoli. Ridefort hated Tripoli, and no doubt calculated that his own influence was greater so long as Tripoli was persona non grata at court. In short, it suited him to have Tripoli disgraced and hated. The Constable had confided to Ibelin that Ridefort had been behind the King's ridiculous decision to attack his most important and powerful vassal in the first place. The sense of impending disaster that had overtaken him when he first learned of Tripoli's separate peace was hovering over him again.

In the refectory, Ibelin was greeted with obvious relief by the Archbishop of Tyre. "Ibelin! Thank God you have made it! I feared something must have happened to you."

"Nothing serious: only a series of petty accidents. My squire was thrown and we had trouble recapturing the horse."

"I wish you had been here last night," the Archbishop admitted as Ibelin joined him at the high table. "Master de Ridefort seemed to completely forget our mission. He was fire and flame for halting this 'insolent' incursion—although the Count of Tripoli sent us word that it was only reconnaissance and we should avoid it."

"*What*?" Ibelin did not want to believe what he had just heard.

"You see, Salah ad-Din sent word to the Count of Tripoli about this reconnaissance in force, asking permission to cross his territories peacefully."

"Jesus God!" Ibelin muttered, his blood starting to run cold.

"He had to agree, of course, because of his truce with Salah ad-Din, but he sent a messenger warning us to stay away. Only Ridefort would hear none of that, not after the citizens of Nazareth asked for protection. He was determined—"

"To make Tripoli look the fool!" Ibelin burst in.

"Do you think that was his motive?" the Archbishop asked, sounding surprised.

"God help me," Ibelin answered, "I do not know the mind of Master de Ridefort, but what do you think? By attacking these Saracens, he makes Tripoli look like he has broken his word to Salah ad-Din. Even if he only succeeds in inflicting light casualties on them, he will still have undermined Tripoli's standing with Salah ad-Din."

"Is that such a bad thing?" the Archbishop asked with raised eyebrows. He clearly disapproved of Tripoli's relationship with Salah ad-Din and saw no harm in undermining it.

"It is *always* a bad thing to give your enemy reason to doubt your honor, your eminence. The Saracens outnumber us ten to one. Even when we defeat them, they remain stronger than we are. We *have* to be able to treat with them—and we can only do that if they respect us and trust our word. I can't believe Ridefort did this!" Ibelin burst out, and sprang to his feet, the last shred of apetite gone. "It would have been enough to send his marshal with some men to reinforce Nazareth. There was no need to attack the raiders—certainly not in person!"

It was impossible to just sit here and wait to find out what had happened. Returning to the ward, Ibelin ordered Thor saddled and mounted the young stallion himself. He left Ernoul behind, still nursing his bruised back and shoulders, and set out with Gabriel, armed and armored.

They made for Nazareth with the sun now low behind them. The entire countryside appeared abandoned. No one was tending the fields, and the villages, too, were empty. They stopped a shepherd boy and asked where everyone was. "With the Templars!" the boy answered eagerly and gestured toward the east. "They went to destroy a Saracen raid," he told them with a grin.

Ibelin clamped his jaw down. Only the King had the right to call up the commons.

A quarter of an hour or so later, they spotted a lone rider approaching them. He hunched forward over the pommel of his saddle, and the horse walked with his head almost dragging on the ground. Ibelin glanced at his squire, then took up a canter to close the distance faster.

Before they had crossed half the distance, it was possible to identify a white surcoat with the red cross of the Temple, but the surcoat was badly torn, soiled, and bloodied. At closer range, it was clear that the knight's chain mail was torn in several places, and blood had soaked his right side. The horse was covered in cuts, some of them gaping open. He was limping, too.

"Sir!" Ibelin called out, and the man lifted his head enough to see the knight and squire who were almost upon him. The Templar just waited until Balian had closed the final yards and drawn up beside him. "Sir! You rode with Master de Ridefort?"

The Templar nodded. His eyes were dull, Ibelin noted, and even his gray-blond beard was flecked with blood. Blood had gushed from his nose at some point.

"What news?" Ibelin asked urgently.

"Bad."

Ibelin shivered as if the sun had abruptly set. "How bad?"

"They're all dead."

"Who?"

"My brothers. The Hospitallers. I think some of the secular knights were allowed to surrender. We were not. They slaughtered us."

"How? Where? Start at the beginning."

"In the Beginning there was Light, and the Light asked—"

"You know that's not what I meant!" Ibelin cut him off furiously. "What happened this afternoon? Where is Master de Ridefort? Master des Moulins?"

"Dead. I saw Moulins unhorsed and set upon by dozens of Saracen. They trampled over his body again and again. Marshal de Mailly built a wall of corpses with his sword, but they eventually overwhelmed him. Just as he had predicted, he proved his courage."

"What do you mean, 'as he predicted'?"

"When we saw how many they were, Marshal de Mailly told the Master it would be madness to attack, and advised pulling back to Nazareth to defend it from behind the walls. Moulins agreed, but the Master scoffed that Mailly was only afraid of losing his 'pretty blond head.'"

Ibelin stiffened at the insult. He did not know the Templar Marshal well, but though Mailly was a handsome man, he was not a vain one. If anyone was vain, it was Ridefort himself!

"Mailly answered that he was not afraid to die a martyr's death, as he would shortly prove, but questioned whether Ridefort would join him in heaven. And then we charged."

"How strong was the enemy?" Ibelin asked with trepidation.

The Templar shrugged. "Too strong. Does it matter by how much?"

"Guess?"

"A thousand, maybe two thousand."

"How many were you?"

"Eighty Templars, ten Hospitallers—plus the two Masters, of course—and about forty secular knights and squires."

Eighty Templars was a fifth of the Templar total strength in the Holy Land! They couldn't afford to lose eighty Templars at a time like this! Ridefort was mad. "My God," Ibelin muttered, too shocked to even pray coherently. "My God."

Tiberias, April 30, 1187

"You didn't know Marshal de Mailly well, did you?" Tripoli asked, his face a ghastly mask of shock on which the horror of the day had frozen.

Ibelin shook his head slowly. He had ridden straight for Tiberias after learning of the catastrophe at the Springs of Cresson, sending Gabriel back to inform and collect the Archbishop of Tyre and Ernoul.

"He was a distant relative, you know," Tripoli continued. "His mother was from Toulouse. When the Templars sent him to the Holy Land, she wrote me, asking that I keep an eye on her beloved son. Naturally I did, and I rejoiced to see him making a name for himself inside the Order." Ibelin wondered how much of that success was due to the influence of the Count of Tripoli, but he said nothing. What did it matter now?

"He, not that idiot Ridefort, should have been made Grand Master!" Tripoli protested vehemently. "He lost by only two votes!" Tripoli added, suggesting a knowledge of the Templar Grand Chapter that no outsider was supposed to have. "Two votes that you can be sure were purchased by Ridefort—or rather by Lusignan!"

Again Ibelin chose to remain silent. There had been ample rumors of bribery when the news of Ridefort's election had been made public. It made little sense to outsiders that a knight of such modest connections and so little experience in the Holy Land should be elevated to the highest office of the Knights Templar. Ibelin himself had not been free of his suspicions, but he had no proof.

"And now dead—so pointlessly dead!" Tripoli intoned. "I saw his head, Balian." Tripoli looked across the table separating them, past a single candle that cast a halo of gentle yellow light, and fixed his dark eyes on Balian's. Then he repeated, in a voice that cracked with emotion, "I *recognized* his head on the tip of a Saracen lance!"

The triumphant Saracen raiding party had ridden past Tiberias on their way back to their own lands. Lookouts had rapidly recognized that they were leading captives and riderless horses, as well as bringing wounded with them, all of which spoke of an engagement. Tripoli had rushed to the town ramparts and managed to get a good look at the Saracens, who mockingly bowed from their waists in their saddles and gestured triumphantly to the "trophies" on their lance tips.

"They must have had a hundred Christian heads speared on their lances, and they waved them over their heads like banners of honor," Tripoli reported, his eyes focused on the images in his memory. Then he closed them and covered his face with his hands.

Balian said nothing, letting Tripoli grieve.

The Count lifted his head sharply and focused on Ibelin. "Moulins' gray, tonsured head was there, but not Ridefort's. The man responsible for this senseless slaughter! How did he survive? How does the *leader* of such an attack survive?

There were at least two hundred riderless horses, Ibelin! And many Saracen wounded. There was a vicious fight, you can be sure of it. It was not a one-sided slaughter; we killed at least two for one. But the *leader* of this charge survived? How is that possible? I'll tell you how. *He ran away*!" Tripoli said it slowly and all the more intensely. "He led them into the battle, but he just kept riding, never turning back to actually engage. He must have realized his mistake so soon that he had time to just abandon his brothers, and the Beauséant itself. He took himself to safety and left the rest to die."

This was pure speculation. Tripoli had not been at the battle any more than Ibelin had been. But there was a certain logic to what he said.

"And that *coward*—because he survived—is *still* Master of the Temple!" Tripoli reminded Ibelin. "That ignorant, arrogant, grasping *bastard* is still Master! He still controls the resources of the Knights Templar! He still commands them! He still sits beside Guy de Lusignan, whispering poison in his ear!"

Ibelin could hardly deny this; it was true.

"And there is no one to take him to task for what he's done. The Templars, in their rigid hierarchy, cannot even question him! They will not criticize him or blame him for throwing their lives away senselessly. No, they'll just sing the Te Deum and ask to be the next sheep to the slaughter! They don't care about saving Jerusalem, Balian. They are more interested in their own souls. No one will hold a mirror in front of his ugly face and declare: 'See Christendom's greatest foe!'"

"No," Balian agreed, collecting his courage, "but there are many men who will blame *you*, rather than Ridefort, for what happened today."

"Me?" Tripoli asked, stunned and defensive at once.

"You let the raiding party into the Kingdom—"

"I had no choice! And I warned you about it! I sent word that it would be here, and I warned you not to attack."

"The Commune of Nazareth sent to Le Fève begging for Templar protection," Ibelin told Tripoli bluntly. "*Your* territories may have been covered by *your* truce, but Nazareth was not. How could the Templars and Hospitallers refuse such a request? They have vowed upon the surety of their souls to protect the Holy Land—no matter what their motives."

"They could have protected it from inside the city. There was no need to attack!" Tripoli pointed out defensively.

While Ibelin shared Tripoli's tactical assessment of the situation, he felt he must remind Tripoli that not everyone would see it that way. "My lord, the decision to attack was a military one, and no matter what you or I would have done differently, the people of this Kingdom expect protection from us—the knights and barons of Jerusalem. They will view the dead of Cresson as martyrs—and they will blame you for letting the Saracens into the Kingdom."

Tripoli's face drew together in an expression of extreme distress that suggested he *was* blaming himself. He glanced at his stepsons, and Sir William backed Balian. "It's true, father. I've been out walking around, and the garrison is in turmoil. They have supported you up to now, but the sight of those lances with the tonsured heads of Templars and Hospitallers . . ."

Tripoli looked to Ralph, and the younger knight met his eyes, his cheeks flushed with inner emotion. "Will speaks the truth, father. They say the dead are on your conscience."

Tripoli closed his eyes for a moment, and then opened them and looked straight at Ralph. "What does your mother say?"

"She is in the chapel, praying for the souls of the dead."

"And forgiveness?" Tripoli asked, his eyebrows raised.

Ralph looked down and mumbled, "Yes, she said she would pray for forgiveness to the end of her days."

Tripoli turned to William. "So, what do you want me to do? Pay homage to Guy de Lusignan?" he asked pointedly.

Sir William nodded and murmured, "For the sake of the Kingdom."

"Ralph?" Tripoli asked his younger stepson.

"Yes, father. It is the lesser evil."

Tripoli looked again at Ibelin, sitting opposite him at the table; the single candle between them still offered gentle, wavering light. "You have succeeded, Ibelin," he declared, facing him with both his fists on the table. "You can tell Guy de Lusignan that I will bend my knee before him and pay homage to the Crown of Jerusalem, stolen though it is."

Balian was aware of some of his tension easing, although he was still far too distressed to feel any jubilation or triumph. Instead he reached out a hand and laid it on Tripoli's balled fist. "Raymond, with this you have helped put Jacques de Mailly's soul at rest, for he will surely think his martyrdom worthwhile if it has effected your reconciliation with the Crown."

Chapter 18

Sephorie, July 2, 1187

Ernoul was having trouble with Thor, as usual. The stallion was trying to bite or kick every other horse that came near him, and Ernoul could barely hold him back. Thor's jerks on the lead as he tried to break free of Ernoul's hold caused the muscles of his bruised shoulder to cramp and burn with pain.

"I'll take him," Gabriel offered, turning over the aging Centurion to his fellow squire.

"Where the hell does he get the energy to fight?" Ernoul complained, happy to turn over the young stallion to Gabriel. Salah ad-Din had crossed the Jordan with an army allegedly fifty thousand strong. In answer, King Guy had called up his entire feudal host and issued the *arrière-ban.* The Templars had even released the money King Henry II of England had deposited with them for his planned crusade, and King Guy had used it to hire a thousand mercenaries, including nearly two hundred knights who wore the livery of the English King. After mustering in Acre, the army had marched out for Sephorie—and the squires, like the rest of the cavalry, had been riding all day in the baking heat of high summer. Balian's two destriers, the young Thor and the aging Centurion, were led by the two squires and carried neither rider nor equipment, but it had still been a long, hot, and dusty day.

Gabriel didn't answer directly. He took Thor's lead and threaded it over and around the nosepiece of the halter to give himself more leverage before leading him to the springs. These were broad and shallow, the water seeping up randomly between the rolled stones and pebbles of the riverbed, and running deeper where it had cut gullies between larger rocks. Usually, grass and weeds grew thick on the banks and in tufts on the pebble islands that formed and re-formed in the lazy current. By now, however, any blade of grass had been trampled under or torn up and devoured by passing horses. The mud was fetlock deep from hundreds of horses churning it up on the way to and from the springs.

Despite Gabriel's better control of the destrier, Thor was still more interested in kicking at other stallions, his ears flat on his head, than in drinking. "Why doesn't he drink?" Ernoul asked irritably, watching Gabriel yank Thor's attention away from the stallion he was trying to kick, squealing his challenge as the other stallion swung his haunches and kicked back. Meanwhile, Centurion plunged his head down and sucked the cool water up his throat in loud, satisfied slurps.

Gabriel shook his head in incomprehension as he patted the black stallion and tried to calm him before circling around for another approach to the springs.

"I just hope we stay here now," Ernoul continued.

"Why shouldn't we? Wasn't that what they decided in Acre?" Gabriel asked, looking up sharply.

Ernoul explained, "A messenger rode in about an hour ago. The Saracens have overrun the town of Tiberias, driving the population into the citadel. The Countess of Tripoli has requested relief, and her sons are hotly urging the army to go to their mother's aid, while Châtillon—of all people!—is saying it would be 'unchivalrous' not to assist a lady in distress."

"But Tiberias is fifteen miles away—and there's not much water between here and there!" Gabriel protested.

"That's what Tripoli is trying to tell the King," Ernoul confirmed.

"How do you know?"

"Lord Balian ordered me to fetch a map from his tent and bring it to the King's tent, where the barons are in council."

Gabriel gave Ernoul a reproving look, noting, "And, of course, you stood around eavesdropping as soon as you finished your errand. No wonder I couldn't find you anywhere and had to set up the tent by myself!"

"But listen!" Ernoul answered, not bothering to deny the accusations. "They're at each other's throats in there! Châtillon and Ridefort have all but accused Tripoli of being in Salah ad-Din's pay, and Tripoli has told them he'd rather see his wife in Saracen hands than move a foot farther from the coast. He said in this heat it would be wiser to withdraw to Acre and make Salah ad-Din come to us. He says whichever army takes the offensive will have to find fodder and water, while the army that takes up a strong defensive position can just sit back and watch the enemy melt away in the heat."

Gabriel frowned. "That's all very well for Tripoli to say. His lands are north of here! What do you think would be left of Nablus or Ramla if we just hole up in Acre? If we don't face Salah ad-Din here, he'll let his horde spread out and plunder everything. We've got all the fighting men with the army now. The cities and towns are practically defenseless. What's the point of calling up the army if we're not going to fight?"

"That's what Châtillon said," Ernoul agreed.

"What did Lord Balian say?" Gabriel asked.

"You know him," Ernoul remarked with a shrug; "he held his counsel until the Constable specifically asked for his advice."

"And?"

"Well, he said it would be madness to withdraw to Acre, leaving the rest of the country open to plunder and exposing the farmers and burghers to capture."

"You see!" Gabriel declared, delighted to have his lord agree with him.

"But he called the relief of Tiberias equal madness. He said the only reason Salah ad-Din had taken the city was to lure us away from the springs here and force us across the high, arid plateau between here and there. He said we should stay where we are now and force Salah ad-Din to take the offensive. From here, he argued, we can block attacks on either Nazareth or Acre, or if necessary put ourselves across the road to Jerusalem. The key, he said, was to force Salah ad-Din to commit himself."

Gabriel nodded, satisfied. "And did the others listen?"

"Most of them did, even the Constable—but Ridefort and Oultrejourdain were still arguing in favor of going to the relief of Tiberias when one of the King's knights chased me away."

Centurion had had enough to drink, and he lifted his head to nuzzle Ernoul for the carrots that he knew the squire kept tucked inside his gambeson. Gabriel had not yet succeeded in watering Thor, however. With an exasperated sigh, he decided he should give up for the moment and return later when there were fewer other horses around. Leading the stallions, the squires returned side by side to their lord's tent.

Guy was finding it hard to sleep. An army of this size was never entirely quiet. Sentries paced, horses nickered, men moved back and forth to the latrines on the edge of the camp. . . . Guy was annoyed and wanted to shout at everyone to be quiet. He needed his sleep.

But even if they had all been silent, the camp bed was uncomfortable. The air was still and oppressively hot. It stank, too—of smoke from the campfires, horse manure, the pork fat his squires had used to oil his chain mail, garlic from someone's dinner, and urine from some sentry too lazy to go the latrines. Guy kicked off his sheet and tried to make himself comfortable on his belly, but a mosquito was soon tormenting him. Exasperated, Guy sat up, swatting furiously at it.

"Annoying, aren't they?" said a voice out of the darkness.

"Who's there?" Guy challenged in alarm, his heart pounding. He was the King! People were not supposed to enter his tent unannounced. He had two knights posted outside to prevent this.

"It's just me. Ridefort," came the answer.

Guy did not see why the Templar Grand Master should have been allowed into his tent any more than anyone else. He frowned, determined to reprimand his knights at the first opportunity. Right now he had to deal with the Templar Master, who had moved closer to stand directly over his bed. "We need to talk," Ridefort announced.

"Now? In the middle of the night?" Guy challenged him petulantly.

"Yes."

"Why?"

"Because you cannot let the decision made in council stand. It is dishonorable, dangerous, and discrediting."

Guy was in no mood for this lecture. They'd argued for hours, and no matter how vigorously Oultrejourdain and Ridefort had presented their case, the overwhelming majority of the barons had sided with Ibelin.

Ridefort sank down on his heels to be at Guy's eye level. He kept his voice very low. "Tripoli is a traitor. Everything he says is to Salah ad-Din's advantage."

Guy rolled his eyes and groaned slightly. "Stop it, Ridefort. I know you hate him, but he has paid homage to me, and he has brought his troops here. I'm tired of you nagging at me all the time just because *you* want your revenge on Tripoli for some girl! It discredits *you*, not me."

"All right; don't believe me. But how can he be so certain no harm will come to his lady if he didn't arrange all this with Salah ad-Din in advance?"

Guy shook his head to indicate this argument convinced him no more than the rest. "No one thinks the lady herself is in great danger. Even her sons conceded that."

Ridefort shrugged. "Perhaps, but that's not really what's at stake here, is it?"

"What do you mean?"

"Well, the Lady of Tiberias is one of your vassals, and you are honor bound to assist her if she is in need. It really doesn't matter what will happen to her personally if you don't—your inaction reflects poorly on *you*. It was your inaction four years ago, remember, that made King Baldwin take the Regency away." Ridefort had hit a nerve, and he saw Guy stiffen in the darkness. He pressed his advantage. "You're the King, aren't you? Why do you let your barons tell you what to do?"

"Every king has a council," Guy retorted irritably.

"Yes, and they listen to the council—but then they make their own decisions. They don't let their barons dictate what is to be done."

"I'm not letting anyone dictate to me!" Guy retorted defensively, and Ridefort smiled in the darkness.

"No?" the Templar Master asked.

"No!" Guy insisted.

"But what did *you* want to do when you received the plea for help from the Countess?" Guy had jumped up, full of chivalrous energy. He'd been on the brink of ordering the army to march at once, through the night, to reach Tiberias. Now he frowned, remembering that, although he said nothing. "Your instinct was to relieve Tiberias, wasn't it?" Ridefort pressed him.

Guy still didn't answer, but his scowl was deeper.

"You are the King," Ridefort repeated. "Don't make the same mistake twice. Don't lose everyone's respect by inaction. Do what your instincts tell you to do. Take this army to Tiberias and crush Salah ad-Din!"

"His army is bigger than ours," Guy complained, still uncertain.

"But we have God on our side. We have the True Cross with us. How can you doubt our victory? Do you not think Christ is intimidated by the hordes of Mohammedans?"

Guy caught his breath.

"Lead this army to Tiberias, your grace, and with the grace of God you will win a great victory! You will forever be remembered as the savior of Jerusalem! Your name will eclipse that of Godfrey de Bouillon and Henry Plantagenet. Why, if you shatter Salah ad-Din's army, what is to stop you from taking Damascus? Or Cairo? Or both?"

"We march at dawn!"

The confusion in the predawn darkness was considerable. Men had slept poorly, and many had only just entered deep sleep when the horns roused them. The orders to strike camp and form up took everyone by surprise, and men kept asking one another what had happened. Why had the King changed his mind? But their lords and sergeants didn't give them much time to speculate. Men hastened to get something into their stomachs and wash it down with water. If they were going to Tiberias, it was going to be a long, hot, thirsty day, and the prospect of imminent battle hung in the air. Throughout the camp, men knelt in the dirt and hastily confessed their sins to the priests who swarmed out to provide absolution.

"I want extra water for the horses!" Ibelin ordered his squires, and the bleak expression on his face made them run to obey as much out of fear as obedience.

"How are we supposed to carry extra water?" Ernoul asked Gabriel once they were out of hearing of their lord.

"The goatskins on the wagon. Fill them up."

"But how can we carry them?"

"We'll saddle the destriers and attach two goatskins apiece," Gabriel answered.

By the time they had filled and hung the goatskins on the saddles, the Ibelin tent had been struck, and Lord Balian was giving orders to his bannerets and sergeants. "With the Templars, we form the rear guard," Ibelin announced. That made sense, Gabriel thought, nodding in approval. Because Ibelin commanded the men from his brother's, his wife's, and his own territories, he contributed the third largest contingent to the army after the King and Tripoli. His more than two hundred knights made up fully one-sixth of the total cavalry, although the eight hundred Turcopoles and roughly twenty-five hundred infantry of the Ibelin/Ramla/Nablus contingent formed a smaller share of the whole, because the coastal cities contributed higher numbers of foot soldiers and light horse than the rural baronies Balian held.

Ibelin continued with his orders. "The wagons and destriers stay with the main body under King Guy; only fighting men remain with me."

Ernoul and Gabriel looked at one another uneasily: Ernoul because that sounded like Lord Balian expected heavy fighting in the rear, which he didn't understand, and Gabriel because he felt he was being treated like a noncombatant, which he resented.

There was obviously no arguing with Ibelin in his present mood, however, so Ernoul and Gabriel joined the squires of the other knights of Ibelin, Nablus, Ramla, and Mirabel as they formed up around the wagons, including one carrying the Bishops of Acre and Lydda and some ten canons from the Holy Sepulcher with a huge gold-plated cross containing a fragment of the True Cross.

The squires were leading the precious chargers, surrounded by the infantrymen of the royal domains and the other barons. The Count of Tripoli had been given command of the vanguard, and he had already set off with his two hundred plus knights and thrice as many Turcopoles, protected by some four thousand infantry.

The sky was cloudless, and the gentle coolness of dawn rapidly gave way to intense and burning heat. Not that the men of Outremer weren't used to it, but the road ahead was utterly without shade, and the passage of so many men and horses churned up the dry surface soil so that it floated in the air up to ten feet or more overhead. It wasn't long before men started coughing. Sweat dried almost instantly if exposed to the sun, but under armor—whether made of metal, leather, or just quilted linen—it collected, saturating undergarments, and made them heavier and ranker than ever.

At about ten in the morning, four hours into the march, the first wave of Saracen cavalry struck the rear guard. Ibelin had been expecting and watching for them. His Turcopole scouts had indicated that Salah ad-Din had moved the bulk of his army away from Tiberias to the west in anticipation of a Frankish relief effort. The center of the Saracen army was concentrated at Cafarsset, blocking the southern route to Tiberias, which was why Guy had ordered his army to follow the northern road by way of the small springs at Tourran. It was only to be expected that the Saracens would attack the Christian right (southern) flank as a result, and Ibelin had kept his eyes peeled toward the wooded slopes that rose to the south. When he saw movement and color among the trees, he shouted a warning to Gerard de Ridefort, who commanded some two hundred Templar knights and five hundred sergeants on his right, closer to the enemy. Inwardly he cursed the Templar Master for his evident inattentiveness.

The Templars looked over as a man, and then in answer to shouted orders, turned to face the horsemen who poured out of the woods and thundered across the shallow valley between them with wild cries and fluttering banners.

"Shields up!" Ibelin ordered his own troops as he recognized the Turkish horse archers of the enemy. These were galloping forward with their reins loose on their horses' withers, preparing to fire their arrows at a gallop. A moment later a shower of arrows followed. Those who had followed their lord's orders and raised their shields over their heads were unharmed. Only here and there, where a man had been slow to react, did the arrows find flesh.

The problem was that no sooner had one squadron of Turks expended their arrows and turned to gallop away, than a second and a third squadron rushed at the Christian rear guard. These were well-organized and well-planned attacks, with little time between charges. Within minutes the Christians found their arms and shoulders aching from holding their heavy shields overhead. After an hour of these assaults, the men began to lose strength altogether. More and more men were letting their guard down at the wrong moment. As they advanced, they were trailing dead and dying men—like a snail leaving a wet trace behind, Balian thought.

Around noon the Saracens changed tactics and started to press home their attacks, coming within a hundred yards to fire directly at the Christians, rather than into the air. They took the Templars by surprise the first time they charged in close, and between a dozen and a score of horses went down to the piercing screams of horse and man. The Templars had no infantry, so Ibelin ordered infantry from Ramla around to cover the Templars' southern flank.

Immediately the Saracens swept behind their lines and fell on their northern flank. Ibelin, fortunately, still had the infantry of Nablus and Ibelin, and so was able to protect both flanks and his rear as well, keeping his knights in the center. The problem now, however, was that they had to stop each time a Turkish charge was launched to let the infantry plant their shields and drop down behind them, while keeping the horses inside the shield wall. Progress slowed to an unbearable crawl. With the sun now directly overhead, they started losing men to sunstroke as well as to the enemy.

Ibelin ordered his infantry to walk backward and sideways to keep moving forward without losing the formation, but this proved virtually impossible. The infantry needed to prop their shields on the ground to have any stability, and after only a half-hour or so Ibelin gave up. They reverted to moving forward in fits and starts, just a few dozen yards at a time, between the unrelenting attacks. Ibelin felt helpless as he watched his infantry shrink man by man.

By early afternoon they had covered less than eight miles, or barely half the distance to Tiberias. Worse, word was passed back to them that the springs at Tourran, where the army had hoped to water their horses and refresh themselves, had been poisoned with slaughtered animals and murdered prisoners. Furthermore, Salah ad-Din had moved the bulk of his army north to block the road east.

They were either going to have to fight their way through or else turn even more to the north, heading not for the already visible—but still distant—waters of the Sea of Galilee, but instead for the village of Hattin. Ibelin was too far back to be involved in the short war council, but he was sent word that Tripoli had urged making for Hattin, which was just three miles away and had ample water supplies. That was assuming, of course, that the Saracens had not poisoned them. King Guy, according to the messenger, already appeared to regret his decision to leave Sephorie and so agreed.

The shift in direction, however, meant that the Christian army left the road and started cutting across country. That made walking much more difficult for the infantry, as there were frequent gullies, rocks, and thorns. That was bad enough for men just walking forward; it was much harder for men trying to stay in formation under unrelenting attacks. As a result, the rear guard was slowed down even more, and a gap threatened to open up between the main body of Christian troops and the rear guard. It was a gap the Saracens were bound to exploit—and if they did, the rear guard would be surrounded and cut to pieces.

As that threat loomed larger with each excruciating step forward, Ibelin rode over to consult with Gerard de Ridefort. The latter proposed charging the enemy to drive them back, but Ibelin angrily rejected the plan. It was too obvious that the enemy would simply fall back before the heavy cavalry, and then attack again as soon as the charge was spent. "That's a waste of energy," Ibelin told the Templar Master bluntly.

"You're just afraid to charge!" Ridefort retorted hotly.

"Don't try that crap on me, Ridefort. I'm not a frightened dandy like the King you made! Charging light Turkish cavalry is idiocy—and if you do it, you do it alone." Ibelin let his eyes sweep the Templars around the Master, hoping to find a man like Jacques de Mailly, willing to challenge their Grand Master and support him. But the men with Ridefort today only dropped their eyes and would not look at him.

"God is on our side!" Ridefort barked belligerently, making his own men sit up straighter in their saddles.

"Really? As he was with you at Cresson?" Ibelin shot back.

"Do you doubt Christ is with us?"

"It is blasphemy to confuse your own will with the will of God."

"We charge!" Ridefort spun his horse on its haunches and spurred it forward, ordering the Templar standard-bearer to fall in beside him.

Ibelin rode back to his own knights and announced grimly, "The Templars insist on charging."

"That's madness!" Sir Bartholomew protested, and Balian noted how haggard the old man looked. His eyes were sunken in his skull, all but lost in shadow in the depths of his helmet. He shouldn't be here, Balian registered. He should be enjoying his old age in peace on his manor, not facing certain death. Then again, he had only daughters, and the feudal duty fell next to his eldest grandson, a boy just eleven years old. So on second thought, the old man was probably prepared to die to save that boy and his younger brothers.

Out loud, Ibelin retorted curtly, "This whole march is madness!" and added before anyone else could protest: "We hold formation, and take advantage of the relief the Templars will temporarily give us to jog forward as far and as fast as we can."

Then he reached down, unfastened his goatskin, and took several gulps of water before demonstratively pulling Rufus' head around to offer the water to the chestnut palfrey. Rufus gratefully closed his lips around the spout of the goatskin, and Balian upended it so that the water flowed into his horse's mouth until the skin was about half empty. Then he took it away, closed it, and tied it again to his saddle. Around him, his knights followed his example of sharing their water with their horses, while the infantry drank deeply. While they drank, the Templars burst through their infantry protection screaming "Vive Dieu St. Amour!"—head-on into the next Saracen attack.

The Saracens just wheeled their horses around and galloped away like the wind. Their fleeter horses, with lighter gear and riders, easily outdistanced the Templars. The latter, armed only with lances and swords, could not hope to inflict the slightest damage and soon drew up, turned, and began to trot back to Ibelin's division, which was jogging as fast as the tired limbs and dehydrated bodies of the infantry would let them. Only Ibelin remained immobile, his horse facing backwards, his eyes squinting against the sun as he awaited the next attack. It came even before the Templars had rejoined the rest of the rear guard. Ibelin shouted a warning, and Ridefort wheeled his knights around and charged again.

This repeated itself four or five times, until the Templar horses were swaying from exhaustion, the sweat dripping from their bellies, their heads hanging in utter dejection. Only then did Ridefort recognize—but not acknowledge—that Ibelin had been right. Furiously, he ordered Ibelin to send one of his knights to the King to demand that the main army wait for the rear guard.

"No," Ibelin answered.

"They must wait for us! If they don't, we'll be cut off and slaughtered. If we're slaughtered, the army doesn't stand a chance. A third of our forces are right here!"

"I agree, but *you're* the one who brought us here, so *you're* going to be the one to tell your puppet King that you were wrong. *You* tell him to stop before he reaches water. *You* tell him we can't make Tiberias tonight. *You* tell him the entire Christian army is trapped in the middle of a wasteland with no water and completely surrounded by the enemy. *You* tell him!"

They stared at one another, and for the first time something like doubt crossed Ridefort's eyes, but he blinked it back. "I don't have a horse that can trot, let alone canter. You must send one of your knights."

"Oh, I'll lend you a horse," Ibelin answered, "but only you! Not one of your sacrificial lambs," he gestured toward the silent Templars around them. Balian had never been so acutely aware of how young many of these bearded men were.

Behind their beards and their tonsures, behind the façade of their white robes, half of them were little more than boys. He noted with poignancy that many of them had faces the color of cooked crabs and peeling skin—clear indications that they were newly come from countries with cool, rainy summers. Why, many of them might have arrived only weeks or days ago, replacements for the men lost at Cresson. They were, he knew, suffering more in this heat than any of the men from Ibelin, Ramla, or Nablus. He could sense that they were frightened, too. They had believed in their cause, their virtue, and their invincibility. And they were starting to ask themselves what had gone wrong.

"Damn you, Ibelin!"

"What for, Ridefort? For pushing your nose in your own shit? You made this King, and you made this catastrophe. Tripoli warned you. I warned you. By God, half the barons of Jerusalem warned you! But you thought yourself cleverer than all of us together. This is your dung heap, and you are going to lie in it. I only pray to God that He will not punish the rest of us for your stupidity, arrogance, and hubris!"

"I'll kill you, Ibelin!"

"You already have, Ridefort. You've killed all of us. Now, do you want my stallion or not?"

Ridefort's eyes flashed with hatred so intense that he refused. Dragging his own poor, tired mount around, he dug his spurs into its flanks, forcing it to lumber forward in an exhausted, miserable lope.

Ibelin let his eyes sweep across the faces of the remaining, still-stunned Templars and shook his head. Then he rode back to his own men to face the next Saracen onslaught.

As dusk fell, they rejoined the main army. Taking stock as best he could in the growing gloom, Ibelin estimated that although casualties among his mounted troops had been negligible, he had lost nearly one-third of his infantry, or close to six hundred men. In contrast, the Templars' rash attacks had killed so many of their horses that many knights and sergeants had no choice but to walk. Men raised to fight on horseback could rarely keep pace with the infantry, however, particularly when weighed down by chain mail. Many Templars had fallen behind and been butchered by the pursuing Saracens as a result. The Saracens consistently straddled them, then hauled them halfway off the ground by their hair to slit their throats as if they were slaughtering sheep.

The main army was camped on a sweeping plain behind two hills that separated them from the Sea of Galilee, known colloquially as the "Horns of Hattin." From the west they were simply two hills joined by an oval valley, but seen from the Sea of Galilee they reared up much more sharply and dramatically and did, somewhat, remind the viewer of ox horns.

There was no water here whatsoever. Anyone who had already depleted the water he carried with him had nowhere to replenish his supplies. As Ibelin made his way through the camp to take part in a council in the King's tent, he saw men lying about with their tongues literally hanging out. Other men were sucking on objects to try to force saliva into their mouths. Still others were gagging on bread, unable to get it down their parched throats.

Ibelin paused beside his squires and admonished them not to give more than half the water to his destriers tonight. "We're still three miles from Lake Tiberias."

"I thought we were going to Hattin," Ernoul replied, surprised.

"Through that?" Ibelin gestured to the hills around them that were literally crawling with Saracen men and horses. Even as he spoke, the muezzins began wailing out the call to prayer and the sound surrounded them, drowning out the chanting of the canons kneeling before the great gold cross containing Christianity's most holy relic.

The canons were not alone; thousands of troops had gravitated toward the wagon with the golden cross and were now on their knees behind the priests. Ibelin had to pick his way through their ranks, conscious of the unnatural intensity of the prayers murmured all around him. Men were crossing themselves, muttering Pater Nosters, or saying the Ave Maria, a new prayer that was rapidly gaining popularity. Balian could smell the sweat and other fluids on their dust-caked bodies. These men were praying for their souls more than for their bodies. They understood their situation.

When the Muslims' prayers ended, their drumming started. Deep, muffled drums beat a slow dirge that continued through the night. As silence settled over the Christian camp, however, laughter and music wafted from the campfires surrounding them.

The enemy thought they had already won, Ibelin reflected, returning from a council that could not reverse the fatal decision of the night before. They were trapped, surrounded, exhausted and parched, while their enemy was fresh—and caravans of camels brought cool water from the Sea of Galilee.

"Do you believe in miracles?" the Archbishop of Lydda asked Ibelin, as the latter paused beside the wagon with the True Cross to say his own prayers and confess his sins before facing the morrow.

Balian thought about that. "I don't believe in counting on them," he answered after a moment, and moved on.

Horns of Hattin, July 4, 1187

The smoke was getting worse, and throughout the Christian camp men were coughing. Lack of water made their coughs harsher, drier, and more persistent. The horses were unsettled, too, nickering and moving uneasily. Balian dragged himself to his feet and squinted. The sky was graying to the east, but clouds of smoke darkened everything west and south of them. At first he thought the enemy campfires had simply gotten out of control—but the longer he looked, the more convinced he became that these fires were far too neat and too equidistant to be out of control. Salah ad-Din had built a ring of fire around their rear and flanks and had drawn up his army ahead of them. The fires had a following southwest wind to drive them toward the Christians and herd the latter onto the spears of the waiting Saracens.

"Tack up Thor and Centurion," he ordered his squires, "and give them what is left of the water. I'll ride Thor. Keep Centurion near at hand in reserve."

"We'll be with you today, then?" Gabriel asked anxiously.

"We are fish in a barrel, boys. Commend your souls to God, if you have not already done so." Balian gestured toward the priests again moving through the host.

Salah ad-Din waited until the sun was high enough in the eastern sky to be blinding—and to cast a brilliant, taunting sheen on the ruffled surface of the Sea of Galilee. While the Saracen troops on the flanks emptied skins full of water onto the earth to demoralize the thirsting Christians, the center launched an attack. Within minutes their arrows were falling with devastating effect among the dense ranks of the Christians. Many men were by now either too tired or too dispirited to raise their shields, and the casualties began to mount correspondingly. Ibelin, his knights and squires on horseback around him, started cursing in a steady stream, and no one dared interrupt him.

It was idiocy to just sit here and let themselves be slaughtered!

Fortunately the Constable agreed, and with a trumpet blast he ordered the attack. Ibelin thanked God and led his men into position, his shield still over his head to catch the falling arrows. The problem they had now was that they would be charging uphill, but anything was better than just sitting under the pouring arrows.

At the Constable's signal the Frankish cavalry started to extricate itself from the protection of the infantry and lumber forward, slowly gaining momentum. A cavalry charge is exhilarating, and it has a contagious euphoria about it that now swept through the men of Outremer. Despite their parched throats, they found the strength to shout "Jerusalem!" as they crashed into the enemy with lances leveled, cutting deep into the enemy lines.

Ibelin saw the Constable decapitate a high-ranking emir with the first stroke of his sword after his lance broke. Then he had no time to pay attention to anything but the men trying to kill him as he continued forward, slashing left and right. Thor was his best weapon, lashing out with his teeth and feet, kicking anything that came near him from behind. Although the horse's kicking often upset Ibelin's own aim, it assured him he would not be attacked from behind, either. Together they were making progress.

Gradually, however, Ibelin realized that the momentum had gone out of the charge and they were stalled. They were only halfway up the slope and surrounded by the enemy. Around him horses were going down with appalling regularity. The Saracen infantry was among them, stabbing the horses in their chests, bellies, and necks. The horses screamed and crumpled. As soon as one went down, the rider was pulled clear and hacked to pieces. He saw that happen first to Sir Walter and then Sir Arnulf.

Over the noise, the Constable was screaming at them to withdraw. Ibelin swung Thor about and leaned forward, shouting into his ears for speed. The stallion responded as much to his own terror as his master's, and they galloped back toward the Christian army, leaping over dead and dying men and horses.

As they crashed through the line of Christian infantry around the supply wagons and the True Cross, Ibelin made a quick head count. He had lost a quarter of his knights in this futile charge—but far more terrifying, the Christian infantry was cracking. He saw men flinging themselves face down on the ground, their arms outstretched in a gesture of surrender, and many more were starting to stream due east in the direction of the Sea of Galilee, visible between the "horns" on either side. It was as if the lure of water had become so compelling that the infantry ignored the enemy still massed at the foot of the hills on either side.

With a start, Ibelin realized that the enemy must have opened a gap between two of their divisions intentionally to lure the Christians into a trap. The enemy would fall on the Christians from both sides as soon as they were between the open pincers. Ibelin shouted and waved at the infantry, trying to warn them and call them back—but orders had little effect on men who felt they had been so poorly led up to this point. He shouted himself hoarse, but it was mostly the men of Ibelin, Ramla, and Nablus who took heed.

Farther east, Reynald de Châtillon recognized the same danger Ibelin had. He, too, shouted for the infantry to stand. When they ignored him, he rode in among them and began flailing at them with the flat of his sword, trying to force them back. Most of the men dodged his sword, protected their head with their arms, or took the blows on their backs, but continued eastward. Abruptly Châtillon's horse collapsed and the Baron of Oultrejourdain sank down among the infantry, completely lost to view. The infantry continued to stream eastward, apparently stepping right over Oultrejourdain. Ibelin shuddered as he registered that their own men that killed his horse — and possibly Oultrejourdain himself.

Moments latter, the enemy launched their crushing pincer movement against the Christian infantry. Thousands were slaughtered in a matter of minutes, while those who could, avoided the slaughter by scrambling and clambering, too exhausted and dehydrated to run, up onto the higher ground of the southern horn.

Tripoli shouted furiously at the King: "We have to break out to the north! To Hattin! The slope is too steep on the east flank!"

King Guy didn't answer. His eyes were blank, his jaw slack. The magnitude of the disaster appeared to overwhelm him. Before his eyes his Kingdom was dying, sinking man by man and horse by horse into hell.

As Ibelin watched the stunned King, Thor abruptly crashed down onto his knees and began to slowly fall onto his right side. Balian barely managed to jump free before his right leg was crushed. The great black stallion's eyes rolled back into his head and his tongue hung out. Balian could see no evidence of a wound; the stallion had died of heart failure and thirst in the heat. The charge had taken the last ounce of strength out of him.

Meanwhile, however, Tripoli's knights were already in motion. Ibelin had not heard the King give the order, but then he'd been preoccupied by the collapse of his destrier. He didn't have a chance of joining the charge, unhorsed as he was, and his knights remained with him out of ingrained loyalty—a lifetime of feudal values that had been drummed into them since childhood until it sat in the very marrow of their bones. He glanced up, and his eyes met those of the aging Sir Bartholomew. The man was sixty if he was a day. He had fought for more than forty years to keep the Holy Land Christian, only to come to this. He nodded to Balian, and seemed to say, "Onto death, my lord, we're with you."

Suddenly Ernoul was beside him, smelling of sweat and urine. He was trembling violently, but he held Centurion's reins, and dutifully jumped down from his own horse to hold the off stirrup for his lord. As he tried to mount, Balian realized his own strength was waning. It took him two attempts to drag himself into the saddle, but around him men were shouting in excitement. The mood had shifted abruptly from despair to exhilaration. Following their excited gestures, Balian saw that Tripoli was through the enemy lines and Reginald of Sidon was reinforcing. They had broken out of the encirclement!

He collected his reins and glanced at the King. The entire army had to reinforce immediately! They had to pour every man and horse left alive through the gap Tripoli had torn open and hope the infantry would follow.

But King Guy only gaped, his jaw still slack, his eyes glazed. It was as if he could no longer grasp what was happening around him, even when it was to his benefit. His brother was beside him, gesturing toward the gap opened by Tripoli and toward the True Cross, the infantry. He was clearly urging a breakout. Oultrejourdain staggered forward on foot to likewise point at the gap, giving the same advice with a vehemence Ibelin could sense although he couldn't hear. Still the King was too stunned to respond.

And already the opportunity was past. The enemy had closed ranks again, flooding like water into the opening Tripoli had cut. Not only that: they now surged toward the Christian ranks around King Guy. They were firing their arrows at close range again, and horses were going down with sickening screams.

"Pull back behind the infantry!" Aimery de Lusignan ordered, while his brother stared at the carnage, apparently too paralyzed with shock to think or give orders. "Retreat up the southern slope!" He pointed to the southern "horn," where the infantry, or what was left of it, crouched around the wagon carrying the True Cross. It was hard to tell who was protecting whom. While the soldiers had planted their shields in front of the wagon, the Bishops of Acre and Lydda could be seen standing on the wagon with their arms upraised, evidently imploring God for succor.

"No!" Ibelin contradicted, pushing Centurion forward until he was directly beside the Constable. "There is Salah ad-Din!" Balian had spotted the glitter of gold and jewels as a knot of men in yellow turbans moved steadily forward through the host opposite. "If we kill him, the battle's over!"

The Constable followed Ibelin's finger and then glanced at his mentally lamed brother, the infantry huddling around the True Cross on the hill to their right, and said simply, "go with God, Ibelin. If I survive, I swear I will care for your widow and orphans as the kin they are!"

Ibelin ignored the remark. He did not see this as a suicide charge. Rather, this was a God-given last chance to salvage what was left of the army—maybe ten thousand of the eighteen thousand infantry and one thousand of the five thousand cavalry they had set out with yesterday. He looked around for the Templars and Hospitallers, who would normally have been tasked with a mission of this sort. There were only a handful of Templars still mounted, in a pitiful cluster around the Beauséant and Master de Ridefort; most of the remaining knights and sergeants were horseless and so acting as infantry protection for King Guy. The Hospitallers might have mustered a hundred mounted men—but they were too far away, guarding the slope up to the hill on which the gold reliquary containing the True Cross glinted in the afternoon sun.

Ibelin raised his voice to the men still around him. "That is Salah ad-Din!" he shouted, pointing again. "If we kill him, the field is ours!"

Sir Galvin took a firm grip on his bloody ax, while the other knights called for lances from their squires and formed up around their lord. Sir Bartholomew held the banner of Ibelin. Many squires also pressed their horses between and behind the knights, evidently sharing Ibelin's assessment of the situation rather than the Constable's—or preferring martyrdom to slavery.

Ibelin couched his lance and shouted "Jerusalem!" Centurion sprang forward, astonishing his rider, who did not know Thor had refused to drink at Sephorie while the older horse had drunk his fill. Around and behind him his knights picked up his call and pressed together, stirrup to stirrup, seized this time less with euphoria than desperation. Or was it a sense of destiny?

Ibelin broke his lance on first impact and it splintered in his hand, but the Saracen who had taken it toppled backwards off his horse into a second rider, knocking the latter down as well. By then, Ibelin had his sword out and was killing with the kind of efficiency that struck terror into the hearts of his opponents. He had no sense of his own vulnerability, nor did he feel the blows that rained down on him. His chain mail blunted most of the hits, and while several slashes severed the metal links and drew blood, none bit deep enough to reach his obsessed brain with a cry of pain.

Ibelin had his eye fixed on Salah ad-Din, and his entire being was focused on closing the distance between them for the sole purpose of executing the great Sultan. He was close enough to see his target's face. The Kurdish leader turned toward him with a look of alarm followed by recognition. Just another seven yards and Ibelin would have him.

And then something slammed into their left flank with so much force that the horses screamed and staggered. Centurion momentarily lost his footing and stumbled, jolting Balian so violently that he lost one of his stirrups as he was pitched forward onto the stallion's neck. Ibelin felt himself slipping to the left, losing his seat and with it his life—for if he hit the ground he would be trampled to death. Instinctively he let go of the shield grip and grabbed at Centurion's long, flowing mane with his left hand. He struggled to stay in the saddle, while the stallion scrambled to get his feet under him. Balian was still half out of the saddle and barely holding on as Centurion spun on his haunches and joined in a stampede of other horses, running away from the Saracen cavalry that had so forcefully attacked from the left.

It was all Ibelin could do to pull himself back into the saddle and collect the reins as Centurion galloped. He could not recover his lost stirrup, but once he had the reins he started to check Centurion's headlong charge. Looking around to assess the situation, he realized that the threat to Salah ad-Din had drawn men not only from the left but from the right as well. Ahead of them, between the horns of Hattin, a gap had opened up again. Not only that, he could see infantry surging down the southern horn, running to follow them out—as they had so singularly failed to follow Tripoli.

Ibelin checked Centurion a second time to enable the remnants of his cavalry to close around him again. Then he pointed with his sword at the gap, and that was all.

They crashed over the edge, and suddenly their horses were whinnying in fear as they slipped and slid on the gravel of the steep slope. Balian leaned back and Centurion sat on his haunches, still skidding and scrambling. This was madness, Balian registered. Tripoli had been right about the slope being too steep for horses—but there was no return.

Around them Christian infantry was running past, sliding and tumbling, even rolling down the hill as they lost their footing. They set off cascades of gravel and avalanches of sand that crashed and clattered down the slope. Balian flung his right leg over Centurion's rump and tried to stand, but he lost his footing on the rolling stones and his knees crumpled up under him. He slid several feet on his knees in the gravel, clinging to Centurion's reins just to stay upright. Finally he came to a halt and got his feet under him. He took hold of the reins right behind the bit so he could steady the stallion, and then led him down the gravel-filled gully. Around him, his men and utter strangers did the same thing.

With each step, the sound of battle receded behind them. Ibelin looked back several times, hoping to see, if not King Guy, the Constable or the Hospitallers reinforcing the gap and cresting the lip of the hill. Instead, the flood of infantry turned into a trickle and then stopped altogether.

He stopped and looked up the steep bank, now silhouetted against the bright afternoon sky. Men appeared on the crest and began shooting arrows at them. The Saracens had managed yet again to close the gap before the bulk of the Christian army could escape.

Ibelin only realized he was weeping when his vision started to blur. He had no articulate thoughts—just a sense of complete and utter loss. He did not know what was happening behind him on the Horns of Hattin, but he was certain that it was the end of the Christian army and with it, the Kingdom of Jerusalem. This was a defeat from which they could never recover.

Then he stumbled and got a grip on himself. He and the men around him were still in mortal danger. For the moment the Saracens had contented themselves with firing a single round of arrows, but once they had captured or killed King Guy and the men still with him, they would come after the men who had temporarily escaped.

Ibelin looked back down the slope. He could count about seventy knights, maybe thirty squires, two hundred-some Turcopoles, and, at a rough estimate, maybe three thousand infantrymen. How many men had made it out with Tripoli? Maybe twice that many knights and Turcopoles, but no infantry.

One by one, they reached the foot of the steep slope. It seemed dark and cool and quiet here. No one spoke. Men just kept stumbling forward, drawn irresistibly by the water of the lake. Many men were wounded, Ibelin noted, and the horses were in terrible condition. He looked with concern at Centurion's bloody hocks, and then tried to take stock of which of his men were still with him. Amazingly, old Sir Bartholomew was still alive, and he gave Balian a weary smile. Three other Ibelin vassals were with him as well. Twice as many of his household knights had also made it out. The mighty Sir Galvin was carrying an unconscious Sir Sylvester in his arms. Ibelin recognized several of the knights of Nablus and Ramla as well, nodding to them to acknowledge them one by one as their eyes met. But half the men were strangers.

Ibelin caught sight of Gabriel walking beside a horse that still had a rider slumped on it, and a moment later recognized the limp body of Ernoul on the horse Gabriel was leading. "Is he badly hurt?" he called to his squire.

"Yes. It's a neck wound, and he's passed out," Gabriel answered.

Ibelin could only nod. There was nothing he could do for anyone at the moment. They had to get to the Sea of Galilee. There they would water the horses, wash the worst of the blood away, and then take stock.

Ibelin looked toward the waters that had shimmered and beckoned all day long. They did so no longer: the sun was too low and the great lake was in shadow. It was so near they could smell it. It smelled fresh and clean and restorative, but that was deceptive, Balian knew.

When he reached the lake, like the others who had reached it before him,

Ibelin walked straight in, letting the comparatively cool water seep through his chain-mail leggings, his surcoat, hauberk, and gambeson. Centurion, like his fellows, walked until the water reached his sweat-dripping belly and then lowered his head to drink loudly. Ibelin saw several men cup water to their mouths to drink as well, and he shouted: "Don't drink! It could kill you! There are springs less than a mile away! Let the horses refresh themselves, but not drink too much or too fast. Then we'll proceed to the springs!"

While the men closest to him obeyed, Ibelin saw that many farther away did not. They would regret it later, but he could not help them if they ignored him.

God—he caught himself and looked back toward the Horns of Hattin. It wasn't just King Guy and the bulk of the barons and fighting men of Jerusalem that were caught up there—it was the True Cross as well. Since the relic had been discovered, it had never before been present at a Christian defeat. And now? Now it was almost certain to fall into Saracen hands. Balian had no illusions about what they would do with it. The Muslims viewed Christian reverence for relics as something between idiocy and idolatry. They would either just toss the fragment of the Cross away or, worse, spit and piss upon it to show their utter contempt.

Ibelin felt rage surging up in his chest at the thought of that, but it was a rage that encompassed Guy de Lusignan and Gerard de Ridefort. The Saracens had only taken advantage of their own weaknesses. If they captured the True Cross, it was not because God had abandoned them, but rather because Ridefort and Lusignan had abandoned God in their arrogance and hubris!

With difficulty Ibelin waded out of the Sea of Galilee, his exhausted body hardly able to drag the weight of his water-soaked clothes, armor and reluctant Centurion. At the bank, he staggered and then sank down onto his knees. He folded his hands and started praying aloud. "Christ, forgive us our sins and the sins of our brothers. Forgive us our foolishness and our arrogance. Forgive us for our weaknesses, and have mercy upon us, such as we are. Amen."

To his astonishment, scores of voices seconded his amen, and when he looked around he saw that many men had followed his example. Was it them—the way they were gazing at him for reassurance and leadership—or was it the figure walking across the water toward them that gave him strength?

What care I for the wood on which I shed my mortal blood? a voice asked in his head. *The blood of mortal man holds not the spirit. Immortality is with me, and he who liveth and believeth in me, though he be dead, yet shall he live. Rise up and lead my people out of the jaws of slavery.*

So Balian dragged himself to his feet and started organizing the roughly three thousand three hundred survivors of the great Christian army into a coherent force, putting the wounded on litters or sledges behind what horses they had, and surrounding the horses with infantry. Then they dragged themselves north along the west bank of Galilee, angling up into the hills making for the Templar castle of Safed.

Chapter 19

Damascus, July 6, 1187

Waking or sleeping, Humphrey kept reliving that moment when the True Cross had fallen. The Saracens were clearly targeting it with their arrows. Spread out before the wagon with the True Cross, the corpses of the Christian dead had lain like slaughtered porcupines, while a half-dozen canons of the Holy Sepulcher lay sprawled upon the wagon itself, their limbs limp and their heads hanging lifelessly as blood soaked their white robes. Then the Saracen infantry surged forward, walking on the bodies of the dead and dying. With one horrible whack, a big turbaned man dropped his sword on the junction of the Bishop of Acre's neck and shoulder. The blade cut halfway to his heart and stuck so fast the sword was wrenched from the Saracen's hand when the bishop's body keeled over like a felled tree.

The Bishop of Lydda was still clinging to the golden cross containing the precious relic, but the Saracens swarmed around him and pulled the cross down from the wagon, bishop and all. As it toppled, a wild cheer of "Allahu Akbar!" went up, followed by the ululations of victory.

The sound seemed to wake King Guy from his trance, and with a roar like that of a wounded beast, he lunged forward. His brother tried to hold him back, but King Guy was faster, and a second later the Saracens had swarmed around him and dragged him from his saddle. It looked at first as if they were tearing him to pieces—until Henri d'Ibelin, although he'd been unhorsed hours earlier, plunged into the horde of Saracens on foot with a violence that sent heads and arms flying through the air. He was able to reach the fallen King and pull him to his feet. Guy, however, was staggering as if he'd taken a blow to his head, and he offered his sword hilt-first to the nearest Saracen.

Instantly the shouts and ululations of triumph rose to a great crescendo, while behind them the King's great red tent collapsed as the stakes were yanked out. Around the wagon on which the True Cross had stood, the Christian infantry fell on their faces in abject submission.

Humphrey saw the Constable throw down his shield and sword and raise his hands over his head in surrender. He hastened to imitate the Constable as the Saracens rushed forward. He was grabbed on all sides by what seemed like dozens of men. They dragged him from his horse and then buffeted and pulled him this way and that, shouting at each other over his head in Arabic.

They were squabbling over whose prize he was. "I got him first!" "No, he's mine!" "Get your paws off my prisoner!"

Humphrey had been limp and helpless, disinterested in who claimed him.

Eventually all the Christian leaders and men had been dragged, stumbling and dazed, back to the Saracen camp. Humphrey saw many men crumple up or vomit from exhaustion and despair, while the shouts and ululations of triumph continued all around them. He had been too confused to take note of very much. Someone had handed him a pottery mug filled with hot, murky water. It tasted foul, but he'd drunk every drop. A moment later his bowels started working and he'd had to crouch and drop his braies.

He was taken to a tent and (not knowing he spoke Arabic) they just pointed for him to sit on the floor. He did as he was told; he seemed to have no will of his own.

Nor did he have any sense of how long he had been there when they came for him and led him toward a larger, more luxurious tent. Just before the door of this tent, a spiked pole had been thrust butt-end into the earth. It was sagging and leaning to one side from the weight of the head stuck on it. Humphrey caught his breath in horror and then staggered as he recognized the bald head and staring eyes of Reynald de Châtillon. Much as he hated Châtillon, he was still shocked into paralysis by the sight of his severed head. From behind, someone roughly shoved him forward, causing him to almost trip over the headless body of the Lord of Oultrejourdain that lay just beyond the pole—still bleeding from the stump of the neck and a stomach wound.

Inside the tent Humphrey found it hard to focus at first, and then he realized that King Guy was seated beside Salah ad-Din, looking ghastly white, as he held a goblet wet with condensation in obviously trembling hands. Henri d'Ibelin was still beside him, a bloody cloth tied around his sword arm, and Aimery de Lusignan stood behind his brother the King, looking nearly as shaken, but not trembling. The old Marquis de Montferrat, father of Sibylla's first husband and grandfather of Baldwin V, had been offered a seat, apparently on account of his white beard and hair. He sat with hunched shoulders and slack arms, clutching a goblet in both hands. Standing behind him were Hebron and his eldest son, the latter nursing a dislocated shoulder, and Walter of Caesarea with a ugly gash on the side of his face. The lords of Bethsan, Nazareth, Haifa, Jubail, and Scandelion, were here as well, filthy and drenched in sweat, but apparently without serious injury. And Gerard de Ridefort. The Templar Master was the only one among them who still looked defiant.

"Who is this?" asked Salah ad-Din.

"Humphrey de Toron," Hebron answered the Sultan, and someone shoved Humphrey from behind so that he fell forward onto his knees.

"There's no need to be rough," Salah ad-Din admonished whoever had given the push, adding to Humphrey: "You have nothing to fear. You are my prisoner." Then to a slave he ordered again in Arabic, "Give him something to drink."

That water had been chilled and clean, but it had been the last courtesy Humphrey had received since his capture. When they were taken from the Sultan's tent, their hands had been bound behind their backs, and they had spent the night like that, bound, with no food. On the morning of July 5 they were untied long enough to relieve themselves in a pit and then given bread, but afterwards their hands were bound again. The knights and lords were put on packhorses, and their feet tied together by a rope leading under the belly of the horse. The horses were on leads, and around them were mounted archers, grinning and pleased with being assigned to escort duty, because it would take them back to the pleasures of Damascus while their colleagues continued with the conquest of the Christian kingdom.

Humphrey caught sight of thousands of Christian foot soldiers being herded together by men with whips. Their legs were bound together so that they could only shuffle, and many stumbled. As he watched, Nubian foot soldiers started tying ropes around their necks to lead them like camels in a caravan. He shuddered as he realized they were all now slaves: thousands and thousands of Christian men. Men who yesterday had been prosperous shopkeepers, master craftsmen, and sturdy journeymen were now nothing but property. And their wives and children . . . He couldn't bear to think of them. Who would defend them, with the entire army dead or enslaved?

The escort, eager for Damascus, gave their prisoners little rest. They were barely given time to relieve themselves and drink. There was no food until they reached Damascus, and that only after they had run the gauntlet of cheering crowds, hooting and mocking them. Humphrey, who understood the insults and taunts, suffered more than the knights and squires who did not speak Arabic so well.

They were taken to the citadel, and here the noblemen were separated from the less important prisoners, including Henri d'Ibelin, who had not left the King's side since their capture. They were put into what appeared to be some kind of storeroom, for there were barrels in it and some dusty chests, but the windows were high above their heads and had heavy metal grilles to discourage thoughts of escape—not that any of them had the strength for it. Here they were given a bowl of rice with pieces of spiced lamb in it. They were also given some wine with their water, and straw pallets to soften the stone floor.

Guy de Lusignan grumbled about "hardly bedding for a king," but his brother hissed something at him that sounded to Humphrey like "good enough for a defeated king!"

"He said he would treat me like a king!" Guy protested.

"He said, 'A king does not kill a king'—that doesn't mean he has to give you silks and feather beds. Have you forgotten our father *died* in a Saracen prison?" Aimery reminded him sharply, making Guy catch his breath and stare in horror at his brother. It was as if it were the first time this possibility had ever occurred to him.

Without guards for the first time since their capture, the tongues of the Frankish prisoners were loosened, and Hebron asked, "Do we know who got out?"

"Tripoli!" Guy snapped bitterly, harvesting silence from the others.

Then Hebron pointed out bluntly, "If you'd given the order to follow him, we would *all* be free."

"But the True Cross—" King Guy started to protest in self-justification.

His brother broke him off: "—is lost anyway."

"Did anyone see what happened to the Bishop of Lydda?"

They looked around at each other. He should have been with them if he lived; he too was a nobleman. They noted another missing face: Gerard de Ridefort. But no one mentioned the latter, and William de Montferrat suggested, "If Lydda was badly wounded, he might have been unfit to ride, and left with the other wounded."

Caesarea crossed himself in silent prayer, and the others followed his example. Then Jubail picked up the conversation. "I saw Caymont go down, trampled to death."

"Wasn't his son killed on the march?"

"Yes. He took an arrow in the throat and died in camp."

"Who is his heir, then?"

Aimery laughed harshly, "Salah ad-Din."

They looked at him, a little shocked, but no one contradicted him.

"So Tripoli, Sidon, and Ibelin are the only barons of Jerusalem still free."

"And Edessa."

"Of course, how could I forget the brave Edessa!" Caesarea commented sarcastically. Edessa had never left Acre on account of his gout.

"There's no point bickering among ourselves," Aimery advised. "Let's try to get some sleep."

But all Humphrey saw when he tried to sleep were the Saracens surging forward and the gold reliquary with the True Cross toppling over into their bloodthirsty arms, as the Bishop of Acre's partly dissected body sank down among the corpses of the canons of the Holy Sepulcher.

At some point his dreams started to mutate. He saw Oultrejourdain's head talking to him, calling Humphrey all the names he'd called him as a boy, mocking him for his weakness. He saw Balian d'Ibelin striding towards him across a green field that was lush with fresh, soft grass, but when Humphrey started towards him, he turned his back and walked away. Humphrey ran after him. "Don't leave me here! Take me home! Take me to Isabella," he begged. Ibelin spun about, but suddenly he had the face of Oultrejourdain, blood running from his neck and coating his surcoat, and he sneered, "Afraid to be without your protectress, little boy?"

Humphrey almost dreamt of Isabella, but then she turned into the girl in the desert, only the men raping her were Saracens shouting "Allahu Akbar" and ululating in triumph as she screamed for them to stop. No, Humphrey could not sleep, and he was grateful for the dawn—until they were rounded up and dragged outside.

They were taken to a large square flanked by fine buildings, including an impressive mosque with three minarets. Here they were made to stand together, surrounded by a heavy escort of armed men. A huge crowd had already gathered, filling most of the square and even spilling into the side streets. Youths had climbed up on buildings for a better view. Soldiers were having difficulty keeping a space about two hundred by three hundred feet clear in the center.

"I don't like this," Hebron muttered, and no one voiced a contrary opinion.

Men in long white robes and turbans filed out of one of the beautiful buildings, which had an elaborate façade at right angles to the mosque. "Sufis," Humphrey muttered, and the others looked at him. The most prominent of these men were quite old already, with long, straggling beards, but they were surrounded by twoscore or more younger men with bushy black beards and eyes burning with passion.

Opposite the Christian prisoners something was roiling the crowd, and it became clear that a large column of people was slowly forcing its way through the throng, squeezing the people already lining the route closer together. At last the head of this column emerged out of the crowd, and behind the leading emir and his lieutenants were men with shaved heads and beards.

"The Templars and Hospitallers!" King Guy exclaimed.

He was right. The men, shuffling forward with bound hands and feet, all wore the tattered and filthy surcoats of their respective orders: white with red crosses or black with white crosses. Their guards lined them up opposite the Sufis, making it easy for Humphrey to count them: there were four and a half rows of fifty men each, or something short of two hundred fifty surviving Knights of Christ.

The emir gestured for silence, and his lieutenants shouted for it. Gradually the crowd settled down and waited with craning necks and uneasy anticipation for the next act. The emir turned to face the captives from the military orders and raised his voice to speak in fluent French. "Christian captives, as the avowed enemies of Islam, you have earned death, for it is written that he who denies Allah and tries to destroy the community of the Faithful must themselves be destroyed."

The crowd chanted their approval, dissolving into a chorus of "Death to the infidels! Death to the Unbelievers!" Eventually the emir silenced the crowd with his gestures, and the crowd again waited with bated breath.

The emir continued, "The Sultan Salah ad-Din, in his infinite mercy and profound wisdom, offers you a chance to save your lives. All you need do is embrace the True Faith."

The nobles of Jerusalem looked at one another, and then back at the lines of Templars and Hospitallers. Humphrey couldn't help wondering if they were going to be next.

"Is there not one of you who would save your soul as well as your body by accepting that your beliefs are infantile and it is time to embrace the Prophet?" the emir asked in a voice thick with mock kindness.

There was some stirring in the ranks of the Templars and Hospitallers—but it was more, or so Humphrey thought, a sigh of resignation. One or two of the knights dropped their heads, their lips moving in prayer. If their hands had not been bound, more than one man might have crossed himself.

"Are you all blind, deaf, and dumb?" the emir asked, in a voice pitched to the crowd and intended to drown out the murmurs of the condemned.

"We hear better than you!" a Hospitaller called out from the front rank, "for we hear the angels of heaven already."

"You hear the demons of hell!" the emir sneered back.

From the second rank, some of the Templars started singing the "non nobis," and William de Montferrat whispered in horror, "God in heaven, they are going to die unshriven! There's not a priest anywhere."

Meanwhile the emir turned and exchanged words with the leader of the Sufis, an old, white-haired man with a frail body, who nodded vigorously before he reverently grasped a sword handed to him by one of the emir's men. The emir than turned back and pointed at the Hospitaller who had dared to speak up.

Two of the emir's men grabbed the Hospitaller and brought him forward, forcing him to kneel at the emir's feet. The Hospitaller did not struggle. He bowed his head and closed his eyes in preparation for death. But it wasn't one of the soldiers that stepped forward to strike his head from his shoulders—it was the ancient Sufi.

The old man could hardly raise the heavy sword over his head. His arms were accustomed to writing, not fighting. He staggered as he tried to swing the sword down. The blade fell short of the Hospitaller's neck and landed on his back instead. It knocked the bound prisoner forward onto his face and drew blood, but did not come close to killing him. The crowd shouted advice and encouragement as the Sufi raised the sword again and now hacked at the back of the Hospitaller's neck. Blood was gushing all over the square, but the Hospitaller was still writhing in agony, his face covered in his own blood, as the Sufi made a third and then a fourth attempt to kill him. It was not until the fifth blow that the old Sufi at last hacked through the Hospitaller's neck and was able to lift up the severed head to show the crowd. He was splattered with blood and grinning proudly.

The crowd went wild with delight, shouting with rising fervor: "God is great! God is great!" Humphrey vomited into the street.

The spectacle was now repeated, with each of the Sufis, one at a time, being given the "honor" of killing a bound and kneeling Christian prisoner as a reward for his devotion to Islam and Allah. Around them the spectators shouted encouragement to the scholars and teachers of the Koran, while others in the crowd took bets on how many blows it would take for them to kill each victim. Once or twice the show was halted so that the bodies could be dumped upon wagons pulled by oxen and the heads collected in burlap sacks while the swords were whetted. Half-starved stray dogs were already trying to lick up the blood running between the paving stones, and flies were swarming so thickly that the bystanders were plagued by them—particularly the steadily diminishing ranks of the Hospitallers and Templars, who with bound wrists could not bat them away.

The entire massacre took almost five hours, and by the end, the Templars and Hospitallers had to be dragged forward, not because of resistance but from debilitating shock and weakness. Many had soiled themselves with vomit or urine, and three actually ended up crawling on their bellies to the emir, praising Allah.

But three out of nearly two hundred fifty wasn't worth thinking about in Humphrey's mind. Instead, he held in his memory the face of a knight too young to grow a proper beard, with a sunburned face and bright blond hair making up the tonsure encircling his peeling scalp. He must have come newly from the West, Humphrey calculated as the young man knelt in the blood of his brothers, and the stench of their bodies made him gag once or twice. Then he looked up at the Sufi, approaching with a sword that had been only inadequately wiped off after the last execution, and said in a voice loud enough for Humphrey to hear: "Forgive them, Father, for they know not what they do." And then he started reciting the Lord's Prayer.

Humphrey and the other barons joined in with him, and they said it to the end, even after the young Hospitaller's voice had been severed by the sword after the words, "Forgive us our trespasses."

The very last of the fighting monks to be brought forward was Gerard de Ridefort. He no longer looked defiant, Humphrey thought, and he stumbled and then slipped in the blood. He would have fallen if the emir's men had not held him upright. He was brought to the emir in the very middle of the square; a dozen bodies and severed heads still lay bleeding in the burning sun, the flies all over them.

A new hush fell on the crowd.

"Master de Ridefort," the emir addressed him. "Now that you have seen where your pride and arrogance have led you, are you prepared to accept that your faith was misplaced? That you have prayed to idols and pieces of rubbish and ignored the call of Allah?"

Ridefort did not speak, but his head moved ever so slightly, from side to side.

"You persist in your folly?" the emir asked him as if astonished.

Ridefort nodded, swallowing visibly.

The emir shrugged. "So be it. You will rot in hell in your own time."

The lead Sufi, the old man with the hawk-like nose, who had been leaning wearily on his sword (killing men was such hard work in the heat of the day), straightened and raised his sword. Clearly he felt it was his right to kill the head Templar, but the emir gestured for him to stand down. Instead, the emir pointed to the other Christian prisoners, and his men escorted Ridefort to them.

As he joined them, the other barons drew back in instinctive horror and disgust. They all knew that he was to blame for the debacle at Hattin and the slaughter they had just witnessed. They moved away from Ridefort, and in their eyes was contempt, but it was left to Guy de Lusignan to mutter, "On your head, Ridefort, on your head are all these souls."

Ridefort started slightly and then looked squarely at King Guy. "They are martyrs for Christ. What could be a better end for them?"

"And all the other dead, wounded, and captured?" Aimery snarled.

"Ask your brother," Ridefort answered; "he's the King."

"I'll kill you!" Guy shouted furiously. "You were the one who told me to leave Sephorie! You were the one to urge me to ignore the advice of my barons! You! You are to blame for everything!"

Before Ridefort could answer, William de Montferrat stepped between them, hissing furiously: "Stop giving the Saracens a spectacle!"

The others looked around at the grinning guards and the curious crowd, while Aimery drew his brother away from Ridefort. Guy continued to swear, "I'll kill him! I'll kill him!"

Aimery answered, "Maybe, but not here and now."

Nablus, July 7-12, 1187

Word of the disaster at Hattin seeped out across the Kingdom on the tongues of deserters and the smoke of burning villages. The former spoke of the mad decision to abandon the springs of Sephorie and clad themselves in the robes of prophets, claiming to be the only clear-sighted men in an army seized with collective blindness. The latter spoke only the irrefutable language of ominous and approaching danger.

Maria Zoë was not prepared to believe the word of deserters. Men who fled before a battle were neither men of good character nor the most knowledgeable about a battle's outcome. Many an apparently lost battle had been won in the end. One had only to remember Montgisard.

Sir Constantine agreed in principle, but he was uneasy nevertheless. There was ample evidence from victualers and whores that the army had left Sephorie and marched toward Tiberias—and then it simply disappeared. That was impossible in high summer in the middle of Palestine. He decided to send riders to Nazareth and Tiberias to try to get more information.

Meanwhile refugees began streaming through Nablus, heading south. At first it was just a trickle, but the numbers increased steadily. Most of those passing through with carts crammed high with household goods and loaded pack animals could report only rumors. No one had actually seen anything, but they had *heard* that the Christian army had been annihilated. They had *heard* the King and the True Cross were captured. They had *heard* that Tiberias had fallen and Acre was under siege. The more people Sir Constantine questioned, the worse the stories became.

Maria Zoë still refused to believe the rumors. "These people have panicked," she insisted. But Sir Constantine started to make preparations for their own withdrawal to someplace defensible.

It was three days after the scouts had been sent out that one returned in a state of nervous agitation. He galloped into the city on a near-foundered horse. He was unkempt, dirty, and wild-eyed. "They've slaughtered the whole army! There's nothing left of it at all! Tens of thousands of corpses are rotting unshriven on the Horns of Hattin—feeding the vultures and the wild dogs!"

"Pull yourself together!" Sir Constantine ordered the youth of barely sixteen.

"I'm not exaggerating!" his young messenger shouted back, too agitated to respect authority. "I *saw* the vultures in the sky—more of them than you can imagine! They were like a swarm of gnats! And you could hear them screaming at one another!"

"Did you verify it was Christian and not Muslim dead?" Sir Constantine asked.

"You're not listening to me!" the panicked young man shouted. "There *is* no Christian army! If anyone survived the slaughter, they have been taken away in chains—slaves! There are nothing but Christian corpses from Sephorie to Hattin!"

Sir Constantine dutifully reported this account (in more sober terms) to the Dowager Queen—but it was not until the other scouts returned the next day, reporting that Acre too had fallen, that he put his foot down and insisted that Maria Zoë withdraw to Jerusalem. "Nablus has no walls, my lady, and with the men we have, we cannot hold the citadel for long. Besides, without an army to relieve us, what would be the point?"

Maria Zoë gazed at him without answering. She was not blind or simple-minded. She had refused to accept that the rumors were correct, but that is not the same thing as dismissing them. She had spent every minute, when she was not actively engaged in doing something else, imagining and weighing the consequences. The very fact that there were no counter-rumors and no confusion, and the fact that Balian had not sent her any kind of message whatsoever, strongly suggested that the Christian defeat had indeed been devastating—and that Balian was dead or captured. Every time she thought of her husband, she said a prayer for his life. Yet even as she prayed, she recognized that survival alone might seem a poor substitute for heaven if he had lost a limb, been blinded, or otherwise crippled. So she prayed again, begging that he be of sound mind and body, and then forced herself to think beyond his condition to her children, her household, her people. She was not, therefore, unprepared for Sir Constantine's announcement. She answered him: "My children are at Ibelin. We will go there."

Sir Constantine cursed himself. He should have anticipated this reaction. "My lady," he spoke as forcefully as he could. "The information we have suggests that there is absolutely no Christian force capable of deterring but less preventing Saracen actions. Salah ad-Din's forces can move about the Kingdom at will—and that's exactly what they're doing. The only—I repeat, the only—defenses we have are the walls of our cities and castles."

"Ibelin—"

"Is not defensible with the garrison it has, and Master Shoreham knows that! Shoreham will do what we—and most of the burghers of the Kingdom—are doing: he will take your children to a more defensible place, either Jaffa or Ascalon."

"Then we will join him at Ibelin and fall back to Jaffa with him," Maria Zoë answered.

"My lady." Sir Constantine paused, considered a more flowery, more diplomatic, more Greek response, and then opted for the brutal reality: "No."

Maria Zoë started. She was not used to being contradicted by a subordinate.

Before she could reprimand him, Sir Constantine continued, "I cannot and will not risk the trip to Ibelin. We have far too little intelligence about where the Saracens are, but sufficient information to know that Salah ad-Din has more than enough troops to be able to divide his forces. If Acre has indeed fallen, as the rumors suggest, he has already cut the Kingdom in two, and he will probably try to re-establish his lines of communication with Egypt. He is most likely to move south along the coast. It would be madness to run into his arms. Jerusalem, on the other hand, is unlikely to be threatened immediately, and it is by far our most defensible inland city. The brothers and sisters of the Hospital have already departed, taking the sick, destitute, and children with them to the safety of Jerusalem. If Christ has not completely abandoned us, it is the city we are most likely to hold—until relief comes from the West, if need be. I will escort you to Jerusalem—and nowhere else."

They stared at one another. Maria Zoë very much wanted to say, "Then I will go without your escort," but she didn't dare. The truth was, she was afraid to ride across a kingdom in which there was no longer anyone to enforce order. She was afraid to ride straight into a Saracen patrol—or a pack of deserters—without an armed escort. A woman alone or with only a handful of servants would be prey for common thieves and brigands no less than for enemy. Instead, she appealed to Sir Constantine's conscience. "And my children? Do you expect a mother to abandon her children?"

"No, I trust Master Shoreham to see to their safety as best he can—just as your lord husband did when he left his children in Master Shoreham's care."

"Sir!" Maria Zoë was starting to lose her temper. "My husband is in all probability dead. My son John is therefore Lord of Ibelin, Ramla, and Mirabel! He and his younger brother and sisters cannot simply be abandoned to the care of a sergeant—no matter how loyal or courageous! Either I go to my children, or they must be brought to me!"

"My lady! My lady!" The voice surprised both Sir Constantine and Maria Zoë. It was Georgios. Neither of them knew when the youth had come into the hall, but a strange man in a filthy aketon, baggy hose, and an unshaved and haggard face was standing next to him.

Sir Constantine frowned at the groom and started to rebuke him, but Maria Zoë laid a hand on his sleeve. She was relieved at the interruption, as it gave her time to think and collect her arguments and her nerves. To Georgios she asked, "What is it?"

"This man!" Georgios exclaimed excitedly, indicating his companion. "He was at the battle!"

"Personally?" Sir Constantine asked skeptically, his eyes looking the man suspiciously up and down. Stocky but with massive shoulders, he had a short sword at his left hip and a bow slung over his back.

"Yes!" Georgios assured the knight, but it was the man himself who answered steadily, "I'm a master mason, sir, from Nazareth. I have my workshop and my family there. I mustered with the army at Acre and marched first to Sephorie and then on to the hills just before Hattin, above Tiberias."

"Under whose command?" Sir Constantine asked sharply.

"The Lord of Nazareth, of course."

"And where is he now?" Sir Constantine wanted to know.

The man shrugged. "I presume he is a captive."

"You presume? Presume? When did you run away, abandoning him?"

"Who abandoned whom?" the mason shot back. "The King ordered us to march in the heat of summer, across arid countryside where we had nothing to drink. Even the springs of Tourran were poisoned! And he led us straight into a trap. We were surrounded by Saracens who mocked us by pouring water on the ground. Then they set fires that drove us mad with smoke in our eyes and throats and forced us forward into their arrows and spears. They were all around us, shooting at us and howling out their chants and curses! And the lords? They did nothing! Just sat there, letting us die in their defense! The Count of Tripoli finally broke out, but he cut his way out to the north, and none of us were close enough to follow him. We were on the southern hill surrounding the bishops and monks with the True Cross. At least up there we were out of range of their arrows, but the King and lords kept ordering us to come down and protect them! Why?" he demanded defiantly of Sir Constantine.

Then abruptly he turned and looked directly at Maria Zoë. "Your husband, madame, was the only one who gave us a thought. He tried to kill Salah ad-Din, but when he failed, he turned east and led his knights across in front of us. He broke a hole in the Saracen encirclement right at the foot of the hill. Any of us with an ounce of strength followed him."

"My lord husband broke out of the encirclement?" Maria Zoë asked, so anxiously that she half lifted herself out of her chair in tension.

"Yes, madame. He not only led us out, he saw to the wounded and organized us into a fighting unit again."

"Dear God!" Maria Zoë gasped, crossing herself and muttering thanks to Christ, Mary, and St. George.

Sir Constantine looked at her a little askance. He still didn't fully believe this man or his story. He suspected he'd concocted the whole thing to win Maria Zoë's trust and then cheat her in some way. "And where is the Lord of Ibelin while you stand here before his lady?" he asked the stranger sharply.

"He is probably in Tyre by now," the man answered evenly. "We made first for Safed, and there we learned that Salah ad-Din was taking his army straight to Acre. In fact, the Count of Edessa had already agreed to surrender Acre—"

"What?" Maria Zoë and Sir Constantine exclaimed in unison.

"Yes," the mason answered steadily and confidently. "The Queen's uncle promised to deliver Acre in exchange for his own life and the retention of his treasure. The citizens of Acre started burning the city, preferring to see it ruined than fall intact into Saracen hands, but then Salah ad-Din offered them all their freedom and movable goods in exchange for the city—"

"It is just as I feared, my lady," Sir Constantine broke in. "Salah ad-Din has cut the Kingdom in half. We must make for Jerusalem at once—"

Maria Zoë ignored him and focused on the mason. "What of my husband? Why is it you are here, but my husband is not?"

"The enemy controls the land between Tiberias and Acre, madame. With just three thousand men, there was no way my lord of Ibelin could have broken through. He had to take the small force he had to the most defensible city north of Acre, and that is Tyre. Tyre they will be able to garrison and hold. But my family was in Nazareth and I chose not to go with them. By darkness I slipped through the Saracen lines and made for Nazareth, reaching it just hours before it was occupied by Salah ad-Din's men. I barely escaped with my wife and two babies."

"Where are you headed?"

"Jerusalem, of course."

"What did I tell you?" Sir Constantine told his lady.

Maria Zoë ignored him. She held out her hand to the mason. "Go with God, good man. We will not delay you any longer."

The mason bowed to Maria Zoë. "And may the Lord be with you and with your lord husband, madame. He is more fit to be King than Lusignan!"

Sir Constantine frowned at that, but he held his tongue. The man turned and hastened out of the hall, clearly in a hurry to be on his way, but to Sir Constantine's annoyance Georgios did not go with him. He was on the brink of dismissing the presumptuous groom when Georgios forestalled him by speaking up.

"My lady, let me go!" he pleaded.

"Of course, Georgios," Maria Zoë replied absently. "You will want to see to your mother's safety. No one will keep you here."

"No, my lady. I meant, let me go to Ibelin."

"Ibelin?"

"Yes. When I interrupted, you were saying that either you would go to your children or they must be brought to you. Let me go to Ibelin and bring them to Jerusalem."

"Don't be ridiculous—" Sir Constantine started, but Maria Zoë silenced her with a hand on his arm. Georgios had been trained at arms by one of the finest knights in Christendom. He was a good rider, and he spoke Greek, French, and the usual survival Arabic of the natives. Most important, he had been raised in circumstances that had taught him humility. Georgios was the kind of young man who could appear and act insignificant, even dumb, if he ran into Saracen patrols. He therefore stood a chance of actually reaching Ibelin. Once there, it would be up to Shoreham and the garrison to get her children to safety. If Salah ad-Din did concentrate his army to take the coastal cities, then Shoreham would surely be able to bring the children through to Jerusalem. If instead the Sultan turned on the Holy City, then Shoreham could be trusted to take the children to Ascalon or Jaffa, whichever he thought safer.

She nodded. "Yes, Georgios. Take the best horse in the stables and a remount as well, in case he goes lame. While you prepare to depart, I'll write a letter for Master Shoreham and Father Angelus telling them we have withdrawn to Jerusalem. The most important thing is the safety of the children, Georgios, but to the extent possible, we should remove everything of value from Ibelin as well. If we abandon it, we will lose everything in it—things we may later need to survive." She turned to Sir Constantine. "The same goes for what we have here. Prepare our departure in such a way that our greatest valuables are packed with our riding horses. Place things of lesser value on packhorses, and things of least value on carts. That way we can jettison carts and packhorses successively, if necessary, and still salvage something."

Sir Constantine smiled faintly at this order; his lady's hard-headed practicality was something he admired, even if it sometimes took him by surprise.

Jerusalem, July 16, 1187

The city was flooded with refugees. Some said as many as twenty thousand people had been admitted at the gates in the last fortnight, and there was no end in sight. Sister Adela did not particularly care. An obsession with numbers detracted from the humanity of each individual—and she tried to treat each patient, one at a time, as one of Christ's children.

On her arrival from Nablus, Sister Adela had been called immediately to the Grand Hospitaller, the most senior surviving officer of the Order. He had entrusted her with the command of the two women's wards in the Hospital of Jerusalem. Her predecessor, he explained, had been frail and ailing for some time, and the flood of refugees following Hattin had overwhelmed her. She had taken to her bed and refused any food, dying within three days.

This left Sister Adela with the responsibility for not only the nearly 400 women and 42 sisters she had brought with her from Nablus, but also the Jerusalem women's wards—housing some 300 women with infectious diseases, and another 400 women suffering from non-contagious illnesses and a variety of injuries, along with the more than 200 sisters, both lay and clerical, that made up the female staff of the Hospital in Jerusalem.

The number of patients suffering from broken bones, twisted ankles, burns, and dangerously deep cuts had exploded with the refugee population. As a result, Sister Adela felt compelled to be very strict about who could occupy a bed. Too many women liked to spend a few nights at the hospital for the solid meals they got—and for the break from husbands and children. Under the circumstances, however, she couldn't afford to have women taking up beds if they didn't absolutely need them.

The situation was even worse in the men's wards. There were scores of men who had arrived after harrowing skirmishes with Saracen patrols. The Saracens appeared to be everywhere at once, but Sister Adela supposed that was just because they heard about where they were, not where they weren't. Still, there was little doubt that the roads were becoming increasingly dangerous. Christians were safe only if they had strong walls around them—and not necessarily even then, as the fall of Acre, Toron, and most recently Sidon showed. To be sure, these cities had surrendered to avoid a futile defense that could only end in slaughter, sack, and slavery. By surrendering their cities, the citizens saved their lives, their freedom, and their movable goods, but for what? To be refugees and strangers somewhere else? Where?

Tyre was the only city on the coast of the Kingdom north of Acre that had successfully defied Salah ad-Din—and that was because the Barons of Sidon and Ibelin had brought the fighting men they'd led out of the trap at Hattin there and had taken over command of the defense. An estimated three thousand fighting men and three hundred knights was a credible defense. One could not say the same about Jerusalem, Sister Adela noted.

As in Nablus, Sister Adela was considered an officer of the Hospital, and as such was included in the daily meetings with the Grand Hospitaller. He was a priest, as were the next most senior officers, the Treasurer and the Quartermaster. There was no Knight of the Hospital in all Jerusalem, and the situation of the Knights Templar was worse. The Templars were a fighting order without a large hospital function, and all their senior officers had been with Master de Ridefort. Not one had been seen or heard from since July 4. There were, of course, still Templar garrisons at various castles, but those few knights in command could not possibly leave their posts; their most urgent mission was to hold the castles entrusted them until reinforcements could arrive from the West. That, Sister Adela knew, could take a year or two. Meanwhile, in Jerusalem there was not a single Hospitaller or Templar Knight, nor even a senior sergeant, who could speak with authority and command respect.

So Jerusalem was on its own, under the command of Queen Sibylla and the Patriarch. Not the most confidence-inspiring duo. The former was foolish and egotistical, the latter corrupt and licentious. Neither had the slightest military experience. The leading citizens, the guild masters, and the representatives of the communes of Pisa, Genoa, and Venice had therefore formed an ad hoc committee intent on organizing the defense of Jerusalem, but they were constantly squabbling among themselves, their jealousies spilling over into every debate about command structures, provisioning, and strategy. Sister Adela sighed and wondered if men would ever learn.

Her thoughts were interrupted by the breathless voice of Sister Patricia running between the beds from the entranceway. "Sister Adela! Sister Adela!"

Sister Adela could still remember the day Sister Patricia had arrived at Jaffa from Ireland. Of the five women who'd come ashore that day, she alone had shown a genuine vocation for looking after the sick. She was intelligent and diligent, and indifferent to hardship without reveling in it. She had the kind of practical faith in God that did not entail constant prayer and undue penance. Best of all, Sister Patricia was the kind of sister who spread cheer and optimism rather than fear and doubt. This display of distress was quite out of character and required a sharp rebuke.

"Shhh!" Sister Adela admonished sharply, "and stop running! You are disturbing the patients and spreading alarm!"

"Sister Adela," Sister Patricia repeated breathlessly as she slowed her pace and stopped before her superior. "A couple has just arrived with almost a hundred children!"

"A hundred children?" Sister Adela asked in obvious disbelief.

"Abandoned children! They must have been in an orphanage, but they had been left without any oversight or food—locked in a cellar—apparently for days."

"Dear God," Sister Adela whispered. "Take me to them."

Sister Patricia led the way out of the ward and across the cobbled courtyard to the southern entrance of the hospital complex. Here lay brothers screened all people seeking admittance, sending them one way or another based on the nature of their needs. As Sister Adela approached, the lay brothers gestured to an elderly couple just inside the door. The old woman was holding an infant far too young to be her own, while the man had a little boy by the hand.

"I am the Head Sister," Sister Adela introduced herself, Patricia at her heels.

"God bless you, sister," the man opened. "My name is Nicolas, and this is my wife Anne. I owned a cooperage near Qasr, east of the Dead Sea. On our way to seek refuge here, we came upon these children—they were locked in a cellar, with no one looking after them. They would all have starved to death, if we hadn't freed them!" As he spoke he opened the door to the street and gestured.

Sister Adela gasped. Sister Patricia had not been exaggerating. Clustered in the street outside, blocking the road entirely, were scores and scores of children. They were filthy, ragged, bony, and too dazed and exhausted to do more than stare at her. Children that looked no more than seven or eight were holding smaller children, while half the children seemed to be clinging to crutches. They had to be from an orphanage, but what had become of the nuns and lay sisters who should have been looking after them?

Her eyes scanned the pitiful herd of children again, and confirmed her fears. Not one of them was older than ten or eleven. In all probability, Saracen slavers had taken away the nuns and any girl old enough for a harem or brothel and any boy old enough to work, but left the rest to their fate.

Nicolas was still speaking. "They must have been locked up for at least a day, and the compound had been plundered, too. All the storerooms had been broken open, the chests and cupboards smashed, even the bedding stripped off the beds."

Sister Adela nodded knowingly. "Thank you both for your Christian charity and for bringing them to us. We will look after them from now on."

As the couple departed, Sister Adela turned to Sister Patricia. "We're going to have to find someplace to put these children, but first they need to been cleaned up and fed."

Sister Patricia gazed at her superior in despair. "We're already bursting at the seams. How can we look after a hundred orphans as well?"

"Would you leave them in the streets, sister?" Sister Adela snapped back. "Go at once to the Grand Hospitaller and tell him what we have here!" Sister Adela ordered, before turning and gesturing for the children to come inside.

As they shuffled past, Adela looked for one who looked older, brighter, or more alert than the others. Her eyes settled on a girl carrying an infant in her arms. "Child! Come here! What is your name?"

The girl stopped and stared at her, but did not come closer. Adela was beginning to think she either didn't understand or was too frightened to speak when she at last announced, "Mary."

Sister Adela sighed with relief. "Come here!" she ordered again, and the girl shuffled forward to stand before her warily. Sister Adela bent down to ask her gently but firmly, "Mary, can you tell me what happened?"

"Men killed Peter, Father Francis, Cook, and Mother Beatrice, and the other sisters ran away," Mary told Sister Adela solemnly.

"Ran away?" Sister Adela asked, scandalized.

Mary nodded solemnly. "The men chased them and they ran away."

Telling herself not to judge women facing rape and slavery, Adela focused on the issue at hand: "Did the Saracens harm you or the other children?"

Mary shook her head. "Not Saracens. Franks."

"I know you're Franks, but the Saracens, the men who—who killed your priest and frightened the sisters away, did they harm you or any of the other children?"

"They *weren't* Saracen!" Mary insisted. "They were *Franks*! That's why Peter let them in—but then they killed him and Cook and robbed us of everything."

Sister Adela felt the hand of fear clutch at her heart and her blood ran cold as she realized that, with the King and all his nobles in captivity, law and order was breaking down across the Kingdom.

Jerusalem, July 18, 1187

"The Patriarch, madame," said the pageboy solemnly, "has sent a priest requesting an audience."

Maria Zoë was in the loge of the Ibelin palace with Isabella and Eschiva. Like the rest of Jerusalem, the Ibelin palace was overflowing with residents. In addition to the households from both Nablus and Ibelin, Maria Zoë had taken in Isabella and Eschiva (with their women, servants, and children), as well as her sister-in-law Eloise, who had arrived in a near-hysterical state from Kerak—although (in Maria Zoë's opinion) she would have been much safer there. The horses were doubling up in stalls, and everyone was sharing beds. Isabella shared her mother's bed, and Eschiva and Eloise slept on pallets in the same room. Not only was there no privacy anywhere, but most rooms were stifling in this season. The loge was thus the most comfortable place in the entire palace, and Maria Zoë had retreated here to get a little respite from all the pressing problems of the household and the cacophony of excited children, quarrelsome servants, and frightened women.

"Heraclius?" Maria Zoë answered the page in astonishment.

"The Patriarch," the boy repeated, uncomfortable with calling such an exalted personage by his first name.

"Indeed, and there is he is," Isabella exclaimed, getting to her feet to see better over the railing of the loge. She had rightly discerned that the commotion at the corner of the Street of the Holy Sepulcher and the Street of Spain could be attributed to a litter carried between two horses and surrounded by liveried servants. Sitting in the litter was the Patriarch of Jerusalem in his full ecclesiastical regalia, white with gold embroidery. Inevitably, many of the people in the streets stopped to gawk or to beg a blessing.

"What can he possibly want of me?" Maria Zoë asked rhetorically before telling the page she would receive the Patriarch here, on the loge. "Fetch a large armed chair for him," she added.

As soon as the page was gone, Eschiva looked up from her embroidery. "Maybe he has word of our husbands. The Sultan might send his ransom demands to the Patriarch."

"Why would he do that?" Maria Zoë countered, anxious to protect Eschiva and Isabella from false hopes. Although rumors consistently reported that Aimery de Lusignan had been taken captive beside his brother the King, the reports about Humphrey de Toron had been far more contradictory. Eschiva worried where she was to find a ransom for Aimery, with no lands of her own and no access to the royal treasury unless Guy ordered his Chancellor to pay for his brother; Isabella, on the other hand, spent much of her time simply praying for Humphrey's life. She had chewed her fingernails to the quick, and the dark circles under her eyes testified to her sleeplessness.

Maria Zoë didn't need a mirror to know she looked little better than Isabella. To be sure, there was no longer any doubt about Balian's survival. With respect bordering on awe, men had reported how he'd preserved the fighting capabilities of his cavalry while the Templars wasted their strength and were whittled down to insignificance. They spoke, too, of the force of his final charge, which had struck at a point where the infantry could join him—not like Tripoli's earlier charge, which had been too far away from the infantry for them to take advantage of the breakthrough. Last but not least, the survivors spoke with wonder of how Ibelin had then rallied them and led them to safety. To hear these men tell it, the Lord of Ibelin was the only baron in Jerusalem who had retained not only his freedom, but his honor, after Hattin.

But while it was certain that Balian lived, it was equally certain that he was *ipso facto* in command of the remnants of the fighting forces of the Kingdom. He was *de facto* Constable and Marshal and Regent all in one. The defense of the realm, such as it was, fell automatically to him. Not only was that a crushing burden—it was fraught with danger.

The commotion in the street had reached the entrance to the Ibelin palace, and some of Maria Zoë's servants went out into the street to clear a way for the Patriarch through the importunate crowd. A moment later, the ladies on the loge could hear a dull thud as the wooden gates fell shut, and the noise in the street started to subside.

Several moments later, the Patriarch was escorted out onto the loge, two boys lugging a heavy armed chair in his wake.

The women dutifully got to their feet and sank down into deep curtsies out of respect for his office. Heraclius held out his ring to each in turn, ending with Maria Zoë. "Your grace," he addressed her, with upturned lips that might have been intended as a smile.

"Your eminence," she answered without the pretense of a smile, although she indicated the chair with carved arms and Saracen cushions that the pages had manhandled into a position beside her own.

Heraclius bowed his head in thanks and sank into the chair. He was still a handsome man, Maria Zoë noted, remembering that day a dozen years ago when she had seen him for the first time across a crowded room at the Royal Palace. Aimery de Lusignan had pointed him out, and in a low voice informed her that he was the lover of the Queen Mother, Agnes de Courtenay. She had been shocked by his morals, but remembered thinking he was as lovely as an angel, with blond locks, bright blue eyes, and perfectly regular features. The blond hair was turning gray and his jowls were squarer, though not really fat, but his eyes were still a bright blue—and his morals as bad as ever.

"Madame," the Patriarch started, clearing his throat a little nervously before plunging ahead, with a smile that seemed (at least in Maria Zoë's jaded eyes) all too practiced. He must have used this smile effectively on many women, she found herself thinking cynically. "We have seen far too little of you."

"We?" she asked back with raised eyebrows. "Just who do you mean by 'we,' monsieur?"

"Well, myself, for one—and, ah, Jerusalem."

"Jerusalem," Maria Zoë echoed with an indecipherable expression. Until she had sought refuge here three weeks ago, Maria Zoë had not set foot in Jerusalem since the usurpation of Sibylla and Guy.

"Yes, Jerusalem," the Patriarch repeated. "I am told that we now have as many refugees in the city as residents—forty thousand men, women, and children—and still they come, daily and from every part of the Kingdom. Soon we will have nowhere left to put them and insufficient food to feed them."

Maria Zoë raised her eyebrows. "Then I suggest you discuss the situation with the Queen."

Heraclius cleared his throat and squirmed uncomfortably in his chair, while Eschiva and Isabella exchanged an amused glance. There was still no love lost between Maria Zoë and Sibylla.

"The Queen, my lady—the Queen is in considerable distress."

"Is she ill?" Maria Zoë almost sounded hopeful.

"In a manner of speaking, yes. She is in great distress over—over what has happened, and particularly the uncertainty of her husband's fate."

"Her husband is alive and well. She has nothing to worry about—unlike my daughter Isabella. We are not even sure Humphrey de Toron is still among the living."

"Ah, on that point at least I can offer you reassurance." The Patriarch looked distinctly relieved to have some good news to share. "I have had word from Stephanie de Milly that the Sultan has opened negotiations with her for the release of her son."

Isabella choked down an exclamation and half reared out of her seat. Her mother and the Patriarch turned to look at her. The Patriarch was astonished by her expression, which did not look relieved and grateful, as one would have expected, while Maria Zoë cast her a warning look. Isabella pressed her lips together furiously while her mother responded graciously, "That is indeed welcome news, your eminence. We will say Mass in thanks before dinner. Can we expect the Lord of Toron to rejoin his wife anytime soon?"

"Ah, um, yes," Heraclius replied, "yes, I think you can look forward to greeting the Lord of Toron before All Saints," he guessed, "which is more than can be said for the King," he brought the conversation back.

"Yes, a king who loses his entire kingdom is in an awkward situation indeed. Who, after all, should pay his ransom, if the entire royal domain has been overrun by the enemy?" Maria Zoë noted acidly.

"That's not entirely true, madame," Heraclius pointed out, licking his lips. "Jerusalem has not yet fallen, nor Tyre, nor Jaffa, nor Ascalon, not to mention many of the most important fortresses—Safed, Kerak, Gaza, and Montfort."

Maria Zoë stared at the Patriarch for a few seconds and then pointedly asked, "Tell me, your eminence, just how does the Queen intend to defend Jerusalem? To my knowledge, there is not a single Hospitaller or Templar knight left in the city, while the garrison consists of old men and untried boys."

"My lady," he licked his lips, "Madame, the Queen—the Queen—is not in a state to organize the defense of Jerusalem. She is, as I said, distressed over her husband's fate, and too agitated and distracted to deal with—with other matters."

"The *Queen* of Jerusalem is more concerned about her miserable husband than her Kingdom?" Maria Zoë asked pointedly, with a glance at Isabella.

"Yes, my lady, I'm afraid that's the case." The Patriarch had the decency to look embarrassed.

Maria Zoë let him stew in his own juice for a few seconds before remarking in a low voice, "Agnes de Courtenay must be turning over in her grave." Whatever else Maria Zoë thought of her late hated rival, she had not been the kind of woman to collapse into self-pity when a crisis was at hand. "And what do you want of me, your eminence?" she asked bluntly.

"My lady, I thought—you are a Dowager Queen. You have authority. You enjoy the respect of the population. Now, more than ever, since your husband successfully escaped Hattin. I thought—I thought—perhaps you would be willing to assist me. We have to do something about the sanitation and the water before the wells are contaminated and disease breaks out. We are nearly sinking under refuse already!"

"Does the Queen know you are here?" Maria Zoë asked sharply.

"I—no. There was no point in telling her. She can talk of nothing but Guy and how he must need her now. Every time I see her, she begs me to ask the Sultan to give her permission to join her husband."

"*In captivity*?" Maria Zoë could hardly believe her ears. "The anointed Queen of Jerusalem would give up her own freedom and put herself in enemy hands just to be with her husband?" She couldn't fathom it. How could anyone—even a stupid goose like Sibylla—take so little consideration of her status, her dignity, and her symbolic importance to the Kingdom?

The Patriarch sighed and looked down at his hands. "I made a grave mistake, my lady. I know that now. I should not have crowned Sibylla queen. I pray every day for forgiveness, my lady. Believe me!" He looked up and met her eyes, his own full of pathos. "I am in hell every day, every minute, because of what I did."

Maria Zoë nodded. No doubt Heraclius did regret his role in crowning and anointing Sibylla and Guy, but not because he regretted the power games he had played at the time. His regret came from feeling overwhelmed by the current situation—and terror for his life. As he watched the city fill up with refugees it would soon be unable to house and feed, he was starting to recognize that he did not have a clue about how to defend Jerusalem. He was beginning to realize that they might soon be dead or enslaved.

"I will think about what you have said," Maria Zoë told the Patriarch—although she knew perfectly well that unlike Sibylla, she would not flee from her responsibilities. There was a great deal that could be done to put Jerusalem on a better footing, at least with respect to sanitation and food. She would contact Sister Adela at the Hospital to discuss options, and put Sir Constantine in command of the defenses; some of the Latins would resent his leadership, no doubt, but there were many Greek and Armenian Christians in the city who would welcome him. Most sensible men would welcome *any* kind of leadership!

Maria Zoë held out her hand in dismissal, and the Patriarch got to his feet and bowed to her. "I will await your answer anxiously, my lady," he assured her, but his expression suggested he had seen through her. His smile was both sincere and touched with relief.

Maria Zoë nodded. She saw him to the door into the interior, where he bowed to her a last time and then withdrew.

As she turned around, Isabella pounced. "How *dare* the Sultan send to Humphrey's mother rather than me? How dare he!"

"Hush, sweetheart," Maria Zoë answered, crossing to her daughter to take her in her arms.

But Isabella, at fifteen, was beyond being coddled by her mother. "I'm his *wife*! The Sultan should have asked *me* for his ransom!"

"And what do you have to give?" Maria Zoë asked wearily, dropping her arms in resignation.

"I don't know. Our income was from Acre, and it's fallen. But there must be some way to raise a ransom! What does Stephanie de Milly have that I don't have?"

"Kerak."

"What?"

"Kerak. She holds Kerak—and Salah ad-Din wants that castle as much—if not more—than he wants Jerusalem itself."

Isabella stared at her mother in horror. "Stephanie de Milly would *never* surrender Kerak for Humphrey. She doesn't love Humphrey at all! She'd rather let him rot in a dungeon for the rest of his life than surrender Kerak!"

"But she's probably quite happy to play Salah ad-Din along for a while—long enough for her to restock supplies and build up defenses. In her shoes, I would denude every other castle I have to concentrate my entire fighting force—every able-bodied man left in her barony—at Kerak. And then I'd prepare to sit out a siege so long that Salah ad-Din—or at least his troops—loses patience." Secretly, Maria Zoë would have far preferred to be behind the powerful, nearly unassailable walls of Kerak than here in Jerusalem.

"But then Humphrey will remain in captivity!" Isabella pointed out, tears in her eyes.

Maria Zoë opened her hands in a gesture of helplessness.

Isabella stared at her, torn between fury at her apparent indifference and despair at the sheer logic of what she was saying. "It's not fair!" she burst out at last. "Humphrey doesn't deserve to rot in a dungeon!"

"I daresay few of the men rotting unshriven and unburied on the field of Hattin deserved *their* fate, either," Maria Zoë reminded her daughter.

It was Eschiva who broke the tension. She rose and slipped her arms around Isabella, holding her close as she murmured, "At least our husbands are together, Isabella. And they say Salah ad-Din can be a gracious host when he wants to be."

July 20, 1187
Sultan Salah ad-Din's Camp before Tyre

The Sultan rode back into the camp just as the muezzin started calling for prayers. He dismounted and at once threw himself down on his prayer rug. When prayers finished, a slave held out a silver bowl for him to wash his hands. He dipped his hands into the cool water and the scent of roses wafted up to him, for a moment obliterating the less pleasant scents of an army camp. He rubbed his hands together in the bowl and then removed them, shook off the drops, and dried them on a linen towel provided by another slave. When he was finished, he took the damp towel and rubbed it over his face to remove the worst of the sweat and dust. Then he shoved the towel at the slave and turned to sit cross-legged opposite his nephew Farrukh-Shah, who had been patiently awaiting him in his tent.

"So?" he asked. "Are the troops grumbling yet?"

"No, not yet. You've given them enough loot to forget the harvest for a little while longer."

"Acre, Sidon, Beirut, Gibelet, and Jaffa ought, indeed, to be enough," Salah ad-Din noted a little sarcastically.

His nephew shrugged. "It has been a great triumph for Believers, uncle, Allah be praised." They bowed their heads in respect.

"Tyre has been reinforced," Salah ad-Din noted with a sour twist to his lips. "Perhaps I should have stayed to reduce it immediately."

"It still would have been reinforced," Farrukh-Shah reminded him. "The reinforcements came by sea."

"Who is this Conrad de Montferrat?"

"The son of the Marquis de Montferrat, the old man whom we hold prisoner, and the younger brother of the man who was married to their queen before she was seduced by Guy de Lusignan."

"It is fitting that people who allow their women shameless liberty be punished by Allah, praise to his name, through the lust of a lewd woman. It was the slut's lust for Lusignan that has delivered the Kingdom of Jerusalem to us. The Baron of Ramla would not have fallen into my trap at Hattin."

"No, our spies say his brother argued vehemently against it."

"Ibn Barzan."

"Yes."

"He escaped the field; do we know where he is now?"

"Yes. He is awaiting your pleasure."

"What do you mean?"

"He rode into the camp under a flag of truce while you were away, and requested an audience."

"Why didn't you tell me?" Salah ad-Din reproached his nephew.

Farrukh-Shah smiled. "You were keen to speak of other things."

"Where is he?"

"In my tent."

"Do you know what he wants?"

"No," Farrukh-Shah admitted, before adding with a cynical smile, "but somehow I do not think it is to accept the True Faith."

His uncle laughed. "No, I do not think that, either. Go fetch him. We have much to talk about."

Farrukh-Shah bowed his head in agreement and got to his feet. Behind him, the Sultan clapped his hands and ordered his body slave to bring him a clean turban and tunic.

When Ibelin was brought into the tent by Farrukh-Shah, Salah ad-Din looked immaculate, jewels glinting on his fingers and his turban.

By contrast, the Baron of Ibelin definitely looked the worse for wear. His surcoat had been cleaned and ironed, but it was also darned in several places. Likewise, his splendid chain mail with the bronze trim had been hastily repaired with wire to bind together the cuts sliced in it at Hattin. The number of places where such repairs had been required testified to how hotly he had fought. Salah ad-Din was not certain, but he thought Ibelin also looked older than the last time they had met. He could not remember the streak of gray that grew out of his right sideburn and that he wore tucked behind his ear.

For all that, the Baron of Ibelin was not broken. He bowed formally to the Sultan, but when he righted himself he stood straight and yet at ease, his exceptional height giving him a certain sovereignty.

"So we meet again," the Sultan opened, gesturing for Ibelin to sit where Farrukh-Shah had sat only moments earlier. Ibelin dutifully folded up his legs to sit cross-legged on the floor opposite the Sultan. The latter clapped his hands and iced water was brought to Ibelin, who took it with a faint smile that suggested he had somehow heard the story about the ice water offered Guy de Lusignan—but not Reynald de Châtillon—after the Battle of Hattin.

The Sultan considered his guest with his head tilted slightly to one side. "It pleases me to have you as my guest," he remarked, adding, "I had hoped it would be sooner."

Ibelin smiled faintly. "I cannot honestly say I am sorry to disappoint you."

Salah ad-Din threw back his head and laughed before conceding, "Well said. Tell me one thing, though. When you charged, did you truly intend to kill me?"

"If I could have reached you with my sword, absolutely—even if it cost me my life, as it surely would have."

"Why?"

"Because then your army would have collapsed in confusion—at least long enough for more of my compatriots to escape. Furthermore, the succession squabbles would have kept your empire preoccupied with itself long enough for us to recover. At least there was a chance of that happening. It was well worth the risk."

"Um," the Sultan answered noncommittally before pointing out, "the death of Guy de Lusignan, on the other hand, would have been more to your advantage than mine."

Ibelin could not deny it, but he hesitated to confirm it, so he held his tongue. After waiting a few seconds for an answer, Salah ad-Din moved on. "You asked for this audience. What can I do for you?"

"I have heard rumors that you have requested the surrender of Jerusalem."

Salah ad-Din raised his eyebrows. "Does that surprise you?"

"No," Ibelin admitted. "The rumors say that you offered very generous terms."

"And does *that* surprise you?" Salah ad-Din asked again, evidently amused.

"No," Ibelin admitted a second time.

"I do not want to see the holy sites damaged," the Sultan explained voluntarily. "Trebuchets and mangonels are far from accurate weapons. Even if I tried to avoid it, damage might occur to the Dome of the Rock or the Al-Aqsa mosque."

"Indeed," Ibelin concurred.

"Unfortunately," Salah ad-Din continued, frowning, the annoyance in his voice too intense to be concealed, "these fools who claimed to represent Jerusalem, a collection of tradesmen and churchmen," the Sultan dismissed them in disgust, "could not see reason! They would not think of surrender, although they have no chance of defending the city against my army. Fools and fanatics!" he spat out furiously.

"Fanatics are always dangerous," Ibelin agreed cautiously.

Salah ad-Din looked over at him with sudden interest. "Do you think you could bring them to reason?" he asked hopefully, suddenly seeing a chance to use Ibn Barzan to get what he wanted: the intact surrender of Jerusalem.

"What exactly did they say to your offer of safe-conduct out of the city?" Ibelin asked back.

"They said they would never surrender the city where Christ had shed his blood for them! They said if they did, they would be damned for eternity. Or some such nonsense." He dismissed the argument contemptuously.

Ibelin smiled wanly and, shaking his head, told the Sultan, "In that case—no, I will not be able to change their minds."

"Why not?" the Sultan asked, annoyed. He was very angry about the refusal of the Franks to surrender Jerusalem, and he liked the idea of Ibn Barzan delivering it to him.

"If that was their answer," Ibelin explained simply, "then they were not bargaining with you. They are preparing for martyrdom."

"Martyrdom!" Salah ad-Din scoffed. His tone of voice was colored by his utter conviction that beyond death, no Christian could ever find anything but hell. Ibelin said nothing and waited for the Sultan to calm down. Salah ad-Din narrowed his eyes. "I have vowed to kill them all—just as you Franks killed all the inhabitants a hundred years ago."

"We didn't kill all the inhabitants," Ibelin countered. "The Count of Toulouse saved many, and others survived as well—after the initial blood lust had slacked." They stared at one another, neither willing to back down on this point. Finally Ibelin continued, "I do not think you will besmirch your name by insisting on the slaughter of women, children, and old people—after an example has been made, of course."

"We will see." Salah ad-Din was not willing to let any hint of possible mercy get into the enemy camp—at least not yet. "Why are you here, my lord? I do not think it was just to pass the time of day with me." Salah ad-Din smiled courteously, but he clearly wanted Ibelin to come to the point.

"I wish permission—a safe-conduct—to travel to Jerusalem and bring my wife and family out—*before* you lay siege to it."

"Ah." Salah ad-Din considered his adversary. He honestly could not understand him. This man was undoubtedly intelligent and courageous, and at no previous time had he been as powerful as now. He was virtually King of Jerusalem. The Count of Tripoli had scuttled back to Tripoli, by all accounts a broken man. Edessa had taken his treasure and run to safety in Antioch. Sidon had sent word secretly that the great victories of the Sultan's armies had convinced him that God favored Islam. He admitted that Christianity was "obsolete" and asked for instruction in the words of the Prophet. This Conrad de Montferrat was of good family, but the Sultan's spies suggested he had fled Constantinople in fear for his life after some mysterious falling-out with the Emperor; he had neither followers nor titles here in Palestine. Ibn Barzan was the only man with any credibility, standing and authority in the entire Kingdom. And here he was, asking a favor of his enemy so he could secure his wife? Ridiculous. Wives were replaceable commodities and largely interchangeable. One was very much like another—at least, good, obedient wives were.

Then he remembered something. "You are married to the Dowager Queen, are you not?"

"Yes."

Salah ad-Din thought about that. The Dowager Queen was a Greek princess, and he was anxious to remain on good terms with the Emperor in Constantinople. The Greeks, like the Arabs and Kurds, often killed their own brothers, uncles, and cousins in their power struggles, but they did not take kindly to *other* people killing their kinsmen. Letting a princess of the Eastern Roman Empire come to harm would not be politic, particularly if it was so easy to prevent. "All right," he decided. "I will give you a safe-conduct to go to Jerusalem and remove your wife and family, under the following conditions: that you go unarmed and with no armed men in your train, and that you remain only a single night."

"I accept those terms, your grace, and give you my word before Christ the Savior that I will uphold them." Ibelin answered so rapidly and fervently that the Sultan sensed he had not expected to be successful. He was anxious to accept these terms before the Sultan changed his mind.

Salah ad-Din smiled and rose to his feet. "Go with my nephew, who will provide you with more substantial refreshment, while I have a scribe prepare the safe-conduct. I will also send a troop of my bodyguard to bring you within sight of Jerusalem and await you there."

Ibelin bowed his head and smiled wryly. The escort would be very valuable getting him through the territory between Tyre and Jerusalem, as without them he might be dead long before someone bothered to read the safe-conduct. At the same time, the escort was also a way of reminding him that he moved at the Sultan's pleasure—and that any violation of the terms of the agreement would be reported or punished immediately.

But that didn't worry Balian. He had no intention of breaking the agreement.

Chapter 20

Jerusalem, July 24, 1187

JOHN HAD ESCAPED THE TEDIUM OF the classroom, the prattle of his siblings, and the droning of Father Angelus for the kitchens. It wasn't that he was hungry—but it was in the kitchens that he learned the most about what was *really* going on. His mother and aunts, his tutors, and even the servants all wanted to "protect" him by not telling him what was happening. They treated him like a baby and kept telling him "everything will be all right," when obviously it wasn't!

Nablus, Ibelin, Ramla, and Mirabel had all fallen. Everything he had ever known as home was overrun by the enemy. Salah ad-Din's forces controlled the countryside all around Jerusalem, and there were no knights left in the city. John understood perfectly that that meant there was no way they could defend themselves. He and his siblings, his mother, his aunts and tutors and servants—they were all trapped within the city, with no hope of relief.

What was more, John knew what happened to women and children when a city was sacked. They were rounded up and sold as slaves. The women would be violated and ravished—like Beth had been—and the children would be made to work, just like the kitchen boys turning the spit before the fire or the boys that scrubbed out the latrines. John shuddered—and couldn't stop thinking about it.

He tried to picture himself defending his sisters and little brother. He imagined saying, "My father is Balian d'Ibelin! And—" And what? They would laugh at him, because his father could not rescue him. His father could not even buy his freedom, because his father had nothing. With the loss of Ibelin, Ramla, Mirabel, and Nablus, they had lost all their land and income. Of course his mother and Master Shoreham had managed to bring most of their movable treasure here, but when Jerusalem fell that would all be seized as plunder by the Saracens.

"Master John!" It was the stern voice of Father Michael. John jumped and then looked over his shoulder with an expression of guilt mixed with rebelliousness on his face. "You're supposed to be at your lessons, young man!" Father Michael admonished.

"What's the point of learning Greek when the only language I'm going to need in the future is Arabic?" John flung furiously at Father Michael, his pent-up terror erupting in defiance.

Father Michael was taken aback for a second, but then reproached himself. John wasn't a fool, and an eight-year-old could reason. The tutor went down on his heels to be at John's eye level and looked him squarely in the face. "It is your Greek blood that might just save you. Your mother's cousin is Emperor of the Greeks." He was stretching the point somewhat—the Emperor Isaac II Angelus was only distantly related to Maria Zoë, but for John's sake he was willing to exaggerate at little. He continued, "And he has made a truce with Salah ad-Din."

John just stared at him, his lips a grim, defiant line.

Father Michael laid a hand on his shoulder and spoke in a gentler voice. "John, what good does it do to get in people's way here?" They were very much underfoot at the moment, for dinner was over and the serving boys were trying to clean up and put things away. Several women were soaking rags in warm, sudsy water to wipe down the tables, while other servants were preparing to sweep out the hall. The cooks were busy sorting out the leftovers into things for reuse (such as the wine), alms for the poor, and bones for the dogs. Just outside the kitchen door, the usual crowd of beggars was waiting in the street for alms. They seemed louder than usual, even more aggressive.

Someone was shouting, "Ibelin! Ibelin!"—as if that would get them more food or fed faster, Father Michael noted with irritation.

Then the noise spilled out of the street into the kitchen itself when one of the scullery servants started squawking in a high-pitched voice: "A rider with the banner of Ibelin is approaching St. Stephen's Gate."

"A rider?"

"It must be a ruse!"

"There's nothing but Saracens north of us!"

"It's the Ibelin banner! Clear as day!"

"How many riders?"

"Just two."

"That's madness! If Ibelin were coming to our relief, he'd bring his whole three thousand men."

"I tell you," the scullion insisted. "They've seen it!"

John ducked down and darted for the door while the others were distracted. He dodged past the cook and the excited scullion and was outside before Michael could stop him.

In the street the crowd was more agitated than the scullion. Everyone was talking at once. "I told you he'd come!" someone kept repeating. Other people were asking more skeptically how he could have gotten through the enemy alone, and while holding his banner upright on a lance. Others were sure it was a trick. "If we open the gates to this rider, they'll flood in!"

"How? He's alone, with just one squire."

A rider forced his way through the crowd, calling for them to make way. "I have a message for the Dowager Queen!" the man kept shouting. But they blocked his way, surrounding his horse and demanding his news.

"The Baron of Ibelin is approaching! Let me in!"

The crowd erupted into even more agitated discussion, but they let the rider continue to the main entrance, where he jumped down and disappeared inside. John was too far away to follow. Instead, he was trapped with the rest of the crowd, and from farther up the street the shouting had grown much louder. More: the shouting had turned to cheering. They were still shouting "Ibelin!" but it had become a chant. "Ib-lin! Ib-lin! Ib-lin!"

More people poured out of the houses and shops lining the street and crowded the balconies and the rooftops, trying to see what was going on. The cheers were coming nearer, growing louder. Everyone seemed to be shouting and waving, and John couldn't see for all the people ahead of him. He pushed and squeezed, stamping on people's feet and clawing his way forward, until he fought his way clear to the front. He looked up the street and could just make out two mounted men. The second held upright a lance with the banner of Ibelin, but John had eyes only for the lead rider: it *was* his father!

John understood at once. His father had come to rescue them!

John wanted to run to him, but the crowds stood in his way. He shouted his father's name and jumped up and down, but he was just one small child in a city awash with refugees and desperate residents. They all stood between him and his father: beggars and shopkeepers, refugees and priests, rich merchants and nuns who didn't normally rub shoulders with the poor.

His father, meanwhile, was so completely surrounded by people that he was unable to advance another step. Scores of hands held his bridle so that the faithful Centurion fretted and tried to shake them off, while people clung to his father's stirrups and Centurion's trapper as well.

John could not hear what they were saying, but he understood their gestures. They did not understand that his father had come only to rescue his wife and children. They saw in the lord of Ibelin a nobleman, an experienced battle commander, the only lord to have fought his way out of the encirclement of Hattin with honor—not a father and husband. They saw him as the savior of Jerusalem itself.

That made John angry and frightened—because if his father stayed to defend Jerusalem, then he, his mother, his sisters, and his little brother would not be able to escape. His father had to say "no" to the others! He had to ignore them, and instead sweep John up onto his saddle and ride with him out of the city to safety.

John shouted and jumped up and down, trying to make himself seen and heard, until tears of frustration ran down his face. But it did no good.

Countless glass lanterns burned at the Patriarch's palace, and the massive candles marked to measure the hours were burning, too. The gold halos around the Virgin Mary's and saints' heads on the wall murals caught the light and seemed to glow in the semi-darkness. When the candlelight wavered in the night air, the life-sized figures appeared to move, as if the saints and the Mother of God were taking part in the council. From outside came the restless murmurs of a crowd that would not disperse.

"I will absolve you of your oath!" declared Heraclius with a dramatic gesture. Light from the candles and lamps glinted off the rings on his fingers. "What is an oath to a Saracen anyway?" he asked rhetorically. "Worthless! Meaningless! You owe it to Christ to remain here and take command!"

"Amen!" echoed the representatives of the guilds and merchant companies, crossing themselves emphatically.

The only one in the room who appeared to have the slightest sympathy for Ibelin's situation was the Grand Hospitaller. The Hospitaller priest met Balian's eyes with a look of great sorrow and shook his head to say he could not help him.

"There are more than sixty thousand people in this city, my lord!" the Pisan representative pointed out. "You cannot just abandon us!"

"Salah ad-Din offered you generous terms," Ibelin reminded him.

The men around the table looked baffled, and Heraclius answered for them:

"You can't be serious! How can we surrender Jerusalem? This is the holiest site in Christendom! You know what happened when the Muslims controlled it. They razed the Church of the Holy Sepulcher. They slaughtered all the monks and priests in the city!" As he spoke, the Greek, Armenian, and Syrian Orthodox bishops nodded their heads solemnly.

"And what does Queen Sibylla say?" Ibelin asked, his eyes sweeping the room in a gesture to draw attention to her absence.

"She says she will not interfere. She will respect whatever decision we make," Heraclius answered. "She has asked to be allowed to join her husband."

Ibelin knew this already from Maria Zoë, so it did not surprise him, but he could not repress a snort of contempt—mostly for Heraclius' sake.

"You should welcome the Queen's attitude, my lord," Heraclius countered. "She has abdicated her role to you—and so do I. I hereby publicly and irrevocably recognize you as the sole and supreme commander for the defense of Jerusalem."

"I have not accepted that command," Ibelin retorted sharply. He did not like being forced into a corner.

"My lord." It was an Armenian merchant who spoke. "We will all die one day. Do you want to face Our Lord as the man who abandoned the site of His passion and left it to desecration?"

Ibelin stared at the man.

"We would all rather die a martyr's death than do that," announced the master of the Furrier's Guild. He was a burly man with a gruff voice.

"And your wives and children?" Ibelin asked back.

"We have agreed among ourselves to kill them rather than allow them to be taken away into shameful slavery."

"You would repeat Masada?" Ibelin asked, his eyes sweeping around the table, making eye contact with one after another. They met his eyes, some defiant, some troubled, but all nodded one after another until Ibelin's eyes came to the master of the Potter's Guild.

This gray-haired master asked in a belligerently reproachful tone, "Do you love Christ less than the Jews loved their Ark of the Covenant?"

Ibelin didn't answer the question. It was obvious that these men were more than disappointed—they were shocked to discover that Ibelin had not come to lead their futile defense of Jerusalem.

Balian considered himself a devout man, but he had never seen himself in the role of martyr. He most certainly could not embrace the idea of killing Maria Zoë, Isabella, and his four innocent children. It was one thing to lead a near-suicidal charge of fighting men; it was something else again to turn his weapons against those he loved. He lacked that kind of fanaticism. "You are trying to impose upon me the decision you took when you turned down Salah ad-Din's generous terms to surrender in exchange for your lives and property. *I* did not make that decision to sacrifice my family for the sake of martyrdom."

"No, you didn't," the master of the Carpenters' Guild admitted. "But we are begging you to stay and help us now." He looked at Ibelin with large brown eyes over a graying beard. He might have been St. Joseph, Balian found himself thinking involuntarily.

"Just what do you think I can accomplish? If you are prepared to die a martyr's death, what difference does it make if you are well or poorly led? Death is death."

"But we can make *them* bleed a little!" the furrier master declared forcefully, pounding his clenched fist on the oak table to underline his point, and the others nodded—even the Orthodox clerics.

"Maybe we can make it so costly that they give up," a Syrian weapons merchant suggested, his eyes fixed hopefully on Ibelin.

So this was their vain hope, Balian registered, and he shook his head. They needed to get that fairy tale out of their heads. "Salah ad-Din has promised his imams and emirs Jerusalem. He does not care what it costs."

"Then by making it so costly that they regret their own intransigence, we can win a victory even in death," the Grand Hospitaller told them solemnly, speaking for the first time.

"What do you mean?" Ibelin challenged him.

"The army of Jerusalem has been obliterated, and the fighting men left here in Outremer are too few and too weak to defend the Holy Places. But even now, ships are flying on the wind to bring word to Rome, to Paris, to London and Cologne. We are weak, but Christendom is strong. I know my brothers in the West—and the Templars, too—will not accept the loss of the Holy Land. King Henry of England has pledged his support and has already raised a fortune. Friedrich Barbarossa is no less committed to the Holy Land. The Christian kings and lords will come as they came before—and the Plantagenet and Barbarossa are not fickle and foolish like Louis VII. They are both tried and proven fighting men. Such men will regain what Lusignan lost. We can make it easier for them by reminding Salah ad-Din here—at Jerusalem—that he has much to fear from Christian knights! He has forgotten that after Hattin, I think."

"Just how many knights are here?" Ibelin asked dryly, for he knew the answer.

"You and Sir Constantine, I believe," Heraclius admitted.

Ibelin looked at him and then back at the Grand Hospitaller with raised eyebrows.

"So much the better," the Grand Hospitaller answered with a faint smile.

"Then we will teach Salah ad-Din to fear all *Franks*—even Franks who are of common birth and not trained to arms."

"I beg to correct you, my lord," the Armenian spoke up sharply. "We will teach Salah ad-Din to fear *Christians*! It is not the Franks alone who will defend Jerusalem!" He was seconded by the Syrians and Greeks at the table.

The Grand Hospitaller bowed his head to them and conceded, "I stand corrected, my lord of Ibelin. We will teach Salah ad-Din that Christian men are not sheep to be slaughtered, but fierce defenders of their faith."

Ibelin looked around the table at the twenty men assembled, and they gazed back at him expectantly and proudly. Heraclius' fingers were drumming on the table. It surprised Balian that the Patriarch was here. He had not expected the self-indulgent luxury lover to fancy martyrdom.

"I will think about it," Ibelin conceded.

Outside, the crowd had thinned, but it had not dispersed. When Ibelin emerged from the Patriarch's palace, a little cheer went up and many people moved forward to touch him, as if he were a saint or a king, while others called out, "God bless you, my lord!" from the back of the crowd. A grinning boy led Centurion forward, having evidently appointed himself to look after the desterier although Balian had left him tethered. Ibelin automatically reached for his purse to tip the boy, but the boy shook his head. "No need, my lord," he said, and then went around to hold the off stirrup as Ibelin mounted.

As Balian took up the reins, he looked down at the boy. "What's your name, boy?"

"Ravon, my lord."

"Are you from Jerusalem?"

"No, my lord, we're from Bethlehem."

"We? Who is with you?"

"My Mum and Dad and my five brothers and sisters."

"What does your father do?"

"He was the gardener at the Armenian seminary behind the Church of the Nativity, my lord."

Ibelin said no more; he just nodded and nudged Centurion forward. What would happen to the likes of Ravon when Jerusalem fell? Ravon certainly had no say in whether or not the city was defended, but he would pay the price, along with the rest of his family.

It was from here a very short ride home, but Balian could feel the dome of the Holy Sepulcher looming to his right and knew he must go there. He dismounted and, looking back, saw Ravon run forward eagerly to take Centurion from him again. With a smile he turned over his faithful destrier and walked back past the Patriarch's palace to turn into the narrow street, lined with souvenir and trinket shops, that led to the entrance to the Holy Sepulcher.

The courtyard of the church was full of people, but they parted for him, a whisper of awe running through the crowd from those who recognized him to those who did not. He passed through the portal into the church itself. This was lit by candles, and the air was heavy with incense. Immediately ahead of him, against the back side of the choir, were the tombs of the Kings of Jerusalem. Balian paused to kneel before Baldwin IV's tomb. "You were lucky to go when you did," he told his former pupil silently.

"But if I'd lived longer, maybe I would have found a way to get rid of Guy," Baldwin seemed to answer.

"Guy and Ridefort together lost Jerusalem," Balian told his dead friend.

"Jerusalem?" Baldwin asked back. "Guy and Ridefort lost *Hattin.* Jerusalem is still Christian."

"Am I to defend it with just two knights?"

"How many knights did you have at Ascalon?"

"You brought me 376 knights."

"I issued the arrière-ban. Do not underestimate the power of people imbued with faith."

Balian looked up at the effigy on the tomb. It was calm and beautiful, unmarked by the ravages of leprosy; it was not a portrait but a symbol. It was the way Baldwin would have liked to be remembered. "What would you have done if you had survived?" Balian asked silently.

"How can you even ask?" Baldwin reproached him. "When did I ever fail to defend my Kingdom? I would do so from the grave if I could. And you are still my knight, Balian. You were always my lance and my sword. Do not fail me now."

Balian stood and proceeded to the rotunda. Here the crowds were thicker than ever; many people knelt on the flagstone floor, praying fervently. Others were lighting candles before the Grave Chapel, while in the choir several hundred people stood pressed together, following the Mass being read by the canons of the Holy Sepulcher. All twelve canons who had accompanied the True Cross to Hattin had been killed. There could not be more than a dozen left, Balian reckoned. But two of these stood as usual at the entrance to the Grave Chapel, controlling access. They recognized the Baron of Ibelin as he approached, and parted without a word; one even bowed his head.

"I wish to be alone," Ibelin told them as he passed into the chapel. They did not answer, but took up their position before the entrance again, ensuring no one could follow.

Balian descended the steep stairs to the grave itself. The grave was cool, almost chilly, lit only by candles. Balian went down on his knees and bowed his head. He recited the Lord's Prayer. Then he sat back on his heels and considered the grave.

"Thy will be done." It was so easy to say, but he was expected to make decisions and take actions.

Balian did not doubt the divinity of Christ even for an instant—but he knew, too, with what conviction and fervor the Muslims too believed that they were doing God's will. Did they not shout "*God* is great" every time they won a victory over the armies of Christ? He had even been told that they shouted "God is great" while executing the unarmed and bound Templar and Hospitaller prisoners after Hattin.

Balian did not believe it was God's will for helpless men to be gruesomely tortured to death, as had happened in Damascus. He did not believe it was God's will that the Kingdom of Jerusalem had been squandered on a single battlefield because of the poor decisions of a usurper. He did not believe it was God's will that Guy was King of Jerusalem at all. And that was his problem. Men made decisions and took actions that were—all too often—*not* in accordance with His will.

Balian laid himself face down on the cold surface of the grave beside the ledge on which Christ's mortal remains had lain more than a thousand years before. The space was too narrow for him to stretch out his arms to either side, so he cradled his head on them instead, and tried to empty his brain entirely. He was not here to plead, beg, or even ask for anything. He was here to receive the Will of God.

The children had been far too excited to sleep, but Maria Zoë could order Nanny Anne and Fathers Michael and Angelus to put them to bed and keep them there. She could hardly do that with Isabella anymore, however, much less Eschiva and Eloise. The other three women sat together in her chamber, as nervous as condemned criminals awaiting an execution.

Eloise was the most difficult. She had broken down very early in the evening and started pleading, "You can't leave me here! You can't!" She whined when she pleaded, and Maria Zoë found it very hard to be patient with her. She hated whiners, and part of her was convinced that Eloise invited contempt by her very weakness. "You can't leave me here," she whined again; "please take me with you."

"I don't know that I'm leaving," Maria Zoë snapped back—eliciting a simultaneous gasp from Eschiva and Isabella that it would have been comic under other circumstances.

"What do you mean?" Isabella asked.

"You saw the reaction of the crowd! And the summons from the Patriarch. They want and *expect* my lord husband to stay and organize the defense of Jerusalem," Maria Zoë told them bluntly.

"But surely Uncle Balian won't do that!" Eschiva protested, horrified. It had never occurred to her that her uncle might choose to remain in Jerusalem. She had been focused entirely on convincing him that "niece" would surely count as "family," or that she could pass herself off as Maria Zoë's waiting woman.

Isabella, on the other hand, had been worrying about exactly that: that her stepfather might decide to stay. She looked sharply at her mother. "What about the children?" she asked, meaning her half-siblings.

"There are thirty thousand children in Jerusalem, Isabella. Maybe more."

"But Uncle Balian can't save them all!"

"No," Maria Zoë paused, reflecting on whether or not she should be honest, and then admitted, "I doubt very much he can save *any* of them."

"But the Sultan gave him a safe-conduct!" Eloise wailed. "He can take you and his children—all of us—" she included Isabella and Eschiva—"to safety!"

"What sort of man would walk away from this?" Maria Zoë answered, gesturing vaguely toward the window. The shutters were open, and even at this late hour of the night, indistinct voices wafted up from the street below. "Where could we ever go where we could look people in the eye again, if he walks away?

"Besides," she added matter-of-factly, "last night we didn't even dream of him coming. Nothing has changed. We are trapped in this city, and when it falls, we will be at the mercy of our enemies." Maria Zoë looked at the other three women, one after another. "You need to face that fact and not keep hoping for a miracle—from my lord husband or anyone else."

"But what about the *children*?" Eloise wailed again.

"I have to believe that the Sultan will not allow the children—or nephews—of a noble opponent to be mishandled," Maria Zoë told her firmly. She *had* to believe that.

"He vowed to kill us all!" Eloise screamed, her terror turning to hysteria in an instant.

Eschiva at once put an arm around her and shushed her. "Hush. Hush. Tante Marie is right. We have to pray—"

"What good is praying? I prayed and prayed—" Eloise broke down into wailing sobs.

Maria Zoë looked at Isabella. "I do not think anyone will dare harm a princess of Jerusalem."

"Princess of a kingdom that does not exist anymore?" Isabella shot back. "Why should anyone care what I once was?"

"Jerusalem has not yet fallen." It was Balian's voice. The women had been too intent on their own conversation to hear him arrive—because, assuming they would be asleep, he had approached as quietly as possible.

Maria Zoë spun about and looked into his face.

"We need to talk," he told her softly, earnestly, holding out his hand.

"Of course." She took his hand and followed him immediately and without hesitation.

He led her to the rooftop. It was flat and enclosed by a crenelated adobe wall, which also provided a running plaster bench around the perimeter. From here they had a clear view: to the southeast, the Dome of the Rock and beyond it the Templar headquarters in the Temple of Solomon; to the southwest, the dome of the Holy Sepulcher and the smaller dome over the Chapel of Calvary.

"I can't go," Balian told her simply.

"I know." She paused. "That was what I was trying to explain to the others."

"Will the children understand?"

"Don't worry about the children, Balian. I will deal with them."

He smiled faintly, because she had not answered his question, but he did not pursue it. Instead he looked out across the city. The sky was lightening, casting the skyline in silhouette against a murky, gray dawn, and diminishing the power of the torches that still burned in the street below. "Do you know a scribe that can write a fine, educated Arabic? I must send my apologies to the Sultan for breaking my word."

Acre, July 28, 1187

Al-Afdal was indignant. He kept insisting furiously that the Baron of Ibelin had broken his word and deserved "swift retribution." Al-Adil, in contrast, just watched his brother's face carefully, but could see neither anger nor indignation there. While his teenage son fumed and threatened revenge on the "perfidious Ibelin," the Sultan calmly asked for the message Ibelin had sent and reached for a goblet with beautiful enameled edging—spoils taken from the Venetian quarter—to sip lemon-laced ice water as he broke the seal with his thumb.

Al-Adil took the liberty of dismissing the escort commander who had brought he message, and telling al-Afdal to calm down.

"Thank you," Salah ad-Din remarked absently to his brother, without even looking up from Ibelin's message.

Al-Adil went to a carved table inlaid with mother-of-pearl, part of the Sultan's traveling furnishings, and helped himself to a goblet of ice water. When he turned back, his brother had finished reading and was folding the message back together.

"What excuse does he give?" asked Al-Adil, his own disgust for Christian perfidy imperfectly disguised, if under better control than his nephew's.

"That the entire city expected him to stay. He says he did not have any choice."

"That's no excuse—" Al-Afdal started to protest, but his father waved him silent.

"Do you believe him?" Al-Adil asked more perceptively.

"All our spies confirm that the inhabitants went wild with enthusiasm on his arrival," Salah ad-Din reminded his brother. "Only a cur would have slunk away at dawn with his wife and children. Ibelin is a Christian, but he is not a coward, and most certainly not a cur."

"But do you think he planned this? Maybe that story about wanting to remove his wife and children was a ruse to get himself into Jerusalem?" Al-Adil suggested.

Salah ad-Din raised his eyebrows. He hadn't thought about that possibility. He gave it a moment's thought, going over in his memory his conversation with Ibelin at Tyre, then he shook his head. "No, I don't think he intentionally deceived me. He said himself that the inhabitants were preparing for martyrdom. I sincerely believe he wanted to spare his wife and children that fate—although he is willing to accept it for himself. Perhaps even welcomes it. It is hard to say."

"Well, now he will have to watch his family die, or die knowing they will be slaves," Al-Afdal declared emphatically and with obvious satisfaction.

"Hmm," Salah ad-Din answered ambiguously, looking into the goblet as if he were searching for something.

Al-Adil sensed that something was bothering him. "What is it?"

"I don't like the fact that Queen Sibylla, Princess Isabella, and the Dowager

Queen are all in Jerusalem. It complicates things. It would be an indignity to negotiate with women, but if their men choose martyrdom, then the women will—according to Frankish custom—actually be in command of the city."

Al-Afdal declared exultantly, "So much the better; then we will take it faster!"

Salah ad-Din raised his eyebrows. "You think so?"

"How can women defend a city?" Al-Afdal answered rhetorically and a touch irritably. His father could annoy him with his obtuseness at times. "They don't understand the first thing about warfare. They will be cowering in their quarters with their children."

"Like Stephanie de Milly?" Salah ad-Din tossed back sourly.

"That's not a woman, it's a demon!" It was his brother rather than his son that remarked this in disgust.

Salah ad-Din didn't bother answering. "I've half a mind to agree to Queen Sibylla's pleas to be allowed to join her husband in captivity. That would take her out of Jerusalem and ensure that we controlled both the King and Queen of the Kingdom."

"Yes, and enable more competent leaders to rise to the fore," Al-Adil warned.

"No one appears to be listening to Sibylla anyway. Even the Christians show no respect for her. It is the Patriarch—and now Ibelin—who are in command in Jerusalem, and Montferrat in Tyre. Sibylla is of little value to them *alive*, but her *death* would be a great boon to them and most *in*convenient for *us*. That would open the way for her sister, Isabella."

"What risk is she? We hold her husband captive."

"She is Ibelin's stepdaughter."

"Ah." Al-Adil caught his brother's drift. "You think Ibelin would be able to rally Christian support around Isabella and rule through her."

"If Sibylla were out of the way, yes. So we need to protect Sibylla, don't you think?"

"I see your point. And hope that Isabella dies in Jerusalem."

Salah ad-Din nodded, but he didn't look convinced.

"Now what?" his brother asked, exasperated.

"I was just wondering if her elimination wouldn't simply invite a strong Christian leader from the West to claim the vacant throne. The English King, after all, is first cousin to both these women. If both died, he could clearly lay claim to the throne—and he is rich in vassals, conquests, and, most exceptionally for these monogamists, sons."

"Why should they both die if we control and keep Sibylla alive?"

Salah ad-Din shrugged. "Allah determines the hour of our coming and our going. I think we would do well to ensure that both these troublesome women are not in Jerusalem when it falls to our troops, and I don't want the Greek woman there, either. I don't want trouble with the Greek Emperor over something so unimportant. I will send fifty men of my personal bodyguard to escort all three of these women and—in the Name of the Merciful Almighty—their children, who are all small and no risk to us, out of Jerusalem. Sibylla will be allowed to join her husband, and the others can go to Antioch or on to Constantinople, if we are lucky."

"I'm not sure your army will understand such generosity," Al-Adil warned in a peeved tone.

"No?" Salah ad-Din looked amused. "I think my generosity will read very well in the chronicles. The chivalrous Salah ad-Din!"

Al-Adil burst out laughing, and his brother joined him.

Jerusalem, August 5, 1187

Apparent chaos reigned in the Ibelin courtyard as servants finished securing saddlebags to all the horses, and the grooms struggled to tie panniers on young, skittish destriers and palfreys unused to this indignity. Meanwhile Nanny Anne settled John, Helvis, Philip, and Margaret into a horse litter and then climbed in behind them, despite the boy's furious protests about being able to ride himself.

Maria Zoë had made the strategic decision that if they were to be allowed out of Jerusalem with the Sultan's escort, then they were going to take every movable valuable with them—and after her own jewels and plate, that included the excellent horseflesh of her husband's stud at Ibelin that Master Shoreham had brought with him to Jerusalem.

The packing had been going on all night, with considerable dissension about what could or could not be left behind, while Father Angelus kept warning them that the Saracens might rob them of everything they had as soon as the women and children were in their power. In the end the girls had been allowed their dolls, Philip his blanket, and John his toy knights. Isabella, after much persuasion, was convinced to leave behind her wedding dress and Humphrey of Toron's second suit of armor. The former she had wanted out of sentimentality, and the latter because she was certain Humphrey would need it when he was freed. Maria Zoë countered by pointing out she would need dresses she could wear, not things she had grown out of, and that freed prisoners were given back their armor.

Adding to the general chaos were the dogs of the household, who were in a frenzy of excitement at so much activity, and the many household members who would not be going, who stood around with envious looks at the lucky few selected to accompany the Dowager Queen. Except for Nanny Anne and Eskindar, none of the servants were going. Eloise had taken the place of Isabella's maid and Eschiva had taken Rahel's place as Maria Zoë's waiting woman. In addition to Maria Zoë's own children, they were taking Eschiva's three children and Eloise's two little boys. The latter five were to travel in a second litter with Eloise. Eschiva had elected to ride one of the brood mares, who was pregnant and quite calm, and Isabella too was mounted.

A crowd gathered in the street, too, for the news had spread like wildfire that the Sultan had sent fifty Mamlukes to escort the Dowager Queen to Christian territory. Curiously, as far as Ibelin could detect, there was not a trace of jealousy among the people. Rather, the news of the Sultan's generosity seemed to fill them with increased awe and respect for their new commander. He'd broken his word to the Sultan, and still the Sultan sent an escort for his wife and children! The Sultan must value him highly.

On the other hand, the news that Queen Sibylla was to go with the Dowager Queen so she could join her husband in captivity triggered a small riot of outrage. Ibelin had been forced to go and speak with the angry crowd. They had sullenly dispersed, but Sibylla's departure from the royal palace to join the Ibelin convoy this morning had been punctuated with catcalls, insults, and rude suggestions of what she should tell (or do to) her husband when she met him again.

At last Maria Zoë and Balian emerged from the upper gallery and started down the broad steps into the courtyard. Maria Zoë was dressed in voluminous layers of white cotton, from her shift to the veils that completely covered her head and face and fell all the way to her hips. They were held in place by a simple golden band around her forehead that suggested a crown. Gold threads were woven into the cotton, a couple inches apart, and the edges of the full, flowing sleeves of her gown were trimmed in purple embroidery, while her doeskin gloves had the crosses of Jerusalem stitched in gold on the back—just like the gloves she had once given King Baldwin. No Muslim could accuse her of immodesty, but her claim to royalty and royal privilege was just as patent.

Balian was dressed in one of his best tunics, and he had changed his own tattered and poorly repaired armor for his late brother Hugh's coat of mail. It was still a little too big for him, but nevertheless in better condition than his own. The oldest palfrey in their stable, Treasure, nearing twenty and graying at the muzzle, had been selected to remain behind, and he was brought forward so

Balian could mount and lead the little convoy to the rendezvous just beyond St. Stephen's Gate.

He swung himself up and signaled for the doors out of the courtyard to be opened. Balian and Maria Zoë rode side by side out into the street with Eschiva and Isabella directly behind them, followed by the two horse litters, four packhorses, and finally Father Angelus and Eskindar making up the rear. Queen Sibylla's party fell in behind them.

Balian and Maria Zoë rode in silence in the brittle morning sunshine. They had said their farewells the night before, and now there was nothing more to say. Except that Maria Zoë was finding it harder and harder to go. She had been amazed and relieved when the Sultan's messenger first arrived. It was the gift of certain life and freedom for her children, for Eschiva, and for Eloise as well. But Isabella, Eschiva, and Eloise had husbands safe outside of Jerusalem. Only Maria Zoë was being torn apart from hers.

Once during the night she had broached the topic. The children would be safe with Eschiva. Maybe she—Balian had cut her off sharply. He would not hear of it or discuss it.

Now he reached out and took her gloved hand in his naked one and raised it to his lips. "I could have died at Hattin, Zoë, ignominiously. Instead, I have the privilege of defending Jerusalem. Be sure my sons remember that: that I chose to defend Jerusalem, even though it was already lost."

Maria Zoë nodded, afraid that if she opened her mouth only a sob would come out. That was another advantage of the gauze veils shielding her face from the sun and the eyes of others: while shielding her face from the sun, they also kept her red and puffy eyes hidden.

"Be sure that they remember one thing more," Balian asked of his wife.

She turned to him and waited expectantly.

"Be sure they always remember that the tomb in the Holy Sepulcher is *empty*. It is empty *because* He rose from the dead. He is not here, in Jerusalem. He is wherever two or more of you are gathered in His name."

They had reached St. Stephen's Gate, and Balian drew up. He would not risk going outside, where—now that he was a valuable prisoner—the Sultan's guard might be tempted (if they didn't have orders) to seize him.

"Go with God, my love, and in the knowledge that He *is* with you."

"But also with you!" Maria Zoë choked out.

Chapter 21

Jerusalem, August 6, 1187

Mathewos could have gone with the Dowager Queen. She had asked him to. But knowing that Salah ad-Din had allowed only one groom and one priest and that all who remained in Jerusalem would die, he had requested her to take his son Dawit with his wife and infant son instead. Beth, however, refused to place herself in the company of fifty Mamlukes. She was certain they would recognize her as an apostate and brutally stone her to death. She said she preferred to die beside her husband fighting in Jerusalem than to allow herself to be slaughtered by people who despised her. So Mathewos had asked the Lady of Ibelin to take his youngest son, Eskindar, instead.

Eskindar had been furious. He wanted to prove he was a great warrior. He wanted to show his older brother Dawit that he would have been a great knight, if only he'd been given the chance. Eskindar had shouted and protested vehemently, but in the end he had done what his father ordered him to do, because he was a good boy and obeyed God's commandment to honor his father.

Mathewos looked around at the little family that was left with him, and tears of pride filled his eyes. Dawit was a splendid young man, as tall and strong as any knight, but a gentle and loving husband and father. Even now, he sat beside Beth as she rocked the cradle with their son and he held her other hand entwined in his own. Mathewos' eyes shifted from her lovely face, framed by a clean white wimple, to his little grandson, sleeping contentedly in the cradle, and he was sad to think they would both soon be dead, yet proud to have had such a dutiful and respectful daughter-in-law.

His eyes shifted to his own daughter, Tsion, who had greatly disappointed and hurt him by her disobedience. He still could not grasp that she would willingly give her body to a man not her husband, and he still felt shamed by her willfulness. But he could not stop loving her, and after she married her Gabriel, she had continued to look after her old father as well as—if not better—than before. Even now, she felt his gaze and smiled over her shoulder at him as she warmed a hippocras over the little tack-room brazier to help him sleep.

He frowned, because he did not want her to think she had been wholly forgiven or that he was going soft. What she had done was wrong, and God was punishing her; she had been barren ever since she lost the baby conceived in sin.

Then again, he thought sadly as she brought him the mulled wine and smiled pleadingly, she was perhaps the lucky one, since she would not have to live with the thought that her baby would be murdered by Saracen soldiers. Mathewos knew the Saracens might spare children old enough to work as slaves, but infants and toddlers were considered noisy and troublesome and would be quickly slaughtered. Mathewos sighed deeply and glanced again at his little grandson, Menelik. He had been named for the Ethiopian king who had, like this little Menelik, been conceived in the City of David, the offspring of the Queen of Ethiopia (more commonly called the Queen of Sheba) and King Solomon himself. Mathewos had had great hopes for his little grandson, but God had decreed otherwise.

Beyond the door opening into the stables, something bumped followed by a chorus of nickers, alerting them that someone was coming, even before the door to the tack room was pushed open so hard it cracked against the nearest empty saddle rack. In the door stood Tsion's impulsive and self-confident husband, Gabriel, the sight of whom always brought a scowl to Mathewos' face.

Gabriel had returned with the Lord of Ibelin when they thought they were coming for a single night to bring the Lady of Ibelin and her children out of Jerusalem. Because Ernoul had not yet recovered from the severe wounds he had taken at Hattin, Gabriel had not had much choice in the matter, but he had come willingly, thinking he would be able to rescue Tsion as well. When Balian decided to remain in Jerusalem, he had sent Gabriel with his written message to Salah ad-Din so that the squire at least could honestly say he had kept his word. The escort commander, however, had been so furious with the treachery of the Lord of Ibelin that he'd held a sword to Gabriel's throat and threatened his life. Only the warnings of cooler heads (suggesting the Sultan might not appreciate a mere slave killing a man enjoying his safe-conduct) had prevented Gabriel's summary execution. After that experience, Gabriel had no intention of traveling in the company of the Saracens; as soon as he'd handed over Ibelin's message, he'd dashed back to Jerusalem.

Now he burst into the tack room with unnecessary force, calling out to his father-in-law: "Mathewos! My lord wants you to attend on him at once!"

Despite Gabriel's evident excitement, Mathewos remained calm. In his opinion, his son-in-law was far too excitable. Instead he asked phlegmatically, "Now? At this time of night?"

"Yes. He's sent for both you and my own dad. You're to go to him in the chapel at once."

"The chapel?" Now Mathewos frowned. "What is this about?" he asked, getting to his feet and setting aside his mug of mulled wine.

"I don't know," Gabriel admitted. "He's spent the whole day with the Patriarch and the council. He only just got back, ate standing up, and then asked me to fetch you and my dad."

Mathewos nodded and gestured for Dawit to stay sitting, while Tsion urged her husband to sit down and spend some time with her at last. Mathewos hated to hear her beg for her husband's attention. It was undignified and it made him dislike his son-in-law more; he was too young and restless to be married. He had only been interested in sex with Tsion, and he would never have married her if the Baron of Ibelin had not forced him. As was to be expected, Gabriel begged off, saying he had to go find Sir Constantine.

Mathewos made his way up to the Ibelin family chapel, a very small room on the first floor overlooking the Street of Jehoshaphat. That the Ibelins felt the need for their own private chapel, in a city bursting with churches built on the most sacred sites of Christendom, was not something Mathewos entirely understood—except that the churches of Jerusalem were almost always flooded with pilgrims.

As he approached the little chapel, he saw Father Michael hastening in the same direction wearing his vestments; apparently there was to be a Mass. The Baron of Ibelin was in the chapel already, but he was not kneeling in prayer. In fact, he was fully armored except for his helmet. His face, which had been earnest, lightened at the sight of Mathewos—but before he could explain what was going on, Roger Shoreham arrived, looking decidedly worried. "You sent for me, my lord?"

Ibelin responded by asking almost jovially, "I hope you don't mind confessing to your own son? He was the priest closest at hand."

Shoreham looked at Michael, and Michael looked back, equally surprised. Then Shoreham asked warily, "Why should I need to confess now?"

"It is customary, that's all. It is, of course, also customary to spend the night in prayer and bathe at dawn before confession—but frankly, I would rather you got a good night's sleep. You see, tomorrow at Prime there is to be a muster of all men in the city who think themselves capable of bearing arms. The parish priests are even now going door to door and making a head count of men, women, and children, both residents and refugees, while spreading the word about the muster. The men are to muster wearing whatever armor and bearing what arms they have. Once I have a better idea of just how many fighting men there are in the city and their age, health, and equipment, I will start organizing them into units. Each unit will be assigned a sector of the city for which they will be responsible—both for keeping order and, when the time comes, for defending the adjacent wall segment."

Shoreham nodded agreement. It was what he expected and what was necessary.

"My problem at the moment," Ibelin continued, "is a lack of experienced men capable of commanding and organizing those units. Sir Constantine," he indicated the Greek knight who had joined them silently, "will, of course, take command of the Greek and Armenian contingents, which we estimate to be about three hundred strong. Roger, I want you to take command of the Franks, which will be the strongest contingent on account of the refugees. Right now we guess it could be as many as five hundred men."

Shoreham again nodded earnestly, but he stood a little straighter, too. He had commanded at Ascalon and Ibelin, but nothing like these numbers. Besides, to command at Jerusalem was the greatest honor yet—one that made him proud, even if he was conscious of how difficult the task would be.

"To ensure that your authority is fully recognized and you are shown due respect, I intend to knight you here and now."

"Me?" Despite his confidence in his own abilities as a sergeant, Shoreham had never expected the accolade of knighthood. He had been delighted by Daniel's knighting and nursed hopes that Gabriel, too, would be honored soon, but he had never seriously thought to attain the honor himself; he was too conscious of his humble origins.

"Yes, you; and you, too, Mathewos," Balian added with a smile to the Ethiopian.

"Me?" Mathewos echoed Shoreham. "But why?"

"Because I need a fluent Arabic speaker to command the Syrians, Copts, and Ethiopians. There are between three and four hundred of the former, maybe one hundred Copts, and a half-hundred or more Ethiopian fighting men who—I have been told—did not go back to Ethiopia with your Prince Lalibela."

Unlike Shoreham, Mathewos did not appear flattered by the unexpected honor. He was silent for a moment before venturing cautiously, "Are you sure these men will accept me as their commander?"

"You come from princely blood, Mathewos, and you have shown great courage. I should have knighted you a decade ago."

"But the Syrians and Copts do not know that, my lord—and the Ethiopians here are mostly followers of King Harbay, a Zagwe, while I am descended from the marshals who served the last Solomonid Emperor."

Ibelin had no time for the politics of a kingdom on the other side of Egypt and answered firmly, "They have all, through their respective representatives, vowed to follow *my* orders, and at the muster they will take an oath personally. By then you will be a knight, and I will publicly designate you my lieutenant. If you have any difficulty, report it to me at once. Meanwhile, the first job for both of you will be sorting out your own men and identifying any youths of good birth and character with training in arms. Sir Constantine tells me he has been approached by a least a half-dozen youths claiming to be younger sons or younger brothers of knights slain or captured at Hattin. If you find anyone like that among your troops, let me know. I intend to knight everyone suitable."

Shoreham and Mathewos looked at one another somewhat blankly.

"Do not underestimate the power of pride," Balian admonished. "Now which of you wants to go first?"

The leprosarium of Jerusalem lay beyond the northern wall, between the St. Lazarus Postern and the "Leper Pool." It had been founded by the Greeks or the Armenians—in any case, before the city fell to the Muslims, much less was liberated by the Latins. It had been much expanded after the restoration of Christian rule, and it had benefited particularly from the patronage of King Baldwin IV.

No less than sixteen knights of St. Lazarus of Jerusalem had joined the royal muster and fought at Hattin. The knights that mustered were either men diagnosed with leprosy but still capable of bearing arms, or knights who had joined the Order to treat ills of the soul rather than the body. They had been accompanied by almost all the healthy brothers of the Order, the men who normally looked after the lepers. None of them had returned.

The leper community that remained in Jerusalem nevertheless consisted of nearly two hundred souls, men and women both, who were seriously afflicted with the disease. With the knights, sergeants, and serving brothers who had guided and looked after them gone, the lepers met to decide what to do next—and to elect their own leaders, as was common practice in the leprosariums across the Greek empire.

After only a short debate, the lepers decided that until the enemy was at hand, they would remain in the leprosarium. The decision was dictated by practicality. In the leprosarium they were directly beside one of Jerusalem's larger water reservoirs, with plenty of water for both drinking and washing. Furthermore, the leprosarium was a solid and spacious building with men's and women's wards, large kitchens, adequate sanitation, and a fine church.

There was more debate about what to do when the enemy actually came. Some lepers argued that the Muslims would leave them alone, but others pointed out that, like it or not, the very location of the leprosarium put them at risk; they were in the way of any assault on Tancred's Tower or the northern wall. As a result, they would be removed forcibly if they didn't go voluntarily. "They might just kill us all—as we're no use as slaves. When the enemy comes, we must take refuge in the city," a middle-aged leper, whose fingerless hands were wrapped in bandages, declared forcefully.

"What makes you think the citizens of Jerusalem will let us inside?" a little man without ears or nose asked back bitterly. He had been expelled from his native Cologne and had walked all the way to Jerusalem in hope of a cure. Instead, he found himself segregated with his fellow lepers, albeit in better circumstances than in the Holy Roman Empire.

"We can appeal to the Grand Hospitaller," a woman with deforming ulcers on her face and neck answered. The Order of St. Lazarus was an offshoot of the Knights of St. John.

It was at this point that Sir Daniel straightened and raised his voice. "No—Ibelin is in command now, and I will go to him."

The congress of lepers fell restlessly silent as they turned to look at the speaker. Sir Daniel was one of them—and he wasn't. He had never really fit in, and then he had gone off to serve the King. When he returned, he had kept himself apart, as if he thought he was better than the rest of them. Yet the leprosy had rendered his left arm useless; it was ulcerous and the fingers were rotting away. Because he could no longer hold a shield, he had not been allowed to go with the knights that mustered with King Guy, despite his protests and pleading.

Now he stepped out of the side aisle to stand directly in front of the altar (the lepers were meeting in the church) and reminded them: "Listen to me. I once served the Baron of Ibelin. If I go to him, he will grant what we request."

Several in the audience, who didn't like Daniel very well and thought him arrogant, grumbled to themselves that he shouldn't be so sure about what the Baron of Ibelin would or would not do. The majority, whether they liked him or not, nodded and agreed that what he said made sense.

"But first we must decide what it is we *want*," Daniel's voice rang out, amplified by the acoustics of the church. His audience grew still, surprised and captivated by something in his tone.

"Do we want to cower behind the walls of Jerusalem like piteous rubbish, waiting for our fate?" He paused, but no one answered him; most of his audience, in their rags and rotting limbs, didn't see what choice they had.

"Or do we want to follow in the footsteps of the late King Baldwin?" Again he paused, but now an intangible excitement had gripped them. The lepers toward the back or behind taller people squirmed and strained to get a better view of Sir Daniel.

Sir Daniel was still a surprisingly impressive figure. His face was not yet marked by the disease, and he stood tall and straight, a habit from his years in the King's service. His rotting arm was wrapped in bandages and hidden from view in his cloak.

"King Baldwin never stopped fighting for his Kingdom, for this city, for Christ. Even when he was too weak to stand, when he could not use his hands, when his sight was dim. To the very end, he fought. Three times, the *Leper* King threw back Salah ad-Din's armies! It took a *healthy* man to lead the Army of Jerusalem to defeat!" he reminded them, and suddenly they were nodding and congratulating themselves.

"I say if he could fight in his condition, then so can all of us!"

"He had others to do his fighting," one of Sir Daniel's detractors grumbled. "All he had to do was command."

"Well, if you want to just whine and act like an infant, then do so!" Sir Daniel sneered. "But I know that I can be useful—and so can you, Tom, and you, too, Molly!" Daniel began addressing them by name. "In fact," Daniel continued, "there are things we can do *better* than the healthy! With less feeling in our limbs, we can handle hot cauldrons with boiling oil and water, or even stamp out fires with our senseless feet. And who knows better than we how to prepare strips of cotton or how to wind them firmly? Why, then, who better than we to wrap arrows with cotton strips and dip them in tar and oil so they can be sent flaming over the ramparts to the enemy?"

His enthusiasm and conviction were contagious. Particularly, the younger and healthier of his colleagues were with him. "Yes, yes!" they started to shout. "We can help!"

"We can tend fires—"

"And put them out!"

"We can remove the dead!"

"We can throw the enemy dead back at them!"

"We can!"

"We can!"

All doubts, voiced and unvoiced, were soon drowned out in the euphoria of newfound purpose, and Sir Daniel was elected "Master" of the Lepers of St. Lazarus at Jerusalem by popular acclaim.

August 10, 1187

Although they left the Ibelin palace very early in the morning, Beth and Tsion had to worm their way through a large crowd that had already gathered on the street before the Church of the Holy Sepulcher. "My husband is to be knighted!" Tsion explained proudly as she squeezed past, while Beth said more modestly, "We're part of the Ibelin household!"

They finally reached the courtyard before the south entrance to the church and managed to find places on the steps up to the Chapel of the Trinity, where they could, by straining their necks and standing on tiptoe, see the youths kneeling in neat rows in the courtyard. The young men selected for knighthood had held their vigil all night in the Calvary chapel, had confessed to the canons of the Holy Sepulcher, and now, dressed in white surcoats (donated by the Templars) and red cloaks (donated by the Patriarch), awaited the accolade.

From their position, Beth and Tsion could see only the backs of the eighty-one youths, and because they were now all dressed the same, it was almost impossible to find their respective husbands. Eventually Beth found two young black men side by side and knew Dawit had to be one of them. She decided Dawit was the youth on the left, but she couldn't be 100 per cent sure. Tsion had a harder time finding Gabriel until she realized he was in the very front row at the far right.

The crowd was getting restless by the time the Patriarch, followed by the Baron of Ibelin and his three deputies, emerged from the Church of the Holy Sepulcher. The Patriarch was in full regalia, the baron and his knights in armor. The Patriarch raised his arms; a gold processional cross glinted in the morning sunlight as he intoned a benediction. Then Ibelin stepped forward and raised his voice so it could be heard at the very back of the crowd. "Do you swear before Almighty God to defend Holy Church, even if to do so you must lay down your life?"

A chorus of "I do!" answered Ibelin.

"Do you swear to defend the weak, whether women or children, the old, or the infirm, and to aid them to the best of your ability, even if to do so you must lay down your life?"

A second chorus of "I do!" answered even louder than before.

"Do you swear to be honest and loyal, abhorring lies, injustice, and treason, for as long as you shall live?"

A final chorus of "I do" followed.

Ibelin took the sword handed him by Sir Roger and, to Tsion's delight, approached her husband Gabriel before all others. To her horror, Ibelin back-handed his former squire hard enough for the burly youth to visibly sway to one side; then he bent and kissed him on both cheeks, before lifting him off his knees and girding the sword around his hips with the words, "Rise, Sir Gabriel."

Ibelin repeated this procedure eighty times, the swords handed to him and the names whispered in his ear by one of his three deputies as he went along the lines, until the last, eighty-first knight had been made. Then at last the crowd could cheer.

As Beth made her way through the crowd of other celebrants and their proud womenfolk, she was struck by how young and untried most of the other knights looked. Most were not old enough to grow a beard; many were still marked by pubescent acne and their bodies thin from teenage growth. Dawit was a like a father among them, she thought admiringly, taller and stronger, and so calm amidst all the excitement. He had rejected this honor before, he told her, because he had no desire to watch horses killed nor to kill himself, but now it was different. Now he would be defending her and their infant son, his father, and his sister. That, he said, he was proud to do.

As she reached him, Dawit smiled and introduced his companion, the other Ethiopian who had been knighted. "This is Sir Kassahun; he only arrived in Jerusalem this spring, escorting his grandparents on pilgrimage. He speaks only Amharic and a little Greek, so I must translate." Dawit switched to Amharic to introduce his wife—and then with Beth on his arm, he indicated they should follow the rest of the crowd to the banquet that the Patriarch was hosting in celebration of this mass knighting.

In the Patriarch's great hall a long table had been set up for the new knights, at right angles to the high table where the Patriarch, Ibelin, the Grand Hospitaller, and other leading men of the city were seated. Dawit found a seat for his little party near the top, and Beth settled on to the bench, somewhat agog at all the splendor laid out for them. In addition to the linen tablecloths, each place setting had not only a trencher but a light-blue glass beaker and a pewter spoon, although guests were evidently expected to provide their own knives. There were silver and pewter pitchers containing both white and red wine at every second place. Big pewter bowls filled with fresh, clean water for washing one's hands and linen towels for drying them were being brought around by little boys in the Patriarch's livery. At the high table the meal was being served entirely on plates of silver, and instead of plain glass beakers, the guests had enameled glass goblets.

Soon the Patriarch's servants filed into the hall carrying huge platters laden with roasted birds, haunches of pork, and legs of lamb. Other servants followed with sauces enriched with raisins and spiced with cumin, nutmeg, and cinnamon. There were brightly patterned baskets full of bread for the Franks and brass bowls filled to overflowing with rice for the Syrians and Armenians. Smaller glazed pottery bowls offered figs, black and green olives, apricots, and almonds. Pottery plates were heaped with hummus soaked in olive oil and sprinkled with red peppers and fresh sliced cucumbers. Later there were sherbets, glazed oranges, candied lemons, and marzipan in the shape of crosses with red and yellow glaze.

Beth had eaten well in the Ibelin household, but nothing like this feast. She couldn't get over the abundance—until she heard someone remark that the Patriarch evidently preferred to use his great stores to feed Christians rather than Muslims. The remark sent a chill down Beth's spine.

Sir Kassahun was deep in an earnest conversation with another new knight and Dawit was diligently translating in both directions, so Beth's eyes wandered farther. She noticed the intricate pattern of the colored floor tiles and the magnificent wall mosaics depicting Christ's entry to Jerusalem on Palm Sunday. Tiny gold mosaic chips depicted Christ's halo, and mother-of-pearl pieces decorated the robes of high-ranking Roman spectators on the edge of the scene. The gold and mother-of-pearl gleamed and glinted in the sunlight pouring through the glazed windows. There was surely no palace in Damascus as fine as this, Beth thought, and her stomach churned as she wondered what the harem of the Sultan was like.

Fortunately, her attention was distracted by the Grand Hospitaller descending from the high table to collect a Hospitaller nun, whom he led to the high table and introduced to the Baron of Ibelin. The latter politely rose to his feet and bowed his head before making a place for her next to him.

Beth thought she looked familiar, but couldn't place her. She nudged Dawit and pointed to the nun. "Who is that, and why is she with my lord of Ibelin?"

Dawit paused in his conversation to look over at the high table. "That's Sister Adela. Don't you remember? From Nablus."

Now everything clicked into place. Beth had sometimes volunteered to help at the orphanage for children before she got pregnant herself.

Dawit was continuing, "Lord Balian wants her to organize the women of Jerusalem—you know, field kitchens and first-aid stations, nurseries to keep the children out from underfoot, and the like."

"The women will be helping in the defense?" Beth asked, a little breathless at such a radical thought.

"Indirectly—as you did at Kerak," Dawit reminded her.

Yes, of course, Beth thought, but that had been different. Or *she* had been different. She had not volunteered to help then, but she would now—if Dawit would let her, of course. "Dawit?"

"Yes, my love?" he answered patiently, although he was clearly more interested in the conversation of his fellow knights. With his head cocked, he was listening to them more than to his wife.

"May I—may I tell the good sister—that—that I—I mean, maybe I can help in some way?"

"Of course!" Dawit assured, giving her hand a squeeze. "You and Tsion can take turns looking after Menelik and helping to prepare for the siege."

August 11, 1187

Although it was ten years since her conversion to Christianity, Beth still found it somewhat frightening to go out into the streets of a busy city like Jerusalem without a male escort of any kind and with her face uncovered. At least in Jerusalem there were no Muslims, she reminded herself, but she kept her eyes down and stayed in the shadows at the side of the street nevertheless.

At the entrance to the Hospital she requested an audience with Sister Adela, but was told she might have to wait a long time. Beth almost lost heart, but then she squared her shoulders and announced that she would wait. The Hospitaller lay brother shrugged and indicated a bench under the arcade on the side of the courtyard, which was already lined with other people waiting for one thing or another.

Beth sat down primly, careful not to touch the man on the bench next to her. It wasn't just innate modesty; the man was crawling with lice, and his breath was so foul it made her want to gag. In fact, the entire complex was laden with unpleasant odors, from the latrines along the south side of the compound under the hospital wards to the smoke from a fire in which old bandages and other rubbish were being burned. Beth shuddered a little as she realized that for all her *will* to help, she was not very well suited to work in a place such as this.

Beth turned her thoughts away from her surroundings to her mission. She had not been able to sleep for nervousness and excitement. Jerusalem seemed so large and strong that she refused to believe it could not be defended. She knew what her father-in-law said, and she knew that the Baron of Ibelin had sent his wife and children to safety. But Beth was *certain* Jerusalem could be defended.

Ibelin town had been overrun because it had no proper walls, just earthworks, she told herself, but the castle of Ibelin had not even been attacked. Kerak had not fallen to Salah ad-Din either, she reminded herself, and all the unpleasantness during the siege resulted from overcrowding and limited water in the middle of the desert. Jerusalem had plenty of water, and just this morning Dawit had told her the Lord of Ibelin would be making armed foraging sorties into the surrounding countryside to round up the herds of cattle and sheep abandoned by their owners in the initial panic.

Beth *had* to believe that Jerusalem was defensible, because she could not face the alternative: capture by the Saracens. It was not death she feared so much as what they would do to her *before* they deigned to kill her—and what they would do to Dawit when he tried to protect her and little Menelik. She had told Dawit more than once that she would prefer he killed her with his own hand rather than let her fall into Saracen hands, but she did not think he would have the heart to actually do it.

No. They *had* to defend Jerusalem, even if it meant surviving a two-, three-, or four-year siege until the Christian princes in the West came to their relief. It had to be possible!

A pretty young Hospitaller sister was in front of her. "You asked to see Sister Adela?" she asked Beth.

Beth nodded vigorously and sprang to her feet to follow the Hospitaller nun. She was led across the huge courtyard, through the billowing and evil-smelling smoke, past a large and bustling kitchen complex that opened on to the Street of Vegetables, and into a narrow, cobbled alley flanked by St. Mary Major and St. Mary Minor. Finally she was led through a low dog-toothed portal into a lovely little cloister around a blooming garth with a bubbling fountain in the center. It was like an oasis in the desert, Beth thought.

Sister Adela was talking to a Hospitaller lay brother who nodded several times, bowed, and then withdrew with only a short glance at Beth. Then Beth was led forward, and Sister Adela turned to her expectantly.

"My lady," Beth started eagerly but nervously. "I don't know if you remember me. I'm in the household of the Dowager Queen, the Lady of Ibelin, and we met several times in Nablus. I—I used to help in the orphanage."

"Of course I remember you!" Sister Adela assured her with a smile. Beth had not only been good with the children, her story had greatly impressed not only Sister Adela but the other nuns as well.

"I—have come because I—I wanted to offer my help."

Sister Adela smiled. "Of course! You must have heard about the one hundred orphans that were abandoned by their caretakers and brought here—"

"No," Beth corrected her, her nervousness making her bold. "I was told Lord Balian has asked you to organize the women to help defend the city."

That took Sister Adela back a little, but she didn't show her surprise, suggesting instead, "Come, let's sit in the shade." She indicated a bench under the cross vaulting of the cloister. As they settled themselves Sister Adela continued, "It is true that Lord Balian has asked me to organize the women—"

"What are the things we can do?" Beth broke in eagerly.

"Well," Sister Adela started, "we will need women who can look after the children in a collective place so the other women are free to do other tasks." She paused and looked expectantly at Beth.

But Beth didn't want to do what she had always done. She wanted a more active role. She asked, "What else?"

"We'll also need women who can administer first aid to the wounded and then send them back here." Beth tightened her lips. She knew she wasn't suited to that, and Sister Adela read her expression correctly and continued. "And we'll need women who can cook hot meals." Still Beth did not respond, so Adela added, "We'll also need women who have the courage and strength to take drinking water to the men manning the ramparts, and women who can soak cotton in oil and wrap it around arrows so our men can fire flaming arrows at the enemy—"

"I would like to do the last!" Beth declared, breathless with excitement.

"Prepare arrows for being set alight?" Sister Adela asked skeptically.

"Yes," Beth declared firmly, lifting her chin.

"Why is that?" Sister Adela asked, puzzled.

"Because the Muslims believe that if they are killed by a woman, they will not go to Paradise! I want to make the arrows that will kill as many of them as possible! If I could, I would shoot them myself!" Beth admitted, with so much passion that it took Sister Adela aback for a moment. But then, on second thought, she understood, and she laid her hand on Beth's and nodded to herself. For the first time in her life, Beth saw a chance to take revenge on the men who had so brutally humiliated her—and all their brothers-in-faith, who despised her simply because she was not their sex.

August 12, 1187

During the public muster, Heraclius had melodramatically placed himself (and so the entire organization of the Church) under Ibelin's command, but already the Patriarch was regretting it. The first thing Ibelin had done after knighting eighty-one youths was to order all decorative gold stripped from the facades, domes, and even the altars of the churches. "Gold," Ibelin told the shocked Patriarch, "will not protect you from the arrows of the Saracens; men who have been *paid* in gold will."

"You would defend this city with mercenaries?" Heraclius asked back, in a voice vibrating with moral indignation.

"No. But even the soldiers of Christ need to eat and drink—and they need to pay for both, and for their arms and their armor, too. The knights I made yesterday have nothing but what we give them, and where should we better find the means to pay them than from the churches they have vowed to defend with their lives? Strip the churches, your eminence!" Ibelin had ordered, and it was being done.

While the senior clergy, with long faces, set about carrying out Ibelin's command, the more humble parish priests and monks were charged with the comfort of men's souls and the burial of the dead. When the siege came there would be many dead, and there would be no access to the cemeteries beyond the walls. The dead would have to be interred in catacombs or crypts. After much discussion, it was agreed that the dead would be placed in the deep, cavernous chambers that ran under the Temple of God and were presumed to have been part of the Temple of Solomon. The Templars had used these chambers as stables for their horses, but the bulk of the Templars' mounts had been with their masters at Hattin, which meant they had been slaughtered or captured. There were almost no Templar horses left in Jerusalem, and the few remaining beasts could easily be stabled elsewhere.

Once this had been decided, the Templars agreed to let lay brothers from other religious orders enter the Temple to clean out the stables and prepare them for use as a mass morgue. Father Michael was one of many priests who volunteered to assist in this operation.

With the Ibelin children gone, Michael's days were empty except for saying morning and evening Mass for the Ibelin household and hearing his lord's daily confession. The empty hours left him far too much time for imagining what was to come—and truly, "idle hands were the devil's playground." Michael preferred to keep busy.

If he were honest with himself, he was also curious about the mysterious "Temple" that had been guarded so assiduously by the fierce militant monks. Although he had been to Jerusalem many times since taking service with the Baron d'Ibelin, he had not once before this set foot across the threshold of the Temple.

The first thing that struck Father Michael, along with the other priests and monks with him, was that the Temple was empty. Not literally, of course, but it was so much too large for the few men remaining that it felt as if they were entering an abandoned complex. Everywhere was evidence of the Order's former strength: a massive refectory that could easily serve five hundred men at a time, dormitories of similar dimensions, a parade ground long enough for knights to joust on, an armory with lances still stacked against the walls, and bins full of arrows (which would be distributed, a Templar sergeant assured them, as soon as the siege commenced). There were tattered black-and-white banners hanging from the roof beams as well; a Templar sergeant proudly identified each banner by the great victory at which it had been carried. The Beauséant was apparently only carried once and then retired here.

And then there were the stables themselves, deep and dark, not the kind of stables Mathewos (now *Sir* Mathewos) would have wanted for *his* horses, Michael noted with amusement. These stables had vaulted ceilings ten feet high, and the stone arches stretched deep into the bowels of the mountain, but the air was stale and the atmosphere gloomy.

Father Michael found himself working beside a middle-aged Syrian priest deep inside the stables. The Syrian was wiry and dark with an impressive beard. They raked the straw together and then loaded it on a handcart to take it out. The straw had once been dirty, but the manure had long since dried out; it was disintegrating and almost odorless. Michael did not find the work particularly unpleasant, but there was something intangibly creepy about the place. He felt the weight of history and the eyes of the dead upon him. The feeling was clearly shared by his colleague.

"My grandfather was a young man during the last siege," the Syrian abruptly announced in a low voice.

"When the Great Armed Pilgrimage liberated the city?" Michael asked, amazed, stopping his work so the scraping of his rake on the stone floor did not drown out a single word.

The Syrian nodded, and he too stopped to rest on his rake.

"What brought him here?" Michael asked.

The Syrian shrugged. "We have always lived in Jerusalem. Probably since it was taken by King David. My grandfather used to joke that one of our ancestors was probably in the crowd calling, 'Give us Barabbas!' to Pontius Pilate."

That seemed an odd thing to joke about, and Michael frowned.

The Syrian smiled faintly. "He said that to explain why we have never had much luck, although our forefathers were converted by St. Peter himself and my family belonged to the first Christian community that met here"—he stamped his foot on the rock as if he meant this very place—"at the risk of their lives under the Romans."

"Do you mean you met *here*, under the Temple of Solomon?" Michael asked, looking about him at the echoing chamber.

"After the Romans destroyed the Second Temple of the Jews, we met here," the Syrian insisted. "And elsewhere," he added, "until Constantine became Emperor and we could build churches and meet openly. But then the followers of Mohammed came, and the church bells were silenced and the churches desecrated. We were humiliated and taxed, and again could not meet to read the Mass in public."

"But aren't there churches throughout the lands held by the Saracens?" Michael asked, surprised. "I mean, I know Christians are subject to persecution, but surely you could remain Christians, couldn't you?"

The Syrian shook his head. "Only at a very high cost! My grandfather used to tell us stories of what it was like before Palestine was liberated by the Latins. He said that in addition to the taxes, Christians were subject to extra duties, and whenever some misfortune befell the city, whether it was drought or floods, snow or pests, the Christians were blamed. Sometimes they would take the priests and drag them through the streets so the followers of Mohammed could spit and throw filth at them. Sometimes the priests were imprisoned and their parishioners were forced to pay huge ransoms to set them free. He said no Christian woman was safe in the streets because the followers of Mohammed, if they knew the woman was Christian, would seize her and use her like a whore for their own pleasure, without remorse or mercy, because only women of their own faith are considered virtuous and worthy of respect. For that reason, in his day the Christian women also went about completely veiled, and dared not show even an ankle in public."

Michael was so fascinated by his companion's story that he completely forgot the work they were meant to do.

"When he learned about the Christian army coming to our relief, my grandfather says he was not at all glad—he was frightened. He says he did not believe that any Christian army could ever cross through the territories held by the Turks, and he was sure he and his fellow Christians would be punished for the effrontery of the Westerners. He says the Egyptians took pleasure in telling them how the armed pilgrims were obliterated, crushed, and utterly destroyed—first near Nicaea, and then near Dorylaeum, and again at Antioch. The Egyptians told the Christian community in Jerusalem that the Western pilgrims had all starved to death in Antioch. By then, however, after being told the Christians were 'slain to the last man' three times, my grandfather and other Christians had come to believe that the Latin pilgrims truly came from Christ, because they had been able to rise from the dead not once but three times!

"Meanwhile, however, each time the Christian armies were 'destroyed,' the anger among the Egyptians grew greater and the taxes increased. When the Christian army actually appeared and set up camp before the walls, the Egyptians gave up all pretense of legality and broke into our houses at will to take anything of value. They abused the women as well."

"I thought the Christians had been expelled from Jerusalem before it was taken," Michael broke in.

"After the first Christian assault failed, the Egyptian commander ordered all the 'useless mouths' to depart, and so the women and children and old people were sent out of the city even if—as in the case of my grandfather's old parents and his sister—they had no place to go. But the young men, like my grandfather at the time, were forced to remain and work on the defenses of the city. They were watched over by men with whips, just like slaves."

"So he was in the city when the final assault came?" Michael asked anxiously.

The Syrian nodded sadly. "Yes."

"And he survived?"

"He and the other Christians knew about these chambers," he gestured to the echoing arches overhead. "We all shared the tradition of the early years. When the Egyptian defense broke and people started fleeing for their lives, he and many other Christians came here." Again he tapped the solid stone floor with his sandal-clad foot.

"And they were not discovered?"

"No; they stayed here until the light of day had faded, and then they waited again for the dawn before they dared to show themselves. By then the blood lust of the conquerors had turned to frenzied piety and the Latins were wandering the streets of Christ's passion, shedding tears of gratitude and kissing the paving stones—if they could find any. For you see, when the native Christians emerged from these chambers, they found a city paved with corpses and severed body parts, the gutters clogged with drying blood, and a sky filled with vultures, crows, and flies. It was, my grandfather said, worse than any image of hell he had ever imagined." The Syrian stopped speaking. For a moment both priests were lost in images of carnage, colored luridly by the knowledge that they were likely soon face the same again.

Michael shook himself free of the mental pictures first. "Will your family seek refuge here again—I mean, if the dead are here. . . ." Michael looked around and shuddered.

"Now you understand why the Syrian Patriarch was so reluctant to agree to the plan. But then, last time, we knew that once the invaders' blood lust had cooled and they were willing to listen, all we had to do was identify ourselves as Christians and they would embrace us as brothers. As they did. This time it will do us no good to survive the first onslaught. Even if we hide for days or weeks, our fate will be the same when we emerge: slaughter or slavery."

"But you lived under the Saracens before. There are still Jacobite communities living in Salah ad-Din's territories," said Michael, returning to his earlier point.

The Syrian shrugged and resumed his raking. "They live as my grandfather says *we* lived before the liberation of Jerusalem: oppressed, taxed, despised, and humiliated. They can endure it because they have never known any other fate. But we have known freedom, and we will have defied the Sultan. He will not forgive and forget. Remember what he did to the Nubians who rebelled against him?" The Syrian seemed to concentrate on his raking, but he was thinking about something, and he nodded to himself. Then he looked up at Michael with a faint smile. "Why do you look so distressed? Don't you believe in the Resurrection and the Life? If He so wills that we should have the privilege of dying in the same city where He, too, was killed by nonbelievers, shouldn't we rejoice? Death is not such a terrible thing, for it is the gateway to Paradise for those who live and believe in our Lord Jesus Christ."

Father Michael felt compelled to answer "Amen!" but he couldn't help adding, "Yet for many who have sins on their conscience, death will mean the gateway to everlasting hell. And who among us has not sinned?"

"That is where we come in," the Syrian priest answered with a smile, "for we can give absolution of sins and assure the dying that they have nothing to fear." He leaned on his rake and considered the man-made caves. "The men brought here will be the lucky ones, for they will be those for whom we have had the time to pray. In the final slaughter there will be no time for us to do our offices, but we must believe that He himself and his ever merciful Mother will give absolution to all who truly repent. That is what I will tell my flock."

"Thank you," Father Michael whispered, for now he knew what he, too, could say in the days ahead.

August 19, 1187

The forge was oppressively hot, and the crippled boy pumping the bellows wore nothing but a loincloth. His misshapen, skeletal legs were exposed and dripping sweat, like the rest of his frail body. The fire glowed red and black, and so did the exceptionally long sword that the armorer was working on. He had been working on this same sword for a fortnight now: heating and hammering, reheating, honing, reheating. He had etched words with the greatest care into the fuller of the blade just below the hilt, and with bronze wire he had inlaid the etching, hammering and melting the bronze into place, before scraping away and collecting the excess for reuse. The hilt had been wrapped in bands of twisted wire to give it a secure grip, and the disk of the pommel had been fitted with two large enamel medallions commissioned from a master craftsman in the Street of Goldsmiths. Now the sword was almost ready; he heated it one last time.

"Are you still here?" a female voice called loudly and impatiently from the entrance. "Your dinner is getting cold."

"I'm almost done!" the armorer answered, his eyes on the sword.

"It's not fair keeping Sven from his supper," she answered with a nod to the cripple at the bellows, her hands on her ample hips.

"I *said* I'm almost done!" the armorer answered crossly.

"It's that same damn sword you've been working on all week, while all the other orders stack up!" his wife complained. "Why waste your time on something so fine, when what this city needs is as *many* weapons as possible—cheap and simple—that's what we need now. It's too big for most men, anyway," she noted professionally with a glance at the fully three-foot blade, "and who can afford a fine sword with bronze inlay in times like these?" she grumbled.

Her husband only grunted in answer, grasped the sword in both leather-gloved hands, and thrust it deep in the vat of water. A loud hiss and a jet of steam erupted from the vat, and then he stepped back with the sword in both hands, admiring his work. His crippled son gaped in wonder at the marvelous weapon his father held, his eyes aglow with admiration.

"Come get your supper," the armorer's wife ordered the boy curtly, then turned and disappeared back into the kitchen. The boy picked up his crutches, but rather than lurching for the kitchen, he swung himself beside his father to join him in admiring the sword.

His father smiled down at him and showed him the blade. "Can you read that?" he asked.

Sven craned his neck and bit his lip, but then he smiled up at his father. "Defender of Jerusalem!"

His father nodded. He then gestured with his head for the boy to go get his meal as his wife shouted again from the kitchen.

The kitchen opened right off the forge, using the same chimney for the bake oven, but in summer the family fled the heat to eat in the cobbled courtyard behind the forge. Here a wooden table was set up, flanked by two wooden benches. Chickens pecked between the cobbles while a cat sauntered over to beg for leftovers. Two little girls waited wide-eyed for their mother to bring out the evening stew.

The armorer's wife clunked the heavy iron stew pot down on the table and reached out her hand toward her daughters. "Don't just sit there staring. Give me your bowls, girls!"

Sven dropped his crutches beside the end of the bench opposite his sisters and used his hands to move himself to the far end, where a wooden bowl waited for him. He handed this to his mother as soon as his sisters had their portion. He was very hungry and he spooned the thick barley, onion, and carrot broth eagerly into his mouth, burning his tongue. At once he started sucking in air to cool it.

"Stop making those sucking noises!" his mother snapped with a deep frown.

"Leave the boy alone," her husband countered, coming up behind her. He had removed his leather apron and was wiping his hands dry on the front of his cotton tunic, and although he had "washed" his hands in a bucket of water after leaving the forge, they were still black with ingrained dirt.

"I don't want my children eating like pigs!" his wife retorted indignantly.

Her husband sighed. She was probably right, but he found it hard to criticize his crippled son. It was bad enough that he had to work so hard. They had sold all they had to pay for the trip to Jerusalem eight years ago, right after the accident. It had been a hellish trip, and his wife had miscarried a child on the way. It had taken almost eight months to reach Jerusalem, and by then they were nearly destitute, but they had still believed that a miracle would happen. So they had followed the Via

Dolorosa on their knees with Sven between them, praying at each station of the cross for Christ to have mercy on their child.

There had been no miracle, and no money to return home. So Godwin had taken work as a journeyman (although he was a master at home), and his wife had worked as a laundress, hoping to save up money for a forge of their own. That wasn't easy, not after the girls were born, and things had been going from bad to worse until Easter four years ago. That was when Godwin met an armorer, one of the Christian craftsmen from neighboring Syria who had answered the King's call for settlers. The man had just had a falling-out with his son-in-law, and after seeing Godwin's work had offered to make Godwin his heir. The only condition was that he work in his forge and look after him in his old age. Just being able to live here over the forge had been an improvement, but it wasn't exactly independence. As the Syrian aged he needed more and more care, so Godwin's wife had to give up working in the laundry. To make up for the loss of that income, Sven started working the bellows. Yet Godwin found himself learning new skills and techniques from the Syrian, which he had combined with his knowledge from home in Oslo. The Syrian had finally died four months ago, and they had barely had time to celebrate the start of a new life of independence when the disaster at Hattin struck.

Godwin sat down and handed his bowl to his wife. She filled it and then filled her own bowl before sitting down beside him. "Just why have you been working on that fancy sword?" she asked in a less querulous voice, now that they were all getting their supper. "No one ordered it, did they?"

"No," Godwin admitted, "but when the Baron of Ibelin got Salah ad-Din's safe-conduct to come to Jerusalem, it was on the condition that he come unarmed. He had to leave his sword behind."

"I'm sure the Baron of Ibelin has lots of spare swords," the armorer's wife told her husband in exasperation. Godwin was such a dreamer! It had been his idea to come out to Jerusalem to cure their Sven, and look where they had ended—trapped in a city that was about to be besieged by heartless heathens!

"None with the arms of Ibelin on one side of the pommel and the arms of Jerusalem on the other, and inlaid with the words 'Defender of Jerusalem' in bronze," Godwin answered proudly.

His wife gazed at him, appalled. "Why did you do that? No one else will buy it with the Ibelin arms in the pommel!"

"I don't *want* anyone else to buy it. I've made it for the Baron of Ibelin, and I'm going to take it to him tomorrow."

"You'd better ask a fair price—or you'll get stuck with it!"

"I'm not going to charge him," Godwin answered, jutting out his chin in defiance of the protest that was sure to follow. "I'm going to *give* it to him."

September 17, 1187

There was considerable rivalry among the new knights. Not with Dawit and Gabriel, of course; they were older and belonged to the Ibelin household, while Gabriel had the added aura of having fought at Hattin. Among the others, however, there was a natural tendency to want to show off and attract the attention and praise of their lord. The opportunities to do so were limited, however, because in the month since he had knighted them Ibelin had been busy with many matters; he had not spent much time with his knights, who were being housed in the royal palace.

Orders to prepare for an armed foraging party therefore ignited a frenzy of activity. Over the last five weeks, there had been a number of these and they were welcome breaks in the bordom. The young men, most of whom had no squires under the circumstances, rushed to help each other into their armor and then ran down to the stables to tack up their own horses.

Sir Alexander, the Armenian who claimed to be related to one of the Armenian kings, was one of the few among the new knights to have a servant, and Sir Galeran greatly resented the Armenian's wealth and airs. He felt it was inappropriate for an Armenian to look down on someone like him, descended from one of the men who (no matter how humble) had freed the Holy Land from Saracen oppression eighty-eight years ago. Just because he had servants, Sir Alexander was finished sooner than the others and was mounted and waiting for the Lord of Ibelin, making a false good impression, Galeran thought bitterly.

In his haste to follow Sir Alexander, Galeran didn't tighten his girth enough, and his saddle slipped the moment he tried to mount. He had to step down, readjust it, and tighten the girth again. By the time he was finished, almost all the other knights were mustered, and Sir Galeran had to take a place toward the back. From here he couldn't hear what Lord Balian was saying to the leaders (including the damned Armenian), and all he could do was follow in their wake.

Lord Balian led them to the south, out the Beaucayre Gate toward St. Mary of Zion. St. Mary's had been built in the last century in the form of a basilica surrounded by a graveyard. It was mostly used for funerals, and the graveyard was very popular. It was still and stately now, abandoned ever since news of Hattin had reached the city.

Beyond St. Mary's they descended the steep slope into the valley, and there they paused at Lord Balian's command to water their horses at the spring of Germain. When all the horses had drunk their fill, they toiled up the opposite hill, taking the road to Bethlehem. The land was parched from the long, hot summer. The grass was dry and rustled in the wind. The passing of more than eighty horsemen churned up the dust of the road, and Galeran, near the back, was soon breathing it in. It made him cough and coated his surcoat with a thin film of dirt.

"What are we looking for?" Galeran asked the youth next to him.

His companion shrugged; he hadn't been able to hear what Lord Balian said, either.

Galeran let his eyes sweep across the familiar countryside. He knew it well, for he had been born and raised in Hebron and frequently traveled to Jerusalem, but it looked strange now that it was devoid of traffic. This road was usually choked with convoys carrying goods from Galilee to Hebron and from Oultrejourdain to Acre, not to mention the hordes of pilgrims that usually clogged it on their way from Jerusalem to Bethlehem and back. It was odd, too, not to see any herds of sheep or goats on the surrounding hills. The grazing wasn't particularly good in late summer, but there should have been the odd shepherd with a small flock on its way to market.

The heat of the sun was starting to make Galeran sweat under his armor. The surcoat prevented his chest and back from overheating, but his arms felt like they were burning up, and his feet were swelling inside his chain-mail chausses. That had been one good thing about being a squire, Galeran admitted to himself; he had never worn more mail than a short-sleeved hauberk, and he preferred low ankle boots for his feet at this time of year.

After they had jogged along at a steady pace for almost an hour, the city of Bethlehem came into view. It was a jumble of white buildings punctuated by towers and domes spilling down from a round hilltop. The imposing Church of the Nativity dominated the skyline, easily recognizable even from this distance.

As they entered the orchards and vineyards that skirted Bethlehem, the lack of movement and human presence was even more eerie. Only an abandoned, lame donkey stared at them from the side of the road, shaking his long ears at flies. The shops lining the road as it started the curving climb to the city were boarded up and abandoned. These were the shops that usually catered to pilgrims. Some sold trinkets and souvenirs, others specialized in more valuable keepsakes like carpets, shrouds, and relics, and there were the many roadside shops selling refreshment in the form of fresh pomegranates, oranges, or apples, whatever was in season, or hot meat pies and honey pastries. Galeran recognized the pastry shop that had sold the most delightful fig bars he had ever tasted; it, too, was boarded up and empty. A stray dog with its tail dragging darted into the next alley with a guilty look over its shoulder.

Lord Balian slowed to a walk as they entered the city itself. The stillness sent shivers down Galeran's spine. There was not a soul in sight, and the only things that moved were chased by the wind: a dead palm leaf, a puff of dust, a rag caught on a nail flapping against the side of a house. And yet Galeran felt as if they were being watched. He looked nervously over his shoulder and then forward toward Lord Balian. He was riding with his right hand on his hilt. This wasn't your usual foraging patrol, Galeran thought with sudden clarity, and looked around at his fellows. Several had followed Lord Balian's example and had dropped their hands to their hilts.

They clattered into Manger Square before the Church of the Nativity, and Ibelin drew up. Ordering the others to remain mounted and vigilant, he swung himself down and approached the western portal. The wooden door set in the pointed stone arch of the modern entrance was closed, and Ibelin raised his fist and pounded on it. There was no answer and he tried the door, but it was locked. He stepped back and looked right and left toward the entrances to the Armenian and Greek monasteries. Galeran looked nervously over his shoulder again. Ibelin returned to the main door and again pounded his fist on it. This time he called out: "This is Balian d'Ibelin. My knights and I are here to escort you to Jerusalem."

Somewhere something clicked. Galeran started and looked around, as did his fellows. Then with a creak the door cracked open, and a man looked out through the slit. Ibelin stepped forward to speak with him and, as the door opened wider, slipped inside. "Who's inside?" Galeran asked generally.

"The monks," someone answered.

"And other idiots who think Christ will save them," someone else answered.

"Don't we all expect Christ to save us?"

"After death, yes; not before."

They seemed to have been waiting for a long time. Galeran had gradually adjusted to the silence, and he was starting to get bored. He dropped his reins and let his horse rub the side of his face on his foreleg. The flies had found them, and Galeran swatted at them in annoyance.

At last the door to the church opened again, and Ibelin called for Sir Constantine. Sir Constantine jumped down and disappeared inside the Church of the Nativity.

"There must be a well somewhere here," the haughty Sir Alexander remarked. "I'm thirsty."

"There's one just down there," Sir Galeran answered to show off his familiarity with Bethlehem, pointing to the road opening off the south side of Manger Square. "On the road to Hebron," he explained.

"Shall we go there?" Sir Alexander asked generally.

"We were ordered to stay here," Sir Dawit reminded them sternly.

"Yes, but it's not as if I'm *going* anywhere," the Armenian prince retorted. "I'm just getting a drink of water. How far is the well?"

"Just a couple blocks. I can show you," one of the other knights, Sir Gautier, offered.

"We won't be gone long," Sir Alexander assured generally.

"You should stay here," Sir Dawit insisted.

"I don't take orders from the likes of you!" Sir Alexander retorted, making Sir Galeran catch his breath. He was a little disappointed when Sir Dawit made no retort, preferring to shrug and look the other way.

Sirs Gautier and Alexander picked up their reins and trotted casually across the square to disappear down the street indicated. The others looked at each other, some longing to follow the disobedient knights and others filled with disapproval.

Voices were raised in anger inside the church, but since the argument was being carried out in Greek, few of the knights in front understood what was said. They guessed, however, that the monks were still refusing to go.

Suddenly a shout came from the south, the direction in which Sirs Alexander and Gautier had disappeared. The knights looked at one another. It wasn't just one shout—there were suddenly dozens of alarmed voices. A second later they heard the clatter of hooves on cobbles, and Sir Gautier burst into the square, shouting at them: "Saracens! Saracens!"

Sir Alexander was lagging behind him, and hot on his heels were dozens, scores, hundreds (or so it seemed to the astonished Sir Galeran) of Saracen horsemen. Sir Gabriel spun his horse around and drew his sword in a single motion, and Galeran, his heart in his throat, struggled to follow his example.

Saracens poured into the square in hot pursuit of the Christian knights. Their swords were drawn, and the bright silk ties of their turbans flew out behind them. Before any of the Christians could intercede, the lead Saracen caught up with Sir Alexander. With a loud shout the Saracen stood in his stirrups and raised his sword over his head. A split second later it sliced down on Sir Alexander, spewing blood and sending Sir Alexander's arm spinning through the air. With a howl the Armenian fell off his horse, gushing blood from his empty arm socket.

But other leading Saracens registered that they were facing not two but more than fourscore knights. They sat back and tried to rein in. Their horses skidded and slid on the cobbles, causing the press of Saracens rushing from behind to collide with them. Horses started whinnying and men shouted in confusion.

Sir Gabriel put spurs to his horse and, raising his sword, shouted: "À Ibelin! À Jerusalem!" Then he spurred forward, his sword leveled as if it were a lance.

Sir Galeran and his colleagues tried to follow, but they had not been formed up and prepared for a charge. They had no experience in charging, and their horses found it difficult to gain traction on the cobbles. The result was a disorganized, sloppy, and rather slow advance that had none of the impact of a Frankish charge. Within seconds the entire square was covered by a chaotic melee. Christians and Saracens were moving every which way, pirouetting around each other as they tried to gain an advantage. It was a senseless and disorganized fight—but one that was still deadly, as the more numerous Saracens were being steadily reinforced.

When Ibelin burst out of the church, he experienced a moment of sheer panic. Everything was lost. He was about to be cut down here on Manger Square, and Jerusalem would be without a commander and knights again. But then Dawit led Centurion forward, shielding Ibelin with his horse from the frantic skirmish in the square. Ibelin lifted his right leg and swung himself into the saddle from the off side, rather than waste time going around to the more exposed side. He didn't bother taking up the reins, but instead grabbed his sword and shield. Centurion was a veteran, and his ears were already flat on his head; he knew the enemy when he saw it, just as well as Balian did. He turned toward them without any urging, while Dawit and Constantine flanked their lord as he plunged into the fray.

It was far too late to try to organize his knights, and there was no room for a charge. Ibelin's only hope was to eliminate the leadership of the enemy. He had not had time to identify the commander, however, so he just started killing, in the hope that his opponent would identify himself by his reaction.

This was Ibelin's first opportunity to use his new sword in combat, and he was astonished what a difference three extra inches made. He was noticeably reaching his enemy sooner and faster, before they really had a chance to close, and without the loss of balance or control. What he couldn't see was the way the bronze in the sword was catching the sunlight, and how the combination of brutal efficiency and glittering blade was starting to strike unnatural fear into the hearts of his opponents.

The Saracens had not expected to encounter any Christian cavalry in Bethlehem, because they had been led to believe there *was* no Christian chivalry left alive and free—south of the city of Tyre. The Kingdom of Jerusalem, they had confidently thought, was utterly denuded of knights. They had been on loose reins, chatting about what a nice town Bethlehem was and what a pleasant night they would spend here, when they had come around a bend in the road and seen two Christian knights at a well. Their surprise had been so great that they had gaped in sheer astonishment, giving the knights a chance to flee.

As the knights ran away, however, the Saracens had become ashamed of their unpreparedness, while the obvious panic of the knights suggested they were two "strays," lone knights who had somehow slipped out of the trap at Hattin. The Saracens set off in pursuit like hunters after a hare—only to crash into an entire squadron of knights. That, too, had been a shock, but the disorganized fight that ensued had restored their confidence. The Christians could not bring their heavier horses and armor to bear in the confined space of the paved, city square. Or so they had thought.

Then suddenly a knight burst out of nowhere, cutting through their ranks as if they were rag dolls. His horse was literally tearing the flesh off the smaller Arab stallions, while the knight slew with his sword and unhorsed men with his shield. The flash of bronze on his sword made him seem strangely superhuman in that instant—as if they were confronting some kind of demon, fighting with the fires of hell in his sword.

As men began to quail before the advancing knight, the commanding emir shouted furiously at them to stand, spinning his horse around to cut off the Christian before he could do more damage. The emir was fired not only by indignation at the cowardice of his men, but by the chilling knowledge that he had let his guard down. The Sultan would be furious to learn that he had allowed his troops to get ambushed like this! There were so many men vying for the Sultan's favor that one little mistake like this could cost him his current status as one of the Sultan's inner circle.

The emir's horse found it hard to gain a footing on the cobbles, but the square was small enough for him to intercept the Christian killer. He called on Allah and raised his sword confident that he was more than equal to anyone who did not recognize the Prophet.

Ibelin registered the green silk brocade, broken only by glittering bands of green satin on which were stitched gold Arabic lettering. He recognized subconsciously that he had an emir opposite him. Sayings from the Koran embroidered by a loving wife caught the sunlight as the emir raised his sword—and Ibelin, knowing this was his one and only chance to extricate his knights and live to fight another day, struck with the power of panic. He swung Defender of Jerusalem horizontally, at the same time spurring forward to lend his arm the strength of momentum. The sword struck just below the emir's rib cage and continued clear out the other side. The emir's upper body flopped onto the cobbles, and the lower half continued riding across the square. But the skirmish was over.

With shouts and screams, the Saracens spun their horses and galloped for the safety of the street by which they'd entered. Sir Constantine and Sir Dawit shouted orders not to follow as Balian sat back in his saddle, dropped his head, and gave thanks to Christ.

After a moment Balian took a deep breath, lifted his head, and re-sheathed his sword. He looked around at his troop. Two knights lay on the cobbles unmoving, two were trying to right themselves, and one was writhing in evident agony. "Sir Dawit, see to the wounded."

He turned Centurion around, reaching down to pat his neck and mutter "well done" as he did so. The horse snorted satisfaction. Ibelin rode straight for the tall portal of the Church of the Nativity. It stood wide open, and one could see across the narthex into the long nave of the church. Crowding the doorway were scores of monks staring wide-eyed at the scene before them.

Ibelin drew up before the portal, but this time he did not dismount. He leaned on the pommel of his saddle and looked down at the intransigent abbot. "Those were men of Salah ad-Din's advance guard," he told them, pointing behind him in the direction the Saracens had fled. "Ascalon has fallen. The siege of Jerusalem is about to begin."

Chapter 22

Jerusalem, September 20, 1187

The Sultan had enough men to surround Jerusalem, something the men of the First Crusade had not been able to do, but it wasn't necessary. The Christians in Jerusalem had no one who could possibly relieve them or send them supplies. Therefore, instead of surrounding the city, Salah ad-Din drew up his army on the hills to the northwest, where the terrain provided no natural aid to the defenders.

Throughout September 20, the defenders had watched as contingent after contingent of Saracen troops arrived with banners flying to set up a neat encampment, protected by a palisade. Speculation on the exact size of the besieging army ran rampant on the walls and in the streets of Jerusalem, but Ibelin didn't participate in it. He knew what he needed to know: the Sultan's army was more than sufficient to overwhelm Jerusalem's defenses.

At dusk the wailing call to prayers wafted over the ramparts to the defenders from the throats of scores of muezzins, and the fires of the enemy came to life as far as the eye could see. Ibelin, reminded of Hattin, turned his back on the sight, and descended from the wall into the city.

There were more people on the streets than usual, and a tangible excitement stirred the crowds. The people behind the high white walls of Jerusalem had expected a Saracen army to surround and besiege them ever since the news of Hattin had arrived more than two months ago. For ten weeks they had lived in anticipation of this event. Ever since Ibelin's arrival they had been consciously preparing for it. Now, finally, it was reality, and everyone felt the need to talk about the fact, to show off how much they knew, and to bolster their own courage with talk of their future deeds. Ibelin understood that—but he refused to be drawn into any conversations, and only nodded greetings to those calling out to him.

At the Ibelin palace, Balian forced himself eat a hearty meal, and then he called for Father Michael so he could confess his sins before retiring to bed. He left orders to be woken at Matins.

September 21, 1187

Father Michael did not sleep, so that he would not fail his lord by missing that morning call. He prayed until Matins and then woke Lord Balian and Georgios, who was serving as his squire since Ernoul was still in Tyre and Gabriel had been knighted. Georgios had been well trained by William Marshal. He was efficient as well as eager, and he knew when to hold his tongue. This morning was no time for chatter; he assisted Lord Balian without a word.

Ibelin left his residence while Matins was still being read in the many churches, but not before meeting with Sirs Constantine, Roger, and Mathewos in the courtyard of the Ibelin palace to give them their orders. He then made his way through the darkened, lifeless streets to Tancred's Tower in the northwest corner of the wall.

Just to the side and at the base of Tancred's Tower stood the Postern of St. Lazarus. As agreed earlier, this quarter had been turned over to the lepers when the arrival of Salah ad-Din's army made it necessary for them to abandon the leprosarium beyond the wall. At Sir Daniel's request, the Order of St. Lazarus had been given the task of defending the St. Lazarus Postern from the inside.

At the sight of his former lord, Sir Daniel strode forward in evident agitation. "My lord, I was just about to come for you. We believe the enemy is preparing to attack here. At this very tower."

Ibelin nodded. "I expected as much. I have already sent Sir Constantine to draw half the Greek and Armenian defenders off the southwest and southern walls. Sir Mathewos will take some of his Syrians off the eastern wall as well. They will reinforce the defenses here." He turned to mount the stairs to Tancred's Tower.

Daniel stopped him, stammering out, "My lord, remember King Baldwin—"

"There is not a second when I do *not* remember him," Ibelin countered coldly; he felt his former squire was being presumptuous.

"I mean, remember what he *did* despite his illness, his disfigurement!" Daniel pleaded for understanding.

"Yes," Balian answered impatiently; the Saracens were about to launch their first assault on the city, and this was no time for reminiscing. "And I intend to do the same." He started again up the steps.

Daniel had no choice but to call after him, "So will *we*, my lord. That's all I'm trying to say. So will *we*!" With his good arm he took in the misshapen, crippled, and disfigured band of almost two hundred lepers clustered around him.

The chorus of voices that fell in with him made Balian pause and look back down on a sea of deformed and misshapen faces—men and women without lips and noses, old and young with missing fingers and crippled feet. Yet they were here in the dark of the pre-dawn to fight for Jerusalem. Ibelin stopped. All they were asking for was recognition of their humanity. He drew a deep breath and took the time to look them in the eye, one after another. Then he nodded, "Thank you and God bless you!"

On the wall walk, the watch also greeted Ibelin excitedly. "My lord, we were just about to send for you. Look! There and there! It's hard to see in the darkness, but if you listen you can hear them. They are forming up opposite."

Ibelin glanced over his shoulder toward the east, trying to judge how long it would be until dawn. Maybe another hour before the sky lightened. Then he turned back to the men of the watch and asked, "Can you make out any siege engines?"

"Not that we can see or hear."

Ibelin nodded. Salah ad-Din was testing them, hoping that they didn't have the heart or means to truly defend themselves. He would, Ibelin guessed, send in some of his best shock troops, probably motivated with large promises of rewards from the spoils. ("All the gold of Jerusalem." "Forty virgins in a single night.")

Well, the Sultan would discover that they certainly had the *heart* to fight.

He looked back into the city and was pleasantly surprised to see that Greeks and Armenians that Sir Constantine had sent were starting to collect at the foot of the stairs leading onto the walls. As ordered, Sir Constantine had brought his men through the darkened streets without a light, and he was enforcing strict silence.

Ibelin signaled for Sir Constantine to join him on the roof of Tancred's Tower, and directed him in a low voice to integrate the Greeks and Armenians into the Frankish line all along the northwest ramparts rather than deploy them as a separate unit. Sir Constantine nodded and returned to give his orders to his men.

No sooner had the Greek and Armenian troops dispersed along the wall than a heavy wagon lumbered up carrying a huge cauldron filled with tar. While half the team set up a ring of stones covered by a grill, the others, carefully and with much whispered bickering, offloaded the cauldron and placed it on the grill. Behind them a second wagon pulled up, full of wood for the fire. The driver clambered on to the back of the cart to start tossing the wood onto the pavement beside the cauldron, and the sound of the wood clattering on the flagstones made Ibelin jump. He leaned over the wall to hiss down to the man: "Stop that racket!"

The man looked up, annoyed, and then amazed when he realized he had just been addressed by none other than the Baron of Ibelin himself. While he gaped, Ibelin snapped, "Get down and offload the wagon quietly!"

The wagoneer bobbed his head deferentially with an awed, "Yes, my lord!" Then he dutifully dismounted and started to offload his wagon an armload at a time.

Meanwhile, two other wagons driven by Templar lay brothers drew up in the street. These were laden with arrows. The lepers clustered around to offload and then prepare these as flaming arrows. They worked in teams of four, men and women both: one cut strips of cotton cloth, one wound the lengths of cotton around the arrow behind the head, a third dipped the prepared arrow in the now slowly bubbling tar, while the fourth stacked the arrows in bundles to be passed up to the wall. Other lepers took braziers of glowing coals up to the ramparts so the archers could light the tar-soaked arrows just before firing.

Sir Constantine, his men now deployed, returned to join Ibelin on Tancred's Tower, reporting that the Greeks had supplies of Greek fire that they would bring with them. Burning tar was unpleasant; Greek fire was deadly. Their supplies, however, were limited. "Today is only the beginning," Ibelin reminded the Greek knight as he turned his attention to the enemy again.

It was definitely getting lighter, making it easier to see the enemy's preparations. There could be no question that the Saracens were forming up opposite Tancred's Tower, but they had separated their forces into two divisions. Apparently they intended to strike both to the west and to the north of Tancred's Tower, probably in order to divide the attention of the defenders, particularly the archers on the tower itself. Although the Saracen formations were quite dense, they remained well out of bow range.

Ibelin returned to the inside wall of the tower and looked into the city again. He was pleased by how much activity was evident although noise was minimal. In strict obedience to his orders, the fighting men not on watch had mustered without lighting torches and were being careful to make as little noise as possible. From David's Gate to St. Stephen's Gate, they were filing silently up the various stairways to the wall walk with their bows on their backs, axes and swords at their hips.

By the time the Saracens started to advance, the Christians were not only in position, they had been so for nearly a half-hour and the tension was almost unbearable. Ibelin pulled his coif over his head and secured the aventail over his throat and chin. He slipped his hands into the mail mittens hanging from the sleeves of his hauberk, and pulled his helmet over his head. He was wearing his older open-faced helmet with the nosepiece, rather than the visored helmet he'd worn at Hattin. He felt it was important to make eye contact with the men he was leading.

Still believing they had the advantage of surprise, the Saracens jogged forward without the usual fanfare of shouts and calls to Allah. Behind them from their camp the muezzins started calling the Faithful to prayer, as if to disguise the fact that the Saracen army was now rushing toward the walls of Jerusalem.

Ibelin could hear the men behind him squirming and fidgeting in nervousness, and it took considerable control to restrain his own instinct for action, but the longer the enemy thought they were approaching a sleeping city, the more careless they would be—and the more of them would come in range of the archers, crouched behind the battlements with arrows already notched in their bows.

Ibelin murmured in a low voice to the sentry beside him on the corner of Tancred's Tower. "Give an alarmed shout—like you just noticed something and are panicked."

The man stared at him and then started shouting with every appearance of panic. "Attack! Attack! We're under attack!"

Unfortunately, his "attack" was misinterpreted as an order by many of the over-tense men along the wall, and these sprang up and started firing at the Saracens. Ibelin would have preferred to wait another thirty seconds, but it was impossible to call the arrows back. All he could do now was reinforce, calling: "Fire!"

Although not as perfectly timed as Ibelin would have liked, the Christian volley still took the attackers by surprise. Instead of a sleeping city, they found themselves racing toward an enraged beast. Arrows poured over the side of the city and rained down on them. Many of the arrows were tipped with flaming tar. The screams of wounded and dying men mingled with shouts of anger, so that the attacking army seemed to roar like a wounded lion.

But these Saracen soldiers were hardened veterans, and even if taken by surprise, they did not falter. They rushed forward, faster and more determined than ever to get the siege ladders up against the walls.

Ibelin shifted his gaze from the base of the walls to the wider situation, and saw Saracens jogging out of the camp in good order to reinforce the attackers. Some units must have been told they could stay behind for morning prayers, but to join the assault thereafter.

Looking down again, he saw the enemy oozing along the base of the wall to the left and right of Tancred's Tower, looking for weakness. Ibelin was not concerned. Men along the western wall all the way to the citadel of David sprang into action as soon as targets came into range. Along the northern wall the Saracens spread out as far as the Leper Pool, still out of range of the men on St. Stephen's Gate—although one or two over-eager archers from that gate tried their luck before their sergeants made them stand down and save their arrows.

Ibelin pulled back from the outer edge of the wall and crossed the roof of the Tower to look down into the city again. There were more carts filled with arrows lined up in the street below, and young boys and women had formed a chain to pass the arrows up from the wagons to the ramparts. Other wagons loaded with water were also visible, and women were dunking tin pitchers into the barrels to fill them before passing them up by the same method to the men manning the wall. Ibelin nodded his satisfaction. The weeks of preparation was paying off.

Jerusalem, September 24, 1187

Salah ad-Din kept up the attacks from dawn to dusk for two solid days, but the Christian resistance did not crack. Then he deployed his siege engines.

Massive mangonels hurled both boulders and smaller stones and sometimes flaming material: twigs woven together and wrapped in oil-soaked rags, then set alight. All were equally deadly. The boulders were directed mostly at the gates and upper portions of the walls, with the objective of weakening the masonry to the point of crumbling or collapse. The stones were "anti-personnel" weapons that killed anyone unlucky enough to be in their path. The flaming materials were intended to set roofs alight inside the city and create havoc, thereby dividing the attention of the defenders.

Movable siege towers were also rolled forward. These wooden towers, mounted on wheels, contained multiple platforms from which archers could fire on the city walls from roughly the same or greater height as the defenders on the wall. This effectively eliminated the advantage of the defending archers. The attacking archers were partly protected by woven mats covered with animal hides, soaked in vinegar to reduce flammability. From these platforms the Saracens could rain death upon the defenders—and if they got close enough, they had drawbridges that could be lowered on to the walls, so that foot soldiers could pour on to the ramparts and take possession of walls, gates, and ultimately the city. Although Ibelin had smaller siege engines mounted on Tancred's Tower and the Tower of David to answer Salah ad-Din's larger ones, with the deployment of the siege engines Christian casualties began to mount dramatically.

Sister Adela had been a Hospitaller sister for a quarter century. She thought of herself as a professional, but nothing in her life had prepared her for the casualties that flooded the Hospital of St. John at Jerusalem after the mangonels went into action. By nightfall on September 24, 1187, after two days of bombardment, the courtyard of the Hospital was paved with wounded, and bands of lay brothers moved systematically and continuously between them to identify and remove the dead. In the wards, the brothers worked feverishly to remove arrows protruding from profusely bleeding wounds, stop the hemorrhaging opened by the missiles, and set or amputate the limbs of people partially crushed by the flung stones. Their habits were drenched in the mixed blood of dozens of patients, and their hands were so covered with it that when they went to wipe the sweat from their brows, they left smears of scarlet on their faces.

Most of the casualties were fighting men, but some of the helpers—women bringing water, boys bringing arrows—had been hit, too. The sight of a young boy writhing in agony from an arrow in his guts made even Sister Adela taste vomit in her throat, while many of the younger sisters were openly weeping and shaking. They were all seeing and hearing things that would haunt them for the rest of their lives.

Beth returned to the Ibelin palace at dusk. As usual, her face and hands were black with soot from standing near the boilers of tar all day long. Her shoulders ached, her back hurt, her feet were swollen and sore, and her throat was parched so badly she could hardly swallow. Just as on the previous four days.

But this evening when Tsion opened the door for her, preparing to welcome her home to a hot meal and wine, she gasped. Beth looked so terrible that at first Tsion thought she had been wounded. "Beth! What is it? What happened?" the Ethiopian teenager asked in wide-eyed alarm as she pulled her sister-in-law inside.

"Nothing," Beth told her dully because she had no words to describe what she had seen: a bundle of burning rags had landed squarely on one of her co-workers. The woman had been set alight. Mad with pain, she had started screaming in agony and running about in panic. One of the men had to tackle her so they could smother the flames with a blanket, but by then her face was a charred wreck. She'd screamed like she was being gutted when they tried to carry her to the Hospital.

Like Sister Adela, Father Michael found himself overwhelmed despite all the preparations. There were too many wounded! If he stopped to hear one man's confession, another died while waiting for him. The sight of a little boy with a crushed chest that left him wheezing and breathing frothy blood, his head rolling back and forth in pain, made him want to scream in rage at the injustice of it all. His only comfort was that the little boy surely had no sins on his conscience, and Christ would receive him with open arms.

The same could not be said for many of the men and women who grabbed at his ankles, begging for absolution with terror in their eyes. Father Michael went down on his heels beside yet another—was it the fiftieth or one-hundredth?—and tried not to hear the sins he had committed. He did not really want to know what his fellow Christians were capable of. Somewhere here, he thought as he made the sign of the cross and moved on, might be the very men who had plundered an orphanage and left little children locked in a cellar to starve. But he would give them absolution if they asked for it. What else could he do?

Sir Daniel finally caught up with Ibelin at the Cattle Market. Ibelin had been ceaselessly patrolling the city for four days, apparently without stopping to sleep, since he seemed to be everywhere: on Tancred's Tower and at the Citadel, of course, but also inspecting the men holding the Armenian sectors of the wall to ensure they maintained their vigilance, encouraging the women running the field kitchens, and even visiting the wounded. That he also took time to check on the livestock struck Daniel as somewhat obsessive—even if the pig market was within range of the Saracen siege engines and Ibelin had ordered the pigs moved to the cattle market, which was not under bombardment.

As Ibelin left the market, Daniel intercepted him. "My lord, there's something we lepers want to propose to you. If you would just come with me?"

Ibelin stopped. Up close Daniel could see the strain of the last four days written on the baron's face. "Is this important?" Ibelin asked, in a tone that suggested he did not believe it could be.

That hurt, and Daniel became slightly resentful. Ibelin still saw him as a runaway baker's apprentice, he thought. But he was going to change that. He drew himself upright and answered firmly, "Yes, my lord; it's about the siege engines." When Daniel could detect no reaction, he added, "We have a plan to destroy at least some of them."

"So do I," Ibelin countered. "And I need to implement it." He glanced to the west, where the sun had now set, leaving only an orange smudge on the underside of a large cloud bank. He had come to the cattle market in part to pass the time until darkness, when he planned to lead an attack on the siege engines.

Daniel took advantage of his silence to speak up. "My father says you plan to attack the siege engines tonight. You must hear us out before you do that!" Daniel insisted.

Ibelin turned back to Daniel. He should have guessed that Sir Roger or Father Michael would keep Daniel well informed of his plans. "All right. Tell me."

"Not here, my lord; I want to you to hear it from all of us."

Ibelin raised his eyebrows, but Daniel did not detect the gesture because Ibelin's eyebrows were hidden under his coif. All Daniel saw was that Ibelin nodded. Together they started for the long covered market that led from this quarter of the city near the southern wall, due north to the Syrian exchange just east of the Church of the Holy Sepulcher.

It was rapidly getting dark, and the bells were ringing Vespers as they entered the market. Normally the shopkeepers would have been locking up their stalls or sweeping away the rubbish in preparation for going home, leaving the narrow, paved alley almost abandoned. Instead, Daniel was startled to find himself amidst masses of people, as if it were the middle of the busiest day in pilgrim season. The entire covered alleyway stretching out before them as it scaled the hill ahead of them was lit up by brass and glass lamps swaying in the arches of the shops.

Then it dawned on Daniel that these weren't shoppers, but rather the families of the shopkeepers. They were sheltering from the enemy bombardment behind the stone walls and under the stone vaults of the market. Children cried and laughed, infants squalled, old men gossiped, and women chatted—all cut off from the sight and sound of incoming boulders, the screams of combat, and the flames and smoke of the fires. It was like being in a womb—or a tomb, Daniel thought, as they made their way up the alleyway punctuated by steps between the shops in the flanking vaults.

They emerged at the Syrian exchange and turned into the street between the Hospital and the Church of the Holy Sepulcher. They walked past the courtyard where Ibelin had created eighty-one new knights, and on between the shuttered souvenir shops. Here the air was heavy with smoke from fires that had been ignited all around, and as they came abreast of the Patriarch's palace they encountered the charred remains of a half-dozen shops that had burned before the fire could be put out. The ashes blew in the light evening wind, and some embers winked at them in the darkness.

Beyond the Patriarch's palace, they reached the corner of the wall beside Tancred's Tower now occupied by the lepers. It stank badly because the latrines were inadequate for the numbers crowded together in this awkward, cramped space. But at the sight of Ibelin, the lepers struggled to their feet and stood upright. They seemed strangely excited about something.

When a hush had fallen over them, Sir Daniel spoke. "My lord. If we don't destroy the Sultan's siege engines, they will surely destroy us." He gestured vaguely across the city where several fires were still burning, but he did not try Ibelin's patience by pausing. "But the Saracens guard them well, both day and night. Furthermore, they will expect attacks from the flanks by men sallying out of the other gates of Jerusalem."

Ibelin said nothing. Daniel not only appeared to know his plan, he was right. Ibelin just didn't have any alternative.

"But, my lord, what if we were to sally forth from here?" Daniel pointed at the heavy postern gate almost lost in the shadows behind him. "Just out there are *two* of the enemy's siege towers. If we could set them on fire, the enemy will be distracted and partially blinded as well. If the siege towers go up, they will light up this entire sector of the wall—and the perimeter, where the mangonels are, will be cast in greater darkness. While all attention is on the burning siege towers, you can lead the attack on the mangonels!" Daniel got his plan out all in one breath, eager for approbation.

Ibelin drew a deep breath to keep calm. "Sir Daniel, the idea of a diversion is a good one, and I thank you for it. But the men out there defending the siege towers are some of Salah ad-Din's best. If we so much as crack this postern to let troops out, they will rush forward and overwhelm us, possibly gaining entry. The city would be lost almost immediately."

"No, my lord, it won't! I mean, if *fighting* men tried to sally out, you are right. The enemy would joyously slaughter them and storm the postern. But we're suggesting that *we* go out."

Ibelin stared at Daniel for a second, and then let his eyes sweep over the nearly two hundred lepers collected around him. They were nodding vigorous assent.

"If we go out in our rags and bandages, begging mercy and saying we have been expelled," Daniel hastened to explain, "they will be shocked and cast into confusion. Meanwhile, other men from the garrison can slam the postern shut and secure it. But each of us will carry a pot of Greek fire hidden in our bandages. As soon as we are in range, we will start pelting the siege towers with them to set them alight. When the towers go up in flame, you can launch your attack on the mangonels."

"You'll be trapped between the burning siege engines and the closed postern!" Ibelin protested. "You will all die."

"We will *all* die, my lord," Sir Daniel answered steadily, adding with passion, "but rather than dying limb by limb in shame and poverty, we will die so others might save Jerusalem for Christ."

"This is what you have *all* decided to do?" Ibelin asked, directing his question to the other lepers, searching their misshapen and deteriorating faces for some sign of dissent or doubt. He found none—at least not in the poor light of this confined space. They all seemed to be nodding, and several ventured to call out "Yes, my lord!" until someone shouted "Deus le Volt!" The battle cry of the First Crusade was rapidly picked up by the others and became a chant. "Deus le Volt!" God wills it.

"But you need to supply us with enough Greek fire," Daniel hastened to point out in a low voice as the others chanted.

Balian met Daniel's eyes. He knew this was Daniel's idea, although he could not know how he had convinced the others to join him. He sensed Daniel still wanted to atone for the sins he thought he had committed: letting Ibrahim get expelled from Baldwin's service, not stopping Guy de Lusignan from wrenching the Regency from a browbeaten Baldwin. . . . But did he really have the right to lead the other lepers to certain death?

"I think King Baldwin would want this," Daniel played his trump. "I think he would *want* lepers to destroy the siege towers."

Balian capitulated. "God wills it!"

So far the burden of the defense had fallen to the archers. The knights had been positioned on the wall, ready to fight any Saracen who actually made it to the ramparts, and once or twice the enemy had succeeded in getting ladders laid up against the side of the wall. When it happened on Sir Galeran's salient, he'd rushed forward with several of his fellows to push the ladder back or kill the man at the head. Yet even as they drew their swords and readied themselves for glory, a team of aging and far from slender Armenians upended a huge ceramic pot filled with boiling pitch over the side. This cleared the ladder of assailants and left them screaming at the base of the wall. Sir Galeran was pleased with the effectiveness of the defense—but slightly disappointed that he had not yet played an active role in it.

And then they were ordered to muster on foot in the inner ward of the Citadel.

Again the new knights helped each other arm, asking in anxious voices what this was about. If this was a sortie, surely they would have been asked to mount up?

They made their way on foot the short distance up the Street of the Armenians from the Royal Palace to the tower that gave access to the Citadel of David from the city. Overhead the sky was still lit up by occasional incoming balls of flame, and across the northwestern quarter fires burned with various grades of intensity. The fires seemed particularly intense in the vicinity of the Church of the Holy Sepulcher, and Sir Galeran was sure that was intentional. The Muslims were trying to hit the dome of the Church to destroy it, but the dome reared up proud and defiant against the backdrop of wavering firelight and billowing smoke, as people worked feverishly to put out the fires in the Street of the Money Lenders and the Street of Bad Cooking.

The knights were admitted at the gatehouse and passed through it to cross by drawbridge over the dry ditch surrounding the Citadel. Just as Sir Galeran started across the wooden bridge, a boulder pounded against the David Gate with such force that it made the drawbridge jump. Sir Galeran caught his breath, then looked at his fellows sheepishly. Several others looked back, as alarmed as he felt. They hurried together across the drawbridge and into the somewhat cramped courtyard of the Citadel. Yet no sooner had Sir Galeran gained the apparent safety of the inner ward than another boulder boomed against the adjacent gate, and someone cursed under his breath. The very earth seemed to shake beneath them.

Sir Galeran glanced upwards to the ramparts, thinking maybe they had been summoned to reinforce the defense at this critical point, but he could make out a substantial number of men silhouetted against a sky lightened by fires. Then another boulder pounded against the masonry, and Sir Galeran shook his head. How long could the walls take that?

The low muttering of his colleagues drew his attention to a figure coming down the stairs from the Tower of David; Sir Galeran realized it must be the Baron of Ibelin, trailed by Sirs Constantine, Roger, and Mathewos. Ibelin stopped on the second step so that he was raised slightly above his knights and could be seen by all. "Sirs." He gestured for them to come closer. When they were all standing in an eager pack at his feet, he announced: "Sirs, we need to destroy the Saracen siege engines."

Sir Galeran had already nodded agreement before he registered that when the baron said "we," he didn't mean the Christian defenders generally; he meant the men he was addressing. Suddenly Sir Galeran felt cold, although the night was warm.

Ibelin was continuing. "We will divide into two groups, so that if one party is discovered and destroyed, the other party will still stand a chance of attaining part of our objective. Sir Constantine will take half of you out the Mount Zion Gate and circle back to take the Saracen siege engines opposite this citadel from the south. Your principal objective will be that mangonel hammering David's Gate." He gestured as yet another boulder smashed against the wall, making the earth shake.

"I will lead the second party out of the Postern of St. Mary Magdalene, and we will attempt to destroy the mangonels opposite Tancred's Tower. Both parties will be accompanied by Greek engineers with pots of Greek fire." He gestured toward a half-dozen men wearing leather armor and heavy leather gloves with large leather satchels over their shoulders.

"The siege engines are heavily defended, and the enemy is expecting us. He knows we must make an effort to destroy his engines. The only thing he doesn't know is when and from which direction we will attack, but he will expect us to attack under cover of darkness. He probably expects us now."

Sir Galeran was getting more nervous the longer the baron spoke.

"The Brothers of St. Lazarus have offered to provide a diversion. They are going to sally out of the St. Lazarus Postern and make a direct assault on the two nearest siege towers that have Tancred's Tower under crossfire." He paused. "They have no chance of regaining the safety of the city, as we must close the postern behind them. We, on the other hand, will strike our targets and then race back around the back of the city to the Tanner's Gate and the Gate of Jehoshaphat respectively, where the watch will be expecting us and ready to open the gates. We will be mounted, and I expect some of us will be able to outrun the pursuing enemy. Any questions?"

"Do we mount up at once?"

"No, we will attack after Matins—when, hopefully, the enemy has become tired of waiting for us and has started to doze in weariness." Ibelin turned to Sir Constantine. "Pick your men."

Sir Galeran wished they had attacked at once. They had been told to "catch some sleep" as soon as they were sure their horses and equipment were ready, but how could you sleep in advance of such an action? At least in Bethlehem they had been taken completely by surprise and had had no time to get nervous. Like many others, he sought out a priest, confessed his sins, and then lay down on his pallet in the great hall of the palace and thought about his short life.

Sir Galeran had no idea what had become of his father or his elder brothers. They simply hadn't returned from Hattin. His mother had died when he was very small, and he had never gotten along with his stepmother. She was staying with the sisters of St. Anne and hadn't even come to his knighting. If he died tonight, he wasn't sure anyone would even notice, much less care. Unless you counted his father's steward, who had brought him, along with the rest of the manor household, from their smallholding near Hebron to the alleged safety of Jerusalem. Only he hadn't seen anything of the steward since his knighting. Sir Galeran turned over on his other side, trying to make himself comfortable, but it was no good. He couldn't sleep.

Shortly after midnight, Sirs Gabriel and Dawit came to the great hall to wake the knights. Most, like Sir Galeran, had been unable to sleep and quickly got to their feet. Only a handful had to be shaken awake.

Thanks to the hour of the night, even those knights usually prone to chatter and boasting were silent. Sir Galeran was glad of that at first, but then he missed the joking. Maybe some stupid wisecracks would have taken the edge off the tension.

Sir Galeran tacked up his horse, careful to tighten the girth sufficiently this time, collected a lance, and joined the party led by Sir Gabriel that was joining Ibelin. They mounted but kept to a walk, the horses unsettled by the smell of smoke that hung in the air—although most of the fires had by now been quenched, and there were no incoming fireballs at the moment.

Ibelin did not join them until they had reached the Postern of Mary Magdalene. Sir Galeran was amazed by how fresh and rested he looked; he had even shaved. He was accompanied by three of the men with the pots of Greek fire. "Maintain absolute silence during the advance," Ibelin ordered in a low voice that carried surprisingly well. "Keep behind me; and remember, no one is more important than the engineers with the Greek fire. If every one of us dies ensuring they can deliver the Greek fire, that is acceptable. The lepers are giving their lives tonight. I presume than none of you wish to be less valiant than they."

Then he closed the aventail of his hauberk over his mouth and chin, pulled on his helmet and mittens, and turned his gray charger toward the postern. With his lance propped upright on his right stirrup, he raised his hand and the gate opened.

They rode out into the darkness, and then down into the ditch that surrounded the city. The dry moat was not deep enough to completely conceal them, but it did greatly reduce what the enemy could see, particularly in the darkness. On the other hand, it was darker there, and the surface was uneven and littered with stones. The horses were unnerved by the novelty of the experience and they nickered, snorted, and shied.

Ibelin led at a walk to reduce both noise and the chance of stumbling. They rode under the arches supporting the bridge that led to St. Stephen's Gate, and then Ibelin had them dismount, lances in hand, and lead their horses back out of the ditch to the backside of the Leper's Pool. Here they paused to remount, right beside the main road to Ramla.

They were now between the main camp of the enemy, on the hill to their right, and the units protecting the siege towers at the base of the wall to their left. Their targets, the three mangonels targeting the north wall, were clearly visible, about two hundred yards behind the siege towers and higher up the slope. There were a least a hundred men around them, some of them diligently loading, winding, and firing the great machines, others watchfully protecting them.

Ibelin sat on his great gray courser, his head swiveling from left to right as he watched for any sign that the enemy had sighted them. All remained still and silent.

Suddenly a shout went up to their left. It was echoed by other excited shouts. Sir Galeran wasn't sure, but he thought he heard "St. Lazarus!" shouted out, and then came the screams of people in pain. He heard the Baron of Ibelin suck in his breath, and Sir Galeran became aware that he was holding his own.

The shouts and screams continued, punctuated by the occasional clash of steel. But most of the lepers were unarmed, untrained in warfare, and incapable of fighting anyway. They were being slaughtered, and there was no indication that they had succeeded in setting even one of the siege engines alight.

Ibelin's stallion stirred uneasily, stamped his foot on the stony earth, and flicked his tail in irritation, the only indication of his master's distress. The other knights looked at one another, but dared not speak.

And then suddenly a flash of light startled all the horses, making several leap sideways. Something had ignited after all.

The shouting increased in intensity and volume. Flames were devouring the *inside* of the nearest siege tower. Someone had managed to get past the protective vinegar-soaked hides and into the tower itself. The unprotected wooden steps leading upward to the fighting platforms were apparently tinder-dry, as were the woven mats behind the hides. In alarm, men started to rush down the hill from the mangonels to try to save the siege tower.

"Now!" Ibelin ordered, and his stallion leapt from a standstill into a canter as he raced forward, leaving the Greek engineers behind on their less well-trained horses. Ibelin soon recognized his mistake and checked Centurion's stride enough for the other knights and Greek engineers to catch up with him.

They were more than halfway to their target when they were sighted. With a new shout, the Saracens turned and started running back uphill toward the mangonels, leaving the siege towers to burn. Although Sir Galeran had not seen the moment when it happened, the second siege tower had also caught fire and was now burning, too, albeit less spectacularly than the first. He couldn't watch what happened there, however, as he had to focus on their own target.

As soon as the Saracen soldiers started running back toward the mangonels, Ibelin ordered Sir Gabriel and the Greeks to continue while he wheeled around, shouting for the knights to join him in cutting off the Saracens. Sir Galeran, however, noticed that the crews of the mangonel had grabbed their weapons and were rushing toward the Christians. He made a split-second decision to reinforce Sir Gabriel rather than follow Ibelin.

Galeran lowered his lance, holding it firmly under his right arm, while his stomach did somersaults. He had charged a quintain hundreds, maybe even thousands of times, but never in his life had he aimed at a live human. The man running toward him held an enormous ax—probably used for cutting the ropes of the siege engine rather than for fighting. Luckily. It slowed him down. Galeran lowered the tip of his lance and spurred forward. His aim was off and it wasn't a clean kill, but it was enough to make the man drop to his knees with a howl of mixed outrage and agony. He was not mortally wounded, but he had dropped the ax. Galeran was past him, drawing his sword in time to bring it down on the back of a man trying to stab the horse of one of the Greeks with the pots of Greek fire.

Again Galeran's aim was less than perfect and he failed to kill his victim, but he succeeded in knocking him away from the Greek. The latter was free to ride up beside the mangonel and start smashing his pots of Greek fire on the base, the coils of rope, and the wheels. A second later the fire ignited explosively, causing Daniel's horse to bolt in terror. He found himself galloping downhill toward the fight between Ibelin and the Saracen guardsmen, but Ibelin was shouting for them to withdraw.

There were still two intact siege engines standing ominous and brooding a couple of hundred yards away, but beyond them the orange glow in the sky suggested that Sir Constantine's squadron had also been successful. Ibelin apparently decided they had achieved enough to live to fight another day, and Galeran was not arguing with him. He sheathed his sword and leaned forward as he turned and then urged his horse to greater speed.

The Saracen guards around the siege engines had been infantrymen, but by now the entire Saracen camp had been raised by the burning towers, and Saracen cavalry began to charge down on their left flank. They were too numerous to count, and Daniel knew nothing would save him but speed. He had to get around the northeast corner of the city and into the—hopefully open—Gate of Jehoshaphat.

Galeran was praying blindly and mindlessly. Praying that his stallion wouldn't stumble on the uneven ground. Praying that he was fast enough. Praying that the gate was open. Praying that the Saracens weren't archers. But before he finished this prayer, the first arrow slammed into the horse of the knight on his left. The stallion reared up with a squeal of pain, tossing his rider.

They couldn't stop for him.

The next instant an arrow sliced into Galeran's thigh and embedded itself there as he screamed, "Jesus God!" The shock and pain both blinded and winded him. He found himself clinging to his horse's mane with both hands, sobbing in terror and agony as the horse just kept galloping, the herd instinct of the beast driving him forward with the other knights.

They careened around the corner of the wall and another horse went down, apparently breaking his leg in a rabbit hole or gully. His rider rolled away, tried to rise, and then flopped back, either injured or in despair. They couldn't stop for him, either.

On this side of the city it seemed abruptly dark. The light from the burning siege towers and engines was blocked by the massive height of the wall. But Galeran at last registered that men were shouting to them, encouraging them. "Come on! Come on! We're holding them, my lord!" a voice shouted. "Keep coming!"

Only then did Galeran register that during their mad dash along the northern wall, Christian archers on the ramparts had been providing a barrage of cover, showering arrows at their pursuers.

The Jehoshaphat Gate yawned open: a blacker patch in the dark wall. With a last effort, the horses bunched together, bumping against one another as they charged over the bridge and then through the narrows of the gate in a close-knit pack.

A cheer went up from all around them. The men on the walls, the Syrian shopkeepers, and even the nuns of St. Anne's were jumping up and down, shouting and cheering. Some shouted "Ib-e-lin! Ib-e-lin!" while the nuns were singing a Te Deum in a frail soprano chorus.

"Here, I'll give you a hand, lad," someone offered, and Galeran passed out as they pulled him from his blood-soaked saddle.

Jerusalem, September 25, 1187

On the following morning, Sir Roger led a sortie of almost four thousand infantry out of David's Gate. The Saracens, still dazed by the loss of two siege towers and three mangonels, responded with sheer panic. They fled for their camp, abandoning much of their equipment, including wagons loaded with arrows. Sir Roger chased them all the way to the wooden palisade surrounding their camp, but then wisely withdrew. However, he took the opportunity to vandalize the still-intact siege engines, and to drag the carts loaded with arrows inside the city wall on his way back down the hill.

A pause followed.

At first Ibelin hesitated to reduce the men on the walls even a little, expecting a rapid sally, perhaps under the personal command of the Sultan. He surmised that Salah ad-Din would be furious with his troops and emirs and would not accept this result. But after waiting in the burning sun for over an hour, Ibelin gave the order for the bulk of his troops to stand down and get some rest and refreshment.

Ibelin remained on the walls for another hour, vigilantly watching the enemy camp for the first indication they were about to sally forth for a new assault on Jerusalem. But then exhaustion overwhelmed him, and he knew he had to lie down for a bit. Leaving orders to wake him at the first sign of movement from the enemy camp, he withdrew to the Ibelin palace, and he was asleep before Georgios could pull his boots off his feet.

Balian awoke feeling stiff, aching, and cold. His shirt and braies had been soaked with sweat, and as the air cooled, the wet clothes were clammy and chilling. He turned over on his bed with a groan and sat up, trying to judge the hour of the day. It was dusk, almost dark. He must have slept nearly seven hours. Since the start of the siege, he had never managed more than a couple of hours' sleep at a stretch, mostly just snatching short naps of thirty minutes or so. Until now.

Georgios jumped up from the window seat and came to him at once. "Can I get you anything, my lord?" he asked eagerly.

"Help me out of my filthy underclothes," Balian answered, determined to change and even sponge himself down if he could. "Still no sign of the enemy?"

Georgios shook his head vigorously. "No, my lord!"

Ibelin didn't entirely believe it, but he was prepared to deceive himself long enough to get out of his stinking braies, shirt, and gambeson. Pointing, he told Georgios to find him clean undergarments and his spare gambeson (one Barry had left behind, actually) in one of the carved chests beside the window, then sent him to fetch water, soap, and a sponge.

It felt wonderful to get out of armor for the first time in five days. Balian felt refreshed by the sleep, and invigorated simply by not dragging the weight of his armor around with him. When Georgios returned, the squire wet and soaped the sponge and then vigorously scrubbed him down. When finished, Balian pulled on the clean underwear, Barry's gambeson, and soft leather boots, over which he pulled a clean calf-length surcoat with wide, elbow-length sleeves and fur trim against the chill of the late September evening.

By the time he was dressed, his brain was fully functioning again. Salah ad-Din was clearly trying to lure them into a sense of complacency. He would almost certainly try a surprise attack at night. But Balian also noticed he was famished. As with sleep, he had only snatched bits and pieces of food over the last five days. He decided to risk indulging in a meal and sent Georgios to the kitchens with his request.

"Where do you wish to be served, my lord?" Georgios asked intelligently.

Balian opted for the solar, adding, "I'll go there at once."

He left his bedchamber and walked the length of the tiled floor past the other chambers, which had been overflowing until his wife's departure. The nursery and schoolroom offered scenes of desolation, since no one had bothered to clean them up after the hasty departure of the Ibelin children. The toys they were not allowed to take were scattered on the floor. The trunks were open, disgorging abandoned clothing. The beds were left unmade. The sight stabbed hard at Balian's heart, reminding him of all he had lost: not just the children themselves, but the chance to watch them grow up.

He shook his head against the melancholy and forced himself to stride vigorously to the end of the hall and down the flight of stairs to the first floor. Here he found Sir Mathewos patiently awaiting him. "My lord," he bowed, but when he straightened he was grinning. "I bring you good news."

Balian raised his eyebrows skeptically.

"We have sent scouts up to the Saracen camp. It is empty."

"Empty?" Balian couldn't believe his ears.

Mathewos grinned more broadly still, his whole dark face split by the white of his smile. "Yes, my lord. Not a man, horse, mule, or goat is left—just discarded clothes and broken pieces of equipment."

As Mathewos spoke, Balian registered that singing was coming through the windows from the street. He turned and crossed the hall to exit by the far doors onto the loge. He went to the corner, where an ancient Roman pillar supported the floor above, and looked first to his left. Coming up the Street of Jehoshaphat behind a raised processional cross were the sisters of St. Anne; behind them the citizens of Jerusalem were falling in, joyously joining in their hymn. Looking right, he saw an almost identical sight on the Street of Spain, only here the procession was led by the brothers of St. Stephen's. Directly below and opposite, excited citizens lined the streets, chattering as they waited to join the processions, which would clearly meet at this corner. Laughter frequently punctuated the steady murmur of the crowd, until all talk was overlaid by the approaching singing.

At the junction of the two main streets in front of the Ibelin palace, the two processions merged and turned together to continue down the Street of Furriers until they could turn right into the Street of the Holy Sepulcher. Behind him, Sir Mathewos explained, "The Patriarch is reading a Mass of Thanksgiving at the Holy Sepulcher. Do you wish me to tack up Treasure?"

Balian shook his head. "*If* I go, I will go on foot."

"You don't want to go?" Sir Mathewos was surprised.

Balian shook his head. For Sir Mathewos he added, "My presence might be disruptive. I will give thanks in the chapel here."

Sir Mathewos saw through him. He cocked his head slightly. "You think we are celebrating too soon?"

"It is never too soon, or too late, to thank the Lord. I am thankful for this respite. We all needed it."

"But you think Salah ad-Din will be back," Mathewos finished for him.

Balian only sighed in answer.

The bells of the Holy Sepulcher started chiming, and from across the city the other churches answered, until the whole city was deafened by the triumphant sound of pealing bells. Balian stood with his hands on the railing, and reminded himself he had thought just this morning never to hear such a joyous sound again. It was beautiful.

Then he went inside and gave orders for a feast. He told the cook to take the very best things they had left in his cellars and to make a meal for the entire household. He told them to spare neither flesh nor sugar, spices nor wine. Then he went out to inspect the walls.

The sentries left on duty were, understandably, not very alert. Some were drinking. From the walls, furthermore, Balian could clearly hear rowdy singing coming from some of the taverns down near Tanner's and Mount Zion Gates, as well as more pious singing from the Patriarch's quarter and the Armenian cathedral.

He found Sir Roger at the Citadel. Apparently he shared Ibelin's assessment of the Saracen and was prowling around trying to ensure a minimum of preparedness—or was he just trying to keep his grief at bay?

"What do you think Salah ad-Din will do next?" Sir Roger asked his lord before Balian could get a word out—as if forestalling condolences for the loss of his son. "He's not going to just give up! He can't afford to leave us here, and he didn't even try to negotiate with us."

"I think he will redeploy his forces opposite the Postern of St. Mary Magdalene," Ibelin answered truthfully.

"Why there?" Sir Roger asked.

"Because that is where Godfrey de Bouillon forced a breach eighty-eight years ago."

Sir Roger grunted as he registered how much sense this made, but then asked, "Why didn't he attack there in the first place?"

"Because he didn't want to risk harming the Dome of the Rock with his siege engines. From his previous position he only had the Holy Sepulcher in range, and it suited him fine to risk setting that alight or bashing it down altogether. If he deploys siege engines north of St. Mary Magdalene, or on the Mount of Olives, it will be almost impossible not to cause damage to the Dome of the Rock."

Sir Roger looked at his lord, amazed. "How do you know all that? How can you be so sure Salah ad-Din won't risk damaging the Temple of God just because it was once a mosque?"

Ibelin paused as he thought about this, and then realized the truth. "He told me so. He said the reason he offered the residents of Jerusalem freedom in exchange for surrender was that he did not want to risk damage to either the Dome of the Rock or the Temple of Solomon, which was also formerly a mosque."

"In that case, maybe he'll try to attack from the southwest," Sir Roger suggested hopefully. There was a steep hill to the southwest, offering natural advantages to the defenders.

"Maybe," Ibelin agreed, but they both knew he was still convinced the assault would come from the north. Balian hesitated. He couldn't just walk away, ignoring Daniel's sacrifice. "Roger." He dropped the "sir" intentionally.

Roger seemed to wince; he'd heard the change in Balian's voice.

"I—I don't know how to express my condolences. What Daniel did—what the lepers did—"

Roger had been repressing grief with work for almost twenty-four hours. Now it welled up from his chest with such force it took him by surprise. It overpowered him, making him speechless.

Balian had no choice but to continue. "Daniel was—you must be very proud of him."

Roger nodded, and then croaked out, "He was the best of them!"

At a loss for words, Balian embraced Roger. The older man dropped his head to cover his face and stood biting his lip to keep from crying. They stood like that for several seconds, and then Sir Roger got hold of himself and stepped back out of the embrace. He still avoided Balian's eyes, but he admitted, "I tried to find his body when we returned from our sortie. I wanted to give him a proper burial. To let Michael say a Mass over him. But I couldn't find any of the lepers. I think they burned them."

"No, I think Daniel was the one to get inside the siege tower and set it on fire. I think he and the others burned *themselves*—and in so doing, they have evaded the fires of hell. I think they are with King Baldwin and Christ, restored to health, strength, and beauty."

Roger nodded, because if he opened his mouth he would sob. Balian turned away quickly to let Daniel's father cry in privacy.

Gradually the city quieted down. Most people had been strained to the limits of their endurance, and rapidly fell into an exhausted sleep after the first euphoria had worn off. Although the hospital was still crowded, the fact that there had been no new wounded all day long gave the sisters and brothers a respite as well. The dead were removed, and they even managed to do a little cleaning up while sleeping in shifts. Sister Adela took to her bed and was out cold for twelve hours.

Sir Galeran, his leg wound freshly bandaged, and the other new knights bedded down again in the great hall of the palace, feeling like the heroes of a *chanson de geste*. Sir Constantine, having slept earlier, replaced Sir Roger on the wall. Beth nestled deep and content in Dawit's arms, while Gabriel and Tsion made love in the loft over their heads.

Balian withdrew to his bedchamber. Someone, probably the loyal and discreet Georgios, had thought to lay a fire for him, so he pulled up the great armchair and tossed two of Maria Zoë's silk cushions into it. He poured himself wine from a silver pitcher into one of the glass goblets with the crosses of Jerusalem enameled on them that Maria Zoë cherished but had been unable to take with her. He sank down onto the chair and stretched his legs toward the fire. The folds of his long surcoat fell to the floor.

If only Maria Zoë were here, he thought. It would have been so good to talk to her, to share his doubts and misgivings and hear her common sense rebuttals. It would have lightened his burden just to be able to talk about it. It would have been heaven to hold her in his arms, to breathe in her always sweet-smelling flesh and hair—much less lose himself in her embrace.

He looked down into his goblet, holding the pale yellow wine from Ibelin that he loved so well. They had opened the last cask of it for the feast tonight, and when he finished this last pitcher he would never taste it again. He'd been all but weaned on this wine, he thought. It was as much a part of him as the blooming pomegranate orchards—which he would also never see again.

Abruptly he was seized by fury. For ten weeks he had been too busy surviving—and helping others survive—to think about everything he'd lost. He had been too numbed by the sheer magnitude of the collective disaster to feel the personal loss he had endured. Suddenly it was all so vivid: he was about to die for nothing because his death would bring no one any good. Without Ibelin he was nothing. Without Ibelin he had nothing to bequeath his sons.

In a sudden rage he flung the empty goblet into the fireplace. The shattered fragments burst in all directions, cutting the back of his hand and dousing a corner of the fire. He burst into hysterical laughter. He was baron of nothing in a kingdom that no longer existed.

Jerusalem, September 26-28, 1187

Salah ad-Din's army returned on September 26. It now curled around the northeast corner of the city, and the Sultan's large, handsomely embroidered tent crowned the Mount of Olives directly opposite the Dome of the Rock. The Christian defenders could only watch helplessly as the Saracens felled the olive trees under which, it was said, Christ had once slept. Far worse, the Sultan's army had been reinforced; it now contained at least one trebuchet and more than a score of mangonels.

While the mangonels and trebuchet remained directed at the Patriarch's quarter rather than the Syrian quarter in the northeast, no less than ten siege towers were concentrated around the northeast corner. By September 27 it was obvious why: Salah ah-Din had brought battalions of engineers to undermine the walls of Jerusalem. The engineers advanced under the cover of shields and a furious arrow barrage to the dry ditch. There they nestled down under substantial wooden roofs, supported by the edge of the ditch, to dig under the foundations of the wall.

The defenders could see timber being brought up and rock being transported back. Unless they could stop the digging, it was just a matter of time before the foundations were carted away and the wall collapsed. But Salah ad-Din was taking no chances of a new sortie. Not only were there infantry guards around the miners, a body of cavalry was also kept constantly mounted and within sight. The Christians could mark the end of each watch when one troop of cavalry was replaced by another. The troop on duty was always alert and ready—and just out of range of the Christian archers.

Meanwhile the bombardment of the city continued to take its toll of casualties, and the city's water supplies were being drained at an exceptional rate by the constant need to put out fires. After the false sense of redemption that had overtaken the city on September 25, the sense of futility was all the more intense now. Morale began to crack.

The number of women reporting to the field kitchens fell off sharply, to the point where several of the kitchens had to be abandoned. Even fewer women were prepared to risk going up on the walls to bring water to the archers, and men started to drop due to heat stroke and dehydration. The boys, so eager just a few days before to help carry arrows up to the ramparts, had disappeared into the dark back alleys of the city whence they'd come, and those that remained were at the end of their juvenile strength.

Likewise, fewer and fewer volunteers came to help wind cotton around the arrows, and all the lepers were dead. Beth found herself working with just three others. The work had always been hot, dirty, and exhausting; now she found herself full of resentment towards those who didn't help—like Tsion, who stayed safe inside the Ibelin palace playing with little Menelik.

Beth's anger was only a weak defense against her growing sense of desperation. They had done everything they could! They had fought so gallantly. The lepers had sacrificed themselves, becoming human torches to destroy the siege towers. The Baron of Ibelin had led his knights, including Dawit, on a daring sortie. Her father-in-law never seemed to sleep at all. They had done their best and more. Why didn't God help them? Why were the Saracens stronger than ever? Why? Why? Why? she asked, near to tears as she dipped another arrow in the boiling tar.

Father Michael had become numb. He literally did not hear the confessions any more, although he absolved everyone. His mind was elsewhere, trying to grasp the will of God. Just because we pray "Thy will be done" doesn't mean we mean it, he thought to himself. Or was that what he meant? What he meant was surely that just because things happened didn't mean they were God's will? The Antichrist was powerful, too. And people who denied the divinity of Christ never prayed to Him, and so could not be guided by Him. And they were surrounded by men who denied the divinity of Christ; so all those men were not doing God's will, but they were systematically destroying Jerusalem and the Christians trapped inside. But if God wanted, then surely he could come to the aid of His people? But maybe too many of His people were terrible sinners, even if Father Michael was giving them absolution. Was it really God's will that he give absolution to terrible sinners just because they happened to be defending Jerusalem? But that wasn't why he was giving them absolution. He was giving the absolution because they repented. Wasn't he?

Sister Adela was numb, too, at least with respect to the wounded. Her worries were shifting to her sisters. With each passing hour she was becoming more and more convinced that the city was going to fall. She had not left the Hospital compound since the start of the siege, and she had consequently lost a sense of how many healthy fighting men were still left. From her perspective, the fighting capacity of the city was draining away—in the blood they flushed out of the yard every morning, and the endless cortege of corpses that moved steadily between the Hospital and the bowels of the Temple. With each dead man, the moment when the enemy would flood into the city to claim the victor's spoils drew nearer.

Sister Adela had no illusions about her fate and that of her sisters. Nuns, unlike noblewomen, would be part of the spoils. Even Christian soldiers had been known to violate nuns, usually in blood lust or when besotted with drink—but such actions were condemned by secular and sacred authorities, and the perpetrators were usually punished. Muslim soldiers, on the other hand, would not be acting in violation of law and tradition, but with the full approbation of their leaders. Nuns were viewed as whores by the Saracens because they were married to three men at the same time: the Father, the Son, and the Holy Ghost.

When the city fell, she and all the sisters of the Hospital would be brutally raped, probably multiple times by a variety of men, and then sold into a slavery that would entail perpetual rape for the rest of their lives. That was the reality they were facing. Did any of them want to live under those circumstances? Knowing that there was no hope of rescue?

Sister Adela knew she did not want to live like that. She knew she would rather die. But to turn a weapon on herself would be a terrible sin—and worse, a sin from which she could not repent. To ask one of her brothers to kill her and the other nuns was to ask him to commit a sin, albeit one for which he could receive absolution. The sortie of the lepers kept running through her mind. They had not taken their own lives; they had simply taken actions that led to certain death. Wasn't there something similar that she and the sisters of the Hospital could do? An act of heroism that fell short of taking their own lives, and yet ensured that they would be dead before the first Saracen soldier could brutally batter his way through their fragile maidenheads to leave them bleeding in their own tears of shame?

Godwin Olafsen had not allowed his forge to go out for over a week. Sir Mathewos had told him from the start that his job was not on the walls, not fighting with his grandfather's great ax, but keeping the weapons of the others serviceable. And there had been so much work to be done! In a city with twelve hundred fighting men struggling day and night, there were always swords, axes, daggers, shields, helmets, and hauberks in desperate need of repair.

The young Armenian soldier who pounded on the door, dragging Godwin from an exhausted sleep, was desperate. The head of his ax had become loose when he used it to hack away at the bridge of one of the siege towers that had dropped on to the wall. Now it wobbled uselessly. The terror of the nearly successful assault made just before dusk was audible in his voice, and detectable in the stench he gave off as well. Godwin guessed the young man hadn't been out of his clothes since the start of the siege and that he'd lost control of his bowels at some point.

Godwin nodded and let him into the forge, telling him to sit on the bench by the door while he stoked the fire. "When was the last time you had something to eat?" he asked over his shoulder.

"I don't remember," the soldier mumbled.

"If you work these bellows, I'll go fetch you something," Godwin offered.

The soldier numbly took over the bellows while Godwin went into the kitchen and rummaged around until he found an old loaf of bread and a bit of hard cheese. He put these on a wooden cutting board and brought them back out to the soldier. He then took the ax and examined it. Nodding, he put it down, and went back to the bellows.

The door from the kitchen banged open, and Sven stood in it on his crutches. He was wearing nothing but his nightshirt.

"Sven!" his father called. "Go back to bed! I can manage."

"No," Sven answered stubbornly and swung himself over to his stool, where he sank down, dropping the crutches. The Armenian soldier gaped in amazement as the little boy took over the bellows and his father set to work on repairing the ax.

It didn't take more than a half-hour, but by then the Armenian soldier had fallen asleep and was snoring loudly with his head against the wall. Godwin smiled and hesitated to wake him, but then he realized he'd sleep more comfortably in his own bed. He shook him by the shoulder and handed him the ax.

The Armenian came out of his deep sleep disoriented and still half-dreaming. Seeing a man leaning over him with an ax, he mistook Godwin for the enemy. He reared up with a roar, lunged for the ax, lost his footing, and fell headlong onto the floor with a groan. Then he realized where he was and apologized profusely as he pulled himself onto all fours and then to his feet, dusting himself off. "Sorry, sir! Sorry! I was dreaming!"

"No harm done," Godwin answered with a weary smile as he handed him the ax.

"Thank you! Thank you! How much do I owe you?"

Godwin shook his head. "Go with God, young man. What good is money to me now?"

The Armenian thanked him again and departed, but no sooner was he out the door than Godwin faced a more dangerous being: his wife. Standing with her hands on her hips she mocked him, "What good is money to me now?" adding: "First you give the most valuable sword you've ever made—a sword that cost you half a fortune to forge—to a baron—a baron who could have paid for it tenfold! And now you're doing work for every Tom, Dick, and Harry for free!" As she spoke, she was working herself into a frenzy. "Where are we supposed to get coin to put bread on the table, if you give away your labor for free? Don't you care about me and your little girls?" In her hysteria she kept raising her voice until her cries were loud enough to wake the dead. "You bastard! You bastard! I wish I could kill you!" she screamed and then fled, slamming the door behind her.

Jerusalem, September 29, 1187

On September 29 at about 5:15 in the afternoon, the attackers set fire to the timbers holding up the tunnel that ran for roughly thirty meters under Jerusalem's northern wall between St. Stephen's Gate and the Postern of Mary Magdalene. The excited shouts of the Saracens as they poured out of the far end of the tunnel gave the Christians a fifteen-second warning, and some of the defenders manning that sector of the wall managed to get away. Many more were sucked down by the collapsing masonry and were crushed or suffocated in the rubble as the wall collapsed.

Ibelin had been on the Gate of Jehoshaphat at the time. He heard the sound of rolling thunder coming out of the earth, then the crashing of stones and the screams of men, and he started running in the direction of the sound, oblivious to the arrows aimed at him. Even before he reached the breach, he was screaming orders for archers to pour fire into the gap, and shouting down into the streets for men to rush into the breach to stop the inevitable Saracen assault.

Sir Roger, who had been on St. Stephen's Gate, converged on the breach from the opposite direction, shouting identical orders. The dust had not yet settled before Sir Mathewos arrived with a troop of crossbowmen who had been held in reserve for this event, while from St. Mary Magdalene Sir Constantine brought the last of his Greek engineers.

The Saracens, of course, had prepared an assault troop just behind the head of the tunnel. As the wall collapsed, shouts of "Allahu Akbar!" went up from across the Saracen camp—and thousands of jubilant Saracen troops, whether Turks, Kurds, Egyptians, or Nubians, pumped their swords or bows over their heads in triumph.

The troops selected for the honor of being the first to enter Jerusalem rushed forward with élan and elation. This was their moment of greatest glory yet. Hattin had been a victory, to be sure: they had humiliated the Non-Believers and crushed them once and for all. But this—this was a moment that would live in history forever. They would repay the outrage of the Christian massacre of their brothers eighty-eight years ago and make them drown in their own blood. They would liberate the Dome of the Rock from the filth of the Franks.

They surged up over the rubble, which was still encased in clouds of dust and billowing smoke from the burning timbers of the tunnel underneath. Because the stones had been dislodged but not settled, they foundered and scrambled as the blocks shifted under their weight. They fell as the broken masonry gave way under their feet, and the leading men started small landslides that knocked down the men behind them. And all the while, death rained on them, loosed by Christian archers on either side of the breach.

Just as they crested the highest part of the rubble and were ready to run down into the city, they were hit head-on by a barrage of crossbow bolts and flaming arrows. The defenders were at such close range that when the bolts struck the Saracens they went clear through their first victim, and some killed the man behind as well. Behind the crossbowmen came slingers releasing pots full of Greek fire. Within a quarter-hour, the breach in the wall was a burning graveyard.

But Salah ad-Din did not have a shortage of fanatical followers ready to take the place of the failed first assault team. The second wave rushed forward, calling on Allah as they charged. These had an easier time mounting the north-facing slope of the debris, but met the same barrage of crossbowmen and Greek fire at the crest. So did the third and fourth assault wave. By then the sun had set and the muezzins were calling the Faithful to prayer.

Ibelin stood on the corner tower, watching the survivors of the last assault drag as many of their dead comrades as possible out of the flames and back down the slope of rubble. Then he turned and strained his eyes in the direction of the Sultan's tent. He thought he saw a flicker of motion: the tent flap opening or closing. Salah ad-Din had no doubt been watching just as he had. Hopefully he had had enough for today.

People were shouting all around him, trying to get Christian wounded to the Hospital and Christian dead to the improvised catacombs. Men had collapsed against the inside of the ramparts and were sobbing from exhaustion, terror, relief—who knew. Somewhere a woman was keening as she discovered her husband or son or lover among the dead. And then the bells of the Holy Sepulcher began to clang. Balian lifted his head and looked across the rubble, through the smoke and dust, toward the dome of the great church, and wondered how many more times it would be allowed to raise its deep, comforting voice.

Ibelin was beginning to regret he had called the leading citizens together. They had gathered in the ward of the royal palace—which, being in the southwest corner of the city, was out of range of the enemy's siege engines. The new knights—the sixty-odd survivors—were there, along with the heads of the guilds and the merchant companies, the Grand Hospitaller, the Patriarch, and the heads of the Syrian, Armenian, Greek, and Coptic churches.

He should have known that at this stage there would be no consensus. The merchants, particularly the Syrians, clearly favored surrender. They argued that Salah ad-Din had shown mercy to other cities. Yes, he'd vowed to destroy them, and he would surely want to humiliate them, but he was a hard-headed man who knew he'd ultimately gain more by letting them live and taxing them hereafter. The Armenians, on the other hand, had memories of many bitter slaughters at the hands of the Seljuks, and insisted there would be no mercy and it was better to go down fighting. Meanwhile, the example of Masada was raised by some of the Frankish leaders: if they were all going to be slaughtered anyway, then why not slaughter their wives and daughters before they could be dishonored and abused, and then kill each other as well, to leave the enemy a city of corpses?

Ibelin was relieved when Heraclius came out firmly against this proposal, insisting that it was not Christian to slaughter themselves. Suicide, he reminded them, was a sin one could not repent, and would lead inexorably to damnation. He added indignantly that it was even more against the teaching of Christ to slaughter, as he rightly put it, "those innocent women and children whom God entrusted to our protection."

"But we can't protect them anyway!" someone retorted in exasperation.

"Let us ride out to martyrdom!" one of the young knights shouted passionately into the crowd. "If we are to die, let it be with a lance in our hands!"

The knights around him cheered their approval.

"Yes, and while *you* ride to martyrdom, our women and children will be dragged off to slavery!" Heraclius retorted furiously. "We must try to negotiate!"

"Negotiate? How? It's too late!" a chorus answered him.

"My lord of Ibelin," the Grand Hospitaller cut through the noise. "What say you? We have recognized your authority, and you have made us stronger than ever we thought we could be. You have enabled us to inflict great damage on the enemy, and you have led us wisely ever since you came to Jerusalem. What do *you* advise?"

Ibelin drew a deep breath. He had hoped they would make a decision without him, but he should have known they would not. "We have only a few pots of Greek fire left. We will not be able to defend the breach tomorrow—or not for long. Nor will darkness come in time."

His words were met with stunned silence—as if, despite everything, they had believed he would give them new hope.

"There is, of course, one last thing we could try. . . ."

They waited with bated breath.

"We could try to penetrate the Saracen camp to the Sultan's tent and kill him. If we did," Balian repeated the argument he had used to the Sultan's face, "there's a chance that his many heirs will become so preoccupied with fighting each other that they will leave us in peace—until such time as one of them has established dominance over the others. By which time, by the Grace of God, help may have come from the West."

Ibelin was surprised by the enthusiasm that greeted his plan, but he had not really doubted his knights would embrace it. They were mostly young men without wives or families. They were still fired by idealism, as well as undiminished naive faith in the righteousness of their cause. It was a little like leading lambs to the slaughter, but it was also a way of sparing them—and himself—the indignity of execution at the hands of the enemy, as the Hospitallers and Templars had suffered after Hattin.

The shouting had not yet died down, and the archers were still exchanging fire in the darkness, when al-Adil burst in on his brother. "You were right, Yusef. Again," he conceded.

The Sultan smiled wanly. "What is the expression? Fool me once, shame on you; fool me twice, shame on me."

"Meaning?"

"Ibn Barzan caught us sleeping with his night attack on the siege engines—"

"Only because he was willing to slaughter lepers like cattle!" Al-Adil protested indignantly. "How could we expect such heartlessness towards the most benighted of God's creatures, even from Christian pigs? To force the most miserable of souls to burn themselves alive is beyond the imagination of a Muslim!"

"Hmm," Salah ad-Din answered. "But who forced them?"

"The Christians!"

"I mean, after they were outside the city, they could have just thrown themselves on our mercy. Why did they go through with the attack?"

Al-Adil shrugged. "I presume because they had been led to believe we would kill them."

"Perhaps; but wouldn't you have at least *tried* to plead for mercy rather than burn yourself alive?"

"What are you trying to say?"

"That I believe they were volunteers. The Christians, too, have fanatics."

"Yes! Men like the Templars and Hospitallers. But these were lepers, including many women."

"And we all know how irrational *women* are!" his brother countered with a smile, before continuing, "Besides, I was not just referring to the raid on our siege engines, but to the fact that Ibn Barzan tried to kill me once before in a desperate situation."

"At Hattin, yes."

"So," Salah ad-Din shrugged, "I expected it."

Loud voices outside the tent disturbed them, and Salah ad-Din looked toward the tent entrance, expecting what followed. One of his Mamlukes bent through the opening and bowed low. "My lord, we have captured one of the Christians alive."

"Ibn Barzan?" Salah ad-Din asked hopefully.

"No, my lord, one of the other knights."

"Bring him in."

His brother looked at him sidelong, wondering what he would have done if it *had* been Ibn Barzan.

The knight had his arms tied behind his back at the elbows, and his ankles had been bound, too, but he still struggled. It took one Mamluke on either side of him to drag him into the tent. The Mamlukes forced him to kneel by kicking the back of his knees, and once he was down, they pushed his head right down into the carpet of the tent and held it there until he was so short of breath he went limp.

The Sultan gestured for the Mamluke holding his head down to lift up his face, which he did by taking a fistful of the Frank's hair and yanking the knight upright, holding his head so he looked straight at the Sultan.

The young man was bleeding from his nose and mouth, and he also had a gash on his forehead, but Salah ad-Din started in surprise. "I've seen you before! Who are you?"

When the young knight didn't answer, one of his guards kicked him hard in the kidneys.

He crumpled up with a gasp of pain, and Salah ad-Din frowned and gestured to the Mamluke that that was enough. "Come, tell me who you are."

"Sir Gabriel."

The name meant nothing to the Sultan, and he racked his memory. Did the boy just resemble one of the Frankish prisoners from Hattin, perhaps? "Who is your father?"

"Sir Roger Shoreham."

That, too, meant nothing to Salah ad-Din. Where else might he have met him? And then it came to him. "You accompanied Ibn Barzan—Baron Ibelin—to Damascus when he came about the truce!"

It was no longer a question, and Gabriel saw no point in denying it. He nodded.

"So you are still following Ibn Barzan around. Tell me, was he trying again to kill me?"

Gabriel decided not to answer that, and was surprised when the Sultan laughed, and then gestured for one of his slaves to bring water. The slave brought it to the Sultan in a silver chalice with a deep bow. Salah ad-Din took the chalice and walked over to Gabriel. "Would you like some water?"

Gabriel looked him in the eye.

"You understand the significance?" the Sultan asked.

Gabriel nodded.

"So." Salah ad-Din offered him the chalice. Since his hands were tied, Gabriel would have to bend forward and drink from it like a dog. Gabriel shook his head.

"If you reject my hospitality, you remain my enemy."

"And if I accept, I am your slave," Gabriel countered.

Salah ad-Din could see that Gabriel was breathing very hard, but he wasn't sure if it was just the aftereffect of combat, or fear.

"Unless someone can pay your ransom," Salah ad-Din countered with an indifferent shrug.

Gabriel did not doubt that his father would sell everything he owned to pay his ransom, but his father owned little. Lord Balian would pay his ransom, too, but his lord was unlikely to live through tomorrow. Should he trade martyrdom for a few hours of hope and a lifetime of slavery? He shook his head. "There is no one to pay my ransom."

"Then you have the choice of slavery or death," Salah ad-Din answered matter-of-factly.

Gabriel swallowed. "Make it swift."

Salah ad-Din shook his head in incomprehension, but he stepped back and returned the chalice to the slave. "I am sorry. You are a brave man. You would make a fine Mamluke." Salah ad-Din indicated the guards on either side of him.

"If you convert to Islam, you could rise high, maybe even become an emir one day."

Gabriel stubbornly shook his head. He was thinking of Daniel. His brother, with one arm rotting away already, had set an example.

Salah ad-Din sighed again, genuinely sorry to waste such a fine young man, but he had given him a chance and had wasted enough time on him already. He gestured for the Mamlukes to remove him and execute him, adding mercifully, "Make it swift."

Jerusalem, September 30, 1187

The city was no longer defensible, and the sortie of the night before had been crushed by Saracen cavalry almost before they were out of the gate. The only good thing about that was that most of the knights had made it back inside the still-open Jehoshaphat Gate, and the Saracen horsemen foolish enough to pursue were slaughtered in the street before St. Anne's. Only eight knights were lost.

That one of those was Sir Gabriel weighed heavily on Balian. He found it nearly impossible to look the young man's father in the face.

Roger took the loss with a wooden calm. "No matter, my lord. I will see him all the sooner—should God grant me grace to join him in heaven." He then crossed himself and pulled on his helmet before shouting at his men to move closer to the breach in the wall. He commanded the troop before the breach and he diligently dressed the lines of the crossbowmen and archers in preparation for the first assault of the day.

Balian took a deep breath and prepared to put on his helmet as well.

Someone caught his arm. Annoyed, he turned to see who it was.

The Patriarch of Jerusalem was beside him. Heraclius might not look as exhausted and filthy as the soldiers, but he had deep, dark circles around his eyes, his lips were chapped, and he looked thinner than a week ago.

"Your eminence?" Ibelin asked in a tone bordering on mockery. The Saracens were already shouting their battle cries and beating their drums. The first assault wave of what was sure to be many was about to come over the crest of the ruined wall. This was no place for the Patriarch to be, and no time for a discussion.

"My lord—you *must* negotiate with Salah ad-Din!"

"It's too bloody late!" Ibelin snarled. "You could have negotiated in July! You could have negotiated in August! You could have negotiated ten days ago! But not now! Not after Salah ad-Din has suffered thousands of casualties and broken down the walls!" Ibelin could not understand how Heraclius failed to grasp this simple fact.

"Try," was the churchman's answer.

"Try what?"

"Try to negotiate! Not for my sake, my lord. Nor for the innocent women and children." He made a dramatic gesture that included the women—who had, strangely, come out again today in force, apparently determined to share martyrdom with their menfolk rather than face a lifetime of sexual abuse, humiliation, and contempt. "Do it for the Holy Sepulcher! Do it for Christ! If they take this city in fury, they will not stop at razing the Church of the Holy Sepulcher. They might very well destroy the Grave of Christ itself!" The churchman's horror was real. He was shaking with emotion, and his voice was so strained it broke. "Save the Holy Sepulcher from destruction!" he pleaded.

Ibelin stared at him. Then he crossed himself as he thanked God. Without a word to Heraclius, he turned and started running, gesturing for Sir Mathewos to follow him. They plunged into a side street just as the first wave of Saracens came charging over the pile of rubble.

"My lord?" Mathewos called, trying to catch up with him. "What is it?"

"Have Georgios tack up Centurion and a horse for yourself while you secure a large white banner and attach it to a lance."

"You're going to try to negotiate?" Mathewos asked, amazed.

"Yes! We exit by the Jehoshaphat Gate."

Mathewos started running faster, motivated.

The Ibelin palace was only around the corner, and conditions in the palace were chaotic. It was in range of some of the mangonels, so the staff had set up buckets of water in the courtyard and on the roof to be ready to fight any fires that started. However, only half the staff was still here. Most had joined the defenders, although for the first time Beth was not among them. Beth was trying to comfort Tsion for the loss of Gabriel, and the Ethiopian girl's keening penetrated to the farthest corner of the house.

Balian took the stairs two at a time to reach his chamber. He tore off his dirty, blood-stained surcoat and rummaged in a trunk until he found one with gold edging. He had no time to bathe, but he hastily brushed his hair. When had his sideburns gone gray? He washed his hands, taking a scrub brush to his nails so vigorously that it tore open some of the cuts on his hands. He found his signet ring, which he usually didn't wear when he expected to use his sword. He thought briefly about taking a leather cloth to Defender of Jerusalem to clean away some of yesterday's blood, but then decided that the sword was far more eloquent if he left it bloody.

In the courtyard, Georgios waited with an excited Centurion. Only the night before, the horse had yet again extricated his rider from what seemed like certain death; Georgios had been in the midst of grooming him but had not yet finished. The hair between his thighs was still matted and he had stable stains on his knees, but he seemed eager. He nickered at the sight of Balian.

Balian swung himself into the saddle and signaled to Mathewos to ride ahead of him with the white banner on the lance. "They may kill you, Mathewos," he warned.

"They will *certainly* kill me if we do not get a truce," Mathewos answered.

The Street of Jehoshaphat seemed abandoned. People were either trying to hold the enemy at the breach, or were already attempting to barricade themselves in hiding places. As they passed the Convent of St. Anne, they could hear the nuns singing with tangible desperation.

Ibelin called up to the men on the gate tower to signal the enemy by waving the banners of Jerusalem and blowing horns. When they reported they had the attention of some of the troops opposite, he ordered them to open the Jehoshaphat Gate.

The first moments were the most terrifying. Sir Mathewos rode out with Ibelin behind him, and they kept expecting arrows to rain down on them. They could hear the noise of the battle from the breach in the wall off to their left, but immediately in front of them all seemed deathly still.

"Now what?" Mathewos asked.

"Keep riding, straight for the Sultan's tent."

They had just come abreast of the Church of Gethsemane when a troop of Mamluke cavalry rushed down the hill to block their path from about thirty feet away. "Who are you and what do you want?" a voice shouted in Arabic.

Ibelin let out a sigh of relief. They were willing to talk.

Ordering Mathewos to remain where he was, he continued forward until he was near enough to speak without shouting. "You know perfectly well who I am," he told them, seeing the way their eyes scanned his surcoat and even looked at the hilt of his sword. When he was satisfied that they did indeed know who he was, he continued, "I wish to speak to the Sultan Salah ad-Din."

"Do you surrender?"

"No. I have come to discuss terms."

This provoked an eruption of angry exclamations from some and laughter from others, until someone said, "The only terms you can negotiate are converting to Islam or death!"

"That," Ibelin answered sharply, "is for the Sultan to decide—not one of his slaves!"

"Well said," the Sultan's voice answered, and the riders parted, bowing their heads to him and backing their mounts out of his way.

Salah ad-Din rode forward until his horse's head was level with Centurion's tail and the two men were exactly opposite each other, but a good eight feet apart—too far apart for a sword to reach.

The baron bowed his head to the Sultan.

Salah ad-Din looked Ibelin in the eye. "You want to negotiate for yourself or for Jerusalem?"

"For Jerusalem."

"You're too late," Salah ad-Din told him with a dismissive gesture. "No one negotiates for the possession of a city he already holds." As he spoke he stretched out his arm and pointed, making Ibelin turn around in his saddle. Behind him, on the corner tower at the junction of the eastern and northern wall, one of the Sultan's banners was fluttering proudly.

Balian felt his heart stop.

Dawit, fighting at the breach, saw a handful of Saracens break off the assault to scramble from the rubble up to the edge of the broken wall. In horror, he saw them gain the wall and start to hack and slice through the archers, who were so focused on the men still contesting the breach that they failed to see the Saracens who had scaled the wall behind them until it was too late. Several Syrian archers fell backwards over the wall into the city as they spun to face this new danger and lost their footing. And while most of the Saracens cleared the top of the wall, one rushed to plant the Sultan's banner on the corner tower.

The sight of that banner flying over Jerusalem sent Dawit into a berserker rage. It symbolized for him total destruction—the slaughter of his wife and infant son. He roared and flung himself up the mound of rubble, running with so much force that even his enemies ducked out of his way. His strides were long and he was possessed of superhuman strength as he flung himself onto the wall, still bellowing in fury and oblivious to the surge of comrades behind him. He lunged for the banner and with all his might flung it down again into the ditch, even as three Saracens closed around him and stabbed him from all sides.

The Baron of Ibelin and the Sultan of Egypt and Syria were still staring at the banner when it was thrown down, followed by the bodies of a dozen men—evidently tossed over the side by a ferocious Christian counterattack.

Ibelin noted coldly, "No, you are not yet in possession of the city. And before you do take possession, we will kill every Muslim prisoner, every woman and every child, and then—before we sally forth on our last sortie—we will enter the Dome of the Rock, and with pickaxes we will destroy the foundations right down to the grotto underneath. We will—"

He didn't have to continue. Salah ad-Din had blanched. "You would not dare!"

"Oh, yes, we would, your excellency. Oh, yes, we would." Everything depended on the Sultan believing him. And in that minute, Balian was completely prepared to carry out his threat. "We would rather destroy the Holy Sepulcher ourselves than let you do it. We will destroy every monument sacred to your faith and mine before we leave you a city full of rotting corpses! And then we will come out of the city and we will fight without any fear. Not one of us will die without having killed several of you!" By the time he finished, Balian meant every word of it.

Salah ad-Din glanced again to the ramparts, but the banners of Jerusalem flew from every tower along the length of the entire wall, and from the shouts coming from the unseen breach it was clear that the most recent assault wave had also been repelled. The shouts of "Jerusalem!" and "Ibelin!" were too loud and too distinct to mean anything but that the Christians had again repulsed the assault.

Salah ad-Din looked back at Ibelin and studied his face. He did not think the man was bluffing. Furthermore, he recognized his mistake. He had told him he did not want the sacred sites damaged. That Ibelin exploited that knowledge now was only to be expected, and it was his own fault.

Still he hesitated. He looked again to the ramparts, hoping that by some miracle his own banners would reappear, but they did not. Instead, the remnants of the last assault on the breach limped into view, carrying their dead and wounded.

This was crazy. He had wanted to take the city intact, and he'd already damaged much of it and sacrificed thousands of lives. "You will surrender the city and withdraw? Every single man, woman, and child?"

"Yes." Balian didn't dare breathe. He didn't dare believe the Sultan was seriously considering his offer.

"No," Salah ad-Din answered.

Balian let the air out of his lungs and waited for the next blow, utterly without hope.

"Not after the casualties you have inflicted. If you surrender the city intact, then I will guarantee there will be no *slaughter*—as your forefathers perpetrated—

but every citizen must *buy* their freedom. In exchange for a ransom of ten dinars per man, five per woman, and two per child, the citizens will be permitted to purchase their freedom and withdraw with as much as they can carry. Those who cannot raise the ransom will remain my slaves."

Hope took hold of Balian's heart in a grip so fierce it seemed to almost crush the life from him. This offer could mean life for nearly sixty thousand Christians, but ten dinars was more than the poor of the city could possibly pay. "The city is full of refugees, your excellency. Some thirty thousand men and women with their children, fled here in terror for their lives after the Battle of Hattin. They came here with nothing, and so have nothing with which to buy their freedom."

Salah ad-Din nodded solemnly. "No doubt. And no doubt the treasury of Jerusalem is still largely intact. Or your Church, I am certain, will be moved by pity to sacrifice some of its infamous wealth for the sake of the poor the prophet Jesus so eloquently championed." The sarcasm in his tone was unmistakable. "With one hundred thousand dinars, you can buy the freedom of them all."

Ibelin wanted to accept, but there was no way they could scrape together a hundred thousand dinars. "Look at the dome of the Temple of God," he countered, pointing behind him. "The gold has already been stripped." Salah ad-Din's eyes shifted to the dome and back to Ibelin, but he said nothing. Ibelin was forced to be explicit. "We do not have one hundred thousand dinars in the whole city."

"How much can you raise?"

Balian had no idea what Heraclius might have or if there was anything left in the royal treasury, but the King of England had deposited thirty thousand bezants with the Hospitallers. He took a chance that the Grand Hospitaller would be more concerned with the poor than his Order's honor and declared: "Thirty thousand dinars."

Salah ad-Din shrugged. "That will buy the freedom of three thousand paupers."

This is surreal, Balian registered. I am bargaining like a customer in a bazaar with the Sultan of Egypt and Syria for the freedom of thousands of Christians. "Most of the refugees are women and children. The sum of thirty thousand dinars should cover fifteen thousand refugees."

"Six thousand," the Sultan countered.

Balian strained to keep his nerve. "Twelve."

"Nine."

"Ten."

The Sultan nodded. "Done. You have two days to prepare the city to receive us. Once we occupy the city, you will have forty days to raise the ransoms. At the end of that time, anyone still in the city and not in possession of a receipt for a ransom payment will become my property, along with all the goods and property still in the city."

"Agreed," Ibelin answered firmly.

Salah ad-Din nodded and started to turn his horse's head away.

"I would ask one last favor," Balian stopped him.

Salah ad-Din looked over, and his expression suggested he thought Ibn Barzan was going too far. The whole deal hung by a silk thread.

"We will turn over the Dome of the Rock in perfect condition, clean and empty of our symbols, if—in exchange—you promise not to destroy the Holy Sepulcher."

"Of course," Salah ad-Din agreed with a shrug. He had never intended to destroy the Holy Sepulcher; pilgrim traffic was far too lucrative. He spurred away at a canter, already shouting orders.

Balian did not have that much energy. He felt utterly exhausted and stunned. He swung Centurion around and started back for the open Jehoshaphat Gate at a walk. As he came abreast of Mathewos, the Ethiopian fell in beside him.

"What did he say, my lord?" Mathewos asked anxiously. From the Sultan's energy and Ibelin's listlessness, he presumed the worst.

"I have surrendered Jerusalem."

"In exchange for our lives?" Mathewos asked anxiously. He did not know that Dawit was already dead; he thought the surrender would save Dawit, along with Tsion, Beth, and little Menelik.

"Yes, and our freedom to the extent that we can pay a ransom of ten dinars per man, five per woman, and two per child."

Mathewos quickly calculated that he would need thirty-two dinars for his little family. It was a lot of money, but it was life and freedom that he had not dared dream about even an hour ago.

"I will pay for everyone in my household," Ibelin assured him, mistaking his silence. "And I believe the Grand Hospitaller will open his coffers for the refugees and the poor. Maybe even Heraclius will be moved to pity."

"This is a miracle, my lord!" Mathewos exclaimed in wonder as he grasped that this was real. He and his family were being granted life and freedom!

"Do you really think so?" Balian asked, drawing up to look hard at Mathewos. "I have surrendered the City of God, Mathewos. I have put the Holy Sepulcher in the hands of men who do not think Christ was the Son of God and do not believe He rose from the dead. Do you think He will ever forgive me for that?"

"There are more than fifty thousand people in this city, my lord," Mathewos pointed to Jerusalem. "Fifty thousand people who—but for you—would be dead or enslaved. You cannot think that He, who let himself be crucified that we might live, would value this *place* over their lives."

"And King Baldwin—whose tomb I have also surrendered—will *he* forgive me for surrendering his city and his grave?"

Mathewos didn't have a clue what the Leper King would have thought of this surrender; he had not known him well enough. But he knew the answer he had to give to the man who had saved fifty thousand lives against all the odds. "I do not believe he would have wished his city or his tomb washed in Christian blood."

"No." Balian pulled himself together. "I suppose not. And that was the only alternative, wasn't it?"

"Yes, my lord. It was."

Suddenly men and women were streaming out of the Jehoshaphat Gate toward them in a loud, tumultuous horde. They had seen from the wall the way, spreading out from the Sultan, Saracen unit after Saracen unit stood down and returned to their tents. They had seen the siege engines go still. They had seen the air empty of missiles.

They rushed around Ibelin so closely that Centurion flattened his ears and snapped at them, kicking out halfheartedly.

"Have you secured terms, my lord?" "Have you negotiated a truce?" "Will they let us live?" "Is the siege over?"

Ibelin lifted his hand for silence, and they stopped speaking long enough for him to confirm: "We will be allowed to buy our freedom. We have forty days to—"

They burst into such enthusiastic cheering that he did not have a chance to explain the details. Already men and women were running to tell their friends and family that their lives were spared, that they would live. Yet others still blocked his way, begging for confirmation, or simply blessing and thanking him.

By the time he reached the gate, the streets were flooded with hysterically cheering people. They had forgotten that they had brought this upon themselves by refusing to negotiate terms two months earlier. They had not yet had time to think about a future without homes or property. At that moment, their naked lives were all that mattered to them.

They pressed in so close that they overwhelmed even Centurion's defenses. Boys were trying to touch the Lord of Ibelin as if he were a talisman. Women were kissing his feet. Priests were calling out blessings. The nuns of St. Anne's had issued from their convent to fall on their knees beside the road, their hands clasped in prayer as they gave thanks for their redemption. Secular maidens, on the other hand, were blowing Ibelin kisses and waving their veils as if they were at a tournament. It was a mad outpouring of emotion that swept away all reason.

Balian reminded himself that Christ had once entered this same city by this same gate to the cries of "Hosanna"—only to be condemned to death by the same crowd less than a week later. Tomorrow, when they found out the cost of their freedom, they would probably curse him, he thought.

Then he caught sight of Sister Adela pushing her way through the jubilant crowd. She too had aged in the last ten days, and her habit was soiled and stiff with dried blood. Indeed, her hands were streaked with it, for the news of the surrender had reached her even as she was helping one of the younger sisters change the bandages on a badly bleeding patient. Ibelin had the greatest respect for this woman; he had watched her untiring service to the wounded throughout the siege. He called to the men ahead of him who blocked her way, ordering them to let her through.

Sister Adela pushed past the astonished archers and reached Ibelin's side. She grasped his mail-clad calf in her wiry fingers, as much to keep herself upright in the jostling of the crowd as to hold him still.

"Thank you, my lord!" she gasped over the surrounding noise, her eyes fixed on his to ensure he heard her. "Thank you from all the sick and wounded who would surely have been slaughtered in their beds. And thank you from the little orphans, too young for slavery, and so doomed to slaughter as well. And thank you from all the women of Jerusalem. Christ will bless you for not putting your honor, your glory, or your chance of martyrdom ahead of the welfare of the helpless entrusted to your care!"

Epilogue

When the fighting ended and the paying started, greed and corruption replaced magnanimity and joy. To be sure, the Sultan kept his word about not harming the citizens of Jerusalem during the forty days granted to raise their ransoms, but the gates were sealed to prevent anyone from leaving without payment. At the end of the forty-day grace period, anyone in possession of a receipt for the ransom would be allowed to leave a free man or woman; anyone without the receipt would be enslaved.

Enterprising Saracens of all ranks found endless means to extract bribes for helping Christians out of the city—and then sometimes recaptured them. Others made out fraudulent receipts for ransom payments that, if detected, resulted in the Christians being enslaved or forced to raise the ransom a second time. Emirs and other officials of the Sultan extracted extra payments for providing the official receipts, thereby increasing their incomes—and the ransom sums. Powerful leaders such as Mozaffar al-Din blithely claimed a thousand Armenians were "runaway" slaves exempt from the entire agreement, although the claim was clearly fabricated.

The behavior of the Christians was hardly better. The Patriarch Heraclius preferred to "rescue" Church treasure, particularly relics, rather than contribute to the ransoms of the poor. Other rich citizens followed his example. Cheating, stealing, extortion, blackmail, demanding and selling sexual favors, and every other method, savory and unsavory, were employed to obtain the necessary money for ransoms—while the value of everything, from jewelry and silver plate to silk and sex, fell due to the glut on the market.

The Hospital of St. John in Jerusalem, however, did turn over King Henry's treasure for the ransom of the agreed ten thousand paupers—and the Templars, too, relinquished *some* of their treasure to ransom *some* of the poor. Other private citizens did the same.

When the forty days were up, the citizens with ransom receipts formed into three columns with all their portable goods and chattels. The lay-brothers from the Temple formed an escort for those who wished to proceed to Alexandria and these lined up in front of the Zion Gate and were let out on presentation of their receipts. At the Jaffa Gate, the Hospitallers escorted those citizens bound for Jaffa to take ships from there to Christian lands. The Hospitallers took with them all the orphans as well as the wounded, paying the ransoms of the sick as part of the lump sum they had provided. Sister Adela rode in the lead wagon, surrounded by her sisters. One of those, Patricia, was sobbing as she remembered that day, now so long ago, when she had first seen Jaffa full of wonder and joy. . . .

Those who chose to travel north to the Christian territories that had not yet surrendered—Tyre, Tripoli, and Antioch—departed by St. Stephen's Gate; this convoy was to be escorted by the Baron of Ibelin and his remaining forty-eight knights, including Sir Galeran and the one-armed Sir Alexander. All of Balian's household was in this column, including the widows Beth and Tsion, Sirs Mathewos, Roger, and Constantine, Father Michael, and Georgios.

By noon everyone with a receipt had departed the city. The gates were closed again, and the process of rounding up the slaves began. Just as no Muslims had been allowed to live in crusader Jerusalem, no Christians were to be allowed to remain in Muslim Jerusalem. All remaining Christians were to be taken to the slave markets of Damascus and Aleppo.

Godwin Olafsen had discovered he had need of money after all—just as his wife had warned. When everything was scraped together and they had sold everything they could sell in a city flooded with superfluous goods, he had the equivalent of just ten dinars. With that he paid the ransom for his wife and his daughters, but there was not enough for Sven, much less himself.

Cursing him roundly, his wife had joined the column bound for Jaffa, preferring the protection of the Hospital to that of the Templars or the secular knights, and hoping for a passage home to Norway from the coastal port. She could dream of returning home, because she had a secret store of seven dinars about which her husband knew nothing. Of course she could have bought Sven's freedom with that, but she did not want to be weighed down and hampered by the cripple any longer. What man would marry a woman with a crippled son? She had sacrificed enough for him already, she reasoned, and she owed it to her daughters to give them a new start and a better future.

When they came to round up the slaves and drive them out of the Jehoshaphat

Gate, Godwin was found in the courtyard of the Holy Sepulcher with several thousand others. The Saracens shouted and pointed and then, when people didn't move, they began kicking people into motion. Godwin lifted his terrified son on his back and started out of the courtyard with the others. Some children were crying, and here and there a woman sobbed, but most of the throng was still, too overcome by their fate for any outward lamentation. They had, after all, seen it coming for forty days.

The column of slaves shuffled forward slowly. What was the point of rushing into misery? Why weary oneself when there would never be an end to the journey? Godwin could feel his son trembling, and he would have liked to comfort him, but what could he possibly say?

They reached the Jehoshaphat Gate and Godwin, like many others, slowed to cast one last look over his shoulder at the City of God. He had come here with such high hopes, and all had been disappointed. Not only was Sven still a cripple—now his family was torn apart, and he had lost everything except life itself. Tears were streaming down many faces, silently, but Godwin had no tears. He cursed God for betraying him.

Beyond the gate the road dipped down sharply toward Gethsemane, and Saracen horsemen with fluttering silks and bejeweled turbans sat upon their gleaming horses, watching the slaves trudge by. Many laughed and joked and patted their prancing horses in obvious high spirits. Godwin kept his eyes down, too ashamed of where he had ended.

Sven tugged at his hair. "Father! Look! Look! Isn't that the Baron of Ibelin?"

Godwin caught his breath and looked up. To his horror, he saw that sitting directly beside the most splendid of all the Saracens was indeed the Baron of Ibelin. He was mounted not on his gray charger but on a bay stallion already gray at the muzzle, but he was wearing a splendid surcoat of marigold and scarlet silk. His chain mail gleamed, and at his hip was the beautiful enameled pommel of Defender of Jerusalem.

Godwin looked down at his feet and bounced Sven higher on his back. His wife had been right: he was a fool. The sword was worth his ransom twice over—and he had given it away to a wealthy man.

The Saracens were shouting something, but Godwin had never learned Arabic and just kept plodding forward, until one of the Saracens grabbed him roughly by the arm and shouted something in his face. The man shoved him to the side so roughly that he almost lost his footing and Sven called out in alarm, clutching at his neck hard enough to nearly choke him.

"I'm going already!" Godwin protested, but he didn't know where he was going. He just tried to evade the man, who chased him with blows and kicks, until he was suddenly thrust in front of the horses and looked up again at the Baron of Ibelin at close range.

"Forgive me," the baron said. "I have forgotten your name, but you made my sword."

"Yes, my lord," Godwin mumbled.

"If I had known your circumstances earlier, I would have ensured your ransom was paid before you suffered this indignity, but I will pay it now. The boy is your son?"

"Yes, my lord."

"Do you have other family?"

For a moment Godwin hesitated, but then he shook his head. "Not anymore."

Ibelin nodded, turned to the Sultan, and spoke in a rush of Arabic. The Sultan smiled but shook his head, making a gesture which provoked a flood of Arabic from the man beside him. Godwin could understand none of what was spoken, but he had seen the Sultan shake his head, and he dropped his own head in despair. The forty days were up; the Sultan was sticking to the letter of the agreement. He was still a slave.

"Shall I take the boy up behind me on my saddle?" the baron broke into his thoughts.

"My lord?" Godwin looked up, puzzled.

"Your son? Shall I take him behind me on my saddle so you can catch up to the rest of the column faster? They have a fair start on us. Once we catch up, he can ride on one of the wagons."

"But—I thought—the Sultan refused you—"

"He refused *payment*. Instead, he has turned over five hundred slaves as a *gift*."

"I am free? Sven and I are both free?" Godwin wanted to be absolutely sure he had not misunderstood. He did not want to rejoice too soon.

"I may have lost Jerusalem," Ibelin answered, "but I have not yet lost my heart or soul—and with both, I intend to keep on fighting for the things I love."

Historical Note

BALIAN D'IBELIN WAS AN IMPORTANT HISTORICAL figure, and his name and deeds are depicted in the contemporary chronicles of both Christians and Muslims. Yet while his contributions to history are part of the record, many facts about his personal life went unrecorded. Given the gaps and contradictions concerning many key aspects of his biography, this novel has opted for a lucid story line that is not inconsistent with key known facts and in no way violates the important features of the historical record, but may condense some events to make the story more coherent and dramatically effective.

Before focusing on the things I've changed, let me highlight the key events of Balian's life covered in this volume that—surprising as they may seem—are historical fact.

- Guy and Aimery de Lusignan's father, Hugh VIII, died in Saracen captivity. Aimery came to the Holy Land in the early 1170s. He was himself captured, but was ransomed by King Amalric, and he thereafter married Eschiva d'Ibelin, the eldest daughter of Baldwin d'Ibelin (called Barry throughout this book to avoid confusion with King Baldwin).

- According to the Chronicle of Ernoul, a document that has since been lost but which was quoted extensively in later chronicles, Baldwin d'Ibelin (Barry) allegedly courted (or had an affair with) Princess Sibylla after the death of William de Montferrat.

- The Christian forces met with a large Saracen army, led by Salah ad-Din's nephew, on the Litani and initially routed it, only to be forced to retreat when the Templars broke and fled before Salah ad-Din's main force. King Baldwin was unhorsed in the engagement and was carried off the field by one of his knights. Balian's elder brother Baldwin (Barry), Baron of Ramla, was taken captive in this battle.

- Apparently because it was assumed Ramla would soon marry Princess Sibylla and thereby become "heir apparent" to the Kingdom of Jerusalem, Salah ad-Din demanded a king's ransom for Ramla's release—and the Byzantine Emperor was prepared to pay part of it.

- When Ramla's ransom was finally paid and he returned to Jerusalem, however, he found his place in Princess Sibylla's affections had been taken by Guy de Lusignan, who (according to Ernoul) had seduced her. Ernoul goes on to claim that the King wanted Lusignan hanged for "debauching" a princess of Jerusalem, but was persuaded by his sister and mother to let Sibylla marry Guy instead. Ernoul was a squire to Balian d'Ibelin, and historians question his account of events, suggesting they are an attempt to cast Ramla's later refusal to take an oath of allegiance to Guy de Lusignan in a favorable (chivalric) light.

- William of Tyre, the most reliable and only contemporary chronicler, claimed that Baldwin IV feared a coup d'état by Tripoli, Antioch, and Baldwin of Ramla at Easter 1180, and so married off his sister "in haste" to the adolescent (sic) Guy de Lusignan to prevent Ramla from marrying Sibylla and laying claim to the throne. Tyre admits that King Baldwin later intensely regretted this hasty decision.

- The accounts of Ernoul and Tyre are not necessarily mutually exclusive. Without alleging seduction or illicit relations, Tyre's account suggests that Baldwin of Ramla had reason to believe he would marry Sibylla—and Sibylla's later loyalty to Guy, even after he had been utterly disgraced, suggests her feelings for him were stronger than mere sibling obedience. Thus my account of the events at Easter 1180 merges both accounts into a coherent story.

- On July 15, 1182, in intense summer heat, the Christian army fought Salah ad-Din to a standstill at Le Forbelet; the monk carrying the True

Cross did die of sunstroke during the battle. The exact sequence of events at the battle is not recorded.

- Isabella was taken away from her mother at the age of eight and sent to live with her future husband and in-laws at Kerak. This was done, historians contend, to remove her from "the evil influence" of Maria Zoë Comnena and "the Ibelins." Why Maria Zoë and the Ibelins were such an "evil" influence is hard to explain, given the historical record of both. However, they certainly opposed Agnes de Courtenay, her policies, and her protégé Guy de Lusignan, so the move was certainly political, with the eight-year-old a pawn.

- Reynald de Châtillon did lead a raid deep into Arabia during a truce in 1181.

- Reynald de Châtillon launched six galleys in the Red Sea in late 1182. They caused immense havoc until Salah ad-Din's brother brought an Egyptian fleet overland to challenge and eventually defeat them. Although Châtillon is almost universally given sole blame for this, Professor Bernard Hamilton argues very persuasively that the costs would have been beyond Châtillon's means, and the advantages to the Kingdom were enormous. I have opted, therefore, for Hamilton's version of events, which makes the enterprise a strategic one designed to undermine Salah ad-Din's standing and sanctioned (secretly) by the King, rather than an irresponsible plundering raid by a rogue baron. The fate of the crews is recorded; the survival of the fictional Henri d'Ibelin is equally fictional.

- The Christian army under Guy de Lusignan thwarted another Saracen invasion in the fall of 1183. The only recorded action in this campaign was the skirmish between Salah ad-Din's forces and Aimery de Lusignan, "reinforced by the Ibelin brothers," over the springs at La Tubanie. Very little else is recorded about the campaign, but it is clear that the army returned hugely dissatisfied with Guy de Lusignan's leadership. Professor Hamilton suggests that inadequate provisions and the sacking of monasteries were the principal grounds for the dissatisfaction, and I have followed him here. While the issue of provisions may sound like a minor point, Napoleon allegedly said an army marched on its stomach, and

Richard I of England was in part successful because of his meticulous attention to provisioning his army.

- The siege of Kerak in the midst of Isabella's wedding to Humphrey of Toron is also a historical fact, as is the refusal of the barons to march to the relief of Kerak until the succession had been settled and Baldwin V crowned co-monarch. Whether Stephanie de Milly really offered Salah ad-Din part of the wedding feast is doubtful—but it is recorded in the Chronicle of Ernoul, a contemporary document written by Balian d'Ibelin's real-life squire, so it is not my invention. The lighting of a fire on the Tower of David is also fact, not fiction.

- The ensuing back-and-forth struggle between Baldwin IV and Guy de Lusignan is, tragically, history rather than fiction. Baldwin gave Guy the Regency in exchange for Jerusalem and ten thousand bezants a year. When asked to exchange Tyre for Jerusalem, Guy refused. He also refused to come to Jerusalem in the spring of 1184, he refused Baldwin admittance to Ascalon, and he finally attacked Bedouins under Baldwin's protection. Baldwin formally and publicly excluded Guy from the succession and the Regency of his nephew, and he consulted clerics about how to dissolve his sister's marriage to Guy. Shortly before his death, he made his barons swear to seek the advice of the Kings of France and England, the Holy Roman Emperor, and the Pope rather than accept Guy de Lusignan as King in the event Baldwin V were to die before his majority. In short, the historical record makes it clear that by 1184 the relationship between Baldwin and Guy was acrimonious, and the pleas of others for reconciliation fell on deaf ears.

- It was during this period that William of Tyre was excommunicated by the Patriarch Heraclius. The date and cause are both unknown, and the cause is the source of much speculation.

- The second siege of Kerak is also historical fact, as is the siege of Nablus and the fact that *not a single Christian was killed* in Nablus. Since Balian was with the army at this time, historians presume Maria Comnena was in command of the defense of Nablus. While it is known that Nablus had no walls and that the people must have taken refuge in the citadel, there is no remaining archaeological evidence of a citadel at Nablus, and so the conjecture is that it was not a very substantial building.

- Patrick, Earl of Salisbury, was killed in an ambush by "the Lusignan brothers" that was intended to capture Queen Eleanor. William Marshal's biographer describes how Salisbury first put Queen Eleanor on his fastest palfrey and was then run through by a lance from behind as he went to mount another horse. Marshal's biography stresses that Salisbury was not wearing armor. Marshal allegedly fought valiantly until he was wounded in the thigh, and his poor treatment as a prisoner of the Lusignans is described by his biographer, as well as the kindness of a lady of the house. What is unclear is which of the Lusignan brothers (or their retainers) actually drove the deadly lance into Salisbury's unprotected back. The English chronicler Roger of Howden says it was Geoffrey, the second of the Lusignan brothers, older than both Aimery and Guy. Furthermore, if it was Guy rather than one of his older brothers, he would have been very young at the time. However, his very youth might explain his impetuosity and stupidity at killing a prize worth a large ransom. It would also explain why Guy was persona non grata in the Plantagenet lands, and so why Guy found it advantageous to go to the Holy Land. Although some chroniclers make the claim that he was the murderer of Salisbury, there is ultimately no evidence. I have chosen to make Guy guilty for dramatic purposes.

- Humphrey de Toron's hereditary barony was turned over to the Crown in exchange for a money fief. William of Tyre suggests the swap was part of the marriage contract with Isabella, but subject to "certain conditions" that he did not divulge. If it was part of the contract, then the swap was made over his head by his mother and Reynald de Châtillon—very much to his disadvantage.

- Balian did carry Baldwin V on his shoulders for the ceremony at the Church of the Holy Sepulcher. This mark of royal favor for such a minor baron is not adequately explained by his being "exceptionally tall."

- Sibylla and Guy seized the throne in 1186 in a clear violation of Baldwin IV's arrangements and without the consent of the High Court of Jerusalem. Whether these acts constituted a usurpation is perhaps debatable, but certainly their actions were "irregular" and of dubious legality. Equally clear is that Sibylla only managed to gain support from a minority of the baronage and prelates by promising to divorce Guy and marry another man—only to then go back on her word and chose Guy as her consort. Sibylla's only known supporters were her uncle Joscelin of Edessa, Reynald de Châtillon, and the Grand Master of the Knights Templar, Gerard de Ridefort. While the Grand Master did not have a seat on the High Court, he commanded more knights than any single baron and had access to more resources from the West. Allegedly the Templars took control of Jerusalem in the critical weeks, and so their support was vital to Guy's success.

- The High Court, or those members of it collected at Nablus, did plan to crown Isabella and Humphrey as rival (legal) Queen and King of Jerusalem, but Humphrey de Toron slipped away in the night to pay homage to Guy de Lusignan. As Isabella could not rule without a consort, this ended the baronial opposition to Guy de Lusignan's usurpation of the throne.

- Baldwin (Barry) d'Ibelin refused to swear allegiance to Guy de Lusignan as King of Jerusalem, turning his lands and titles over to his son Thomas and naming Balian Thomas' guardian until he came of age, before leaving the Kingdom to start a new life in Antioch. He is never heard of again. There is also no other trace of "Thomas," so the dates of his birth and death are unknown—but since I have postulated that Ramla would not have abandoned a young child that he loved, I have invented the older boy and made Thomas an infant too small and sickly to have yet earned his father's affection. Also unexplained in the story of Baldwin's (Barry's) renunciation of his baronies is what happened to his wife. Again, since she did not appear to figure in the equation at all, I have presumed she too was dead. However, some sources suggest she lived long enough to be widowed and remarry one of Tripoli's stepsons.

- Balian tried to reconcile Raymond de Tripoli and Guy de Lusignan in 1187, allegedly talking Guy out of a full-scale attack on Raymond in the fall of 1186. The negotiations dragged on. The next year he set out with the Templar and Hospitaller Masters to try to negotiate an agreement between the two men, but due to a short detour for personal business, he avoided the disaster at the Springs of Cresson.

- The slaughter of eighty Templar Knights, including the Marshal, and the Hospitaller Grand Master in an ill-advised attack on a much larger Saracen raiding force (some sources claim it was seven thousand horsemen) at the Springs of Cresson is historical fact.

- Accounts of the Battle of Hattin are both incomplete and contradictory to some degree. Undisputed is the fact that Tripoli commanded the advance guard (leading units) and that Balian d'Ibelin and the Templars made up the rear guard during the advance from the springs of Sephorie. It is clear that the bulk of the army was caught on the plateau behind the Horns of Hattin, more or less surrounded by Saracens, although it is not clear how dense the troops were to the west and south.

- All accounts agree that Tripoli led a charge toward Hattin (i.e., north), whether on his own initiative or on the orders of King Guy, but that his charge was not reinforced, and the Saracens again closed the encirclement after he and "his knights" got out. Some sources speculate that only a handful of mounted men escaped with Tripoli.

- Since Joscelin de Courtenay was not recorded at the Battle of Hattin but shortly after the battle negotiated the surrender of Acre, there is good reason to assume he was not at Hattin at all. He commanded no troops, after all, and was already an elderly man.

- There is no question that Balian fought his way out of the encirclement on the Horns of Hattin and reached Tyre with some of his knights. Some sources say he was part of Raymond de Tripoli's charge—but other sources, notably the "Lyon Eracles," which are the most comprehensive and detailed chronicles for the period 1184-1197 and are probably based on eyewitness accounts, assert that Balian made a separate breakout. Furthermore, Arab sources speak of charges by Christian knights *after* Tripoli had broken out. One of these charges threatened Salah ad-Din himself. Therefore, I have opted to put Balian in command of one of these later attacks, leading to a separate breakout. After all, if Balian had come close to capturing Salah ad-Din, it might explain Salah ad-Din's respect for him in the months that followed.

- Historians estimate that approximately three thousand infantry also survived the battle, but no source I have found explains how they broke out of the encirclement. It seems most reasonable that some infantry managed to fall in behind one of the cavalry charges and escape through the gap torn in the enemy lines by the cavalry. Since it is widely reported that none of the infantry got out with Tripoli, I have described them as following Balian's charge. This makes sense if, as I hypothesize, Tripoli led to the north and Ibelin led to the east, past the slopes on which the Christian infantry had retreated.

- Following the battle, Salah ad-Din did order the execution of the approximately 230 surviving Templars and Hospitallers, with the exception of Grand Master Ridefort. The Sufis were given the "privilege" of carrying out the executions, and it is recorded that it sometimes took five blows to sever the neck of the victim. It is unclear where the executions took place, and some claim they took place near Hattin (with Salah ad-Din standing by, grinning and showing his approval). Other sources place the executions in Damascus, in which case Salah ad-Din could not have been personally present. I have opted for the latter version as the more plausible. There were many madrassas in Damascus from which to draw the Sufis, and the execution spectacle was for the "masses" and the civilians, not for the fighting men, who had probably had enough slaughter by then. Last but not least, Salah ad-Din ordered the executions because he saw the Templars and Hospitallers as dangerous fanatics, but it is not particularly in character for him to want to watch—much less enjoy—the executions.

- Balian obtained a safe-conduct from Salah ad-Din to remove his wife and "family" from Jerusalem after Hattin. Salah ad-Din granted the safe-conduct on the condition that Balian go to the city unarmed and stay only one night.

- Balian was greeted in Jerusalem like a savior, and he was begged to take command of the defense of the city. Balian sent word to Salah ad-Din, explaining the situation, and Salah ad-Din responded by sending fifty of his own men to escort Maria Comnena and Balian's children to safety in Tripoli.

- When Balian discovered there were only two knights in the city (including himself, presumably), he knighted approximately eighty youth "of good family"—probably from both the merchant class and the feudal elite that had taken refuge in Jerusalem.

- Although it is frequently asserted that Orthodox Christians were "better off" under the Muslims and were not loyal to the Latin Kingdom, there is no evidence of this. On the contrary, the First Crusade was launched because of the oppression of Orthodox Christians, and from the beginning the Latin rulers repealed the extra taxes leveled on Christians, ended the periodic massacres and indignities they had suffered under the Muslims, and allowed Orthodox Christians to practice their religion openly under their own leaders, with the exception of appointing Latin bishops to previously Greek Orthodox sees. The native Christians responded with loyalty, providing troops for the Christian army and contributing to the defense of Jerusalem.

- Despite the lack of trained fighting men, Balian organized a highly effective defense of Jerusalem, including early foraging expeditions into Saracen-controlled territory to ensure the city had enough provisions to withstand a siege.

- During one of these sorties, the Christians clashed with a Saracen patrol and a famous emir was killed; neither the location nor the names of the commanders are recorded.

- After the siege was established, Balian led successful sorties against Salah ad-Din's siege engines, and one Christian sortie drove the Saracens right back to their camp.

- On September 25 Salah ad-Din withdrew his army, and many Christians in the city thought they had been saved. People took to the streets singing hymns, and thanksgiving Masses were read in all the churches.

- When Salah ad-Din returned, he focused his attacks on the same section of the wall (the northeastern wall) where Godfrey de Bouillon had breached the defenses in 1099. He is said to have had a trebuchet (then a new invention) and twenty mangonels, but at this point he concentrated his efforts on undermining the walls.

- After the walls of Jerusalem had been undermined, the nerves of some of the defenders (understandably) cracked, and Salah ad-Din used a close adviser of Syrian Christian faith to try to coax the Syrian population into betraying the defenders. Before anything came of this, Ibelin negotiated the surrender. The fact that Syrian Christians were ready to negotiate after almost ten days of siege does not prove that they had been traitorous or disloyal all along.

- Ibelin led a mounted sortie out of the Jehoshaphat Gate on the night of September 29. Historians can only speculate about the objective, but as it was directed at the Mount of Olives, where Salah ad-Din had set up his command tent, it is not unreasonable to think the objective was to kill the Sultan.

- Ibelin did force Salah ad-Din to negotiate terms of surrender after the Saracens had breached the walls by threatening to kill all the Muslim prisoners in the city, and all the Christian residents as well—after destroying the holy sites of all religions. The bargaining about the height of the ransom and how many poor could be bought by what lump sum was, allegedly, even more lengthy than I have made it here, with the Sultan consulting his emirs and other advisors.

- Salah ad-Din agreed to ransoms for the residents of Jerusalem, and when at the end of the forty-day grace period thousands were still in the city unransomed, he "gave" a thousand to his brother and five hundred each to the Patriarch and Ibelin. Balian offered to remain as a hostage for the payment of ransoms for the rest, but Salah ad-Din refused. According to Arab sources, the number of Christians Ibelin rescued from slavery through payment of a lump sum varied from eight thousand to eighteen thousand, but all sources agree that roughly fifteen thousand Christians whose ransoms could not be raised went into slavery.

- Last but not least, Balian really did have a squire named Ernoul (possibly a variant of Arnuld/Arnold), who was with him at the Springs of Cresson and Hattin, and who later in life wrote an account of the events leading to the loss of Jerusalem in the vernacular. This original source, however, has since been lost, and all we now have are later chronicles that were in part based upon the original account written by Ernoul. The depiction of events credited to the lost "Chronicles of Ernoul" is colorful and contains many details about people that the more serious Church chroniclers skip over as irrelevant. Ernoul is therefore considered by modern historians to be a "lightweight," but also an invaluable, source. He is also presumed to be shamelessly biased in favor of the Ibelins. While it is correct to assume that he understood the Ibelin perspective on historical events, it is wrong to assume that that bias makes everything he said a mirror image of reality. The Ibelins, and specifically Balian d'Ibelin, just might have had a very valid view of what was happening in the Kingdom of Jerusalem! The fact that Arab sources—which are not inherently biased in his favor—also attribute nobility and wisdom to Balian d'Ibelin suggests that Ernoul's version of events might be a lot closer to the truth than the revisionist histories of more recent historians that attribute shameless ambition and evil intent to the Ibelins without a shred of evidence. In any case, this novel is based on the Ibelin view of history and so relies heavily on Ernoul.

Let me now turn to the features of the novel for which more literary license was necessary:

- As I noted in Book I, the character of Henri d'Ibelin is completely fictional, and so is his role in Reynald de Châtillon's raids and in the Red Sea.

- The death of the Greek Emperor Manuel I occurred one year earlier than noted in the novel. There was simply too much going on in 1180 for me to give proper attention to it between the marriage of Sibylla and Guy and the betrothal of Isabella and Humphrey, so I moved it back one year to a point in the novel where I could give it the kind of attention it deserved. This means that it was not Manuel I, but the young Alexius II or his Regent (Maria Comnena's uncle), who paid Ramla's ransom.

- Baldwin d'Ibelin (Barry) actually married twice after his suit of Sibylla failed, but I have merged his wives into a single character to reduce confusion and simplify the plot.

- Humphrey's age at the time of his marriage to Isabella is sometimes given as seventeen, but the fact that he was still living in Kerak under his mother and stepfather's tutelage suggests he was either very immature, even backward, for his age—or that he was, in fact, younger. Since I have found no hard evidence of his date of birth, I have elected to make him just fifteen at his wedding to Isabella.

- William, Archbishop of Tyre, was excommunicated by the Patriarch Heraclius most probably (although accounts differ) in the spring of 1183 or 1184. The reasons for the excommunication are obscure. Ernoul claims it was because of an attack on Heraclius' unchaste lifestyle, but historians suggest it was more likely a conflict over the independence of his see. Neither theory is supported by strong evidence. Since this was the time when Baldwin IV was seeking an annulment of Sibylla's marriage, and William of Tyre was an unwavering opponent of Guy de Lusignan while Heraclius was a client of the Queen Mother and so the Lusignan faction, conflict over this crucial question between the two most prominent churchmen of the realm is almost certain. Hence, while not historically documented, an attempt by Tyre to annul Sibylla's marriage to Guy de Lusignan is entirely plausible. The "arrangement" between Ramla and Sibylla would likewise have been the most obvious grounds for such an annulment, given the fact that the Byzantine Emperor and Salah ad-Din both thought Ramla was the designated next husband of Sibylla at the time of his capture on the Litani.

- The historical record is unclear on when William of Tyre ceased to be Chancellor to Baldwin IV. I have chosen to make this break at the time of Heraclius' appointment to increase the dramatic tension: the sense of Baldwin being torn between his mother, sister, and their clients and the traditional elite including Raymond de Tripoli and William of Tyre.

- While we know that William Marshal was in the Holy Land during the period in which he appears in this novel, no one knows exactly where he was, who he met, or what he did. His role in the siege of Nablus is thus completely fictional, albeit based on a real incident when Henry II was fleeing from his son Richard and Marshal alone turned to face the pursuers, covering Henry's flight. In that incident he killed Richard's horse under him, but wisely refrained from killing the unarmed heir to the English throne.

- Eschiva of Tiberias had four sons by her first marriage: Hugh, William, Ralph, and Odo. To simplify things, I've reduced them to two, William (to avoid name duplication) and Ralph.

- Salah ad-Din received the delegation from Jerusalem during his siege of Ascalon, not Tyre, but Balian received his "safe-conduct" at Tyre. To keep the story moving, I elected to move the date of the delegation forward so I could cover both events in a single scene.

- William of Tyre describes the blood bath in Jerusalem in 1099 in vivid detail, and then a few pages later talks about the Christians "dwelling in Jerusalem" giving "heartfelt thanks to Peter the Hermit." He does not explain how these Christians had managed to escape the slaughter. I have hypothesized that the Christians had knowledge of some places to hide—which they later revealed to the Kings of Jerusalem, who in turn passed these on to the Templars.

- While Balian did lead sorties out of Jerusalem that damaged or destroyed some of Salah ad-Din's siege engines, the leper sortie is my own invention.

- Salah ad-Din actually consulted with his leading commanders after Balian threatened to destroy the holy sites and kill everyone in Jerusalem, and they agreed with the idea of letting the Christians ransom themselves. I eliminated this step in the negotiations for dramatic effect.

- The dialogue (with the few exceptions noted in the text), the physical descriptions, and the supporting characters are all fiction. This is a novel—one based on historical fact—but a novel nevertheless.

Note on Leprosy

Baldwin IV of Jerusalem suffered from leprosy from the time he was a boy. He was diagnosed by his tutor William, later Archbishop of Tyre, while still a schoolboy, and he was recognized as a leper by contemporary society.

In writing this book, where Baldwin IV is a central character, it was important to understand both the disease as we know it today and what medieval man knew and thought about leprosy. I have relied heavily on Piers D. Mitchell's essay titled "An Evaluation of the Leprosy of King Baldwin IV of Jerusalem in the Context of the Medieval World," which appears as an appendix in Bernard Hamilton's *The Leper King and his Heirs: Baldwin IV and the Crusader Kingdom of Jerusalem*, and the excellent study of attitudes toward leprosy published by Timothy S. Miller and John W. Nesbitt, *Walking Corpses: Leprosy in Byzantium and the Medieval West.*

It was important to me that the actual evolution of the disease as depicted in this novel be consistent with both the historical record and the stages of the disease recognized by modern medical knowledge. For example, we know from William of Tyre that Baldwin's leprosy first manifested itself as a lack of feeling in his right hand, but we also know that Baldwin was an agile rider as a young adult. It is further recorded that he commanded his armies in person at Montgisard, on the Litani, at Le Forbelet, and even as late as the relief of Kerak. However, his body was in fact decaying progressively and noticeably. William of Tyre also noted a particularly dramatic deterioration of his health in the year 1183, and by the time he died in 1185 just short of his twenty-fourth birthday, he had gone blind and did not have the use of any of his limbs.

Based on the historical descriptions of Baldwin's initial illness, which state he had lost the feeling in his arm but that there were no other symptoms such as discoloration or ulcers, Mitchell suggests that Baldwin IV initially had primary polyneuritic tuberculoid leprosy, which deteriorated into lepromatous leprosy during puberty. There was, according to Mitchell, nothing inevitable about this deterioration—however, puberty itself can induce the deterioration, as can untended wounds (going unnoticed due to loss of feeling) that cause ulcers to break out. Historically, Baldwin led the dangerous campaign against Salah ad-Din that led to the surprise victory at Montgisard when he was in puberty, just sixteen years old. I hypothesize that it was in part because of this campaign—which required camping out in the field and going without the usual bathing of his feet and hands—that his disease took a turn for the worse. According to Mitchell, children who develop lepromatous leprosy are likely to die prematurely, and so once Baldwin's leprosy had become lepromatous, it inevitably took its course through the gruesome stages of increasing incapacitation to an early death.

The degree to which the disease is contagious is another critical issue in this novel. Modern medical research suggests that although during an epidemic as much as 30 per cent of a population can catch the disease, once leprosy has become endemic to a population (as it was in the Levant in the twelfth century), only about five percent of the population has a genetic proclivity to the disease and hence a high risk of contagion if exposed to the disease. Furthermore, if a person is susceptible to leprosy, he or she is most likely to develop it between the ages of ten and twenty—exactly the age at which Baldwin IV became ill. The adults in attendance upon him, however, such as the Archdeacon of Tyre and, in the novel, Balian, had less than a 5 per cent chance of becoming ill.

Just as important as an accurate depiction of the course of decay caused by leprosy, however, is a depiction of medieval beliefs about leprosy. We know today that less than 5 per cent of the population is likely to contract the disease if exposed, but medieval man believed the chances of contagion to be much, much higher. Medieval medicine suggested, at one extreme, that just breathing the same air as lepers could result in infection. Yet, because the disease was widespread, medieval man also knew that many men and women washed, cared for, and even kissed lepers without themselves suffering from the disease. I have chosen, therefore, to have my characters subscribe to a non-scientific but plausible "enlightened" view of leprosy's contagiousness that is consistent with the fact that Baldwin IV was never completely isolated from society. Those closest to him evidently thought that by taking certain precautions they could remain healthy, while the majority avoided intimacy and maintained some distance without avoiding Baldwin altogether.

Medieval attitudes were not governed by the state of medical knowledge alone. Religion played a critical role. Leprosy was *not* seen as a sign of sin, but rather as a sign of grace—particularly in Byzantium. Indeed, the Byzantines came to call leprosy "the Holy Disease," and there are a number of Greek Orthodox legends in which Christ appears as a leper. Miller and Nesbitt note that the harshest views on leprosy came from pre-Christian Germanic tribes and the Jews. Crusader Jerusalem, however, was far more heavily influenced by Byzantium than by the Germanic tribes or Judaism. This fact is underlined by the creation of the Knights of St. Lazarus in Jerusalem, probably in the second decade of the twelfth century, as an outgrowth from an earlier Byzantine or Armenian leper hospital.

In short, while the progression of the disease depicted in this novel is based on modern medical knowledge of leprosy, the attitudes and treatment provided Baldwin in the book are based on what we know of medieval remedies and attitudes toward leprosy during the twelfth century.

Glossary

Abaya: a black garment, worn by Islamic women, that completely covers the head and body in a single, flowing, unfitted fashion so that no contours or limbs can be seen. It leaves only the face, but not the neck, visible and is often supplemented with a mask or "veil" that covers the lower half of the face, leaving only a slit for the eyes between the top of the abaya (which covers the forehead) and the mask or veil across the lower half of the face.

Aketon: a padded and quilted garment, usually of linen, worn under or instead of chain mail.

Aventail: a flap of chain mail, attached to the coif, to cover the lower part of the face, secured by a leather thong to the brow band.

Battlement: a low wall built on the roof of a tower or other building in a castle, fortified manor, or church, with alternating higher segments for sheltering behind and lower segments for shooting from.

Buss: a large combination oared and sailing vessel whose design was derived from Norse cargo (not raiding) vessels. Busses had substantial cargo capacity, but were also swift and maneuverable. They could be two- or even three-masted.

Cantle: the raised part of a saddle behind the seat; in this period it was high and strong, made of wood, to help keep a knight in the saddle even after taking a blow from a lance.

Cervelliere: an open-faced helmet that covered the skull like a close-fitting, brimless cap; usually worn over a chain-mail coif.

Chain mail (**mail**): flexible armor composed of interlinking riveted rings of metal. Each link passes through four others.

Chausses: mail leggings to protect a knight's legs in combat.

Cincenelles: Apparently some kind of fly. According to the *Itinerarium Peregrinorum et Gesta Regis Ricardi* (Book 5, Chapter 44): "At Ibelin flies called cincenelles ravage[d] the faces of the army with their stings, so that they look[ed] like lepers." I have not been able to find a modern word for the insects.

Coif: a chain-mail hood, either separate from or attached to the hauberk.

Conroi: a medieval cavalry formation in which the riders rode stirrup to stirrup in rows that enabled a maximum number of lances to come to bear, but also massed the power of the charge.

Crenels: the indentations or loopholes in the top of a battlement or wall.

Crenelate: the act of adding defensive battlements to a building.

Emir: Saracen rank or title similar to barons in the Frankish armies. Emirs controlled territory or administrative units that generated substantial income and were required to raise troops to serve under the Sultan. Unlike barons in the feudal West, however, their fiefs or *iqtas* were not hereditary, but held only at the pleasure of the Sultan. In theory, the Sultan could dismiss them, but he was also dependent upon them and the troops they could muster, making the relationship much more complex. Emirs had no religious function.

Faranj: Arab term for crusaders and their descendants in Outremer.

Fief: land held on a hereditary basis in return for military service.

Fetlock: the lowest joint in a horse's leg.

Frank: the contemporary term used to describe Latin Christians (crusaders, pilgrims, and their descendants) in the Middle East, regardless of their country of origin. The Arab term "faranj" derived from this.

Destrier: a horse specially bred and trained for mounted combat; a charger or warhorse. These horses had to have the strength to carry a man in full armor at a gallop, but sprinting (for a charge) was more important than endurance, and high spirits and temper were valued. Over time the horses were increasingly trained to take part in battle by kicking and biting, thereby becoming an additional weapon of the knight.

Dromond: a large vessel with two to three lateen sails and two banks of oars. These vessels were built very strongly and were consequently slower, but offered more spacious accommodation than galleys.

Garderobe: a toilet, usually built on the exterior wall of a residence or fortification, that in rural settings emptied directly into the surrounding ditch or moat, or in cities into an external pottery drainage pipe leading down to the city's sewage system.

Hajj: the Muslim pilgrimage to Mecca, one of the five duties of a good Muslim.

Hauberk: a chain-mail shirt, either long- or short-sleeved, that in this period reached to just above the knee.

Iqta: a Seljuk institution similar to a fief in feudal Europe, but not hereditary. It was a gift of land or other sources of revenue from an overlord to a subject that could be retracted at any time at the whim of the overlord.

Imam: a Muslim religious leader and scholar who leads prayers in the mosques.

Jihad: Muslim holy war, usually interpreted as a war against nonbelievers to spread the faith of Islam.

Kettle helm: an open-faced helmet with a broad rim, common among infantry.

Lance: a cavalry weapon approximately fourteen feet long, made of wood and tipped with a steel head.

Madrassa: A Muslim theological seminary.

Malik Rik: Saracen term for King Richard.

Melee: a form of tournament in which two teams of knights face off across a large natural landscape and fight in conditions very similar to real combat, across ditches, hedges, swamps, streams, and so on. These were very popular in the late twelfth century—and very dangerous, often resulting in injuries and even deaths to both men and horses. The modern meaning of any confused, hand-to-hand fight among a large number of people derives from the medieval meaning.

Merlon: the solid part of a battlement or parapet between two openings or "crenels."

Muezzin: The man who calls Muslims to prayer, usually from a minaret, five times a day.

Outremer: A French term meaning "overseas," used to describe the crusader kingdoms (Kingdom of Jerusalem, County of Tripoli, County of Edessa, and Principality of Antioch) established in the Holy Land after the First Crusade.

Pommel: 1) the raised portion in front of the seat of a saddle; 2) the round portion of a sword above the hand grip.

Palfrey: a riding horse bred and trained to be calm, with comfortable gaits, and capable of traveling long distances.

Parapet: A wall with crenelation built on a rampart or outer defensive work.

Quintain: a pivoted gibbet-like structure with a shield suspended from one arm and a bag of sand from the other, used to train men for mounted combat.

Rampart: an earthen embankment surmounted by a parapet, encircling a castle or city as a defense against attack.

Saracen: a collective term meaning "easterner" that referred to any of the ethnically diverse Muslim opponents of the Franks.

Scabbard (also sheath): the protective outer case of an edged weapon, particularly a sword or dagger.

Snecka: a square-sailed warship or galley that was very swift and maneuverable but had only a single bank of oars in addition to the sail, and so a very low freeboard. These evolved from Viking raiding ships. Some, however, appear to have had battering rams, as is described in the attack of Richard I's galleys on an Arab ship off Acre.

Sufi: Members of an Islamic mystical sect; Islamic scholars.

Surcoat: the loose, flowing cloth garment worn over armor; in this period it was slit up the front and back for riding and hung to mid-calf. It could be sleeveless or have short, wide, elbow-length sleeves. It could be of cotton, linen, or silk and was often brightly dyed, woven, or embroidered with the wearer's coat of arms.

Tenant-in-chief: an individual holding land directly from the crown. A baron.

Turcopoles: troops drawn from the Orthodox Christian population of the crusader states. These were not, as was often claimed, Muslim converts, nor were they the children of mixed marriages.

Vassal: an individual holding a fief (land) in exchange for military service.

Additional Reading

FOR MORE READING ON THE HISTORICAL Balian d'Ibelin, the crusader states, and the crusades, I recommend the following sources:

Barber, Malcolm, *The Crusader States*, Yale University Press, 2012.

Barber, Malcolm, *The New Knighthood: A History of the Order of the Temple*, Cambridge University Press, 1194.

Barber, Richard, *The Knight and Chivalry*, Boydell Press, 1970.

Bartlett, W. B., *Downfall of the Crusader Kingdom*, The History Press Ltd, 2010.

Brand, Charles M., *Byzantium Confronts the West*, ACLS Humanities E-Book, 2012.

Boas, Adrian J., *Crusader Archaeology: The Material Culture of the Latin East*, Routledge, London, 1999.

Conder, Claude Reignier, *The Latin Kingdom of Jerusalem, 1099 to 1291 AD*, Committee of the Palestine Exploration Fund, 1897.

Edbury, Peter W., *John of Ibelin and the Kingdom of Jerusalem*, The Boydell Press, 1997.

Edbury, Peter W., *The Conquest of Jerusalem and the Third Crusade: Sources in Translation*, Ashgate Publishing Ltd., 1998.

Edbury, Peter W., *The Kingdom of Cyprus and the Crusades, 1191–1374*, Cambridge University Press, 1991.

Edbury, Peter W., and John Gordon Rowe, *William of Tyre: Historian of the Latin East*, Cambridge University Press, 1988.

Edge, David, and John Miles Paddock, *Arms & Armor of the Medieval Knight*, Saturn Books, 1996.

Ehrenkreutz, Andrew S., *Saladin*, State University of New York Press, 1972.

Folda, Jaroslav, *Crusader Art: The Art of the Crusaders in the Holy Land, 1099-1291*, Ashgate Publishing, 2008.

Gabrieli, Francesco, *Arab Historians of the Crusades*, University of California Press, 1969.

Hamilton, Bernard, *The Leper King and His Heirs: Baldwin IV and the Crusader Kingdom of Jerusalem*, Cambridge University Press, 2000.

Hamilton, Bernard, "Women in the Crusader States: The Queens of Jerusalem 1100–90," in *Medieval Women*, David Baker (ed.), Basil Blackwell, 1978.

Hopkins, Andrea, *Knights: The Complete Story of the Age of Chivalry, from Historical Fact to Tales of Romance and Poetry*, Collins and Brown Ltd, 1990.

Jotischky, Andrew, *Crusading and the Crusader States*, Pearson Longman, 2004.

Maalouf, Amin, *The Crusades through Arab Eyes*, Schocken Books, 1984.

Miller, David, *Richard the Lionheart: The Mighty Crusader*, Phoenix, 2013.

Miller, Timothy S., and John W. Nesbitt, *Walking Corpses: Leprosy in Byzantium and the Medieval West*, Cornell University Press, 2014.

Morgan, Margaret Ruth, *The Chronicle of Ernoul and the Continuations of William of Tyre*, Oxford Historical Monographs, Oxford University Press, 1973.

Nicolle, David, *Hattin 1187: Saladin's Greatest Victory*, Osprey Military Campaign Series, 1993.

Pringle, Denys, *Secular Buildings in the Crusader Kingdom of Jerusalem: An Archaeological Gazetteer*, Cambridge University Press, 1997.

Robinson, John J., *Dungeon, Fire and Sword: The Knights Templar in the Crusades*, Michael O'Mara Books, 1991.

Riley-Smith, Jonathan, ed., *The Atlas of the Crusades*, Facts on File, 1991.

Runciman, Sir Steven, *The Families of Outremer: The Feudal Nobility of the Crusader Kingdom of Jerusalem, 1099-1291*, Athlone Press, 1960.

Stark, Rodney, *God's Battalions: The Case for the Crusades*, HarperCollins, 2010.

I also recommend the following websites/blogs:

http://DefenderofJerusalem.com
http://defendingcrusaderkingdoms.blogspot.com
http://Tales-of-Chivalry.com
http://helenapschrader.com
http://schradershistoricalfiction.blogspot.com
http://crusadesandcrusaders.com
http://realcrusadeshistory.com

Also by Helena P. Schrader

A landless knight,
A leper king,
And the struggle for Jerusalem.

A Biographical Novel of Balian d'Ibelin, Book I

Buy Now!

Balian has survived the catastrophe at Hattin and walked away a free man after the surrender of Jerusalem to Saladin, but he is baron of nothing in a kingdom that no longer exists. Haunted by the tens of thousands of Christians now in Saracen captivity, he is determined to win back what has been lost.

Buy Now!

Lightning Source UK Ltd.
Milton Keynes UK
UKHW012118290520
364120UK00001B/20

9 781627 872737